"A MASTER STORYTELLER ...

A deeply moving American story of the conflicts that threaten a marriage, the love of a father and son, and the fabric of a great nation."
—DAN WAKEFIELD

"Carroll captures a commitment to principle and fierce, bewildered bravery emblematic of a generation."
—*Publishers Weekly*

"Remarkable ... Illuminates the flow of American history, from the depths of the Depression to the triumphs of World War II to the pain of Vietnam. Written with a brilliant attention to detail, MEMORIAL BRIDGE creates an unforgettable cast of characters who live long after you finish the book."
—DORIS KEARNS GOODWIN

"One of Carroll's best novels. He has always been a remarkable storyteller, with a strong sense of the moral dilemmas underlying the exercise of power; here he combines those gifts in an engrossing portrait, personal and official, of the national director of American military intelligence.... A spellbinder."
—WILLIAM GIBSON

MEMORIAL BRIDGE

James Carroll

IVY BOOKS • NEW YORK

Ivy Books
Published by Ballantine Books
Copyright © 1991 by Morrissey Street Ltd.

For information about permission to reproduce selections from this book, write to Permissions, Houghton Mifflin Company, 2 Park Street, Boston, Massachusetts 02108.

Library of Congress Catalog Card Number: 90-28730

ISBN 0-8041-1274-6

First published by Houghton Mifflin Company. Reprinted by permission of Houghton Mifflin Company.

Manufactured in the United States of America

First Ballantine Books Edition: March 1995

10 9 8 7 6 5 4 3 2 1

I gratefully acknowledge the help I received from my friends Don Cutler, Robert Baer, Jody Hotchkiss, Deborah Olson, Paul Buttenwieser, Richard Goodwin and Bernard Avishai. For their continuous support and encouragement I thank especially my wife, Alexandra Marshall, and my brother Dennis Carroll.

For Joe, Brian, Dennis & Kevin

PART I

CANARYVILLE

ONE

The idea of the place was one thing. It had been laid out fifty years before in a perfect square, a mile on each side, one border the south fork of the river, another the outer boulevard that marked the limit of the city. It straddled the terminal points of three great railroads. Its multitude of activities, all designed to turn flesh into coin, were organized according to the rigid grid formed by fifteen miles of railroad tracks and half a dozen of paved avenues. Each intersection formed the corner of a smaller square that repeated the pattern of the great one, and one quarter of the tract was marked further by the lines of countless fences and stone walls so that the section formed a huge maze. These were the animal pens built to corral fourteen thousand head of cattle, twice that many sheep and fifty thousand hogs. The pens were subdivided further into sections by loading platforms, ramps and long rutted chutes leading to one of two mammoth packinghouses from each of which tall graceful chimneys rose like the fingers of a woman drying her nails.

The packinghouses were themselves divided into killing beds, hoisting platforms, disassembly lines, cold-storage vaults, pickle rooms and canneries. Smoke from the chimneys streamed neatly into the sky, the only unused vestige of cattle, hogs and sheep whose flesh, hides, bristles, blood and bones had been so efficiently—the rate was eleven hundred carcasses per hour—turned into hams, bacon, dressed beef, fresh mutton. And glue, brushes, leather, margarine, gelatin, lard and fertilizer.

Several thousand men—mostly Irish, but also Germans, Poles and Bohemians—filed through the Stone Gate at Section

3

Five before dawn each morning. They moved purposefully, each to his exact station. They were railroad men and livestock men and knifemen. They were skinners, butchers, gutters, choppers, trimmers, boners, luggers and wool pluckers. They were cookers and tinners. They were ham sewers. They were pipefitters and fertilizer makers. They were squeegee men whose job was to keep the slaughter room floors clear of blood and offal, and trap cleaners who made sure the pipes carrying the runoff—blood mostly, but also vast quantities of urine and internal discharge—did not clog. Each man had his function, just as each square foot of the perfect square mile had its designated purpose.

On the face of it, in other words, from a distance or on the paper of the market reports, all was order in the Chicago stockyards. The stockyards were an emblem of a larger order. Chicago's Pride, they called it, a wonder of the industrialized world. Not even the Depression, now in its ninth year, had slowed the yards' activity, although every man who carried a lunch pail through the great Stone Gate lived in terror of losing his job. Outside the stockyards Chicago was an employment desert, and on the far side of Halsted Street where the taverns and boardinghouses stood, desperate men gathered daily by the hundreds in the hope that the Swift or Armour agents would pick them as replacements for the knife wielder who'd sliced his finger off or the vat tender who'd fallen into his steaming kettle or the trainman who'd lost a foot in the unforgiving clutch of an iron switch. The stoop-shouldered jobless looked longingly across the walls toward the well-ordered acres of pens and tracks and the structures that loomed above them, the wooden-staved water tanks, the brick carshops with cloudy Gothic windows and the enormous packinghouses with their chimneys; toward the stockyards, Chicago's Pride, because to them, as to everyone, the idea of the place was one thing.

The stench was something else.

The stench was the other thing about the stockyards. Even people who depended on the place for wages, even people who could discourse on the idea of the place as an industrial wonder—the stench made them hate it. Those elegant chimneys, for example, pouring tons of ash and gas into the air, loosed a suffocating cloud of sulfur dioxide into the prevailing southwest winds that carried it over Canaryville to Hyde Park where the packinghouse owners lived and even, on some days, to the Loop itself where the owners had their offices. Countless lesser odors rising off mountains of urine-soaked manure, piles of wet wool, rotting innards, congealed spillage, albumen and lye combined with the overwhelming stink of the rendering required for the manufacture of fertilizer and glue. Discharge sewers poured steaming tankage into the south fork of the river, which so reeked of eye-stinging alkaline that city engineers had found a way to reverse its flow to keep stockyard effluent out of Lake Michigan and the stench away from Chicago proper. Putrid railroad cars carrying livestock to the yards and loads of fertilizer away fanned the odors out through Englewood and Lake and New City.

The yards themselves and the neighborhood behind them—Canaryville—were the concentration of all the foulness, the dead center of it. The stink was in the wood of the frame houses the workers lived in. It was in their clothes. It was in their skin. It was in the felt of the pool tables in the taverns. It was in the cheap beer they drank. Newcomers to the yards went to work with dabs of Vicks Vapo-Rub stuffed under their noses. Eventually their sense of smell would simply cease to function. Children who were born and raised "back of the yards" experienced their first olfactory shock when finally they traveled to other parts of the city—a trip on the El to Grant Park—and smelled nothing.

So the idea of the place was one thing. And the stench was another. But on that day what got to the men in the Swift killing beds was the blood.

Blood like they had never seen before, or smelled. Blood like the Nile River scenes in a Bible movie. Blood as if all those slaughtered animals had found a way to come back and get them. They were used to blood, but not like this; so used to blood that only such an eerie freak happening would make them notice it, would make them think, in fact, about what it was they did. They were skilled butchers, far from squeamish, and their work on the animal disassembly lines hardly encouraged introspection. But the blood this time was different.

These were men whose routine involved precision slitting of jugular veins, beheading beasts with three swipes of the knife, quartering carcasses with exactly aimed cleaver cuts, skinning animals without wasting meat or lard or damaging hides. But this blood was something else.

Instead of running off from the gutters into the floor holes, the holes themselves, like wounds, began to spurt. The blood began to run back up through the drain holes in the floor of the slaughter rooms. It was such a reversal of what they were used to—of the *order* on which everyone in the stockyards depended—that they were aware of the seepage at once. It wasn't only that the new blood spurting from the animals they'd just killed did not drain away, but that the blood from the bowels of the building itself began coming back at them like the reversed flow of the Chicago River. It was an offense against the *idea* of the stockyards, and not only that. There was a sudden new stench too. That quantity of already decomposing blood and offal brought with it an escalation of stink that even those noses registered. Some raised their kerchiefs to just below their eyes to dull the fresh assault. Soon every waste hole on the first level of the building gurgled with the dark foul liquid. The blood kept gushing until, one by one, each drain disappeared beneath the flow. Within minutes the bubbles above each hole dispersed. Then the blood seeped across the floors quietly, quickly overspilling the rutted gutters that were supposed to carry the stuff away, rising to the level of the concrete platforms on which the knifemen stood. Hundreds of drain holes overflowed at once in a dozen different cavernous rooms. The blood splashed onto the slaughtermen's boots and soon covered their ankles. Still it kept coming.

Traps in the smaller waste pipes often clogged with meat scraps or gristle or became fouled with animal hair or chunks of bone, and discharge occasionally backed up through one hole or another. But the entire drainage system? The individuals on the lines never imagined that the cold floors of all the huge slaughter rooms everywhere in the building were covered with rotten fluid just like theirs was. No one saw the horror entire, but every drain hole across thousands of square feet of work space was pumping with blood as if the huge building was suddenly endowed with a mammoth heart muscle, as if the Swift packinghouse itself had at last become a living thing, but one in acute distress, an animal about to die.

Sean Dillon was in the shower when he heard about it. It was the end of his shift, and as always he stood under the scalding water, taking the pain to mean that the effect of another day's work was coming off his body. Other naked yarders clustered under a dozen other shower heads in the tiled, steaming room, but they kept away from Dillon's shower. No one else could stand it that hot, but no one else hated the stench of the stockyards on his body like Dillon did. He rubbed the gritty soap up and down his arms and legs until his skin glowed like an Indian's. He stood with the jet of water pounding his black hair. Because of that, the first words he heard were muffled, unintelligible, and he ignored them.

"Goddammit, Dillon!" The flow of his water was abruptly cut off and Dillon looked up to see in the steam the fully clothed form of Jack Hanley, his boss. "I'm talking to you."

Dillon was too startled to reply. Behind him the other workers continued their showers. He stared at Hanley, whose right sleeve was drenched from reaching into the stream for the spigot handle. Hanley said, "Get your overalls back on. We've got a job." He adjusted the crushed felt bandless hat on his head. Hanley was never seen without it.

"My shift is over, Jack." Dillon moved toward his towel as much to cover himself as to dry his skin. "Besides, I finished the—"

"This is something else. Get dressed. Get the tools." Hanley turned to leave, but Dillon grabbed his sleeve, the dry one.

"What is it?"

"The lines are down, all of them. The killing gangs have stopped working."

Dillon's first thought was, Strike! But it couldn't be. The endless Depression had destroyed the union. Any man who talked of strike—or was caught listening to talk of one—was canned on the spot. But what else would shut the lines down? And what could it have to do with Sean Dillon, a three-dollar-a-day steamfitter's helper whose job kept him mainly on the tanks floor two stories above the slaughter rooms or in the boiler rooms which occupied their own separate wings on three sides of the packinghouse? "I've quit working too, Jack. I'm a measly wrench holder. Whatever it is, it doesn't need me."

"It needs me, boyo, and I need you."

"Where's Flaherty? Where's Lonergan?" Dillon toweled his hair vigorously.

A voice from behind Hanley in the room beyond yelled, "Shut the damn door!" The steam was pouring from the shower room into the changing room. Dillon tied the towel around his waist and went through so that Hanley could close the door. At his locker a dozen yards into the room Dillon reached for his shirt, the clean one he wore to work that morning, the one he was going to wear now.

"Didn't you hear what I said? The fucking line is down. Don't you know what that means? A thousand beasts, maybe two thousand right now, all bunched up at the feeder corrals, crashing against the posts and walls. Those animals are jammed up and every minute they get more so. You know what that means, don't you?"

Cattle, sheep and hogs stymied in narrow pens with too little room, pressed by more and more stock, the air charged with ever mounting animal anxiety. Yes, Dillon knew what it meant. He was a city boy, but he'd grown up in the foul shadow of this place, and he knew what its nightmares were. If the mass of cattle, sheep and hogs panicked in their pens, there was no place for them to bolt to. Yet the stampede impulse was still a danger, a greater one, they said, inside the yards than on the open plain. A crazed but penned-up herd would simply maul itself, hogs butting at walls, cattle tearing into each other with their horns, slamming bone against bone, breaking heads, stomping the fallen, a fury unleashed but leashed still by the very pens and therefore all the more furious. Once the animals were seized by that frenzy, nothing would relieve it until they were all dead. Uselessly, absurdly, cruelly dead. And if the frenzy struck, for as long as it lasted the animals would send up a rough piercing squeal of terror that would carry out across Chicago. Dillon himself had heard that sound once years before when a fire had set the animals off. It had so chilled him—he was twelve years old—that he'd vowed never to work in the stockyards, that awful place, that hell. When later he'd found that it was to be a job there or nowhere, he'd swallowed his qualm and put in for steam so that he would have less to do with the animals.

The pipefitters were not kings of the place, or even princes. The kings were knifemen; the princes were livestock handlers and the buyers. By most definitions the pipefitters weren't ranked with the stockyard royalty at all, but they were organized nevertheless according to their own rigid caste, and they regarded themselves—whatever the shit-kickers or cutters said—as an elite. Jack Hanley had accepted Dillon into it because he'd needed a helper at the time, and because Dillon was fresh out of the seminary where he'd been friends with Hanley's nephew.

That was six years ago. By now Hanley had taught Dillon damn near everything he knew, and though the older man would never have admitted it, their relationship had in fact subtly changed. Dillon was a savvy worker, but he was more than that. He had an agile, strong body and an even more agile brain. Mostly the job of steamfitters was to solve the incessant problems of three dozen burdened, aging boiler systems which generated not only steam heat for the huge buildings but also heat essential to the manufacture of margarine, lard, dressed beef and tinned hams. Finding leaks, repairing cisterns, sealing joints, rerouting pipes, maintaining huge cookers and hooking up new water lines to those already in place all involved a feel for systems you could never fully see. Dillon could picture how the steam works ran in the Swift packinghouses better than the old-timers who'd helped lay them out. The old-timers had of course been better fitters than draftsmen, and the drawings they left behind were often useless even to the men, like Hanley, who had learned directly from them. So Hanley, in drawing *his* rigs, as in plumbing his holes and applying his sealers, had come to depend as much on young Dillon's intuition as on his own memory of what some old fool had taught him back near the turn of the century. Hanley was grateful that it suited Dillon to stay on his slate, though Dillon could have had a slate of his own for a long time now. He had a fierce ambition but, lucky for Hanley, it had nothing to do with the hierarchy of Swift's plumbery.

But that didn't mean Dillon couldn't understand why all stockyarders, even plumbers, lived in dread of a panicked herd. The herd's order was the goal toward which all the other levels of order in the yards were directed—the physical order of the grid layout, the political order that elevated handlers, the ceremonies of stately animal procession through the chutes behind the Judas cow. And the main function of all that order was to keep the animal victims blind to the truth of what awaited them. And wasn't that semblance of order, in turn, how the men kept *themselves* blind to what the yards were doing, day in and day out, to them?

"Yes, Jack, I know what it means if the animals snap. But that's the handlers' problem. A dead killing line is a knife-man's problem. Or it's the top boss's problem; tell Moran to call Mr. Swift." Dillon had put his clean shirt on and now began to button it. "We're pipefitters, Jack. Remember? Humble pipefitters."

"It's pipes that caused the problem. Blood pipes."

"Blood pipes! Jack, blood pipes are the trap cleaners' job, not ours." Trap cleaning was the scum job of scum jobs.

"It's not the traps. They've checked the traps. Blood backed up a foot deep in *all* the killing rooms. No single trap blocks that much blood. The amount of it is what shut the lines down. Blood is over their boots down there."

Dillon studied Hanley's soft face. The familiar stale odor of alcohol poured off his breath. His rheumy eyes didn't move from Dillon's. The plea Dillon saw in them made him uncomfortable. "Jack, I've got to get downtown. I have to be there by five."

"Moran's the one who called me. He's waiting for us."

"Why is Moran on it?"

"The whole fucking line is down. Nothing's moving anywhere! Of course the boss would be on it. They expect the cows and hogs to break out any time. And the boys are coming out from State Street. Moran wants the fix before they get here. They're on him, and he's on me."

"And you're on me."

"We have to figure which pipe is clogged."

"Did they check the tanks? Are the holding tanks full up? That would do it."

"Moran must have checked the tanks first. He says it has to be the pipes. Jesus, Mary, and Joseph, there are probably fifty miles of cast-iron pipe—"

"Then it's a box basin, Jack."

"What?"

"If the runoff is backed up everywhere, and if the tanks aren't full. A clogged pipe by itself wouldn't do it. If it was one lousy pipe, the flow would only reverse as far as the nearest junction and find another way to run. You'd get backup in one section, maybe two, but not everywhere. But if the downpipe of the box is fouled, it backs up equally through all four feeder pipes, and then you get tankage all over the place."

"But the downpipe, that's three feet across! What could clog a downpipe?"

"How many box basins are there under the house?"

"Four."

"And which one is closest to the lines?"

"There's one at the pickle rooms."

Dillon took his shirt off. For a moment he stared at Hanley, who touched a hand to his own bristly cheek. Dillon saw his fingers shake. Dillon wanted to say, Jack, it's not that complicated. If you'd thought about it for a minute instead of running to me, you could be there already, cleaning the thing.

Dillon faced away to reach into his locker for his rank overalls. How he hated them and how he hated this place and how he hated, for that instant, the pull of his own unexpressed affection for this dumb bastard. He glanced at his watch where it lay on the top shelf of his locker. Still with his back to Hanley, pulling on his work clothes once again, he said, "I'll get you started, Jack. But I can't see it through. I've *got* to get downtown by five."

"You said that."

"I just want you to know I mean it." Dillon braced himself. It had been a while since Jack had given him shit about school, but he sensed it coming now. Hanley wanted Sean Dillon holding his wrenches forever.

But Hanley said simply, "I appreciate it." And then he moved away.

When, after dressing, he turned to look for Jack, all he saw were the other fellows who'd drifted in from the shower room. They were at their lockers, too, weary to talk to each other, too indifferent. They showed no sign of the emotional lift Dillon felt at the end of every shift. Of course Dillon rarely showed any sign of such a feeling either; around the stockyards he was as expressionless as any of them. The Stone Gate, he'd often thought, turned men who entered it to stone, like Eddie Quinn there, sitting motionless on his bench, his towel across his middle, apparently unable even to reach for his clothes. Beyond him Pat Riordan was picking his fingernails with a skinner's knife, as if he were ready to turn his skill against his own parts, to carve the stench from his skin.

Jack Hanley was at his own locker. Dillon watched as Hanley pulled furtively on a bottle of hoochinoo. Like a lot of yarders, maybe most of them, Jack needed more than a double shot at the tavern on the way in and another on the way out. The rotgut got him through his shift, but the rotgut was also why Jack was less and less able to remember on his own which way the pipe screws ran. As he watched Hanley drink, Dillon fixed on the familiar tattoo on the back of Hanley's hand, what Dillon knew to be a faded Celtic cross with a lily sprouting from its base. Years ago members of the stockyards branch of the Ancient Order of Hibernians had made the mark a sign of membership until the priest from St. Gabriel's had condemned tattoos as self-mutilation. Dillon had often fixed his gaze upon the gaudy cross while Jack used that hand to apply his wrenches. An image of the resurrection, with its lily, yet the thing always seemed full of grief to Dillon.

When Hanley had wiped his mouth, returned the bottle to its shelf and closed his locker, he faced Dillon from across the room, ignoring the others, and he intoned, "Praised be His Holy Name." Even at that distance Dillon was struck by how bright Hanley's eyes had gotten with the sudden jolt of alcohol, and he saw his partner for an instant as one of the big-eyed animals outside, holding off panic while waiting in the crush of the pens for what it thinks will be release.

Hanley left the changing room. When Dillon caught up with him in the dingy corridor he was at the phone. "Give me Mr. Moran," he was saying. He looked back at Dillon, raised a clenched fist and grinned. A moment later he leaned into the mouthpiece again, turning away from Dillon, his voice excited and youthful. "Mr. Moran, I think I've got it figured. Forget the traps. Forget reaming the pipes. If the jam was one pipe, we wouldn't have backup everywhere. It's got to be a box basin, Mr. Moran . . . Yes, sir. Thems where the several horizontals meet the whatcha-call downpipe. That's what runs to the cookers—" Hanley stopped abruptly and swung back to look at Sean. Alarm showed on his face, and a question.

Dillon took his arm and whispered, "Tell him you'll check out the pickle room box. Tell him to get his fellows to the other ones. Tell him where they are." Hanley did so and then, dismissed, hung up.

Moments later the pair of them pounded down the dimly lit stairs to the long low corridor that led to the pickle rooms where, in great foul vats of steaming brine, countless slabs of hind-cut beef were soaking. Dillon walked behind Hanley carrying the cumbersome wooden toolbox. Usually, on his way to a job, he liked to picture what they would find, but now his mind was blank. He knew that if he was right, they were about to open the lid on a car-sized pit full of blood, but he couldn't imagine it.

They came to the cast-iron disk on the floor.

Without a word from either, Hanley put his hand out and Dillon slapped a foot-long crowbar into his palm. With one swift jerk of the rod Hanley had the heavy cover open, and he expertly pried it up with a flip so that it twirled for a moment like a coin, then fell clear. The stink blasted out, pushing them back, the odor of death, a fetid tomb.

Dillon tied his soiled handkerchief around his face.

Hanley pinched his nose and craned over the hole. "Boy, oh boy, give me the light, Sean, will you?"

Dillon slapped the flashlight into his partner's hand. When the beam of light hit the hole, they saw what seemed to be its floor, a gleaming dark asphalt surface only a foot below the lip of the basin. But it wasn't the floor; it wasn't asphalt. The utter lack of movement—no ripples, no bubbles—made the liquid look solid. They both knew at once that this was it, but as if to be certain Hanley moved his hand away from his nose and spit into the hole. His oyster splashed. He looked up at Sean and nodded.

Sean stared back at him, understanding that Jack Hanley expected him, the helper, to hoist himself down into the pit. Each man was over six feet tall. The blood would reach at least to the level of their shoulders. In order to free the downpipe it would almost certainly be necessary to go under. Dillon shook his head, his voice muffled by his bandana. "I took my shower, Jack. Remember?"

Hanley looked around at his feet. "What if we had a pole-and-hook?"

"You could go up to supply and get one, maybe run into Moran, or you can get this thing over with."

"I'm not sober enough to get in there."

Dillon, who was too sober, laughed, but the space closed in on him. A single dim bulb protruded from a wall socket a dozen yards down the corridor. If he stretched out his arms he could have touched both walls.

Dillon thought suddenly of the catacombs, the tunnels under Rome. Once such an association would have come into his mind with sharp alacrity. He'd have taken comfort in the sense of his own membership in the great communion, for the catacombs were the womb of the Church. But wasn't the womb what he had left? Now he thought of the tunnel-like sub-basement under the residence building at the major seminary. In its cubicles were the side altars where the faculty priests said their private Masses before dawn with cassocked boys like Dillon himself in holy attendance.

Dillon chided himself. It wasn't the womb he'd left, but only training for the priesthood. He rarely welcomed memories from that long, futile phase of his life, and he didn't now. This one had caught him off guard, and he stood there in the dark corridor staring at the unseen with hollow eyes. At moments like that it seemed to him he could feel the blood moving inside his body, but now—blood!—that was an image he wanted no part of. What he wanted was some visual detail on which to fix his concentration, but he saw nothing, save the light bulb itself, with which to stave off his moroseness. The catacombs were where the martyrs lived and where they buried each other. It probably stank like this, he thought.

"Here goes nothing," Hanley said as he plopped down onto the lip of the hole. He stared into it for a moment, removed none of his clothing and swung down feet-first. "I hate this fucking job. Oh, it's warm!"

"I'll hold your hat, Jack." Dillon plucked Hanley's hat from his bald head. That baldness was always a surprise, and so was the recognition that gruff Jack Hanley wore his hat out of vanity.

"Oh, Jesus, Mary, and Joseph." Hanley had himself braced between the walls of the box basin, and was working his feet. "Something squishy is what it is. Something's there, though. Oh, Jesus, God, this is awful."

Clotted blood, Dillon thought. A slimy concretion had blocked the downpipe. Coagulation.

But he dismissed the idea. The diameter of the pipe was too large.

Hanley sank deeper into the ooze.

But what was it? Nothing solid could come into this basin. Not unless it came, instead of through the feeder pipes, through this hole here.

Dillon looked up when he heard the men barreling down the corridor toward them. Moran was in the lead, a short, fat man with a cigar in his face, a man Dillon had made a point of staying clear of. Behind him were two others, each wearing a bandana around his nose, like holdup men. They were dressed in business suits—the boys, therefore, from State Street.

Hanley said, "Keep the light on me." Then he ducked into the hole, disappearing in the black liquid.

"What'd you find?" Moran demanded.

"This is it, all right," Dillon said. "Jack had it figured."

"So is it clear?" Moran peered down into the hole. The liquid swirled now with Hanley's movement. The two Swift's executives stood warily back. Each man's eyes above the stretched material of his kerchief danced wildly.

Hanley burst from under with an explosion, and the foul liquid splashed up onto all of them. Hanley collapsed onto the lip of the pit, gagging. "It's a carcass!" he croaked before a fit of coughing overtook him.

"A carcass?" Moran stooped down to him. "What do you mean? A whole carcass?"

Hanley ignored Moran for Dillon. He stared right up into the beam of the flashlight, and once more Dillon saw his eyes as those of a near-panicked animal. "It's whole," Hanley gasped. "A hog, I think. Really jammed. I can't get it out alone."

Dillon stepped back, thinking, Hell no. But Hanley's eyes held him.

And Moran swung to look up at him. "Get down there, you. Help him haul the goddamn thing out of there."

"How would an entire hog get in this pit?" It was one of the boys from downtown. No one answered his question or acknowledged hearing it.

Nor did Dillon acknowledge Moran. As always, it was something in Hanley's mute plea that tore at his defenses. Still he did not move. He thought of the stupid cattle following their Judas to the slaughter.

"What's your name?" Moran demanded.

Now Dillon looked at him, and he saw that this crisis was his excuse, only his latest, to lash out at underlings. Stuff yourself, Dillon thought. He felt the freedom of a man who was quitting soon anyway. But Moran would hold Hanley responsible for the impudence of his helper. Hanley wasn't quitting, and Dillon knew he'd be a fool to make enemies at Swift's.

"Who me, sir?" Dillon said, Charlie Chaplin coming to.

"I said get in there and help him."

"Oh yessir, I see, sir," he said, fluttering the handkerchief that covered his nose and mouth. Dillon handed the flashlight to Moran and indicated the toolbox at his feet. "Watch me tools, would you kindly?" He spoke with a stagy brogue, suddenly one of those Irishmen who clothed his hatred thinly in mock ingratiation. He stooped to untie and remove his boots, then quickly unbuttoned his overalls and slid out of them, abruptly naked. When he'd removed the handkerchief from his face, he grinned stupidly at Moran. "Whatever you say, sir." And he climbed into the pit gingerly, like a lad into the lake on a cold spring morning. In fact, Dillon hated going into water.

Dillon's feet nearly slipped out from under him when they landed on a soft squishy mass. He looked at Hanley. "This is one you owe me, Jack." Then he gulped air and went under. Despite his tightly closed mouth, the sharp taste of blood revolted him beyond what any foul odor had done.

Together they tugged at the beast that was jammed head-first into the downpipe. Blood had coagulated around the head in the ring of the pipe, sealing off the tankage flow completely and holding the animal fast. They had to force it loose.

"Animal" was the word Dillon used in his mind, but he knew better. He knew better when his feet first touched the thing.

"Oh, Jesus," Hanley gasped when they broke into air again.

They had to work to maintain the hold they had on the slippery carcass. The pit full of blood had become a whirlpool, sucking the liquid downward and out at last through the opening below. They had only to stand there, straddling the downpipe, as the level of the blood dropped, exposing them and the naked white hulk they were holding.

"A man!" Moran gasped.

"Oh, Christ!" one of the boys from downtown muttered, while the other one fell back against the wall, then down to the floor in a dead faint.

Moran aimed the flashlight beam at the figure slumped between Hanley and Dillon. He stooped down for a handful of the dead man's matted hair, to pull its head back, to see the face. But when he laid eyes on the swollen black mass into which all of this body's blood had run, he gagged. He straightened up and stepped back. "Get him out of there."

Hanley and Dillon had to lock their arms around the corpse to heave it up to the floor. The side of Dillon's face pressed into the dead man's buttock. Hanley seemed to be in shock, and Dillon had to lift him out too. Hanley collapsed on the cold concrete next to the carcass, gasping. It was Moran, the cigar still in his face, who then reached a hand down for

Dillon. Moran hauled him up easily, and Dillon understood for the first time that the superintendent's toughness was real.

While Dillon got back into his overalls, Moran satisfied himself that the blood pipes were running freely now, then he slid the heavy iron cover back into place without help. It clanged shut.

In the silence it was Jack Hanley's inability to catch his breath that the others focused on. The front-office man who'd fainted came to slowly and got to his feet, leaning on his colleague. Moran ignored them, waiting for Hanley to compose himself. Finally he said, more to Dillon than Hanley, "You two wait here. I'll send a wagon down for . . ." He looked at the maggot-like corpse and winced. ". . . this thing."

Dillon asked, "Who is he, do you think?"

Moran shook his head. "His own mother wouldn't know at this point. Whoever he is, he crossed the wrong people, that's sure." He shifted his glance to Dillon. "He was flogged."

Dillon looked again and saw the grid of slivered skin on the corpse's back. Drained of blood, the welts were white, like the slats of Venetian blinds.

"You know whose mark a flogging is, don't you?" Moran seemed to be testing Dillon. When Dillon only shook his head, Moran said, "You wait here until my blokes come." He turned abruptly toward the pair in business suits. When he pointed along the corridor they went obediently, as if they too were his inferiors. Here—and at this—they were.

When the others were gone, and when Hanley was sitting up against the wall, having put some space between himself and the cadaver, Dillon said quietly, "I have to go, Jack." He began wiping his hands on his kerchief.

Hanley looked up at him helplessly.

"I told you before. I have to get downtown. It's not just a routine class tonight. It's an exam."

"Exam?" The word had reference to a world Hanley had nothing to do with.

"I have to go right now."

Hanley made his plea with his eyes.

For once Dillon had a plea of his own, if no way to make it. The exam was the last thing standing between Dillon and the other man it was long past time for him to be. This was the end of his fifth year of night school. He was nearly thirty years old, and if he didn't get out of the pit soon, the blood was go-

ing to swallow him. He said quietly, "Moran's people will be
here before you know it, Jack. You'll be all right with . . ."
Dillon's voice trailed off.

"Who is the guy, do you think?" Hanley had roused himself
to stare blearily at the corpse.

Dillon shook his head, but his eye fell upon a blue mark.
The pasty, wrinkled body was lying face-down, but its puffy
arm, clearly out of its socket, was bent perversely back across
its own shoulder blade. Instead of the palm of that hand, such
was the break that the back of it was showing. And that was
where Dillon saw the mark, a blue tattoo. The taste of blood
shot into his mouth again, and he retched violently, as if, finally, he was going to vomit. The tattoo was of a Celtic cross
with a sprouting lily. Whatever the creature was now, once
he'd been a man; once he'd been one of Jack Hanley's boys at
St. Gabe's.

Dillon looked back at his partner. The dumb bastard's
clothes were soaked through, and now he was shivering. Dillon
reached down to the tool chest onto which Hanley's hat had
fallen. He picked it up and crossed to him, wishing it was a
bottle of booze. "Here's your hat, Jack."

Hanley took it and put it on. Dillon saw something in the
way he did so—covering himself, hiding his baldness, hiding
his face—that seemed as hideous as anything he'd seen in that
grotesque hour. His old friend, to whom in fact he had never
spoken the word "friend," felt ashamed.

Dillon leaned his shoulder against the rough cinder wall and
slid slowly down it, to sit by Hanley, to wait with him who
said nothing.

TWO

At the beginning of the century the Union Elevated Railroad had built a continuous double-track line that made a closed rectangle above Lake, Van Buren, Wabash, and Wells streets. This elevated ring was called the Union Loop when it opened, but before long it and the urban core it served were commonly referred to simply as the Loop. Every store, office building, and theater in the heart of Chicago was within a short walk of one of ten Loop stations, and at first the downtown Elevated was regarded as an absolute boon. But it brought such a concentration of building within its limits that eventually the Loop began to strangle itself. By 1939 pedestrian and automobile traffic inside its boundaries was always congested, and at rush hour it barely moved.

So now, late on that August afternoon, as the warm sun mellowed, a Chicago redhead had to cut through the tides of the crowded sidewalk on her way home from work. From an office window above the street, from a passing bus, from the United Cigar Store on the corner, from within the throng itself, men and women noticed her. Mainly they noticed her flashing crimson hair, the downpour to her shoulders, which from a distance, set against the sea of dark fedoras, seemed the center of a moving circle of light.

She was slender, but her body wasn't punctuated with angles, and she had no need to lead with her elbows like others, because the rough crowd parted slightly just ahead of her. It would have seemed a presumption to bump her, as if she were Maureen O'Hara or the Luxite Hosiery Girl. She walked with a steady serenity, oblivious, taking for granted the small deference that others unconsciously showed her. She had the vibrancy of a woman on the brink of her first society curtsy.

Her name was Cassie Ryan, and she wasn't what she seemed. She had never made a curtsy in her life, much less a movie. She was a working girl, and except for what she saw in films and magazines, she knew nothing of society. If she arranged her hairstyle, clothing, and makeup to imitate the looks of screen stars and the lovelies of soap ads—Djer-Kiss Talc and Mum Cream were the Guardians of Her Personal Daintiness—that was because she was just like all the other girls who worked for a living in the Loop, where the sweethearts of the dress balls and cotillions wouldn't be caught dead.

Cassie was glad for the summer air and glad to have her face back after its eight-hour stint inside the wire-and-leather headset of a telephone operator. She was only twenty-four years old, but she had eight years seniority with the phone company. That and her easy way with her fellow switchboard girls had led to her appointment as supervisor of her shift, with thirty operators on her rotation. They were would-be Myrna Loys and Janet Gaynors, but they were unmusical Kate Smiths too. After a day of tending to her girls, checking on the old-timers, cajoling the new ones to be peppy, being peppy herself; after a day of taking the public's complaints—Cassie's trick was to be half again as courteous as the malcontent was rude—it was a relief to be out and moving toward the El. She was unaware that the eyes of others were unrolling a carpet for her; she walked on it nonetheless like it was hers.

Cassie Ryan's office, the stolid American Bell Building, was on North La Salle Street near the intersecting train line. Most girls regarded having the El so close as an advantage, but she hated the way the hulking mass of steel cast its shadow on the street like a permanent tent. In the summer, as now, that shadow made the street cooler, it was true, but who would want to tarry there? Cassie remembered from excursions downtown as a child that the Loop's boundary streets were blighted even before the Depression, but now those streets were full of cheap stores, flophouses, and deteriorating buildings. In their alcoves panhandlers huddled between forays out into the crowd, and they were a particular problem for Cassie.

Most commuters seemed able to push through those outstretched, palsied hands as if they were the branches of bushes, but Cassie could not. The respectably dressed office workers and shop girls, in their refusal even to see the derelicts, seemed certain of their superiority, but she knew better than to feel that way. She knew how desolate those men were from the way they looked at her when she gave them coins. Her girlfriends chided Cassie for doing that, and more than once her mother had forbidden her to give money to men on the streets. Handouts, she said, were what enabled them to stay away from home. Which of course was the point. Cassie's mother wasn't stingy. Her bitter attitude came from the hurt of what had happened in *their* home.

And not only theirs. By that phase of the Depression most of the girls Cassie knew had lost men to those alcoves and those alleys and those eerie circles around oil-drum fires. Cassie's loss—her mother's—had come early. She had had to go to work in the first place when her father disappeared way back in 1932. She hadn't finished high school and had had to lie about her age to get the switchboard job. When, after her first raise, she'd begun putting pennies into the chapped hands of beggars, it was to make them look at her. She wouldn't release her coin until the man looked up. Then she would stare carefully into his face, hoping it was familiar. Her green eyes had been her father's first.

And she was still doing it. She always had her coins ready, to enact what by now was a ritual from which she expected nothing for herself. She was giving those men pennies and nickels because they needed them.

"God bless *you*, Miss," one derelict said, raising his eyes to her.

Cassie sensed that the man wasn't nearly as old as he looked. His face, what she saw of it beneath his lumpy felt hat, was etched with that familiar shame. But nothing else about him was familiar, and she hurried by.

She hopped onto the first step of the stairway going up to the El. The iron structure shook with the weight of all the people. As she climbed with them, it seemed to Cassie she could feel the sadness of her fellow commuters.

As if to change her mood, she swung her shoulder bag from her right side to her left as she took the last steps up to the platform. A man tipped his hat at her, and she smiled unselfconsciously. There was always more to be glad about than sad.

God bless *you*, she said to herself, repeating the derelict's words, but as a prayer.

Halfway down the crowded platform she found her usual waiting place by the cloudy, cracked window from which she could both watch for her train and look back down on the street. Her eyes went automatically to the beggar in the felt hat a few paces beyond the stairway. From there, seen through the hazy glass, he seemed a figure in a mournful side window at church. God bless *you*, she said again. And then she added with a sharp, unexpected pang, All of you.

A few minutes later her train came. Cassie always welcomed the jolt of departure, the sensation at the base of her spine as the car began to accelerate. She thought that riding the El above Chicago was as close as she would ever come to flying. That was why, despite her weariness and the perennial crush of the other riders, the time it took to go from North La Salle to Canaryville seemed sometimes to be the best of her day. She never refused a gentleman's offer of his seat if it let her face the window, especially the window on the right side of the car from which she could stare out over the western stretches of the city as the sunset approached. Chicago was so flat and, once away from downtown, the buildings were so low that, even lifted above the rooftops only that much, it was possible to see for miles. The sight of the squared-off ribbons of roadway soothed her with its familiar uniformity. The dwellings of working people were all alike, and to look out above them was to see a checkered plain of tar paper and asphalt. Only the sharp upward thrust of church spires and factory chimneys broke the horizontal monotony, and those towers glowed in the kindly light of the early evening.

When the train jogged off Archer Avenue to turn due south onto the branch of tracks that ran down Halsted, the Elevated began its slow descent to the level of the street, and Cassie strained to get a last glimpse of the distant city. Between the jagged rooflines of tenements and warehouses she saw flashes off the sheen of the south fork at the point where it met the old canal, the Illinois and Michigan, that joined the waters of the lake and the Mississippi thirty miles away. She'd read in one of the books her supervisor had given her—Ellen Flynn thought she should be educating herself—that the linking of those two great waterways was what had made Chicago happen in the first place. The city would have developed in a straight band westward, straddling the canal, if the whole water system hadn't been made suddenly obsolete by the invention of the railroad. You just never know. Trains had come into Chicago mainly from the south, so it was southward the city went. The South Side, Cassie's world, was built around the railroad, and that seemed fitting, since it was the Irish enclave, and most Irishmen, including her own father, had made their way west from Ellis Island as laborers on those railroads. Cassie Ryan was quite aware that her part of Chicago, instead of straddling water which never tired of flowing, straddled iron which never moved. She herself was more like water than iron, but she could not imagine that she would ever leave her family, her neighborhood, or her parish behind. But neither could she imagine that Halstead Street and North La Salle would be the boundaries of her world forever.

"We Feed The World," the huge billboard read as the train—now the streetcar, not the El—crossed Thirty-ninth Street, into the yards district. The big sign had been there on top of the five-story corner building for as long as Cassie could remember. It was the slogan of Armour and Company, but South Siders generally took it as their motto. Cassie could not read that sign anymore, though, without immediately dropping her eyes to the Halsted sidewalk where the ragged line of men in torn jackets and battered hats always waited. It was the laborers' line outside the Armour jobs office; the men there now were hoping for something on the night shift. Cassie saw them as a hiring agent might: desperate, unsteady men, half of them cradling brown paper bundles, the bottles they brought with them everywhere. We Feed The World, she thought harshly, not for the first time, but who feeds us?

When Cassie stepped off the streetcar onto the island in the middle of the broad avenue, she took a deep breath, as if daring the stench of her own neighborhood to offend her nostrils. She chided herself for even noticing it, but that was the great disadvantage of leaving St. Gabriel's each day. For years stockyard odors had bothered her no more than the smells of her own body. She looked across at the Stone Gate and beyond. The chimney-ridden yards even then at the end of the day were pumping clouds of burnt offal into the wind.

Above the street noises she heard the sound of a voice on the air, someone calling her name. She turned toward it, knowing right away that something was wrong.

Cassie had six brothers and sisters, only two of whom were still at home. But her family was bigger than that, even, for in the flat upstairs lived her aunt and uncle and their four young daughters, the eldest of whom, Molly, was standing on the far curb now. She was waving frantically. Molly was thirteen. She was still wearing the white blouse and blue skirt of her uniform. Why hadn't she changed clothes after school? One tail of her blouse overhung the front of her skirt.

Molly cried Cassie's name again and stepped from the curb into the street. But immediately an automobile screeched to a halt just short of her. The driver honked violently and Molly jumped back. A beer truck swerved away from her, cutting off a car in the next lane. Rush hour traffic had thinned out just enough that the cars were traveling at speed again, whipping along in the three lanes between the cousins. Molly froze, her hands at her mouth, staring across at Cassie.

Cassie could see that her eyes were nearly blind with tears. "Wait there!" she called with the authority of a parent. "Get back on the sidewalk!"

Cassie's legs twitched to be moving, but she forced herself to wait on the streetcar island until the traffic broke. She never took her eyes from Molly, her darling, clever Molly. Molly whose mind gave her no peace, who fussed forever over pencils and foot rule, over lists of state capitals and the great dates of history. Of all her cousins, or even sisters, Molly was the one most like Cassie herself.

"Molly, Molly," Cassie said, enfolding her when finally she'd crossed the avenue. "What is it, hon?"

But Molly only sobbed into Cassie's body. How thin she is, Cassie thought, pressing her own long fingers into her cousin's bony back. Molly was a girl who had nightmares over and over, but who on waking could never say what had so terrified her.

"What is it, darling?" Cassie gently pushed the girl out of the corner her arms had made.

Molly opened her mouth but could not speak. She seemed retarded or mute. A wave of worry washed over Cassie. This was the child, more than the others, to whom she'd given herself. Molly's intelligence had been evident early, and one of the things Cassie's salary had always meant to her was that Molly was not going to have to drop out of school. But Molly was as fragile as she was smart. She stared into Cassie's eyes now, a look of pure terror on her face.

Jerry's face flashed into Cassie's mind. Jerry? Her brother, two years her junior, was the only one of her siblings who had a steady job, but it was a job Cassie had never liked. He worked in the carshops where the meat packers' refrigerated railroad cars were repaired. How many collections had been taken up at St. Gabe's for carshop men whose legs or arms had been crushed under the huge iron wheels of—

"Pa's dead, Cassie." Molly's face collapsed around her mouth as she forced the words out again. "Pa's dead."

Cassie's elbows stiffened, an involuntary reflex which pushed Molly away the length of her arms. It was like pushing off from the ground, a seesaw.

"Ma sent me to wait for you. I didn't know—"

"What?"

"Pa's dead."

"Pa? *Your* Pa? Uncle Mike?"

Molly shook her head up and down, making the tears fly from her cheeks.

Cassie pressed her cousin's shoulders, but really it was into herself that she was pressing, to force calm into her voice. "Tell me, Molly. You've been waiting here to tell me."

But already Cassie knew she was not going to believe her. Uncle Mike? Dead? It couldn't be. Uncle Mike was the man who'd taken over the place in Cassie's heart, what her own Pa had left empty. But then an image shot into her mind of her poor, soft Uncle Mike sprawled facedown on the sidewalk outside Dooley's. Like most of his kind, Mike Foley was long unemployed and by now beaten down by the sense of his own failure. Unlike so many others, he had never turned that frustration against his wife, and his daughters loved him. Cassie loved him.

She shook her cousin. "What happened?" And while she waited for the stunned girl to speak, she repeated to herself, It can't be.

Sean Dillon stared at the cross. The figure of the crucified Christ seemed tidy, a man in vertical repose, a positively tranquil image compared to the bloated cadaver from the blood pipes. Moran's knuckle-draggers had taken their time getting to the box basin, but when they came they plopped the corpse

onto an iron-wheeled hand truck and took it away without a
word, as if they were carting off the remains, say, of a disease-
ridden rejected hog. Where were the police? Where was a doctor to pronounce the body dead? Those questions had occurred
to Dillon, but he had to get downtown.

Now he was sitting in the anteroom of the dean's office at
Loyola. His restless fingers jitterbugged on his knees. To his
great regret he was still wearing the threadbare shirt and trousers he had changed into at the slaughterhouse, not having
dared take the time to go to his room. Not the rancid overalls
he'd worn to and from the blood pit, true, but not the suit and
tie he usually wore to night school either. He was nobody's
idea of a professional-in-training now. The skin on the backs of
his hands and on his face glowed even more from the ruthless
scrubbing he'd given himself in the shower again. If he'd
scraped away whole layers of skin, exposing nerve endings and
pores, perhaps that was the reason for his strange, unsettled
sense of vulnerability. He saw himself as a rube, hadn't felt so
ill at ease in years. How long had it been since he was publicly
rebuked by a professor. "Get out!" the man had screamed.
"Get out!" As if Dillon was an obnoxious janitor come too
early to clean the classroom.

Dillon's eyes went from the dean's secretary's vacant desk
to the wall behind it where a clock showed that it was nearly
eight, which was when his classmates would finish the exam.
He'd found it impossible to explain himself to his stern professor, and the dean would be worse. If he told him the unvar-
nished truth—lifting the swollen, rotten corpse had been like
lifting a mass of congealed lard—would the Jesuit think him
mad? What would justify tardiness, even to a final exam, if not
such a grotesque event? But Dillon had sensed shame in
Hanley, and he knew he was uneasy now because, however
unaccountably, he felt ashamed too. Why? For being one of a
species that would do such a thing? The poor bastard had been
stuffed into the blood pipe like a cork.

He focused again on the crucifix which hung on the wall directly opposite his chair. He had never beheld the sacred object
as a source of consolation, and in the seminary that had come
to seem like a failure of faith. Always the corpus's gnarled
boniness—the ribs like teeth, the knees like fists—had seemed
a rebuke to him for his not being in pain. The figure's hollow
eyes were grottoes out of which accusations flew. Turning

away from the crucifix, in fact, had been like turning away
from the sight, on the street, of the desperate characters whom
the years had reduced to human offal. That Dillon had long
ago given up even imagining that he could help them had
come to seem like both the height of his new realism and, still
and always, the serious sin a pious boy sees in his furtive
omission. He had concluded that the most insidious thing
about the Depression was the way in which people who were
barely scraping by—most of the people Dillon knew—felt that
their survival, such as it was, came at the expense of those—
the rest of the people he knew—who'd been chewed up by the
age and spit out.

The man in the pipes: Why do I feel ashamed? Someone
else did that, not me.

He remembered Moran's reference: Whose mark was it, the
shredded skin of a flogging?

Dillon shook the questions off, but he was still unable to
look away from the cross. What the cross proves, he thought,
is that if you befriend a leper, as Jesus did so famously, you
become one. No wonder the religion could be so bitter. The
cross was pure warning, a clenched, stingy gesture. No wonder
most of what it promulgated served mainly to keep people in
their cramped, dark corners. Normal Catholic piety had been
impossible for Dillon since before he'd abandoned his vocation
to the priesthood, and doubly so since.

The dean was a priest, and he could blast him the way Professor Corrigan had, but the dean would know no more about
what had mattered at the yards than the dandruff-ridden torts
professor had.

"Tort," Dillon recited to himself, "any wrongful act not involving breach of contract, for which a civil action will lie."

Wrongful act, as in walking out on a helpless friend. Dillon
would simply explain about the cross, that other cross, the poor
bastard's Celtic cross tattoo.

"Tort," he recited, "the breach of a duty imposed by law
whereby some person acquires a right for action for damages."
Tort, from the Latin *tortus*, past participle of *torquere*, meaning
twisted, wrung, or, as in the English, tortured.

As in the cross. He stared at it hard. The symbol of a tortured people. The symbol, whether he liked it or not, of who
he was. The Son of Man flogged, His skin shredded, His body
left to rot through all history on a pair of beams. Dillon could

not stifle his old question, the one he had been told never to ask: Are we supposed to be *consoled* that God has joined us in this?

The door beside him banged open, and the lean stooped figure of Professor Corrigan stumbled in, burdened with a stack of books and examination papers. Inside his rumpled brown serge jacket the point of one shirt collar was bent up above his tie, like a flap. His tie was askew. The sight of Dillon had obviously startled him, and now he peered over the rims of his glasses, his eyes flaring as they had when Dillon entered the examination hall nearly two hours late.

Dillon stood, eager to show the man the deference he seemed to require. But Corrigan turned brusquely away and crossed to the door of the dean's inner office. He knocked, and from within came a muffled sound which the professor took as permission. He went through the door, clutching his books and papers. It closed with a bang behind him.

Dillon sat again. He brushed the back of his hand against his nostrils, whiffing it. He smelled nothing.

The dean's door opened. The black-robed Jesuit stood there holding it, but not for Dillon, as he first supposed. Professor Corrigan, still with his armload, brushed by the priest without a word. Three paces took him across the anteroom, his eyes rigidly avoiding Dillon. When he fumbled at the knob, Dillon sprang to his side to help him, but the professor managed the door on his own and, without a word, was gone.

"Come in, Mr. Dillon," the dean said coldly.

As Dillon crossed in front of him, he picked up the man's faint body odor. Away from the yards Dillon was a connoisseur of odors, and he put this one at two parts tobacco, one part the smoke of incense and one part stale perspiration pouring off an unlaundered cassock. A priest's odor, it automatically summoned Dillon's potent memory of the seminary rector. Once when Dillon was serving as an altar boy a consecrated host had fallen from the gold lip of the ciborium to the profane linoleum of the sanctuary floor, and when Sean Dillon, age eighteen, had instinctively reached for it, the rector had stomped on his hand with the heel of his stout, black, ankle-high boot.

Dillon took up his place facing the cluttered desk while the dean crossed behind it to sit. On the near edge of the massive mahogany desk Dillon read the Gothic letters of the nameplate: "Reverend Aloysius T. Ferrick, S.J."

"You have a problem, Mr. Dillon, a rather large problem."
It had been more than fifty years since the priest had come as
a child from Ireland, but he had an accent still.

"I understand that, Father."

"Professor Corrigan was more than a bit incensed at your
interruption. You caused a major distraction, he says."

"With all due respect, Father, it was his reaction that did
that. I was intending to slip quietly into my usual chair, which
isn't far from the door. Professor Corrigan—"

The Jesuit silenced him with an abruptly upraised hand.
"That isn't the issue anyway. The commotion isn't the issue."
Father Ferrick leaned forward to pick up a thin, black volume
from his desk. "Your problem, Mr. Dillon, is that regulations
of Loyola Law School"—he began leafing the pages, the book
of rules—"define absence from a terminal examination as ipso
facto cause for failure of the course in question."

"I was not absent, Father. I was late."

The Jesuit raised his eyes to Dillon. "Professor Corrigan has
failed you."

Dillon had to resist an urge to look behind himself; to whom
could this priest be talking?

"Failed?"

"Yes." Father Ferrick snapped the regulations closed and sat
back in his chair, relieved to have done his duty.

"But, Father, I hoped for a chance to explain myself."

"Loyola College Law School procedures require no explana-
tions of you, since none would mitigate the ruling. 'Ipso Facto'
is the operative phrase, Mr. Dillon."

"But if I fail this course, that means I can't take the bar next
month."

"I know that. I said as much to Professor Corrigan. He was
adamant."

"Can't I take the exam tomorrow?"

The dean shook his head. "Professor Corrigan's position is
that there is a principle here that must be upheld."

"But if I—"

"You will have to repeat the course next year. It is offered
again beginning in January."

Dillon thought his melting knees were going to collapse
under him. Next year! Impossible!

The stinking monstrosity he and Hanley had hauled out of

the blood pipes had finished him for working in the yards. Another year in the slaughter pits—impossible!

To stiffen his quaking legs, his quaking self, he used them to step toward the priest. "Father, you have to listen to me—"

But he stopped himself, afraid of the emotion he felt stinging the backs of his eyes. A voice in his brain instructed him, "Like a lawyer. Do this like a lawyer. You are a lawyer for yourself."

The lawyer's first idea is that discipline takes the place of feeling. Dillon forced a quality of detachment into his voice. "Father, I was late for the examination, too late to reasonably expect to take it, because a man was dead at my feet. I am speaking quite literally here. And my choices were two— either to abandon him before authorities arrived to deal with him or to maintain the vigil proper to the deceased despite the delay it caused. For the crucial time, it fell to me and me alone . . ." Was that true? Was it wrong to omit mention of Hanley? But Hanley might as well have been absent. The Jesuits themselves had taught Dillon the principle of the Pertinent Truth. ". . . to care for the dead, which I took to be my serious moral obligation. When help came I left at once and got downtown as fast as I could. I'm sure my rough appearance was part of what put Professor Corrigan in such a state."

"You work at the stockyards." The priest's hand went unconsciously to a closed manila folder, Dillon's own file, he realized.

"Yes. I am a steamfitter's helper." Jack Hanley's helper, he added to himself, and with a shock he realized that, moving with a lawyer's instinct to the best possible case for his behavior—with this Jesuit, a moral case based on the absolute Catholic obligation to respect the dead—he had, despite his careful rationalization about Pertinent Truth, just told the priest an explicit lie. He had stayed so long beside the corpse not for the dead man's sake, or for God's, but for Jack's. To someone else these distinctions might have seemed innocuous in the extreme, but to Dillon, a line had been crossed.

"And you say a man was dead?"

"I helped pull the body out of a blood sewer."

A stricken look crossed the dean's face. "I know what a hard place the stockyards are. It doesn't take much of a slip . . ."

The priest thought it was an accident. Dillon felt impelled to protect Father's innocence, as if murder were some kind of sexual sin the clergy should not hear of. He shrugged noncommittally. "It happened just at the end of my shift. There was no possible way for me to get here by five."

Dillon paused. Knowing the value of seeming to concede, how it undercuts an opponent's sense of power and makes him generous, he said, "I've offered my explanation not as an excuse, but because I want you to understand that only a conflict of conscience could have kept me from being here. I understand now that there is nothing you can do—"

The upraised hand again. "It is I who apply the regulations. Professor Corrigan . . ." And an upraised eyebrow, a hint of condescension which Dillon grasped at once. No one knew better than his students that Corrigan was a mediocre lawyer for whom teaching was a refuge. ". . . has done his duty. Now I must do mine. And my duty is to decide whether the intention of the lawmaker is served by applying the law in a particular case. It is a question of . . . ?" Now both the dean's eyebrows shot up, indicating the interrogatory.

"Epikaia," Dillon said at once.

"Precisely." Father Ferrick sat back, satisfied. "The truth, Mr. Dillon, is that you are quite well prepared for your torts exam, aren't you?"

"I believe so, Father."

"You haven't missed a step here in five years." He indicated the file. "You have compiled an excellent record. It would be an understatement to say that your professors, until now, have rated you highly."

"I appreciate that."

"It's not what they did; it's what you did." Father Ferrick paused, not troubling to conceal a glint in his eye that was at once admiring and self-satisfied. "It would have reflected badly on what we teach here if you had failed in your duty as a Catholic. The human body is the temple of the Holy Ghost and must be treated as such, even after the immortal soul has departed from it."

The pieties breezed by Dillon, familiar and meaningless.

"There's something else, Father," he said without meaning to. Suddenly it felt as if the grill of the confessional were between them, and now his words came unbidden, in a guilt-stricken rush. "I also stayed at the yards because my partner needed me to. That is"—here it was, an admission of the lie, the only way to undo it—"my partner was there. I wasn't alone."

Father Ferrick waved his hand dismissively. If this was a hollow spot in the wall of the case that had just convinced him, it was not a hole he cared to open.

Dillon felt relieved, but also foolish for being so easily teased by his own conscience.

Father Ferrick had picked up a page of Dillon's scholastic transcript. "You did your college work at seminary."

"That's right."

"But you left?"

Dillon answered, but only to himself. Of course I left. I'm sitting here, aren't I? He could feel the color coming into his face.

"You left after third theology."

"Yes, just before ordination to the deaconate. Just before vows."

"Do you mind my asking why?"

"Why I left?"

"Yes."

Dillon wanted to look out the window, to see the beauty of the evening, the shadows on the street, the men and women going out to shows. What could he possibly say?

For an instant he was back in the rector's office, the rector staring harshly at him, waiting for an explanation. Sean Dillon had been selected to go to Rome for his doctorate, and *this* was his response? Sean Dillon had been housed, clothed, fed and educated from the age of twelve, and *this* was his response? But Sean Dillon had had no response.

Now he said simply, "I left because I'd lost the sense of my vocation."

The Jesuit sighed dramatically. "Well, it's too bad. We hate to see the Church lose a good man." His teeth squeaked as he inhaled through them. "Do you ever reconsider?"

Dillon shook his head.

Ferrick dropped the transcript and folded the file shut. "The law is a noble calling too." He smiled. "I hope you can keep your sense of *this* vocation."

"I hope so too, Father." But then it hit him that he had just done the same thing to himself. He'd come within an inch of ordination, and now he'd come within an inch of the bar. Only to fall short? The nightmare was that his first failure to follow through would repeat itself again and again through his life. Dillon knew that that was exactly what the rector and all his disappointed seminary teachers expected would be his pattern. Or was it only that they hoped so?

Was this the real reason he'd stayed with Hanley, undermining himself without knowing it?

Father Ferrick surprised Dillon, cutting through the glue to say abruptly, "I want you to take that examination right away. Did you say you can do it tomorrow?

"Yes."

"I will speak to Professor Corrigan. He won't like it, but if you answer all the questions correctly, he won't have a move against you, will he?" Father Ferrick smiled suddenly. "And after the bar, what?"

Dillon shrugged. "I have six years in at Swift's. That should give me a shot at a job in their law department."

"Why not a law firm?"

Dillon looked quizzically at the dean. They both knew that the law firms, after a decade of steadily laying off their own lawyers, weren't hiring new graduates even out of the prestigious law schools, certainly not out of Loyola.

The Jesuit said quietly, "I have a contact at Lambert, Rowe . . ."

Dillon waited. Lambert, Rowe was one of the top State Street outfits.

"I could get you an interview." Loyola was at the point where it had to start placing graduates with better firms or accept permanent consignment to the ranks of the fly-by-night law schools that trained ambulance chasers, JPs and pols. Dillon was the best prospect Father Ferrick had seen in a long time. He turned his hand over, brandishing his palm. "The rest you'd have to do for yourself."

Dillon laughed with surprise. "One minute, Father, you're flunking me. The next minute—"

"The next minute I'm seeing in you a good example of what we try to do here. Is Swift's really what you want?"

"No."

"You'd have a little extra . . . work . . . to do if you wanted a real shot at Lambert, Rowe."

"What do you mean?"

"That you don't go into a State Street law office whistling 'The Bells of Saint Mary's.' "

"It's not a tune of mine, Father."

"Your first name is Sean. Jack Benny's real name is Benjamin Kubelsky. Did you know that?"

Dillon cursed himself for being unable to think what to say. Perhaps he lowered his eyes out of a sort of despair, but they fell upon the desk nameplate. "And yours is Aloysius."

"That's right. But if I wanted what you want, it would be Allen."

Dillon saw it then. "But you do. You just want it for Loyola, that's all." Dillon laughed at himself for thinking this priest was out for *him,* for thinking his reprieve could come without a price.

Father Ferrick leaned across the desk. "There's a bit too much of the harp, lad, in the likes of us."

"I don't lead with my Irishness, Father. But I don't disavow it either."

Ferrick opened his hands. "As you wish. I was only interested in your seeing the thing for a minute the way the managing partner at Lambert, Rowe would see it. He'd never be so crude, of course, as to display discomfort at a candidate's overly ethnic name. Only a fellow Mick on the make would raise the issue." He grinned. "Let's say I considered it my job."

"And the managing partner's job is to make sure the firm's first Irish Catholic doesn't seem like one."

The priest nodded. "*John* Dillon has just the right ring to it."

"And after I changed my name, you were going to send me down to Moss Brothers Outfitters for a new suit."

"I was going to lend you the money."

"Is it so important to you, Father?"

"You're a young man, Sean. When you get to be my age you'll have grown weary, I'll wager, of the border turf they leave to us."

"When I'm your age, Father, I'll be in the middle of the field, and I'll be there as myself." Sean knew that to any other priest such a statement would have seemed like rank arrogance: Who do you think you are? "I'm Sean Dillon, Father."

"And you live in Canaryville."

Dillon laughed. "Where no one raises the question of my name. It's one advantage of working for a fellow named Gustavus."

"Swift would be lucky to get you for a lawyer. I want you

to think about what I'm offering you. But your given name is an obstacle. I'm serious about your changing it. If you want out of the cramped, unpromising world you were born to—it's either that or go back and finish up your studies for the priesthood and get sent to Rome." Father Ferrick leaned back in his chair. "Or stay in Canaryville, Sean, with the sparrows."

Dillon eyed the priest steadily, aware that he was not only "offering" something, as he claimed, but exacting something too. After a moment Dillon said with bemused casualness, "You know about the sparrows?"

The Jesuit laughed. "I know that the birds around the yards aren't canaries, and never were."

The two men smiled at each other, thinking of the same story. In the last century the population of English sparrows feeding on bits of grain in the ubiquitous piles of dried dung had become so large that the area had become known as Canaryville.

Father Ferrick said, "But when I think of sparrows I think of St. Bede's sparrow."

What was this? Dillon raised his eyebrows.

The priest leaned toward him, his large hands entwined. "The story is in Bede's *Ecclesiastical History,* the story of the conversion to Christianity of what we now know as England."

Father Ferrick's intensity pulled Dillon in.

"The Druid king, Edwin, called a meeting of his councilors to hear what they had made of the preaching of the monks who had come over from the Continent. The king and his barons gathered in a great stone hall illuminated by the flames of torches and candles, warmed by a massive fire at one end. They sat around a table, each man giving his impressions while the king listened.

"St. Bede says that the king and his advisors achieved no understanding of what they were groping toward until one councilor—we don't know his name—stood up when it was his turn to speak. Instead of talking about what he'd heard of the Christian preaching, he said something about human life."

Father Ferrick paused here, as if to plunge into his story. But surfaces to him were a sea to move across. Dillon saw the sea shimmering in his eyes. His story was a ship in which to cross it. Dillon waited, listening.

"He said human life is like a sparrow coming by accident into a great lighted hall in winter. It flies frantically in through a doorway from a world outside that is cold and dark, and it soars through the bright air of the illuminated hall which is so warm . . ."

Dillon too, in the trance of the old man's description, began to see it.

". . . with its flickering candles, its tapestries, its stonework, its quiet fellowship, so beautiful. The sparrow flies quickly through, a perfect arc, and then, like that, goes out again through another opening into the merciless cold, the wind, the dark."

What am I hearing? Dillon wondered. Who am I to have the sea within me, a feeling of the ocean inside my throat?

"King Edwin's councilor said that human life is that interval of warmth and light and peace within the hall. Human life is the sparrow's flight. What comes after life and what goes before it is the winter darkness outside the hall. 'Therefore,' he said, 'if these new preachers have some certainty on these matters, it behooves us to receive it.' "

The Jesuit leaned back, unfolding himself into his chair, moved.

"Did they?" Dillon asked. When Father Ferrick failed to respond he said, "Did they have some certainty?"

"Of course."

"What was it?"

"Why, our certainty."

And Dillon sensed that *this* was the test, and if he was now required to take it, he would not pass.

"Our certainty," the priest said, "is that *outside* the hall it is light, True Light of True Light. *Here*, inside, is where it is dark."

"I'm not sure I believe that, Father."

"I know. That's why you stopped short of the priesthood, isn't it?"

"Yes."

"What you believe in is the sparrow's flight."

Dillon answered carefully, unsure now whether this man was a professor or a spiritual director. "Instead of a certainty of faith, what I have is eagerness, Father. I want a flight of my own. Is that wrong of me?"

"No. But you don't get off the ground by hesitating, lad. You came so far in the Church and hesitated. Now you've come so far in the law, and I fear you're hesitating again."

"Because I won't change my name?"

"Because you won't *act* on your eagerness and get out. Why are you still in the stockyards? Why would you even think of working for Swift? Because it's so familiar to you, that's why. And because for the likes of us it's so safe and comfortable."

"I pulled the rotting corpse of a man out of a blood pit at Swift's this afternoon, Father. From the mark on his hand I know he was a Hibernian. That's how safe the stockyards are for the likes of us. You assumed before it was an accident, but he'd been flogged. That corpse was a little warning against thinking too much of yourself. If so, it's a warning I reject. I don't know who the fellow was, but maybe his offense was a Canaryville version of refusing to change your name simply because your betters don't like the ring of it, if you receive my meaning, Father. Besides, it took a hell of a lot—" Dillon's anger surprised him. Was there something true in what the priest was saying? Hesitating? Again? Dillon shook the question off. "I'm not talking about narrow loyalty, Father. I broke more rules of the tribe in leaving the seminary than I would in changing my name."

The priest nodded, accepting Dillon's point. After a pause he said softly, "The sparrow's flight through the hall, whatever else one believes or doesn't believe, is all too quick, gone in a flash. I'm sorry about the man you found. I'll pray for him. I'll pray for you too, if you don't mind. Don't waste another moment of your time, that's all I'm telling you. Be what you can be, Dillon."

"It's not advice I'm used to getting, Father. Didn't Jesus say His Heavenly Father watches over the sparrows—not the ones that find it possible to fly, but the ones that fall? Isn't that what I'm supposed to do now? Get off the ground so that I can fall? *Then* God will love me? Then the Church will take me back?"

The priest shook his white head slowly. "I had the impulse to send you over to Lambert, Rowe because I didn't think you would fall. I see now . . ." He hesitated. ". . . that I was more right than I knew." He slapped his desk and stood abruptly. "Now go home and study your notes. Start from scratch with them. I don't want you embarrassing me in that exam tomorrow after I stick my neck out for you."

A few minutes later, after leaving Loyola, Dillon was riding the El, rattling south away from the Loop, looking out across the western stretches of the hard-ass, indifferent city. The last glow of twilight faded above the silhouettes of the round-houses and smokestacks and grain elevators and mills. This had been a day on which the slow coming of summer darkness seemed for once completely wrong. The darkness should have come hours ago.

He'd left Father Ferrick feeling the way, as a boy, he'd felt leaving the confessional. He'd wanted to savor that sweet catharsis, but the feeling didn't last. The image of what had sullied him intruded, and with it a wholly different, and unwelcome, set of feelings.

The dead man.

The murdered man.

The darkness.

Against the darkness outside the window, against the shocking image he saw reflected in the darkness of his own pupils, Dillon closed his eyes. He had left the dean's office resolved to go directly to his workman's bare room in a boardinghouse on Halsted Street and study through the night—a perfect exam!—as he had so many times before.

But what were the requirements of school now if not a mockery of what Dillon knew to be the truth about himself? Something irresistible was drawing him back toward that foul abyss into which, for a moment, naked as the day he was born, he had plunged. No mere idea or hope or feeling or metaphor—the darkness outside King Edwin's castle—that blood pit was a fact, a fact about the world, like it or not, to which he—"Sean"—belonged. It wasn't over yet.

The train accelerated as it hit the downward slope at Archer that marked the end of the elevated section of the line. Now the train rumbled into his home neighborhood, and Dillon felt a rare dose of longing for it. This *was* his place. These *were* his people: the canaries, the yarders, the Irish, the Catholics, the human beings. He was involved with them. He was not alone.

THREE

Doran's was one of a dozen saloons on Exchange Avenue in the block across from the Stone Gate. It was like other back-of-the-yards taverns in its dinginess and in the thick, layered odors of cigar smoke, hoghouse, and stale booze. The men who came to Doran's before and after work were not coming for decor.

They weren't coming just for booze either. Like many pubs, Doran's had a back room the door to which was open during the day. The back room men, wearing headphones and punching tabulators, could be seen then from the tavern proper. The room was a betting parlor. Discarded gambling tickets covered the floor of the entire saloon.

Now the back room was closed. Affixed to its door was a poster featuring a bespectacled orator in clerical collar whose twisted mouth and extended fist indicated the heat with which he was speaking. On the wall behind his pulpit was the carved legend "Christ Crucified," and text above and below the priest's image read, "I have taken my stand," and "Social Justice."

It was Father Coughlin. The bread-box-sized Philco on which Doran's customers had listened to the radio priest every Sunday for most of the decade stood on the near end of the worn shiny bar that ran the length of one wall.

Arranged along the bar at intervals were a complimentary jar of pickled pigs' feet, a salt shaker, a half-empty bowl of boiled eggs and the donation box from the St. Vincent de Paul Society. Tarnished spittoons stood at like intervals along the footrail. Against the opposite wall were benches and narrow tables, hardly more than hoisted planks.

Most customers began their serious drinking standing up, but by now the benches were crowded with woozy, indifferent day-shift men who'd come in hours ago. More recently arrived drinkers at the bar, in contrast, tossed back ale and whiskey while talking energetically, or even arguing, pounding the smooth wood or each other's shoulders. These had mostly come in since supper.

As in all taverns that had betting parlors in back, the windows were papered over to keep passersby outside from indulging their curiosity, although not patrolmen, since the bookies operated, in effect, in partnership with police. The blanked windows fixed the place in the constant artificial nighttime that daylight drinkers liked. But now, since it was nearly nine o'clock and finally dark outside, the tavern door was open to the authentic night. For once a balmy breeze wafted through the crowded room, swirling the smoke and carrying the noise out to the street.

Cassie Ryan stood in the doorway. Most young women in such a threshold, and ordinarily Cassie herself, would have felt afraid. The roughness of the room and the crudeness of the men, with their brutal faces, loose jaws, and bloodshot eyes, were not lost on her, but Cassie forced herself to recall that these same men with this same brainlessness crowded the vestibule of St. Gabriel's every Sunday. The wave of feeling that had carried her this far was not going to break now on girlish timidity. Cassie Ryan had come with a question and she was going to ask it, no matter of whom.

She watched the yardmen in the tavern gesticulating at one another, indifferent to their filth; it was their liveliness that struck her. These men were so reserved in the presence of their women and children—she thought of them mutely hunched over one knee in the back of St. Gabe's—that it was a shock to come upon them in a moment of their vigorous camaraderie. How they prefer each other! How they sting each other's shoulders with their slaps, these fathers and sons who never so much as stroked a cheek at home. No wonder they love their whiskey and beer if this is what it does for them.

A barrel-chested off-duty policeman pushed by her, turning his broad shoulders sideways to enter, touching his cap at her and letting his eyes hesitate on hers for a moment. She recognized his concern at once, his assumption that she was one form or another of the perennial waif sent by an irate mother for an oafish drunken father. She deflected the policeman's gaze, but not before it called up a choking sensation she hadn't felt in years, which was how long it had been since she or anyone had bothered to haul Mike Foley home from one of these dives. To her knowledge her uncle had never done his drinking at Doran's.

The policeman went in. Cassie hesitated only a moment longer before following him. When she stepped into the tavern the thick air clogged her nostrils. To the warmth and joy of the room was added suddenly a fresh attentiveness as the men became aware of her. The tone of their banter shifted. Those nearest the door who had closed in behind the policeman made way again, opening her an avenue as the commuters on the North La Salle sidewalk had.

Cassie nodded at them as she pressed on through to the bar.

The bartender saw her coming. He held a finger up at the policeman, meaning Wait, and slid along his side of the rail to intercept her as close to the door as possible. He leaned toward her, quite obviously not to take an order but to hear whom she'd come looking for.

"Jack Hanley," she said.

In the din he hadn't heard. He cocked his ear at her. His face grew twisted and savage-looking.

"Jack Hanley. I'm told he's here."

The bartender drew back. Cassie saw the vein in his temple swelling and she sensed he was deciding whether to point him out. Cassie had no idea what Hanley looked like. She had gotten his name from the night supervisor at Swift's only by threatening to call the priest at St. Gabriel's. From Swift's she'd gone to Hanley's house. Hanley's wife had told her at once where she'd find him, but this bartender was like the supervisor in being a man. She was still at the point of taking this reticence as a simple part of how these men habitually dealt with women. Cassie felt she knew them. She felt a rush of resentment. She knew them all.

The weight with which she'd packed her expression gave the bartender no choice. He turned and craned, looking across his room. His eyes stopped and Cassie followed them to the far corner where half a dozen overall-clad men were sprawled at one of the narrow tables.

As she moved toward them the drinkers once more cleared the way for her, some unsteadily, some eyeing her with bleary shock. More than one man inhaled quickly at the sight of her. Now the shift in the room's tone was more pronounced as the others became aware of her. Even those young enough or sober enough to be struck by her rare green eyes and bright auburn hair, by her red lips even in that hard-set mouth and by the sure, certain way she carried herself, like a dame in the movies—even they reacted first to the intrusion she was. Gradually they stopped talking as she cut through the aisle they opened for her. In silence they watched as she approached the corner. When they saw that it was Hanley slumped there with his back to the room, they all guessed that she'd come because of the blood pipes.

Those at the table with Hanley were the last to sense her presence. When finally they stopped talking—two froze with mugs nearly to their mouths—it was to peer upward quizzically. Jack Hanley was dead last to turn. His hat was cocked to one side, forgotten. When he looked up at Cassie the grief and fright she saw in his unfocused eyes seared themselves into her brain and she knew at once that this was him.

"I'm Mike Foley's niece," she said.

"Oh." Hanley started to get up, but he couldn't. He fell back into his chair. He reeked of alcohol. "Oh, darling," he said weakly.

"I've come to find out what happened."

Hanley looked quickly at his nearest companion, as if for guidance. The man was also drunk. He tossed his head toward Hanley's hat, which Hanley then took off. Now when he faced Cassie again a satisfied expression filled his face; by doffing his cap he had discharged what responsibility he had toward her.

But Cassie repeated herself coldly, "What happened to my uncle?"

Again Hanley cast his eyes about, but no one would meet them. He stared at the hat he clutched between his beefy hands. "He died."

"I know he died. I've been to Riordan's. I've seen his body. But what happened to him? They told me he drowned in a vat at Swift's. But what was he doing at Swift's? What happened to make his head like that? Where did he—?" Cassie stopped abruptly as the rampant emotion began once more to overtake her. She had become hysterical at Riordan's. The undertaker had felt free to put his arms around her. Now she hugged herself hard, choking off the violent shudder she felt coming. If she held herself in the vise of her own arms she could do this. "You have to tell me," she said. Only she knew how close she was to weeping.

Hanley's lips were set in a line. He thought if he didn't move she would go away. But she stood where she was above him, a grim statue. He said quietly, to soften her, "I knew him." He felt a fresh hit of the shock with which he'd heard who that pulpy mass had been.

"Then tell me, please."

Hanley brought his face up. "I mean years ago, I knew him years ago. I didn't know him now." Hanley clenched and unclenched his hands. "I don't know what happened."

"But you found him."

"I'm just a pipefitter, Miss. Your uncle was in the pipe. They made me go in for him."

"Pipe?"

Hanley realized he'd told her something she did not know. Stay out of this, he told himself. Stay out! Even drunk as he was, he knew enough to turn his back on the poor girl.

"Pipe?" Cassie repeated. She took Hanley by the shoulder, to force him to look at her, but he wouldn't budge. She heard the screech of emotion in her own voice; she hated it. "They told me *vat*. He fell into a giant vat. He took a short cut across a slippery cutting table, lost his footing and slid into a giant pickle vat. That's what they told me at Swift's. They said it was his own fault."

"Well then, what's your question, Miss?"

Cassie was surprised by the sober, calm voice behind her. When she looked she saw the policeman she'd followed in. His tunic was open at the throat. His hat was off now. His head was shiny bald. He held a shot glass in one hand, a beer mug in the other. A black cigar poked out from the glass, between his fingers.

"My question?" Cassie stared at him. She became aware of the press of stinking men. Why couldn't they give her room? They were all glaring at her as if it were an offense that she should want to know what happened to her uncle. The man at Swift's had concocted that story, she just knew it. When she'd challenged him, he'd as much as admitted it. He had told her he wasn't sure what had happened. My question, she repeated to herself. My only question.

Her real question had little to do with the famous dangers of the slaughter pits. What had made her dear uncle's sweet, loving heart so weak? And, before him, why had her father disappeared? That was what she wanted to ask someone, but these stewed prunes were too much like her uncle and her father, as her stoical mother and aunt were too much unlike them.

She looked at the policeman with a sudden incredulity, as if snapping out of a trance. "My uncle died at Swift's. But he didn't work for Swift's. He hasn't had a job in years."

The policeman shrugged. "An odd-lot day laborer, Miss. Lots of fellows never tell them at home if they pick up a shift here or there." He lowered his voice to emphasize its Irish warmth. "Though usually they keep day workers away from the cutting tables. I'm sorry for your troubles, Miss."

The policeman's sympathy took Cassie by surprise. She deflected her emotion by turning back to Hanley. "I asked to talk to someone who saw it happen. I told them I wouldn't leave until they said who I could talk to. Then they told me you."

Hanley shot bolt upright. "I never saw it happen! I never saw anything happen!" He looked wildly about. "I just found him, is all. This has nothing to do with me. The blood was backing up into the slaughter rooms—"

"Jack." One of the men next to Hanley tried to silence him by squeezing his forearm.

But Hanley grabbed the man roughly in return. "You tell Buckley this has nothing to do with me! Moran sent me down there—"

"Shut up, Jack!" The man pushed Hanley back into is chair.

Cassie Ryan saw what a weary, frightened man he was. The onlookers were mainly expressionless, though at the mention of the name Buckley she'd seen the furtive rustle of their anxiety.

Buckley? Cassie tried to grasp the relevance to her uncle's fate of Raymond Buckley, if that's who they meant. He was the local Kelly-Nash ward boss, the man in charge of South Side disbursement of city jobs and of the dole. Everyone knew who Buckley was.

But to Cassie's knowledge Buckley had nothing to do with her uncle. Certainly he'd never helped him find a job.

Instinctively she knew not to pursue it. She leaned down to

put her face by the fading Hanley's, despite his odors. "Then who *did* see what happened? Who can I talk to?"

Hanley twisted his head away, as if Cassie Ryan were the one who reeked.

"You should go now, Miss." The policeman touched her elbow.

Cassie didn't move.

Hanley's pale eyes told her nothing until, finally, his dazed look gave way to one of recognition. "Dillon," he said abruptly. "Talk to Dillon."

"Who?"

"Sean Dillon. My helper. He was with me. He saw what I saw." A shudder curled through Hanley's body. "Which you don't want to hear about."

Cassie glanced at the policeman and at others nearby who shrugged. They'd never heard of Dillon. She turned back to Hanley. "How can I find him?"

But his face had clouded over already.

Sean Dillon was standing by himself near the bar. He'd come into Doran's after the woman had, but for the same reason, as he'd understood by listening, with everyone in the room, to her interrogation of Jack.

He watched as she drew herself up over Hanley, then turned, tossing her hair back, and looked into the eyes, a pair at a time, of the men she had to squeeze past to leave.

She moved steadily across the room toward the door, toward Dillon.

When she got close to him he did not step out of her way. "I am Sean Dillon."

She stopped before him, startled.

"I was with Jack. I'm sorry about your uncle."

Cassie put her hand to her lips. When Dillon noticed her fingers trembling, he realized she wasn't as tough as she pretended.

"Can you tell me what happened?" She spoke quietly, but the policeman who'd followed along behind her had heard.

Before Dillon could answer, the policeman stepped between them. "Don't go into the terrible details, son. It isn't what the lass needs. Her poor uncle died by an accident in the yards. That's all you need tell her."

Dillon found it easier to face the burly cop than the raw

young woman. How *could* he speak to her of the grotesque pulpy mass who had been her uncle? He felt an incoming wave of what the priest had called his hesitation, but it wasn't about protecting the girl. Like others in the room, he had heard the name from Hanley's lips—Buckley, Raymond Buckley. Would he be the one now to splash that name with the blood of this woman's uncle? What about protecting himself?

Dillon knew very well what it meant then when he checked his hesitation. It almost surprised him that he could. He said to the policeman, but pointedly aware of speaking more to her, "It was no accident."

"What do you mean?"

"A man doesn't fall into a blood pipe, then haul the cast-iron cover closed above himself."

"Blood pipe?" Cassie said, revulsion in her voice.

"You see what I mean?" the cop said.

But now Dillon was fixed on the woman who had come into this place to hear the truth. "We found your uncle's body in the box basin where two large drainage pipes meet. The pipes draw blood out of the slaughter rooms."

"They told me he fell in a vat from a cutting table."

"He was nowhere near the cutting tables. There was no vat. It was the box basin near the pickle rooms—"

"Pickle rooms?" Cassie felt bile spurt into her mouth.

The policeman took Dillon's forearm and squeezed it hard, intending to hurt him. "You don't want to put your mouth where your feet shouldn't be, my friend. You should check your facts with the man at Swift's before you go upsetting people."

Sean was far from indifferent to the threat he heard in the cop's voice, felt in the vise of the cop's grip, the cop who had nothing to do with any of this, but who also knew instinctively the importance of sticking to the official story, whatever it was.

The men in the tavern moved away from Dillon and the cop, pointedly not listening anymore. Dillon recognized their unsubtle distancing as a form of what he had been doing for years. He might have moved away too at that moment, but the policeman was still holding on to him.

He said, "I don't know what the man at Swift's said. I came here looking for Hanley, to find out what happened."

"Well now you know. The bloke slipped."

"He was flogged," Dillon said, but under his breath so the woman would not hear.

"He still slipped."

It was like offering his soft throat to the wolf astride him when Dillon muttered, "If that's what Hanley says . . ."

"It is."

The woman interrupted, "But what about what *you* said?"

Dillon looked at her briefly, but his eyes went involuntarily back to the cop, who said easily, "Don't open that closet door, McGee."

But now, instead of a door, Dillon thought of the iron lid on that downpipe. Before he could respond to the dead man's niece, the policeman released his grip on Dillon's arm and faced her.

"Shall I be taking you home, Miss?"

Miss Ryan refused the policeman by shaking her head. When she glanced around the awful room one last time, it was as if Dillon weren't there. She moved between him and the cop to the door, where she turned and said, "You should all be ashamed of yourselves." Then she walked out into the blue-black night alone.

Dillon followed her.

When he hit the street, she was most of the way to the corner. "Hey, wait up!"

She ignored him.

He began to run after her.

The night air, even here, a mile from the lake, had turned clammy. Dillon was suddenly aware of the sweat on his shirt, his filthy shirt.

The sound of his own hurrying feet faded in his ears as he picked up the sound of hers. He called out again, but she only went faster, not quite breaking into a run. At the corner, across from the Stone Gate, she was swallowed by a throng of night-shift workers streaming out of the yards. Dillon had to cut through them, skipping like a halfback.

When he saw her figure out in the street, crossing toward Walgreen's, he leapt into traffic too. But the drivers did not yield for him as they had for the pretty young woman. The spectacle of his crossing Peoria Street—horns blaring, tires screeching, curses—had the effect, at least, of stopping her.

"Are you crazy?" she asked when he joined her on the sidewalk. "You wouldn't even answer me back there. And now you're getting hit by a car to catch up with me?"

He saw that her face was covered with marks like bruises, and it took him a moment to understand what had happened. Tears pouring freely from her eyes had flooded her makeup. He felt color rising in his own face, and he retreated. "I'm sorry."

"Don't tell me you're sorry!" she said. "I don't care if you are sorry. This has nothing to do with you."

This pain, she meant, this grief. This mess on my face which you have insisted on exposing!

She wasn't finished. "Nothing to do with you! Isn't that what you just said?"

"It was Jack Hanley who said that, not me."

"But it's what you meant."

And of course it was. Dillon had to look away from her. His eyes fell on the old Stone Gate.

"And you know what?" The woman pushed Dillon's arm, to make him look at her again. He saw how angry she was. "It's true. It has nothing to do with you! So leave me alone! Do you hear me?"

"I think the whole South Side hears you."

"Well, do *you*?"

"Yes."

At that Cassie Ryan turned and stalked away.

Dillon didn't move, but knowing he had only a moment more in which to reach her, he called out very loudly, "But you wanted to know what happened to your uncle!"

She stopped cold.

Customers went in and out of the all-night drugstore, pointedly ignoring them. If their spat was different from other arguments that were carried so frequently into those streets, it was in their being so young, in his not being drunk—though to passersby, didn't it seem that she had, like a Canaryville wife, just dragged him from his tavern?

At last she faced him. A dozen yards of open sidewalk separated them. Those passersby were staying clear.

"But you won't tell me."

Dillon slowly closed the distance. "I don't know what happened to your uncle. I came to Doran's like you did—to hear what Hanley knew."

"What they said happened—about him falling into the vat—something told me that wasn't possible."

"You're right."

"You made it sound, at first, like someone . . . killed him. Is that what you think?"

Dillon glanced toward the blinking neon of the Walgreen's sign.

"But then you took it back."

Dillon nodded, but his silence thickened, becoming his positive statement, despite himself.

He broke it, aware of the change this was. "I'm not taking it back now. I won't take it back again. Something awful happened to your uncle. I became involved in it because I was one of the people to find him. If you want to find out what happened—"

"Of course I do." Her feeling brought her right against him, her hands pressing into the sleeve of his shirt.

"Then I'd like to help you."

"What happened to crush my uncle's head like that?"

She asked the question coldly, so that was how he answered it. "We found him head-first in the downpipe. He had been stuffed into it. When his head swelled up . . ." Dillon let a shrug finish for him.

"Was he already dead, do you think?"

"An autopsy would show that. Will there be an autopsy?"

Cassie stared at Dillon with yet more horror on her face. "They dissect the body, don't they?"

"Partially."

"Well how could we—?"

"If you want to know what killed him, you do an autopsy. It would show if he choked, if he drowned, if he was hit . . ."

The girl's eyes had clouded over. She was seeing those panhandlers downtown, the men into whose upturned eyes she had for years now poured her hope and her despair.

"You say he's at Riordan's?"

"Yes."

"Who in your family is in charge of—?"

"I am."

"Do you know . . ." Dillon softened his voice for the unspeakable again. "Have they started the embalming?"

Cassie nodded. "Mr. Riordan said they do it at night." Her

hand went to her lips, an abject gesture. "He said it would be disrespectful to wait."

"Who's paying him?"

"Mr. Riordan? Why I—" Bewilderment got the better of her. Paying? What did paying have to do with this? Cassie forced herself to focus. "He hasn't mentioned it yet."

Dillon shook his head. "They mention it first." He took her arm. "Why don't we go back over there and see what Mr. Riordan says."

Cassie fell easily into step with him, but because, really, since getting off that streetcar hours before to have her cousin hail her with the news, she had been operating in a kind of trance. Her aunt and her mother both had surrendered all initiative to her, and making one decision after another had protected her from her grief and anger, as moving with this stranger now protected her from having to decide what to do next. She only half heard what he was saying.

"If they haven't started the embalming, you can ask them to wait. There's no hurry. Embalming can wait until tomorrow."

Sean was aware of her emotional drift, and he was relieved that their movement through the streets made further talk impossible. He felt her thin arm in his hand, and at one point he imagined his fellow pipefitters ragging him about the canner he was with last night. A canner is any animal too thin for the butcher's block.

They left the Stone Gate and the glaring, pole-lit abyss of Section Five behind, and the soft yellow lights of the broad avenue too, its confusion of cigar stores, shuttered newsstands, boisterous taverns, and pushcarts covered for the night. They passed into the tranquil reserve of the neighborhood itself, coming finally, in ten minutes, to the block of Forty-fifth Street in the middle of which stood the squat, reddish-brown church of St. Gabriel the Archangel. Only its tower, a pseudo-Tuscan belfry, had any boldness, and in the dark it loomed above the plain of grim rooftops like a sentry looking out for the mellow hills of the former countryside.

Across from the church was the funeral home, a converted residence, one of the few brick houses in an area famous before the Depression for its modest but well-kept wood frame dwellings. Now those houses were run-down, even dilapidated, because money was so short, of course, but also because so many of the men who'd have kept those clapboards scraped and painted had disappeared. Buildings that had housed one family before now housed three, and the patches of soil in front, where squares of grass once grew, were now planted inexpertly with tomato vines and poles of beans.

"Riordan's Funeral Parlor," the tidy sign read. With its green awning overhanging the sidewalk directly opposite the pillared entrance of the Romanesque church, Riordan's was as much a part of St. Gabe's as the nuns' school farther down the block. Parishioners were always taken aback to be reminded, and at the worst time, that funerals, unlike the other functions of the parish, were conducted for a fee. No wonder Cassie hadn't thought to ask who was paying. Maybe *she* was.

Sean Dillon led the way up to the door which, under the awning, was the darkest on the street. When he glanced back at Cassie, only to see her wiping her cheeks with her handkerchief, he froze. Were her feelings of devastation taking her under?

But instead of dabbing at fresh tears, she was repairing her ravaged eyes. She brought them immediately up to meet his and he saw a depth of cold determination.

He knocked, then knocked again. They waited.

The tall bespectacled bald man who opened the door was familiar to them both, as to every parishioner, despite his collarless shirt, the sleeves of which, like Dillon's, were rolled past his elbows. He was drying his hands with a ragged towel. The stench of formaldehyde clung to him. Usually they saw Riordan in his charcoal suit and gray gloves, leading the casket down the aisle like death's father. Usually he reeked of cologne; this chemical was why.

"Mr. Riordan, I'm Sean Dillon, and this is Miss Ryan."

Riordan nodded, but his voice was thick with negation when he said, "Miss Ryan and I met earlier tonight. I'm closed now. I told you, Miss, we can make arrangements in the morning."

"Miss Ryan and her family want you to delay preparing the body." Dillon had unconsciously assumed the air of the family representative, as he did this. "The family is going to have an autopsy performed."

"An autopsy!" Riordan faced Cassie. Light flashing off his glasses underscored his amazement. "Why?"

"To find out how he died."

"You don't need a postmortem report for that, Miss. I've al-

ready begun on him. Your uncle drowned. Do you imagine he
was poisoned or something?"

Dillon noted that the man's surprise, and mystification,
seemed genuine. Perhaps he *wasn't* in a hurry to hide something.

With an eyebrow arched above the wire rim of his glasses,
Riordan said, "Your uncle unfortunately found himself where
his anatomy meant he shouldn't be. His lungs were full of . . ."
His pointed hesitation flagged the next word as euphemism.
"Fluid."

"You mean blood," Cassie said.

"Yes. Blood wastage. He drowned in it. He was still breathing when he went under. Otherwise—" Riordan checked himself and turned brusquely to Dillon. "Why are you letting this
girl subject herself to this?"

Dillon replied in the calm but insistent tones he'd imagined
himself using in court. "She wants to know what happened to
her uncle, beyond his having drowned. What do the man's
bruises reveal?" What was he flogged with? he added to himself. "The man was found in blood pipes, Mr. Riordan, not in
a vat of pickle fluid, as Miss Ryan was told. And not in Lake
Michigan either. An autopsy—"

Riordan cut him off to hiss, as if the girl wouldn't hear him,
"An autopsy would show how much alcohol was in the man.
Is that what you want? Talk about pickle juice! That man was
too baffled from drink to know *where* he was. Is that what you
want established?"

"Yes," Cassie said, startling Dillon and Riordan both. When
they looked at her she added in an undefiant voice, "If that's
the truth of it. No one needs to know but me."

Riordan draped the towel over his shoulder and folded his
arms. "You're a little late, as it happens, Miss. Your uncle's
fluids are all but drained, if you'll forgive the indelicate detail.
There'd be no question of a proper autopsy now."

"Nevertheless . . ." Dillon wasn't sure what his point was,
beyond helping this girl take some control over things. "Your
instructions from the family are to cease the embalming of Mr.
Foley's remains. A doctor will be in touch with you tomorrow."

Riordan pointedly waited for some endorsement from Cassie. She gave it with a nod. Riordan smiled the thin, empty
smile of his profession. "I'll have to talk to Mrs. Foley."

"But stop the embalming," Cassie ordered.

"As you say, Miss." He stepped back from the door to close it.

Dillon stopped him. "One more thing, please."

"What?"

"Who's paying you?"

The firmness in Dillon's voice as he asked the simple question stirred in Cassie a deep sense of gratitude. Where had this man come from?

"The ward committee," Riordan answered.

"What?" Cassie was aghast.

"Your uncle is a beneficiary of the Democratic Party. He—"

"The party? My uncle had nothing to do with the party."

"The committee pays for a lot of funerals, Miss."

"Who gave you your instructions?" Dillon asked.

"Arthur Nolan. He works for Mr. Buckley."

"Buckley?" Cassie touched Dillon. "Jack Hanley mentioned Buckley."

Dillon stepped back from Riordan's door, but the mortician leaned after him. "*Now* do you see? You'd better butt out of this, Mister."

"See what?" Cassie asked. She grabbed Riordan's arm.

"Ask him," he said, jerking free. Then he fell back into the darkness of his funeral home, and he closed the door.

"See what?" Cassie repeated, now to Dillon.

Instead of answering, Sean drew her down the stairs and out from under the awning. They crossed the street to stand in front of the entrance to St. Gabe's.

"My uncle was nobody to Mr. Buckley. Why would—?"

"He must have owed them money," Dillon said simply. "They had him killed, and now they're having him buried. They want everyone to know what happened. That's why they brought the stockyards to a halt. They're making an example of your uncle."

"But he doesn't gamble. He couldn't have owed them that much money."

"It doesn't take much. And gambling is less what snags them than drinking." Dillon was speaking coldly now. These were realities which he, like every yarder, knew very well. But he'd kept them at a distance. "A dollar a bottle. Two bottles a day. Fourteen, fifteen dollars a week. Could your uncle afford that?"

Cassie lowered her eyes pitifully. "I gave him five a week. I thought it was enough."

Dillon shook his head. "Saloon keepers advance them credit to a point. Of course, it isn't *their* credit they're advancing. And once the debt is on the poor sap, then in addition to the cost of booze every week, he has to come up with interest payments. A quarter a week per ten dollars owed is the usual rate. That's the 'vig.' It's not that much for any one guy. There's the genius of it, keeping a man's payment due within his ability to get it, while keeping the total owed high enough that he can never fully pay it off. Interest payments—every bum on the South Side is making them to somebody, but most of every nickel and dime goes to one guy, who fortunately is very generous and lenient." Dillon stopped, then added quietly, "To a point. The point at which the discipline of the system has to be enforced."

"Is that what happened to my uncle?"

Dillon stared at her. The girl's skin, even in that pale light, was the color of her striking hair. "It's not that often that they kill people for—"

"Are you saying somebody killed my uncle because he didn't pay his quarters?" A baffled fury had made her face savage. "How do you know all this?"

Her question landed like an accusation. "Everyone knows it, Cassie. You and I saw as much back in Doran's. *They* knew, the policeman knew, Riordan knew. And the monsignor who will conduct your uncle's funeral knows."

"*I* don't know."

Dillon looked away from her, up toward the shadowy church. He remained silent.

"You're telling me everyone submits to—what did you call it, 'the discipline of the system'? Everyone allows it? Everyone supports it?"

"Not everyone submits," Dillon said slowly. "I think your uncle fought them, and that's why they killed him so brutally. *That* is the point they are making: don't resist."

"You said you would help me."

Sean didn't answer her at first. If he wanted some version of the "Count me out" he'd said years before to the Church, and had been saying ever since to his chums in the yards, and was trying to say now to Swift and Company itself, he could not summon it. But neither could he summon its opposite, a restatement of his enlistment in this woman's struggle. What exactly *had* he said to her? And how had it bound him?

He had been "submitting to the discipline" for a long time. If he was somehow now to set himself against the corrupt system of generalized overlordship that had so efficiently and ruthlessly replaced the mob—Capone was dying of syphilis in Joliet; his mantle had fallen to Frank Nitti, but not his power—Dillon knew that his own habit of passivity implicated him. He had fixed his attention on the law books at Loyola in part as a way of avoiding a confrontation with Chicago's radical lawlessness. Yet he knew very well that the Kelly-Nash precinct captains and bosses, the aldermen and commissioners and supervisors, the party chairmen, were in reality pimps, gambling moguls, loan sharks, and killers. The true measure of their skill was the respectability the men of the Chicago machine had achieved, for it stretched from the parish to the nation as a whole. Roosevelt owed his recent election to the illegal manipulations of these very pols, and he continued to depend on them. Their alliances with and control over every level of law enforcement, including apparently the federal, made them more immune from legal challenge than Capone had ever been. They cultivated the image of local philanthropists, and in Canaryville they liked to act like the Irish songbirds that Roosevelt and the bankers and the packinghouse owners were happy to pretend they were. But they were vultures feeding on the spillage of human need. And unfortunately, first for Mike Foley, and now for Cassie Ryan, one of those vultures was Raymond Buckley.

And unfortunately, Dillon added to himself, for me. "Yes, I did offer to help you. And I meant it. But in all honesty I'm not sure what else there is to do."

"Well, to begin with there's telling Mr. Riordan that my uncle was not a derelict. We won't need Buckley's generous help in paying for the funeral."

"You don't need to use Riordan at all. You could use Gibson's on Halsted Street. That would make a point everyone would understand. I know Gibson."

"Would you arrange it?"

"Yes."

"And the autopsy. What about the autopsy?"

Dillon cursed himself for that bold, earlier impulse of his. It was one thing to refuse to submit to Buckley, but to go after him?

He studied Cassie carefully, but the shadows obscured her face. He wanted to search her eyes for fear. He felt ashamed of the fear he sensed in himself. He said quietly, "Riordan's right about the autopsy. I didn't realize it was Buckley when I suggested that. As long as you understand . . ."

She said nothing. She was not going to release him from this. He said, "Before crawling into pipes, steamfitters ask each other, 'How far in shall we go? Far enough in to tell the boss we've been there? Or far enough in to get the job done?' "

"What doctor would do an autopsy if Buckley didn't want it?"

Despite himself Dillon smiled at the way she'd refused to be deflected. When had he last beheld such nerve? "Don't worry about the doctor," he said, resigning himself, the way he did when he went into a hateful pipe. "I'll get the doctor."

Dillon registered the charge enlivening the field between the woman and himself, and he recognized—belatedly, but look how new this was to him—that her anger and grief had released into the air an energy that was somehow essentially sexual. They were Irish Jansenists, and neither would have openly acknowledged their connection as the first stirring of an erotic emotion. Yet there it was, and Dillon recognized the thing viscerally. Cassie Ryan's pert body, even shadowed, revealed itself to him suddenly, from the lift of her hair to the line of her throat to the simple fall of fabric over her womanly curves. It was her passion that had drawn him, his intuition that her intensity of feeling might complete him somehow. Now here was a first hint of passion of another kind.

Cassie stepped away awkwardly, as if aware of the shift in Dillon's preoccupation. She moved toward St. Gabriel's. "I haven't even said the prayers yet, prayers for the dead." And with that, only that, she turned and went up the stairs to the empty, dark church.

FOUR

Sean Dillon was back at the yards at dawn, lost in the swarm of austere men funneling through the Stone Gate into Section Five. Above them the last stubborn stars refused to leave the sky. On this morning Dillon differed from the others not only in the purposefulness of his step, but in his being dressed in a dark suit, a collar and necktie. The workers wore the usual overalls and brogans, carried toolboxes and lunch sacks. Dillon walked with his arms moving at his sides, his fingers curled lightly into fists. His fellows seemed to ignore what set him apart, except for the automatic way they gave him room, like cattle ovaling a rider.

They moved through the morning haze as they had for years, blind to the forms and shapes around them, the stout pen walls, the looming chimneys; deaf to the scrape of their own thick-shod feet and to the rough hum of the yards' cold engines and to the drum sound of railroad cars bumping, of coupling chains snapping to; not smelling the congealed-guts stench exploding from every drop of moisture in the fog.

But Dillon was different here too. His senses were far more concentrated than usual, but instead of smelling the generalized offal, he smelled that particular putrid odor of the blood pit, he saw the naked human carcass, white and wrinkled. He heard his own stomach groan in revolt. He tasted that wave of vomit that he'd only barely been able to swallow back. It was not the outrageous stockyards, so familiar in their vastness, that he was entering, in other words, but the narrowly perverse scene that had spiked the heart of the day before. As a pipefitter's helper he had often come across long-drowned rats in tunnels. He had helped clear the cadavers of sheep from runoff gutters.

57

He had seen maggots crawling through the muscle folds of fouled meat. Every yarder had seen such things. But this—he recalled how the slimy film coating the object's swollen skin had made his own hands and fingers useless in gripping. He and Hanley had been able to hoist the corpse only by locking arms around it.

When he had crossed through Section Five and turned onto the broad asphalt-covered tractor way that would take him to Swift's, he awakened to his surroundings. Suddenly the pitch of sensation, until now so internal, extended to the brightening sky and a flock of welcoming sparrows wheeling down from the roofs of the packinghouses.

Sparrows! Dillon tried to see the birds as emblems of a world he wanted. How had Father Ferrick put it? Human life is the sparrow's flight.

But what about Cass Ryan's uncle's human life? Dillon felt a fresh rush of the anger and shame. Not canaries or sparrows, he thought, but vultures!

His emotion fueled his energy, sharpening his reactions. Now when he looked around at the knifemen whose caps hid their eyes, at the cattle scraping their filthy hides on the board walls of their pens, at the forklifts and tractors jolting into motion, spewing exhaust, his old sense of dislocation came back more acutely than ever. He remembered walking in an endless stream of men like this, but then it was black-robed lads filing from the refectory to the chapel. At the seminary they had always moved in a flock, a herd, and that enforced massing had always left Dillon feeling, ironically, completely isolated.

But those kind-hearted, pious boys, soft as the satin vestments they hoped to wear, had not been scavengers.

Dillon looked at the hard, clomping bodies around him, and it struck him now that these men weren't scavengers either. They were losers like Mike Foley had been, sparrows in St. Bede's sense, frightened creatures who had no understanding of what brought them here, where they'd come from, where they were going.

Dillon felt a rare urge to protect his fellow yarders, to save them—here he was apart again—from themselves.

He had been awake all night, mostly at his table, bent over his books, but he had taken in nothing of the law. His mind had been tethered to the image of Cass Ryan. He had bounced through the chutes of a dozen different approaches to the mystery of her uncle's death, but they all, like the corridors of a labyrinth, took him to the wall of Raymond Buckley.

The wall's shadow overspread most of the South Side, but it was very unlikely that a penny-ante deadbeat, if that's what Mike Foley was, would have come to Buckley's explicit attention. Buckley would have insulated himself from the harsher operations of his machine, and in that he'd have been like Gustavus Swift III, who made a point never to come near his own reeking slaughterhouse. Swift's namesake grandfather, the founder, had been a butcher who knew what it was to have blood on his arms up to his elbows. Capone had been a butcher too, but Buckley was a businessman and politician. Times change.

Dillon's night had been an ordeal of doubt and second thought. He knew nothing, really, about how a system like Buckley's worked, and he admitted finally that what he had effectively promised to help Cass Ryan do—lay responsibility for her uncle's death at Buckley's feet—was impossible.

When he got up from his table, Dillon had washed and shaved and dressed in his best clothes without knowing why. He looked better, but his head was ringing with pain. He had scorched the remains of day-old coffee and forced himself to swallow it, a potion to get him through the day. It had only sickened his stomach.

And now he had joined the throng of first-shift automatons, although he might better have been one of the dumb animals filing out of a railroad car into the chutes that would take him—where? Dillon may not have slouched along like the zombies around him, but his purpose was in fact far cloudier than theirs.

He found Jack slumped on the bench in front of his locker, his head in the clamp of his gnarled hands. His hat was on the floor in front of him. Other workmen were moving through the room in their usual early morning stupor. A knifeman named Smitty bumped Dillon, noticed his clothing and said gruffly, "Who died?" He didn't wait for an answer.

Dillon touched Hanley's shoulder. "Jack, it's me."

Hanley slowly hauled his face out of his hands. His skin was gray, his eyes were red. He looked old.

"Christ, Dillon," he said hoarsely, and then he fell silent.

"Jack, I want you to do me a favor. I need some help from

one of the docs. You have a friend at the yards' dispensary, don't you? What's his name?"

"Doc Riley?"

"Right."

"What's wrong? You sick?"

Dillon stooped for Hanley's hat, picked it up and handed it to him. "No, I'm all right. How about you, Jack?"

"I'm sick. Real sick." He put his hat on his lap as if it were a basin.

"You look it."

The shift whistles sounded in the yard outside. The noise carried shrilly even into the building, and the other workers in the changing room snapped up their overalls and hurried away. But Hanley stayed where he was, and so did Dillon. Gradually the whistles faded. Then silence filled the room the way the noise had.

Hanley looked around and realized their privacy. His shoulders settled, relaxing in it, then he said, "I'm going to quit the booze, Dillon. That's what."

The slur was still on his words, and Dillon realized that his boss was far from sober even now. The poor bastard. "Good for you, Jack." He sat down on the bench next to Hanley, feeling the weight of his own exhaustion. We're all poor bastards.

Hanley then mumbled a few words.

"What?"

"Mike Foley was a friend of mine."

"I know he was." Dillon watched as Hanley stared into his hat, and he saw the complete futility of the only idea he'd come up with. Without Hanley, he would have to approach the yards doctor himself, but what was the point of that? The doctor wasn't going to risk offending Raymond Buckley because a pipefitter's helper he'd never heard of asked him to.

"If it was you, Jack, instead of Foley, I wouldn't let it go at this."

Hanley turned toward Dillon, an expression of drunken self-pity on his face. "What would you do?"

"For starters, I'd find out what the hell happened." Dillon paused to light a cigarette, wanting the air of detachment. He knew how easily spooked Hanley was, like a skittish animal. Dillon's part in all of this had begun the day before with Hanley's panic, but not only that. It had begun with his own feelings for Hanley, his own inability on the lip of that blood hole to let Hanley confront it alone. Dillon was standing now before a feeling he had not articulated before, for he was a South Side Chicago man, a man of the yards, and they could make the simple statement of such a truth only when drunk. Nevertheless, then he said, "You're a friend of mine, Jack."

Hanley felt the force of his partner's statement, but apparently as a blow. He crushed his hat angrily. "But what can I do? Mike's dead!" He'd spoken much too loudly. When he glanced around the empty locker room, he registered what it meant that the others had gone. "Jesus, Mary, and Joseph, we're late." He put his hat on and started up.

Dillon held him down. "You can go to Doc Riley, Jack. You can get Doc Riley to check Foley out. He could do an autopsy."

"A what?"

"A postmortem exam."

Hanley shook his head. "Not Doc Riley. He's just a doc. You need a, a . . ." He didn't know the word.

Dillon supplied it. "A pathologist. That's right, we do need a pathologist. But we don't have one. What we have is a doc."

Hanley snorted.

"Any trained doctor can do a postmortem on Foley, to find out what killed him."

Hanley yanked his arm free. "We know what killed him. The blood pit killed him."

"They are saying he fell in the pickle vat, Jack. We should get it on record what really happened, what really was in his lungs, and it wasn't pickle."

"On whose record? For what?"

"On my record, for now."

"Are you off your trolley?"

For a long moment neither of them moved.

Then Hanley stood. "You've got your head in the Bible, Dillon. You know nothing."

Dillon was stunned by the contempt he sensed in Hanley, and he realized Hanley had just given expression to something his fellow yarders felt about him.

Dillon forced a laugh. "Not the Bible, Jack. Goddamn Justinian Code, maybe, but not the Bible."

"You're on your own, because you've always been on your own."

"Not with you I haven't been, Jack." If Hanley was not his friend, he had no friend.

Hanley seemed to understand that, and he softened. "What's your plan?"

"No plan, Jack. Just a couple of moves I thought I'd make this morning. First the autopsy."

"Doc Riley will never do it."

"He's a Hibernian, isn't he? Haven't I seen that tattoo on his hand?"

Instead of answering, Hanley stared glumly back at Dillon.

"I thought you fellows took an oath to watch out for each other."

"Doc Riley does what the bosses tell him."

"So you tell him, Jack. You're a boss. Tell him that the family wants him to do an autopsy. They'll pay his fee. Tell him that."

"You say you know what's what. You know that the fee isn't it. There are some things you just have to leave alone. This is one of them. That's what the doc will say."

"When he does, you tell him Mike Foley was a Kerryman who had it too hard here, and now his widow has it hard. What's wrong with wanting to ease the grief she feels with a little direct knowledge for her own private use of what the hell happened to the man?"

"Her own private use?" Hanley grasped at the phrase as if it were a raft.

And Dillon realized what a fiction he'd just concocted. His instinct was to back away from it. Is this what lawyers do, dance around the truth until they find the lie that works?

"What do you mean, her private use?"

Dillon dropped his cigarette, crushed it under his shoe. "Just what I said, Jack."

"It's not for the police?"

Dillon laughed. "The police! You think you take on Raymond Buckley by going to the police? The police are the rats in his wall. You know that. They feed on the scraps he leaves out for them. That's the point, Jack. Buckley won't be afraid of Mike Foley's widow, not that he knows she exists. Why should you be? Why should Doc Riley be?"

Hanley eyed his helper, but obliquely, as if he didn't want to be caught at it. He knew Sean Dillon better than anybody. He knew that when Dillon put his wrench to a frozen pipe joint, no matter if the grooved metal of the pipes and coupling had long since oxidized into one solid piece, that joint eventually was going to come loose. "I wasn't thinking of Mrs. Foley," Hanley said, "as somebody to be afraid of."

"Who then? Who were you thinking of?" Answering his own question, Dillon saw what he himself was after: not the police, but the coroner's jury. An autopsy contradicting essentials in Swift's posted cause of death could force Foley's case onto the coroner's docket. Even if the coroner belonged to Kelly-Nash, his jury wouldn't. How much leeway did that jury have? It was law he'd have to check on.

Hanley was shaking his head. "Nobody. I wasn't thinking of nobody. If you say the autopsy is just for the widow to know about, that's good enough for me."

"For the family," Dillon corrected, thinking of Cass, relieved to have found a way to nudge back toward the literal truth.

"Then okay, I'll do it."

"Do it this morning, Jack. Gibson is the undertaker, and he's waiting."

Hanley nodded. He turned and moved toward the door, then stopped and indicated Dillon's clothes. "You dressed for the wake already, or what? You better get your dungarees on."

"I'm off today, remember?" Dillon spoke as if they had agreed on this. "I missed that examination last night. I have to go downtown this morning to see if the priest will let me take it now." Another lurching to the side of what was so. Father Ferrick had scheduled him for late afternoon. These subtle deceptions were coming easily.

"You already look like a lawyer, Dillon." Hanley checked himself before adding, And you act like one. "You going to the wake, though?"

"Sure."

"Good. The Hibernians are doing the rosary. Doc Riley will be there. All of us will be. Mike Foley was a Sinn Feiner, one of the first. He left the old country with a price on his head."

Hanley's eyes had filled, reminding Dillon that he was still slightly drunk. The green fog was rolling in. Next he'd be cursing the Black and Tans. Dillon thought of his own father, a streetcar driver who'd been silent as stone, except on the subject of the British rape of Ireland.

Dillon deflected Hanley. "Can I tell Mike's widow she can count on you then?"

Hanley replied with a forced energy. "Indeed you can. I'm going to the dispensary right now." But then he sagged. "I don't feel so hot anyways. Maybe the doc can give me something before he goes to Gibson's." He paused, then added with sharp sobriety, "Doc Riley will do it for Mike Foley. I'll make sure of it." Hanley turned and left.

But Dillon had intended to ask him one more thing: where to look for Buckley.

Confronting Buckley early, before he was surrounded by lackeys, was the second of the two moves he had determined to make. Hanley had asked him for his plan, and now it struck Dillon what a thin set of impulses he had. What was he doing anyway? Would going to Buckley's unannounced be any more productive than half an autopsy performed by a company-owned—Buckley owned?—sot doctor? And where, anyway, would he find Raymond Buckley at this hour of the morning?

Dillon checked an urge to call after Hanley, to ask him. There were half a dozen other fellows he could ask. He would pretend he wanted to approach Buckley for a loan. Simple enough. Better to leave Hanley out of it.

The fiction he and Hanley had just implicitly agreed to hold by opposite ends, like a pair of herders holding rope, was that they would leave Raymond Buckley alone, no matter what he'd done to the once heroic Mike Foley.

Not fiction, Dillon said to himself as he left the slaughter-house changing room, but lie.

There had been an essential weakness about her uncle, and Cass couldn't deny it; a weakness like her father's. Her uncle was dead, but it was an ache for her long-gone Pa that had wakened her.

She lay in her bed listening to the sounds of the coming day, glad for them. She heard an automobile engine coughing in the street outside. She heard water running in the bathroom. She heard her mother's tea kettle blowing in the kitchen like a near version of the yards' shift whistle, which was floating faintly all across the neighborhood.

She remembered how her father had always roused himself at the sound of that whistle. He would dress in his rough clothes. After eating his pancakes and molasses in silence, except for the click of his utensils, turning the plate twice to cut the cakes in quick squares, which he speared into his mouth on the tip of his knife, he would stand in the doorway of the kitchen looking back at Cass's mother, as if *today* they would speak. After a moment he would disappear behind the dotted muslin that hung in the threshold as a door. It would fall in after him with a *swish, swish,* which to Cass sounded like a slam. She would go after him, down the dark hall, to see his exit from the house. "Got to hustle down to Halsted Street," he would say back to her with a wink. "With any luck, they'll give me a job beheading hogs."

Outside her window, the gray light moved. A summer morning. The curtains stirred.

Sometimes when she was a girl, her father's hand would rest easily on her head as they walked to or from the streetcar, and she would feel as though the canopy of heaven itself—blue satin ardent with stars, Our Lady's veil—had settled on her.

Sometimes when he was reading the paper, she would sit on the edge of his chair, smelling his leather and tobacco, studying the deep lines on his face, which in repose was always grave and sad. The sadness in him was the clue to his weakness, she thought now.

She heard the muffled argument of her brothers a room away—a shirt they both wanted. She looked over at the cot in the corner of her own room: the tidy mound of Molly still sleeping soundly. The night before, when Cass pulled the sheet to cover her cousin, the pillow was still damp from her tears.

Molly's father had had that same sadness reading the paper. Cass remembered how, often, when she went upstairs to the Foleys' flat, Uncle Mike would be sitting in the wing chair, with the job ads open in front of him, nothing to apply for.

Cass rolled over in her white bed and crushed the pillow between her arms. Her heart sank again with the knowledge that her uncle was nothing but a victim. History's victim—Ireland, the Depression; whiskey's victim; his wife's. The weakness Cass sensed in him, and in all her men, was a weakness for victimhood. That was what she saw when they weren't looking, in the deep lines around their mouths, but she had just called it sadness. Sadness. A pathetic, weak word, it seemed to her now, which did not remotely describe the agonies or the furies that had taken her father away and destroyed her uncle.

Cass felt herself sinking fast. Now was she to think of her Uncle Mike as the victim, finally, of a brutal slayer who stuffed him in a blood sewer?

She squeezed her eyes shut against this train of thought.

I am not a victim, she told herself.

But she was. She was a victim of the ache behind her breastbone. "O God," she whispered, "not my will but Thine." She repeated the familiar phrase once, then twice, reaching for the strength and peace that always came to her when she prayed.

But nothing.

The prayer had left a metallic taste in her mouth, and she felt afraid that in this hour of need her faith was deserting her. She pulled her right hand free of the pillow to touch her forehead, crossing herself, as if that gesture would release the wave of solace for which she longed.

But the sensation of her own fingers lightly on her head released instead a memory of that other hand on the very crown of her head, but now it was her uncle's hand, a large, rough workman's hand. He was touching with outstretched thumb and little finger both her ears. Her uncle had replaced her father as the man who touched her head like that, but now, instead of the canopy of heaven, the memory of that loving touch felt like the weight of an unwanted hat.

After washing and dressing, and greeting her mother, Cass went upstairs to sit in her aunt's kitchen. Her cousins had all finished with breakfast and were either gone now or elsewhere in the house. Cass was not going in to work. She sat at the kitchen table, drinking coffee. Her aunt was kneading dough at the floured heavy board, her back to Cass. This was the first time the two of them had been alone.

Mrs. Foley was a large woman. The flesh above her elbows made her upper arms look like thighs. In her summer dress, those arms were exposed now, and the sight of them, quivering as she pounded the dough, filled Cass with embarrassment for her. Mrs. Foley's most prominent feature was not visible from behind, an unfortunate goiter the size of a golf ball that protruded from below the right side of her jawbone. The swollen thyroid was harmless, the doctors said, but the sight of it never failed to stir Cass's sympathy.

"Have you called Andrew, Aunt Flo?"

"Yes, last night. He's coming up today."

"By train?"

"Yes. Hannah too, he said."

They were silent for a moment, then Mrs. Foley said, "Monsignor Sweeney is postponing his retreat to stay here, thanks be to God. If he wasn't at the wake, those foolish Hibernians would expect to lead the rosary."

"It doesn't matter."

"It does to me."

The determination in her aunt's voice surprised Cass and alarmed her, for now she was going to have to tell her what she had done. The best thing to do was just to come out with it. "I ordered an autopsy last night, Aunt Flo."

"What?" Mrs. Foley's entire body registered her surprise, as she turned to face her niece.

Cass suddenly felt dizzy, and she pressed her fingers against the rim of her cup, as if that would keep her voice from shaking. "I ordered Uncle Mike's body moved from Riordan's to Gibson's, and I told them we would want an autopsy, to learn what happened."

"We know what happened."

"No, we don't. Uncle Mike didn't die the way they said he did. It may not have been an accident. That's why an autopsy—"

"What are you talking about?"

To Cass's surprise she couldn't remember the name of the man who had made her think this way—or what he had said the night before that she'd found so convincing.

She could see his face clearly, though, and remembered very well his earnest and generous eyes as he'd looked back at her on the street outside St. Gabriel's. He had made the autopsy seem so important, as if a doctor's dissections would tell them everything. But would it tell her where her father had gone when he disappeared? Would it explain what went so horribly wrong for her uncle?

"I don't know," she said vaguely.

"Then don't ever say such a thing again, to anyone. Do you hear?"

Only now, in the light of this fierce imperative, did Cass see what her aunt thought, and she stood up at her place, jolting the cup. "He didn't kill himself, Aunt Flo. That's not what I meant."

"Are you sure?" she asked, so weakly. Mike Foley wouldn't have been the first of the defeated fathers they knew to embrace that final defeat, that mortal one. Suicide would have consigned his soul to hell forever.

But no, that wasn't what she was saying. Cass put her arms around her Aunt Flo's shoulders. Mrs. Foley leaned into her, the goiter pressed warm against the side of Cass's throat. Oh, Aunt Flo.

Mrs. Foley kneaded her niece's thin body, weeping quietly. Cass stroked her.

After a few minutes Cass said with the simple authority that had now fallen to her, "The undertaker will almost certainly call you this morning to ask for your approval. I want you to give it to him."

"But won't an autopsy show if your uncle was drinking?" Mrs. Foley pulled abruptly back, applying the corner of her apron to her eyes. "Oh, look, I'm sorry, darling."

Cass's dark dress was covered with flour. Both women brushed at it.

"It doesn't matter if he was drinking, Aunt Flo."

"People will laugh at him if it was his own fault."

"But it wasn't his fault." Cass took her aunt by the shoulders again. This was the core of it for her. "That's the point. Not that he was drunk. Not that he was where he shouldn't have been. Not that what happened was his fault at all. That's the point. It's what we owe him, finding out what happened."

"If he was drunk, though"—she was a child at the mercy of a night fear—"even if it wasn't suicide, that means he died in mortal sin, without confession. Do you want *that* put out for your cousins and your brothers and sisters to know?"

The phone rang.

Both women faced it where it hung on the wall near the window, opposite the icebox. Mrs. Foley wiped her face with her hands and, crossing, wiped her hands on her apron. "Hello."

Mrs. Foley looked helplessly at her niece, who was slowly moving toward her. "What?" she said to the mouthpiece.

Cass drew steadily closer.

"Dr. Riley? I don't know him."

Cass heard the impending collapse in her aunt's voice. She put her arms around Mrs. Foley's waist, thinking, If we stand together with each other, we can do this.

Sean Dillon was his name. This call was proof that he'd meant what he said, that he was helping her. If we stand together—

Cass moved her head up and down, supporting her aunt, but

also commanding her. "Say yes. Say yes. You tell him yes, Aunt Flo."

Sean Dillon, she thought again. How could she have forgotten that name? To have recalled it now exhilarated her. The sun hadn't risen above the eaves of the parish church yet, and already he had produced a doctor for the autopsy.

Mrs. Foley saw in her niece's will, as she had so many times, her complete refuge. She did as she was told, letting go of her own impulse, which was so much easier to do than it ever would be letting go of her Mike.

The Stockyards Inn billed itself as the finest example of authentic Tudor architecture in the Midwest. With its multiple gables and finely wrought leaded windows, its mortar-and-beam siding above a first story of tawny brickwork, its clumped hedges, perfectly shaped spruce trees, regimented garden flowers and swarded lawns, it had the air of a well-kept Elizabethan manor house, or perhaps of an English Benedictine monastery, or, at very least, of a New England boarding school. But in fact it was a two-hundred-room hotel facing rough-and-tumble Halsted Street on the east side of the yards. Designed originally for the yards' owners to accommodate leaders of the livestock industry, now it also served patrons of the mammoth exposition building, the Kelly-Nash monument to itself, the site of FDR's triumphant renomination. Stockyard workers like Dillon had no occasion to enter the inn, and for the Irish among them it had come to function as an oversized Chicago version of the Big House, to which, in the old country, they had access only as servants.

Meals at the inn were served in the Sirloin Room, and even at breakfast, steak was the feature of the menu. The waiter whose job it was to enforce the rules of this sparkling universe did not bother to mask his disapproval when Dillon ordered only coffee and toast. He lacked enough money for anything else.

When the waiter left, Dillon snapped his newspaper open and went back to watching Raymond Buckley.

He was distracted by the entire scene before him, for here, on the very edge of the slaughter fields, which Dillon identified with everything he wanted to leave behind, was a display of opulence such as he'd rarely seen. The room could seat several hundred diners and was perhaps a third full. The waiters

wore tuxedos. The guests, almost all of them men, wore dark
suits and waistcoats, the tailoring of which put his own poor
suit to shame. Gleaming shoes and flashing cufflinks and sleek
oak wall paneling and polished silver serving trays bounced
the light around the room while patrons talked softly to one
another or read their papers with a show of well-being and as-
surance. Dillon read a message of order, harmony and perma-
nence both in the nobly proportioned room and in its
self-satisfied occupants that clashed utterly with the message—
violence, death, stink, greed—of the yards outside.

Buckley was sitting with a pair of companions at a table in
a far corner. Dillon's view of them was wide-open. From behind his spread newspaper he could watch without fear of
drawing notice. But soon it was apparent that Buckley, so at
ease, so expansive with the men before him, wanted to be
watched. He was performing for the brilliant room the role of
a great captain of business, and that required an exaggerated
bonhomie that would carry out across the tables.

But the two men with Buckley held themselves in check before him. The one on his right was apparently a clerk of some
kind, fixed as his attention was on an oversized ledger in front
of him. In the more than ten minutes that Dillon had been
watching, the clerk had said nothing, confining himself to jot-
ting notes. The man across from Buckley had only just sat
down, replacing another, and another before him. They had
conducted their business with gingery agitation. This one too
wore the demeanor of pure underling, a man in unrelieved
haste to be about his orders. His orders now had brought him
here.

Dillon surmised that a supply of men was waiting in a small
chamber off Buckley's corner of the dining room, each to be
brought for his moment with the ward boss. This was a routine, Dillon saw, and it was easy to grasp what was going on.
The tavern owners, policy runners, and gamblers who operated
in or around the stockyards—canaries, Dillon thought, picking
grains out of manure—came to Buckley at regular intervals to
be informed of adjustments in their assessments. No money
changed hands. Dillon saw how that would be pushing it, but
he also saw that the public character of this obeisance, offered
no doubt by every petty operator in the district, was essential
to Buckley's hold on it. The hearty arrogance of the man;
Dillon sat there and, despite himself, admired it.

Raymond Buckley was thin and, Dillon guessed from the reach of his bony legs under the table, taller than average. He wore a dark gray suit and an out-of-fashion celluloid collar that made the knot of his black tie ride high up on his gaunt neck. From where Dillon sat he could see a two-thirds profile of Buckley. Behind him the gray glass of a narrow window filtered the sunlight in such a way as to highlight something somber in the man. His pinched face, slicked hair, and rimless eyeglasses gave him the prim look of a schoolteacher which contrasted sharply with his expansive manner. He had continued to eat his breakfast, cutting morsels of food with arch fastidiousness, but then plunging them into his mouth with sudden gusto. Dillon was seeing the man now in his contradictions, and he sensed how difficult it would be to penetrate to the truth of who he was. Buckley's highly mannered behavior was intended to satisfy the curiosity of onlookers while revealing nothing.

When the waiter brought Dillon his coffee and toast, served prettily with fresh parsley sprigs, he touched the man's sleeve and pointed across the dining room. "Isn't that Harry Booth, the Union Transit man?"

"Who, sir? The man in the corner?"

"Yes."

"Why, no, that's Mr. Buckley," the waiter said easily, without a trace of the fear with which Hanley and the other yarders spoke the name. Buckley was a big tipper, no doubt. In this realm he sauntered more than swaggered.

"I took him for Booth because he seems to be interviewing those fellows. What's he hiring for?"

"Oh, I don't think it's hiring. Mr. Buckley is an iron dealer."

"An iron dealer? What's that?"

"Used iron. Scrap iron."

"You mean a junk dealer?" Dillon didn't even try to keep the surprise from his voice. He smiled blithely, like a harmlessly curious stockman.

"He's very successful. A place like the stockyards moves a lot of iron. Anyway, most of his breakfast business is about the Democratic Party. He's also the ward committeeman here. He brought the mayor here for lunch last month."

"Who, Mayor Kelly?"

"None other." The waiter glanced toward Buckley. Furtively? "The party does a lot of business in this ward. He always has people who need to see him."

I need to see him, is what Dillon wanted to say, but the waiter moved away.

Should I be posing as a commission man, a buyer, a valve salesman? What if I was a lawyer for Swift and Company? Or for Lambert, Rowe. Dillon's mind stalled at that thought.

If I did dare approach him, would it be with the direct set of my questions? Who was Michael Foley to you? What more than nickels and dimes? Why the brutality of how you killed him? What were you avenging? What could such a nobody possibly have done to you?

Dillon turned back to the *Trib*, tugging uncomfortably at his tie. He felt the falsehood of his presence here, not only that he was pretending to be a member of this circle, but that he could never close the distance across this room, bridge the gulf of what he did not know. He sat hunched over his paper, moving nothing but his fingers which absently stroked the crisp linen tablecloth, aligned one ornate piece of silverware, pushed at his untouched plate of toast. He lifted his gaze to let it float around the bustling room. The breakfast trade was picking up as more and more of the hotel's guests—the real buyers and sellers, the real lawyers—presented themselves at the maître d's rostrum. The heavy mix of aromas—steak, leghorn eggs, fried potatoes—wafted off the platters on the trays of passing waiters, yet Dillon had no appetite. In truth, he could not imagine eating ever again.

The futility of his thrust at Buckley struck him. Thrust? A flaccid wave of a hand was more like it. Raymond Buckley could ply his trade, a barely hidden system of loan sharking, influence peddling, protection, and extortion, in this most opulent and open setting in Canaryville because, on this narrow but well-tended turf, he was invincible. Buckley had made himself essential not only to the petty hoodlums who ran the local gambling houses and brothels, but to respectable businessmen right up to the packinghouse bosses, and to the neighborhood police and magistrates who were on his payroll, and to the political big shots downtown who used him as the lever of their vise grip on the entire South Side. Dillon could see, as he and everyone else were intended to, the full reach of Buckley's power. What had ever made Dillon think he could take on this man? That he could penetrate the stockyards-wide collusion that protected him? That he could link, before the law, this dapper big shot with the grotesque pulpy mass found head-first in the blood pit?

Was that only yesterday? No wonder he had no appetite.

He stared at Buckley as his first question—What did you do to Foley?—gave way to a new one: What am I going to say to Cass Ryan when she asks me what we can do to you?

A large man in a suit made of sheeny cloth approached Buckley from another table. Dillon leaned back casually, watching closely. The man's face had a bashed-in look, and Dillon recognized him as a famous boxer. A diamond flashed on the hand he held out. Raymond Buckley rose from his chair, waved his napkin in welcome, delighted to be so acknowledged by a genuine celebrity.

This move gave Dillon a fresh view of Buckley as he swung around to shake the boxer's hand, and something new struck him. A bandage had been applied to Buckley's right ear, the ear which until now had been hidden from Dillon's view. The white cloth and tape covered the ear like a muff. A swimmer's infection? Such a mundane infirmity so contrasted with the impression Buckley had made on Dillon that it drew his absolute attention. But his curiosity about Buckley's ear faded as quickly as it had been aroused when the ward boss took his chair again and that side of his face once more disappeared.

Dillon stayed for most of another half hour, watching as the string of cohorts continued unbroken. Buckley's lackey ushered them in and out efficiently.

When Dillon stood, crushing his napkin onto his plate, he felt a wave of disgust at himself for not having seen an opening in the wall around Buckley. Thus, without having planned to, he touched the waiter's elbow as the waiter collected the check. "That man's iron company," he said.

The waiter looked at him quizzically.

"What's it called?"

"Shamrock," the waiter said. "Shamrock Scrap Iron."

"Where is it?"

"Why don't you ask Mr. Buckley?"

Dillon grinned. "I wouldn't want to trouble him, not yet." And now he winked. "I may have something for him later, though. And I'll tell him you sent me. What's your name?"

"Malloy. Mick Malloy."

"Good fellow, Mick." Dillon slapped his shoulder and started off, then stopped. "But where is it?"

"South Bryant Avenue. Near the carshops. You'll see the sign. 'Shamrock Scrap Iron and Metal Company.' Big green sign."

Dillon thanked the man, winked again and left the Sirloin Room under the steam of his fresh impulse. By the time he got to South Bryant Avenue he had already imagined what he would find there, a scene similar to the one he'd witnessed in the opulent restaurant. Everything on this sooty street was shoddy, of course, and the supplicants lined up outside the ramshackle office of Buckley's junkyard were not tavern owners or politicians but two-bit debtors whose elbows showed through their sleeves. But they were in a line of Buckley's, just like the others, even if here it took them to a table inside the office at which a mere collector sat. The office windows were clouded over, and as each man entered, the door was firmly shut behind him, so Dillon had no glimpse of the transactions inside. But he didn't need it.

The waiting men reminded him of stunned cows in the slaughter chute. They were clutching bills or coins, not trusting their pockets with their puny weekly interest payments. Dillon saw the men for the grovelers, drunks and losers they were, and in the fear in their faces he read the key to Buckley's success. In his unflinching willingness to squeeze even these husks, squeeze them ruthlessly, Buckley's power lay. These men would all know very well what had happened to Mike Foley the day before. They were the exact point, Dillon saw, of what had happened.

The shadow of Buckley's presence overspread the day, chilling Dillon despite the summer heat as he traveled downtown. He went to the law library intending to study for the torts exam, but in the dark reaches above the cone of light at his table, he kept seeing the images, in turn, of those stooped men, of the corpse in the blood sewer, of Cass Ryan's face looking up at him as if he could help. This was the first time in Dillon's life that he found himself unable to push through a tangle of emotions to the inner calm of his concentration. As the hours passed and the time of the makeup exam approached, he began to feel a mounting sense of panic. Rifling through his notes and books, he could not break his mind free. Eventually he succeeded in putting Mike Foley and Buckley aside, but that only enabled the stronger image of Cass Ryan to take over the entire field of his consciousness. Finally he surrendered to it, forgetting the exam.

He put his head down on the table, closed his eyes and allowed himself to think of her. His mind came back to one scene in particular. She kept turning in place on that night sidewalk outside Walgreen's, her hair swirling across her perfect cheek, her legs shifting the weight of her perfect body, shifting it toward him. That picture of Cass, like a hypnotist's fixture, calmed him. The storm of what had followed his dashing after her that night—*last* night—simply went away. No woman's image had ever so soothed him before. He clung to it. Soon he felt strangely at peace. And then he was asleep.

He woke up seven minutes before four o'clock, just time enough to get to Professor Corrigan's office. The professor wouldn't even look at him. He gestured toward the narrow table in a corner of the small room. The table was cleared of everything except a pencil and the examination booklet. Dillon sat and opened the booklet, marveling at how this scene differed from the classroom trauma the day before. Professor Corrigan pointedly buried himself in the tome on his desk. Dillon picked up the pencil and began to read the first question. Nothing else existed for him but breaches whereby persons acquire a right of action for damages. He took the test with the detached efficiency—the infallibility also—of a veteran sleepwalker.

As he approached the Ryan house at dusk, his heart sank at the sight of the knot of men in front. They were the spillover from Michael Foley's wake, an informal throng, but the line of Buckley's supplicants was what Dillon thought of. How awkward his fellow yarders were in their collars and suits! They looked better when their elbows showed, he thought. He sensed in their uneasiness something else, however: the accuracy with which they'd registered the warning Mike's death was. This wake would not be raucous.

Dillon drew closer and saw that the house itself was jammed with people, mostly women. These men would have dutifully passed in pious silence before their friend's casket, then eased out onto the porch and into the warm, twilit street for their smokes and furtively passed bottles. Dillon read their anxiety more accurately now, understanding that they thought they were risking something by coming to Foley's wake at all.

As Dillon joined the cluster, a man in a green martial tunic and Sam Browne belt leapt at him. It was Hanley, and in tow behind him was another bedecked figure, although he was too stout to fully button his tunic, and the breast belt of his Sam Browne was extended with a piece of rope.

"This is the doc," Hanley said urgently.

The doctor, too, eyed Dillon with rampant worry.

They drew away from the others. "We haven't told anybody," Hanley said.

"Good, Jack. Told them what?"

Hanley's eyebrows shot up as he deferred to the doctor.

The doctor began a rambling report on what he'd found in the autopsy, and as Dillon listened he focused unprofitably on the man's half-drunken state, on his ludicrous Hibernian get-up, on the Celtic cross tattooed absurdly on his wrist.

Suddenly, as if the doctor were aware of Dillon's perception, he stopped. Then, in clipped language he made the statement that enabled Dillon, in turn, to make the crucial connection.

It came as an upward surge of recognition, a miracle of obviousness, the ground of a second mystery, but the absolute obliteration of the first. Doc Riley told Sean Dillon that in his examination of Michael Foley's corpse he had found lodged in the cavity of its thorax a half-dollar-sized, teeth-severed piece of what could only have been a human ear.

FIVE

Darkness. South Bryant Avenue in darkness. Sean Dillon walked rapidly along the rough edge of the street. Despite the designation "avenue," there was no question of curbs or sidewalks here, for this was a ragtag trucking district, and the unfriendly buildings were marked more by loading platforms than doorways. Dilapidated lorries and carts were parked at uneven angles, and Dillon had to cut between them, zigzagging, to stay in deep shadow. He was lugging a roll of cloth on his shoulder, like a cowboy's bedroll, and as he went first this way, then that, he had to keep an arm hooked on the roll to steady the thing. It was three o'clock in the morning. The warehouses and factories loomed over the deserted street like walls of a canyon. A faint mist hung in the air, what remained of a midnight rainfall, and Dillon had to hop occasionally to keep his feet dry.

Two blocks away the grim walls on the left side of the street gave way to stockade fencing, and that clued Dillon. When he'd come here in daylight the broad gate had been wide open, but he had noticed the formidable wooden pickets and the strings of barbed wire topping them. Now the gate was closed, locked. He picked his spot, the midpoint between two barbed-wire stanchions, then stood below it in silence for a moment, to listen.

In the distance were faint night-city sounds, but here on this street, and over the fence, inside the junkyard, nothing disturbed the night's tranquility.

The wooden pickets were seven feet high, and the two strands of barbed wire added another foot above that. Dillon shrugged the cloth from his shoulder, a section of heavy canvas tarpaulin. He bent to refold the tarp into a thickness of four layers, a yard square, and in one swift, leaping movement hurled it up to the top of the fence. It fell across the wires like a horse blanket, and in clambering up the rough fence, hooking his leg over the barb-smothering tarp, he felt like the star of an Old West movie.

In seconds he was over the fence and down.

Once more he froze, listening. He was ready for a watchman, but who would steal this junk? The forms of the iron wreckage cluttering the yard—rods, engine blocks, automobile fenders, radiators—poked eerily through the mist. Nothing moved.

The one-story building into which the line of coin-clutching supplicants had filed two mornings before was dark too. From his vantage now, it looked like a gas station shack. He made for it.

Halfway there he heard a cough.

He dropped behind the rusted hulk of a tractor motor.

Someone coughed again.

Not coughed. Only after the fact did Dillon recognize the sound of snoring.

Again he heard a loud, satisfied snore, then the lip-smacking grunt of a happy sleeper.

Dillon could still get away. He could retrace his steps to the fence and get up and over. Even if the sleeper woke up, he would never catch him. The smart thing would be to take off, now.

But instead he came out of his hiding place and crept forward. Near the building, to the left of the door, was the form of a man prone on a low cot. Not a cot, but the upholstered backseat of a car, propped now in the open air between a pair of crates. Dillon ignored the voice in his head that warned him not to approach.

The man was sound asleep on his stomach, his face turned aside, his arm hanging from the seat, his hand still clutching an empty bottle of hooch. Not asleep, but passed out. A pool of spittle had soaked the fabric by his mouth, and even now strings of drool blew in and out with each breath.

Dillon bent over, ready to hit the man if he woke, but then saw the flash of metal on the man's collar, a small silver pin, the letters "C.P.D." At the sight of the uniform Dillon straightened. The man's hat was on the ground near his feet. Dillon picked it up, eyed the badge, then dropped it. "Christ," he muttered. The cop had a ring of keys on his belt, and a flashlight. Dillon took them both, thinking, Someone must want me to succeed at this.

At the door, even in the dark, it was a simple matter to find the key that opened the lock, and without thinking more about it than that, he went inside. Once in the shabby dark room Dillon realized he had no idea what to do next. The plan in his mind hadn't even taken him this far, and the fact that the passed-out cop's key ring had solved his largest problem only emphasized the absurdity of his having come here so unprepared. The outrageous violation of his act hit him, not violation of the law or of Buckley's code, but of his own history. When had he ever behaved so impulsively? To have come here equipped only with a piece of tarp seemed suddenly childish, a caper from the Keystone Kops. He could not have justified himself to anyone at that moment. What *was* his purpose here? What did he hope to find? His uncertainty now, after having so easily slipped past the watchman, sparked an unprecedented bolt of fear, as if the threshold he had just crossed had in fact brought him into a trap. Buckley's office a trap?

He shook the thought off. The true threat—what *could* ensnare him—was the rampant set of his own feelings, utterly uncharacteristic, what had brought him here like this.

Now what? To move into the room and against it? Or slip back out and be gone? He crossed to the oversized, littered desk; the movement itself was his choice, and it made everything obvious. He removed the top desk drawer and placed it on the floor, below the level of the window, so that he could use the flashlight without being seen. After examining the desk drawers, he would move to the cabinets that lined one wall. He had time, he told himself. The cop was dead asleep. There were no other hitches. Someone *did* want him to succeed at this. He was here to learn whatever secrets the room would give up to him. It does not matter, he told himself, if I don't know ahead of time what they will be.

As he removed the second desk drawer, he froze again on instinct, to listen.

No sound anywhere, not even the stoned cop outside. All Dillon could hear was his own breathing, and to his surprise it was steady, regular. His body was attuned, his hands dry. His fear was completely gone. He had come here on the power not of his rational mind but of his intuition. His rational mind had given him pause, but now, by intuition again, he knew, even before finding what he did not know to look for, that he'd been right.

Someone wants me to succeed at this? Yes, *I* do.

Sean had approached her in the cemetery itself. To do so had seemed not quite decent, and he'd been full of apology, but he was only proposing that they talk when there was a chance. Cass knew she'd surprised him by abandoning her unfinished prayer to say, Let's talk now. They had—just down the hill from her uncle's hole in the ground, in the company of, once the others had departed, only the merciless grace markers. While listening to Dillon she had focused on those tombstones, measuring them like a farming lady might her crop. The idea that the granite slabs might keep growing, like cornstalks, was no more offensive against nature than what Dillon had told her.

Now, the day after the funeral, she was walking just ahead of him, up the stairs of a dark building in the Loop. They were having to climb four flights in the airless sweltering stairwell because the elevator was broken. What kind of a law school is it, she wondered, that can't keep its elevator working? Compared to her own building, American Bell, two blocks away, Loyola was dreary and ill-kempt. Was it the Depression that had so wearied the place, or was this the way downtown night schools always were? At the phone company, stairwells were brightly tiled. Here the unclothed, corrugated-iron structure shook with each step. These were hardly the tranquil tidy halls of learning one saw pictured in the magazines. But what did she know about such places, of whatever stripe? She never admitted being bothered that she hadn't finished high school—a dozen girls she was in charge of had—but she felt like an interloper even in this unappealing building.

At the landing Cass turned back to Dillon. A shortness of breath from the climb keyed her anxiety. "Who will it be, again? Besides the priest?"

"Someone Father Ferrick knows, a man to trust." The unreality of their situation hit him. They were two lively young people whose picture could have been on a subway poster, pointing to the amusement park at the World's Fair or to the lakefront beach with a gang of chums. Especially her picture, selling Wrigley's or Palmolive. I should be taking her to a movie, he thought, or, if she feels fancy, to the nightclub at the Drake, where we could ask each other questions about where we learned to dance so wonderfully. Dillon had to laugh as he turned away because he did not know how to dance. He couldn't afford the Drake. God, she's pretty, he thought.

"Father Ferrick has friends in the police department who went to Jesuit schools, men we can trust," he said again, as if she'd asked for this point of reassurance. "Father Ferrick was anxious to help. This meeting was his idea. He was one of the leaders of the reform, one of the people who helped break Capone."

Those words jolted Cass. How could he imagine that such a statement would reassure her? Capone? What could the gangland monster of her childhood have to do with her? She felt dizzy, and looking at Dillon didn't help. He was a stranger. Why had she allowed him to bring her to this frightening place? When he touched her arm as he opened the door, Cass felt, rounding through, that she was spinning on a tilted axis.

They walked side by side down a long corridor. The gleaming brown linoleum, splashed with light from ceiling fixtures, made Cass feel better. Stout wooden benches sat against one wall. The other wall was divided at intervals by doors with carefully lettered numbers and nameplates. At the end of the corridor, Dillon led the way into the office marked simply "Dean." At the sight of that word, Cass felt her racing pulse ease up somewhat, but then she found herself confronted by a white-haired secretary.

As Dillon talked to the woman, Cass's eyes went automatically to the crucifix on the wall behind the secretary's desk, and all at once she ached for the cool, hushed consolation of shadowy St. Gabe's. That church had always been her heart's one refuge; and God's too, she thought, where if He was condemned to claw at His nails, at least He could do so before people on their knees instead of behind surly clerks ignoring Him for their typewriters and telephones. By the time the dean greeted them, Cass's anxiety was peaking like a fever. The sight of his kind eyes above his crisp priest's collar broke it, and she felt at once that now things would be all right.

Dillon's reaction as they entered the dean's office was different, for what he saw were not Father Ferrick's kind eyes, but the blue uniform, all braids and stars, of a senior Chicago policeman standing stiffly beside the desk. Instead of taking him as the trustworthy figure of the help they needed, Dillon held back. "C. P. D."—the silver letters rode cockily on the man's collar. And Dillon thought of the cop in Doran's tavern, whose main function—an act of pure boss-protection—had been to squelch Jack Hanley's panic-driven ranting about Raymond Buckley.

"This is Deputy Superintendent Eddie Kane," Father Ferrick said, "an old friend of mine." The priest winked at the cop, a showy affirmation.

After the introductions they sat, the priest behind his desk, the policeman on an adjacent wooden chair, Sean and Cass on the cracked leather couch against the wall. Sean sat forward over his knees, aching to say what Doc Riley had found, but listening also to the warning voice in his head which said, Go slow.

Father Ferrick's gray eyes came gently to rest on the young woman. "I am sorry for your family's trouble, Miss Ryan."

"Thank you, Father."

"How's your aunt?"

"She's holding up."

"Would you tell her that I offered Mass for Mr. Foley this morning? I'll be making the novena for him."

"I will, Father." Cass dropped her head. "Thank you."

Dillon sensed a concentration of feeling in the priest that he had never noticed before; how the old man was flowing toward her. Dillon thought what a rare thing it was for the Jesuit to have such a woman in his presence. Then he thought, glancing at her, what a rare thing for me.

The policeman said, "It's terrible, what happened to your uncle."

That heartfelt acknowledgment made Dillon chastise himself for his initial reticence. The yards have gotten to me; this cop is Father Ferrick's friend. What else do I need to know about him?

When the policeman looked at him, Dillon saw his gaze harden. "Father tells me you're the one who puts two and two together here."

Dillon weighed the moment, having to decide once again to go forward. He said carefully, "Mr. Foley was murdered by Raymond Buckley. Do you know who he is?"

Kane's eyelids dropped, becoming hoods. "I know of him. That's quite a charge you've leveled. But does it make sense?

A well-connected party boss brutally killing some nobody? As I'm given to understand it, this Foley was hardly ..." He shrugged awkwardly, aware suddenly that this "nobody" was the man for whom he'd just expressed his sympathy. Truth was, his sympathy was for the girl. ". . . in a position to cause a man like Buckley a lot of trouble."

"Buckley is a usurer," Dillon said. "It's how he started out, and he's still at it. He crawls all over men like Foley. His system depends—"

"A what?"

"A loan shark."

"That's not the sort of thing you say about a man like Raymond Buckley unless you can prove it."

"Would a loan ledger constitute proof?" Dillon paused, then added, "A full record of principal and interest payments on dozens of loans, including a set to a man named M. Foley?"

"And where would I get such a thing, Mr. Dillon?"

"In the top right-hand drawer of the desk in the office of Buckley's iron company on South Bryant. On page two-seventeen of the ledger you will find Foley's name, and next to it a scrawl of arithmetic, the number five followed by seven hash marks. Foley had missed his interest payment seven times running. At seven Buckley's collection agents get very serious."

"Which means what?"

"As you stand facing that desk there is a file cabinet to the left. It's on wheels and rolls out easily. You'll find a section of wall that has an iron ring embedded in it at the perfect height for shackling a man. When Jack Hanley and I hauled Foley's body out of the blood pit, the flesh on his back was shredded. He'd been flogged." Dillon nearly choked on a feeling of revulsion, that such an image had anything to do with him. "You go to Buckley's office now, and you'll find a long-handled leather whip like the drovers use in the yards. It's in the bottom drawer of that file. I saw it there last night."

Eddie Kane grimaced at the Jesuit. "Don't you teach these guys over here that breaking and entering is against the law?"

"I didn't break. I used a key."

"Where the hell did you get a key?"

"From the watchman's belt. He was asleep. He is a Chicago police officer who works at Buckley's place in uniform."

"You have his badge number?"

"Nine-three-seven."

Kane had to deflect the feeling that he'd fallen too far behind this guy to get in front again. He shook his head. "Loan sharks don't kill people. What they want is to get paid."

"I think Mike Foley would be alive, but he fought them when he felt that lash on his skin. He broke away from the thugs and jumped the man in charge."

"You're still miles from Buckley. So some punks in his organization use the junkyard to squeeze oranges on the side. Buckley wouldn't go near the rough stuff himself."

"He must like to watch, because he was there, all right. When Foley jumped the man in charge, it was Raymond Buckley. They became locked in a death struggle with each other. I know that for a fact."

"Were you there, or have you talked to someone who was?"

"No."

"Then would it be too much to ask how you know that?"

Dillon glanced at Cass. She had laced her fingers together, was staring at them. He wanted her to look his way, to indicate she was all right with this.

As if she'd read his mind, Cass looked at him then with an unshaken expression, which he read as, This is *my* breaking loose from Buckley's thugs, *my* fighting back.

Right, Dillon said to himself, and he faced the policeman again. "The Foley family had a doctor examine the corpse. He found a piece of a human ear in Foley's throat. The court will find in checking it that that piece matches what's missing from Raymond Buckley's ear."

"Good God!" Father Ferrick's head jolted backward in disgust.

Kane asked calmly, "What doctor?"

Dillon calculated: the police could easily identify him by asking the undertakers. It gave away nothing to tell Kane now. "Dr. Richard Riley, head of the stockyards dispensary."

"And where's the . . . specimen?"

"He has it."

"What's the coroner's—?"

"The coroner knows nothing about this. The coroner is on Buckley's list." At that, Dillon reached into his jacket. He handed a piece of unlined yellow paper to Kane. "I copied these names from another ledger in Buckley's office, one labeled 'Special Friends.' You'll see the Cook County coroner's name two thirds of the way down the second column." Dillon gave him a moment to read, then added, "Your name isn't there. If it was, we wouldn't be talking to you."

"Most of these people run for office—aldermen, ward committeemen, judges." The policeman dropped the paper on Father Ferrick's desk. "The coroner runs for office. Buckley solicits contributions for the party. A list like this means nothing. In fact, most of what you've said means very little in a court of law, where you'd have to back up the very serious charge you've made."

The priest had picked up the list, was perusing it, and said now with studied offhandedness, "Come on, Eddie. A piece of one man inside another?" He looked up sharply to fix his friend with a stare. "Your crack surveillance unit should be able to determine if Mr. Buckley's ear is missing."

"Even if it is—"

"It is," Dillon said. "Buckley's right ear is heavily bandaged. That and everything else I've said is easily verified. You could have the warrants you need by lunch. Then you could force a formal inquest. The coroner would have to call his jury. That's step one. They rule for homicide, and then the grand jury has to take it. We bypass the men on Buckley's list."

The superintendent hesitated, glancing at Father Ferrick for support. The Jesuit stared back at him impassively. When at last the priest spoke, it was as if to a mulish student. "What seems to be the problem, Eddie?"

Kane's eyes had softened. "What's that saying, Father? About taking on the king?"

" 'When you strike at a king, you must kill him.' Holmes."

"That's the one."

"Buckley's no king," Dillon said. "He's a Canaryville thug."

"Maybe." Kane picked up the yellow paper, showing more interest in it now than before. "But he's a thug with friends. Who says this is the whole list?"

"It surely isn't."

The cop looked up at Dillon. "So I could be on it after all."

"Yes."

"But I'm not." He folded the list and put it into his coat. "And neither are the people I depend on." He stood up. "South Bryant, you said."

"That's right."

Cass startled them all by standing up abruptly. "Can I say something?"

"Certainly." The policeman took a step toward her, as if to catch her when she fainted.

But Cass Ryan wasn't fainting. "My uncle was a 'nobody,' as you put it. But not to us, he wasn't."

"Of course not. You—"

Cass raised her hand. "I'm a nobody too. But I'm not invisible. That I haven't spoken here doesn't mean that I'm invisible. My uncle was invisible, and you think he might as well stay that way. Raymond Buckley is who you see, and the list of his powerful partners. I saw your eyes widen as you read it. You *see* those people; they are the opposites of 'nobody.' Well, now you have to see me too. I'm not disappearing until you punish him. Do you hear me?" Cass had closed the space between them. Her face was level with the policeman's broad chin, pressing up at him. "Do you hear me?"

"Yes, ma'am." It seemed to take his entire effort not to back up. He had misunderstood. He'd thought the man was the one with the dogged will. Now he saw they both were. "Yes, ma'am, I hear you."

Only a few blocks away, across the river and outside the Loop proper, past the Water Tower and the Wrigley Building and the *Trib*, just beyond the intersection of Michigan Avenue and Lake Shore Drive, was the Oak Street Beach. The calm waters of the lake lapped at the crescent of sand like a pet's tongue. The beach was thinly populated, despite the warmth of the bright morning. On a weekend, it would be crowded with thousands of Chicagoans, but today only ladies from the nearby luxury apartments had spread their blankets. A few jobless men in tattered suitcoats and scruffy street shoes, as isolated from each other as from the privileged bathers, walked along the packed sand or sat on the edge of the boardwalk. A ranting old scavenger woman tugged at a battered baby carriage that was loaded down with scraps, the wheels rattling the planks of the boardwalk.

When the old woman had passed, Dillon broke their long silence. "So you ever come here?"

They had been walking steadily since leaving Loyola, but with no destination. Their purpose had become, apparently, the simple one of not stopping. Now, on the boardwalk, their footsteps sounded loud to Dillon, like the questions in his mind.

"I did," Cass said, "when the boys were younger, before they could come without me."

What about now? he wanted to ask. Do you go to the beach? Do you go to the movies? Dillon had taken careful note of her friends, men and women who had rallied to her during the wake. Mostly they had looked like telephone operators and clerks, chums from St. Gabe's, neighbors. She was the center of a lively, affectionate circle. It hadn't closed around her for the funeral itself, though. Perhaps because of her role inside her family as the strong daughter on whom both her mother and her aunt leaned—in the church they literally had leaned—her friends had kept their distance. No man had taken her arm or touched her shoulder reassuringly.

"What about you?"

"Not in years," he said. "Though when I was a kid, I used to come down here on Monday mornings to collect the milk bottles out of the trash baskets."

Cass stopped abruptly and faced him with an expression of pure shock. "You did that?"

Dillon thought he was being accused of something. What, of being poor? "Yes, I did."

"So did I." Her face broke into the largest grin. "I collected bottles one whole summer."

Dillon laughed. "I never saw you." He remembered how the boys and girls going from trash barrel to trash barrel had refused to look at each other. It was hard to imagine it now, when everyone took the Depression so for granted, but poverty had once been a dirty secret. The milk bottle collectors at the Oak Street Beach a decade and a half before had been like first friends, even if they never spoke to one another. "Then we got our jobs." Dillon was still laughing. "You did better than I did."

"No, I didn't."

"You got out of Canaryville."

"Just during the day. I go back at night, like the birds."

"Those are sparrows, the birds at twilight. Not canaries."

"Do you know about the canaries, though? What gave the place its name?"

"Sure." The English sparrows eating seeds from cow shit.

Was she going to refer to that unseemly part of their native lore?

But Cass announced with pride then, "My grandmother was one of the canary ladies."

"What?"

"The women who kept the canaries."

"I don't follow you."

"I thought you said you knew."

"Maybe you'd better tell me."

"The place was dubbed Canaryville because so many women that close to the rail links raised canaries in their homes."

"When was this?"

"My grandmother's day, turn of the century. They sold them to the B-and-O railroad men whose lines took them down to West Virginia and Pennsylvania where the coal mines are." Cass could tell from Dillon's expression that he'd never heard this before, so she went on with energy. "The miners took the canaries into the tunnels with them because canaries stop singing when the oxygen gets low, and the miners know they have to get out."

"The canaries die."

"That's right. Maybe that's why they don't use them anymore. They haven't in years. But we still live in 'Canaryville.' "

He'd taken her for such a knowing girl that this display of naïveté charmed him. Did she really believe miners would stop using canaries because their function killed them? Did she really believe, for that matter, that Canaryville had taken its name from such a poignant cottage industry? He liked her and showed it when he said, "It's a sweet, melancholy story."

"It's true! I've seen pictures of my grandmother by her cages!"

Dillon laughed. "Now those I know about, the cages."

"Well, why do *you* think it's called Canaryville?" She stopped walking and waited for him to stop too. A new, high-toned pleasantness had bloomed between them.

Dillon knew better than to spoil it by offering his far cruder—and, to him, truer—explanation. Seeds in manure was for the blottos in Doran's, who loved to emphasize that the shit eaters were English. He answered lightly, with the first other thing that came to mind. "I thought it must have been Capone or Dillinger or someone. Don't the hoods use the word 'canary'? Of course, when they do, they mean rat."

Cass's face darkened, a sudden shift in mood, which Dillon regretted. She said, "They would say that's what you are."

"Except they never heard of me."

"They will now."

He shrugged. "Another reason to blow Canaryville. I shouldn't have gone back once I started coming up here for those bottles. You were smart."

"But you're the one who's been going to school all this time."

"Just another way of collecting bottles."

"But how did you do it? You've been working at the yards all this time? And you made it to law school?"

Dillon resumed walking. She was asking where he'd gone to college, what had qualified him for Loyola. And he did not want to tell her.

Cass followed, perplexed that he'd hopped away like a skittish cat.

It was Dillon who stopped again. He would not treat the largest part of his own biography as shameful, even if everyone else who knew him did. He said, "I did my undergraduate studies in theology and philosophy at a place called Quigley."

Cass looked at him blankly.

"That's the seminary."

"I know it is."

"I was studying to be a priest. The Church gave me my entire education; it's why I have one. At the last minute, just before my vows, I quit." He waited for her to flinch or blush or look away. But she did none of those things. "I got my job at the stockyards, and started at Loyola the next year."

Cass smiled. "And you've been collecting bottles ever since."

Dillon nearly blurted out, You mean you're not shocked?

She touched his arm. "I used to think I would be a Sister when I grew up." She felt closer to him than she had before, the generosity his story implied, and also the suffering. Her eyes glinted when she added, "But then I realized I *was* grown up. I mean, I am."

"You are."

Now, because of the affection she saw in him, affection for

her, she did blush. "What next? You're almost finished, aren't you?"

"I'll take the bar. But there are still no jobs, not even for lawyers." His mind flew for an instant to what the dean had promised, the interview with Lambert, Rowe.

Would he call himself John? Well, hell, maybe he should.

He turned from her and stared back at the wall of downtown buildings. The nearest was the pyramid-roofed Drake Tower, where he had thought to take this woman dancing, only he couldn't dance, he couldn't pay the cover.

In his face, as he looked back at the city, Cass saw the hint of the ache that made her want to understand him. All that he'd been through, all that he had done and failed to do—but what Cass saw was an image of him as a young boy collecting bottles here and wanting only, as she had herself, to be close to God.

She had hardly given a thought to his situation, so full of her own grief had she been. It shocked her to see only now what this man was doing for her. "And your chances of getting a job are even worse, aren't they?"

"What do you mean?"

"As a lawyer. That list of Buckley's 'Special Friends.' They're the people who hire lawyers in Chicago."

It was true, of course. Not even Swift's would hire a man who'd made enemies of Kelly and Nash. Dillon was as capable of feeling the job-panic as anyone, and it amazed him now to realize how unprotective of his future he had been. What he wanted to protect was this woman.

Touching her arm, he turned her back toward the city, to walk. "I can always collect bottles."

"Are you really so unafraid?"

He did not know what to say. They continued to walk, Sean holding her arm. As man and woman, they had no training in speech of this kind. But Cass had broken the silence even as it had begun to flow back toward them. He was unprepared to feel this connection, a connection of common history and of wanting to break out of it.

"I am afraid," he said finally, "but not in any way that presents me with decisions. I'm not afraid of a man like Buckley. And I'm not afraid of losing a job I haven't been offered yet."

"So?"

Dillon laughed. "You want me to say what I am afraid of?"

She laughed too. It did seem ridiculous, as if they were school chums daring each other into some display of intimacy. But she had the sense also of standing with him on the edge of a very real taboo. In moving into an active assault against Buckley, they were violating the rule of their kind: at work and on the street and even in church, the message was, Suffer in silence.

But it was more than what they'd just begun with Buckley. They were close to some violation with each other too, something personal.

"I'm afraid of the water," Dillon said as he grabbed her hand and forced her into a run with him. At first it took a great effort, running through the sand. Cass pulled her hand free—to refuse his impulse, he thought. But she stooped quickly and removed her shoes, then took hold again, and they were off, heading for the gentle surf. He hadn't run like that in years, and soon it was as if they had left the ground together.

Running hand in hand, with the same wind in their faces, the same sand springing beneath them—it was a purgation, a ritual action dividing the first phase of their relationship, when a focus on who they were to each other was out of place, from the second, when nothing else would be as important. No wonder gravity fell away! No wonder it felt like flying!

At the water Dillon stopped, but Cass, letting go of him and veering away, kept running along the shallows, soaking her stockings, splashing the hem of her dress. Dillon was aware all at once of how much farther into the moment she had gone. He was still in his damn shoes. He was still dry.

She came back laughing. "You are afraid of water?"

"I never learned to swim."

The simple admission jolted Cass. She heard it for the preamble it was. She stopped laughing.

"I was out there on a boat once, a measly rowboat. My friend"— Sean stared out at the very spot—"my friend stood up and the boat tilted. He fell out. I tried to pull him back into the boat. Then I fell out. I thought we both would drown."

"But you didn't."

"No." Dillon had never described that event to anyone, not even his mother. His friend and he had not mentioned it again. "We hung on to the boat until somebody came along. We didn't drown because it wasn't that dangerous. But you asked me what I am afraid of. You're standing in it."

Cass looked down at her feet. "Oh, my . . ." She stepped out of the water, wringing her hem with her free hand. She looked up at him. "Are you afraid of drowning, or only of getting wet?"

She meant nothing by the question, but its relevance slapped him. Despite appearances, he *was* getting wet, with her. He did not answer.

The sudden gravity of his silence drew her. She straightened again, aware that, after all, he had something more to say.

"Back there at Loyola, I listened to the priest and the cop tell you they were sorry about your uncle. I realized I had yet to tell you that I am sorry too. I sensed how important he was to you." His words hung in the bright air between them. The breeze flapped Dillon's tie up into his face. He caught it and buttoned his jacket.

Cass caught her breath, to be back to that. "He'd become my father to me, my second father. Now I've lost him too."

"I know what you mean. That is, I . . . I wanted to tell you how, about a hundred years ago when I was maybe ten—it was the same summer I was out here in that boat—I came home and found the breakfast dishes still in the sink. My mother wasn't there. My sister told me she was at the trolley shed on Archer Avenue where my father worked. I ran there. I found my mother sitting on the step of the shed's main door, dry-eyed, stunned-looking. Before I could ask what had happened, she told me to get home and watch my sister. I asked her what had happened. She wouldn't answer me.'"

"What was it?"

"My father had gone to work sick. He took a nap in the shade of one of the idle trolley cars. He was asleep when some other driver got in to move it, not knowing my father was underneath." Dillon looked sharply away. His eyes went to the skyline, the Drake, the huge Palmolive Building topped by the Lindbergh Light.

When Cass touched his arm, it seemed she could feel the blood pulsing through the sleeve of his coat.

"I never saw him again. I never saw the . . . remains." He looked back at her. "I think that's why I felt . . . Maybe I sensed your uncle was someone's Pa, and I could do for him what I never got to do for my own. I don't know," Dillon closed his eyes.

Cass could have touched his chest, which moved, just perceptibly, as he breathed. He seemed the very soul of self-possession to her. She said quietly, "I wondered why you are with me in this."

"Now you know, and now I know too."

Sean put his hand on her shoulder, pressed it lightly, the most natural thing in the world, a chaste communion. If they had broken something, it was no taboo, but the habit—the false taboo of their kind—of solitude.

"You are a good man, Sean," she said. He did not answer.

They stood like that, in the wind, at the edge of the lake, her feet wet, his not, the weight of the city accumulating against them.

After walking Cass Ryan to the Switchboards Building, Dillon set off for the stockyards, intending to work the rest of his shift. Not that he thought he could slip back into his old routine, but he had yet to imagine an alternative to it. His long-standing fallback plan to stay on at Swift's remained in place, the beam of his ambition, even if he had sawed half through it. For now that meant donning his overalls, holding Hanley's tools, breathing through clenched teeth; the years had given him nothing if not will.

The South Side El was uncrowded in the middle of the day, yet its run out of the Loop, past Soldier Field and the fairgrounds, down to Archer, seemed to take forever. Approaching his own district, Dillon couldn't help but see the rickety wooden rear balconies of the tenements lining the tracks as the slatwork, yes, of cages. He felt like a pigeon compulsively heading home—pigeon, canary, sparrow, rat—without a thought as to whether it was where he wanted to go. When he saw the great, familiar billboard, "We Feed The World," he imagined those scrawny brown birds, a wing of them, darkening the sky, swarming down on the dried crusty piles overflowing the collection pens.

He laughed at what Cass had said. He had seen the "canaries" with his own eyes, would see them this afternoon. They were the opposite of the martyr birds whose memory the martyr women of St. Gabriel's revered. He chastised himself for the rush of disdain he felt, as if the extremes represented by Cass's story and his weren't the limits of the world to which *he* was born; as if its people were only either scavengers or victims. What about St. Bede's sparrow?

Dillon's mind went at last to Dr. Riley. *When you strike at a king, you must kill him.* He felt a pang that the blunt, avenging weapon he and Cass had raised above Raymond Buckley—how bold of them!—was the timid, wet-eyed Riley himself.

He checked his watch. It would add less than half an hour to his tardiness—tardiness again!—to go to the yards dispensary first, to put a firm hand on the man's shoulder. Dr. Riley, more than any of them now, was the sparrow. And if he was the sparrow—Dillon wished for a way to say this to him—he was soaring.

The dispensary was housed in a low, one-story whitewashed building behind the looming fertilizer factory. A pair of brick smokestacks towered over the medical hut, spewing gas. As Dillon went through the flimsy glass-paneled door into the clinic itself, the stench of an ammonia-based disinfectant hit him. But it smelled sweet compared to the air outside.

A man in a black rubber butcher's apron and knee boots was sitting on one of the benches in the hallway, cradling one arm in the other. Blood showed through the heavy gauze bandage below his elbow. Dillon caught the poor bastard's eye and nodded as he passed. The nurse was behind a table near a door that led to the examining room, but she was fingering through a drawer of folders. Dillon went by without her seeing him.

Dr. Riley was alone in the room at a small metal desk in the corner. He was bent over a sheaf of forms, pen in hand. One wall was lined with shelves holding various-sized bottles, cartons, and packed bandages. On another was a pair of charts, one showing the entire human anatomy, the other a page of text labeled "Eight Kinds of First Aid That You Can Do."

"Hello, Doc."

Riley started. Fresh blood splotched the left sleeve of his frayed white coat. As he capped his pen, his hands shook. "What happened? What'd they say?"

"It went the way I hoped. Father Ferrick—"

"Did they arrest Buckley?"

"Not yet. Cass Ryan made the charge. They'll have to get a statement from you first. They'll want the . . ." He glanced over at the shelves. Which bottle? Which beaker? "Specimen."

"They can have it. Then I'm out of this, right?"

"You'll have to say where you got it. They'll take your

statement now, and then they'll ask you to repeat it at the hearing."

"I thought all I had to do was give it over." Riley scraped his chair around to look at a small white cold-cream jar on the window sill. His voice cracked when he faced Dillon to ask, "When will this hearing be?"

"Soon, I hope. That's up to them." Dillon's crossed to the window and picked up the white jar. "Is this it?"

"It's formaldehyde."

The heft of the jar reminded Dillon of a baseball. "Who ever heard of such a thing?"

"I'll tell you, if I'd of known who that piece of cartilage belonged to, I'd of flushed it down the toilet."

"You could still do that. You could have done it anytime." Dillon reached a hand behind his own neck to rub it, aware of the tension he felt. He saw how scared Riley was. "Why didn't you?"

"I wish I had."

The man's fear so openly displayed made Dillon see his simple courage, and Dillon realized that this was nothing new. Riley had been living by it somehow all his life. Otherwise he would not have been able to swallow his terror now.

Dillon turned back to the window sill, to replace the jar. He looked out at the broad cinder-paved avenue that ran between the fertilizer factory and the Armour cannery. In the distance he saw the top of the Stone Gate, that Druid dolmen that so weighed on all those Irish. A tractor was hauling an overloaded offal cart toward the bins, and had to swerve when a forklift backed out of its shed. Up the wall of the nearby factory, he saw a Negro coughing at a small window on the third floor.

And then he saw the two coming. The policeman was no surprise. Dillon didn't know him, but even from the distance of fifty yards he read the rank insignia that marked him as a captain at least, one of Eddie Kane's deputies, no doubt. It was the sight of the other man, the civilian, that set off the alarm, for Dillon remembered at once where he had seen him—at Raymond Buckley's elbow at the Stockyards Inn. This bastard had ushered Buckley's vassals in and out of the Sirloin Room.

Dillon turned back to Riley and forced himself to speak calmly. "I see them coming now, Doc, the policeman and a lawyer or somebody. I've had a second thought about how this thing should go. Will you play it my way?"

"What do you mean?"

"I'm not ready to trust these people yet." Or you, he might have added. Dillon knew better than to say that their bold move against Buckley had already been betrayed. So much for Father Ferrick's old friend.

"How are we going to do this thing if we can't trust somebody? What are we supposed to do, bring Buckley to trial by ourselves?"

"I'm asking you to trust me for now, Doc. Just me."

Dillon slipped the cold-cream jar into his coat pocket, then took his coat off and slung it on the bentwood rack in the corner. As he loosened his tie and unbuttoned his shirt, he squinted at the door. "What would you be checking me for? Maybe I've got a bad cough or something."

Riley's eyes slowly focused. "A cough?"

"Maybe my chest hurts bad when I cough. What would that be?"

"Pleurisy, maybe, or TB. We've had TB, you know."

Dillon picked up the stethoscope. "Check me over, Doc. We want them to think you're just checking me out. I'm nobody to these two."

Riley deftly hooked the stethoscope around his neck.

"But what can we give them? They've come for the evidence, that's what they'll be interested in."

"Evidence?"

"The piece of cartilage, the ear." Dillon's eyes bounced off his coat on the rack. "We can't give that to them yet. While we see how they're playing this, we have to give them something else."

"A base on balls."

"Sort of, yes." Dillon openly surveyed the various bottles. "Something they can look at as the thing you took from Foley's throat." Something, he added to himself, they can throw down the gutter and think it's gone.

Riley's hesitation lasted only a moment. He moved Dillon aside to get at his counter. "This is what we want," he said, reaching for a quart-sized metal canister. He twisted the lid off, then fished in the vinegary liquid with two nicotine-stained fingers. He pulled out a shriveled walnut of flesh and held it up in triumph.

"What is it?"

Instead of answering, Riley put the thing in his mouth, swelling his cheek to a knob, and chewed. Riley loved it when Dillon went pale, and he fished in the canister for another. Instead of eating this one, he snipped at it with scissors until he had a crescent of raw flesh the size of the first digit of his finger. He held it up for Dillon to admire, all the while gnawing away at the one in his mouth.

"What the hell is it?"

"Pickled pig's foot." Riley laughed out loud. "Knuckles," he said. "I'm a sucker for them."

Dillon slapped the doc's shoulder, craning to look into the canister, Riley's snack supply. Dillon had seen the awful things in jars on tavern counters, but he hadn't tasted one in years. When he and the doc grinned at each other, Dillon felt a blast of the fellowship that took men like them into those taverns together.

While Riley found just the right small container, Dillon removed his shirt and hopped onto the examining table.

Riley washed his hands, then applied the cold disk of his stethoscope to Dillon's chest.

Each relaxed into the role he would play now. He's trusting me, all right, Dillon thought. Who am I trusting?

Dillon was surprised at the doctor's steadiness. His hands moved over his body easily. I'm trusting Riley, he thought. Their bond made him feel powerful. If we have to, we *will* bring Buckley to trial on our own.

When the knock came, they were ready.

"You're Dr. Riley?"

"Yes." The doc stood aside as the cop and the civilian entered.

"I'm Captain Gallagher. I've come for the . . ." The policeman was a large, self-sure Irishman, but he hesitated and glanced at his companion. Buckley's man was staring at Dillon, who was still bare-chested, seated on the table, his legs dangling. Sensing that the man was trying to place him, Dillon kept his eyes on the floor, like an intimidated yarder. He noticed the man's highly polished shoes, the cuffs of his fancy suit riding them just so.

". . . the evidence in the Foley case," the captain said.

"The cartilage."

"If that's what it is."

Doc Riley moved away from Dillon toward the cluttered table that served as his desk. "It's about time you got here. I don't want the thing." He picked up a tin canister and turned back to the policeman with convincing readiness.

Gallagher crossed to Riley, prepared to take the canister. But the doc shook his head. "Where's my receipt?"

"Your what?"

Riley looked quickly toward Dillon, who inwardly groaned, What's this? Just give it over.

"I'm not releasing evidence to anybody without a receipt. What if you—?"

"You needn't bother yourself about it, Doc. There's no question of a receipt." Gallagher smiled, but without friendliness.

Buckley's henchman forgot about Dillon, and went to the other side of Riley. "Listen, you—"

"Never mind," the policeman said, and he put his arm out to block Buckley's man, as if to prevent the rough stuff. But then, without warning, he himself seized Riley by the wrist, twisting his arm so violently that Dillon thought it would break. He checked the impulse to protest. Riley cried out in pain and dropped the container.

The civilian picked up the tin canister and opened it. He winced at the sight of the piece of flesh, the stink of the chemical soaking it. "Jesus."

Gallagher, in releasing Riley, shoved him aside. Riley fell against his desk, spilling papers and folders. While he struggled to regain his balance, the two men left the room. Riley rubbed his arm, staring at Dillon. The boozer's cloud had swept out of the doc's eyes, replaced by the cold, sharp glint of fear.

SIX

On the morning of the inquest Dillon went to Doc Riley's rooming house to pick him up. What alarmed him first was that the guard was gone. After today, but only after, Riley was not going to need protection. Once his finding was formally endorsed by the medical examiner—a piece of the killer's ear in the victim's throat!—the coroner's jury itself would replace him as the accuser of Raymond Buckley. The case wouldn't hinge on Riley anymore, and more to the point, the Kelly-Nash machine's commitment to its South Side overlord would evaporate. Buckley, not because of his brutality but because of its being exposed, would be finished.

But that was *after* today. Dillon hurried up the stairs of the by now familiar stoop. Every other time he'd come here this week, the uniformed sheriff's deputy had been sitting in his car right in front, but now the car was gone, the deputy nowhere in sight. Was the Sheriff's Office the same as Eddie Kane's after all?

When Father Ferrick had learned from Dillon that his old pal Eddie was in league with Buckley, he had immediately reached for his phone, announcing, "It's time to get serious about this shit." The crudity had surprised Dillon, and so had what the Jesuit did. He called up Cardinal Stritch on the spot, and then so bluntly demanded the cardinal's intervention that for an awful, paranoid moment Dillon thought the entire phone call was a show for his benefit, that the cardinal was not on the other end of the line at all, or that, if he was, Father Ferrick was a secret Buckley ally and was trying to get the cardinal to dismiss him. But not so. The cardinal matched Ferrick's indignation and went to work. By the end of that day, the state's attorney for Cook County, a prosecutor named Tom Courtney, had launched his own investigation into the death of Michael Foley, and the sheriff's men had been dispatched to protect Riley.

But now the sheriff's men were gone. Dillon hopped steps all the way up to Riley's room. The boardinghouse was a dark, overcurtained place, essentially like Dillon's own. Several times that week, Dillon had felt a pang of pity for the doc, that he had wound up living alone in such dilapidation. And not only that: Dillon had more than once bumped against the cold wall of his own fear that he too would be in such a place when he was old. But now his only feeling was a screeching anxiety. Where are you, Doc? Where are you?

At Riley's door he knocked, and knocked again. "Doc! Doc!" His voice died against the wood. The door was locked. He put his ear to it, then banged it. The doorjamb hardware was as flimsy as that on his own door, at his house in another corner of the same rotten neighborhood. Without a further thought, Dillon bumped the door with his hip, a swift concentration of his full weight. The door burst open and Dillon went through so easily that he thought at once, with stark incredulity, This is where I let Courtney leave him?

The room, with its gray, twisted bed linen, its clutter of chop suey cartons and empty whiskey bottles, was an expression of the surrender Riley had made, not to Dillon but, long before, to the inertia of an unhappy life alone. The room was wreckage, but of a normal sort for a man like him. Riley was gone, but Dillon saw nothing to suggest that he'd been forced from the place against his will.

One corner held a dark old wardrobe. Dillon sidled between the bed and a basket of soiled clothing to open it. Riley's suitcase and the rest of his clothes were there. On the bureau was his black medical bag. If Riley had left the place of his own accord, intending to flee Dillon as much as Buckley, surely he'd have taken some of this with him, or all of it. Dillon examined the bed sheets, but they were dry, unslept-in. The doc had promised Dillon repeatedly that he would not leave the room, not even to walk around the block for air. Only the evening before they had grinned at each other, feeling they had made it through the chancy week. Dillon had finally decided he'd been obsessive in insisting that the sheriff's men protect Riley around the clock, but now he saw he hadn't done enough. Everyone in Chicago had his price, the sheriff too. If goddamned Buckley knew that already, why didn't I?

"Trust me," he'd said so glibly to Riley. Dillon felt a surge of a coming panic as he began slamming the drawers of the bureau, rifling Riley's belongings, desperate for some clue to explain what happened.

That he found nothing was the clue.

Buckley's men had come for Riley at some point the night before, after Dillon had departed and after the sheriff's deputy had been taken care of. Riley would have had no choice but simply to go with them. He was no Mike Foley, had never claimed to be.

Now Riley was—Dillon pictured this as if he knew it for a fact—at the bottom of Lake Michigan. He banged a drawer shut, a lamp fell over. He pounded his fist on the bureau top, bouncing the lamp again.

When he had quit the seminary, the rector had told him contemptuously that he was a man with no follow-through. The red margin between the rector's lips had narrowed to nothing, a thin white line of suppressed fury. He had treated Dillon as if he had broken a vow when, out of respect for a vow's solemnity, he had refused to make one.

But a vow was what he'd made to Riley. "Trust me." The words in his own voice would haunt him, he knew. But then he heard them in Riley's voice, now as, "I trusted you."

Dillon crossed to the window and snapped the shade. The sound of its recoil around the spring tube was like a gunshot. Morning light flooded into the room and, suspended in it, a fleet of dust particles.

Maybe not Lake Michigan; an incinerator someplace, a grinder. Dillon knew very well that Doc's body would not turn up incriminatingly in a drain box at Swift's. Not this time. When had he ever failed so utterly? Now instead of Riley's face or the rector's, Dillon saw his father's.

He closed his eyes, turning away from the room, then opened them. On the street below he saw a thin man in a dark suit, alone, staring up at him.

The sheriff's deputy?

The deputies were all in uniform. They never left their cars.

The man did not disguise his interest, and that refusal of the surreptitious, with its presumption of invulnerability, infuriated Dillon. His rage vied with his self-loathing, an emotional turmoil he had not felt before. He braced himself against the frame of the window, as if to keep from leaping out, aiming his own body, like an arrow, at the bastard's throat. The man's cocky presence was one last message from Buckley.

Dillon backed away from the window, moving slowly for as long as he thought himself visible to the man below. Then, at the door, he exploded through, hurling himself down the stairs, as if bringing Doc Riley back were a simple matter of moving faster than Buckley's man did.

Dillon knew from books and movies that the reward for whipping down to the street and confronting the watching hoodlum and forcing him to confess would be the discovery of where his friend was being held. Having magnified humanity with his righteous indignation, he would go at once to his friend and free him.

Even crashing down the boardinghouse stairwell, his mind a frenzy of aggression, Dillon knew very well the difference between this moment and the golden time of movies. One difference was that these bastards would stuff a man into a blood sewer. Another was the despair he already felt, the certain knowledge that Riley was already dead.

And the man on the curb was already gone.

Dillon stood there, breathing painfully, staring at the vacant place by the lamppost. Now he was a sparrow to himself, a South Side pseudo-canary, not flying through the bright warm hall of a movie screen but skittering in the dark, pecking at grains of real food but eating what was around it, shit.

"German Army Attacks Poland; Cities Bombed, Port Blockaded; Danzig Is Accepted Into Reich."

Cass Ryan stared at the newspaper in her hands, trying to take its headlines in.

"Hitler Gives Word."

She looked up from the paper, startled, as if Aryan boys were trooping down the main corridor of the Cook County Courthouse. The wide hallway was crowded with citizens and functionaries striding past in both directions: jurors, witnesses, plaintiffs, defendants, lawyers, bail bondsmen, magistrates, marshals, and police. There were secretaries, clerks, and messengers too; yet they seemed, every one, figures of immense authority to Cass Ryan. Mature women in their dark brown pumps and old-fashioned stifling wool suits, and girls in cloche hats and colorful light dresses, men with gray hair and men with dazzling shoes, zoot-suited boys in custody and an old derelict under escort, trailing the odor of his own stale urine. Cass watched them all, wondering if Hitler was more to them than he was to her. She sat alone on a bench opposite another bench, which was vacant and which, with hers, seemed a kind of sentry for the ornate doorway of the hearing room. She wanted to hail one of those prim ladies—they reminded her of Switchboards senior supervisors—for an explanation *for her* of what she was reading.

"British Children Taken From Cities."

Cass could hardly imagine such a scene. What, millions of boys and girls in flight from German bombs? She pictured her own Aileen and Jerry. But her sisters and brothers were no longer children. They were like the fleet of ships that had left the harbor, each on its own, before the war began. But what of her cousins? What of Molly?

"Roosevelt Warns Navy; British Warships Mass."

Each clerk and magistrate moved along the corridor in his own way. Some read papers as they walked. Some carried rolled newspapers and used them to gesture with. All of their mouths were moving at once.

Cass felt that her ears were stoppered. The corridor hummed with talk, but she could make out nothing. She knew that events on the other side of the world—"Hitler Vows Fight"— were as awful in their way as what had brought her here, but it made her teeth ache right to her eyes to think that, because of Poland, the coroner's jury would not convene.

It was five minutes before ten, the appointed time. That none of the others had arrived fueled her worry. She felt as if she had been camping there, awaiting an apparition, like a woman in the Bible. When the young man in white arrives, he denies being the Lord. He is one sent to say that the Lord is not coming; the Lord has been called to Poland.

Cass thought of the Paroffs, who lived on her block of Forty-fifth Street, though they belonged to St. Stan's, the Polish parish in Englewood. She had only the vaguest notion of what the war would mean to them, for it confused her that Mrs. Paroff was one of the women who regularly came to Cass's own house on Sunday afternoons to listen to Father Coughlin. The radio priest thought well of Hitler. Cass hated the things he said, but her mother and her mother's friends always sat at the radio, nodding in agreement. What now, though? What if Father Coughlin said the Poles had somehow asked for this invasion?

Cass looked down at her hands, which were black with newsprint. She saw the coiled outlines of her fingerprints. Her palms glistened with perspiration. She folded up the paper and put it beside her on the bench. Poland would have to take care of itself today. She opened her purse for her handkerchief. I'm taking care of my Uncle Mike.

While wiping the smudges from her hands, Cass failed to notice the man approach her. She felt his shadow sweep over her, though, as he blocked the light from the ceiling lamp.

"Miss Ryan?"

"Yes?"

"I'm Raymond Buckley."

He hovered above her, a lean man with leathery features and flinty eyes which sparked behind rimless glasses. Cass had never seen him up close before, and his appearance surprised her. He was younger than she expected, and in his drawn face there was nothing to suggest the pampered life she had assumed was his. He was wearing an expensive dark suit and a laundered shirt with a high formal collar, that was true, but in his bent shoulders and bony hands Cass saw the signs of a man who had worked hard. A line of moisture made his forehead glisten, and Cass's mind tossed up a picture of him hunched over the wheel of a forklift tractor. If she was disappointed that he was not one of those overweight, soft-skinned bosses, it was because she sensed in him at once the capacity to survive the rigors of prison.

He was about to speak when he turned his head slightly, and she saw the bandage on its side—not what she expected either, a little white cap on his ear, hardly anything. But the sight made her quiver, and she felt her pain and rage afresh.

"I'm sorry for all of this," Buckley said, but not at all smoothly. He spoke with a near lisp.

It was as if he were standing in the sweltering air of a summer dream she was having. He would not go away. She was powerless to speak to him.

A man with a briefcase tugged at Buckley from behind. Buckley allowed himself to be drawn away. "You're the kid I feel for. Did your aunt get the flowers I sent, the wreath?"

Cass watched him, as if a curtain had fallen across his face, and in her mind she watched herself. She was a doe in an open field, aware of the hunter aiming at her, convinced he would fire only if she moved.

Buckley took a seat in the middle of the bench opposite, his lawyer next to him. Then the lawyer deftly moved to Buckley's other side, to whisper in his unbandaged ear.

That ear. It reassured her. How could he deny what it implied? She knew nothing about the laws of evidence, but the white tape on the side of Buckley's head seemed a certain flag of his guilt. She worked slowly back from her paralysis, and what she came to first was gratitude that her uncle had found a way to mark his murderer.

Buckley shook a cigarette from a pack. The lawyer snapped a lighter in front of his face. When Buckley guided his eyes back to Cass, she saw him flinch behind the flame.

Sean Dillon and Mr. Courtney arrived, but before they could tell her anything, an official called them all into the hearing room. Cass nudged Sean as they went through the doors. "That's him."

Dillon hadn't even looked Buckley's way and did not now, but he nodded. "I know."

"Where's Doc?" Cass asked as they made their way up the aisle. The raised table at the far end of the room was vacant, as were the witness chair and a dozen jury chairs to the side. Ceiling fans beat the air, but the room felt smothered, and Cass touched her wet forehead.

Instead of answering, Dillon shook his head.

Cass stopped him. "What do you mean?"

Again he shook his head. He took her elbow. Choking for air, she let him direct her toward the chairs. It was like a phone line going dead in her ear. When that happened, even if she knew linemen were testing splices, she always felt it was her fault.

Cass and Sean sat in the front row on Courtney's side. Behind them, seats were taken by two dozen spectators, including the pair from Swift's who had introduced themselves at her uncle's wake. Cass realized that most were sitting on Buckley's side of the room, like a wedding. They had chosen sides.

Just before the coroner and his jury were ushered in, Jack Hanley arrived, hat in hand, looking like a frightened cow. Somewhere he'd found the nerve to walk right to the front and take a seat directly behind Cass. She reached her hand back to him, to let him squeeze it. Suddenly she felt sure that Doc Riley would make it too. She turned in her chair, scanning the room steadily until her eyes came around to Buckley, who, staring back, chose that moment to moisten his lips with a slick tongue.

The coroner was a stout, red-faced man dressed in a rumpled linen suit. Cass had expected someone more like a judge, those robes at least. The jurors were striking only in their ordinariness. Of the twelve, four were women. They looked like people Cass saw every day on the El.

As the coroner banged a gavel on his table, unnecessarily, since there wasn't a sound in the room except the whirring of the ceiling fans, he used his other hand to wipe a gray handkerchief across the back of his neck. "The matter of Michael J. Foley, deceased," he read, then squinted up toward the state's attorney. "Mr. Courtney?"

Courtney stood at his table. "I'd like to call Dr. Ferguson for testimony."

The coroner shook his head and brought his palm down on a folder in front of him. "I have the medical examiner's report." He glanced at the jury. "My people have had it read to them. There's no need for Ferguson here."

Buckley's lawyer stood. "Mr. Blodget, we stipulate the medical examiner's finding without objection. The point of contention is not the tissue match but where Dr. Riley obtained his specimen. The question is, What exactly happened by way of injury to my client's ear?"

The coroner nodded and peered at Courtney. "That is the issue, is it not?"

Dillon shifted to look at Cass, displaying his worry by raising his eyebrows.

Cass whispered, "Where is he?"

"He's not coming. He won't be here."

"Where is he?" she repeated more loudly.

But Dillon's gaze had gone past her. He saw, standing in a rear corner, the man who'd been watching Riley's place from the street. He reined an abrupt impulse to cross the hearing room and seize the bastard, to choke him until he said what he'd done to Doc Riley.

But Cass repeated her question more loudly still.

The coroner banged his gavel at her. "I expect the demeanor of a court of law here! This *is* a court of law!"

Cass dropped her eyes, focused once more on the smudges of newsprint on her fingers.

The coroner aimed the handle of his gavel at Courtney. "You have witnesses to call besides Dr. Ferguson?"

"Yes, sir. One. Dr. Richard Riley." Courtney could not bring himself even to look at the coroner. From the glow of his thick neck, Cass realized how he was blushing.

"Then call him."

Courtney did not move.

Sean Dillon stood and closed the short distance from the spectators' section to whisper in Courtney's ear. He slid into the vacant chair next to Courtney, who said, "Dr. Riley's sworn statement, taken by the Cook County Sheriff's Office, is that he removed the specimen in question from the Foley cadaver's throat."

"So where is he?"

"I don't know. He has disappeared."

Cass came half out of her chair. Disappeared! Her question formed itself as, "Where am I?" She reached a hand toward Dillon, saw it was impossible, then folded back into her seat.

"Disappeared?" the coroner said skeptically. "You mean he didn't show up."

"No, sir. I mean disappeared. My associate here went to his house. The man has disappeared."

"This entire hearing was called to enter the family-commissioned postmortem into the record. Mr. Courtney, you told me yourself it was grounds for an overrule of the cause-of-death finding."

"We believe it is, sir. And we have entered the report—"

"I've seen the report. I've seen Dr. Ferguson's report. What we need is Dr. Riley. His report does not stand without him. The Sheriff's Office does not rule on the cause of death. My office does."

Courtney was mute. Dillon leaned toward him and whispered. Courtney hesitated, then, clearing his throat, said, "On the grounds of the Riley autopsy and the medical examination, the county moves—"

The coroner slammed his gavel down.

As the clap reverberated, Cass raised her eyes to the blades of the ceiling fan, which was up there slicing away at all of these absurd disputes. She saw the fan as the wheel of an old cart, and she thought, British Children Taken From Cities.

"You are out of order!" the coroner said.

"May I move postponement, sir?" Courtney glanced at Dillon for support.

But Dillon's thought was, No wonder Kelly rules this city like Genghis Khan, if this is the opposition.

The coroner was about to deny the motion, thought better of it, then looked across at Buckley.

Buckley's lawyer slowly came to his feet. He had a patrician calmness that contrasted with the layered-over tough-guy impression that Buckley had made on Cass. Buckley's lawyer, with his manicure and his watch fob, was what she had expected of the boss himself.

"If you please, sir," the lawyer said, "my client is entitled to this hearing now, at least to the extent of answering the slanderous charges that have been made against him."

"This is an inquest, counselor. Not an arraignment, and not a trial. Our concern is limited to the cause of death of one Michael J. Foley. The Cook County state's attorney is unable to bring forth testimony pertaining to that cause, therefore we have no further—"

"But charges have been made, sir, and spread abroad. Those charges are efficiently answered. Mr. Buckley would like an opportunity to do so. We don't want this hearing postponed. We want it terminated."

"Your witnesses are present?"

"Most assuredly. Four of them, including Mr. Buckley himself."

The coroner nodded and shifted slightly in his chair. Cass was certain his eyes made brief contact with Buckley's; a quick glint of the man's subservience.

Buckley went to the witness chair first, was sworn, took his seat and, prompted by his smooth lawyer, identified himself.

"And your occupation?"

"I am an iron dealer. I own the Shamrock Scrap Iron Company on South Bryant Avenue, back of the yards." Now, as he spoke up across the room, Buckley's slurred sibilants seemed a full-blown speech impediment. It was possible to imagine his playmates teasing him as a child. Cass pushed that thought aside, though. She would not sympathize with him in any way.

"And where did the injury to your ear occur?"

The question, put so directly, shocked Cass. Wasn't that the one question he wanted to avoid? She leaned forward to hear.

"There, at my place, at the Shamrock."

"Would you describe how it happened?"

"Sure." Buckley touched his bandaged ear lightly and began to address himself to the jury.

Cass wanted him to look at her, but he wouldn't.

"I have a diesel hunker at my yard, for hauling heavy loads like, say, an industrial radiator, or for pulling the engine up out of a wrecked car. You know what I mean, a hoist operation." He waited until a juror or two nodded. "I don't work the thing myself like I used to. It's not work for an Irishman." He grinned. "It takes brains." He waited for a laugh. "I have some Bohemian fellows who help me."

The lawyer interrupted. "Isn't it so, Mr. Buckley, that since your business began to prosper you have given more and more of your time to charitable work?"

"I try to pitch in."

"You are a past chairman of the St. Vincent de Paul Society of your parish."

"That's right."

"You serve as the Democratic ward committeeman for your precinct?"

A spectator snorted, a Republican's contempt for the lawyer's linking of a party job with charity.

Buckley, glancing toward where the sound had come from, said, "Yes, I do. And I serve for nothing."

"Go ahead about your ear."

"Anyway, I guess I got rusty on the hunker, because one day last week, when I go to add in my shoulder, my fellows were having a deuce of a time getting the engine out of an old brown Packard, a twelve-cylinder job, a monster, I've done it a hundred times, but I make a big mistake. I lean down over the engine to adjust the hauling chains, it's here, see?" Buckley hunched out of his chair to demonstrate, eyeing the jury with the air of a man who knows his story is good. "I should of leaned over from this side, because over here, opposite, is where the pulley and gears are. Those gears are vicious and you have to keep clear of them. Two sets of gears, up here and down here, primary, secondary. These are the ones to watch for because they're shoulder high, they can snag your clothes easy."

"You had a man lose his fingers in those gears once?"

"That's right. His thumb and two fingers."

"And what happened to you?"

Buckley startled everyone in the room by smiling broadly. "Like I say, I got rusty. I was leaning over on the wrong side. We get the engine up. I'm down on the thing to keep the chains in sync. The engine tilts unexpectedly, and oil gushes out of the block and shoots all over my legs and down onto my shoes."

"And the oil made the floor slippery."

Buckley nodded. "My feet went right out from under me. I would have been fine except for that oil. I fell."

"Where did you fall?"

"I fell into the open gearbox. That is, I hit it with my head, the side of my head."

"Your ear?"

"Yes, sir. My goddamned ear." Buckley's hand went gingerly to his bandage. He looked at the coroner with mock sheepishness. "Forgive my French, your honor."

There was such open intimacy in the glances they exchanged that Cass expected someone to point it out as proof, right then. She looked at Courtney, who was idling a pencil on a pad, and at Dillon, who was staring gravely across at Buckley. Well? Well? She wanted to shake Dillon. It's all lies! Outright lies and deceit! What hunker? What gear?

The jurors were staring at Buckley with a kind of sad fondness, and Cass grasped that they were believing him. But it's fake! she wanted to shout. His tale of homey clumsiness is fake, like his condolences to my aunt. How can a man be sorry for the family of someone he stuffed into a pit? Her eyes burned into Dillon's neck. Why aren't you saying something?

But Dillon didn't even know she was looking at him.

"And then what happened?"

"Nothing. I mean not at first. I couldn't move. The gearbox had me. They shut the hunker down. I was stuck."

"By your ear?"

"Yes. My ear was stuck in the gear."

"And then?"

"One of my boys ran to get the doctor. Another one held a rag to my head, to stop the blood. Oil all over my bottom half, blood all over my top. I was a mess."

"Are your workers able to verify this story?"

"Sure." Buckley pointed across the room. "Schevsky and Karlov. They saw the whole thing."

"And one of them returned with the doctor?"

"Yes."

"Who then freed you?"

"Yes."

"How?"

"By cutting the top of my ear off. It was pretty much gone anyway."

"So the cut was clean? With scissors?"

"He used a doctor's knife, but the cut wasn't near clean. The thing was half chopped through already by the gear."

"So there were teeth marks on your ear?"

"From the gear, yes. Plus, his hand shook so bad he sliced right into my skull. I would never have let that lush touch me with a knife, but he was the closest doctor."

"Can you identify the doctor for us?"

"Doc Riley."

The lawyer swung around to see the jury's reaction to this revelation. "Dr. Richard Riley?"

"Yes."

The eyes of the jurors had gone to Courtney and Dillon for *their* reaction. Courtney was perspiring visibly, leaning over his table, apparently reading what was printed on the side of his yellow pencil. Dillon's face had grown vacant. He was staring at Buckley, but Cass sensed that he had gone inside himself. Say something, she thought. Stop this.

"And then what?"

"Doc Riley took me down to the dispensary, to put medicine on me."

"And presumably he saved the severed piece of your ear."

"I guess he did. I never gave the thing a thought. Who would?"

The lawyer walked away from Buckley, toward the jurors. "Mr. Buckley, why would Dr. Riley make up the story about finding that piece of your ear in Michael Foley's throat?"

"Because he saw it as a way out of the money he owes me."

The only sound was the *whir-whir* of the ceiling fans. Everyone was staring at Buckley except his lawyer, who was staring at the jury. "Dr. Riley owes you money?"

"Yes. Eleven hundred dollars."

"Can you prove that?"

As the lawyer turned and crossed back to him, Buckley calmly reached into his pocket. "Here are his IOUs." He held a packet out to the lawyer just as the lawyer reached him. The lawyer passed it over to the coroner in one motion, an act almost of choreography.

Even the coroner, Cass thought, has been part of the rehearsal.

"That's all."

"Thank you, Mr. Buckley," the coroner said.

While Buckley returned to his place, and the coroner flicked through the IOUs, Courtney glared at Dillon and hissed, "Did you know Riley owed him money?"

"Never mind that. Demand to cross-examine."

"There's no cross here. Forget it."

"Move to postpone again."

Cass had joined them. "Yes, postpone it," she said too loudly. "Doc Riley will show what lies these are."

But when Dillon looked at her, it was with a futility so abject it jolted her. "It *is* lies, isn't it?" she said.

Dillon nodded. "But Riley's gone. Everything they just did depends on his being gone."

"Gone?"

Dillon said nothing. When she grasped that Buckley had done to Doc Riley what he had done to her uncle, she thought unaccountably of Poland. "Why are you letting them do this?"

Before Dillon could answer, the coroner struck his gavel one last time. "This inquest is hereby—"

Cass whipped away from Courtney and Dillon to do what Poland had done. "No!" she cried, hurling herself into the open area in front of the coroner's table. "You can't stop yet! Ask him—"

The coroner banged his gavel. "You sit down, whoever you are. You are out of order."

"Ask him what he did to Doc Riley!"

They were all looking at her as if she were hysterical, but inside she had turned to ice. The outburst was an ax she was taking to the jam of feelings that had clogged her for days now. "Ask him!" she screamed. "Ask him what he did to Doc Riley!"

The silence that rushed in after her came dangerously close to being a silence of recognition. One by one, each person turned toward Buckley, but Buckley had fixed his stare on the coroner.

The coroner shook his head, but tentatively. "Obviously, Dr.

Riley knew his testimony was going to be impugned. That's why he failed to show up."

"Not 'failed to show up,' " Cass said with crisp exactitude. "He *disappeared!* He disappeared because he is dead." Her hand shot out at Buckley. "You killed him, just like you killed my Uncle Mike!"

"Someone get her out of here!" the coroner ordered. Officials began moving from the corners. Jurors were up and backing away, but their eyes remained fast on her.

Now she wheeled on the coroner. "And tell us who else owes Buckley money! Do you? Is that why you are doing this? And what about the mayor?"

He banged his gavel twice more. "This inquest is adjourned!" he cried, then made quickly for the door.

Cass moved toward the jurors, but they scattered. The officers were about to grab her when Dillon put his arms around her, turning her so that he was between her and the burly men. "I have her," she heard him say. "I'll take care of her."

Dillon welcomed it when Cass went to the women's room. Once she'd turned the corner, he went quickly down the crowded hallway to the coroner's office, and he was there when Raymond Buckley and his lawyer came out, grinning like businessmen. A few steps brought Dillon into their path. They stopped abruptly.

"Mr. Buckley, I want to tell you something."

"What's that?"

Together the three men automatically retreated to the wall. Dillon was not making a speech—he differed from Cass in this—and it would not serve his purpose any more than Buckley's to be overheard.

The lawyer put his arm between Dillon and his client. Dillon swatted it away. "You aren't finished with this yet. That's all I mean to say. Don't think you are finished with this."

In fact, Dillon had no conscious idea what such a statement could mean, but he knew it embodied the core of his own truth now. He was not, however, simply putting his determination on display, a self-indulgent defiance. He was instinctively moving to draw Buckley out.

"And who the hell are you?"

"Leave it," the lawyer said.

But now it was Buckley who swatted the lawyer's arm, as he closed on Dillon. "Who the fuck are you?"

"I was a friend of Mike Foley's." Dillon had forgotten that this was untrue. "I was a friend of Doc Riley's."

"If you are the prick who brought that old fool into this, you did him no favor. I wouldn't wait by the phone for his call, if I was you."

"In your testimony, you referred to him in the present tense, as if he were still alive."

Buckley laughed and winked at his lawyer, who'd coached him, obviously. "I did very well, didn't I?" The ingratiating self-deprecator of the witness chair was gone.

"Ray—" The lawyer took Buckley's arm, but Buckley shook him off and grabbed Dillon's shirt. The man's wiry strength jolted Dillon as he felt himself lifted free of most of his weight.

"And I'll fucking kill you too, if I ever see you again."

Dillon now had his moral certitude, and he saw all of his important choices sweep into line. "That is what I wanted to hear you say."

Buckley laughed. "My saying that won't mean shit. Don't you get it, Mac? When I go into court I deny, deny, deny! That's all. The law works for me. Jesus, don't you get it yet?"

"The law works for a lot of us, Mr. Buckley." The law was Dillon's church now. He took Buckley's wrists and forced them apart, like freeing a rusted pipe joint. He squeezed until he saw Buckley wince. "I made a mistake with you," he said quietly. "I told Doc Riley I'd take care of him, and I didn't. I trusted the wrong people. I feel very bad about that, and one of these days you will too. I owe Doc Riley, see?" He dropped Buckley's arms abruptly.

Despite himself, Buckley began to back away.

But Dillon wasn't finished. He thought of it as flogging when he said, his voice at a whisper, "I owe Doc Riley as long as I live. I owe him you."

"That's it," Buckley's lawyer said. Now when he took Buckley's arm to lead him around Dillon, Buckley did not resist. The lawyer said over his shoulder, "Not a chance, Mister."

Dillon remembered Father Ferrick's claim to have a contact at Lambert, Rowe, and he realized he could be a lawyer like this man, professionally unintimidated by all that frightens clients, unoffended by all that clients do, regretful at what winning for clients may require. At Lambert, Rowe, Dillon would be a credit to Loyola, and he would be free of the yards, and his name would be John.

Dillon was still a young man, but as he watched his first enemy moving down the corridor, supported by his high-class lawyer, he felt the impossibility of what he'd set for himself. He felt the impossibility of his own life again.

"Mr. Dillon?"

When he turned, he saw Buckley's thug behind him, the man from the street below Riley's room. Dillon tensed; now the blood would flow, but it would be cleaner.

"You carried it as far as it goes here." The man held up a credentials folder, a badge.

Sean looked at it, unable to grasp its meaning. "You're the FBI?"

Light glinted off the small gold shield. Dillon stared at the thing. The blindfolded lady, Justice. But he couldn't make his mind function. When he looked in the man's face, he saw the tiny reflections in his eyes of all that was moving around them. He saw one moving spark in particular. Cass.

Dillon perceived her approach, as he was perceiving everything suddenly, like someone in a trance, a survivor of a car wreck.

"I'm Leo Fitzgerald, Miss Ryan." The man held his folder up for her, then put it in his pocket.

Cass did not react.

Facing back to Dillon, Fitzgerald spoke with the flat accent of a man from somewhere else. "I want to come right to the point."

Dillon pressed his arm. "You were watching Riley! You must have—"

"No, we weren't watching Riley."

"But I saw—"

"We were watching you."

"Me!"

"We picked you up the night you broke into Buckley's place. We know from Father Ferrick that you have the makings of a good lawyer. And now we know we have this case in common with you. Raymond Buckley has been near the top of our list for a while, but he is very careful to stay off the turf where our rules apply." When Fitzgerald paused, Dillon sensed that he was measuring him one last time. "We could use a patient, thoughtful lawyer who understands how it goes in Chicago."

Cass interrupted, "He killed my uncle!"

"We know he did. He has killed a lot of people. But you understand about jurisdiction—"

"You don't have jurisdiction over murder?"

"You just saw what happens in these courts." Fitzgerald looked at Dillon again, the one he wanted. "We have to get him into federal court, *our* court."

"Why are you telling me this?"

"Because you're inside, and we're not. We want you to join us."

"I'm inside!" Dillon nearly laughed. But then he realized in what simple way it was true. His feeling had put him inside. And so had Cass. He glanced at her, but what he saw was a way, finally, to be the man he had told her he already was.

"Will you?" Fitzgerald asked.

Dillon heard the question as, Will you, for once, finish something?

"Yes," he said, facing Fitzgerald, but he was speaking to Cass.

SEVEN

Poland fell. President Roosevelt immediately declared a so-called "limited national emergency," and limited was how most Chicagoans experienced it. The first shock of Hitler's aggression faded when several months passed in which the Nazi appetite for territory seemed sated. Newspaper wags began calling that period of lull the "phony war." Coughlinites wished Hitler well, and to them the disappointing German inaction was the "Sitzkrieg."

Unlike the émigré professors in Hyde Park and the Anglophiles in Riverside, back-of-the-yards Chicagoans resumed their habit of paying little attention to that part of Europe east of Wicklow. The parishioners of St. Gabriel's were more anxious that year about how the White Sox would do without Luke Appling than they were about Hitler.

In Washington during the same period, however, there was a profound if untouted urgency, as FDR maneuvered the fickle government into a state of readiness. And Washington, beginning after his taking the bar and completing his training, was where Sean Dillon was. He had joined the Bureau to be part of the move against the wily Chicago pols like Buckley. Especially Buckley. But the FBI war against the new breed political hoodlums was the real Sitzkrieg, as events in Europe forced the Bureau, too, to reorder priorities.

The FBI training facility in rural Virginia was a sprawling complex of buildings, athletic fields and firing ranges deep inside the huge Quantico Marine Corps post. The sky boomed with the sound of ordnance as leatherneck gun crews drilled in the surrounding hills, while Bureau recruits put in hour after hour shooting at human-shaped targets and practicing live-

ammo assaults against mock-up gangster hideouts. They were
taught how to interrogate and how to interview, and they
learned the latest in techniques of eavesdropping and surveillance. Dillon had never been much with his fists, but now he
became adept at throwing opponents and pinning them. He
qualified early on the pistol range, and in the classroom displayed the acute intelligence that had always marked him as a
student. One hastily organized course emphasized the activities
of the German-American Bund, and another laid out basic
principles of cryptanalysis.

The training lasted two months. By the time Dillon's class
was presented with its agent's credentials and personal weapons,
the men's morale was high. They felt ready, even, for war. And
by then, war seemed imminent. That's why most of the new agents were assigned to Bureau headquarters or to the beefed-up
D.C. field office, and at first Dillon was one of the few who did
not see it as a privilege to remain in the nation's capital during
a time of national emergency.

It was in Sean's absence, and with a sharp sense of
disappointment—almost betrayal—that Cass began going to
see Father Ferrick at Loyola. Because Sean's letters described
his duties only vaguely, they did little to help her share the
powerful patriotic urge with which, finally, he threw himself
into his work. Soon it wasn't only the war that was a distant
abstraction to Cass; Sean himself was. But there was nothing
abstract in the offense she felt as the months passed; as the
missing Doc Riley never turned up; as rough grass grew over
the oblong plot of her uncle's grave; as snow covered it. And
as Raymond Buckley still went unchallenged.

She looked less and less well to Father Ferrick. Her reports
of sleeplessness and of night-long bouts of weeping filled him
with inept worry. He was a teacher, even a lawyer, more than
a priest, and her plight chastened him. His attachment to her
grew, though; and that was what she needed—a father, an uncle. Often, instead of going home after work, Cass would go
directly to the Jesuit residence at Loyola, not far from the
Switchboards Building. She would curl up in the stiff chair by
the parlor window while Father Ferrick sat in silence, watching
the evening light softly fading until the shadows were as dark
as the dresses she habitually wore. She would periodically
start, as if recalling his presence, and then she would apologize
for saying so little. But the priest considered their speechless-

ness his failure, not hers. They were enacting an all too familiar Irish melodrama, for he was, to himself if not to her, just another in the ever growing line of flawed men who'd let a good woman down.

They had put Sean in that line, but too soon. In fact, his assignment at headquarters had been to the newly established office responsible for coordinating Bureau policy with war-readiness measures taken by other federal bodies, particularly Congress. All that year, unbeknownst to Cass or Father Ferrick—and, for that matter, to his superiors—Dillon was stalking Raymond Buckley through the thickets of the burgeoning Washington bureaucracy. The decisions arrived at, the directives issued, and the laws passed, when taken together—and, owing to Roosevelt's discretion, few did take them together—represented the most massive expansion ever of federal jurisdiction over the lives of ordinary Americans.

Over the life, therefore—and here was the core of Dillon's insight—of his own Buckley.

Dillon had quickly recognized his advantage over gumshoe agents in Chicago. Even as a low-level neophyte, he was one of the first to see the implications for law enforcement of the new national situation, and that was never more true than the day after Hitler moved on Denmark, Norway, and France. On that day, emergency legislation was introduced in Congress to call up the first peacetime draft in U.S. history. Through that summer, Congress debated the conscription bill and took testimony from any experts, including J. Edgar Hoover.

Hoover was drawing on recommendations that Dillon himself had had a hand in shaping, and he succeeded in influencing the legislation in ways that matched the Bureau's own broad agenda. Now, for example, instead of waiting for bail jumpers or prison escapees to cross state lines, Hoover's agents could come into any unlawful-flight case on the wonderfully simple grounds that fugitives, by definition, fail to notify their draft boards of changes of address. The draft law would authorize the FBI to stop any male on any street and demand to see his registration card. Every American man between seventeen and forty-five was about to come under the personal authority of J. Edgar Hoover, and of those, Hoover had his special attention fixed on the big-city political hoods who had so successfully eluded him.

Sparked to the idea by Dillon's office, Hoover argued that

the bill's proposed penalties were too lenient. An unprecedented national conscription, he said, would work only if it
was backed up with merciless sanctions. Anyone convicted of
draft dodging or of abetting it should face up to, not two, as
proposed, but ten years in federal prison. The *minimum* should
be five. "This is the survival," he said, "of our beloved nation."

The U.S Congress, in its Selective Service and Training Act
of September 16, 1940, set the general penalty for failure to
comply at up to five years—not ten, but not two either. Hoover
groused, but in fact the new law was his dream come true.

Sean Dillon, for his part, wanted a stockyard cutter's knife
with which to make his long-postponed thrust, but this law
would have to do. Unlike his colleagues, he did not have an
eye fixed on an entire class of criminals, but on one man
alone.

"Ecce Agnus Dei," Father Ferrick said, turning to face the
scattered congregation and holding the host above the ciborium
like a small torch. It was the early morning Mass at the Jesuit
chapel at Loyola, a weekday in November. The chapel glowed
eerily with its candles and votive lights. As the old dean recited the triple plea for mercy, the people on their knees, heads
thrown toward him, thumped their breasts. *"Domine non sum
dignus,"* they repeated. His vestments swirled as he descended,
and the communicants rose like a stirred undersea animal, a
single creature now instead of urban hermits, curling to the
bright rail like a tide. The click of their shoes on the linoleum
was one of the eternal sounds of the church, like the swish of
the confessional curtain, sounds which instead of breaking the
peculiar silence of the religion, floated within it.

Father Ferrick dispensed the wafers rapidly, moving along
the row. Their beady, moist tongues were what he saw, not
their faces, the old ladies in their hats, the shopkeepers on the
way to work, the odd Loyola student, the nuns who smelled
of soap. But Father Ferrick always noticed Cass. Unlike most
of the communicants, she kept her eyes open when she received, a violation of the piety, but a welcome one to him. Her
face, framed by the slanting thin visor of her hat, offered a
tiny, warm greeting which slipped between the stones of the
impersonal.

The dean would remember that particular morning because

of who else came to the rail: one of the last to do so, a scoured man in a dark suit, elbows just so at his waist, a stranger to the priest there, on his knees, with his tongue waiting. Sean.

Does she know you're here? Even as Father Ferrick put the host on Dillon's tongue, he glanced toward the pew in which Cass always knelt, saw her bowed head. As Sean blessed himself, and stood and turned away, never having raised his eyes, the priest watched to see if she would notice. Sean moved down the side aisle to a place in the distant rear—the hard men always took pews near the door—but she never brought her face out of her hands.

Father Ferrick's hesitation threw off the student serving as altar boy, who nearly bumped the priest when he didn't glide back across the sanctuary. *Sean is back!* He stood there watching the two of them, separated and unaware, aching that they should find each other. *Sean is back, Cass!* He wanted to cry out to her.

Sean's eyes flashed in the dim light when, instead of burying them in the postcommunion depths, he looked across at Cass, knowing exactly where in the dark church she was. *He's back for you!*

He waited for her on the steps of the chapel, and when she came out, eyes on her feet, belting her coat against the chill, he was afraid that she would pass without seeing him. He stepped into her path.

"Sean!" She was as surprised as he was to hear the weight of harshness with which her voice had automatically loaded his name.

"Cass," he said, but softly. He twirled his snap-brim awkwardly between his hands. He never used to wear a hat.

"You're in Chicago?"

"I just arrived. Literally. I took the Nighthawk. My train came in an hour ago. I came here hoping to see you."

"How did you know to do that? I never used to come to daily Mass down here."

"Father Ferrick told me."

"You talk to him?"

"In letters. He mentioned you."

Cass turned half away, afraid for a moment of what Dillon knew, of what the priest had told him.

"Your letters were nice," she said.

He knew, if she didn't, how little of what he'd wanted to express had made it into those thin envelopes. "There's been a lot I've wanted to tell you, but I couldn't."

"Why?"

He looked away and said nothing. The air between them might have been the same blank paper he'd been unable to fill.

He fell into step beside her as they began to walk up the crowded street toward La Salle and her office building. Now when Dillon spoke, it was with a certain impersonalness. "I came to you first, Cass, because I wanted to tell you what is going to happen with our friend."

His words only made her want to go faster. What she regretted most about the way time had so undercut them was that, apparently, he thought her sole passion was the hatred she had for Buckley.

"Would you stop a minute?" When she did, he added, "You're always walking away from me."

"That's not true. For more than a year I've hardly taken a step, but how would you know?" She didn't care a damn suddenly if he saw how hurt she was. "You've been busy in Washington."

"Right. And now I'm in Chicago, without knowing for how long. And the first thing I do is check my suitcase in a locker at the train station and come to you. What I have been doing in Washington is setting a trap for Raymond Buckley, and I thought you had a right to know about it before we laid it out in front of him."

"I do want to know."

"Then let's find a place where we can talk."

"I can't now. I have to get to my job."

"But I have to talk to you before I report in. The first order they'll give me is to talk to nobody. I've already said too much."

Cass laughed harshly. "I know Raymond Buckley better than they do. How could they say something is secret about him from me? How could *you*?"

"I didn't, Cass. That's why I'm here."

"Then meet me after," she said coldly.

"What time?"

"Five o'clock. You're really going to get him?" With a rush of feeling she touched his arm. But the feeling *was* hatred.

"Did you think I wouldn't?"

She had to look away. Of course, that was what she thought.

"I'm here for the homestretch and the finish, Cass. I've had my binoculars on Buckley the whole year. And now . . ." He shrugged. "Leo arranged my TDY."

"Your what?"

"Temporary duty. I won't be here for long." How to explain that he wasn't in charge of himself anymore, of a schedule of time that reflected his own priorities. Buckley, for one. This woman, for another.

Her hand closed on his arm, pressing it hard, and her eyes sparkled as she said, "I have something of my own to tell you, a secret. That's another reason to wait until later."

"Where should we meet? I can't come to the Switchboards."

"But you'll be downtown?"

"Yes."

"Then Oak Street Beach."

Dillon remembered that afternoon—was it really more than a year ago? At the lakeside, the scene of their youthful bottle collecting, their hearts had opened to each other for a moment.

"At that pavilion," she added, "where the polka bands play."

"Polkas?" Dillon laughed with a pleasure he hadn't felt in years. He saw himself cavorting on the margins of those summer concert crowds, one of a gang of Irish kids pretending to know the dance, jerking around the slatted floor, mocking the thick-legged Polacks, but also themselves.

"We won't be dancing," Cass said.

She should be here by now, he thought. He lit a cigarette, but even in cupping his match, he kept an eye scanning across the sweep of Lake Shore Drive to the buildings beyond. He stood alone in the shadow of the weathered pavilion. From the shabby look of the place, he guessed it was years since bands had really played there. He had not anticipated the lakefront's autumnal desolation.

He had no way of knowing that Cass Ryan's impulse to meet there had come automatically because of the countless hours in the last year she had walked those boards, that sand, alone.

The wind blustered in from the lake, fluttering the brim of Dillon's hat. He leaned against a bench with his back to the water, staring now toward the stout, backlit skyline, then toward the tiny people moving along the distant promenade.

All those thousands within range of what he saw, and not one remotely aware of him.

Damn, she should be here.

He took a last drag on his cigarette and let it fly. It soared toward town with all the other litter.

"Hello, Sean."

Her greeting startled him. He whipped around to see that she had just stepped out from behind the bandstand, having approached from the direction of the water, and not from downtown at all. The hulking pavilion had blocked his view of her.

She had been carrying her shoes in one hand, crossing through the sand in her stocking feet. Over her shoulder was slung a large, dark woven bag, too big to be a purse. She put it on the bench, and leaned over to slip on her shoes again.

Her slim ankles struck him, the curve of her legs.

When she stood up straight again, she tightened the belt of her trenchcoat and pulled the collar up closer to her throat. She is so beautiful, he thought. Why is it again I have not been with her?

"I got off work early," she said, as if that explained her coming on him from behind.

Sean grinned. "I'm a pushover as a G-man, aren't I?"

"That depends." She picked up her bag again, clutching it with both arms, holding it before herself like a shield. Dillon noticed the bag's rough fabric and realized it was a messenger's satchel.

But what kind of G-man had he become? Raymond Buckley was the one measure of that. Depends? *Everything* depended on what he was going to say.

With a gesture he proposed they should sit on the bench, but she seemed not to notice, as if in her concentration she had been stripped to one thing.

He went forward a step. "We are launching . . ." he began, then hesitated at the stilted word. But argot, the language of his authority, was the point now. ". . . a special operation to bring highly public enforcement action against violators of the new draft law."

"The draft law?" Cass was sure she had missed something.

Dillon repeated himself. "The draft law. A month ago more than a million men registered for the draft. Two weeks ago local boards started issuing classifications and calling men up. You know that."

Cass nodded. Everyone knew it.

"For conscription to work, it has to be fair and it has to be *seen* as fair, which his where the Bureau comes in. Law enforcement is always targeted. Usually the targets are anything but the well connected and the powerful, but this time that's *just* who they are. The men who beat everything else and who people assume will beat the draft too—we have a surprise for them. In several key cities, beginning this week, agents will be nailing big shots who falsified their registrations or used influence with local boards to get exemptions. The point is the *show* of enforcement. The targets happen to include a Chicago fellow named Buckley." At last Dillon allowed himself to smile. "His name near the top of the list is my small contribution to the effort."

If by smiling Sean meant to elicit her congratulations, Cass missed the signal. "The draft?" she repeated with stark incredulity. "What does Raymond Buckley have to do with the draft?"

"He's a thirty-four-year-old male citizen, and therefore subject to the law." Dillon's voice went flat, a briefer's voice. "The Ward Seven draft board, at least two of whose members Buckley himself nominated, just this week classified him S.S. 3-D, based on information Buckley was obliged to furnish under penalties of perjury."

"But what—?"

"3-D grants exemption from conscription due to hardship to wife, child or parent. In Buckley's case, since he's obviously unmarried, the hardship is to his widowed mother, whose address he gives as a La Grange old folks' home; he claims to be her sole support."

Dillon paused, wanting her to say something, but Cass only stared at him, waiting.

"The local draft board found itself disinclined to require proof, and so did not confront openly what everybody in the yards knows very well—that Buckley's widowed mother is dead."

Cass had begun to shake her head. "You're saying he fudged a draft registration? Who cares about that? The draft is nothing compared to—"

"But it's *ours*, Cass. His mother died four years ago. Buckley perjured himself. A federal violation. The draft law puts him on our field, in our court. He'll go to jail, Cass. He'll go to jail for *years*."

"But for the draft? What about what he did to my uncle? I want people to know what he did! What he is *still* doing!" Cass pushed her satchel into Dillon's arms, but it fell, spilling papers, yellow sheets filled with scrawl. The wind ripped several pages away, and Cass rushed to retrieve them, even as she continued frantically, "Anyone might cheat the draft"—she snagged a page, then another—"but only an animal would do what Buckley does. It's all here." She flourished the papers in Dillon's face. "This is what I brought you. It's *everything* about Buckley."

The satchel held manila folders crammed with hundreds of yellow sheets. "What is it?"

"It's Buckley conversations, what he says to people, how he speaks to them, what he threatens them with, what he does to them. My uncle and Dr. Riley were just two. Buckley is an animal! I want people to know about this!"

"His conversations?"

"On the telephone."

"The telephone?" A steel spring snapped open in his mind, an entirely new image of the woman before him.

"The switchboards. It's where I work, remember?"

"*You* did this?" He fingered the pages of transcript, lists of names, dates, paragraphs of tidy handwriting.

"I've been doing it every free moment for a year. As supervisor, I make it a point to relieve the girls myself who handle Buckley's exchange. In front there's an index, a log of dates on which he talks about the killings. There are six separate killings at least. He talks about it like he's ordering sandwiches. It's everything you need."

The shock Dillon felt had transformed his face into something ugly. "I couldn't use it, Cass."

"Why?"

"Because this is illegal. And it's federal, it's FCC. You can't show these transcripts to anyone. Who knows you've done this?"

"Nobody."

"Cass, this is serious."

She grabbed the satchel. "You're saying *I* broke the law? You're saying what *I* did is serious?"

Dillon turned, holding on to the bag. She fought him for it. "Are you going to arrest *me*?"

He held the bag away from her with one arm. When she reached for it, he pulled her against himself with the other. Neither of them moved.

After a long time she spoke, her voice muffled against him, still thick with incredulity. "You think I did something wrong?"

"That's not what I meant, Cass." He held her away, to see her. "It's Buckley I'm thinking of. If a judge knew about this, we couldn't convict him even of the draft violation."

"But it doesn't count, what's in there? What I heard him and the others say? Murder? Gambling parlors? They have slot machines in candy stores! There are police captains who call Buckley every week, and Buckley—"

"That's the problem, Cass. Their system works only if they stick together, and they do. Everyone from Mayor Kelly and the chief justice down will work to protect Buckley. Anyone who comes forward against him will disappear the way Doc Riley did. There have been six hundred syndicate homicides in Chicago in the last twelve years, not counting so-called accidents like your uncle's. Do you know how many convictions? Eleven." Dillon paused to let the number register. "We don't investigate or prosecute murder cases. The DA does, and he's either one of them, like the coroner was, or he rolls over for them, like Courtney did. And the same is true of the grand jury. We can only get Buckley if we get him into federal court. It's that simple."

"But the draft—"

"It's five years in prison if he gets maximum, and I promise you he will."

"That is not enough," Cass said with cold exactitude. "You are rolling over for them too, by thinking it is."

Her accusation was like a blast of wind off the frozen sea of her hatred, and Dillon wanted to turn away from it. But perhaps the chill he felt was from the bundle of pages he held under one arm, not only a record of Buckley's connivance, but evidence of his absolute immunity. *There* was the outrage. Dillon knew damn well the mockery it was to go after Buckley on the draft, like going after Scarface Capone on taxes. But you play the cards in your hand, or you fold.

Thinking about cards, he shifted the satchel to get a better grip on it. "I should look at this," he said.

"Even if it's against the law?"

"Do you want me to read it or not?"

"You were why I took it all down. I thought it would be a weapon."

"How?"

"I don't know." She felt the full force of her disappointment at his scruple, his readiness to strike so weakly at Buckley, and at her own inability to think what else to do. "I have nowhere to take it but to you."

"That's just as well, Cass. No one else should know about it, just us."

They were not standing on the same spot at all; their South Side Irish-Catholic lives, with all they had in common, had made them very different people. Something in Cass Ryan frankly frightened Dillon. The unexamined purity of her perception? Her utter lack of second thought? Selfhood like a flame?

But he had just agreed to throw in with her, no? Now that he was going to read the pages filled with her painstaking handscript, therefore justifying them, he knew that what bound him to this woman was more powerful than what he once regarded as the flame of his own selfhood, his very conscience.

With that recognition, a feeling of amazement flooded him. As if it were the most natural thing in the world, he leaned toward her, bringing his face to hers.

Cass instinctively lay aside her large question about him as she inclined slightly to meet him. It was as much her act, then, as his, their first kiss.

Dillon helped himself to a cone full of cooler-water and downed it like a shot, not to quench a thirst, but for the sheer release of crushing the paper cup in his fist. Then he turned and walked slowly down the long, brightly lit corridor to the room where they had Buckley.

Buckley and his lawyer, both seated on one side of the long table, looked up when Dillon entered. He enjoyed the shock of recognition in Buckley's face, but it went as quickly as it came, and he said nothing.

Dillon also enjoyed the sight of the gnarled pink notch in his ear.

"Aha, Dillon!" Leo Fitzgerald said from his place on the

near side of the table. He was in shirtsleeves, standing with one foot on the seat of a wooden chair, the revolver on his hip on full display.

To the side, at a smaller table, sat a young girl, a Bureau stenographer, hands poised at her machine. A glance was all it took to make her once again invisible.

Fitz swept a hand toward Sean. "This is my colleague, gentlemen. Special Agent Sean Dillon, who came up from Washington to give us a hand."

"Mr. Buckley and I have met," Dillon said as he closed the door. He stepped aside to lean against the wall, pulling cigarettes out of his pocket.

Buckley leaned to whisper in his lawyer's ear, not the man who'd represented him at the Foley inquest. The lawyer listened for a moment, his eyelids lowered. He nodded, then abruptly glared up at Dillon. "My client says you threatened him."

Dillon did not react.

But the lawyer turned back to Fitzgerald. "Which perhaps answers our question? Is this agent's personal vendetta the reason for my client's indictment? Whatever the reason, it amounts to selective enforcement, and it won't stand up."

"Not 'selective enforcement.' Selective *Service*." Fitzgerald began to fuss tobacco into the scorched bowl of his pipe. "The reason for the indictment is right in front of you." He gestured at the photostats on the table. "Shall I recite that last sentence for you again, the one just above your client's signature? 'I fully understand that it is a federal crime punishable by fine or imprisonment or both to knowingly make any false statements concerning any of the above facts as applicable under the provisions of Title 16, United States Code, Section 1032.' "

"Which we deny."

Fitz glanced at Dillon while putting a match to the pipe now at his mouth. "He forgot that his mother died."

"That is not what we asserted." The lawyer slapped the table. "And my client is in no way responsible for the classification rulings of the Selective Service board. If you follow up on these charges against Mr. Buckley, you're going to have to bring charges against a lot of people."

"What is your draft status, counselor?" Dillon asked.

"How is that relevant?"

Dillon pushed away from the wall. "May I see your draft card, please?"

"It's in my desk."

The two agents exchanged a look. Fitzgerald asked, "Have you read the statute?"

"I'm over-age. They're only drafting up to thirty-five."

"Men up to forty-five are required to carry their registration cards on their person at all times. As surely you know."

"How old are you, counselor?" Dillon asked.

The lawyer only stared at Dillon.

Dillon said, "American men may take their obligations under this law more seriously when they learn that the federal grand jury—which convenes, by the way, in *New York*—has handed down this week indictments identical to Mr. Buckley's against seven hundred and twelve men."

"Out of a total of what?" the lawyer was relieved to ask.

Fitzgerald glanced at Dillon.

"Millions, right?" the lawyer pressed. "That proves my point. This is politics, not justice."

"Would it be justice," Fitzgerald asked, "if I arrested you?"

Dillon watched Buckley, who sat with his hand at his eyeglasses, hiding the ear, tilting the lenses slightly to read the form that bore his signature, as if trying to grasp how such a trivial matter—he barely remembered dealing with it—could be coming back at him like this. He was dressed in a dark suit and white shirt. His tie was carefully knotted. A gold cufflink showed at his sleeve.

"The papers said there were forty-seven indictments in Chicago." The lawyer put his hand on Buckley's arm as if to restrain him, though Buckley had continued to read with the equanimity of an accountant.

Dillon was disappointed that he could sense so little of Buckley's reaction, and he realized that by rising to the lawyer's bait, he and Fitzgerald had been suckered. The lawyer's job was to draw the heat away.

Dillon had been imagining this moment for months, and he had gotten it completely wrong. He'd remembered Buckley lunging at him outside the coroner's hearing room, threatening to kill him too, and he'd counted on some similar display here. He never anticipated this cool detachment, what seemed a radical self-control.

Finally, as if in response to Dillon's stare, Buckley shook his head, pulled his arm out from under the lawyer's hand, looked up at the agents and said, "It doesn't matter. It's obvious what you've cooked up, and it doesn't matter."

Dillon had forgotten Buckley's speech impediment, that thick-tongued slurring. Unconsciously, he had eliminated it, as if such unmanly imperfection didn't square with the proper image of an enemy.

"I got to admit, I didn't see it coming." Buckley leaned back in his chair, unhooked his eyeglasses and only then allowed his direct gaze to fall on Dillon.

"Fine or imprisonment or both, Mr. Buckley?"

Buckley shrugged, but could not resist asking, "How long?"

"Up to five years."

Buckley glanced at his lawyer, who shook his head: never.

And then, for an overlong time, nothing happened. Fitz smoked his pipe, still with his leg on the chair. Dillon continued to hold his position against the wall. The ash from his cigarette fell on the floor because he did not want to lean forward to the ashtray. Dillon quite deliberately called up the memory of Mike Foley's corpse dripping with blood on the edge of the slaughterhouse sinkhole. Cass Ryan's uncle seemed more dead than ever because Dillon had no memory of what he looked like alive. It made no sense to him now that, in fact, he had never met the man.

Buckley's face was white, unsmiling, set like plaster.

Dillon realized that Buckley and his lawyer were waiting for an offer, as if what Washington had wanted was a piece of Buckley's loan shark operation to help finance the coming war. The bright room with its four blank walls and overhead light sank into the silence of human refusal.

No one moved or spoke.

Then Leo did.

He tapped the bowl of his pipe on the table, and said, "Take your break, Marie."

The stenographer stood up and, without a backward glance, left the room.

Fitzgerald now took his foot off the chair and sat down, leaning across the table toward the lawyer. "We are pressing for the maximum penalty in this case, and given the importance the government attaches to making the draft law work, I think we'll get it. Your client should understand what he's up against here, and so should you. Do you want to deal with us or not?"

Dillon's surprise took him off the wall. He nearly screamed, Deal? Deal with this bastard? What are you talking about?

Dillon steadied himself by leaning on the table, a standing version of Fitzgerald's craning posture.

The lawyer picked up a pencil and began tapping idly. "What do you have in mind?"

"Not what, who. We want Edward J. Kelly."

The lawyer dropped the pencil.

Buckley continued to sit stone-faced.

But Dillon had to grip the table to keep from challenging his partner: What the hell is this?

"We want John M. Bolton. And we want Jimmy Martin."

Now the lawyer laughed abruptly. "Why stop at the mayor and a couple of aldermen? What about Pat Nash? And Governor Horner? Don't you want them, too?"

"We would take them. We are prepared to quash the indictment against your client in return for his help in developing certain cases."

"What cases?"

"Misappropriation of NRA funds, interstate transportation of gaming equipment, violations of the Mann Act."

Raymond Buckley cut Fitzgerald off simply by raising his hand. "Or what?"

"Or you go to prison as a draft dodger."

"Up to five years?"

"That's right."

Buckley leaned forward to put his face opposite and level with Fitzgerald's. "Federal lockup?"

"Yes."

Dillon was staring at Buckley's upraised hand, as if trying to see specks of dried blood in its swirling pores; he was not ready for it when Buckley turned to face him. It was to Sean Dillon that he wanted to make his declaration.

"I can do five years standing on my head."

It was the exact statement Dillon would have predicted, and his anger was aimed as much at Fitzgerald as at Buckley. Who could ever have expected this callous bastard to break so easily? What was he, a pickpocket? A Canaryville pimp? Toothless as the draft law snare turned out to have been, still its jaws were closed on Buckley. Who was Leo Fitzgerald to offer him a way out of it? Leo had his own strategy, obviously, but to Dillon it felt like betrayal.

But Dillon's anger curled back on himself: How could I not have seen this coming? To bring down the majordomos of the Kelly-Nash machine, Leo would offer Buckley his own stained-glass window in the cathedral; he would make Buckley an FBI agent, if it would help.

Like he did me.

Dillon remembered what Cass had said about their great strategy against the man who had so brutalized her uncle: "That is not enough. You are rolling over for them too, by thinking it is."

Cass Ryan had known instinctively that Buckley would shrug at them.

Raymond Buckley, who, on page after page of the yellow sheets which Cass had so compulsively covered with her nun-pleasing handscript, and which Dillon had by now all but memorized, showed himself to be completely ignorant of the relationship between acts and consequences.

And us? he thought now. What consequence was five measly years in starched denim compared to the swollen hulk of Mike Foley's body?

"Leo, can I talk to you for a minute?" Without waiting for a reply, Dillon moved to the door, opened it and went out into the hallway. Fitzgerald followed him. They faced each other.

"You were going to let that bastard off."

"I'll let the devil off if he gives me Kelly."

"You've misread Buckley, Leo." Dillon poked Fitzgerald's chest, a brisk expression of anger. "And you've misread me."

"We're not just settling scores here."

"What are we doing?"

"Trying to pry these spiders out from under their rocks. You brought me back a sweet set of draft laws from Washington, but it's up to me to use them the best way I can. This is Chicago. The draft law doesn't mean squat here, except as a rod to poke and pry with. That's all it's ever meant to us."

"Tell that to the director."

"Hoover knows how this is played. You're the one who's learning, Dillon."

"Buckley would never give you anything. I could have told you that."

Fitzgerald shrugged. "That leaves me forty-six other rocks

to pry up. And as for Buckley, he can serve five years on his head? Good for him. Let's make sure he does."

Fitzgerald turned to go back into the room, but Dillon stopped him. "That's not enough."

"What?"

"Five years, and with good time it will be three. That's not enough for Buckley."

"So what are you saying?"

"Let me have him."

With those words Dillon had pushed into another realm, the uncertain once, more familiar to Fitzgerald than to Dillon, in which obligations were not spelled out, nor limits; in which famous distinctions blurred over, as between ends and means, as between justice and revenge. It was a realm supposedly forbidden to men like them, but they both knew—now that Dillon knew—that it was also the realm in which they had their true existence.

"What are you going to do with him?"

"I'm going to spend the afternoon sitting in that room with him, letting him stare me down. And then I'll invite him again to help us develop a case against Kelly. And he'll say no. Then I'll let him go. Tomorrow, Thursday and Friday, I'll help you interview the other big shots. A few of them I'd like to take by myself. And then on Monday, I'll want it announced that the draft indictment against Raymond Buckley has been dropped."

Fitzgerald put his hand on the wall, leaned into it. "What do you have, Dillon?"

"Just a feeling, Leo."

"What do you *have*?"

"A feeling."

Fitzgerald sighed wearily. "I don't tell you everything, so you don't tell me—is that it?"

Dillon arched his eyebrows, but in his mind, the long yellow scroll of Cass's transcript unrolled: calls to commissioners, tipoffs to casino operators, bribes to judges, orders to leg breakers, rewards to cops, name after name, secret after secret, more than enough to stun Buckley's colleagues with what he, Dillon, knew. The FBI in possession of reams of information that could only have come from Buckley.

"It won't work, Sean, unless you have something. You've been gone for a year. What could you have?"

Dillon stared back at him. "I want the Buckley indictment quashed, Leo."

"Just as if he talked to us. You're setting Buckley up to get him killed."

"You've seen too many gangster movies, Leo. I didn't spend six years at night school learning to be an accomplice to murder, not even Buckley's. I want to use the force of law against this bastard. I want him faced with what he's done, and I want him punished."

"Forget it. Let's go with what we've got."

"Give me a week, Leo. Let me have him for a week—alone. After that it's all yours. What do you say?"

"You've pulled ahead of me, Sean. What do they teach you guys in Washington now?"

Dillon put his hand on the doorknob, going back to work. "That anyone could forget that his mother died."

Dillon spent that entire afternoon in the interrogation room with Buckley and his lawyer, just the three of them. Except for intermittent protests from the lawyer, no one spoke. Dillon claimed to be waiting for Buckley to cooperate. Buckley was glad for the chance to show that he could wait too. Dillon leaned against the wall, smoking in silence, watching as Buckley resolutely stared at his thick knuckles.

Throughout the day on Thursday, and again on Friday, Dillon interviewed the other draft law violators, a series of small-time Chicago politicians, assistant county commissioners, magistrates, ward committeemen and party functionaries. Dillon emphasized their vulnerability to federal prosecution, and at a certain point in each interview, he asked the stenographer to leave. As Fitzgerald had done with Buckley, he then offered to quash the draft indictments in return for help in developing cases against senior members of the Kelly-Nash machine. As Dillon expected, each one refused.

The following Monday morning the U.S. attorney's press officer announced without explanation that the Selective Service charges against one man, Raymond Buckley, had been withdrawn.

Within an hour of the announcement, Sean Dillon and Father Aloysius Ferrick were shown into Eddie Kane's office at police headquarters. Since their last meeting in the dean's office at Loyola the year before, Kane had been promoted to superintendent, and his large office was an emblem of his new position as Chicago's top policeman. A pair of leather couches flanked a low table at one end. Kane's oversized desk dominated the other. The walls were covered with framed citations and photographs, including one, prominent behind the desk, of the stocky policeman side by side with FDR.

"Congratulations, Eddie," Father Ferrick said once the three had taken seats on the couches. Dillon and the priest sat opposite Kane.

"That's right, Father. I haven't seen you since my promotion."

"No." Ferrick fixed him with a disapproving stare. "You haven't seen me since Doc Riley disappeared."

Kane blushed, and Dillon sensed that only this old priest could cause such a reaction in the man. Kane looked at Dillon. "But I'm not the only one moving up, huh? You're with the Bureau now."

"Yes."

"I hear you guys are pressing hard on the draft thing."

"Maybe too hard. We've had to admit we were wrong with one guy. A friend of yours."

"Really? Who?"

"Raymond Buckley."

Kane eyed Dillon carefully. "We all noticed when you hauled him in. I mean, we noticed it was you. Or I did, anyway."

"Why? You thought it might be personal?"

"But you dropped the charges?"

"An hour ago. In time for you to read about it in the afternoon papers. The indictment against Buckley has been quashed. You look surprised, Eddie."

"You had him for a sure five years, I heard." Kane shrugged. "Not like the Bureau to make a mistake." The policeman leaned back against the smooth leather couch, a man whose new furniture still gave him pleasure. "What can I do for you?"

Dillon took a folder from his briefcase and handed it over. Kane flipped it open, leafing through the dozen pages quickly. "What is this?"

"The summary of what we have so far from Buckley, what he's been putting out in exchange for his release. Look it over, Eddie. See for yourself. Names, dates, records of meetings, descriptions of his arrangements, a list of violations matched up against a nice selection of Buckley's associates, a three-ring circus of life in the new Chicago."

"New? As I recall, you brought me a list like this once before."

"Not quite like this one. Besides, in those days, Buckley was denying it. Now he's giving it to us." Dillon watched Kane read for some moments, then he added quietly, "And this list differs in one other way. Your name is on page eleven, Eddie."

The cop flipped to the page.

Dillon looked across to the priest. "It seems Raymond Buckley recalls in some detail a series of their meetings at Comiskey Park last summer. Eddie and Buckley had adjoining boxes behind the dugout on the first-base side. Buckley had been complaining to Eddie that his payments were lagging, and so the Sox games were set as a series of deadlines."

"What payments?" Surprise snapped out of the priest. "Eddie got into debt to Buckley?"

Kane ignored the two, reading. His lips moved.

Dillon shook his head. "Nothing so crude as debts, Father. Buckley's not just a loan shark anymore. He's an informal banker for the whole machine. He supervises off-the-record collections and disbursements, keeps track of things for Kelly himself. Eddie had to fork over fifteen thousand dollars for his new job, for this nice new office and the clout that goes with it. Five installments, wasn't it, Eddie? Three thousand each time? You met Buckley in the men's room under Grandstand C, wasn't it? Bottom half of the fourth inning each time? Have I got it right?"

At last Kane looked up at Dillon. "What do you want?" he asked hoarsely.

"I want Buckley."

Kane shook his head, in confusion, not negation. "But you have—"

"I have you, Eddie. I have Jimmy Martin. I have Sonny McCue. I have a shot at six judges, a dozen other cops and maybe the mayor. Even given my jurisdictional problems, with Buckley as a ready witness, I can develop federal cases against most of you. And the stuff that isn't federal will become public anyway. It seems Raymond Buckley just doesn't want to go to jail, not even for the draft. He's giving me the whole machine."

"But—"

"But what I want is him, and you know why. It *is* personal. I want you to get him for me. I used the draft to break Buckley for *this*, so that I could come back to you, Eddie, and give you a second chance. You saved his skin once, and this is the thanks you get. He sold you out for bribery, and that's just the opener. What else can he give me about you if I express an interest?" Dillon paused, then said, "I want Buckley, and not just for a measly draft violation, but for racketeering, loan sharking, gaming—everything. I want him for *murder*, Eddie, but I can't get him for it. You can. The mayor can. The D.A. can. The judges named in those summaries can. All the people who've been protecting him can."

"I still don't get it."

"Check with the pols I interrogated at the Bureau offices last week. This is my show. I'm the only one who knows what's in that folder. I typed the damn thing myself. That's why there are hash marks and typos everywhere. I'll trade those pages. You develop the case against Buckley, including murder. You get your pick of his murders, Eddie, but make sure you choose one you can prove. Bring the charges, get the conviction, send him away for life. And meanwhile I forget I ever heard of any of what's in those pages. In fact, I disappear from Chicago. I go back to Washington."

"You want Buckley that much?"

"Yes. You know my reason. Now you have a reason too. And so does Kelly."

"How do I know you'll really—?"

"That's why I asked Father Ferrick to come along." Dillon looked at the priest. "He knows the score. I wanted him to witness my solemn oath. My oath as a Catholic." Dillon faced Kane once more. "I swear that I will never use the material I have from Buckley against you or against anyone. And I swear no one else in the Bureau has seen it or will see it but me. So help me God and my immortal soul." Dillon let a beat of silence fall, then added, "No one but me, with one proviso. If I should have an unexpected accident or, say, if I should disappear, my personal security box at the Bureau will be opened. It holds a copy of Buckley's statement and a description of this meeting, including the fact of Father Ferrick's presence."

Dillon looked at the priest. "Another reason I asked you to come. One sacred reason, one profane."

Kane stared at Dillon and the priest, pale and unsure. His voice cracked as he said, "But if Buckley has talked to you, once we press him he'll talk to everybody."

"You and the Chicago D.A. will control what Buckley talks about, and you'll control who he talks to, the same way Ness hemmed in Capone once they made their case. You can keep the focus on what Buckley did. Anything he tries to give away will be dismissed as the moves of a desperate man. The same system that operated so efficiently to protect Buckley can operate now to destroy him."

Kane closed the folder and looked at Ferrick. "Does that oath he just took mean anything?"

The priest nodded. "The immortal soul is not to be trifled with, Eddie. I'd say Sean's oath gives you a chance to do something about your own soul."

"Check with your bosses," Dillon said. "See if they don't agree. One way or the other, Buckley is a problem for you all. I'm giving you a way to dispose of it. And Eddie?"

"Yes?"

"Buckley in court is the *only* way I want it disposed of. I don't want him hit on the street. Tell that to Kelly. The deal is off if Buckley is killed."

"I could bring charges that would get him the electric chair. You don't want that either?"

"I'll leave that to the jury. My point is, I want it by the law. Do you remember the law? Buckley deserves anything you throw at him, but do it by the book."

Kane laughed nervously. "Is this by the book?"

But Dillon ignored him. "Otherwise I stay in Chicago. I bring the Bureau in, and we go all the way with this."

Dillon held the cop's eyes until Kane couldn't stand it. He stood up. "So in one move we get rid of him *and* you?"

Dillon and the priest stood. "That's right, Eddie. What a deal, huh?"

As Father Ferrick moved toward the door, Kane touched his arm. "And what about our friendship, Father? Does this mean we can be—?"

"You took an oath too, when you got your badge. Fulfill it this time. Then talk to me about friendship."

Dillon and Ferrick left the police superintendent standing in his office, holding the folder. On the street outside the priest stopped Dillon. "Is that true?" he asked. "You got all that from Buckley? He *talked* to you?"

Dillon felt ambushed. How could he lie to this priest? Yet he had promised himself he'd keep Cass out. Her transcripts, the true basis for the document he'd composed, was his absolute secret. He said coolly, "Yes, it's true, Father. Buckley would deny it, of course. But I cracked him. He didn't want to go to jail."

"But now he will. He *really* will. But the rest of them, you meant that? Giving up what you had against them all, not to use it?"

Dillon forced himself to grin. "Of course I meant it. I swore, didn't I? Don't ask me to explain." He slugged the priest's shoulder affectionately. "But I bent the rules with Buckley. I could never have used the stuff in court anyway." Dillon laughed, and then the priest did, not sure why, except that this young man had done it again, made him feel great about himself.

In the late morning of the next day, November 17, 1940, Raymond Buckley finished his usual string of breakfast interviews at the Stockyards Inn, but they hadn't gone smoothly. The ward boss had been nervous from start to finish, as if one of the supplicants across the fancy table from him was going to pull a black rose out from under the linen cloth. At one point he thought that his coffee tasted strange, and he made the waiter bring him a fresh cup, but he couldn't drink that either. The feeling wouldn't fade that something awful was going to happen to him, and he knew why. He'd demanded that the feds drop the bullshit draft-law charges, but when they had the day before—only his charges, and no explanation for it—he knew enough to be afraid. The fuckers.

Now, as he went outside to his canvas-topped coupe roadster, his hands twitched to be on the steering wheel. He longed to be gone from the yards, driving in a crowd of traffic downtown where no one would single him out. And sure enough, as he began to pull away from the would-be Tudor manor house, three sedans converged on Buckley's car, making him stop. He knew this was it. They were going to kill him. From two of the cars men leapt carrying shotguns and drawn pistols. He reached down to the floor for his own gun, but then he saw their uniforms. Cops! His own guys! From the third car came newspaper photographers, whose flashbulbs then blinded him.

Chicago policemen! Not assassins. And not feds. What the fuck—? "All right, Raybo!" one of them cried, grabbing him, knocking his gun away and hauling him from the car. He recognized Dooley, and then Griffen. They slammed him against the fender, cracking his skull, making him think he was passing out. "You're under arrest!"

What? Not dead? Not gunned down? What was happening?

His mind fled his body as they wrenched his arms back, savagely handcuffing him, and he took refuge in the meaning of it all, the epiphany. Buckley instinctively calculated the equation between this moment and the endless afternoon the week before. He pictured that agent leaning against the wall, staring at him through the smoke. That prick's silence had made him almost crazy, but now at last, in the detached spin of his brain, Buckley heard Sean Dillon's voice. He heard the words Dillon hadn't said at all last week, but a long time before: I owe Doc Riley. I owe him you.

"South Side Politician Charged with Murder, Rackets," the headline read. "Mayor Kelly Announces Major New Crackdown."

Framed by the headlines and the story columns was a grainy photograph of Raymond Buckley pinned against the hood of a car, his face twisted in pain, his eyes distended with fear, like a stockyards animal.

" 'The last gasp of gangland Chicago,' " Sean Dillon read out loud. " 'Buckley is a throwback, an exception, a blot on the honor of Chicago's new politics.' So says the mayor in announcing the arrest." He raised his eyes to look at Cass Ryan.

They were on the boardwalk of the Oak Street Beach. It was cold and dank. It had been raining, and would rain again.

"His own people turned against him?" she asked, staring over his shoulder at the newspaper. "*They're* the ones who did this?"

"Yes."

"Because of you?"

"Because of what you gave me."

"But you said that was—"

"I lied about those pages, Cass. No one knows where

Buckley's secrets came from. I lied to everyone. Including Father Ferrick."

Lied? What were lies, compared to what Buckley had done? But she knew what Sean was telling her, that he'd crossed a line here. For her?

"What will happen now?"

"A trial, a sure conviction, a merciless sentence. They need him executed or in jail more than we do."

"No, they don't."

"They have him for murder, Cass. Buckley's finished. We're finished with him." Dillon put his fingers lightly on her lips. "We don't ever need to speak of him again." He smiled, wanting to cut through her mood. "Do you think Adam and Eve ever spoke of the snake?"

"After they were banished?" She stared into his eyes more deeply than ever, aware that what had stood between them was gone now. Not Buckley, she thought strangely, but our innocence. Unable to speak, she wanted him to.

When he did, it was to say simply, "I'm going back to Washington. I'll be there through the war, at least. Will you come with me?"

"Yes," Cass answered without hesitating.

When those two left Chicago, it felt less like banishment than release. It was true, they had finished. Now they could begin.

PART II

WASHINGTON

EIGHT

The Melville Arms Hotel was only two blocks from the quarter of Capitol Hill that included the Library of Congress and the new Supreme Court Building. It had long been favored by less well-connected lawyers and lobbyists, by would-be staffers and fading hangers-on. The step boards and railings of its entryway were warped and unpainted, its masonry façade badly in need of painting, its windows blanked by faded green shades in various stages of disintegration. The alley that ran back from Fifth Street directly beside the hotel led into a warren of no-toilet shacks in which destitute Negroes lived. But now not even the Melville Arms made itself available to just anyone, and it was rare that a room was booked out to the same party for more than a day or two, and unheard-of that one visitor should monopolize accommodations for a period of weeks. Yet that was exactly what was happening in January and February of 1944. In fact, by apparent coincidence, it was happening with two different rooms, two different hotel guests, each a government man of influence.

One was a portly former boiler baron named David Lothrop. His family had made a fortune in steam-works manufacture in Cincinnati, and the Lothrop factories on the Ohio River were one of the great industrial centers of the Midwest. After Pearl Harbor the Lothrop works had shifted to war production and now were a major supplier of the primitive but powerful diesel engines used to power LSTs. A year into the war it had become clear both that the Lothrop Company was a highest-priority manufacturer and that David Lothrop, its president and owner, was incapable of running the concern in its new situation. That potentially insoluble problem was actually resolved

quite handily when Senator Robert Taft proposed David
Lothrop as a candidate for a prestigious senior position in the
War Department. Lothrop was accordingly named deputy undersecretary of war, materiel. He assumed, as did his proud
wife and children, that he was brought to Washington especially to oversee the crash manufacture of the thousands of landing
craft that the Allies would need for their eventual invasion of
the Continent.

In fact, Lothrop's incompetence was as apparent in the co-
lossal new War Department Building in Arlington as it had
been in the converted boiler works on the bluffs above the
Ohio, and even Lothrop himself soon realized that he was surrounded in his fancy offices by people whose entire job was to
keep him occupied with projects that involved careful preparations, elaborate briefings and complicated follow-up summaries, but which finally had nothing to do with fighting, much
less winning, the war.

David Lothrop wasn't the only one with a morale problem.
The news from Europe that winter was all bad. The great
breakthrough landing in Italy had turned into a disaster at
Anzio where tens of thousands of American soldiers were
trapped on a narrow beachhead, an army bleeding to death
week after week under savage German assaults. Every day
brought more news of defeat.

It was under the pressure, perhaps, of seeing his own failure
magnified by the entire army's that Lothrop had begun his uncharacteristic love affair. He had met the woman at the Red
Cross honors ceremonies in the ornate marble Red Cross headquarters mansion near the White House. Her name was Sylvia
Yergin, and though with her shapeless black hair and unstylish
clothing she seemed indifferent to her appearance, and though
she seemed ill at ease in speaking English, she struck Lothrop
as all the more alluring for not being one of the aggressive
Washington beauties who so intimidated him. Their first tryst
took place in the small apartment Yergin shared with another
woman. When on that occasion, to Lothrop's amazement, she
expressed a wish for a discreet place to meet him regularly,
he'd recalled someone in the Senior Mess mentioning the
Melville Arms.

There, at last, with Sylvia Yergin's encouragement, Lothrop
had rediscovered his competence, performing acts of which no
one would have believed him capable, certainly not his thin-

lipped wife or the condescending War Department functionaries who not doubt took his impotence for granted. He had found his place in Washington, finally—in the embrace of an exotic woman who claimed, incredibly, to love him.

The other party to whom the steel-eyed manager of the Melville Arms had let a room without restriction was Sean Dillon, and he was driving there now as fast as he dared. He could make it from Bureau headquarters on Ninth Street to the far side of Capitol Hill in less than ten minutes, but this time even that seemed an eternity. He pushed hard on the steering wheel and cut smoothly in and out of the oncoming traffic, storming the Hill. Washington was as much his city now as Chicago had ever been, and speeding along its axis avenue, aware of his own skill, Dillon felt the familiar exhilaration. To whomever the proud capital's echelons and traditions and, also, social privileges had belonged before, the city now had been put in the power of men like him. He could never have predicted what the FBI would come to mean to him, not only the bold integrity of the self-image it offered, but the sense of a deeper role in protecting the country against what threatened it. That function of the Bureau's was revered almost mystically not only by the agents themselves, but by Washingtonians, or at least by the civilians among them. The city of embassies, branches, departments, commissions and boards was afraid of itself, as besieged in its way as London was, if only from within. The war had started, after all, with a shock of deceit, and from then on the expectation of mortal betrayal would be a near permanent feature of the Washington mind.

FBI agents in the capital of the United States during World War II were, in Dillon's experience, exactly what he himself was—social, political and, despite their law degrees, educational outsiders who had been joined to each other by a common summons to serve the very circle that once would not even have noticed it was excluding them. Dillon had been moved by the tacit bond he felt with his fellow agents, men linked by a spirit of the emergency, but also by a recognition of common ideals; a shared lack of intellectual sophistication, perhaps, but also of pretension. Their virtues were the simple ones of directness and physical courage. They were a modest elite. It surprised Dillon what happiness it was to be one of them.

He slowed his car as he turned onto Fifth Street, not want-

ing to attract notice as he approached the hotel. He pulled over
to the curb, glancing up at the third-floor window of a nonde-
script office building that stood across the street. He saw
Coles, the agent who had called him to say the subjects had
both arrived.

He got out of the car with the air of a bored messenger and
sauntered across the sidewalk and up the stairs to the hotel. He
crossed the small lobby without a glance at the desk clerk and
went through the door to the stairwell. Now unobserved, he
took the uncarpeted stairs in a hurry, but withholding his
weight to keep the noise down. When he'd first ascended these
stairs they had seemed familiar, and it was only on his second
or third visit that he realized they reminded him of the winding, creaking stairs in Doc Riley's rooming house in
Canaryville. It had been years since Riley met his fate, but to
Dillon that failure of his had happened, it always seemed, just
yesterday.

Coles and six others watched the hotel in shifts from their
perch across the street, but Dillon was the only agent who ever
entered it. The others were told this was to keep from drawing
attention with their comings and goings, but the more important reason was that in this operation, only Sean Dillon, the
agent in charge, could know what was going on.

On the third floor he left the stairwell and moved quietly
down the hallway to the last room on the left. Once inside he
crossed to the low chest of drawers on which two machines
sat, a radio receiver and a wire-reel sound recorder. He
snapped them both on and donned a set of earphones. He listened for a moment, then adjusted the volume on the receiver.

He closed his eyes and placed the open palm of his left hand
on the bare wall before him. It was the wall his room shared
with David Lothrop's.

The microphone hidden in the ceiling lamp above the bed in
Lothrop's room picked up every faint rustle of movement. He
adjusted the volume down again because the amplification registered in his earphones almost painfully as Lothrop and the
woman approached the climax of their energetic fornication.
The crude staccato of thumping bed furniture and human
grunts meant nothing to Dillon but that he had arrived in time.
It had been eleven days since the lovers had last met each
other here, an interval which made today's the most important
rendezvous yet.

Dillon had to check a surge of anxiety, and he deflected a simultaneous, rare impulse of curiosity. Nothing of professional interest to him would happen between these two until their postcoital talk began.

He listened with cold detachment, but in a wholly distinct—and personal—part of his brain something else began to happen, a straightforward erotic response, a matter of quick images of a woman's body, not any woman, certainly not the impersonal flirts of magazines or alluring girls on the streets or the woman on the other side of this wall. It was Cass, and he saw her clearly, not in a languid, willed fantasy, as if he had, voyeur-like, observed her too, but in the broken series of partial glimpses, the way he saw her in the throes of their own lovemaking.

It made him feel less like a pervert, perhaps, if this was his association with those sounds: Cass with her lips parted; Cass with her flattened breasts riding loosely back and forth beneath him, like mounds of gelatin; Cass with her painted toenails flailing a small circle by his left ear; everything reduced to Cass, to this moment inside her which in its intensity of pleasure and fearfulness meant more to Dillon, while it lasted, than the idea of all eternity, and *there* was why sex was sinful, how it obliterated for a moment everything else, including God; and *there* was why, with Cass, if with no one else ever, Dillon longed to dive into it, like into the water, as he'd come to think of sex, of which he was no longer afraid.

He tried to come back from that all too personal side of his brain, to listen to Lothrop, but another image—Cass, her hair flogging the damp pillow—popped into his head. He remembered the night after he had first watched Yergin and Lothrop making love. To his own surprise he'd arrived home in the grip of lust. He'd scooped Cass up and carried her into the bedroom and put her, not roughly, on the bed. She'd responded by laughing, "What have *you* been up to?"

"I can't tell you," Dillon had answered with a grin.

She'd grabbed his shirt to pull him down on top of her. "Well, whatever it is, I like it." That exchange had become a joke between them from then on.

He opened his eyes and stared at the fleck patterns in the swirled plaster wall. He tried to focus on what he was hearing, but still his mind faltered.

Cass was now in the last stage of her second pregnancy, due

in a month or so. Her first had ended in a miscarriage shortly
after she'd discovered her condition. It had taken them almost
two years to conceive again, and they were both happy and relieved. Dillon had expected that, pregnant, she would revert to
a typical Irish reticence, but she hadn't. Once she had successfully weathered the uncertain first three months, her physical
ease had returned and, in fact, she had become lustier than
ever. As her belly grew Sean had found her more desirable
than ever too.

"Oh, you are so wonderful! So wonderful!" The woman's
voice crackled in his headset, hollow-sounding, as if the transmission wire ran under the ocean. "Do you know how wonderful you are?"

He brought his face closer to the wall, his left eye closer to
the pencil mark encircling the pinhole. He heard the word as
wunderbar, and he had to remind himself that she was not German. Sylvia Yergin was a Dane. She had been in Washington
for a year and a half, having come from London as a liaison
officer from International Red Cross.

Now he saw her. The pinhole gave him a view of the upper
half of their bed. It was not to watch them fucking that he had
drilled the hole, but only to be able to confirm beyond doubt
every time that the woman Lothrop had brought here was
Yergin. Dillon had seen her often from a distance, going and
coming from Red Cross headquarters, waiting at her trolley
stops, browsing in the Corcoran Gallery on Seventeenth Street,
sitting on a stool in a luncheonette on Pennsylvania Avenue,
shopping at a corner market near her apartment house in
Georgetown. Despite her exotic accent and her success in snar-
ing Lothrop, Sylvia Yergin was no one's idea of a femme
fatale. She dressed frumpily, in thick woolen suits, heavy
stockings and a dowager's stout shoes. Her graying hair made
her look older than the forty years Dillon knew she was. Her
aggressive lack of makeup gave her face an unpleasant sever-
ity.

Yet now, kneeling naked on the edge of their bed, craning
over the spent Lothrop, her breasts folding onto him, her skin
glowing silken pink—her appearance was transformed. To
Dillon, no connoisseur, her head in profile had the finely
wrought line of a woman in a painting, and her full figure had
the erotic appeal of classic sculpture. There was a gentleness
about her as she fondled Lothrop, a vulnerability Dillon asso-

ciated only with a woman cuddling her child. He sensed how an unsuspecting man could find her irresistible.

Over the weeks he had heard the whole range of her passion sounds, and he'd thought Lothrop a fool for so slavishly responding to whores' tricks. Not only her appearance was transformed in this room; her stern bashfulness became a feverish assertion that often threatened to leave her panting lover behind. But also, sometimes, she whimpered with such apparent depth of pleasure that Dillon, despite his resolve, and feeling all at once ripe for submission himself, would put an eye to the pinhole to watch. At such moments her face would take on a pleading aspect that reminded Dillon of the Dutch girl in the famous war-relief poster: "Answer Their Prayers." Dillon thought that Sylvia Yergin wanted Lothrop to see her as the heroine of one of those not incidentally Germanic fairy tales, a girl in a cape lost in the forest, this—to her—foreign, unfriendly war capital. But Dillon constantly forced himself to see her as the one who, when the woodsman lays down his ax, bares her fangs and lunges at the dumb bastard's throat.

Surely she would do that now.

Lothrop looked up at her gratefully. She had succeeded in making him feel that, despite her age and her obvious expertise, he was the first man who had found the way to touch her. "It is not me," he said pathetically. "It's you, darling."

She leaned to kiss him, with more tenderness than passion.

Dillon found Yergin's tenderness more appealing than her sexual heat, but no more believable. He knew that now her thrust would come because she had Lothrop completely at her mercy. Dillon was certain she had a mandatory question, and he knew what it had to be. After a period of two months in which Lothrop had compulsively sought her out almost daily, nearly two weeks had now passed in which he hadn't called her.

They kissed again, lightly, and Dillon strained to hear past the amplified rustle of bedclothes as they readjusted themselves.

"I missed you so." She stroked his forehead, brushing the strands of his thin hair with her fingers. Lothrop was now reclining half against the headboard and half in her arms, lacking only grapes. He seemed to be settling into sleep. An old man's nap would suit Dillon's purposes no more than Yergin's.

"You never told me where you went."

Lothrop looked at her sharply. "Who said I went any-where?"

"I know you left Washington. Or else you would have talked to me."

"I had to stay with my wife. She wasn't well."

Yergin smiled. "You know I don't believe you. Your wife is in Ohio. She has been in Ohio since before Christmas."

"How do you know that?"

Yergin shrugged. "My friends in the Ohio Red Cross."

A look of pure horror crossed Lothrop's face, but then he realized she was joking, and he pushed her shoulder, a bit roughly.

She sat back from him, tugged a corner of the sheet free and draped herself with it. The shadow of an uncharacteristic pout crossed her face. "But now I see you have lied to me. And there can be only one reason."

"What reason?"

"There is someone else. Not your wife. Some other—" She finished the sentence with a weary hand gesture.

Lothrop sat up abruptly. To Dillon, Yergin's complaint had been obvious posturing, and he was shocked to see how it seemed to wound Lothrop. "That's not true. There is no one but you."

"But what shall I think? You tell me you were in Washington when I know you were not."

"How do you know?"

She turned her back on him, shamelessly flaunting her naked spine, reminding him which of them was stronger, ordering him implicitly to grovel.

"I can't tell you where I was. I can't."

She neither faced him nor moved.

"It's too important. It's secret." He put his hand on her shoulder, but she was marble. "It's my work."

"Your work gives you a way to deceive me. I never believed I would be lovers with a man who did not trust me."

Lothrop laughed and rolled away. "Don't trust you! I trust you with everything. You could ruin me."

Dillon thought Lothrop had turned from her in a pout of his own, but he reached across to the nearby chair, fumbling in the pocket of the coat he'd flung there. He rolled back to Yergin and said in an unhappy voice, "Here." Still she did not move. "This is for you." He held a small brown package out.

She faced him, letting the sheet slip, exposing her pearly breasts as she accepted the package.

Dillon marveled at her lack of modesty.

As she unwrapped the paper, Lothrop's face lit up expectantly.

A piece of gold jewelry. Yergin carefully removed it from its wrapping and held it up, an oblong pendant on a chain. The thing seemed to draw to itself what light there was in the room. "It's beautiful," she said.

"It's a cartouche. It's old."

"A cartouche?"

"Those are hieroglyphic figures engraved there, the name of some pharaoh. I mean it's very old. It's real."

Yergin raised her eyes to him, shining with pleasure. "You were in Egypt?"

Instead of answering, Lothrop took the chain and pendant from her. "Here." As she inclined her head toward him, he hung it on her like Caesar bestowing an honor. The flat gold swung between her breasts. Her breasts drew his attention, and he leaned down to them, kissing each one, a gesture of loving tenderness it seemed to Dillon impossible to feign.

Then Lothrop took Yergin into his arms and held her.

"Where did you find it?" Yergin asked quietly. "It is so beautiful."

Lothrop touched his finger to her lips, but then he said, "Cairo. I found it for you in Cairo."

"Cairo?"

"My company has business there, my company in Cincinnati, I mean. I wasn't always in the War Department, you know. I still do a little business."

"Your company? Business in Cairo?" Yergin laughed suddenly. "I thought your company made furnaces. Furnaces in the Sahara?"

Lothrop stared at her, then said, "We did. That was before the war. How did you know what my company made?"

"You told me."

"No, I didn't."

"What does your company make now?"

"You tell me."

"I don't know." She laughed again. "But you are testing me." She tickled his ribs. "Aren't you? You are testing me."

Despite himself, Lothrop began to laugh. "It's ridiculous, isn't it? As if I can't trust you."

"Yes, darling, ridiculous." She held the cartouche up. "I love this. Thank you." And she kissed him, pushing her tongue into his mouth.

When they stopped kissing, she simply rested against him, apparently content.

Lothrop said in the silence, "We make diesel engines, for the LCI."

"LCI?"

"Landing Craft–Infantry, the flat-hulled assault vessels we use to bring soldiers ashore on beaches."

Yergin pulled away from him, to look in his eyes. "And you were in Cairo?"

"Yes. Does that tell you something?" He grinned, a boyish I-know-a-secret grin.

"It tells me perhaps something is happening in the Mediterranean."

"Very good, darling. *Very* good. The truth is, everything depends on landing craft. For want of landing craft, the invasion hasn't happened yet. But not for long. Not to blow my own horn, but my company has turned out eleven thousand LCI engines in the last seven months."

Yergin's eyes had brightened. "I had no idea you were so—" She shrugged happily. "So wonderful."

He laughed again, but then said soberly, "I haven't been able to tell anyone, not even my wife. It's fantastic, what we've done!"

"Tell me."

"My trip was to the staging areas, Cairo, but also Tunis and Nicosia. Soon we'll have thousands of LCIs and LSTs in place all across the Med."

"But everyone says the invasion will go across the Channel."

"Yes, they do, don't they?" Lothrop smiled.

"But it will be the south of France, instead of the north?"

He shook his head. "The Balkans," he announced triumphantly. "The back door to Germany. The door Churchill had slammed in his face in the First War. This will be the vindication of his losses at the Dardanelles. Are you old enough to remember the Dardanelles?"

Yergin grimaced, tugged the sheet free and once more covered herself with it. She left the bed and disappeared from Dillon's line of sight.

Lothrop was too revved up now to stop. "And if we go in through the Balkans, we keep the Red Army out of Eastern Europe."

He grinned at her expectantly: Isn't it brilliant? "The key is Bulgaria. Germany collapsed in the First War only when Bulgaria defected. We've spent all this blood on Italy, but Italy means nothing. Bulgaria! That's the linchpin!"

From her place out of Dillon's view, Sylvia's response, if any, was silent.

"I'll have one of those," Lothrop said, then caught the cigarette pack she threw at him, then the lighter.

The silence curdled the air in the room while the two lit up and smoked.

When Yergin spoke at last, her disembodied voice seemed ghostly. "Will it come soon?"

"The Joint Chiefs just ordered materiel and supplies brought up to the forward staging areas."

"Which are Tunis, Alexandria, Nicosia . . .?"

"Heraklion in Crete, Tripoli, and Valletta."

"Valletta?"

"The port of Malta."

"And where is the headquarters?"

Lothrop's head snapped as if he had just taken a blow, and for a long moment he could only stare at her. Color rose in his face. Finally he cleared his throat nervously. "That's an overly interested question, Sylvia. If you don't mind my saying so. You make me nervous all of a sudden." Lothrop inhaled his cigarette compulsively.

Yergin came back to the bed, and Dillon could see her again. She laughed. "Oh, darling, I do not care. Tell me nothing more. I am only interested because it involves you." She stroked his arm, tracing the line of it with a crooked finger. "I had no idea your work was so . . . near the center . . ."

"Yes, well . . ."

She had lost her advantage and saw it. She knew enough not to push. Instead, she took his cigarette and put it with hers in the ashtray on the bed table. Then, letting her sheet fall, she reclined alongside Lothrop and began to plant kisses on his torso. At first he refused to respond, like a pouting adolescent. But then she began to fondle him blatantly, and he became

aroused. Abruptly, angrily almost, he pushed her over onto her
back and mounted her.

Dillon pulled back from the wall, aware suddenly of his
parched throat. He wished Coles or one of the other watchers
was with him so he could turn with a "Christ, you won't believe these two."

He had no choice but to stay there and listen on the chance
that Yergin would resume her sly interrogation. She did not.
Their exchanges now were limited to Lothrop's stifled yelps of
surprise and delight as he found himself sustaining his rare
second erection, and to Yergin's whorish cry of ecstasy, that
abject lie with which, apparently, she'd leashed him like a
puppy.

Cass didn't know whom else to call, and that seemed to sum
up her problem. She had called Patty and Norma, her two
friends in the apartment house, but neither was home. She'd
called Mrs. Connor, the head of the sodality at St. Thomas
More's, but the parish line was busy, and busy again.

If she were in Chicago, she'd have had a hundred others to
call, beginning with her Ma. The thought of her mother lower-
ing a chipped cup of steaming tea to answer her phone made
Cass want to weep. *Oh, Ma! Who shall I call?*

For three years they had been living in Barcroft, a garden
apartment complex off Glebe Road in Arlington. The buildings
at Barcroft were only three stories high, and had a crisp, colonial feel unlike anything in Chicago. There were lawns and
flower beds, forsythia bushes and dogwoods, but the Dillons'
neighbors were all government workers from elsewhere and
they kept to themselves. A few FBI agents lived in Barcroft,
though, and others had places nearby. Every few months, they
got together for a picnic at Four Mile Run, if the weather was
good, or in winter, for canasta parties. But even at those gath-
erings, the men stayed to themselves, playing horseshoes or, on
card nights, poker in the other room—always talking shop. The
women, young mothers all, it seemed, went on and on about
their babies. No one seemed to notice or care that Cass did not
have a child. If they had a clue about how desperately she
wanted one, would they have tortured her so with their endless
talk of diaper-rash ointments and formula? The FBI claimed to
be a family, but where were Cass Dillon's sisters and brothers

now? All she knew was that she was in trouble, and she was alone.

She had called Dr. Lyons, who wasn't in his office. The woman who answered wasn't even a nurse. She had listened from behind the counter of her silence, then had said, "You just lie down, Mrs. Dillon. The pain will pass. Doctor will call you when he comes in."

Now she was on the couch, the phone just out of reach, on the table behind her head.

She was trying to focus on her rosary. The amber beads trickled through her fingers, and her lips moved automatically around the words her heart knew best.

The rote prayer cut her mind loose and it rose to the Blessed Mother herself, how frightened *she* must have been, going into labor in a stable. But Mary had had her husband with her.

Cass joined her hands on her swollen belly, the rosary still entwined in her fingers. She pressed gently against herself. "Dear baby, please," she said aloud, and those words released the nervous incantation of her prayer, "Hail Mary, full of grace," as if she were kneeling with the sodality ladies in St. Gabe's. "Holy Mary, Mother of God . . ."

It was not that Mary was her closest friend, or that ordinarily prayer was such a consolation. She was running these words and images through her mind as a way of staying calm, of staying in control of herself.

"Mary!" she cried, as pain shot through her body, a twisting of innards she had never felt before.

Even with her eyes closed the light in her head blazed. She had never had such a headache. The scalding wire wrapping her stomach turned tighter and tighter until the sensation of pain exploded into something else—a feeling of pure terror. Now her unspoken prayer became, Punish me, but please don't punish my baby!

She tried to get up, but the torment curled through her, cutting off escape, forcing her back down onto the couch.

She reached up for the telephone as she realized that something serious was wrong with her. Something was wrong with her baby.

No sooner did the phone touch her cheek than the operator came on, saying, "Number please," the most familiar, soothing voice Cass had ever heard.

Oh, Helen! Oh, Maisie! She saw the girls lined up along the

switchboards, leather-and-wire headsets framing their faces, her dearest friends waiting there to help.

But it wasn't the girls she wanted.

It was Sean! Her only Sean! He would take care of her. He would take care of their baby. He would make this pain go away. Never mind that she had never called him at work before. Never mind that she had never asked him to think of her first. She would ask him now. He would drop whatever he was doing. He would come for her. He would take her to the hospital. He would save their baby, and he would save her.

"Get me the FBI," she pleaded.

NINE

The new War Department Building was already a year old, but Sean Dillon had never been there. It was impossible not to have seen it from a dozen angles across the river, though, and like everyone in Washington, he'd heard all about the place.

Not one building actually, it was five distinct pentagonal structures arranged concentrically around a five-acre open court. They were called rings and were joined by ten spoke-like corridors. Its five stories (seven, counting the two below ground) were connected by broad ramps. The building covered thirty acres, had three times the floor space of the Empire State Building, was a mile in circumference and was surrounded by vast parking lots with spaces for ten thousand cars. Yet the rings, bays, corridors and ramps of the Pentagon were so efficiently laid out—corridors numbered, rings lettered, the walls of each floor a different color—that no two offices were more than a brisk six-minute walk apart.

Sean Dillon was climbing the limestone steps of the mall entrance which, with its huge columns, rose up above the Potomac River like a Hellenic temple. The architects of the city behind him had reproduced pagan sanctuaries up and down several avenues, but not like this.

Dillon swung his leather satchel into the curl of his own leg to keep from bumping the other men, all uniformed, who were streaming up and down the stairs with self-important urgency. Neither Dillon nor the FBI agent at his side knew the exact litany of numbers—eighteen dining rooms serving sixty thousand meals a day—that made the building a modern wonder of the world. But each man felt on entering it the charge of the spacious silence of the broad vestibule. The war energy of the en-

tire nation was focused in this place. The two FBI agents were
doing their parts in the great struggle and knew it, but they
could not help but feel, *there*, a civilian's humility, and also,
during that war, gratitude.

And Dillon felt something else. As they produced their
"creds" folders, passing through the security funnel, then up
the crowded blue ramp toward A-Ring-Three, he thought of
the chutes and ramps of the Chicago stockyards. But what a
difference! Here the order embodied in a mammoth grid was
real; in Chicago it had been a lie, a veneer laid over every kind
of slaughter. Like the yards, Washington itself had been laid
out at first in a perfect square—ten miles on a side instead of
one—and that order too, in Dillon's experience, had proved
trustworthy. For four years he had seen American
institutions—the presidency, the Congress, the courts, his own
Justice Department, the army—functioning at their best, and it
was the knowledge that he was protecting those institutions,
the order *they* enshrined, that enabled him to do his unsavory,
cryptic work. The effect of Washington, even of the shadowy
side on which he worked, had been to reverse the alienation
he'd felt in Chicago. Washington had restored the sense of his
own worthiness. Here, in this period when the contrast between good and evil was never sharper—Hitler's gift—Sean
Dillon had become what he would be for life, a modest, but
also an earnest, American patriot.

The undersecretary of war, the immediate superior of the hapless David Lothrop, was a New York patrician named Randall
Crocker. A fifty-four-year-old lawyer, he had left Wall Street
after Pearl Harbor to take his position under Henry L. Stimson.
Stimson was a Republican whom Roosevelt had appointed secretary of war in an effort to broaden support, and though
Crocker was a Democrat and a staunch New Dealer, he had
strong social ties to Roosevelt's Establishment enemies, and
his appointment too was a bid for their cooperation.

Crocker was very much a *civilian* overseer of the mushrooming military, but his background gave him advantages that
the politician Stimson and other war administrators lacked.
Crocker had distinguished himself as a young officer in World
War I. He had no need to refer to his record ever, for he wore
the ultimate emblem of valor, having suffered the amputation
of his left leg above the knee in a field hospital at Château-

Thierry. Roosevelt, even more than others, had to find Crocker's lifelong refusal to act the cripple an infallible sign of character. When Crocker walked, his wooden leg clicked rhythmically at the knee joint, making a sound like a metronome that taunted the able-bodied to keep up with him.

Now that leg was stretched out, paired with his good one inside the cavern of his huge mahogany desk. He had just resumed his seat as four men took their chairs in the semicircle in front of him. While waiting for them to get settled, his eye fell for an instant on the pair of leather-framed photographs on his desk, the two most familiar and precious objects in the room. One showed his wife Hillary posing happily with their Irish setter, and the other their son Geoffrey in the uniform of an army lieutenant. In the photo he was smiling broadly as he saluted, amused at himself and slightly embarrassed. Crocker could never register either photo without a pang. His Hillary was dead. The boy was their only child, and now he was in the infantry overseas.

On the wall to Crocker's left was a floor-to-ceiling map, in pale greens and browns, of Italy and the Balkans. Colored pins highlighted various positions; a sinister line of black tacks bisected Italy just below Rome. Behind Crocker was a large window showing the ubiquitous view, a parking lot which in this case stretched toward the hills of Arlington.

Crocker's office was one of the largest in the Pentagon. In addition to his desk, which once belonged to Edwin Stanton, it was furnished with eagle-tipped flagstaffs, a broad blue carpet, two leather couches, an oversized conference table and ten black Windsor chairs, half of which were arranged before him now. The uniformed men were seated in them.

"You know each other," Crocker said with metallic abruptness. He knew that the officers and he were on opposite sides of a classic American divide, and after three years of stalking it, he had no more interest in bridging it than they did. Despite his own record, including the loss of his leg, he was a civilian to the core, and they were soldiers who could not even arrive at his office for a meeting without an implicit resentment at his having the authority to summon them.

Crocker eyed them in turn. Brigadier General Peter Alfred, a white-haired, mustachioed officer, Marshall's exec, saw his job first and last as protecting the chief of staff and the chief's turf. Crocker did not admire such hedged loyalty in a military man, but he often wished his own people had it.

Next to Alfred was Colonel George Cheever, the number two at OSS, a man Crocker had known since Groton. Cheever had stayed on in the army after the First War, and in this one had become famous as Patton's G-2, head of intelligence, in North Africa. Cheever's association with those first American triumphs in the war, and his white-shoe connections, had made him a logical choice the year before when Wild Bill Donovan assembled what wags derided as his "Oh So Social" OSS.

Beside Cheever was Colonel John Lawrence, deputy director of military intelligence. Lawrence's uniform had been made by his Savile Row tailor and looked it. His brown tie was a soft worsted, not the quartermaster's serge, and the twill of his trousers was a shade off regulation tan, just enough to be noticed. In Crocker's primitive view intelligence officers were supposed to collect impressions, and it put him off that Lawrence so obviously liked to make them. Colonel Lawrence wasn't the man Crocker had ordered here anyway, and he had to stifle his impatience. Lawrence's boss, Major General George Veazey Strong, had refused to come to this meeting when he learned that his archrival Donovan was sending his deputy.

Seated somewhat apart from the other three, with a vacant chair setting him off, was Brigadier General Victor E. Forbes, the chief of Joint Security Control, whose job was to make sure that plans for the coming Allied invasion of the Continent remained completely secret. As befitted his job, he was a reticent man famous for sitting through meetings like this one without saying a word.

Crocker smiled slyly and said, "Gentlemen, I know that you are not often around the same table." He put his hand quite deliberately down on his desk. "I appreciate your indulging me by coming to this one."

"What's our agenda, Randy?" General Alfred asked with unclothed impatience.

"I'd like you to meet a couple of"—how to refer to them?— "friends of mine." He leaned toward his intercom and pressed it. "Send those gentlemen in, Harry, would you?"

A moment later, Crocker's door opened and the pair of civilians walked into the room.

Crocker stood, balancing himself with a hand on the edge of

the desk. The others looked up at the newcomers, pointedly not rising.

"This is Walter Dunlop, the assistant director for domestic intelligence."

"Assistant director of what?" Cheever asked sharply.

"Of the Federal Bureau of Investigation," Dunlop replied. He carried his hands at his side. His brown suit was sharply creased. His shoes were polished. Like all members of Hoover's inner circle, he had learned to stop buying his clothes at Robert Hall.

At Dunlop's announcement, a wave of disdain curled palpably through the military men. Crocker saw Forbes's eyebrow shoot up as he exchanged a glance with Alfred, and it occurred to Crocker that the outsiders' arrival, in a single stroke, had eliminated the officers' disregard for one another.

Crocker gestured toward Dillon. "And this is . . .?"

Dunlop introduced him. "Special Agent Dillon, who is supervisor in this case."

Crocker pointed to the empty chair between Forbes and Lawrence while resuming his own seat himself. "Please, Mr. Dunlop."

Dunlop approached the chair but remained standing.

Crocker said, "There is a Dictaphone player on the table. You have the recording?"

"Yes, sir." Dunlop paused, then added, "Although, because of security requirements, I must know who is present."

For a moment no one moved, even to look at him, their surprise was so complete. Then, recovering, the officers made a show of rolling their eyes at each other: Who is this asshole?

"Forgive me," Crocker said ingratiatingly, as if the awkwardness resulted from a lapse of his manners. Inwardly he groaned, More positioning! These spooks and counterspooks never let up. Crocker then introduced the officers to Dunlop, who nodded at each from his position behind the vacant chair. They just stared at him. No one offered to shake hands.

Dillon counted for even less than Dunlop in that room. He took up a position away from the others, at the conference table. When Dunlop nodded in his direction he took the belt of wire out of his satchel and set it up on Crocker's machine.

Crocker eyed General Alfred. "You asked about our agenda, Peter. It begins, uncharacteristically enough, with our listening to something." He waved his hand toward Dillon even while pushing back in his chair, using his good leg to lever his wooden one up onto the edge of his lowermost desk drawer. Suddenly, at that display of his infirmity, his discreetly tailored clothing—the French cuffs, the gray silk tie riding at a precise angle above the V of his waistcoat—seemed incongruous. Who was he to be presiding over this meeting of robust, trained men in their physical prime?

Dillon snapped the machine on and stood away from it, watching the reel turn as if it were the passionate arrival of the man and the woman.

"You never told me where you went," Sylvia Yergin said, a hollow, ghostly version of her voice.

"Who said I went anywhere?"

"Can any of you," Crocker put in quickly, "tell me who these people are?"

"I know you left Washington . . ."

The men listened in silence to the conversation, each more impassive than the other. They were a group of past masters at masking their reactions, especially from one another.

When finally the wire ran through the spool and the sounds of the man and woman talking were replaced not by the sighs of foreplay, but by the loose end of stiff black cord going *flick, flick, flick,* General Forbes announced, "That's Lothrop."

Crocker nodded and readjusted his leg to come forward to his desk. "Right. David Lothrop, deputy undersecretary of war, materiel. He works for me, which is the genesis of my interest here."

General Alfred said, "But he's talking about landing ships. That's the navy's purview. The chief of K-2 should be here."

Crocker stared at Alfred, unable to believe he wanted to crowd this pitch further by bringing in navy intelligence too. But then Crocker realized Alfred was only anticipating Admiral King's raging complaint to Marshall when he learned of this meeting. By declaring the navy's interest, Alfred was covering Marshall's ass. The others simply ignored Alfred.

General Forbes said with steely precision, "Lothrop is off the tickler. Everybody knows that. What the hell is he doing traveling the Mediterranean?"

"He didn't."

"What do you mean?"

"Everything Lothrop told the woman is false. Unknown to anyone in his office or, for that matter, in his family, he spent the last twelve days in a house in horse country, preparing himself for this deception. He has nothing to do with the LCIs"—Crocker swung toward Alfred—"as the navy knows better than anyone."

Alfred rebutted, "Lothrop is a fool, which makes him a goddamned security risk."

"That he is," Crocker replied, "but he was hand-picked for this operation."

"By whom?"

"By the woman." Crocker paused to let his answer sink in. "She picked him up at a party. She didn't know that we don't let Lothrop within a mile of his own factories or of what's real here. Lothrop has been watching shadows on the wall the whole war long. He's perfect for this. The woman didn't know that his title as my deputy means nothing, any more than his own wife knows it. Once the woman had her hook in him, we had to decide what to do about it. As it happened, the timing was perfect for using Lothrop to launch Noah's Ark."

The military men knew that "Noah's Ark" was the name Churchill and Roosevelt, meeting in Teheran six weeks before, had dubbed their deception strategy. Fooling the Nazis into worrying about the Balkans, and therefore keeping a full third of German infantry divisions and half their panzers in southeastern Europe, was the flip side of their final decision to invade through Normandy.

Colonel Cheever sat forward. "General Donovan *has* been traveling the Med. He is in Turkey now, deliberately making his presence known to the Abwehr. *He* is going on to Cyprus and Cairo, as if visiting staging areas. He thinks *he* is launching Noah's Ark."

"Doesn't matter who smashes the champagne, does it?" Crocker asked mildly. "As long as the Krauts maintain their southern front?"

But Lawrence was unable to restrain himself any longer and slapped both his hands down on the polished black arms of his chair. "Noah's Ark explicitly falls under General Strong's purview. Not General Donovan's, and, with all due respect, not yours, Mr. Secretary."

Crocker did not blink. "Lothrop is the man at bat, and he is my explicit responsibility."

Lawrence started to reply, but Crocker cut him off, and all pretense of gentility disappeared. "I've had it with you people!

Joint Security, OSS, K-2, G-2, ONI, CIC, CID, Special Branch—you're all like novice skippers panicked by the warning gun into trying to nose your boats up to the starting line in a yachting race! Don't you know how important it is to hang back? You take what opening you get and *then* move into it!"

The well-bred officers could only stare at this strange lawyer, a cripple giving them a lesson in strategy.

But in the Penobscot Bay of Maine Randy Crocker and his crew of Deer Island boys were famous for always sailing away from the fleet, looking for their own wind and often finding it. Crocker hated jostling, because to him the race was never against other boats but against nature and against himself.

"Who is the woman?" General Forbes asked.

"I thought you'd never ask," Crocker said. "The woman is the point, gentlemen. And like it or not, the woman falls outside the 'purview' of each of your organizations for the simple reason that none of you uncovered her. Which is why I'll let the people who did introduce her to you, as they did to me." He raised his eyes to Dunlop, who in turn looked at Dillon.

Dillon withdrew a manila folder from his satchel, and from that he took half a dozen glossy copies of the same photograph. He passed them out.

"Her name is Sylvia Yergin," Dunlop said. "She is a Danish national, employed by the Central Coordinating Committee of the International Red Cross. In effect, she serves as liaison between Geneva and the American headquarters on Eighteenth Street, where she has an office." Dunlop paused while the others studied the photograph. It showed a stolid middle-aged woman standing at attention in the unglamorous nubby blue uniform, including hat and shoulder patch, of a Red Cross functionary. Only her fierce eyes, fixed squarely on the camera lens, indicated that she was a woman of exceptional energy. "She is an agent of the Abwehr."

"Impossible!" Lawrence blurted out. "A German agent across the way from the White House? Impossible!"

"Why do you say impossible?" Cheever countered. "Isn't CIC responsible for vetting the auxiliaries? That's General Strong's—"

"The Red Cross is an entirely civilian—"

"It is charged with care and support of military personnel, prisoners of war—"

"I won't have General Strong disparaged—"

"Gentlemen!" Crocker barked, but his glare was aimed at Lawrence. "General Strong could be here to defend himself, Colonel, as I asked him to be. But apparently there are other, more important items on his schedule." Crocker let the full weight of his displeasure fall on Lawrence, then he brought Cheever in under it. "You two are out of order. If you have questions or comments, direct them to Mr. Dunlop."

General Forbes said with overelaborate casualness, "Perhaps Mr. Dunlop could tell us who tipped him to the fact that this Yergin woman is a Kraut agent?"

"No tip," Dunlop answered. "Simple police work. My agents tracked her from an Argentine embassy party last April. We found that she frequented social functions at various embassies beyond what a woman in her position would reasonably be expected to do. We also found that she was, shall we say, generous in her affections. In both the Canadian and British chanceries, she has been friendly with cipher clerks and signals personnel. Among Americans, she has had a special knack for cultivating military staff workers."

"That hardly proves—"

Dunlop abruptly held a hand out toward Dillon, who took another set of photographs out of his folder and gave them to Dunlop, who passed them around. This showed Yergin standing next to a man in a crowded public square. The man, dressed in a bowler hat and frock coat, had his hand on Yergin's shoulder and seemed to be admonishing her.

Dunlop said, "That is Major General Helmut Reinhardt, head of the Abwehr regiment which refers to itself as *Amt Ausland*."

"A German general operating in Washington?"

Before Dunlop could reply to Forbes, Cheever said, "Not Washington!" He stood up at his place to peer across Lawrence's head at the FBI division chief. "Where was this photograph taken?"

Dunlop did not answer.

Cheever slapped the photograph. "That automobile behind them is a Peugeot. Where was this? France? No, Switzerland. That license plate is Switzerland." Cheever whipped around toward Crocker. "This is a violation of the President's explicit order! FBI operations are restricted to this hemisphere." Cheever faced Dunlop once more. "Geneva! Your people tracked her to Geneva!"

"Sit down, Colonel," Crocker said icily.

"I will not sit down. OSS by its charter has—"

"Then get out!" Crocker bellowed as his arm shot toward the door of his office. "And when Donovan asks why he wasn't brought into this operation, you tell him you stalked out of the initial briefing to protest the infringement of precious OSS prerogatives. Go ahead!"

Cheever was immobilized.

After a moment, his lips pressed thin and white, he resumed his seat.

Crocker prided himself on an economy of emotional expression, and to have been driven to such a display was even more infuriating to him than the petty squabbling that prompted it. He leaned back in his chair, taking his pipe and tobacco pouch with him. He would reclaim his detachment by pretending already to have it. "And tell us about Lothrop, Mr. Dunlop. How does he come in?"

"As you said, sir, she picked him up at a party."

"Where?" Crocker began popping the flame above his pipe bowl.

Dunlop stared blankly back at the undersecretary, unable to answer.

"The Sulgrave Club," Sean Dillon put in. "On Dupont Circle. The occasion was a New Year's reception for war-relief workers. Mr. Lothrop was present to bring greetings from Secretary Stimson."

"Yes, that's the sort of thing he does."

Dillon continued, "We did not know who Lothrop was. We were outside. When he and Yergin came out together and drove away in his car, we noted the registration. When we ran a check and discovered the car belonged to a deputy undersecretary of war, we realized that Yergin had finally landed her fish."

Crocker said, for the officers' benefit, "And that is when they came to me. I confronted Lothrop, told him who she is and offered him a chance, finally, to join the war effort. A chance, as I made clear to him, he had no choice but to accept. It has taken regular injections of spinal fluid, which, I believe, you, Mr. Dillon, have been administering, but Lothrop has conducted himself more or less admirably. His role, as you have all perhaps gathered, has involved both factual pretense—his LCI oversight, his trip to the Med—and a certain regular display of, what to call it, sexual enthusiasm. The woman seems to have been receptive on both fronts, and now perhaps is even convinced. Lothrop's success has brought us to the stage where we can offer each of you a chance to join up too."

"For sexual enthusiasm, Randy?" Lawrence asked, grinning.

Crocker smiled, but dismissively. "As the President hoped might happen, we have been given a major opportunity to reinforce Hitler's famous paranoia about the Balkans. Think of it, gentlemen. Nine panzer divisions! Forty-three infantry divisions! Sitting idle along the Danube! The balance of power in Europe depends on them staying there. If we do nothing else for the Allied cause, imagine what we do here! What Lothrop's pillow talk may have accomplished is just the start, and we can all be hugely grateful for it." Crocker's gaze fell for an instant on the photograph of his son, who would almost certainly be one of those going ashore at Normandy.

Dunlop said, "Yergin will see herself as providing the intelligence that will enable Germany to win the war. She will look everywhere now for other signs pointing to the Balkans, beginning with her own Red Cross."

"Right," Crocker said, and he aimed his gaze at General Alfred. "The chief has to issue orders to have the Red Cross blood reserve moved to the Mediterranean, incrementally beginning now, and completed by mid-May."

"That's ridiculous," Alfred countered, "the blood reserve—"

"I'm not talking about the blood reserve. I'm talking about *orders*, about paper. Paper that has to cross desks on Eighteenth Street beginning this week. Paper that refers to medical staging areas on Crete, Cyprus, and Malta."

"But how will the woman get access to the paper?"

Dillon answered from his place by the conference table. "She is sleeping with the Red Cross director's assistant too, another man near retirement age named Keith Simon. He's a widower, and she goes with him to his apartment. He expects to marry her in June."

"But if you bring him and others at the Red Cross into this—"

"We do nothing of the kind," Crocker said. "Everyone in the Red Cross remains in the dark about the real blood reserves and where they are. They don't know now. The levers they pull are attached to nothing." Crocker looked at Cheever.

"Which presumably violates the Red Cross charter, George. We're poking holes through charters right and left, aren't we?"

Forbes, the man in charge of security for the real invasion, said, "The Red Cross director hasn't known anything about the blood reserve for a year. When he gets an order from Marshall, he'll suspect it's a ruse, but he'll play along. He's no dummy."

"That's just one example of what we can do now to satisfy Fräulein Yergin's curiosity. We want to give her a full set of collateral indications, documentation if possible, things to take with her when she returns to Geneva in—?" Crocker raised his eyebrows toward Dunlop.

But it was Dillon who said, "Three and a half weeks."

"What if she doesn't buy it? What if—"

"Lothrop will continue to see her," Dillon said with an authority he had not yet displayed. "And I will continue my surveillance. It is my job to assess whether Yergin has swallowed the hook or not. If I conclude that she hasn't, or that she is playing us along, I will call the operation off and arrest her."

"And *your* jobs, gentlemen"—Crocker swept them with the stem of his pipe—"is to provide support to Mr. Dillon. I'll expect an action plan from each of your shops on my desk when I arrive here in the morning."

"What time do you want us?" a thoroughly chastened Cheever asked.

"Not you, George. Just your plan. Tell me how OSS can support us in confirming the Balkans for this woman. Like it or not, until this phase of it is resolved, Noah's Ark is going to be run off of one desk. This desk."

Crocker slapped his hand down and a cup of paper clips jumped. "From here on you are each to be individually responsible to Mr. Dunlop. He speaks on this matter with my authority. Is that clear?"

Cheever leaned back in his chair, lifting its front legs off the floor, craning toward Dillon. "Where does Yergin live?"

"We are conducting this operation on a need-to-know basis, sir."

Cheever went white again, and he exchanged a look with Lawrence. For once they had something in common: neither would find it easy to brief his boss on this shit. Donovan and Strong would have something in common too: a reaction of sputtering rage to this incredible intrusion by Hoover.

General Alfred had his own reasons for finding this turn of

events unbelievable. He said timidly, "Your authority, Mr. Crocker, I understand that. But General Marshall is going to ask me where your authority rests in this matter. Shall I tell him Secretary Stimson's?"

"No, General, you tell him President Roosevelt's. You tell General Marshall to feel free to call me or the President, either one."

Crocker stood up. His leg clicked, and the others seemed to take that as their signal to rise too. Dillon thought of a nun's cricket, these eminences in a Canaryville parish school.

Dillon stepped forward, preempting his own chief. But he was not jostling for position on a racecourse. He simply stood there with his hand extended, facing General Forbes, who hesitated for a moment before understanding that Dillon wanted the photographs back. Forbes surrendered them, saying, "If this works, it will make my job easier. I can admit that."

Dillon went efficiently around the half-circle, silently collecting the pictures. Only Colonel Cheever refused. "I want General Donovan to see these."

"General Donovan will be welcome to see them, Colonel. I will bring them over myself whenever he asks. Or he can call Mr. Dunlop or Mr. Hoover."

Cheever looked to Crocker for support. But Crocker said quietly, "I'm sorry, Colonel."

Cheever turned and started to leave the room, the photographs under his arm. Dillon stepped around a chair to block him. "Colonel, these photographs constitute evidence in a criminal investigation. If you refuse to yield them, I will arrest you for obstructing a federal officer."

Cheever handed the photographs over and pushed roughly past to leave.

Dillon crossed back to the conference table to put the pictures back in his briefcase. He began to rewind the Dictabelt.

By the time he finished, the others were gone. Dunlop was waiting by the door. Crocker, from his desk, nodded at Dillon once.

Dillon started for the door.

"Mr. Dillon?"

"Sir?"

"Can David Lothrop hold himself together?"

"Yes, sir. I believe he can."

"You did a good job getting him ready."

Dillon hesitated, then said, "He's better at it than I would be. When he's with the woman, I almost believe him myself."

"Yes, I know. Lothrop *is* better than you would be. To do what Lothrop is doing takes an emptiness at the core of the man. If we hadn't gotten there first to fill it with our idea, Sylvia Yergin would have filled it with hers." Crocker paused before adding, "You don't have an emptiness like that in you."

The two men looked at each other across all that separated them, each one aware of the strength of their surprising connection.

Dillon, as the junior agent, did the driving. He nosed the heavy Bureau sedan out of the freshly paved parking lot onto the boulevard that ran between the Pentagon and the river. Dunlop had gone within himself, but Dillon felt too exhilarated not to comment. "I thought wars made men pull together. Those fellows are at each other's throats. They were at *our* throats."

Instead of answering, Dunlop pointed at a drive-in restaurant called the Hot Shoppe. It had once served box lunches to travelers flying out of the mud-flat airport that the Pentagon had replaced. "Pull in here. I've got to make a phone call."

Dillon did as he was told, but with an ominous intimation. He'd expected his boss to be roaring with satisfaction. Hoover was going to be delighted at how they'd held the line against Donovan and Strong both. More to the point, a crew of gumshoe FBI agents had a chance now of really affecting the outcome of the war.

But Dunlop was in the grip of an altogether different set of feelings. Dillon would have asked him what was up, but rank separated them. When the car stopped, Dunlop opened the door. "I'll be right back."

Dillon put a cigarette in his mouth, lit it and smoked. A sense of trepidation thickened in his chest.

When Dunlop returned he was positively morose.

Now Dillon did ask, "What's up?"

"Christ, Sean, I hate to be the one to tell you this." He was no longer the man who had coolly made the moves in Crocker's office.

Dillon's mind leapt ahead to, He's taking me off the case. "Tell me what?"

"Your wife called the Bureau this morning. I couldn't tell you before. She's in the hospital."

"In the hospital? What are you talking about?"

"She went into labor."

"When, now?"

"This morning. The baby was born. That's what they just told me. Your wife is all right. She's going to be all right."

Dillon started to speak, then stopped. He looked at his watch. "When was this?"

"She called about ten."

"Ten o'clock this morning? That's six hours ago! Why the hell are you telling me this only now?"

"How could I have this morning? You were en route to the Melville Arms at ten o'clock. What was I supposed to do, summon you back? Cancel the surveillance just when it was paying off?"

"But we've been together all afternoon, and you didn't tell me?"

"I'd have told you if what we're working on wasn't so—"

"What, the damn war depends on *me?* I can't have an hour to go to my wife to make sure she knows—" He stopped, unwilling to say "I love her" to Dunlop. His mind jumped. "And now she's alone?" To start the car, he pushed the ignition button so hard his thumb went white. "She's by herself in the hospital all this time?"

"Mike Packard went over, and I think Packard's wife is there too. She's a friend of your wife's, isn't she?"

Packard and Dillon had trained at Quantico together. Mike should have come for me, damn it. Dillon whipped the car backward out of its space. He shifted into first and gunned away from the restaurant. "You've got a nerve, Dunlop, keeping this from me."

"Calm down, Sean. Get your priorities straight. We made sure your wife got everything she needed today. As soon as it was proper to do so, I informed you."

"Need-to-know, is that it?"

"You're upset, but don't push it. If it's your wife you're worried about, relax—"

"What about my baby?"

Dunlop hesitated, a beat too much, before saying, "I don't know."

Dillon slammed the steering wheel.

"Sean, nothing would have been different if you had been there."

"I'd have *been* there." He circled off the ramp onto the road leading to the Fourteenth Street Bridge, fast. "What hospital?"

"George Washington."

"George Washington, shit! That's the other bridge!" He swung off the approach road as abruptly as he'd cut onto it. As he sped upriver toward Memorial Bridge, he reached to the dashboard to flick the siren switch. The noise seemed to goose the car, which nearly climbed onto the bumper of the car in front. "Move! Damn it!" And the car ahead did.

He drove wildly along the river boulevard, the Pentagon and the cemetery on one side, and, across the water, the monuments and temples of the sacred city. He had stopped thinking of Dunlop, of Yergin, of winning the war. "Cass," he said under his breath, as if the name itself were a password. But what it opened was a memory of running like this before.

But on foot. He was running to the trolley shed to find out what had happened to his Pa. "None of your business," his mother had said, which told him that his father's death was his fault.

His wife in the hospital? His baby—?

Raymond Buckley's face, of all things, came into Dillon's mind. Then Doc Riley's face, afraid. "Trust me, Doc."

"What?" It was Dunlop, reaching across to him, touching him. They were halfway across the bridge, almost into Washington. "What'd you say, Sean? I can't hear you because of the siren."

What siren? Dillon wanted to say. I thought someone was screaming.

When he stepped quietly into her room, she was turned away, facing the wall. He thought she was asleep.

He stood over her, as unmoving as she.

Her red hair was tangled, a mass of knots and snarls spilling onto the pillow behind her. Her hair, the curve of her ear, the ridge of her cheekbone, the hollow of her neck, the lines of her form under the sheet; the simple sight of her was all he needed for a moment.

Then he became aware of the reason for the reassurance he felt. The subtle rising and falling of her body meant she was alive. His Cass was still alive! Now he could begin to believe what the nurse had told him: his Cass was going to be all right. The floor of his heart had turned upside down, was the ceiling, all at once, of his gratitude. When had he ever felt so thankful? And when had he ever been hauled so far beyond his capacity for expression? He was grateful too that, at that moment, she required none from him.

But then, as if reading exactly that in him, she rolled slowly back from the wall. Her weary gaze floated around him for a moment before snapping to, and he understood that she had not been sleeping at all. The black hole in her eyes made him feel that his gratitude had come too soon. She had not died, but he understood at once that something in her had.

"Hello, darling." He took her hand, which was wet and cold and made him shiver.

"Where were you?" she asked dully.

"What?"

"I needed you. You weren't here, and the baby died."

Dillon was stunned to hear the link of causality in her statement. For a moment in the car he had accused himself like that, but it was nonsense. Nothing would have been different if he'd—

"The baby died!" Suddenly she rose up, half out of bed, like a crazy lady.

He sat beside her, to take her into his arms. "I know, darling. I know."

"Where were you?"

"Cass, you know where I was. I was at work."

"But for hours?"

"Cass, they didn't tell me."

"Sean, there was no one to help me. I didn't know who to call!" She was sobbing into him, but dryly, as if she had no tears left.

"You did just right, sweetheart. You called the Bureau, and they—"

"They said you'd get here, but you didn't. The baby didn't die at first. They said she might . . . if you had come . . . Oh, Sean, where were you?"

The baby, a baby girl, had lived for two and a half hours. That news had pierced Sean when the nurse had told him. The baby had been living when he drove across town to the Pentagon. That meeting with Crocker could have been postponed. He pictured the child, undersized and flushed, trying to breathe in an incubator. The little girl had tried to live long enough to meet him, but he had not come. Now her remains had already been taken discreetly away. Her grave would be marked "Baby girl Dillon."

"Cass, Cass," he said, stroking her. He knew better than to try to explain himself to her, as if he could.

But of course he could. For a moment, he rebelled at her blaming him. He had not been on the golf course, for Christ's sake! He'd been laying snares for Hitler!

"Cass . . . Cass . . ." He repeated her name to soothe himself as much as her. Yet he hated how her accusation made him feel. He hated how it forced him to face the choice he had made. He had chosen the Bureau. But what was he supposed to do? It seemed unfair to him that—

He stopped himself, aware of how hurt she was. "Cass," he said, holding her so that she could see him. "I'm just grateful to have *you*. You're all right. I'm so grateful."

"But don't you care about the baby?"

"Oh God, Cass." He gently pulled her against himself once more. "Don't say such a thing to me." And, despite himself, under his breath, as if she were Dunlop, as if she were responsible for what she was saying, he added with exasperation, "Christ almighty, Cass."

"What?" She pulled back from him. "What did you say?"

"Just don't accuse me of not caring about the baby, when all I'm trying to say is how much I care about you."

"If you cared about me, you'd have been here. That's all."

And with that, she pulled away from him and rolled back to her wall.

And now he realized that he'd become furious at Dunlop in the car because he knew in the first instant that she would feel this, taking his unavailability as indifference. But it was not true, not remotely true. Nor was it fair! There was a war on, and lo and behold, without her even knowing, he had an important part to play in it.

How well he knew her. He had understood viscerally that she would blame him. And he knew himself. Much as he hated it, he could feel the temperature dropping in his own heart, a chill coming, even ice. If she could throw shutters open to the freezing wind like this, so could he.

He forced himself to touch her shoulder, and when he did, she fell back toward him again. Now tears ran freely on her face. "Sean, Sean, I'm *not* all right. You said thank God I'm all right, but I'm not."

"The nurse told me—"

"The doctor said I shouldn't have children again. I mean, ever. He said—"

"Cass, hush, we can—"

"No, listen! He said I have hypertension or something. I risk this every time. He said he was going to talk to you about it. Sean, promise me we can have a child! We'll try again, promise me."

"But, darling." Dillon felt buffeted. No wonder she was unglued. The nerve of the doctor, talking to her about this now.

"I want a child, Sean. I don't care what the doctor says. Promise me."

How could he promise such a thing? He could only hold her. He said, "I love you, Cass," but that was not the point, or not enough, and he knew it.

Dillon had wanted to get back to Ninth Street for the shift briefing, but he missed it. He waited in the hallway outside Cass's room until her doctor finally came. Approaching from the stairwell, he was a white-gowned white-haired older man. Though he'd been taking care of Cass since before she was pregnant, Sean had never met him. His name was Bigelow, and now Sean saw in his erect posture, in his cold blue eyes, and in the features of his handsome face the marks of a man long accustomed to thinking of himself as superior. He was taller than Sean. Dr. Bigelow took off his white cap off. Sean understood that he'd just delivered someone else's baby.

They shook hands. "Mr. Dillon, I'm sorry."

"What can you tell me about my wife's condition, Doctor?"

"She suffered a severe bout of eclampsia."

"You told her hypertension."

"I said it's like that, soaring blood pressure, but associated with the trauma of childbirth. She won't have a problem otherwise."

"She'll be all right?"

"Well, she's stable now. But you should understand, she almost died. Her blood pressure had us . . . her numbers were up in stroke range. We really thought she'd have a stroke. But now she's near to normal again. We'll watch her for a couple of days, keep her comfortable. Nature will do the rest. But my goodness, she came awfully close . . ."

"She seems very . . ." What? He could not explain. He'd never seen her at such an edge before.

"I'm not a psychiatrist, Mr. Dillon, but your wife is going to need more than we can give her. A woman might tend to feel like quite a failure after—"

"She said something about not conceiving again. You told her not to conceive."

"Yes. Eclampsia is a condition that we would expect to see again, and she seems susceptible to a severe form of it. She's very lucky not to have had a stroke. I seriously question if she can stand the stress of childbirth."

"My wife wants a baby, Doctor."

"I understand that. There are risks, is what I'm telling you, serious risks. I would frankly recommend at some point, soon, a tubal ligation."

"What's that?"

"Making it so she can't conceive. Cutting the Fallopian tubes."

"Sterilization?"

"Yes."

"Christ, Doctor, isn't that extreme? Why couldn't you anticipate this and get her ready for it? Isn't it your job—"

"We *did* our job, and your wife is alive."

"But my baby is dead."

"Yes, tragically. And now *your* job is to take care of your wife. She can't conceive alone, you know."

Dillon wanted to hit him.

"You're concerned because you're Catholics."

"That is not the issue here."

"If not sterilization, then strict birth control. That's what I recommend. Otherwise"—Dr. Bigelow shrugged, supremely detached—"your religion may well present you with a truly awful problem."

"What do you mean?"

"Don't Catholics believe it's more important to save the life of the baby than the mother?"

"I don't believe that." Dillon had to look away sharply. His anger had become another kind of intense emotion. "I'm grateful to you for saving her."

Even Dr. Bigelow seemed ambushed then.

"My wife wants a baby. It is not a casual wish of hers. I'm not talking about what I want. If my wife can't have a child . . ." Dillon stopped. He had never come this close before to the recognition of how little, in fact, he gave his wife. A child was to have rescued both of them, her from loneliness and him from precisely this sense of failure. "My question to you, Doctor, is, Exactly how dangerous is it?"

"I can't say *exactly*. There are precautions one would take through confinement, watching for swelling and headaches, but once the blood pressure starts to soar, there's nothing we can give her to stop it. We would just have to take the baby, no matter what."

"That's what I'd want. The baby would never come first."

"Then don't go to a Catholic hospital, Mr. Dillon. This condition kills women. You *could* be lucky. Maybe she could get through pregnancy and delivery all right, but I'm telling you she almost died today. Her body threw off the baby to save itself. That could happen again too, preempting us. How would that make her feel? There are, you see, a range of risks. You two will have to decide, that's all."

"My wife has already decided."

"That's how she feels today. That's natural. She's a grieving mother. If she still feels that way later . . ." Dr. Bigelow shrugged. "I just think nature is trying to tell you two something. I think you should listen."

"I'm listening to you, Doctor. I have to listen to my wife too."

"She's devastated. It's natural. You are too, I think."

"Not like Cass is."

"Well, no, of course not. The woman bears the brunt."

Bears the *child*, Dillon heard him say. But he hadn't.

Cass was asleep, so Dillon went downtown. The briefing had occurred and the surveillance teams were set; there was nothing to do. He returned to the hospital. It was after midnight when he slipped into her room, intending just to sit with her, to watch her sleep.

But at once she opened her eyes.

"Did you talk to the doctor?"

"Yes."

"I've been thinking about it, Sean, and I want you to know how I feel."

"Cass, we—"

"No, listen!"

When he took her hand, she squeezed it hard.

"If it's God's will, we're going to have a baby, Sean. That's all."

God's will? Dillon was confused. If God's will is awful, whose fault is it?

TEN

The encumbrance of their love took Cass by surprise as much as Sean. She had never thought of herself as a needy person. Quite the opposite. But after the baby, feelings of competence and independence were like rumors to her of the person she had been. The isolation of her life in Washington became intolerable in large part because, to her, that isolation had caused the loss. Not that she blamed Sean, when she was rational, and not that there was anything to do about it while the war continued. Cass told herself to relax, and eventually, in a way, she did.

When Sean came home, usually she was already in bed, and they still made love occasionally, she nestling into him groggily, the way she always had. But sex was different too; how could it not be? Though she never said as much, she was afraid of it now, not of his body, but of her own. This was what Sean was incapable of understanding—that if she had stopped trusting anyone, it was herself. Whether she trusted him or not was no longer relevant. And so, of course, the act itself, which once had seemed simple and natural, had become a matter of her wincing and him withholding his weight, as if he expected her to break when he pushed in. She didn't know, in those first months after the baby, what frightened her more, the thought of getting pregnant or the thought of not.

The baby died in February. Cass became pregnant again the following August. Her mother came from Chicago, and Cass went to bed in October and stayed there. At last she let herself go, falling back into the feeling that someone was there to catch her.

During that winter and spring, the very world seemed

181

blessed, for the war too came to its head. In early April Cass gave birth to a nearly full-term son. Once more her blood pressure shot up, and once more there was an air of emergency about the delivery. But the doctors were ready this time. They performed an immediate cesarean. Still, nothing they did while she was in conscious distress mitigated the certainty she had, at the moment of going under the anaesthesia, that she was about to die. When she came to, and Sean himself was there to put the healthy baby into her arms, she just cried and cried.

He said to her, about their baby, words she would always remember: "Darling, we have a perfect son." He kissed her. And then, as if he knew all about the terror she'd thought her secret, her private failure, he said, "And you never have to do this again. I won't let you. You are too precious to me." And in reply, all that she could do was squeeze his hand and sob.

President Roosevelt died, but so did Hitler, and just this week the war in Europe ended.

Now the Dillons had come to the crypt-church of the National Shrine of the Immaculate Conception, the half-finished basilica on top of Washington's tallest hill in far Northeast. Cass had been the one to want the baptism here, as a gesture of thanksgiving to the Blessed Mother. During her sojourn in Washington, the Shrine had been a place to which she'd go for solace, and she'd never failed to find it. Now more than ever—she was a mother!—she felt a bond with Mary.

Construction of the Shrine had been discontinued at the beginning of the war, and all it really consisted of was the largest untopped basement in the city. The crypt, even with its unclad stonework and awkward bulking exterior, was nevertheless a point of reference for Cass. The various stone rooms, windowless and cool, linked by raw concrete corridors like catacombs, evoked an air of secrecy that she had learned to associate with the Church's age of glory, but which also gave form to feelings she had about herself in an alien city. The barrel-vaulted chapel itself, illuminated only by candles or the pseudo-candles of dim electric light fixtures, made her want to bow from the waist.

Sean stood by Cass at the baptismal font. Behind him were Mike Packard and his wife Ellie. They looked ill at ease. The light of votive candles flickered on the walls. Cass was holding the baby. She wore brown gloves, a stylish yellow suit and a broad-brimmed hat with a lace veil pinned up into the silk band. Even to those who did not know her well, like the Packards, she seemed a woman who had her happiness back.

Beside her were her mother and, just in from Chicago, her Aunt Flo and Molly. At eighteen, Molly had grown into a striking young woman. She was about to graduate from high school and start a job at Bell, indeed as an operator at Cass's old Switchboards Building. The limit of Molly's ambition was to be like her cousin, but Cass was crushed that Molly was not going to college. Instead of disapproving of her, though, Cass had chosen that moment of letdown to ask Molly to be the godmother of their new baby.

"What name do you give your child?" the priest asked with ritual solemnity. He was Monsignor Barry, the famous rector of the Shrine. Cass regarded it as an honor that he had assigned himself to this christening, instead of one of the assistants.

Cass and Sean exchanged a look. The name of their baby was a grave matter to them. Sean had been the one to suggest it, but Cass had wanted it as much as he.

Sean answered firmly, "Richard."

In memory of Doc Riley, the only Richard they both knew.

Cass and Sean were not the same people who had left Chicago nearly five years before, but in that way they were like most Americans. Their own odyssey was a personal version of what the whole nation had undergone. Those five years, more than any other half-decade in the entire century, altered the meaning and the feel of life in their country. It would never be as hard as it had been, perhaps, but neither would it be as simple.

Sean had made a new place for himself in the work he did. With the Sylvia Yergin operation, he'd enabled the Bureau to play a real part in the most important maneuver of the war, for on D day a full third of Hitler's infantry and a quarter of his panzer force were still uselessly deployed in the Danube Basin. By now Dillon was the deputy assistant director for counterintelligence, an extraordinary position for a man in the Bureau only five years. Since shortly after D day, most of a year before, Dillon had been one of a few top agents supervising the transition of counterintelligence focus from the Nazis to the Soviets. The FBI director had, of course, been famous for hostility to Communists since his days as an assistant to the notorious Red-baiting Attorney General Palmer, but that was before Stalingrad. Everyone knew that without the Russians, the Allies would have lost. For years, therefore, the Reds had had free run of Washington and, though no one knew it or had even heard of the place yet, free run of a desert town called Los Alamos. It was a counterspy nightmare now to track and plot their multipronged penetration, not to mention trying to devise ways to undo it. In those weeks after the Red Army and the GIs met up at the Elbe River, it was far from clear that they were not going to turn their weapons on each other. Washington, having hardly caught its breath after Hitler, was bracing for what Forrestal called "a new barbarian invasion of Europe." One war was only half finished, but Dillon and others like him were already preparing to fight another.

Richard had not protested when Monsignor Barry, using the classic golden scallop shell, splashed his forehead with holy water, but no sooner was the ceremony finished than he began to cry loudly. His complaint echoed in the vaulted chapel, and it was Sean who took him.

Sean loved the way his son fit the crook of his arm like a football. All during Cass's pregnancy, he had anticipated this baby's coming as if it would be an event belonging primarily to her. The obvious and powerful fact that the baby was growing inside Cass had made Sean feel that his relationship to the born child, and the born child's to his, would be equally indirect and abstract. But the birth had jolted him. Whatever the baby meant to his wife, to Sean the baby was the answer to a question he hadn't even known he was asking. The living baby, so physical in its demands, so absolute in its presence, filled up a hole in Sean's heart that he had never admitted having. Now, swinging the baby in the cradle of his arm, Sean felt that happiness again, and it redoubled when Richard's wailing quieted, and peace came over him. What Sean loved most was the simplicity of the baby's needs, and the ease with which he and Cass could meet them. The miracle to Dillon was that *his* presence soothed, and *his* arm cuddled, and *his* love registered as welcome. Dillon was in no way prepared, in other words, for the connection he felt to his son, how it transformed him too. What a surprise to discover in the same moment—a birth—both his huge, unanticipated need as a man and the one thing that could fill it.

"You doll," he said aloud, his face just above the baby's.

Dillon was sure Richard knew him for his father. They were in the corner of the chapel, near a rack of votive lights. The others were chatting quietly at the baptismal font while the priest put away the paraphernalia.

Dillon became aware of someone on the other side of him. He brought his face up from his baby's and turned. A man beyond the last pew began to walk away. His body jerked awkwardly as he pressed the weight of each step down onto the handle of a cane. The sound echoed, the click, click, clicking of his wooden leg.

"I'm so sorry," Randall Crocker said when Sean had caught up with him in the next cavernous hall, a memorial room on the stone walls of which workers had begun chiseling the names of benefactors' beloved dead. "The last thing I intended was to intrude."

"Not at all, Mr. Crocker. Are you here because of us?"

Randall Crocker had never been in the Catholic basilica before. "Because of your baby," he said simply. Dillon was still carrying Richard, and Crocker slid his forefinger inside the curl of the infant's fist. "I *had* to see him."

"I would have invited you."

"I was going to wait outside, to greet you when you came out, but I couldn't resist." Crocker smiled warmly.

Dillon, in an unprecedented gesture, put his hand on the older man's arm.

Cass joined them. Everyone else had remained in the chapel. "This is my wife, sir. Cass, this is Mr. Crocker."

"Hello, Mrs. Dillon. Forgive me. You must think me awfully rude." Despite his lameness, Crocker greeted Cass with a slight bow that was graceful beyond anything she was accustomed to. He held on to her fingertips while he said, "When I learned of your child"—he inclined toward Richard again—"I was entirely happy for you."

"You wrote to me last year . . ."

"Yes, I did. I was so very sorry."

Even now, when she thought of that other baby, her eyes burned. All she could thing to say was, "A beautiful, beautiful letter, Mr. Crocker."

Now it was Crocker who touched Cass. He would never refer to it, but, looking at her face just then, he knew very well what had compelled him to come here.

He knew why he had continued to feel so close to Dillon

even after they'd wound up the Lothrop case, why he'd kept himself informed about Dillon's climb in the Bureau hierarchy and why, when he'd learned that Dillon's wife was pregnant again, he'd asked his secretary to keep track of her due date.

"If I may say so, your son is beautiful."

Cass leaned to kiss Richard. Crocker was pleased to see her happiness, but he was in no way ready for it when she swung back up toward him, saying, "I remember that you have a son."

Crocker looked away.

Sean's heart sank at the flash of pain he saw in Crocker's face. "Mr. Crocker has a son in the army."

The silence betrayed them. Crocker stared off at the shadowy near wall, the names of the dead.

The baby broke them free by beginning to cry. Cass automatically took him back from Sean, and Richard became quiet again, nestling on his mother's heart. Cass asked directly and simply, "Is your son all right, Mr. Crocker?"

His pain was long since fused into place. It wasn't himself he was thinking of, but them. How he hated to have intruded like this, but Crocker was incapable of the greater offense it would be now to deflect these two good people. "My son was killed in February. There was a battle for a bridge on the Rhine. My son was one of the first Americans across the river."

"Oh," Sean said, a gasp. Then, "I remember when he came through Omaha Beach all right."

Crocker nodded. "If we made a mistake, it was in thinking that by surviving D-Day, he had survived. Strange, isn't it? How we arrange our perceptions according to little check-off boxes in our minds that have nothing to do with reality."

Tears had come into Cass's eyes, even as she pressed her infant child closer. "I am so sorry, Mr. Crocker."

"Thank you." Crocker swung toward Dillon. "You look awfully well, Sean." Then he lifted his eyes toward the low ceiling. "Are we allowed to talk in here?"

"You mean is it secure?" Sean grinned.

"No, is it respectful." But Crocker was grinning too.

"Come back with us to our apartment," Cass said. "We have a ham."

"I wish I could, but thank you." He leaned and kissed the

baby, a farewell. Then he said to Dillon, "I have something in the car. Could you walk out with me?"

"Certainly."

"Goodbye, Mrs. Dillon. I'm very happy for you."

Cass dammed the corner of her eye with her gloved knuckle. "Could I write to Mrs. Crocker?"

"My dear wife died many years ago. That's why I'm a man with no manners. My Hillary would be horrified at my showing up uninvited like this. But at least I brought something."

"Could I come out with you?"

"Of course, but I"—Crocker looked toward the chapel—"I hate to take you—"

"It's all right." Cass glanced back quickly. Her aunt and mother were laughing at something the monsignor had said.

They left the hall and took the stairs up to the street. Crocker's car, a big black Chrysler, was by the curb near the entrance. His driver had been leaning against the front fender, enjoying the bright afternoon. When he saw his boss, he dropped his cigarette, moved to the door and opened it. Crocker retrieved from the seat a package wrapped in silver paper tied with white ribbon. He turned back to the Dillons with it.

The driver moved away discreetly.

"I hope this is all right." He gave it to Cass, whose hand dropped with the unexpected weight.

"May we open it?" Cass gave it over to Sean, who unwrapped it.

A black leather-bound Bible, a new one, with gold-leafed pages, a far finer edition than either Cass or Sean had ever held. Sean opened it and saw that the registry page had been filled out in formal Gothic script: his name, Cass's, Richard's and the date, May 19, 1945.

"It's beautiful," Sean said.

"It's the Douay-Rheims version," Crocker said, "which I'm told is the preferred translation." He meant for Catholics, and Sean knew it. The man had thought of everything. "In my family," Crocker added, "everyone gets his Bible at his christening."

Cass impulsively stepped forward and kissed his cheek, an act which parted the curtains on all her lost affection. Jostling her baby made him cry. She managed to say, "I should feed him," then turned and almost ran back into the hulking unfinished church.

The two men stood looking at the door into which she had disappeared.

"I apologize," Crocker said at last, "for intruding with my personal circumstances. I'm not myself."

"But your coming here honors us, sir."

"I've upset your wife."

"No, it's a confusing time. The baby, and our other baby, and her mother and aunt . . . Cass's feelings are all jumbled up, I guess."

"I think the women have a lot more to handle than we men do." Crocker flashed his kindly smile. "We take care of the world. They take care of the people who live in it."

Dillon sensed what a façade Crocker's equanimity was. Crocker might admit to stress or fatigue, but he would not show it. He had himself, even his grief, perfectly under control, and he would until one day he simply died. The compensating fitness of a crippled man.

"Do you know what I think?" Crocker took a step back toward his car, his leg clicking. Dillon realized that he often covered that sound by talking over it. "I think we're all damn near shot with this war." He slammed the flat of his hand against his car. "This goddamned war which has left Europe a charnel house! The dead! Christ, you wouldn't believe the dead! Now that it's over we're beginning to see what it's been."

"It doesn't feel over to me."

"Well, of course, with Japan it isn't yet. But the Japs will settle now. They don't want to be ravaged like Germany was. You wouldn't believe what Hitler's done . . ." Crocker paused, thinking of photographs he'd seen that week of what GIs were finding in the death camps. "I was thinking of Europe."

"I'm thinking of Europe too. I'm no military man, but I have to admit it looks to me like we *should* have gone in through the Balkans. Greece, Albania, Bulgaria, Yugoslavia, Rumania, Hungary, Poland, maybe Austria, most of Germany. If this war began when no one challenged Hitler over a few hundred square miles in the Rhineland, what will come of not challenging Stalin over half of Europe?"

"What do you want us to do, Sean? Set Patton loose?"

"As I say, I don't know strategy, but I will tell you what I do know." Dillon was aware of the transition they were making, back to the world, away from the people who lived in it, including themselves. "Encrypted cable traffic out of the Soviet embassy on Sixteenth Street, back to Moscow, has increased in volume fiftyfold over the last four weeks. Cipher clerks transmit around the clock now. We can't read it, but it's hard not to think they're clearing the decks. They are sending back everything they can get their hands on. They are still our ally, of course. So all we can do is watch. We're watching them pound stakes down the middle of Europe. And we're watching them loot Washington for information."

"What else are you seeing?"

"That isn't enough?"

"I have the impression there's more."

"Perhaps I've said too much already, sir."

"My clearances are in place, Dillon." Crocker's authority thinned the air suddenly.

"It was the founding meeting of the United Nations in San Francisco last month that started things. The Russians used it as a justification for flooding us with NKVD agents."

"Beyond the usual delegation?"

"*Twice* the usual. They sent men as typists who couldn't type. They sent men as chauffeurs who haven't touched the wheel of an automobile. Every member of their delegation was an agent. The State Department granted their every request: double-length visas, freedom to travel, unrestricted telegraph, accommodations requiring the use of an entire hotel. Claiming some connection to the UN, they applied for and got credentials to triple their staffs in New York and Washington. Eighty-two agents with free access to every point in the country, and they are using it. The UN conference is over for weeks, but none of them have left the country. We have them spotted in Seattle, Atlanta, New Mexico, and Maine. They pretend to be sightseeing, although they assume they're being watched and so they make a show of collecting road maps and phone books and photographing National Guard armories and police stations, as if they are after general intelligence."

"And they're not?"

"They're doing it so openly that we have to assume they are up to something else. They pretend to be inept, but when they want to shake us they do. The guess is they're making last contacts with members of a deep-cover network already in place, preparing to activate it when the diplomats are expelled if the U.S. and Russia break off relations. They are getting ready for war with us, and the State Department is helping them."

"The State Department would probably say it is helping them get ready for war with Japan. The Russians have to carry our water in Manchuria, Sean."

"But why can't we restrict their travel in the U.S.? Why can't we limit their use of transmission cables? Why can't we send their UN delegates home with every other nation's? They're playing us for saps."

Crocker, who had listened with such sobriety, smiled as he realized that, though he had practically ordered Dillon to brief him, he had played into Dillon's hands. "You're telling me all this for a reason."

"Just small talk, Mr. Crocker."

"You want me to go to Stimson."

Dillon shook his head. "I've heard you're acquainted with the President."

" 'The President,' to me, is still a phrase that refers to Roosevelt."

"But you supported Truman when Roosevelt was thinking of naming him vice president. Truman owes you."

"How do you know that?"

"Didn't I read it in *Time* magazine or someplace?"

"No, Sean, you didn't."

"My point, sir, is that President Truman should be getting assessments from somebody besides the State Department."

"J. Edgar is surely making this information available, isn't he?"

"I'm afraid with Mr. Hoover it's like the boy who cried wolf. He has sounded alarms about the Reds before. This time it's real. They are getting ready for war with us. The cable traffic alone warns of something. Mr. Truman should hear that from somebody besides the Bureau. What is Donovan saying? Or General Strong?"

"You can imagine what they *would* say if I went to Truman with intelligence provided by the FBI. I'm War Department, remember? You want me to make war on State. As for Donovan, forget it. His standing depended on FDR. Truman has no use for OSS, not that I did. But it's a disgrace how these generals chew each other up, not to mention the admirals. You've probably heard that General MacArthur refused to allow OSS in his theater, and Truman backed him up. Score one for General Strong. No one is in charge over there. That's the biggest problem we've had in this war, competition between army and navy fiefdoms, all those goddamn geniuses, and intelligence is the worst of the lot, a bunch of hot-rodders, and all they want to do is drag-race with each other. If Truman asked my advice, which he hasn't, I'd tell him to get the whole operation out of the Pentagon altogether, maybe give it to you people, but someone should be in charge. Some*one!*"

"It would never be Hoover," Dillon said matter-of-factly. "Not if Truman's doing the appointing. The President has, shall we say, old friends who are old enemies of ours. That's another reason the director can't get Truman's ear on what the Soviets are up to."

"What are you talking about?"

"Pendergast in Kansas City. Truman's sponsor. He's the one who lined up Frank Hague from Jersey City and Ed Kelly from my own Chicago. Among the three of them Truman was launched. I know how machines like those operate, and they always call in their chits eventually. I make certain assumptions, in other words, even about the President."

"Truman is a bigger man than that."

"He is now. Now he's the President. But once he was a ward boss. He's a politician." Dillon didn't bother to hide his disdain.

Crocker sighed with discouragement. "Well, I'm no politician. I've often thought I should be, that maybe with a little more deviousness and a lot more compromise I could have gotten things to work better where I am. No politicians in the damn army or navy, just virtuous men of principle who refuse to give an inch. Given the crap I've seen flying between the services, we're damn lucky to have beaten Hitler. And don't ever forget something, lad, and if it cost us the Balkans, so be it: we would not have won without Stalin. And we still need him."

"Was the war worth it, though, if all we've done is replace one monster with another?"

Crocker shrugged. "Worth it? I can't answer that. I don't know."

"We should know, Mr. Crocker, with all due respect. Isn't that what government service is about? If we can't justify what's happened, who can? And how do we do that if we lose half of Europe?"

" 'Government service'? Christ, it seems like years since I heard that phrase."

"I don't mean to sound pompous."

"And I don't mean to deflate ..." Crocker laughed and slapped Dillon's shoulder. "You remind me of my boy. Did I tell you that? He was a great believer."

"In what you taught him."

"I guess that's right. Maybe it's a function of age, though. My brain has more trouble than it used to with the great abstractions, the noble ideas men fight wars over."

Was that the difference between them? Age? Abstractions? Dillon didn't think so. "In any case, Mr. Crocker, the recent activities of the Soviet diplomats inside the United States are not abstractions. Will you approach the President with what I've told you?"

"Does Hoover know you're asking me this?"

"I didn't know myself. Did I know I'd be seeing you?"

Crocker's silence was pointed, then he said, "It hasn't been announced yet, but Truman is meeting Stalin in two weeks in a suburb of Berlin. It will be a game of bluff, and knowing Harry, he'd like to have an extra card or two to play. He probably hasn't answered Hoover's phone calls because people like me keep telling him the action is all overseas."

"It isn't, not by a long shot."

"Can you give me exact numbers and dates on the upswing in cable traffic? Can you give me exact records on the diplomats' travels and a paragraph on what it might mean? And I want you to give me every detail you have on their interest in New Mexico, don't ask me why."

"I'll have it for you tomorrow. But I have to tell Hoover I'm doing it."

"He'll object to your going through me."

"I can handle Mr. Hoover. I just can't do this behind his back. What I hope is that Truman will take what you give him and want to talk to Hoover then."

"You've been learning how it goes in this city, haven't you?"

"I've had good teachers, Mr. Crocker."

"I guess you have." Crocker absently pulled his pipe out of a pocket. In the silence he notched its stem with his thumbnail. Then he said in a more personal tone of voice, "A minute after midnight on V-J Day, my suitcase comes down from the shelf in my closet. I'm going back to New York to practice law. Wall Street will seem straightforward and honest after this place." He fussed tobacco into the bowl of his pipe.

Dillon watched him in silence.

Crocker went on casually, "What are your plans?"

"I'm sorry, sir?"

"After the war."

"Which war? As I was telling you, it seems to some of us another war is almost under way."

Crocker shook his head. "You have a narrow view. I don't dispute what you report or underestimate its meaning, not at all. But it's only one piece. There are other things you don't know about. We're not going to war with the Soviets. They're destroyed. Their industrial base is gone. And the Japs will settle before the summer is out. The war is over, and we won. We won it all. You can think of yourself for a change." When he noticed Dillon glance back toward the bunker-church, Crocker added, "You can think of them."

Sean nodded as if he knew only too well.

"You'd best get back to them." The men shook hands. "File what I'm saying for later. When the war ends I want you to consider coming to work with me."

"Sir?"

"At my firm in New York. Crocker, Wells. Look it up."

Sean did not have to look it up. He found it impossible to answer.

"It's a new ball game in this country, Sean. The war will at least have done this for us: taught us how to value each other for something besides who our father's tailor was."

Sean laughed. "My Pa's tailor was Montgomery Ward."

Crocker squeezed Dillon's hand one final time. "I want you in New York as one of my lawyers."

"Sir, I . . ."

"Just think about it, will you?"

The word "No" formed itself in his mouth, as his tongue went flat against his upper teeth. But why? "No" was the word around which he had built his life: "No" to Canaryville, "No" to the Church, "No," to Lambert, Rowe in Chicago. To his horror he saw that now his entire future involved a new kind of "No" to Cass. Renunciation, he'd been taught to believe, was the way to salvation.

But did he believe that now? He didn't want to. No? He threw the word back on itself. "Thank you, sir," he said. "I will think about it. Yes."

"Are you awake, sweetheart?"

"Yes, I'm just lying here."

"Me too."

"I think I'm waiting for the baby to start again." Cass laughed. "This is one way to avoid being wakened in the night. Just never go to sleep." She turned on her side toward him. When he opened his arm, she went inside. "What about you?"

"I've been watching the car lights flashing on the ceiling, how they come and go. Like sparrows, I was thinking."

"Sparrows?"

"Do you remember Father Ferrick?"

"At Loyola."

"He told me a story once about a sparrow's coming into a great hall, flying through it, then going out."

Cass hadn't a clue what he was talking about. "Are you sure you're awake?"

He laughed and squeezed her. "I'm a pompous fool, aren't I?"

"Not pompous."

But he'd been pompous with Crocker. "I was thinking about the last time I saw my father. It was that morning when he left for work. He had a hard-boiled egg swelling his cheek when he left the kitchen." Dillon took Cass's hand. "But then I stop seeing my father and I see someone else."

Cass thought he was going to say their little boy. In place of his father, his son.

But instead he said, "I see Mr. Crocker."

"In place of your father?"

"I guess so, yes."

"Why?"

"He encouraged me today to think about after the war, what we would do."

"What do you mean?"

"If we didn't stay in Washington."

"Not stay in Washington?" Cass was so surprised she sat up, adjusting her nightgown as she did. In the dark she could not see what was written on his face. "I don't understand."

"Mr. Crocker offered me a job in his law firm."

"In Chicago?" Cass grasped Sean's hand with an unprecedented burst of joy, and in those two words the entire landscape of what separated them, a flash in the dark, seemed illuminated.

Sean pulled his hand back from her, and he sat up too, against the headboard. He leaned across to the bedside table and snapped on the light to wash out what, with stark clarity, each had already seen.

When he looked at her, she was surprised at how obviously startled *he* was.

"Chicago?" he asked. "Who said anything about Chicago?"

"I thought you did."

"No, New York. Mr. Crocker's firm is on Wall Street. Wall Street, Cass!"

"Oh." She was so deflated—and he so charged with pleasure—that she had to face away. Wall Street? How could her Sean have anything to do with Wall Street?

Perversely, Sean's mind tossed up an image of Sylvia Yergin in that exact posture, that same place on the edge of a bed, the same feeling of disappointment in a thick-skulled man. But Sylvia Yergin was a whore. It shamed him to think of her here. To shut that image off, he touched Cass's shoulder, turning her toward him once more. "You want to go back to Chicago?" he asked with amazement.

"I wouldn't have ever brought it up to you."

"But you do?"

She nodded. Unable to look at him, she dropped her eyes to her hands.

"God, Cass, I had no idea." He leaned forward and took her in his arms. "Is it your mother's being here, and your Aunt Flo's, that brings this feeling up?" If so, he could understand her emotion, he could outlast it.

"Yes," Cass shuddered. "They've both gotten so old." Cass hesitated, then felt obliged to add, "But it isn't just them. Even more, it's our baby, Sean. I don't want to raise him here. We're too . . ." She did not mean to include Sean in her "we," and that, for her, was a summary of the problem. ". . . alone."

"But we're not alone. We have friends. What about the Packards?"

"I love Ellie and Mike, you know I do. But they're Mormons."

"Mormons! What does that have to do with it?"

"Nothing! It has nothing to do with it!" She pulled away as her anger flared. "You asked me about feeling alone. And this is what I mean! Not even you understand. I try to explain, and you make what I say seem silly. Ellie and Mike are Mormons, and so we can't ask them to be Richard's godparents. That's what it has to do with it. We have to ask Molly and my brother Jerry, who can't even get here, so we have a godfather in absentia. In absentia! That's what it has to do with it. And that lovely Mr. Crocker, when he came today, it made me cry because the most thoughtful, sensitive gift to our new baby, to *us*, should have come from a complete stranger."

"He's not a stranger to me."

"Well, he is to me, and that's the difference. You were asking about how *I* felt. How *I* feel counts!"

"I know it does."

"Nobody knows each other here. Nobody talks to each other at the Laundromat. I've been shopping at the same IGA for three years, and they still don't know my name. The grocer doesn't bother to learn it because he thinks when the war ends, all of his customers are going to go home, and most of them are."

Dillon could not think what to say. It was like being brought to the top of a mountain renowned for its view of a lush green valley, but seeing instead a vast desert.

"I don't want to go to New York," Cass said. "And I don't want to stay here."

He stared at her, the only view there was. He was amazed at the directness of her statement. What had they been to each other all this time? Why had she never talked like this before?

"I never thought we'd be going back to Chicago," he said.

"I didn't either." Cass leaned against him again. "It feels like a defeat."

"Chicago's not what it was, and neither are we." Even as he said that, he heard the cry of something dying. Not him, not her, but what they might have been together. Already he understood that their baby had replaced him in the center of her heart, and though he would not have said so, he felt relieved.

She raised her face to him. "Do you mean . . .?"

"The grocer is right. When the war ends, everybody will be making new decisions. We can too."

"Would the Bureau let you go back?"

"If we decide to go back, they'll have to, won't they?" Sean smiled. He pictured himself announcing his decision to Mr. Hoover. He felt a rare relief, a freedom. The director would fire him on the spot for arrogance, or think more of him than ever. Either would be all right. As for New York, so what? Sean Dillon was not fated to wear three-piece suits, a watch fob, and English cordovans. And the truth was, that relieved him too. Maybe all he really wanted—what else could the sudden inner peace he felt mean?—was to pay attention at last to the miracle of what had just happened to them. Their child had made them into a family. Cass was healthy. And now she was asking for something from him that he could give her.

"The day the war ends finally, Cass"—this was a vow, as if sworn upon the Bible Randall Crocker had brought to their son—"you tell me what you want, and that is what we'll do."

She pressed herself against him, gratefully holding on. She already knew what she would say. This place will do something awful to us if we stay. I want to go home, which is not Canaryville but anywhere we ourselves can shape what we become.

Dillon wanted to bury his nostrils in that bright auburn hair, inhaling her scent. He wanted to blank his mind out with the feel of her satin nightgown bunched in his hands, of her naked breast against his, of her legs wrapping his hips.

But he checked himself. Now his love for Cass precluded that expression of it. Was he a priest at last? Whatever in him had prompted the early choice of celibacy—would it haunt him forever? Had he leapt too quickly to this solution? Was he really doing this for her? But he was, of course he was. He had left the renunciations of the Church behind. This was not about renunciation, but love. Or was—

Dillon cut short his rumination and simply moved away from her, stifling his impulse, but also shuddering at the prospect, whatever its cause, of a lifetime of such frustration. What will *this* do to us?

He felt her reluctance to let him go, but also sensed it when her fingers lifted from his skin, then closed, without touching him, into fists.

ELEVEN

Two and a half years later, Dillon looked out the airplane as it angled down along the Potomac River, beginning its sharp descent above Chain Bridge, bringing him back to Washington. Directly below were the autumn reds and golds of the rolling wooded hills, Maryland on one side, Virginia on the other. From the air that landscape of colored leaves achieved a cushion-like suppleness on which Dillon had let his eyes rest unseeing for most of an hour. But when the plane banked and his gaze was drawn ahead to the gleaming city, he felt a jolt in his stomach akin to the sinking sensation of the swooping finish of the flight. He came alert.

He saw the monument in the distance, the white needle shimmering in the late morning light. He glimpsed the rooflines of the marble enclave, the Archives, the Federal Triangle and the Capitol dome itself, before the wing came up to block his view of the city.

Twisting with the river, the airplane banked and turned again, and now Dillon saw immediately below the tidy campus of Georgetown University, with its observatory and its playing fields, its old stone buildings squared around a quadrangle, its neatly lined tennis courts and its boathouse on the river. But above all, the dark Gothic spire of the central building loomed like a black-robed missionary. Dillon was struck as never from the ground by the gritty solidity of that granite spire, how it contrasted with the pristine limestone and marble edifices that came once more into view just then as the plane wheeled. Georgetown slipped under the wing, disappearing, but not before it had reminded Dillon of what made him different here. He had had to leave Washington to understand what it had begun to do to him, and he sensed that a Jesuit dark tower on the margin of that clipped skyline, in contrast especially with the white Masonic monument at the center of it, was the perfect emblem of his former alienation. He had lived in this city as a professional outsider, after all, a man whose role had been not to affect persons and events but only to watch them. He did not know yet what circumstance had led to his being summoned back here now, but he knew he would never willingly become again what wartime Washington had once made him.

The angle of the airplane's glide path did not become constant until it came to the point where the river finally straightened out to run like a highway toward Alexandria and the great bay beyond. But then, dropping into the last phase of its approach, the airplane seemed to pick up speed, and Dillon became all too aware of the water itself rising to meet him. He saw its currents swirling a range of blues and the whitecaps flecking the surface. He had not flown enough, certainly not into airports on the spits of rivers, to feel blasé.

To take his mind off the hazard of landing, he stared across the river toward the imposing pillared dome of the Army War College at Fort McNair. Lining the open green in front of it was a long row of elegant brick mansions, generals' houses, from the backs of which tidy lawns sloped down to the walled bank of the river itself. A beautiful, enchanted place, Dillon thought, a realm of the army romance. It struck him that from the grounds of Lee's mansion at Arlington, their cemetery, to the Pentagon, to McNair and beyond, the military occupied the best land on the river. At the point where the Anacostia flowed into the Potomac—that junction had been the reason George Washington chose this spot for his city—half a dozen decommissioned submarines were gammed at the piers of the Anacostia Naval Station. Below that was Bolling Field, a broad stretch of grass and runways bordered by Quonset hangars and rows of whitewashed barracks buildings. Dozens of airplanes were lined up three deep on the infield between runways. Some of the planes had the protruding igloo-like gun turrets and double fin tails of the workhorse B-29s that had won the war.

Even before he'd become aware of the land below, the plane jolted down, slamming the solid ground. The tires squealed as the pilot applied the brakes. The engines revved so furiously that Dillon braced himself. This is like landing on a damn aircraft carrier, he thought. A moment later it shamed him to realize that his hands were curled into fists, and, when he opened them, that his palms were wet.

As he crossed through the main hall of the terminal building, the soaring *art moderne* room, with its rounded, streamlined surfaces, all chrome and polished stone and leather, struck Dillon as brand-new. In fact, it had been built before the war, and he had been through it a dozen times. It was less bustling, there were fewer uniforms, no slacks on women or bandanas informally knotted in their hair. He associated the smooth music of Glenn Miller with the airport, although piped-in music had never been a feature of the place. Dillon knew that Washington itself was no longer what it was when he had become so familiar with its shadows, yet he felt the old rush of adrenaline—the upbeat strain of "In the Mood"—as he crossed the slick terrazzo toward the baggage claim.

However complicated his feelings about his time here—his resentment, for example, at how Washington had seemed in the end to have irreparably undercut his marriage—he was as keyed as ever to the electric charge in the air. Once having felt that voltage of power and action, of history, no man of Dillon's generation would arrive in Washington again without registering a momentary jolt of the pulse.

"Mr. Dillon?" A man stepped into Dillon's path, cutting him off. His black suit and tie made Dillon think, Jesuit! But the man had raised his hand in half-salute. A chauffeur's cap was wedged between his arm and his side.

Dillon knew he'd seen him before, but where?

"I have retrieved your bag, sir. There was only the one, is that correct?"

"You have my bag?"

"Yes, sir. In the car. If you follow this way—"

Dillon ignored the driver's gesture toward his briefcase. "Would you identify yourself?" Dillon's free hand, from habit, brushed his hip for the familiar feel of his pistol. If a stranger accosted him like this in Chicago, odds were he'd be some gangster's crank-hanger.

"I'm Mr. Crocker's driver."

"Mr. Crocker? Randall Crocker?"

"Yes, sir."

"He's in New York."

"No, sir. Mr. Crocker is here again."

"Since when?"

The chauffeur stared at Dillon impassively.

"I saw you once, two years ago."

"Yes, sir. At that church in Northeast."

"You're with the War Department?"

"No, sir. I work for Mr. Crocker personally."

"Is he with the War Department again?"

Once more the chauffeur pointedly declined to answer.

"Is Mr. Crocker with you now, in the car?"

"No, sir. I'm to bring you to him."

Dillon shook his head. "My business isn't with Mr. Crocker. You're not bringing me to him unless he's waiting for me at FBI headquarters on Pennsylvania Avenue."

Dillon was the agent-in-charge of the Chicago field office. He had been summoned here only late the night before by Tolson, Hoover's yoker. Tolson had refused to offer an explanation, and Dillon had no idea why the director wanted him. What he could not hear, what he could never later announce to Cass, was that he was being transferred back.

"My instructions are to take you wherever you say, Mr. Dillon. Although Mr. Crocker is hoping you will begin by seeing him."

Dillon wasn't due at headquarters for another hour. "Is Mr. Crocker at the Pentagon?"

"No, he's at the Metropolitan Club." When Dillon did not react, the driver added, "Near Lafayette Square."

"All right, let's go."

Moments later Dillon was ensconced in the rear seat of the limousine, like an honest-to-God VIP. To his surprise, it seemed the most natural thing in the world, in that spacious, plush corner, to snap on the gooseneck reading lamp and open his briefcase as if to read stock reports instead of dope sheets on sleazy Chicago hizzoners, the graft ring of judges. But then he found the letter.

He recognized her handwriting on the envelope, the single word "Sean." As he opened it, his fingers tore the paper clumsily.

The letter was several pages long, her tight, perfect handscript, and what Dillon noted first with a sinking heart was the absence, at the top of page one, of any salutation. As he began to read his breathing slowed, a reflex of his discouragement. Moisture came once more to his palms.

* * *

The phone was ringing, and though Cass had already gotten into bed, he wished that she would get up again to answer it.

He was with Richard.

It was after ten o'clock. For most of the hour he'd been home Dillon had been in the boy's closet-sized room, sitting in the rocking chair, his son against his chest. The child had been asleep most of that time, but Dillon did not want to break the spell. Richard was not quite a baby anymore, but the feel of that warm, packed body against his own was still the most soothing sensation in Sean's life; it was what he came home for.

Finally he heard Cass at the phone in the next room, her voice muffled and short.

Even before she appeared, a dark form in the doorway, her slim torso outlined in her nightgown by the hall light behind, he knew it was for him. He managed to get Richard into his crib without waking him. As he slipped past Cass where she'd remained in the threshold, she whispered, "It's long distance."

Dillon winked. "You're still a switchboard gal, Cass." She seemed to flinch, as if there were something barbed in the remark. Inwardly he recoiled at her apparent readiness to take offense.

At the phone, he stood with his back to her, but he was aware of her watching him. Half his brain clung to the image of his wife, her body outlined in the doorway, and the more frustrated he became with Tolson's refusal to explain the summons to Washington, the more Sean deflected his resentment back toward her, wishing to Christ she would not stand there monitoring him like a goddamned supervisor. Switchboard indeed.

When at last he hung up the phone, he stood leaning over it for some moments, not wanting, for one thing, to turn back to her. He was waiting for her to go back to bed. That was how these incipient standoffs ended. Once the mysterious charge of their unhappiness crackled in the air between them, one or the other would leave the room.

But not tonight. "What is it?" she asked.

"Tolson, from Mr. Hoover's office." Sean inhaled deeply, half a sigh, drawing himself up, and he faced her. "I have to go to Washington."

"When?"

"In the morning, first thing."

Neither spoke for a moment, then Cass said, "I'll help you pack. How long will you be there?"

"I don't know, Cass," Dillon answered, but with that edge again. Facing her this way, with the room behind her dark, he could no longer see the outline of her body. Her nightgown was a modest, plain white cotton.

"Don't resent my asking, Sean. I only meant, how many shirts will you need?"

"And the answer is, I don't know. I don't know how long I'll be gone, and I don't know why they've sent for me. All right?"

"There's no need to say that."

"Say what?"

"What isn't true. I wasn't asking you to explain yourself. You don't have to pretend your life is all a mystery to you, just because it is to me."

"I'm not pretending," Sean said angrily, too loudly.

Cass turned back to pull the door to Richard's room closed behind her.

Even that made him angry, as if she were appointed to protect their son from his voice.

She looked at him coldly. "It's how you lie to me, pretending you are as in the dark as I am."

"Lie to you? Lie to you?"

"Yes, lie."

Sean refused to move. He refused to respond to her.

"You don't like that word, do you? You are so honest, so pure." From her place by Richard's door, she was spitting words at him, unable to stop herself now that she had started. "But you are not honest with me."

"What in the world are you talking about?"

"You come and go from here as if you're a shoe salesman. You want me to believe that you are not in charge of your life, that you have bosses everywhere, that they tell you nothing, when the fact is, *you* are a boss. You know everything."

"Not this time, I don't."

"I don't believe you."

"The truth is, even if I did know, I wouldn't tell you. You are a Bureau wife, Cass. You should understand that."

"I'm not talking about the Bureau, I'm talking about *you*. I don't expect anything from the Bureau, but from you I do. I expect you to love me. You're my husband!"

"I do love you." Sean whipped around, away from her, heading for the small kitchen.

"Don't walk away from this, Sean. For once stay here and talk to me."

Slowly he faced her. "About *that?*"

"That?" she mocked. "You mean the fact that you never touch me, never even kiss me hello and goodbye anymore? That?"

"And there isn't a reason? Are you telling me there isn't a reason?"

"For not kissing me goodbye in the morning? Yes, I'll tell you there's no reason for that. I won't get pregnant if you kiss me. Here's the lie, Sean—why you've withdrawn from me."

"I don't know what you're talking about."

"The 'reason.' It isn't that you don't want to get me pregnant"—adding to her fury was that, all at once, her eyes were filling, then water was flowing onto her cheeks—"it's that you don't want me."

"That is not true."

"You don't want me *because* I don't dare get pregnant."

"That is *not* true!"

"Then why? Why?"

"Cass, this is not the way to discuss these things. This is—"

"We *never* discuss them. In all this time, we've never talked about it."

"What is there to say, Cass? The situation is clear enough."

"Not to me, it isn't."

From his place in the middle of the room, he leaned toward her, lunging almost, pointing his arm at her. "You're the one who—" But abruptly as he'd started, he stopped.

"Go ahead," she dared. "Say it. I'm the one who what?"

He shook his head. "What is your complaint with me? I work hard. I bring the money home. I stay out of taverns. I'm faithful to you, even if—" Once more he stopped.

"Even if what, Sean?"

He backed up wearily to the bookcase. "You are out of order, Cass."

"Out of order?" She began to close the distance between them. "What is this, a courtroom? What am I, a lawyer who hops out of her chair at the wrong time? I'll tell you, Sean, I *am* out of order, but like a telephone or a Frigidaire. Broken."

"You hated it in Washington. And now you hate it here. There is no pleasing you."

"What I hated, for your information, was being alone. I'm not alone here, that's true. But in relation to you, I am. And that's what's out of order, if you ask me. You have nothing to do with me."

"I don't want to hurt you, Cass."

"So you stay away? If we weren't Catholics, forbidden to divorce, you'd have left already."

Sean faced away from her. "We are Catholics," he said quietly, as if that summed up everything.

"Don't blame it on that." She collapsed, sobbing, onto the couch, overtaken by the futility of this exchange.

He listened to her weeping, unable to think of anything except, I didn't want to hurt you. Now that this awful laying bare had happened, he realized it was exactly what he'd have predicted. This was why he had instinctively avoided meeting her at this level, because it *had* to be hurtful.

He started for the bedroom, but as he passed her he said, "I didn't want this. I didn't want you to be hurt."

And, more furiously even than before, she snapped up at him, "What about *you*? Aren't *you* hurt?"

Instead of answering—she was impossible!—he crossed into the bedroom, to pack. By the time she came into the room, he had undressed and turned the lights off and was under the covers on his side, facing away, apparently asleep. He was relieved when she did not join him.

Instead, she went back into the living room, back to the couch. And then, when she could not sleep, to the dining room table where she wrote her letter.

"I was just standing there in the doorway looking at you, feeling so angry that you can just go to sleep again, even after what happened. It is always like this, you walking away from what happens, and me being the one left awake all night, like punishment."

Dillon raised his head from her letter with a sigh and looked out the window. How many times had he rolled away from her like that, pretending to be asleep, not asleep at all?

"Maybe I deserve punishment," he read, then stopped again

under the weight of his sadness, raising his eyes once more to watch the passing scene. The car was approaching the bird sanctuary, an inlet of the river halfway between the airport and the bridge. Unlike the rest of the tidy parkway, snaking all the way from Mount Vernon between bands of trimmed lawns and shrubs, the sanctuary had been left wild, a lush Virginia swamp which, with hanging vines knotted in the lace of willow and bamboo, moss like tropical icicles, always made Dillon think of bayous and everglades, the rot of the overgrown Deep South. He saw the skittering birds in and above the trees, and he thought of the birds from *his* world, the sparrows of the yards, the rot of urban scavengery.

He resumed reading. "I've been thinking about how we used to walk along the Oak Street Beach, you in your boater hat and seersucker suit, me with my stockings stuffed in my purse so that I could wade. You used to look out across the blue lake and interrupt whatever you were saying by all of a sudden saying instead, 'God, Cass, don't you love it here?' And I always knew you meant that stretch of beach, not Chicago, and I assumed you felt that way because the Oak Street Beach was where we'd found each other. But we never go there now, have you noticed?

"And I know why. We would talk to each other there, but talking has gone from our marriage, as if the Church had rules against that too. We have become a man and woman apart. And I know that because of how you can't stand it when I try to reach you like this, which is my fault because I so easily become upset. Then my feelings *do* come out, and they make you hate me, though they are nothing but the terrible, painful feeling of how much I love you. I have loved you from that first night outside of Walgreen's. But I made a mess of it then, and I am making a mess of it still, like Richard crushing crackers in the crib he has to sleep in. Nothing matters to me like you do, my darling, dearest Sean. *That* is what I am writing this letter to say.

"But even this letter, which is how I moved tonight from anger to its opposite, is against the rules of what a woman like me is supposed to be. I don't even know if I dare give it to you. How did this happen, that every way I would try to reach to you is wrong? Can I reverse things perhaps, and propose something to you? The man does the proposing, I know. But just this once, a woman does. When you return from Washington, can we talk to each other about all of this? Quietly, without arguing? Can we do that, Sean? Can we stop being blind and mute? Can we look each other in the eye and speak, without hurt and anger overwhelming us? I am going to count on it, may I? And to let you know the spirit in which I ask this of you, I am going to end this letter by asking something else of you. Dear Sean, with all my heart, I ask you to understand and, also, to forgive your sad, sorrowful—Cass."

Dillon fingered the warped spots on the paper where her tears had fallen and dried.

He folded the letter carefully back into its torn envelope, then put it in his briefcase with the pissant grand-theft-auto summaries he had yet to read, and the boner forms, the agent-performance reports he had yet to write. He realized consciously what for years he'd known only as a nagging, unarticulated sense of private failure. If his initial reaction had been, What the hell does she *want?* he knew now that the issue was not want but need. He knew that her need had grown so vast that its object no longer mattered. He simply knew that he, Sean Dillon, could never fill it.

He stared up the river as Crocker's car carried him across the Fourteenth Street Bridge. Georgetown loomed in the distance, that black spire. It struck him that he should never have turned his back on the priesthood, especially since he'd ended up celibate anyway. Cass's letter said he *hated* her, but that was not remotely it, and Sean was at a loss to see how that grave word applied. Hate? Christ Jesus, Cass, nothing like hate!

He saw the fringe of golden leaves on the trees ringing the tidal basin. Near here he'd begun his frantic rush to G. W. Hospital almost four years before, and he conjured the scene as clearly as if it were a photograph he carried, and not a mere memory called up to answer what she had written. Dillon had undergone an epiphany of feeling that day, but feeling radically *for that woman*, and it had not ever fully left him since. Its stirring now refuted not only her word, "hate," but his own flash of nostalgia for the life of the men of the Church. He was a typical Irish husband and knew it, barely more versed in the language of self-expression—not to say romance—than priests. His wife's physical vulnerability was real, and the inhibition that imposed on them was inevitable. Couldn't she see that? He didn't want to kill her. But he was the worst kind of man for such a situation, and he knew it. He could only withdraw. For now he clung to the feeling that that place on the bridge called up—his feeling for her. What he needed to do was keep this memory of that rare emotion as a point of reference—how longing, desire, fear, and pain had combined once to form a measure of love.

He snapped his briefcase shut, snapping shut too the impossible question of what exactly he should do now about his sorrowful, yes sorrowful, wife.

The Metropolitan Club was like an Italian Renaissance palace that had lost its way in the commercial district of that modern city. It was a massive five-story brick edifice with carved Florentine balusters on the roofline and a banked crescent stone driveway slicing across the corner of Seventeenth and H streets. Insurance salesmen and loan underwriters from offices in the prosaic adjacent buildings would expect no access to the realm thus defined. In mundane Chicago the place would have been the cardinal's residence, or Colonel McCormick's, but in Washington it was typical of the houses of dozens of would-be New World aristocrats.

The driver was out of the car, and it took Dillon a moment to realize that he was coming around to open his door. Not my door, you don't. Dillon had authority over a hundred and fifty agents, not to mention accountants and clerical workers, but he had a complete aversion to a chauffeur's routine subservience. He nearly bumped the startled driver with the door as he opened it and got out.

He apologized and thanked him in the one efficient phrase— "Sorry, thanks"—which, all his life, he had heard deferential Irishmen use when cutting through crowds.

In the opulent marble entrance hall a Negro steward greeted him by name and led the way up a curving broad staircase to the second floor. To one side of the landing was a set of elaborately carved doors, two pairs of them, thrown open on a high-ceilinged dining room. The bulbs in the sconces on the oak-paneled walls and those in the two massive chandeliers were all illuminated despite the midday light pouring in the huge windows on the far side of the room. Dillon thought of the Tudor dining room at the Stockyards Inn because it too had sought to combine elegance and masculinity. This room, however, succeeded. Because there were so few people present, the room's features themselves could impress—the carved lintels over three imposing fireplaces, oriental rugs running the length and width of broad crossing aisles, the discreet patina of the aged leather wing chairs, the shimmering chrome of urns and taps along a mirrored wall. It was too early for lunch, and the chairs were still empty as waiters buzzed from table to table, fussing the silverware and linen and cobalt water glasses into the last state of perfect readiness.

"This way, please," Dillon's escort said, and he took Dillon the other way, toward a closed door across the landing from the dining room. It led into a narrow dark corridor off which other doors opened, and it was one of those, a dozen yards along, on which the man knocked briskly.

"Come," a voice said from within.

The steward opened the door and Dillon realized this was a routine of his. He had shown many visitors up here this way. "Mr. Sean Dillon," he announced, then stepped aside.

Randall Crocker was seated alone, in shirtsleeves, at a broad table on which papers, folders, and familiar green-jacketed volumes from the Government Printing Office were stacked haphazardly among two telephones, a Dictaphone machine, and an ashtray the size of a meat platter in which little cones of tapped-out pipe cinders were arranged like burnt offerings. A private side dining room had been transformed into Crocker's office. Dillon's sense of mystification redoubled.

"Forgive me if I don't stand, Dillon, will you?" When Crocker smiled, the room brightened. He reached a hand up to Dillon, who had to lean across the table to take it.

"It's great to see you, sir."

"You too. Take a seat. You're good to come."

"I'm on my way to Mr. Hoover's office." Dillon sat in the single dinner-table chair. It was cushioned, fancy, one of a set, but the others had all been removed from the room. He put his briefcase on the floor beside him.

"I know you are. Once we've had our chat, you'll want to talk to Hoover. I talked to him less than an hour ago."

"What's going on?"

"A lot. A lot is going on." Crocker scraped his chair back. It matched Dillon's, lacking the maneuverability of a wheeled swivel chair, which was why Crocker had not risen. He reached for his pipe. Small talk later, if at all. "Have you followed the debate on the Hill, over the National Security Act?"

"More or less."

"You know the act passed last week?"

"Yes, sir."

"You know what it does?"

"It unites the War and Navy departments under a single chief. Secretary of defense, isn't it?"

"Right, the first step toward unification of the services, or 'centralization,' as the act calls it."

"Which was a recommendation of yours, as I recall."

"Then you'll appreciate the irony when I tell you that I'm involved in the one part of the process that decentralizes. The act creates a third military service, separating the air corps out of the army—the air force, it's called now."

"I read that."

Crocker put his pipe in his mouth and lit it. After letting the smoke billow around his head, he waved the match out and looked up at Dillon. "The President is going to sign the act into law tomorrow. He is going to name me undersecretary of war for air, pending the new law's date of effectiveness; then I become secretary of the air force."

"Congratulations, Mr. Crocker."

"I want you to work for me."

"How?"

"The air force has its airplanes and its bombs and its pilots. What it does not have the day it severs from the army is any organization." Crocker struck the table, bouncing papers. "And organization is what I aim to give it. The air force is not going to be a collection of feudal fiefdoms at the mercy of geniuses who don't trust each other, like the army and the navy are. The whole thrust of this reform is centralized control, and we're going to show them with the air force how it's done." Dillon remembered Crocker from two and a half years before as spent and old, the effect of the war. Now he was a man of striking vitality.

"I have two key areas," he said, ticking his fingers. "I want total centralization of procurement and supply. And I want total control of security." Crocker brought the fingers of his other hand into it, enumerating. "In the army you have CID, Criminal Investigation Division; the provost marshal, who's like a police commissioner; the CIC, Counterintelligence Corps; JAG, judge advocate general; the inspector general; the Special Branch of military intelligence; and God knows what else.

They keep their secrets from the enemy, and especially from one another. They are police and counterspy operations, but they are staffed by infantry officers or engineers, men trained in logistics or whoever the hell gets transferred in that week. By the time they know what they're doing, they're transferred out. The only constant is the determination of the man in charge of each office to keep his command unpolluted by any tendency to cooperate with anyone else. The security system of the army, in other words, is a perfect scaled-down version of what's wrong with the whole goddamned American military."

Crocker stopped to let Dillon comment.

Dillon did not move in his chair.

"You're listening to me, aren't you?"

"Yes, sir, I am."

"I can't tell what you're thinking, Sean."

"Nothing yet. I'm still listening."

"Right." Crocker flared his fingers again, to resume his briefing. "Each one of these directorates has its AAF contingent, and they all think they will be coming over to the separated service whole, just like a Tooey Spaatz bomber wing. But they won't. In the air force we're going to do something new. One agency. One director. One organization to handle both criminal investigation and counterintelligence, an office rigidly controlled, with highly trained, absolutely reliable agents who respond to the authority of an all-powerful director. Ever heard of an operation like that, Sean?"

Dillon smiled. "It sounds vaguely familiar."

"I want the FBI inside the air force, and Hoover agrees with me."

"I'm sure he does. He'd like the FBI inside everything."

"I have informally asked Hoover's assistance in setting this thing up. Once my appointment is official, I will make the request formally. I'm asking for a six-month loan to the new Department of the Air Force of Special Agent Sean Dillon, whose job will be to propose a specific charter for an air force security-investigative organization." Crocker put his pipe in his mouth. That was it.

Dillon dropped his hand to his briefcase which held Cass's letter. To his horror he realized instantly that he was going to say no to this man again. Once more Crocker had flung wide the doors before him, opening the way to an entirely new room, the best in the house, a gleaming, polished room with chandeliers. And Dillon was going to say no.

Before he could, Crocker leaned across the table, pointing with his pipe. "Don't misunderstand what I just said. I was describing to you the *motions* I am going through with Hoover, but I am not really asking him. And I'm not really asking you. This is not an invitation to come on up to Wall Street. This is conscription. This is your country saying it needs you, same as it did to me. If I couldn't say no, neither can you." Crocker reached for a tamper the size of a golf tee and used it on his pipe. The gesture diluted his too solemn tone. "Do you know what the air force is going to be? It's going to be the goddamn A-bomb with wings. Are you going to say no to helping to protect that?"

"Protect it from whom?"

"Uncle Joe, for starters."

"When we last talked, you seemed to think Stalin *was* an uncle. I hate to say I told you so, Mr. Crocker. What we know now is that Uncle Joe has murdered more people than Hitler did. Only he's still doing it."

"But not with the bomb. I'm terrified, the way our army security system operates, that Stalin is going to walk into Oak Ridge and take one. I can admit you saw something coming before I did, but as I recall, that was your job. It's the job I'm offering you back."

"Why me?"

"You already combine expertise in criminal work, fraud investigation *and* counterintelligence. How many, even in the Bureau, have covered the bases you have? How many?"

"I don't know."

"Well, I do. An even dozen agents have records to compare. And of them you're the only one who's run a major office. How old are you?"

"Thirty-seven."

"You're the youngest agent-in-charge in the Bureau, aren't you?"

"I've no idea."

"You've broken a fifty-year-old machine in Chicago. They tell me Ed Kelly didn't run for mayor again because of what you brought to the grand jury."

Dillon laughed. "He didn't run again because he'd been mayor seventeen years and people got sick of him. We've hardly touched the damn machine. I've hardly started in Chicago. I wasn't out to retire Kelly. I was out to indict him."

"The FBI course in Chicago is set. You can turn the wheel over to someone else. I know for myself what you did in Washington. Among other difficult accomplishments, you impressed me. What I want in my air force outfit is an organizational version of *you*."

"But *air force?* I can't land in an airliner at National Airport without my palms getting wet. I don't think you know what you're asking."

"Hell, do I look like a birdman? I'm not asking you to fly a secret mission into Berlin. I *am* asking you to help us keep the Russians from finding out when someone else does, though. Your palms don't get wet at the thought of that, do they?"

"No."

"Good. And that's the last 'no' I'll take from you this time. I told you, this is conscription."

"I'm not saying no, Mr. Crocker."

"You're not saying yes either, I notice."

Dillon had been gripping the handle of his briefcase all this time. He released it. "Six months?"

"That's the commitment. You acquaint yourself with what's under way in the army. You already know some of how it goes. Learn everything. Decide what functions fit and what don't, what activities, what plans, what procedures and what command channels. I want your view of everything but personnel. That will be my problem. Yours is to give me an organizational blueprint that's so foolproof even military men can implement it. Six months. That's Hoover's limit of how long I can have you, but these initial six months before the new service hardens up are all I have anyway. We have to get the new operation up and running before the old ones, especially CIC and CID, can move to undermine it."

"How would they do that, if you're in charge?"

"They'll do it on the Hill. Every feudal baron in the Pentagon has his protector in Congress. And they will *all* be threatened by what you're doing. First they'll whisper, then they'll scream. And some congressman will listen. Like it or not, those knuckleheads on the Hill think they're in charge."

Dillon grinned. "They gave you the law you wanted, didn't they?"

"They're knuckleheads not to know what we are going to do with it. When Jimmy Forrestal and I get finished, the brass are going to be on permanent parade up there, accusing Congress of selling them out, when what they will have done is simply to have put some new men in charge of the American military." Crocker shook his head, imitating the generals' and admirals' stark disbelief. "And the new men in charge are all goddamn civilians! That is what 'centralization' in the National Security Act means. The military, which in the war came to regard itself as omnipotent, is about to be brought back into the corral of the U.S. Constitution. Is that important enough for you?" Suddenly Crocker seemed pissed off, but then Dillon read that as an imitation too, the imitation of a cross-examiner. Never ask a question you don't already know the answer to. "Is that important enough for you to leave Chicago?"

"Yes, sir, it is."

"Do you agree then? Do you accept the job?"

"Absolutely."

Crocker pushed his chair back and hauled himself up. He leaned across to offer his hand. "Great, Sean, great!"

Sean's hand was dry. The sensation of strength in his fingers, his own and also Crocker's, filled him with pleasure.

"Have lunch with me then. We'll celebrate."

"I'm due at the director's office."

"I'll call Hoover. You and I have to talk. We'll have lunch."

Dillon pictured himself walking with this exemplary man into the sterling, exclusive room across the way. He imagined the preening patrician males of Washington looking up from their chats; he imagined a footman announcing his name.

"All right," Dillon said.

Crocker came out from behind his table. When he took Dillon's arm it was partly an intimate gesture with which to lead the way, and partly a cripple's move for support.

"And we can talk about getting your family back here right away. How is your dear wife?"

"She's fine."

"We'll pull some strings and get you a place to live that she will love."

"That won't be a problem, sir." Dillon was crisp. When had he made *this* decision? Life without Cass? Life without his boy? No warm bundle on his chest each night? "Since it's just six months, my wife and son won't need to come out."

"Really?" Crocker let Dillon lead the way into the corridor. "But you'll want to talk to Mrs. Dillon before making up your mind."

"No need, sir." What a surprise, the relief he felt, although it made him feel a bit ashamed. He would not have to deal with Cass or her proposal after all. "I'm sure of it," he said. "They won't be coming to Washington."

TWELVE

The Cold War took its shape from a pair of strange springtime suicides occurring within a year of each other. In both cases a senior government official plunged out a window to a jolting, gruesome end, flattened on concrete far below The first was the death in Prague of Czechoslovakian Foreign Minister Jan Masaryk. It happened on the night of March 10, 1948, and because Masaryk was identified with elements inside Czechoslovakia which had resisted the establishment of a Moscow-run Communist regime, his death was taken as a symbol of the demise of the Czech republic itself. As such, it sent a shock wave rolling west, where Masaryk was assumed to have been murdered by Stalin's agents. Czechoslovakia's fall represented the final consolidation of the Russian theft of Eastern and Central Europe, and was taken as dramatic evidence of aggressive Soviet intentions toward the rest of the Continent. Masaryk's death precipitated what came to be called, in Washington, the Spring Crisis. American generals and admirals sounded alarms on Capitol Hill and succeeded, by the way, in derailing the two-pronged process of demobilization and centralization under civilian authority that had been under way for two years. "Things look black," Truman wrote. "A decision will have to be made. I am going to make it." What he decided was to get ready for all-out war at once.

Such was the "crisis" that no one seemed to notice how useful it was, in fact, both to the President, whose heretofore uncertain election prospects were enormously improved, and to the generals in the Pentagon whose very jobs were saved by the "shocking" events of that spring. Families all over the country understood that the emergency was real when, at

Truman's urging, a new draft law was rushed through Congress. America seemed relieved, really, to look for rescue again to its sons in uniform. And not only sons; the newly empowered civilian commissioners of the AEC were shunted aside as the generals were given custody once more of atomic weapons. A quickly drawn-up defense appropriations bill with huge outlays for increasing A-bomb production was passed without objection. The military budget doubled overnight. Within weeks of Masaryk's death, the United States entered into a formal new pact with the French and the British, committing itself, in what would become NATO, to the defense of nations outside the Western Hemisphere for the first time since 1778.

The pressures generated by this sudden reversal of national direction bore down on the mind and psyche of one man more than any other, hard-driving James Forrestal, the first secretary of defense. Forrestal had been a Wall Street investment banker, and it was he who had prevailed upon Randall Crocker to come back to Washington to help reassert civilian control of the military. Forrestal had served during the war as secretary of the navy, but his role beginning in the autumn of 1947 was to be the architect of a new, streamlined, combined military built around the axis of air power and the atomic bomb. He had expected the navy and the air force to be maneuvering against each other, but not against him. When the Spring Crisis led to the sudden mushrooming of the entire military, with the revitalized draft for the army, the promise of new bomber wings for the air force and the prospect of a new fleet of aircraft carriers for the navy, generals and admirals not only intensified their squabbling with each other, but also began to challenge Forrestal. The one thing they all agreed on was that centralized command was a bad idea, and to hear their version of it, unification of the services would play into the hands of the newly threatening Russians. Forrestal fought the generals, but the lines of his own authority became unclear as Congress and the President himself steadily gave the service chiefs what they wanted.

Having used the spring war scare to defeat the secretary's efforts at consolidation, the military settled back into its old systems of independent fiefdoms which cooperated with each other only when a common enemy forced them to. The Russians were such an enemy, but Forrestal discovered to his horror that he was one as well. For month after month he stalked the labyrinth of the Pentagon, but with increasing ineffectiveness, irascibility and, on occasion, irrationality. Finally, with no support from the all too political civilians across the river, and with no power over the unleashed warlords in the corridors around him, he was replaced as secretary in March of 1949, exactly one year after Masaryk's "suicide."

The war alert of the previous spring had become institutionalized. In one short year public hysteria about the Soviet menace had come to seem normal, but by then James Forrestal's hysteria was also private, and not normal at all. On his last day in the Pentagon an aide found him sitting alone in a small dark room, wearing his hat, his eyes fixed on a point in the empty air before him. After Forrestal was taken away, generals heard and repeated in the corridors that he had run through the streets near his house, crying, "The Russians are coming! The Russians are coming!" The generals knew better than anyone that it had not been Russians who had so undone the first secretary of defense, but even his strange demise, by fueling American fears, which in turn fueled their return to power, served the generals' purposes. Forrestal was admitted as a psychiatric patient to the naval hospital in Bethesda, where within days he opened the window of his room on the sixteenth floor and jumped.

That was the unlikely situation into which Sean Dillon found himself so unexpectedly inserted in the period just before Jan Masaryk's ominous "defenestration." His status as a special assistant to the secretary of the air force amazed him. Bureau work had always seemed important, a defense if not of the great virtues, then of social cohesion or good government. But those had been things at a distance, like clouds passing behind the branches of a tree, compared to the sense of urgency he had now, moving through rooms in which the real fate of the world itself was being decided.

Dillon had nearly been taken under at first by an eerie feeling of dislocation in an unfamiliar postwar Washington. As a civilian in the hypermartial Pentagon, he had no standing of his own, apart from Crocker. It depressed him to return at night to a dreary furnished room alone. Sometimes he was so tired he slept on top of his blankets, fully clothed, and always his last, fleeting, and forever unexpressed thoughts were of Cass and of their son.

He dealt with the unwelcome loneliness by working all the harder, throwing himself into his Pentagon assignment with diligence rare even for that driven place. It was always dark when he left the building at the end of the day, and dark when he returned in the morning. He had become a man without daylight, and why should he not have felt dislocated?

As usual, his was one of the first cars to pull into the remorseless expanse of the Pentagon parking lot on that day in May 1948. He walked up the sequence of broad, gleaming terrazzo ramps to the third floor of E-Ring, his footsteps echoing loudly in the empty halls. After retrieving his papers and charts from his office, Dillon went by himself, well ahead of schedule, into the air secretary's briefing room where he was at last to present his report.

The fact of his having completed his work would alone have accounted for the current of adrenaline, but the prospect of contention had quickened his juices too. He had come into this room early to reacquaint himself with the space, set up his boards and stand at the lectern—not to rehearse, exactly, but to imagine himself efficiently making his points before a group of men who would want nothing to do with anything he said. The predictable resistance of the brass would be Crocker's problem, a new version of the most familiar problem he and the other civilian secretaries already had.

The room was large and appointed like a corporate boardroom. Dillon had attended briefings here, at Crocker's side like a satchel carrier. But he had never stood behind its lectern in the circle of light that washed down from a pair of aimed ceiling cones. The rest of the room was illuminated by the new long fluorescent tubes hidden in valances, soft light spilling on the walls, but also cold and unnatural. A stretch of drawn blue draperies so blanketed one wall it was impossible to know for certain that there were windows behind it. He resisted an impulse to throw those draperies open, to let in the real light of dawn. Instead, he let his eyes drift past the podium to the wall which was entirely taken up with an unclothed movie screen. He remembered watching, weeks before, the grainy images of troops clubbing citizens while the throaty narrator had described the latest purges, arrests, and executions then taking place in Czechoslovakia.

Taking up the long, third wall opposite the draperies was a map of the world, not the usual Mercator projection, but a

view of the globe as seen from above the North Pole. Instead
of Kansas at its center, this map had the massive white bull's-
eye of the ice cap.

Versions of this same map covered walls in the chief of
staff's office and in the Air Staff conference room, and Dillon
remembered the day it had dawned on him that this air force
view of the world, by emphasizing the Soviet Union's ominous
proximity to Alaska and Canada, exploded the Mercator-
reinforced illusion of American invulnerability behind a pair of
protecting oceans. The point was to undercut the navy's claim
to a mammoth share of the new defense appropriations. Dillon
recalled how shocked he was at first by the bitter conflict between the leaders of the two service branches—how it had en-
gulfed Forrestal—but even he had grown accustomed to
Pentagon infighting. Now the argument had shifted to Capitol
Hill where the choice would be made between the new long-
range bomber the air force wanted and the navy's new generation of aircraft carriers.

The fourth wall of the secretary's briefing room was painted
the unlikely blue of robins' eggs, but dominating it were four
dark oil paintings depicting dramatic scenes of warplanes in
combat: a single bomber diving toward a factory complex
amid puffs of antiaircraft fire; a pair of fighters swooping at
each other; a downspinning plane with sharks' teeth painted on
its nose and flames streaming from an engine; a fleet of bombers in formation high above a desolate, burning landscape.

Arranged in formation at that end of the room, like the
bomber squadron, were three rows of five ebony Windsor
chairs, and for a mad moment Dillon thought he heard the
empty chairs roaring at him like warplanes. He faced away and
walked to the empty easel beside the lectern to set up his cardboard charts. He put his binder on the lectern, carefully align-
ing it with the corner of the shelf so that when he opened his
briefing book it would be centered before him. The act was
merely superstitious, though, since by now Dillon was perfectly capable of laying out his proposals without a note. With
a once rare and, to him, offensive resignation, he admitted
again that the perfection of his preparations would make no
difference.

Two and a half hours later he was standing at that lectern,
having just delivered his report, a straightforward description
of what he'd dubbed the Office of Special Investigations.

Dillon's proposals, elaborated with charts and graphs, had seemed so simple and logical that he could not imagine them not carrying, but on another level, the one on which he had been steadily rebuffed by these very men for months now, he knew better. They were generals and colonels, all in their new blue uniforms with silver stars and eagles on their shoulders, and huge, beautiful patches of ribbons on the left sides of their chests, trophies of their harrowing bomber missions over Germany and Japan, badges of valor and of membership in a rare fraternity to which Sean Dillon could never hope to be admitted.

General Thomas M. Eason, the chief of staff, was there. So were the vice chief; the provost marshal; the air inspector; the assistant chief of staff, operations; the assistant chief of staff, intelligence; and the most famous of them all, General Mark Macauley, the bomber command hero of the night raids on Berlin, and now the commander of the fledgling Strategic Air Command.

In the silence that followed his briefing, Dillon understood that the resistance of the men in front of him was so complete they might not raise an objection to what he'd proposed, or ask a question or comment at all. What better way to express their resentment at having been ordered here by Crocker?

As he looked across the room at the faces of the uniformed men staring back at him, Dillon recalled the meeting in Crocker's office years before. Because that had been a Bureau case built around his discovery of Sylvia Yergin, it had not mattered what OSS and G-2 and CIC representatives had made of him. But these were men whom he was supposed to convert to his way of thinking, and he knew that the opposite had just occurred. A wall of glass bricks, one for each word he spoke, had arisen between his audience and his lectern.

Randall Crocker sat immobile and inexpressive in the front row between the only other two civilians in the room, his deputy and one of Forrestal's. Crocker's left leg was stretched out rigidly in front of him. He was dressed in a dark suit, and his breast pocket carried a crisp, steepled handkerchief. Crocker had kept himself aloof from Dillon all winter and spring, but Dillon had chosen to read that as the preoccupation of a man with huge and urgent other tasks. In fact, Crocker had been sucked into the fan of Forrestal's emotional distress. As the conflict between the navy and the air force had heated up,

Forrestal's bias toward the navy had come out and he'd begun
to treat Crocker, his old Wall Street friend, like yet another enemy. But few knew of that intensely personal struggle yet, certainly not Dillon. Randall Crocker's reaction to his briefing,
the one that mattered most, was the one that Dillon had not
dared to predict. It unsettled him that even now he could not
read the man who had brought him here.

"Questions, gentlemen?" Dillon said at last.

No one spoke.

Forrestal's deputy leaned to whisper in Crocker's ear, but
Crocker ignored him.

"Well, I have a question," the gruff, portly Macauley said.
From his chair in the second row he pointed with a dead cigar
at the easel. "I see it on the chart there, and I heard you say
it. But I guess I still don't get it."

"Sir?"

"I would have this OSS operation—"

"OSI, General, not OSS." Dillon smiled self-deprecatingly.
"Most definitely not OSS."

The bomber general waved his cigar impatiently. "OSI then.
I would have it in my command, but the damn thing wouldn't
report to me?"

" 'Report' to you, sir?" Throughout his presentation Dillon's
palms had remained dry. Now he calmly picked up the long,
rubber-tipped wooden pointer and aimed it at the organizational chart. "I would assume 'reporting,' sir."

"I mean reporting in a military sense. The chain of command. This operation, the way you outline it, would be outside
the chain of command."

"No, sir. Simply that the chain of command would run more
directly to the chief of staff." Dillon tapped the chart at three
points. "Regional OSI commanders would, as you say, 'report'
to the OSI director, who would report in turn to the chief of
staff."

"Why not through the IG?" another asked. Then Dillon saw
that the voice belonged, in fact, to the inspector general. If they
had had a common strategy of responding to Dillon with a
monolithic silence, it was broken. As usual with these bastards,
self-interest had prevailed. One at a time, Dillon felt, he could
handle them.

"As I said, sir, there are two reasons for reserving an independent OSI from the regular command structure. First, the

difficulty inherent in an investigative agency whose mission may on occasion involve investigation of persons senior in the chain of command—"

"That's ridiculous," the bomber general barked. "You're saying they might investigate me?"

Dillon eyed General Macauley carefully. "You are familiar, perhaps, General, with the case of General Hill?"

"I know all about Charlie Hill."

"Then you know that while serving as director of the Air Technical Service Command, responsible for the purchase of all army air force's equipment during the war, General Hill used his influence over the assignment of contracts for personal gain."

"I know Charlie was accused of—"

"General, if I may, please." Dillon's voice rose sharply. He was ten, even twenty years younger than these men. They were not accustomed, to say the least, to juniors compelling their attention. Blood burned in Macauley's face. To avoid even the appearance of deference, he began noisily to unwrap the cellophane from a new Garcia y Vega. He exchanged an exasperated glance with the inspector general, then concentrated on managing his cigar. Dillon nevertheless continued to address him. "The investigation into allegations against General Hill was severely hindered by the inability of the relatively junior investigative officers to obtain cooperation from their seniors. As you no doubt heard, General Hill at one point issued orders forbidding the release of his own records, and the provost marshal backed him up." Dillon faced the air inspector. "And the inspector general at the time tried to overrule General Hill, but lacked the authority to do so. Hill's records were not made available until General Marshall himself intervened, and by then the records were incomplete."

The vice chief broke in, "The Charlie Hill case hardly justifies what you've proposed. You don't rearrange the flight plan of an entire squadron because of one enemy ack-ack gun. You take the gun out and maintain course."

"As you know, General, the Hill case was not the only one. There were twenty-seven separate cases developed by CID inside the Air Technical Service Command alone."

"But how many brought to court-martial?"

"My point exactly. It was precisely the knowledge that he would almost certainly *not* be court-martialed, even if accused, that stimulated every officer who abused his trust in that command to do so."

"You did not conduct those investigations, Mr. Gillen. You weren't even here. Where *were* you during the war anyway?"

"My name is Dillon. I was in Washington throughout the war. It is correct to say I did not conduct those investigations, but it has been my responsibility to acquaint myself with the records of those who did. For your information, those records are in the files of seven different Defense Department agencies. Yet taken together they absolutely established that graft in the amount of millions of dollars had corrupted the procurement system even before the war ended. And then after the war, with the project of military surplus disposal, the problem worsened. Tens of millions of dollars of simple theft and bribery are at issue now. Dozens of separate cases involving everything from the illegal consignment of surplus GI clothing to unlicensed profiteers, up to and including the covert shipment of twenty-two decommissioned fighter bombers to the Irgun resistance in Palestine, in violation of the Neutrality Act."

"The air force did not do that."

"It is the air force's job to see that such things don't happen. And if they do, to bring those responsible to justice. Yet to date, almost all charges have been brought against enlisted men and NCOs. In the cases I'm referring to, the variously constituted courts-martial have so far convicted four supply clerks, thirteen mechanics and repairmen, an armorer, a wire technician and two parachute riggers."

Dillon paused to allow the weight of the litany to accumulate, then he found the eyes of the silver-haired vice chief of staff. "The problem toward the end of the war and immediately afterward was not one enemy ack-ack gun, General, but a massive moral sabotage from within, the effect of which continues in the widespread assumption that the air force does not seriously enforce either its own regulations or the law. That assumption, left unchecked, will cripple the entire air force. It must be clear to every man in this service, no matter what his rank or position, that air force justice is efficient and absolute, and that what it is blind to here is what rank insignia a man wears on his shoulder. *That* is why I propose setting OSI outside the chain of command, and it is why I propose that OSI agents, in conducting investigations, will wear civilian clothes and will not be required to identify themselves by military rank."

"What the hell!" Macauley snapped. "Why not just have a civilian agency then?"

Dillon did not answer. He glanced toward Crocker, whose face showed nothing.

General Eason sat two chairs away from Crocker, also in the front row. Four stars gleamed on his epaulets. Speaking for the first time, he said quietly, "Perhaps there is another explanation for why so few officers have been charged in these investigations. Perhaps it is nothing like what you call 'moral sabotage.' "

"Sir?"

"The obvious other explanation, Mr. Dillon, is that our officers for the most part are what they purport to be, men of honor."

"General, we are talking about an officer corps, during the time in question, of tens of thousands of men."

"Is it unthinkable to you that—?"

"I'm a Catholic, General." Dillon slapped the wooden pointer down onto the lip of the easel. "I've been taught to believe in original sin. And I'm a lawyer. I've been taught to believe we *all* need the limits of the rule of law. General Hill's name is known to all of you because he is the only general officer to have been court-martialed, but I am morally certain, given the quantity of misappropriated supplies and arms, that Hill is not the only general officer to have reaped personal financial gain from the improper discharge of his duty. We will never know for certain because, owing to the chain of command and the dispersal of investigative responsibility, generals are not accountable to anyone but other generals who apparently think criminal behavior by their peers is best punished by a snub at the Officers' Club, if that. In the air force right now—this is as good a summary of my conclusions as any—there is less a rule of law than a rule of privilege."

Having said that, and seeing the subtle jolt backward of their heads, Dillon realized why Crocker had brought in an outsider to do this. His job was to drop his bombs on them and leave. With a sudden fresh rush of authority, Dillon pointed at the wall behind them. "Those paintings back there, gentlemen, are glimpses of the past, if you will permit my saying so. A civilian like me cannot look at such scenes without feeling a kind of awe. They feature the heroic action of individuals, pilots like yourselves, men who made the difference for our country between victory and defeat. But that is not all those pictures feature, as no one knows better than you. You who organized air raids involving hundreds of warplanes flying at night over contested territory know the absolute requirement in the modern era for the submission of the individual will to group effort. You've told your men again and again, reining in fighter-jocks and daredevils, that the time for individual heroism is over. The principles you have already so effectively applied to operations I only want to apply to security." Dillon swung his arm toward the polarcentric map of the world. "That's the future, and you created it. In conflict with the USSR one thing will count far more than individual action, no matter how heroic, and you know what it is: clear, effective organization responsive to the will of proper authority.

"At the risk of offending you with the obvious, I am telling you that the opposite of such organization is confusion. It is not that there are large numbers of criminals in the air force, or in the officer corps, but that there are human beings who in a situation of confusion will make bad choices. That is what General Hill did. Those of you who know him personally could surely attest that he would not have compromised himself had he known in advance that an aggressive, unintimidated OSI was going to investigate his activity and bring charges against him if his activity proved improper. The confusion of authority among the CID and provost marshal and the IG and JAG, all subject to local commanders in the chain of command, created an opening in enforcement that General Hill knew he could exploit. An OSI, by its very existence, would close that opening, and otherwise honest men would have a good reason for staying honest."

The assistant chief of staff, intelligence, stood up at his place in the last row. A tall man with a neatly trimmed mustache and a hair part sharp enough to focus a camera on, he reminded Dillon of Colonel Cheever, the OSS officer who had challenged him in Crocker's office nearly five years before. Cheever's aristocratic air had impressed Dillon because it was so clearly uncultivated, and he recognized a like sense of self-assurance in this officer.

"But you are claiming authority beyond the merely criminal." He indicated the diagram on the easel. "I see the word 'intelligence.' "

"*Counter* intelligence, General. OSI would be to the air force what the FBI is to domestic intelligence."

"But there it is, 'intelligence.' "

This was a turf boundary Dillon knew better than to cross. "Air intelligence would not be affected by OSI. Your operation is to the air force what CIA is to worldwide espionage activity. The distinction is not original with me, sir, but is implied by the National Security Act."

"Nonsense. Counterintelligence belongs with intelligence, and whether the civilian sector accepts that or not is of no importance to us. Counterintelligence in the military is a function of intelligence." The general's skin, even the skin showing in the part of his hair, had turned bright red.

"To the extent that is true, it shouldn't be. It is an entirely separate discipline. Experience suggests that when the two functions are melded, counterintelligence always suffers. I must tell you quite frankly"—Dillon stared fiercely at the officer, knowing full well that his statement was armed—"that, after a thorough evaluation of air force security systems, including the carryover CIC, the vulnerability of this service to Soviet penetration terrifies me." Before the intelligence chief could respond, Dillon swung toward General Macauley. "And nowhere is that more true than in the Strategic Air Command."

Macauley slowly took his cigar out of his mouth, studied it for a moment as if reading the tiny words on the paper band, then said calmly, "You don't know what you're talking about."

"No one has clear responsibility in your command for security, General, presumably because you reserve it to yourself. Yet one of your wings, the 509th, has been assigned the atomic mission. Surely you know enough to assume that a Soviet espionage operation is already under way at your present headquarters at Andrews, as well as at Offutt in Nebraska, to which you're moving, and certainly at Roswell, New Mexico, where the 509th is stationed. In the last six months, since the appropriations bill authorized the full establishment of SAC, the number of personnel in your command has increased fourteenfold, everyone from bomber pilots to clerk-typists. I suppose you know all of the pilots and navigators personally."

"I handpicked them."

"And the clerk-typists?"

The general did not answer.

"The secretaries who will be handling correspondence between the Pentagon and Omaha, and between Omaha and your proposed network of—how many bases?"

"Twenty-seven."

"The signal corpsmen, General? The aircraft mechanics, the crews who see to the maintenance of the atomic bombs in your charge? Did you handpick them?"

Macauley tongued his cigar from one side of his mouth to the other.

"Do I need to tell you, General, what Soviet agents— saboteurs included—could do to this country from the inside of your command?"

Macauley withdrew his cigar to study it again. "I have to admit, young man, the Soviets *do* worry me. But what *really* worries me"—General Macauley looked around at his peers, his wide eyes announcing a punch line—"is the navy."

The men laughed, but falsely.

Macauley mugged, "Can you imagine a plane with an A-bomb in its belly missing the wire, trying to land on a flat-top?"

The generals laughed, but still weakly.

That the image of a bomb-laden airplane crashing on a ship seemed horrible to Dillon, instead of amusing, marked him as an outsider more surely than anything he had said.

Of course, the joke was only a way to put Dillon in his place, and once that was done the men fell smugly silent.

Macauley said soberly, "I'll take care of security in SAC, don't you worry, Mr. Dillon."

"By yourself, General, you simply can't. Your base at Roswell, because of its proximity to Los Alamos, falls under the jurisdiction not only of your G-2, but of the army and of the Atomic Energy Commission. Do you think that they will *ever* coordinate security with you under the present setup? The same thing applies now to the globe." Dillon pointed to the map. "You know better than I what the North Pole frontier means for airplanes. But I know what it means for organization. Security in Omaha and in New Mexico requires absolute coordination and control from Washington."

"I'll have that."

"With all due respect, General, you will not. Your security people, no matter who they are, will not have the clearances they would need to know what the whole picture of attempted Soviet penetration looks like. Do you think the FBI will be co-ordinating counterintelligence with your security officer in Omaha? I promise you it will not be. And unless it can deal with an air force organization with integrity, which boils down—as in the Bureau and in the new CIA—to a single director with total control over all aspects of operation, those crucial resources will be permanently unavailable to you. And you will have, on your own, no way of knowing which of your clerks or maintenance crewmen takes his orders not from Moscow but just from the Soviet embassy here on Sixteenth Street or from the Soviet UN delegation in New York or the consulate offices in San Francisco or Amtorg, the Soviet trade organization in Manhattan. The FBI may well know, General, because those are bases we have covered, but we won't trust that kind of information with you or with anybody in the Pentagon because, however well your airplanes operate, your security systems leak all over the place. And when I return to the Bureau next week I am going to make sure they understand that about this place. It won't matter how heroic your pilots are. In the next war, the way things are run here, they will have been defeated even before their planes leave the ground."

A colonel in the back spoke up. "Not everybody agrees that there are Commies behind every bush. What are you saying, first the State Department, now the Pentagon?"

"Alger Hiss is not the issue," Dillon said firmly. "Not even Oppenheimer is. Congress may be hysterical about cell group meetings in the thirties, but that is not what I'm talking about, not 'pinkos' or 'fellow travelers' or people who gave money to the Scottsboro Boys. The threat is from deep-cover NKVD agents who operate freely all over this country. The last thing they would do is attend a left-wing rally or sign a petition or balk at taking a loyalty oath. If you don't think the Soviets have an elaborate, professional espionage network in place in this country, you are not paying attention. And if you think the air force can protect itself from those agents using a set of narrowly conceived, competing systems it inherited from the army, you are doing the work of the enemy."

At last Dillon saw that these heroes of the world conflict to whom he had felt inferior—that *they*, not he, were the provincials. He had lived his entire life in two cities, yet he was the one who understood the real meaning of events in Czechoslovakia. He saw the void behind their great chests full of commendations and awards, and he realized that every ribbon they had won had narrowed them. They were getting ready to fight the last war all over again, and the one thing they didn't want was news that the next war would be different, that it had already begun.

Dillon expected the generals to be angry at him, but it was wariness, not anger, that he sensed in General Eason's voice then. The smooth, white-haired senior commander said quietly, "If you sense some uneasiness in our reaction, Mr. Dillon, I think it's because, as a group of men charged with defending the American way of life, we are very sensitive to proposals that smack of what, given our experience, can only seem like a Gestapo. The OSI you're talking about would range freely and have total unchecked powers over all aspects of the air force mission."

"The OSI, as I propose it, would be totally accountable to you, General."

"I would appoint its director? He would serve at my pleasure?"

Dillon glanced at Randall Crocker, whose mask of neutrality was still firmly in place. Had he settled into the oblivion of a pseudo-objectivity? But the meaning of Crocker's impassivity was clear: Dillon was on his own. He brought his eyes quickly back to the chief of staff. "The director would be appointed by and serve at the pleasure of the commander in chief. That is to say, of the President."

General Eason quite pointedly did not react to Dillon's assertion, and it was evident that he had intended his remarks to be conclusive. No one behind him spoke.

A terminating silence ensued—the OSI was a Gestapo—and that would have been it, but Dillon raised a hand, like a pupil. "If I may add . . . I have come to my conclusions by looking at air force cases and problems again and again, until finally a single abstract idea arose from all the different details. And that is what I presented here, not a Gestapo, not even a police force, but an investigative agency the purpose of which would be to answer *your* questions."

Dillon's words were simply bouncing off the wall of their stolid common refusal. He was blathering on now because he did not know how to end it. His voice trailed off weakly as feelings of anger and disappointment burned in his throat. He had felt so confident for a moment there, as if his arguments *were* swaying them. But he was the one swaying, swaying back and forth—the taste in his throat turned foul—like an animal on the stockyards killing line.

When he looked at Crocker, Dillon's feelings curdled into shame. He had let his mentor down.

Crocker was staring at him over the knuckles of his folded fists. When at last he spoke it was the meager phrase "Thank you, Mr. Dillon," uttered with an exquisite detachment. A bored judge at the end of a meaningless civil trial.

Torts, Dillon thought; from the same root as "torture." He took a seat on the side of the room, apart from the others.

Crocker pushed himself up out of his chair and, without his cane, crossed with a lurch to the podium, which he clutched. He pivoted around to face his audience.

The generals and colonels softened nothing in their expressions as they awaited their dismissal.

Crocker said, "I want to test my impression, gentlemen. Am I correct in sensing that everyone in this room thinks the Office of Special Investigations as outlined here is a bad idea? If I'm wrong, please indicate."

No one spoke.

Crocker nodded. "Well then, I want you to hear from me what I intend to recommend to the President when I see him on this matter later today. First, I will recommend that he issue an executive order establishing the Air Force Office of Special Investigations immediately to supersede and replace AF CIC and CID. I will inform the President, of course, that you oppose my recommendation." Crocker paused. His concentration faltered as he thought of the old barn on his place in Maine. He had tried years before to demolish it, using the time-honored method of hooking a tractor and chain to one post and hauling away, expecting the other posts and the roof to collapse in a heap. When he had gunned the tractor across a dozen yards of field, then looked behind, he was shocked to see the entire stalwart barn intact and dragging along behind him. That's who these bastards were.

"And second, I will recommend to the President that he appoint as founding director of OSI Mr. Sean Dillon, from whom we just heard." Crocker swung toward Dillon. "Providing, Mr. Dillon, you would accept the appointment."

"I would, sir," Dillon answered at once, to his own bottomless surprise.

Several of the officers reacted audibly, but it was Macauley whose shock brought him to his feet. "You can't do that!"

"We're talking about what the commander in chief can do, General. Not what I can do."

Macauley opened his hands toward Eason. Eason in turn raised an eyebrow at Peters, the provost marshal. Peters stood up. "The lines are very clear, Mr. Secretary, both in traditional army regulations and in the air force charter of the National Security Act. Civilian and military spheres of authority are separate and distinct. The organization proposed here is a line organization, under the purview of the chief of staff, manned by military personnel. It is illegal to insert a civilian into that line. Mr. Dillon would have no basis in law for exercising authority over the air force men assigned to this organization."

Crocker leaned across the podium, seeming to peer at the provost marshal, but what he was seeing was his barn. "So the director has to be an air force officer?"

"That's right."

Crocker nodded slowly, full of grudging admiration for a structure that so refused to fall. If they couldn't stop an independent OSI from coming into being, they could stop it from being independent. "What rank would the director properly hold?"

Peters looked quickly toward General Eason, who, with a cock of his head, took over again. He said slowly, "Worldwide command? Responsible directly to my office? He would have to hold the rank of brigadier general."

Crocker was still nodding. "Thank you, gentlemen. That clarifies things for me." He abruptly straightened at the podium. His leg clicked. "My third recommendation to the President today will be to immediately have drafted proper legislation and lay it before Congress at once, commissioning Mr. Dillon an officer in the United States Air Force, holding the rank of brigadier general."

THIRTEEN

A special law was passed by Congress and signed by the President making Sean Dillon the youngest general in America. With Lafayette, he was one of only a handful ever to be directly commissioned at that rank.

Cass and Richard arrived in Washington by train on the morning of the ceremony. It was June 27, 1948.

Sean was waiting on the platform. Cass saw him from the train window. He was dressed like an FBI agent, dark suit and hat, despite the sultry southern weather. She saw the anxiety in him as he stared the length of the slowing train. She had an urge to call out, but the window was closed firmly between them.

Richard was three, and he traveled whenever possible in his mother's arms. His face fell naturally into an expression of wide-eyed curiosity, but it looked at times like pure wariness, and that was the case now.

Cass came off the train carrying Richard. The child, at least, they had unambiguously in common. He wore a clip-on bow tie, a sleeveless sweater and perfectly polished Buster Browns. Like his mother, he watched carefully as his father approached.

Sean Dillon sensed his son's reticence more than Cass's, yet hers was what he'd worried about. As he drew close to them, stopping, he had an impulse to say to her simply, I have not learned yet how to be a husband and a man both.

He said instead, "Hello, Cass."

"Hi, Sean." She quickly and awkwardly kissed him, and he might have returned the kiss, but at that moment Richard burst into tears and buried his face in Cass's neck.

"It's Daddy," Cass said. "It's Daddy."

233

Sean reached to Richard and took him firmly into his hands. For a moment, the boy refused to relinquish his grip on Cass. She looked sadly at Sean, as if to say, It's not you. Then Richard did let go, and he transferred his hold to Sean's neck. Sean felt, as the boy's small arms encircled him, the release of a tension he had not acknowledged. How he loved this boy.

"He's grown," Sean said at last.

Cass smiled. "I hope we all have."

He had expected her to be withholding, but she wasn't. He had expected her to be nervous, intimidated by what was about to happen to him. But she was carrying herself between those bustling tracks like an arriving celebrity.

She was nearly ten years older than when he first saw her in that rancid stockyard tavern, and though the decade had been unkind in many ways, its effect on her appearance had been to fulfill the early promise of her beauty. Was it her persistence in staying with Sean, despite his preference for worlds in which she was unwelcome, that drew out the fiber of her will, solidifying what before had been the erratic, untested core of herself? Sean sensed with fresh gratitude how, despite all that had passed between them, she had refused the Canaryville woman's role of long-suffering martyrdom. On the contrary, at that moment, in the flash of her arrival, she had become to him a woman of rare independence, able, if not to understand a husband's limits, to accept them. Dillon wanted to see her this way, and Cass knew it. And so she let him.

Her integrity, for her own part, consisted now in the firm knowledge that her love for Sean, as for her child by him, was a given, not dependent finally on anything he did to earn it. If he had been through an ordeal by which he had proved himself, so had she. She had learned the secret of real love, was determined to rebuild her life around it.

A porter had collected Cass's bags, and now led the way down the platform. Sean wanted to reach down with his free hand to take Cass's, but he didn't. "We don't have a lot of time. One of the first things you'll notice about my new situation, unlike my old one, is that they like to have wives around for the ceremonies."

"So someone ordered you to send for me?" Cass's stylish brown fedora obscured one eye, but the other held steady with what Dillon hoped was affectionate amusement.

"You are supposed to hold the Bible on which I take my oath."

Cass stopped and so did he. She opened her handbag to reveal the black leather Bible that Crocker himself had presented to Richard three years before.

Sean grinned broadly, realizing she'd been ahead of him, and like that the thick weather broke. "How the hell did you know?"

When Cass smiled, it was to let her pride show, pride in him. "A little bird told me." Her eyes flashed. "A sparrow."

Sean embraced her, and for a moment all three of them were joined in an overflow of feeling.

"I've arranged for Ellie Packard to take Rickie to the Smithsonian this morning. By the way, Mike Packard has come over to work for me at the Pentagon." Sean grinned at the boy. "You'll love the Smithsonian, buddy. They have Lindy's airplane and dinosaurs and Indians. I'll take you there myself one of these days. I'll take you a lot of places."

"Run me, Daddy," Richard said. That game of theirs, Sean carrying him like a football, cutting through the grass like a halfback. He hooked his arm around Richard's waist, and the boy hung at Sean's side. He'd gotten so big! Sean began to sing, "Cheer for the Redskins!" He took off, running down the platform, zigzagging around the posts and carts. Richard's squealing laughter echoed under the canopy.

Cass watched, aware that her terrible anxiety was gone. Her husband had asked her to come, that was all. And she had come. He was going to be sworn into a rare, important realm, and without understanding how such a thing had come to pass, she was going to hold the Bible for him. It was all so simple, suddenly. All he had ever had to do—of course, she always knew this—was ask her.

Cass and Sean came out of the old Willard Hotel on Pennsylvania Avenue, just below the White House, in clear sight of the gleaming distant Capitol. They had dispatched Richard and Ellie, with her two kids, to the Smithsonian, then had showered in turn and begun to dress shyly in opposite corners of the room. At one point their eyes met, and with no more warning than that, Sean had crossed to her. He was wearing his trousers, but no shirt. She was in her slip. They kissed. He lowered the straps of her shift, and it fell. He pressed her against himself, her naked chest against his. It was only a moment, and that was all that happened, but that bare physical contact quickened more in each of them than the old longing.

Now they stood in the bright noon of a hot summer day. Sean, in his best suit and the new tie Cass had brought from Chicago, had never seemed more handsome to her. In her mind they looked like one of the golden couples she had often seen coming out of the Drake.

Cass had chosen her clothing carefully, a dark green crepe dress, stylishly cinched, with sleeves to her elbows. The line of the airy ribbed cloth ran vertically, and she knew that it emphasized her height and slimness. The color of her dress set off the flecks in her eyes; her eyes hovered in what she hoped was the beguiling shadow of the soft wide brim of her new beige hat. When, in their room upstairs, she had finished dressing at last and had turned to face her stolid husband, he spoke his first words in all that time. He had been watching blatantly from across the room, and for a moment she thought he was going to come to her again. If he had, it would not have given her more satisfaction than what he did. He took his cigarette away to say simply, "Cass, you're the loveliest woman alive."

As they strode past the doorman toward the line of taxis, they were cut off by a newsboy, who was fiercely repeating some line of *"Extra!"* gibberish that Cass could not understand. He had a stack of fresh newspapers under his arm and was waving one. The headline, when she read it, hit her: "Russians Blockade Berlin; U.S. Forces on Alert."

Sean snatched the kid's paper and paid him, but he didn't open it until they were inside the moving cab.

"What does it mean?" she asked.

He ignored her to read, rudely, she thought.

When the cab had completed its circle past the Washington Monument, she asked again.

He read for a moment more, then said, "The Russians have shut down all the roads and train lines into Berlin."

"How can they do that?"

"They claim Berlin is theirs. Czechoslovakia last month, Berlin this month. They say they will let the citizens in the western zones of the city starve if we don't yield."

"But—"

Sean cut her off by snapping the newspaper shut. He looked

out the window, away from her. "I'm sorry, Cass." As if the real danger was that Stalin might ruin their day.

A few minutes later, having left the cab, they stood before the building which loomed above them like something out of ancient Egypt. Cass's thought, as they walked up the broad esplanade of the river entrance, was, They'll never let me in here now.

But they did. She had never been inside the Pentagon. Entering, she felt none of the tourist's awe—three times the floor space of the Empire State Building! Instead, she felt a fresh dose of a citizen's wartime gratitude to the men in their handsome tan uniforms. As they brushed by her, she couldn't help but see them as soldiers who would go quickly now to Europe and die.

Far from stopping her, the military men seemed not to notice her at all, or Sean either for that matter. She kept expecting him, after all these months of coming here, to wave at someone or say hello, but the Pentagon men passed him as if *he* were invisible too. She felt a pang for him, as she realized how out of place he seemed here.

She had to move quickly to stay up with him, and at one point, rounding a corner, she clutched at his sleeve, to slow him. He ignored her, and she dropped his arm. Once they had to dodge out of the way of a messenger, who sped toward them on an oversized tricycle. His bell blasted and made Cass jump with surprise, which prompted Sean to take her hand. Even in his haste he smiled at her with what she recognized as the old affection, and for an instant—how little of him she needed!—she felt as though they were walking along the Oak Street Beach. We have been too hard on ourselves, she thought. For years we have been too hard.

"This is Mr. Crocker's office," Sean said, ushering her into a reception area.

Cass knew that Sean's one question had become, What is Berlin for me? But she had far more to take in than he. She quickly surveyed the soft blues of the carpet and drapes, a riotous bouquet of freshly picked zinnias on an end table, an oil painting of rocks along a nasty stretch of shoreline. The gracious room soothed her after the stark, bustling corridor, and the gray-haired, tailored woman at the desk stood up to greet Cass and Sean as if she were welcoming them to her home.

Again Cass expected to be told to wait outside, but instead the receptionist led them both through the inner door.

As they entered Mr. Crocker's office, he was coming toward them from behind his desk, limping. Cass paid his leg as little mind as he did, for to her great surprise, he was opening his arms to her. Without hesitating she went into his generous, warm embrace. Sean had once said he was like a father.

"Mrs. Dillon," he said, his mouth at the brim of her hat. "How *very* good to see you."

She pulled back just enough to search his eyes. "You make me feel like a stranger, calling me that. Please call me Cass, Mr. Crocker."

Crocker laughed at the juxtaposition of their names, its perfect expression of the inequality which was a given between them, but which also failed to preclude their immediate mutual sense of intimacy. "I will with pleasure, Cass."

With a courtly flair, he showed her to one of two wing chairs that flanked a matching prim settee. Then Crocker faced Sean.

Cass waited to see his expression change, as if now, with a man, he would get serious. And indeed the words he spoke did address Berlin, but with an equanimity consistent with the mood of his greeting Cass. "We have an emergency situation in Europe."

"Yes, sir. I understand that."

"It's a moment I've been positively longing for."

Both Sean and Cass were confused by Crocker's burst of eagerness.

Crocker said, "At last the air force will have the chance to do something else besides destroy. We bombed Berlin into rubble during the war. Do you know what we're doing now, as of this morning?" Crocker leaned closer to Sean. "We're bringing in coal and milk and flour by air! *Instead* of bombs!"

"I assumed we would—"

"Break the blockade? Bull through it?"

"Yes."

"Stalin wanted us to, I'm sure of it. And the Red Army would have swallowed us whole. But we're leapfrogging them instead."

"How long can we—?"

"As long as it takes. We saw this coming. Spaatz and Eason had already convinced the President that our fliers *could* supply the city. I've been pushing the idea of an airlift with him since Zhukov first threatened the cutoff. Spaatz and Eason backed me up. Once President Truman had this option, he didn't consider tanks-through-the-turnpikes for an instant. The army, of course, had not given the thing a moment's forethought, and all they could propose this morning was to start shooting. General Marshall undercut Bradley completely by saying if we did that, we'd end up having to use the A-bomb on Berlin."

"To defend it?" Cass asked.

"That's what Truman said." Crocker snorted with pleasure. "We've called Stalin's bluff. The President is going to announce it at noon. C-54s started flying out of Frankfurt two hours ago, loaded with butter. Think of it! We're feeding people instead of killing them! Isn't that wonderful?"

To Cass at that moment Randall Crocker was wonderful. The energy with which he displayed the triumph to Sean made very clear the depth of their bond. Cass thought her husband wonderful too.

"Rhine-Main?" Sean asked.

"Yes, and Wiesbaden."

"But those are fighter bases. What are you flying?"

"C-54s up to now. We've been quietly bringing them up from Ramstein and Evereux. The entire transport squadron based at Essex—C-54s and -47s—is crossing the Channel this afternoon. We'll have a hundred and seventy planes lined up to ferry in and out of Tempelhof by dawn." Crocker pulled his pocket watch out. "It's almost nightfall there now."

"Will you restrict to daylight?"

"To start with."

"What if Stalin just keeps the barriers up? We can't supply a city of three million from the air indefinitely."

"Two million, since we're talking about the Allied zones. And we'll keep it up as long as we have to." Crocker eyed his watch again, then put it back in his vest pocket. "You don't have much time, Sean. General Eason will be here at thirteen-fifteen sharp."

"We're going ahead?"

"Of course. We have to get OSI off the ground too, don't we? Maybe more than ever. Go get dressed." Crocker slapped Dillon's shoulder like a coach.

Dressed? Once more Cass was mystified. Sean *was* dressed. He never looked better.

"Oh, but Christ! Wait a minute, Sean. I almost forgot, you have to call Hoover."

"What?"

"J. Edgar Hoover. You have to call him."

"Why?"

Crocker's face broke into a sparkling grin. "He wants to know why he wasn't invited."

Dillon came back. "Invited to what?"

Crocker cast a look of mock exasperation at Cass, then said soberly to Dillon, "Your formal commissioning."

"You mean this?"

"This plus General Eason."

"What does Mr. Hoover think is happening? No one's invited."

Crocker smiled at Cass. "Not 'no one.' " He said to her, "Your husband's new status is not something we can exactly flaunt. You can have no idea how many 'bird colonels' haunt these corridors, all veterans of the Bulge or Bataan, all desperate for the star they will never wear." Crocker looked back at Dillon. "They will hate you."

Dillon answered, "And I won't blame them."

Crocker turned back to Cass. "A subdued, unnoticed observance is what's called for. Hoover's presence would call all kinds of attention to it, and would be widely misunderstood, to boot. In the minds of some, OSI is already too closely identified with the Bureau."

"That's an understatement," Sean said. "Those colonels out there think I'm Mr. Hoover's foot in the door of the Defense Department, that *he* plans to run OSI and ultimately expand it beyond the air force."

"Those colonels may not be the only ones who think of you that way, Sean." Crocker smiled smoothly. "Perhaps Hoover does. You have to make the phone call. Do it here."

Dillon did not move.

This was a last test. Crocker wanted Sean to refuse Hoover himself. It seemed a meaningless matter, but to the director, Sean's confirmation of Crocker's rejection would seem like betrayal. And to Crocker, it was an essential act of Dillon's independence. The OSI was not to be the Bureau's scouting party.

A thick silence had settled on the room.

Cass broke it. "Why don't I call Mr. Hoover?"

"Cass," Sean said quietly, a plea in his voice.

"Mr. Hoover likes me, Sean."

"Of course he likes you." Sean laughed, as if aware all at once of the absurdity of his situation. Unlike many Bureau wives, and many agents for that matter, Cass had no built-in awe for the men in power, not even Hoover. She had won him over at dinners in Chicago by drawing him out on his own childhood, a subject everyone else had treated as taboo. "We *all* like you, Cass."

Crocker too was laughing quietly. "That's right," he said. "We all do."

Cass could feel herself blushing. Were they mocking her? "Isn't it important to keep Mr. Hoover supportive? You want him at a distance, but you want him on your side, right?"

"That's right." Sean looked at Crocker. "I've learned over the years that the thing to do when the director makes a wrong-headed move is simply to deflect him. It never pays to poke a finger in his chest, much less his eye." Sean closed the distance to Crocker's desk and leaned over it. "I have nothing to prove in relation to Hoover, Mr. Crocker, whether you think I have or not. The way I intend to play it, he will be no problem to the OSI, but he will be very useful. My wife is exactly right."

"What are you saying?"

Cass knew: that Sean's independence as director of OSI would extend to J. Edgar Hoover and Randall Crocker both.

"I'm saying Cass has a good idea. Let her call him."

Crocker let his glance flow from one to the other, admiration in it. "I've never seen this before."

Cass understood what he meant. Sean Dillon's willingness to duck behind his wife was a sign not of the lack of manhood, but the fullness of it. To Crocker, it must have seemed that Sean had nothing to prove in relation to her either.

Without waiting for Crocker's leave, Sean indicated the telephone on her side of the large desk. "Turn on the charm, kiddo." He headed for the door. "I'll be right back." He left.

Cass got up and crossed to the desk. "Can you get Mr. Hoover for me?"

"I can try."

While Crocker directed his secretary and then waited with the phone by his cheek, Cass studied the pair of leather-framed photographs that stood just beyond the blotter's edge. A handsome, sandy-haired woman in sweater-and-collar, cuddling a dog, looked fondly out from one. She seemed about forty. Her eyes were pale but friendly. Her arm draped the dog's neck, but it had been the picture taker toward whom her affection flowed. Cass had never forgotten Mr. Crocker's simple statement at the Shrine that day: My dear wife died many years ago. My Hillary, he'd called her.

Cass wished that she could tell his Hillary what Mr. Crocker had done for Sean, what he was doing that very day for Berlin and for the world. Hillary Crocker would have been a person like her husband: privileged, of course, but decent and good. Cass had had no direct experience of patrician women, but the society pages made it seem that all they cared about, like worried little girls, was being invited to the best parties in the biggest houses. But not this woman. The center of her life would have been her home, her husband and her children.

Her child. Cass corrected herself as she looked at the second photograph, Crocker's son in uniform, saluting. In that picture he would be forever amused at himself, forever slightly embarrassed. His eyes were pale, like his mother's. Then Cass realized it wasn't paleness at all, but the color blue, which lost its vibrancy in black-and-white. The lad, she saw, was beautiful.

"This is Randall Crocker, Mr. Hoover."

Cass was startled to realize how easily she had been drawn away from what was happening. She glanced one last time at the image of Hillary Crocker and thought she was a capable woman who accomplished difficult things. Cass offered a quick prayer—her simple, habitual "Help me"—but as much at that moment to Hillary Crocker as to the Blessed Mother.

"Mr. Dillon still is not here, but Mrs. Dillon arrived, and she asked to have a word with you, sir."

Cass took the phone with one hand while removing her earring with the other. She felt the calm detachment of one of the airport-tower people guiding those transport planes into Berlin. "Hello, Mr. Hoover," she said with a bright lilt.

Her eyes remained fixed on Hillary Crocker's eyes while Hoover's brusque voice filled her ear.

"Hello, Cass. How are you?"

"I'm very grateful, Mr. Hoover," she said. "That's how I am, grateful to you."

"To me? Why?"

"For everything, of course. But especially for what you did today. I wanted to thank you myself, before Sean could stop me. He knows better than I do how busy you are, and he would have told me to just write you a note. But I remembered how you told me one time in Chicago that I should never hesitate to call you." Cass paused. It seemed ominous to her when Hoover did not speak, and she felt the first curl of panic twisting her stomach. Was this a terrible mistake? Was she about to humiliate Sean? Cass hated the obvious tricks of womanly flirtation; Hillary Crocker would have hated them too. But when the time of Hoover's silence lengthened into a positive, chilling act of disapproval, she knew she had to turn it back upon itself. She said, "Unless you tell all the girls to call you."

Her thrust disarmed Hoover. He guffawed with delight, then protested, "Oh, come, come, Cass! What do you take me for?"

"For a good man, Mr. Hoover. That's all I called to tell you."

"You said 'today.' What did I do today?"

Cass relaxed. "Why, you made it possible for me to be here, Mr. Hoover. When Sean told me there wasn't to be a ceremony for his new job, I wanted to come anyway. I don't know if Sean told you, but I've stayed in Chicago, where my mother was sick."

"Oh, I'm sorry."

Cass retreated from the outright lie. "She died a while ago, but I've been attending to family matters."

"I'm sorry, Cass. Someone should have told me."

Cass wanted to smile, remembering that she had received a warm letter of condolence signed with Hoover's name. She had known better than to think he had written it. "But you know what Chicago's like, Mr. Hoover. Sean's friends all told me they were coming to Washington for the ceremony. Then the monsignor from our parish said he was coming. How could I say no to a monsignor? When I said there wouldn't *be* a ceremony, they all said there would be *something*. They are all so proud of him. You know better than anyone what Sean has achieved. They all just *had* to be here. What was I going to do?"

"But I don't—"

"It was only when I told them all that not even you would be here that they gave up. I don't understand these things, but

Sean told me how important you felt it was to be—what was your word?—discreet."

"Well, it behooves us sometimes, you understand—"

"Now I do. Monsignor Barry, our friend from the Shrine, wanted to come this morning, but not even he is here at Mr. Crocker's office." Cass averted her eyes from Mrs. Crocker's. This was shameless of her, but she didn't care. "Monsignor said if J. Edgar Hoover can forgo the honor, then he could too. And that means that I can be here, for the proudest moment of my life."

"The honor is the Bureau's, Cass. Not mine. Your fine husband is a reflection on all of us over here. I didn't give him up to the air force without a mighty large qualm, I'll tell you."

"You didn't give him up, Mr. Hoover. You know how devoted Sean is to you. And how he always will be."

"I always say, it's the woman behind the man, Cass."

"I know you do, Mr. Hoover." Cass paused, then pushed in once more with, "You say it to all the girls."

Hoover laughed delightedly again.

"May I tell Sean you said you're proud of him?"

There was such a sudden silence in her ear that Cass thought for a moment he had left the line. She realized that he had not said that exactly. Hoover maintained his control over the souls of his agents more with threats than with rewards. His letters of commendation were rarely effusive. Had he ever told an agent he was "proud" of him? To Cass's knowledge, no.

So even she was impressed for Sean when at last Hoover said, "Yes, you can tell him that."

"Thank you."

Another silence, and then the director said, "Tell him to call me when he can."

"Yes, Mr. Hoover." When Cass looked at Crocker he was studying her across the tips of his entwined fingers.

"Goodbye," she said.

"Goodbye, Cass." Hoover hung up.

Cass replaced the phone on its cradle, aware that the time for her impersonation was not yet over. As she clipped her earring back on, she eased back on her breeziness just enough. "What is it you fellows say to each other? Mission accomplished?"

"Only in the movies. You handle him well."

Cass sensed his disdain for Hoover. She would not endorse it, and so said nothing.

It was only when Crocker had exhaled a long, steady lungful of air that she recognized the tension with which he had been listening. He might disdain Hoover, but he also understood his power.

Not only Crocker had been listening.

Cass turned to see Sean standing by the door. He was looking at her with pride in his eyes, and no wonder. He had changed from his suit into the tan uniform of an air force officer. Its sharp creases, its brass buttons, the curving flaps of its tunic pockets, the subtle stripe on each sleeve—she stared at him as if she'd never seen such clothing. A peaked hat was riding between his side and his upper arm, the visor just visible. She saw its elaborate silver braid forming thunderbolts and clouds.

This was Sean?

For the first time Cass understood what a transformation was about to be worked in his life, or thought she did.

Pride in his eyes, yes. But what really surprised her then was the sharp recognition, what she had not experienced in a long time, that the pride he felt at that moment was not in himself, but in her.

"It becomes you, Sean," Crocker said, then he smiled at Cass. "Don't you agree? Doesn't a uniform do wonders for a man?"

Cass knew he was thinking of his son, and she could not answer.

Crocker said, "You are going to have to help him." His voice was so soft, it occurred to Cass he might not want Sean to hear. "He's going to need you. He won't have many allies in this building. He'll have many enemies."

"Sean can do it," she said.

The door behind Sean opened and Mr. Crocker's receptionist appeared. "General Eason is here, sir."

"Splendid, splendid." Crocker hoisted himself up from his chair. "Hello, General."

A slim, gray-headed man even taller than Sean entered the room, ignoring both Sean and Cass as he crossed to shake hands with Crocker. He was dressed like Sean, Cass saw, but with a striking difference. His uniform flashed with reflected light and colors, a dramatic winged badge on one side of his chest above a wallet-sized square of ribbons, and on each shoulder four silver stars which sparkled like a woman's sequins.

"Mr. Secretary," he said formally.

"How is it proceeding?"

"Very good, sir. The first group is already off-loaded and in the air again. We will have the second out of Tempelhof before dark."

"And out of the zone?"

"In fifty minutes. The first day will be buttoned up by"—he flashed his wristwatch—"fifteen hundred."

Crocker abruptly shot his arm toward Cass, where Sean had joined her. "General Eason, say hello to Mrs. Dillon. Mrs. Dillon, General Eason, our chief of staff."

Two strides took Eason back to her.

Cass would have had to be made of wood not to mark the man's coldness. She would perhaps have attributed it to a natural resentment at being pulled away from urgent duties, but when Eason pointedly ignored Sean, turning back to Crocker, she realized that his resentment had nothing to do with Berlin.

Eason said, "Shall we proceed?" and he once more pulled his sleeve back, checking the time.

Cass glanced at Sean, who met her eyes with that stark neutrality of his. For once his stolid reserve seemed admirable to her, the thick wall off which the general's insult bounced. Crocker had promised enemies, but Cass knew she was right: Sean could handle them.

"Indeed so," Crocker said. He came out from behind his desk and took up a position immediately in front of the staffed American flag by the large window. Just his standing there transformed the space between the window and the furniture, giving it a slight aura of sanctuary, so that as Cass and Sean approached she felt relieved. Ritual solemnity always rescued her from jumbled feelings, and did so now.

Eason remained where he was, but he adjusted his posture, a subtle coming to attention that indicated his acquiescence.

"Oh, I forgot the Bible," Crocker said and moved toward his desk.

"I have it." Cass opened her shoulder bag and drew out Richard's. "This one is special to us," she said, and when she looked at Crocker, her eyes burned with gratitude.

Crocker touched her hand. "No wonder we all like you."

Without any further elaboration, they observed in its barest
version the form of the rite of Sean's military initiation. With
his hand firmly enough on his baby's Bible that his wife could
feel its weight, repeating after the secretary of the air force,
with the chief of staff as solemn witness, Sean Dillon swore to
God that he would defend the Constitution of the United States
of America as an officer in its air force.

When he had finished, Cass expected the men to shake
hands, but instead Crocker extended his hand toward Eason.
General Eason efficiently handed over a small black box. A
ring box? Was this a wedding? The thought of the self-
important Eason as a ring bearer made Cass want to giggle.
One incongruity after another. One absurdity . . . Was this a
dream?

Crocker shocked Cass by giving the box to her. He took the
Bible and waited while she opened the lid.

Why did she know so little of these things? A dream? If she
awoke now, she would remember none of this.

The box held a pair of silver stars. Now she understood.
This was what wives did for their general-husbands. She
touched the perfectly faceted five-pointed stars, felt their
weight, recognized each one for the wrought sterling piece it
was. She looked at Sean, Sean who had never worn jewelry.
He was waiting for her.

In the sacraments of the Church, the ritual act itself accomplished the saving ontological change, and now Cass felt that
her presenting his stars was what would effect the change in
Sean's life. Nothing he had ever asked of her had made her
feel like this before, not that she was a part of his remarkable
destiny, but that somehow she was actually helping to shape it.

Cass Dillon was famous throughout Canaryville, and even
the FBI, as the unawed woman who was never at a loss. But
now, as she stood on her tiptoes to pin each silver star on its
epaulet, her hands shook. Her full heart overflowed, like both
her eyes.

Cass would not have been surprised if, after the ceremony,
Sean had told her he had to go to work now, he'd see her later.
Indeed, as they walked out of the Pentagon toward the line of
taxis on one of the ramps leading up from the river boulevard,
she decided yes, he's going to put me in a cab.

But they stopped on the curb, short of the taxis.

Now that he was outdoors, Sean had donned his hat, and the sight of him so completely decked out heightened her former feeling of unreality—that dream!

Soldiers of all ranks hustling toward the Pentagon, the very men who had failed even to see him only an hour before, now snapped brisk salutes.

The further marvel was the way in which Sean returned those salutes, his flat hand hitting his brow with complete naturalness.

"Where did you learn that?"

Sean grinned. "You won't tell?"

"Of course not."

He leaned to her ear. "I've been practicing in front of my mirror for a week."

She started to laugh. "You do it great. You really do." And finally her true amazement at the house of chills and thrills into which he'd dragged her poured out in the form of laughter. She leaned against him.

He held her, laughing too. He ignored the passing military men, who were looking for his eye, to salute. It felt like being kids again, larking on the Oak Street Beach, having pulled one off on the swells from Lake Street.

Cass just knew there was nothing left that could surprise her.

But then the long, blue Lincoln pulled up to the curb and stopped. Above the license plate was another plate that displayed a silver star.

The driver hopped out of the car and rushed around to stand before Sean at brisk attention. There were blue stripes on the sleeve of his tan belted jacket.

Sean pulled himself together, returned the man's salute. "Cass, this is Sergeant Hewitt. Sergeant, I'd like you to meet Mrs. Dillon."

"Pleased to meet you, ma'am." He opened the door for them.

Cass got in, and then Sean did.

In the seconds before Sergeant Hewitt resumed his own seat, Cass whispered, "What is this?"

"It's my car!" Sean blurted out with unfettered amazement of his own. "He's my chauffeur!"

Hewitt got in.

Sean and Cass, holding hands, had to look away from each other to keep from screeching.

As they drove across the city, Cass gradually returned to herself. At first, like a schoolgirl salvaging her self-control, she watched the monuments and becolumned buildings for the focus. But then, as if she'd never seen them before, the sights of Washington—Jefferson's temple, Smithson's castle, Mellon's gallery, Grant's equestrian statue—began to thrill her. A schoolgirl's happiness filled her, and she felt free as any tourist. It struck her then, as they cruised along the Mall, that the tourists were pointing at their car. Hot-dog vendors and balloon men waved at her, and policemen touched their hats. The golden city seemed to be opening itself in ways it never had before, and as Cass sat back in the spacious plush seat, an unprecedented exhilaration buoyed her, as if the official car itself were magic.

Soon they came to Bolling Field, the air base on the Potomac just south of the Anacostia. This was a part of Washington Cass had never visited, and the airfield had registered only vaguely in her mind as the busy second airport across the river from National.

The car slowed as it approached the guardhouse at the gate.

Two soldiers wearing white helmets marked "AP" snapped to attention, saluting, as the car went through. Once more Sean returned the salute with what seemed to Cass an effortless panache.

Now as Cass stared out the window, what she saw was an exotic, unfamiliar realm. Only a hundred yards inside the gate the flight line began where a large formation of silver airplanes sat with their noses pointing at the clouds. They reminded Cass of birds bathing in the flow of wind on the edge of a South Side Chicago roofline.

At a low, round-roofed building marked "Base Ops," the car turned onto a road bordered on one side by glistening steel hangars and on the other by a string of pristine white buildings. These were set amid crisply edged lawns with low fences of gracefully draped white chains. That the driver had so slowed the car gave Cass the feeling she was expected now to inspect what they were passing. She could not identify them as such yet, but the diverse structures were barracks buildings, a commissary, the base exchange, the rehearsal hall of the USAF band and the headquarters of the First District Command. One building, from the side, looked like a hangar, but it had a brick façade and a theater marquee which announced *The Third*

Man. Another building's sign read, "USO." Then they came upon a small white church with a steeple, clapboard siding and frosted glass windows. It reminded Cass of churches on calendars, New England churches, Puritan ones, but they were always surrounded by snowy fields and mountains in the distance.

"That's the Protestant church?"

"Everybody's," Sean said.

The unornamented sign read, "Base Chapel. Sunday Services 1100 hours, Catholic Mass 0730 daily, Sunday 0730, 0815."

"They have Mass in there?" There was no cross on top of the steeple. Protestants didn't believe in showing Christ's crucified body.

"There are dispensations in the military," Sean said. "Soldiers can eat meat on Fridays."

Cass looked with surprise at him, but he didn't notice. He was pointing out the window on his side, toward a swimming pool in which a throng of children splashed and cavorted. "There's a pool that Rickie will love."

Cass leaned toward him, to see. It reminded her of pools on the South Side which would be crowded in the same way with ecstatic summer children.

Sergeant Hewitt said from his place at the wheel, "Actually, General, that's the NCO pool. Your pool is up by the Officers' Club. There, see it?"

Cass and Sean watched in silence as the Officers' Club came into view, its broad veranda overlooking a landscaped terrace and pool. The swimming pool here, twice as large as the other, had almost no one playing in it. Didn't officers have children? Women were lounging in deck chairs. Waiters could be seen moving among them with trays of drinks. All at once Cass had the feeling that more than one of those ladies behind the dark glasses were turning their languid eyes up from their magazines toward her.

The car stopped at a corner, then turned, passing by the front of the Officers' Club. It was large, three stories, a Georgian manor house made of brick. A sloping curved driveway led to an entrance defined by an overarching dark blue canvas awning. Cass pictured those swimming pool ladies arriving beneath that awning in evening gowns with white gloves to their elbows. Their hands would be linked to the arms of their handsome husbands, who would pass Sean by without seeing him.

The car kept on, and all at once the very air around them changed, becoming cooler, as they drove into a distinctly set-off enclave. The street was a tunnel of graceful old elm trees the leaves of which stirred shadows in a breeze that until now Cass had not noticed. A sign with the same utilitarian stencil lettering as the one outside the chapel proclaimed, "Off Limits To Unauthorized Personnel." Beyond it Cass saw on one side a line of large brick houses in the Georgian style of the club. Each house was set apart from its neighbors by a broad apron of grass clipped as smooth as a putting green. Not houses, Cass thought, but mansions.

Across from each house, folded into a wooded hillside, was a garage with spaces for three automobiles. In front of each residence were tidy, more formally lettered signs.

"This is Generals' Row, Mrs. Dillon," the driver said.

"Maj. Gen. Cabot," she read, "Lt. Gen. White, Lt. Gen. Davis, Maj. Gen. Ford."

One house was even larger than the others and had an entrance awning like the Officers' Club. Sean poked her as they passed it. "Gen. Eason," she read. A curtain moved inside a window, and Cass saw a woman staring out at them. It seemed to Cass that their eyes met. The curtain fell. Cass shivered to think that here was a female version of General Eason's coldness.

Several houses farther along the car slowed and pulled to the curb.

Mother of God, she thought.

A sign right there, where the car stopped: "Brig. Gen. Dillon." She read it again, pressing Sean's hand. His soaking hand.

"Brig.?" she asked. "What's 'Brig.'?" But she answered at once herself: a military word for jail.

"Brigadier," he said quietly. His lightheartedness was gone. "This is it."

Cass couldn't move.

Sergeant Hewitt had come around to Cass's door and now opened it. Still she did not move.

She looked at Sean. "This is what?"

He shrugged.

"When were you going to discuss this with me?"

Sean glanced awkwardly toward the driver. A screen door clapped shut, and when Cass looked toward the house, two men in white waiters' jackets were coming toward them. Both were smiling. One was colored.

Not waiters' coats, she saw then, for on each man's sleeve were sergeant's stripes, like the driver's.

"Who are they?"

"Our aides, Sergeant Jones and Sergeant Austin."

"Welcome, General," the colored sergeant, Austin, said. He seemed to be in charge. "Welcome, Mrs. Dillon."

And when they both saluted, she realized to her horror—she could never do this!—they were also saluting her.

FOURTEEN

By November of 1948 the Berlin airlift was in its sixth month. More than a hundred thousand flights had been logged in and out of the blockaded city, and more than a million tons of fuel and food had been brought in. Air force fliers, the very men who had savaged German cities only three years before, were now referred to by the children of Berlin as the "bubblegum bombers." The air crews had taken to tying little sacks of gum and candy to tiny parachutes and dropping them by the hundreds out the bays of their C-47s and C-54s each time they swooped in for landings at Tempelhof, Gatow, and Tegel. The laden planes landed every few minutes around the clock, to be off-loaded by squads from among more than twenty thousand German volunteers. Still, it would be another six months and another hundred thousand flights before the Russians would lift the blockade. When that finally happened—and it would happen within a few days of the suicide of James Forrestal—Winston Churchill would say, "America has saved the world."

But in dank November no one could foresee that triumph. To the air force brass who were managing it from Washington, the airlift had begun to seem futile. The Russian impunity in continuing to shut off access to Berlin seemed to prove the point they were so desperately trying to make to the beleaguered Forrestal, and to the House Armed Services Committee—that the American monopoly of the A-bomb was no threat to Stalin without a new long-range bomber with which to deliver the thing to Russia itself. But Forrestal had come fully over to the navy position, whence he'd started, and the committee, long divided, had lately seemed to be leaning that way too: the atomic bomb should be based on a massive new carrier fleet, with a new navy airplane to match, which would not depend on a permanent, far-flung network of air bases on foreign soil. Forrestal was pressing the committee for a decision, one way or the other, before the December recess. Almost surely it was going to be a decision not only against the B-36 but against, really, the future combat role of the air force.

The generals of the Air Staff, Dillon's neighbors, were thus a dispirited group by that November. Early one morning, as they enacted the ritual of their departure for work, it seemed to Dillon more absurd than usual, even as he participated in it. Without ever acknowledging the irony, given their death struggle with the navy, the air force brass traveled every day from Bolling to the Pentagon by boat.

At precisely 0700 a line of more than twenty blue staff cars, each with its plate bearing one, two, three, or four silver stars, cruised passed the Officers' Club onto Generals' Row. The filigreed branches of the bare elm trees laced the sky above the automobile procession like a long canopy. There was a car for each house, a driver for each general. By 0710 the generals had all come out and their cars were all under way again, now each with its lone backseat rider. Instead of proceeding off base through congested Washington, finally inching across the bridge to the Pentagon, the limousines drove directly to the far side of the flight line, to the riverbank and Bolling's one-wharf dock. There the generals left their cars and boarded a fifty-seven-foot-long teak-and-mahogany motor launch, the *Valkyrie*, which President Roosevelt had favored for twilight summer cruises down to Mount Vernon and back. In addition to staterooms below, the yacht features a luxuriously appointed main salon where a crew of air force stewards waited to serve the generals their coffee and hot sweet rolls while the yacht purred upstream to the river entrance of the Pentagon.

From his first experience of it the previous summer, the Potomac River boat had seemed to Dillon a ludicrous way to commute. He much preferred the productive solitude of time in his car. He needed Hewitt and his car available to him at the Pentagon in any case, for the ride home hours after the other generals had departed on the late afternoon launch, if not for one of his many trips into Washington, where the job of selling OSI to various government officials was never finished. The other generals regarded the boat as a perquisite, as did their wives, who, unlike Cass Dillon, had their husbands' staff cars and drivers at their disposal throughout the day. Dillon's intuition was that the members of the Air Staff prized the motor launch because, unconsciously, they too recognized that those who were at ease in and around boats were somehow better. In America farm boys, auto mechanics, and simple tinkerers had become fliers, some had become war heroes and perhaps a few, even, air force generals. But only men of a certain background became admirals. In his time at the Pentagon Dillon had become a connoisseur of condescension, for he was an interloper on whom even a lowly ROTC-commissioned state-college graduate could look down. He had concluded that the argument between the air force and the navy drew its ferocious energy from the old conflict of class. Randall Crocker, as an Ivy League–educated New Deal lawyer known, despite his handicap, to be a successful skipper of racing sloops, was the great exception on the side of the air force, but the generals distrusted him anyway as a former Wall Street associate of Forrestal's. If they wanted proof that Crocker was out to undercut them, they had only to point to Dillon.

Morning after morning he had boarded the motor launch despite himself. This was his only informal contact with his new colleagues, and it was here that they had made their attitude toward him very clear. The OSI was Crocker's brainchild, but it remained an air force *step*child and they had simply not accepted it. Dillon himself, the instant general, was an affront to everything they had all achieved, whatever their backgrounds, and even as he implemented his charter, resolutely extending his authority to OSI field offices in every command, their equally resolute rejection of him was by now undermining his fledgling operation. Dillon knew that, behind his back, the brass referred to him contemptuously as "the cop." To his face they had not hesitated to turn down his various, regular requests for support. Time and again Dillon, to his own chagrin more than theirs, had had to call on Crocker to back him up in disputes with Eason and other commanders. He knew that every such victory over these men was, at a deeper level, a defeat. Their resentment of OSI was choking him. Even officers who had specialized in security and counterintelligence, men whom Dillon was sure he had won over otherwise, understood soon enough that an assignment to his organization was a career killer. Not only were such men slow to volunteer for the

OSI; many already assigned were requesting early transfers out.

"Good morning, Herb." Dillon took a chair next to Herb Dalby, another BG, the deputy for plans, just as the launch pulled away from the dock. Since they were of the same rank, Dillon's use of his first name was not an issue. He tucked his hat under his arm as if he'd been doing so for years, then looked directly at Dalby, forcing him to react. Dillon had decided months ago that he was not going to make it easy for these bastards. That was why he was here instead of in his quiet car. Day in and day out, he made them all do this to him.

Dalby grunted and snapped open his copy of the *Times Herald*.

One of the white-haired senior generals, sitting with a cluster of his own peers, called back to Dalby with a generous camaraderie—a reward, no doubt, for his having efficiently snubbed Dillon. "Turn to page seven, Herb. See what Forrestal said yesterday."

The announcement caught the attention of most of the others, and they fell silent, looking toward Dalby, who scanned the paper until he found it. Aware of his audience, he read aloud, "The secretary of defense said, 'All Americans should be proud of what the air force is achieving in the western sector of Berlin.' "

"Hear! Hear!" a voice called, and another added, "Damn right!"

Dalby paused to grin at his fellows. Mostly they had remained silent, savvy and skeptical, and were now waiting for Dalby to read on, to tell them what *else* Forrestal had said. A steward carrying a tray of Danish had halted to listen too.

Dalby continued, building to a punch line. ". . . and what the airlift proves is that the air force is ideally suited to a primary mission of transport and supply."

Hoots, then groans and real curses. "Fuck Forrestal!" someone said loudly, an extreme expression even for them. It silenced the group for a moment.

A major general, a former bomber pilot named Spike Brown who was famous for his pearl-handled swagger stick, reached that stick across to lay it on Dalby's forearm. He said in a stage whisper, for Dillon's benefit, "And while you're at it, fuck Crocker too."

Dillon stood up, brushing General Brown's stick back. The

boat lurched and he grabbed an overhead rail, back for an instant to the Archer Avenue El careening down the slope into Canaryville. The jolt brought his face closer than he wanted to General Brown's. "Why not include the commander in chief, General? Fuck him too, while you're at it, 'eh? And why not the U.S. Constitution for that matter?"

Later Dillon would chide himself for this—not the display, but the failure to defend Crocker explicitly. What were Truman's prerogatives to him, or the Constitution's? What angered him was the insult to Crocker, pure and simple.

Brown stared blankly at Dalby. "Do you smell something, Herb? Did someone fart?"

Dillon pushed Brown's stick against his chest and held it there. "What is this, high school?"

Brown slowly moved his eyes to Dillon's hand. "As you were, Mr. Dillon."

Dillon moved away from him.

Dalby raised his voice to read a further paragraph from the newspaper story. " 'The committee expects to hear testimony from General Mark Macauley, the much decorated head of the Strategic Air Command, who during the war led the night raids against Dresden.' " Dalby looked up. "It's about time. Mac will tell those bozos. If he can't tell them, no one can."

Dillon moved toward the salon door, through the various expressions of confidence in Macauley, a man whose gift Dillon remembered as more for bluster than for thought. No wonder these fools think well of him.

Just before he left the salon for the deck outside, Dillon's eye caught General Eason's. The chief was sitting alone at a small table in the forward port corner of the cabin, removed from the others, as if judging them. He watched Dillon's exit with cold detachment, and all at once Dillon realized what this room had just become to the others. It was the officers' mess of a combat air group, the place in which hyper pilots vent their anxiety in raucous irreverence—"Fuck Forrestal!"— before and after the most dangerous and destructive activity yet known to man. The gift for thought was not a virtue in such a room. Bluster was precisely what had gotten men like these—*these* men—through the worst nightmares it was possible to have outside sleep.

And who the hell are you, Dillon—here was Eason's question—to feel superior in this company?

The biting wind hit him as he stepped outside to the rails, and with it came a recognition. He had made a huge mistake in becoming vulnerable to such men. He knew he would never win them over. The wind in his face seemed to be blowing back on him from a time when he would remember this as the largest moment of his life, and also as the moment of his largest failure. The boat lurched again, and Dillon saw that their craft had just hit the wake of some bigger vessel which was as invisible to him, and as unsettling, as the future. His stomach jumped, pathetic landlubber that he was. The bile of coffee shot up into his throat, and he thought for a dread instant that he was going to vomit.

Cass Dillon came out of the house on Generals' Row shortly after her husband did, but she left on foot and alone, not in the parade of blue limosines. She blinked up at the slate November sky, trying to read it for rain. A shiver curled up her spine as she thought for the hundredth time how she hated the weather here. But she hated other things more. She decided not to go back inside for her coat because she would have to explain herself to Sergeant Jones, and Richard would start all over again his pleading to come with her.

She turned up the collar of her plain Donegal tweed suit. She wore a simple green hat. Her hair tickled the back of her neck and made her think how she hated that too. Her hair was at an awkward length, neither here nor there, because she was letting it grow out again, having made the mistake nearly two months before of listening to the girl at the base's beauty shop. "The New Look," the girl had said in a thick southern drawl. "I'll make you look like Paris. Paris, France." It was the way the girl had seemed to be responding to what Cass regarded as the secret of her unhappiness that had made Cass say yes. "The change will cheer you right up," the girl had said. By now, at age thirty-four, Cass's hair was the color—her own color—of burnished copper, and even bobbed—it looked like a Chicago flapper's hair to Cass, not some chic fashion model's—her hair was still her glory. But the hairdo had seemed to change her into someone else, as if even the gum-snapping beautician knew that the real Cass Dillon was not good enough for Generals' Row.

She pulled her gloves on and began to walk. She passed the houses of the other generals without seeming to see them, as

if to look would turn her into a statue of salt. She refused to
worry anymore who might be watching at those curtains as she
strode the length of the tidy street. The wives of the other generals had yet to extend an invitation.

It still stunned Cass that the main effect of Sean's sudden reception into the world of prestige and power had been to make
her feel, for the first time in her life, inferior. In his Pentagon
world, she knew, literally thousands of men owed Sean deference, but here, in her corner of Bolling, all of the women out-
ranked her. She could identify the wives of General Eason,
General Cabot, General Polk and a dozen others, having seen
them at the swimming pool in the summer, at receptions in the
O Club, coming and going on the shady street and in the park
at the end of the Row, where Cass went with her son and
where other women went, when their aides didn't, with their
dogs. They acted not only like the wives of gods and heroes
but like goddesses and heroines themselves. And to Cass's true
horror, she had herself begun to think of those women that
way, as if they had been born to a higher order.

Cass might have taken the initiative with some of the generals' wives herself—they were neighbors, weren't they?—but
Sean had drilled her in the protocol that now was supposed to
rule their lives. Juniors, he said, do not extend invitations to
seniors. But Cass wondered, Was protocol his only inhibition?
He never referred to it, but Cass knew very well that even if
it was absurd to think the other women had been born to a
higher order, they were still quite different from her. The pink-
bordered roster of the Officers' Wives' Club, for example,
listed its members not only with the ranks of their husbands in
parentheses, but also in each case with another word that Cass
had failed at first to understand, the name of the woman's
school. The generals' wives seemed all to have attended Vas-
sar, which she had heard of, or places called Briarcliff or
Goucher, which she hadn't. Cass had pictured "St. Gabriel's"
inside such parentheses, and at that had felt her lack of education not as a mere regret, but as a matter of shame. Was Sean
ashamed of her too? That was a question past which she strode
as if it were a blank-windowed officer's house.

Cass Dillon was no fool. She had known right off that she
had to find a niche for herself in her husband's new world. She
had wasted little energy bemoaning her background or lack of
it, or waiting for the Mrs. Generals to call. Instead, she had in-

stinctively pushed open the one door on the entire base that
was locked to no one. She was on her way to open it again
now. As she did every morning, once Sean had left, she was
going to the chapel for Mass. Her devotion here was a measure
not of her piety, but of her savvy intelligence.

She walked briskly out of the generals' enclave, past the
club and its now tarp-covered swimming pool, down the hill to
the corner on which the little wooden church sat with its un-
adorned steeple. The dozen entrance stairs were covered with
cocoa matting. Instead of stone, the steps were of wood and
made a hollow, muffled sound. As she took them she stifled
the usual feeling of foreignness. This was still a Protestant
church to her, not only its prim white exterior, but the interior
too: its amber, unstained windows, its unornamented white
walls, the bright mysterylessness of it. The pews were as white
as the walls, and the carpet was the same pallid blue that covered the floor and chair cushions in the Officers' Club. Cass
knew she would never forgive the place its lack of saints'
statues—no Joseph, not even Mary—or the blankness of the
walls where the Stations of the Cross should have hung.

Two dozen other people, mostly men in uniform, were already kneeling here and there around the chapel with their
heads in their hands. It never failed to move Cass that men
outnumbered women at this Mass, young men, airmen with
stripes on their sleeves and spit-polished shoes. At St. Gabriel's
they would never have come to the early morning weekday
Mass, and she wondered what stresses of barracks life drove
them here now. She crept a third of the way down the aisle and
genuflected, which was not strictly necessary, since the Blessed
Sacrament was not reserved here. There was no sanctuary
lamp requiring the obeisance, but the blank Protestant cross
had been removed from the wall behind the altar, and its framing blue curtain had been drawn back to expose the true crucifix, the Catholic cross with its near-naked tortured body of
Jesus. Cass was genuflecting to Him and to the transformation
His presence worked upon the cold, uninviting place.

She stepped sideways into the pew, fumbled for the movable
little stool—instead of the sturdy fixed plank of a Catholic
kneeler—and settled onto her knees. The stool was covered in
crisp needlepoint, not dimpled leather padding, and against the
stretched skin of her knees she felt the tiny threaded grid.
Flowers decorated those stools, she knew, lilies, roses of

Sharon, palm fronds, all embroidered on the same washed-out spineless blue that the air force splashed everywhere.

Like the others, Cass covered her eyes to pray, but before the consoling shadow of God's presence fell across her mind, the altar bell rang once, announcing the priest's entrance. She stood. The altar boy, leading Father in from the side door, was a robust young man in uniform, not a child in the effete gown of a miniature priest. Her breath caught in her throat as she admitted that some things she liked better here; she preferred the unapologetic manliness of the congregation. She quickly surveyed her fellow worshipers again, the familiar backs of their heads, their butch haircuts, their bright, pulsing necks around which it was so easy to imagine mothers and girlfriends clasping arms. In addition to the airmen, there were two—no, three—men in officers' uniforms, insignia gleaming on the epaulets of their jackets. She had not mastered those various symbols of rank, bars of silver and gold, stylized eagles and leaves, but she knew, since none wore stars, that they were not generals. To her knowledge, Sean was the only Catholic general on the base.

Only four other women were present, and all were familiar to her, especially a middle-aged bespectacled woman who always wore the same out-of-fashion cloche hat and a brown wool coat slightly frayed at the collar. For a while now Cass had had the distinct impression that the woman watched her carefully each morning as she approached the communion rail. The woman herself, Cass had noticed, never received, which was unusual in someone who attended daily Mass. Sensing her interest, Cass had intended to approach the woman, but she was always gone before Cass herself left the church. The other ladies at Bolling avoided Cass because she was not enough of a general's wife. Did this one do so because she was too much of one?

Now the woman seemed intent only on her prayers, and following her example, Cass took out her own rosary. Cass blessed herself, kissed the cross and, putting everyone out of her heart except her Richard and her Sean, placed it so gently in the outstretched hands of God's mother.

After Mass the priest followed the server off the altar into the sacristy. The chaplain's assistant—Cass still did not know the difference between an assistant, an orderly, and an aide—appeared carrying the long-handled brass candle snuffer. After dousing the two candles, he moved easily about the sanctuary, collecting the cruets and altar linens. He then stripped the altar bare, folding the cloths with care, a function which in all parishes was performed by ladies of the altar guilds and sodalities. The masculine cast of religion in the military seemed complete, and Cass found it easy to imagine the priest of this church genuflecting before the makeshift altar of the hood of a Jeep parked on a rough hillside, then raising the sacred host above the helmeted heads of GIs on the morning of a big battle. She did like religion here for the way it included men, but also, always at this moment, the lack of roles for lady volunteers left her feeling useless, which was exactly how she felt at home, where the high-spirited, ingratiating sergeants did all the cooking, cleaning and shopping.

Cass finished her prayers and left the chapel just as the orderly drew the blue curtain back across the crucifix, hiding it. Outside, to her surprise, she found the priest waiting at the bottom of the stairs. He was in his blue uniform, necktie, shoulder bars and all. Only the stark naked cross on his left lapel marked him for a chaplain. He could have been a Methodist.

"Good morning, Mrs. Dillon." He touched his cap. He was a tall man, blond and good-looking, younger than she was.

"Hello Father Boyle."

"I was hoping to have a word with you."

Cass smiled with real pleasure. She admired this priest for his easy way with the enlisted men, the clear sense he and they had that he was there for them. He had rarely addressed more than a few formal words of greeting either to Cass or, on Sundays, to her husband. "I'd be delighted to have a word with you, Father," she said. "Why don't you come back to my house and I'll give you some coffee."

"No thanks, Mrs. Dillon."

"I've been meaning to invite you. Besides, it's cold." She grinned, turning up the collar of her tweed coat.

"It will just take a minute, Mrs. Dillon. I wanted permission to send you a proposal for—"

"Permission! Father, really!" Cass laughed. She noticed the woman standing a dozen feet away near the curb of the street, the woman in the cloche hat. As if aware of Cass's quick glance, the woman looked up sharply. Cass realized that the priest had been speaking to her.

The priest was blushing, which made Cass want to blush

too. She had never felt such deference from a priest before. He said, "It's about the National Shrine. There's going to be a military chapel, dedicated to soldiers, sailors and airmen. We are all expected to help with it."

"The National Shrine! The Shrine of the Immaculate Conception?"

"Yes."

"My son was baptized there."

"Have you been out there lately? It's really coming along."

"I knew Monsignor Barry when he was rector."

"The bishop? Bishop Barry?"

"Yes." Sean was not the only one who'd been promoted. The priest who'd been so nice to them was now the auxiliary bishop of Washington. "I still think of him as monsignor."

"Well, that's another reason. Bishop Barry would be delighted if you took a part in helping with the military chapel."

"Well, *that's* another reason for you to come for coffee."

The priest glanced awkwardly back at the other woman. She pointedly avoided his eyes.

"Oh, I've interrupted—"

"No, I . . . That is . . ." Father Boyle reached an arm toward the woman. "Allow me to introduce you."

The woman raised her eyes and smiled shyly.

"Mrs. Dillon, this is Mrs. Jones."

"Hello, Mrs. Dillon."

"Mrs. Jones?"

"Yes, ma'am."

"Are you Sergeant Jones's wife?"

"Yes, ma'am."

Cass almost blurted out, *My* Sergeant Jones? Instead, she crossed to her and touched the tips of her gloved hands to Mrs. Jones's hands. "My goodness, I think the world of your husband."

"You do?"

"He's a good man. I can tell from the way he treats my little boy. Rickie loves your husband."

Mrs. Jones's eyes went to a spot on Cass's left shoulder. "We have no children of our own."

"I know." Neither woman spoke for a moment. Cass's heart flowed toward her. Now she understood why the woman didn't go to communion. She said, "I didn't know he's a Catholic."

"He's not. I'm the only Catholic."

"Well, he's proof you don't have to be. Your husband has been teaching me all the things I'm supposed to do. Did he tell you how new I am?"

Mrs. Jones nodded. "He likes it, with you and the general."

"I'm glad."

Father Boyle stepped between them. "I didn't know this," he said, and there seemed more than a hint of rebuke in the expression with which he turned to Mrs. Jones. "Your husband works for General Dillon?"

"Yes."

"You could have told me that."

Cass touched the priest's sleeve. Where was his deference now? "Why should she have?"

"Because I was going to ask you to head up the officers' wives' committee."

"I didn't know that," Mrs. Jones said miserably.

"I don't understand," Cass said.

"I already asked Mrs. Jones to head up the NCO wives."

"That's all right, Father. I don't have to—"

"What's the problem? I don't see the problem," Cass said. The priest backed away. "I'm sorry."

"No, wait a minute. You have to explain to me what's wrong here."

"If Sergeant Jones works for you, then it might be awkward . . ."

"I didn't know Father was going to ask you, Mrs. Dillon."

"And what are these committees to do?"

Father Boyle said, "Sodalities and altar guilds see to the finishing decorations for all the Shrine chapels, which mostly commemorate immigrant groups. The servicemen's chapel will be finished by military wives' committees organized through the chaplains. There will be committees from Fort Meyer, Andrews, Fort McNair, Bolling, the marine barracks and Anacostia."

"So why are there two committees from Bolling?" Cass laughed. "It's not like there are that many of us Catholics."

"That's standard, Mrs. Dillon. There will be two separate committees from all the chapels, one for officers and one for enlisted personnel."

"Why not one committee? Aren't we one family in church? I've never heard of this before."

Instead of answering, Father Boyle glanced at Mrs. Jones. *She* knew how these things worked.

Cass said, "I invited you for coffee, Father. And you too, Mrs. Jones. Please come to my house for coffee."

Mrs. Jones's uncertainty disappeared.. "No, that would not be right."

"What, serving a priest and a fellow Catholic coffee in my home? How in the world could that not be right?"

Mrs. Jones replied matter-of-factly, "You would not be serving it." Then she added, "My presence would embarrass my husband."

Cass's visceral and by now habitual impatience with mindless military barriers became something else. What block of the imagination had kept her from picturing Sergeant Jones extending the creamer to his own wife? What's *wrong* with this picture? She had no choice but to turn this moment away. She said to the priest, "I meant it about the Shrine, Father. I'm devoted to that church. If military women are supposed to help with it, I must be a part of that. Mrs. Jones and I won't have any problem, will we?"

Mrs. Jones shook her head.

"So you'd head up the officers' wives' committee?"

"Maybe if it's for the Shrine, then the military protocol could take a backseat to the way, well, to the way the Church works."

"What do you mean?"

"I'd be glad to serve on Mrs. Jones's committee. With her as the head, I mean." The priest hesitated. Cass pushed him. "This is the air force, isn't that the point? Aren't we starting fresh as a service? Who says there have to be separate committees? Maybe at Fort Meyer or Anacostia, but this is Bolling." Cass turned toward Mrs. Jones and addressed her as if they were alone. "I've only been an air force wife for six months, but nobody has been one for a year yet. We're the ones starting the traditions, aren't we? We're the ones setting what is 'standard.' What do you think? Your husband wouldn't be involved. Neither would mine."

Mrs. Jones said simply, "If there was one committee, the officers' wives wouldn't join, and neither would the NCO wives. Where would that leave us?"

Suddenly both women laughed.

Cass felt the jolt of an energy she had not experienced in

months. But at once she wondered, Am I really so hungry for a way into the life here? And what way was this? Do I just want to feel superior to someone? She would not have to worry about Mrs. Jones's school, that was sure.

But Cass Dillon would have offered herself like this to the chief of staff's wife if Mrs. Eason had let her. Uncowed by the requirements of an alien society, Cass was simply being who she was. They stopped laughing finally. For a long moment neither spoke, then Mrs. Jones said, "We could have coffee at my quarters." Her gentle smile brightened the air between them.

Cass understood in a way she would not have only minutes before what a violation of the "standard" even this invitation was. "That sounds lovely." Cass removed her glove and they shook hands, each surprised by the feeling that joined them.

Cass added self-mockingly, "But your 'quarters'? How long did it take you to get used to calling your house 'quarters'?"

"It isn't a house. We have a small apartment in the barracks."

"Oh." Cass felt dizzy to think she'd offended the woman again.

But Mrs. Jones squeezed Cass's fingers. "It's nice, though," she said, with such patent satisfaction that Cass envied her.

Late in the afternoon of that same day, Sean Dillon was summoned to Randall Crocker's office. When he arrived at the anteroom, the receptionist simply opened the inner door ahead of him, with no announcement, which was the first clue that something was wrong.

The second was the presence in Crocker's office of General Eason and General Macauley. Eason was seated in a wooden armchair next to the long leather couch, on which Macauley sat alone. Behind the couch was the familiar wall-sized polarvantaged map of the world.

Even apart as they were, the pair of four-star generals mirrored each other, sitting rigidly, their hands stubbornly capping their knees. Dillon saw them for an instant as perpetrators—"perps" in the old parlance—waiting in a holding cell.

Crocker was loose in his chair behind his huge desk, but for once on Dillon's entrance his face remained as perfectly buttoned as the vest of his brown suit. His pipe was jammed firmly in the side of his mouth.

Behind Crocker stood Lloyd Nevin, deputy chief counsel of the air force, the civilian attorney whose office supervised all air force–related testimony on the Hill. Nevin, a taciturn man, was exceptionally tall, and Dillon sensed that he had remained standing behind the secretary as if this were a courtroom, as if the intimidation of his height would be useful.

Crocker removed his pipe to say, "Hello, Sean." The others barely acknowledged his arrival, but still Dillon sensed how they had been waiting for him.

Dillon nodded toward each man in turn. At Crocker's gesture he took the ebony chair, the twin of Eason's, that was equidistant between Macauley's couch and Crocker's desk.

Crocker said, "You know that General Macauley was testifying before the House Armed Services Committee?"

"Yes, sir, I know that."

"About the B-36."

"Yes, sir."

Dillon glanced quickly at Macauley, who stared sullenly at a spot in the air. Eason was lacing and unlacing his fingers, but otherwise seemed to be in the same trance with Macauley.

"Well," Crocker said, "We have a problem." He leaned to his desk and pushed a set of papers toward Dillon.

Dillon went to the desk to pick the papers up, four pages of closely typed material. He returned to his chair to read it.

The pages were plain, headingless typing paper; at the top of the first was the brisk salutation. "To Whom It May Concern." The typescript was broken into a series of short paragraphs, each separated from the other by a double space.

As Dillon read through the pages he was aware of Macauley's refusal to watch him. What is his problem? Even while reading, half of Dillon's brain stuck to that question.

The document was an enumerative description of the technical shortcomings of the B-36. Most of the first three pages seemed to assert variations of one theme, that because the huge bomber was originally designed as a propeller-driven aircraft, its modification with the addition of a pair of two-engine jet pods made it "an aeronautical engineering mustard cluster." Design flaws were listed in language—"four-blade pitch," "synchronous thrust," "hydraulic constant speed," "radial air-cooled," "in-line liquid-cooled"—that meant nothing to Dillon. Was he supposed to offer an opinion of these assertions?

But on the last page, the tone of the document shifted from

the technical to the polemical, and he suddenly understood why he'd been called in here, and why Macauley and Eason seemed paralyzed.

"The question remains," he read, "why such a patently inferior aircraft should have been chosen for development by the air force. And the answer is simple. Senior air force officials have, for more than two years now, been recipients of secret cash bribes from Consolidated Air, the manufacturer of the B-36."

Dillon looked up sharply at Crocker. "What is this document?"

Crocker swiveled toward Nevin, who answered, "Congressman Newfield of California produced it at the hearing today. He identified its source only as a constituent of his who is an employee of Consolidated Air, an employee, the congressman said, whose conscience would not allow him to remain silent any longer."

"But the committee accepted this? An anonymous accusation?"

"Newfield made it a point of personal privilege. He said if he were to identify the man, the man would be destroyed."

"But the congressman claims to know him?"

"Yes. 'A senior engineer at Consolidated.' Newfield vouched for him absolutely. That's why the committee bought it."

"Was it a public hearing?"

"We had gone into executive session, thank God."

Dillon resumed reading. "The most egregious of many violations has been committed by General Mark Macauley, the commander in chief of the Strategic Air Command, on whose recommendation this year the air force request for the inferior B-36 airplane was increased by a factor of three. General Macauley's request for one hundred and twenty B-36s was made the same week, in April of 1948, that one thousand dollars was deposited in his wife's savings account at the First Nebraska Savings Bank on Ames Street in Omaha, where Offutt Air Force Base, SAC headquarters, is located. Over the next four months, three more deposits, each totaling exactly one thousand dollars, were made to that account. Bank records will show that all four of these deposits were made in cash money. During that same period, General Macauley took four vacation trips in the company of Albert T. Carver, the president of Consolidated Air. These trips were taken at Carver's expense, in Carver's private airplane, and on one of them General Macauley was accompanied by his wife and two daughters, whose expenses were also covered by Carver. Bank records will show that the deposits in question took place on the days subsequent to each of Macauley's returns to Omaha. In addition to moneys already received, General Macauley has been promised by Consolidated a further cash payment of ten thousand dollars, to be made on the day that the full appropriations for the B-36 have been formally approved by the U.S. Congress."

Dillon looked up at Macauley, who was now staring at the pages as if he expected them to burst into flame.

Then Dillon looked at Nevin. "What do you make of it?"

"A disgruntled employee." Nevin shrugged. "Somebody senior. Obviously somebody who has been in on the design process."

"How would an engineer at Consolidated in California know what General Macauley did with the money in Omaha?"

Macauley broke in, "Wait a goddamn—"

"No, *you* wait, General!" Crocker aimed his pipe stem at Macauley, sighting along it.

Dillon was still looking at Nevin, as if they were the only two in the room. "How did you respond?"

But Macauley slammed his knees. "Respond, shit! I wanted to punch that son of a bitch in the—"

"That's enough!" Crocker ordered.

Macauley fell back against the couch.

Crocker turned to Dillon. "Nevin quite properly requested an immediate adjournment. Macauley has made no response on the record yet. The hearing reconvenes tomorrow morning."

"Can't you get it postponed?"

Crocker shook his head. "Vinson smells blood. We're lucky he didn't force a response on the spot. Committee members were livid, wanting to pounce, and those friendly to us— Patterson, Keogh and the others—were as stunned as General Macauley was. Patterson objected, but Vinson wouldn't hear him. He admitted it for the record, that, that—"

"That bullshit," Macauley said.

Dillon dropped his eyes once more to the pages in his lap. "How much of what's written here is bullshit, actually, General?" As he awaited the answer, and then as he listened to it, he continued to scan through the pages.

"Everything it says about the airplane is wrong. Those jet pods don't alter the aerodynamics of the thing one iota. The jets give it five thousand feet more altitude and increase speed over target by twenty percent. The original design foresaw those engines—"

"But are these criticisms within the realm of the technical debate? Do you believe the author, in other words, knows what he's talking about, even if he's wrong?"

"Is he an engineer, you mean?"

"Yes."

"If he's not, he had access to the Consolidated files. Some of those objections have been made. They've all been—"

"What about you, General? How much of what it says about you is true?"

Macauley's eyes went involuntarily to Crocker, then to Eason. Dillon realized that both had been grilling Macauley just before his own arrival. Now Macauley, with his furtive, pathetic glancing, was asking if he had to explain himself yet again, and to this asshole.

Crocker said coldly, "Answer General Dillon's question, please."

"I took my wife and girls once to California on Carver's airplane. Otherwise, I've done nothing—"

"What about the money?"

"Las Vegas. I won that money in Las Vegas. It's just across the state line from Consolidated's desert testing strip. The deposits went into Ginger's account because I always give her the first round number of what I win."

"What does that mean?"

"If I win in the hundreds of dollars, she gets a hundred. If I win in the thousands, she gets a thousand. The money has nothing to do with Consolidated."

"Who else knows about this arrangement you have with your wife?"

"Nobody. You think I brag about it?"

"Somebody knows, General. Will the bank records bear this out, these deposits, each one a day after your return?"

"Probably. But I told you, that money had nothing to do with Consolidated."

"How would a disgruntled aeronautical engineer get hold of your wife's bank records, though?"

"Who the hell knows."

"And the vacation trips?"

"Vacation, hell! Those were serious meetings, every damn one of them! At the flight-test strip, which is where the last phase of developmental research goes on. I've been working on the goddamn prototype. The B-36 is *my* airplane. I'm the one they have to damn well satisfy. *Me!* That's why Carver flew me out there."

"And once your family."

"Yes. A mistake, I admit it. My Ginger and the girls went on with Mrs. Carver to L.A. to see the houses the fucking movie stars live in. I didn't see the harm in it."

"But you do now?"

"Yes."

"And while they went to L.A., you went to Vegas."

"I never went to Vegas until after I worked my butt off in—"

"Who went to Vegas with you?"

Macauley hesitated. "Sometimes Carver. Sometimes other people."

"Your people? Or Consolidated's?"

"Both. Just a bunch of birdmen, you know?"

"Any disgruntled engineers?"

"Not that I know of. The people I dealt with all love that fucking airplane."

"This person calls it a 'flying coffin.' "

"He's wrong."

Dillon studied the pages in his lap for a moment, then looked up sharply to ask, "Who covered your expenses in Las Vegas?"

"What, my hotel and—?"

"Your losses, General." Dillon shifted toward Crocker. "A casino is a perfect place to wash a bribe. We used to see it in Chicago all the time, with judges and police captains. Interested parties would take them down to the open counties in Indiana or Kentucky and bankroll them at the gaming tables. The judge would simply stand there shooting craps or spinning the roulette wheel until he won. The winnings belonged to the judge or the cop, but the losses always belonged to the fellow who needed the favor. They would play until the judge's loot reached a pre-arranged sum. Then he was on his own."

Macauley leapt to his feet. "That's not how it was! That's wrong! I covered my own fucking losses!"

"Even when Carver was with you at the table?"

"Yes! Carver never—"

"How much?" Dillon was as cold now as Crocker. "On those four trips, when you brought back a thousand dollars for your wife, what were your totals? You won every time?"

"*Those* four times, yes. But other times I lost, plenty of other times. Hell, I lost thousands, but that damn letter doesn't mention those times, or the shit I had to take from Ginger." Macauley's voice dropped; here was the admission, the shame. "If there's bribery anywhere, it's what I had to give her to get her off my ass."

"What casinos do you favor?"

"What?"

"In Vegas. Where do you like to play?"

"The whole damn place. The Sands. The Golden Kettle."

"And when you go up to the window on your way in, who pays for your chips, General?"

"My chips?"

"Your gambling chips. Your ponies, your pebbles. Who buys them for you at the teller's window?"

"I do," Macauley swallowed. "I mean, mostly I do. Once or twice somebody might have given me a few. I don't remember."

"You don't remember?" Dillon exchanged a look with Crocker, who then closed his eyes.

"How often were you out there?"

"From last March, when the field tests started, through this past September, I was out there every two weeks at least. How many is that?"

"Fourteen times."

"All right, fourteen times. Fourteen at least. Every time they adjusted something I had to check it. It was my job to check it."

"And you usually came home with cash from Las Vegas?"

"I won more than I lost, but hell, I'm lucky." Macauley grinned at Eason, falsely, but Eason only stared at him glumly.

"General, you just told us that you lost thousands. Now you tell us that you're lucky. Which is it?"

"I won most of the time. But nobody was rigging it for me. Mostly it was in the hundreds. Mostly what I gave to Ginger was a C-spot."

Dillon said to Crocker, "Newfield's source would have seized on the four deposits because of the even thousand-dollar figure."

Macauley, still on his feet, stepped toward Dillon. "Well, do you believe me or not?"

"Believe what, General?"

"That I didn't do it!"

"General, that you didn't do what?"

"That I didn't recommend the B-36 because of bribes!" Macauley led with the wound in his voice. He reminded Dillon of a man who needed someone else to answer for him, as if he did not know *what* he had done.

Dillon had heard the sound of that same wound a hundred times before, and it always angered him. He wanted to say, We all have to answer for ourselves! But he put aside his urge to treat Macauley like a suspect, letting him dangle, prodding at his panic to see what was behind it. Whatever Macauley's violations added up to, Dillon knew instinctively—cop's knowledge—that of this massive, serious crime the general was not guilty. The head of SAC did not need bribes to make him want the B-36, any more than the air force itself did. "No, General, I don't think you recommend the airplane because of bribes."

"Unfortunately"—now it was Crocker speaking—"it can be made to appear that way because you accepted favors—"

"Hell, favors! Per diem is all it was."

"Your per diem comes from the United States government, General Macauley."

Macauley whipped around to face Eason. "Tell them, chief! Goddammit, tell them! I'm not taking this by myself!"

Eason looked sheepishly at Crocker. "Officers on TC—"

Dillon interrupted, "I don't know what that is."

When Eason looked toward him their eyes met for the first time since that morning on the generals' launch. "Technical consultation." Eason went on now to address himself to Dillon, as if he too finally recognized that the OSI director was the one to satisfy in this. "Officers on TC are permitted to draw a per diem from civilian contractors."

"As well as from the paymaster?" Dillon's words floated in

silence. "Are you telling me, General Eason, that the air force permits double billing of expenses?"

"We don't call it that."

"What are the regs defining this policy?"

"It's informal. Not a matter of regulations."

Once more Dillon let the silence build. Then he asked the chief of staff quietly, "Sir, do you remember a discussion we had once, in the air secretary's briefing room, I believe it was?"

"You were a civilian then."

"General Eason, it was a discussion about discrepancies in the way the system of law in the air force applies to general officers."

Crocker interrupted, "Good God, Dillon, double billing isn't the issue here. We have to develop a response to this slander—" He held his hand out for the document. Dillon crossed to give it to him. "I'd like to call it slander, Macauley, but I don't know, given what you've said, if I can. It slanders the airplane, I know that much."

"It slanders me, Mr. Secretary."

"Do you realize how vulnerable you are tomorrow? That minority counsel is going to have you for lunch. You and the air force too! Wait until those committee members hear about your per diem! About Las Vegas!" Crocker slammed the pages down on his desk, and one floated to the floor. Dillon had never seen him angry like this. "You've scuttled the air force here, Macauley. Do you understand that? If you cannot deny the allegations, *all* of them, in one sentence, you're dead! If you can't say it's all a pack of lies from A to Z, the B-36 is dead! And so is SAC, and so is the air force, except as a fleet of flying boxcars. That committee isn't going to sit still for a minute while you start making distinctions between what you won at roulette and what you took in per diem! Jesus! Congratulations, Macauley. You have just bought the navy a new strategic aircraft carrier fleet and a new light bomber!"

During this outburst Dillon had moved to pick up the sheet that had fallen to the floor. Now he stood by Crocker's desk, immobile, studying the page.

When Crocker had fallen silent, Dillon asked quietly, "What do we know about Newfield?"

Nevin answered, "A Taft Republican from Orange County."

"Did he serve in the military?"

"I don't know."

"Is he young enough to have been in the war?"

"Yes." Nevin stepped to the phone. "I know someone who can answer the question." Nevin turned away to place the call. The others waited. After a quick exchange, he hung up. "Newfield was in the navy. He is a captain in the Reserves, attached to San Diego."

Eason grunted. "You don't have to be Sherlock Holmes to know the navy is behind this."

"Can you prove it, General?" When Eason did not reply, Dillon asked Nevin, "What time is the hearing?"

"Ten o'clock."

"So what can we do, Sean?" Crocker seemed to expect no answer.

Dillon brushed the secretary's moroseness aside with the efficient clip of his response: "We have to keep General Macauley from being interrogated on this matter under oath. The way to do that is to shift the committee's concern away from the accusations in this document to its source."

"How do we do that?"

"I don't know yet." Dillon asked Macauley, "Who else could possibly have access to your bank records? An aide? Your exec? A lawyer?"

Macauley shook his head.

"Were you robbed in Omaha? Burglarized at any point?"

At first Macauley didn't respond, then he sat up. "Ginger's purse was stolen, right out of the commissary at Offutt. It disappeared from the cash-register table when she wasn't looking, about six weeks ago."

"Was her bankbook in the purse?"

"Yes, the savings book *and* the checkbook. We changed both accounts."

"Did you file an OSI report on the theft?"

"I put my provost marshal on it."

"Your provost marshal?" If Dillon was cold before, he was ice now. "And did your provost marshal solve the case?"

"No."

"And General, now that you need it as corroboration, do you suppose your provost marshal kept a complete record of the theft report, as the OSI surely would have, with a listing of the items inside the purse, including the crucial savings book?"

"He probably didn't."

Dillon could only nod mutely in frustration.

Crocker said, "Do what you can, Sean."

Nevin added, "Whatever you come up with, there won't be time to prep anyone else. You should come ready to testify."

"My advice to you, Mr. Nevin, is to assume General Macauley is going to have to explain himself. You'll need affidavits from his wife, both about the source of those four deposits in her account and about the theft."

"My wife! I won't allow—"

"General, if you had had the local OSI detachment handle the theft, we would not need the one affidavit, and the other is your only chance to head off a criminal indictment for bribery. You're lucky not to be in a court of law, where your wife's testimony would be inadmissible."

"My wife is in Omaha," Macauley said miserably.

"You're the air force, aren't you? You can have a plane out there and back by morning."

"Sean," Crocker said quietly, "we're *all* the air force here. The future of the air force is at stake in this."

"I understand that. But you will forgive me if I tell you that the fate of the air force is of secondary importance to me. My oath, even as a general office, is to uphold the United States. I don't have a position on the B-36. My position is on how this government conducts itself." He faced Macauley. "And, General, I have no interest in seeing you exonerated if you do not deserve to be. But this"—he held up the page—"is no way for the United States Congress to be making its decisions. If this is bullshit, I'll do my best to expose it as such."

Dillon sensed how the other men had ceded everything to him. He turned back to the desk and began to collect the other pages. "I'll need these overnight."

Nevin said, "You can't take the originals. I'll give you the photostats I had made."

"I need the originals."

Neither Dillon nor Nevin moved.

Randall Crocker said, "I think this is where I came in, Sean." He smiled, thinking of the similar standoff that occurred five years before, between Dillon and Crocker's insufferable old friend Cheever. "Drop it, Lloyd," Crocker said simply.

Dillon then reached farther across Crocker's desk to pick up an odd page of an unrelated report. He held it up to the light, then did the same thing with a page of the accusing document.

"Congressman Newfield said this came from a private citizen in California?"

"That's right."

Dillon lowered the pages. "Then why do you suppose it has a 'GSA–District One' watermark, like every other piece of typing paper in this building?"

Dillon replaced the odd page on Crocker's desk, nodded at the secretary and crossed to the door. Only there did he stop, turn, draw himself up and salute.

FIFTEEN

"General Dillon's residence, hello?"

"Cass?"

"Sean? Is that you?"

"I'm sorry I haven't gotten to you before this. I know it's late. Did you let Jones go yet?"

"Of course I did, hours ago. I thought I'd fry you a cube steak or—"

"That's not what I meant, Cass."

"What time will you—?"

"I won't be coming home at all tonight."

"What?"

"It's impossible to explain."

"I wasn't asking you to explain."

Silence.

Then, "Cass, I need your help."

"What do you mean?"

"Don't ask me to explain."

"I won't."

"I need you to bring the car, *our* car, the Studebaker, to the Pentagon, to the farthest section of the south lot, the side facing Shirley Highway."

"How can I—"

"First, drive to an all-night taxi stand. There's one at the Willard. Tell a taxi to follow you. Then, when you get to the Pentagon, leave the car there. Leave the keys under the seat, and take the taxi back. Tell the driver your husband works the night shift, a maintenance supervisor. Then take the taxi to the Willard. Wait for it to disappear. Then take another cab back to Bolling. The whole thing won't take forty-five minutes."

"You mean leave Richard?"

"He's asleep, isn't he? He never wakes up."

"I couldn't leave Richard alone. How can you ask me to do that?"

Silence.

"What about Sergeant Hewitt, Sean?"

"I sent Hewitt home. I can't involve my people in what I'm doing, and I need the car."

"What will you be doing with the car?"

"I'll be going downtown."

"To the Bureau?"

Silence.

"Why don't you use a Bureau car?"

"Cass, I called you because there are problems with every other way of doing this."

Silence.

"What if I bundle Richard into the backseat. He'll stay asleep, you know him. I could drive you."

"That's ridiculous, Cass. If I'm not going to involve the orderlies, I'm sure as hell not going to involve our child. Never mind. I'll arrange—"

"Wait, I can do it, Sean."

"How?"

"A woman I know from church. She lives on base. I could ask her to come over."

"She would? In the middle of the night?"

"It's only nine o'clock. I'd call her now. She doesn't have children of her own."

"You'd have to lie to her, say there's an illness or something."

"Don't worry."

"But she lives on base? Her husband's air force? I can't allow that. What I'm doing could backfire. The woman's husband—"

"He won't know anything. No one will. This will be between two women who meet at church."

"But she'll have to tell her husband something."

"She helps out at the base infirmary as a volunteer. She can tell him she's going there."

"Will she lie to—"

"It's been known to happen, big fellow. Let this end be my problem."

Silence.

Then, "All right."

"But, Sean."

"What?"

"I'm not taking a taxi home, not right away. I'm going to drive you."

"No, Cass."

"You have to let me."

Silence, and silence.

Then, "Wait for me at the far end of the south parking lot, on the edge near the ramp off the highway. No one will notice you. Sit there with your lights out. I'll show up between midnight and one."

"I'll be there. And Sean?"

"Yes?"

"Whatever it is, be careful."

"Thanks, Cass. I will. Oh, and bring my raincoat. My civilian one."

Half an hour before midnight Dillon left his office. He was dressed in his blue uniform with the star on each shoulder. He carried a leather satchel. Instead of going to his right to follow E-ring around to the massive center well of ramps that would take him down to the river entrance, he went left and circled away from the offices of the Air Staff. He greeted cleaners who were just finishing up, as well as the patrolling night guard, who knew him from his countless late nights. If either noticed that Dillon was going the wrong way, he gave no sign of it.

A few minutes later he was still in E-Ring, but on the second floor instead of the fourth. Here the walls of the corridor were a pale blue instead of green, and the paintings hung at intervals depicted ships instead of airplanes. No one would know him here, especially now. No longer dressed as an air force general, he was a white-smocked member of the night cleaning crew. Under his smock he wore the matching forest-green pants and shirt that were the maintenance workers' uniform. He was pushing a canvas-sided trash dolly. A broom handle stuck up from the cart, and a pair of washerwoman's rubber gloves was hooked on the side.

He cruised along the corridor, whistling faintly through his teeth, the wheels clacking, until he had located each of the three suites he needed. Then he returned to the first door, the fancy double one over which the gold-leaf sign read, "The Secretary of the Navy."

Dillon stood very still, listening. Not a sound came from inside, not a sound from either direction in the corridor. He took from his pocket a palm-sized, hinged set of lockpicks. He hadn't used it since the time during the war he'd covered Embassy Row, but he had also never disposed of it. The lockpicks, more than his gun would have been, or even his badge, were a relic of his time in the Bureau, though he had never expected to use them again. Certainly not on E-Ring.

Stooping, he eyed the door lock, then applied the slimmest of the tiny hooked steel rods. He pushed the pick, pulled it, then removed it altogether and selected another. He tested that one, then began to nudge it past each tumbler in turn until they were aligned. The slightest tug and click! The lock opened. He pocketed the tool, put on the rubber gloves before touching the knob, opened the door and went in. He pulled the trash cart in behind him.

Once he closed the door, the room was pitch dark. He had to stand frozen for a long moment while his eyes adjusted. He used the time to listen.

Nothing.

He reached into the trash cart, pushed aside a layer of rags and crumpled paper to take out a flashlight and a large manila envelope containing sheets of plain, government-issue typing paper. He swept the room with the beam of the light. He saw a spacious reception area, heavy furniture, chairs, couches, four desks separated by low, dark wood railings. At each desk was an adjoining typewriter table, each typewriter with its cover.

He began with the one immediately to his left. At the typewriter he took the flashlight in his teeth, like a football fan holds a hot dog. It filled his mouth, and the taste of the metal casing revolted him, but he was able to aim the cone of light as he uncovered the typewriter and rolled a piece of fresh paper into it. "Underwood," he read, and so he typed that word onto the blank page. Then he punched out every letter of the alphabet, in both cases, a clumsy procedure because of his gloves. He then identified the page, "SON, Recept, left #1." He whipped the sheet out of the machine and covered the typewriter, to leave it as before.

Dillon repeated this at the three other machines in that

room—Underwoods all—each with its own sheet of paper, each with its own ID. One desk displayed a nameplate, "CPO Allen Dietrich," and he noted that too. Then he moved through the five other rooms of the office suite, using his lockpick twice. He took samples from every typewriter, eleven in all.

From the secretary's offices he went to the undersecretary's—seven typewriters—and then to the chief of naval operations'—twelve. Only once was he afraid, and his first impulse then was to reach for the gun that he no longer carried on his hip. In the middle of striking the keys of a typing-pool machine, he heard the footsteps of the night security guard. The sound was like the radio as the guard passed in the corridor outside. He did not alter his pace and was gone quickly, but Dillon forced himself to remain absolutely still for the full count of five minutes.

Otherwise nothing else went near wrong. No one else came even that close to noticing him.

It was ten before one when he came out of the Pentagon, in uniform again, carrying his leather satchel.

He stood on the top step of the river entrance, looking across at Washington. The monument was no longer illuminated—the powerful spotlights which had been developed in the war as antiaircraft beams went out at midnight—but under the clear light of a glowing moon he could see the giant obelisk and the low outline of the other buildings. The hum of a car passing drew his eyes down to the shadows of the nearby river boulevard. He heard the car shift gears as it took the low hill of the bridge over the lagoon channel, but he never saw it.

Sean Dillon wanted that moment to last. He felt no urge to hurry away from the scene of his violation. He was standing at the very heart of what seemed a new nation to him, taking in the silhouette of its capital, but no longer, as he had for years, from outside it. He had come to this city a decade before, when this same nation had seemed bereft. He himself had been full of yearning, but without knowing for what. Now he knew. Yearning for this, a role that mattered, a way to move this world, to affect it, to make it know that he had come here.

Cass was sitting in the Studebaker on the passenger's side. He opened the driver's door and got in, saying nothing. He put the satchel between them, on top of the tan raincoat she had brought. Dillon started the car, snapped on the lights and put it into gear. He drove out of the lot toward the Shirley Highway access road, but at the point where it forked short of the highway, Dillon surprised himself by turning into the dark, abandoned lot of the Hot Shoppe, the small drive-in restaurant long since closed for the night. It was exactly the turn Dillon had taken once years before at the direction of Walter Dunlop, his FBI boss at the time. They'd been coming from Dillon's first meeting with Crocker, the event from which his entire life since had taken its shape. Dunlop had ordered him to stop there so that he could call and find out if Cass was still alive.

Sean stopped the car abruptly and pulled on the brake.

For a moment he stared out through the windshield at the illuminated wedge of blacktop, feeling as if he had just awakened from a dream. He turned toward Cass.

Her eyes welcomed him.

Pushing the satchel and raincoat off the seat, he reached across to her. As if she had somehow anticipated his all but unprecedented impulse, as if she knew the moment of his brimming had come at last and he could not stop himself spilling toward her, she went into his arms. They kissed.

Not even he had known that this was why he'd called her. Not the car, this. They were standing together against Canaryville all over again.

If they had been different people, or the same people in a different time, if the act were not loaded with a fearful, mortal consequence, they would have come out of their clothes right there in the car, but not even sexual intercourse would have been more an act of love than their prolonged, heated and, to them, already dangerous embrace. When finally they pulled away from each other, there was no question of speaking.

Dillon's hand shook as he adjusted the gearshift.

Cass kept her hand from trembling by pressing it on his thigh. She sat close to him, like a high school girl, as they drove into Washington.

Instead of going up Fourteenth Street, past the hulking Bureau of Engraving, Sean turned off on Maine Avenue.

"Why are you going this way?"

"I'm taking you to Bolling."

"But I was going to—"

"Darling," he said quietly, "darling." He fell still, then continued, "You were going to help me." He looked at her. "Wasn't that it?"

She saw in his eyes, in their absolute black center, the first sign that she had ever seen that his desire, his insatiable, mysterious, frightening desire, had been fulfilled.

"You were going to help me tonight, with this thing I have to do. Wasn't that what we both wanted?"

"Yes."

"Well, you have. You already have," he said so simply.

At 10:07 A.M. on November 17, 1948, in Room 340 of the Old House Office Building, Chairman Carl Vinson banged his gavel. The dust flew off the inclined mahogany surface in front of him, rising in the morning light that streamed through the palatial windows to his left. With that, the executive session of the full House Armed Services Committee came to order.

The hearing room was a spacious chamber decorated in florid style, with curved plaster molding on the ceiling and pierced shellwork lining the wall behind the dais. The dais itself, from the center of which Vinson presided, was like a mammoth altar, but with a pair of curved wings behind which sat the other committee members. The wings extended toward the rest of the room, as if to engulf it. Above the dais hung a brightly illuminated three-tiered chandelier, and at intervals around the dark paneled walls, matching crystal sconces glowed in the subdued light of the curtains drawn against the room's four large windows.

The witness table in front of and below the dais stretched across the room from one side aisle to the other, and seated there now were General Macauley, Lloyd Nevin to his right, and a mustachioed, portly air force colonel to his left. Somewhat apart from those three, but still at the long table, another pair of civilians huddled; and at the opposite end, also apart from Macauley, were General Dillon and another civilian. Dillon, like Macauley, was wearing a crisp, fresh uniform with a stiff shirt and a perfectly knotted blue tie. His left breast pocket, compared to Macauley's riot of ribbons, had never seemed more the stretch of blank blue serge. Back of Dillon's chair was an easel holding yard-square display boards.

Behind the witnesses, because the session was closed, nearly all of the spectators' chairs were vacant. One pair of seats was taken, however, by General Eason and his exec, and another pair, at some distance toward the rear, by Randall Crocker, accompanied by Secretary Forrestal's deputy. A lone navy captain sat in the last row, a notepad balanced on his knee. Near the firmly closed door sat the sergeant at arms.

This was an unusual session for any House committee, simply by virtue of every member's being present. Not a chair at the huge dais was vacant. The congressmen leaned forward on their elbows, Vinson of Georgia and Newfield of California, but also Allen of Pennsylvania, Thompson of New York, O'Connor of Massachusetts, and a dozen others. Behind them, on the raised platform, were another dozen stenographers and aides, but none was moving. Vinson had had to strike the gavel only that once.

"General Macauley, you remain sworn. Do you understand, sir?"

"Yes, Mr. Chairman."

"Good morning then, sir."

Macauley nodded. Dillon, glancing sideways, sensed how the bomber general's fingers itched for a cigar.

"We await your statement, sir."

Lloyd Nevin leaned to the microphone. "Mr. Chairman, if it so please, before General Macauley responds to the document introduced into the record yesterday by the honorable congressman from California, the general would like once more to hear the honorable congressman's statement as to the document's origin and authorship."

"Not necessary, counselor. Not necessary at all. Congressman Newfield's statement is in the record."

"I understand, Mr. Chairman. I was thinking of those members not present yesterday." Nevin glanced along the full length of the dais. "I assume their attention has been drawn to the document in question, and copies have been provided."

"That's correct."

"My thought, sir, was to be sure the entire committee understood—"

"Mr. Chairman! Mr. Chairman!" Fuller of West Virginia, a Democrat and an air force ally, took the hint and now had his hand raised. "Point of information, Mr. Chairman. I for one was detained yesterday, and I do note the lack of attribution, which frankly troubles me. Given the gravity of what it contains, I would like to hear about the author of this—"

"Mr. Fuller, we have Congressman Newfield's statement that this document was provided him by a constituent, that there are good reasons for anonymity. We have a member's word here, sir. And that settles it."

"But, Mr. Chairman—"

Down came the gavel.

"The chair entertained objections to the anonymity yesterday. On the strength of a colleague's solemn assurances as to the integrity of the submission, the chair overruled those objections and does so again. Now, General Macauley, if you please, sir."

Nevin once more preempted Macauley. "Mr. Chairman, for the record, sir. These are charges of a most serious nature, both as concerns the national security and the character and the conduct of a distinguished officer who, in leading over two hundred night air raids over Germany, risked his life—"

"Mr. Nevin, if you please."

But now Newfield spoke up. "Mr. Chairman, by your leave. If I can dispose of this by repeating what I said yesterday, I will gladly do so." Newfield was an owlish man whose dark-rimmed spectacles seemed too big for his face. The way he hunkered down on the dais made him seem even smaller than he was. Facing Vinson, he seemed the supplicant waiting for permission.

Vinson nodded impatiently.

"I was provided this document . . ." Newfield held up the dark pages of his photostat. Nothing in him hinted at insecurity or guile. His words were edged with, if anything, the melancholy of a reluctant witness. ". . . by a man personally known to me as a resident of the thirty-ninth congressional district in the state of California, and further known to me as an employee of the Consolidated Aircraft Company. For obvious reasons, given the unprecedented disclosures made in this document, I accept the author's contention that to reveal his identity at this time will result not only in the unjust destruction of a long career, but also in a terrible purging retribution among employees of firms contracted to supply the new Defense Department. We must protect such patriots who put country ahead of self in order to make sure that the Congress is informed of what is really going on in some of these companies."

Nevin had Newfield's eye. "And the manner in which the document was delivered to you?"

"Personally handed to me."

"In California?"

"Yes."

Vinson slammed his gavel. "Counselor, you are not interrogating Congressman Newfield."

Nevin sat back.

"Now, General Macauley, if you please!"

But once more Nevin darted to the microphone. "Mr. Chairman, since the allegations in this document involve not only extensive criticism of the B-36 airplane, but also and especially acts purportedly committed by senior air force officers, which, if true, would amount to numerous felonious violations of the law, the secretary of the air force was obliged by statute to immediately begin an official investigation of those allegations. Therefore, Secretary Crocker ordered the director of the Air Force Office of Special Investigations, General Dillon, to undertake said investigation. The first part of General Macauley's response, which is the air force response, is to be presented by General Dillon."

Vinson shook his head. "An investigation in its most preliminary phases won't tell us what only General Macauley—"

"Not preliminary, Mr. Chairman. General Dillon's investigation is complete. He has conclusive findings and is prepared to present them. I defer to General Dillon."

Vinson peered across at Dillon, made a show of studying him.

The eyes of all those politicians looked down on him, like the eyes of jurors, Dillon thought. He sat straight and still, aware that with his own eyes he had thrown up a solid, unmoving wall.

"All right," Vinson said. He flicked his head at a clerk. "Would you kindly swear the general in."

Dillon stood, raised his hand and, led by the clerk, made his oath in a loud, firm voice.

"For the record, General, would you state your name, rank and present position."

"Sean Dillon, brigadier general, United States Air Force. Director, the Air Force Office of Special Investigations."

"Which is what?"

"Mr. Chairman, the OSI is responsible for criminal, counterintelligence and security investigations within the United States Air Force."

"It's a new agency, isn't it?"

"The OSI was formally established by a directive of President Truman on June 2, 1948."

"Just six months ago."

"That's correct, sir."

"And you already have the capacity for far-reaching overnight investigations?"

"We do the best we can, Mr. Chairman."

"Well, by all means then, General, do us the honor of reporting your findings." The chairman fell dramatically back in his chair.

Dillon turned to the easel behind him and took a yard-long rubber-tipped pointer from its ledge. He removed the covering blank display card and stepped back so that all of the congressmen could see the first exhibit. It was a photographic blow-up of the entire page of Newfield's document on which the explicit accusations against Macauley were listed. Dillon made a point to stand there reading the text to himself, allowing the members to do likewise. Displayed in such a way, the charges against the famous general were more sensational than ever. In the center of the blow-up, in red ink, were the four perfect lines of a box which set several sentences apart.

Finally Dillon took a step closer to the easel. "Gentlemen, you all recognize this page." He tapped it once with the pointer. "Page four of the document in question. I draw your attention to these particular lines, and these words." He made his indication with three swift circles, then, with a practiced flourish, he removed the card and placed it behind the easel, to expose the next, which showed an enlargement of the center section of the four lines inside the box. "I want to draw your attention to the actual characters imprinted on this page by the typewriter keys themselves. This *r*, for example, the notch on its arm, here. This *n*, the blurred foot, here. This uppercase *B*. Notice the break between the two curving halves, which with the naked eye one would never notice."

Dillon removed the card to expose another on which the same letters were blown up even larger. Each character was now the size of a human hand, and at that scale had begun to lose its definition. Dillon outlined each letter, as if to restore its focus, then touched with his stick the same points of detail he had identified on the previous card.

"As you may know, every typewriter machine leaves what you can think of as its own fingerprints, minute but characteristic flaws or eccentricities in the typeface which, when seen under the microscope, set an individual typewriter apart from every other typewriter in the world. Same as our fingerprints do for us. It is possible—"

"General Dillon, you have our attention with your charts and what-not, but . . ." Vinson aimed along his index finger, without adjusting his posture. He remained sprawled back against his chair like a cornerboy at a backroads Georgia filling station. "What do you mean to tell us, son?"

"Mr. Chairman . . ." Dillon braced the pointer with both his hands. "I'm going to tell you who the author of this document is."

"We know that."

"No, sir. With all due respect, you do not. And again with all due respect, the authorship changes the meaning of these accusations materially."

Vinson glanced noncommittally over at Newfield. When Newfield refused to look back at Vinson, Dillon resumed. He reclaimed attention by slapping the card with his stick. "This exhibit was prepared by forensic experts, who at my request conducted an analysis of the typeface of Congressman Newfield's document, here"—Dillon pulled the card half free of the easel—"and found it to match exactly the face of the typewriter which produced these characters."

He took the card away and handed it to the man seated near him at the witness table. The card remaining on the easel showed the blow-up of a page on which only the alphabet was printed. In the left lower corner of the card, four specific letters were lifted out in even larger magnification. "Note the r, the notch on its arm, here; the n, the blurred foot; the uppercase B, the break; the g, the broken tail.

"An exact match of two separate samples, this one supplied by Congressman Newfield, and this one . . ." Dillon paused, touching the letters again while the congressmen had no choice but to hear the potent sound of their own silence. ". . . taken from the typewriter on the desk of one Stephen Warner, a special assistant to Eliot Weld. Mr. Warner may indeed be known to members of this committee, because his job title is special assistant for congressional liaison. Whether Warner is the author of the document in question, it is certain that said document, including the highly incriminating charges made against General Macauley, was typed not in California and not on the typewriter of an unnamed employee of Consolidated Aircraft, but on Mr. Warner's personal typewriter, which sits even now on his desk in Room E-347 at the Pentagon, in Arlington, in the suite of offices belonging to Eliot Weld, whom you all know as the undersecretary of the navy."

Vinson sat slowly forward. The creaking of his chair seemed amplified. "What are you saying?"

"The anonymous document attacking both the B-36 and General Macauley, as well as other, unnamed senior officers of the United States Air Force, comes from the office of the undersecretary of the navy."

"Are you saying Weld is behind this?"

"I restrict myself to matters of fact. The typewriter is in his office. As of now, under my guard."

"How do you know for certain that matching type sample came from the navy typewriter?"

"I took it myself, from the machine on Mr. Warner's desk."

"How did you know to do that?"

Dillon shrugged slightly, his only answer.

"And who did you say conducted this analysis?"

Dillon put his hand on the shoulder of the man seated near him. "Special Agent Erik Simmons, the chief of the Document Section of the Laboratory Division of the Federal Bureau of Investigation. His complete report . . ."

Simmons reached into a briefcase and produced a stack of pages several inches high, which he placed on the table and pushed toward the clerk. The clerk came, collected the copies of the report and began to distribute them among the committee members.

". . . is available to you there, and Mr. Simmons is prepared to testify if you require further elaboration."

For a few minutes there was a lull while the congressmen cursorily reviewed the FBI report.

At last Vinson craned toward Newfield, who was sitting immobile, staring at the square of his handkerchief, which he had stretched between his hands on the wood surface before him. It was as if he were trying to press the wrinkles out of the cloth. Vinson said coldly, "Does the esteemed member from California have questions for the witness?"

Coerced, Newfield sat forward, peering at Dillon through his oversized spectacles. His previous self-confidence was gone. He bunched his handkerchief, twisting it as he spoke. "I'm frankly stunned by what you are saying. The man identified himself to me as, as"—Newfield glanced toward Vinson, then back at Dillon—"as an employee of Consolidated."

Dillon rebutted him immediately. "Congressman, we heard you assert only moments ago that the man was known personally to you."

"Well, yes, personally, but that was after I met him. Obviously if what you say is true—"

"You needn't take my word for it. The evidence is in the FBI report in front of you."

Newfield stared glumly at Dillon. "So you think I was duped?" He applied his handkerchief to his mouth.

"No, sir. I do not think that."

Newfield glanced about at his colleagues, who avoided his eyes.

Finally Vinson said slowly, "Your opinion, General, is that the congressman from California was *not* duped?"

"My opinions, sir, are not material. I am prepared to testify to matters of fact."

"Such as?"

"The undersecretary of the navy recommended to the Naval Promotion Board that Congressman Newfield, who holds a captain's commission in the naval Reserves, be promoted to the rank of rear admiral, lower half."

"When did this happen?"

"The recommendation was drafted four days ago. It was formally submitted to the board yesterday, but not until shortly after this committee's session was adjourned—the session, obviously, in which Mr. Newfield introduced the navy's poison-pen letter."

Congressman Fuller raised his hand slowly, as if pushing it through gauze. "Mr. Chairman?"

Vinson nodded.

"This committee owes an apology to General Macauley." Suddenly Fuller's voice shook with anger. "This is the shabbiest, most outrageous injustice ever done to a patriot, and I demand this committee make its apology to General Macauley!"

"And to the air force too!" another added.

A third congressman slammed the dais. "Be it moved that all materials and documents pertaining to the United States Air Force or its personnel introduced into the record of these proceedings by the member from California be hereby stricken from said record, and be it further moved that all copies of said materials and documents be collected by the clerk of the committee and forthwith destroyed!"

"Second!" half a dozen voices cried at once.

"Call the question!"

"All in favor?" Vinson said.

A chorus of "ayes."

"Opposed?"

Not a sound.

Once more Vinson looked at Newfield. "Carried!" Vinson's face had broken out in red blotches. He shifted toward the open room and pointed his gavel at the lone navy man in the rear. "You, Captain!" He waited until the man looked at him. "You get across the river right now. You tell Weld and this man Warner that before this noon they are going to receive subpoenae from this committee. You tell them to prepare an answer to this question: Why I should not hold them in egregious contempt of the United States Congress."

The navy captain sat there like one of the statues in the hallway outside.

"And you tell Weld he has better promptly reconsider any recent recommendations he has made to any damn promotion board! Did you hear me?"

"Yes, sir!" The captain stood up at his chair like a plebe.

Vinson swept his colleagues with a quick glance. "We will move through this appropriations question tomorrow. I want a quorum, gentlemen. I want to report this matter out and be done with it. And Mr. Newfield, I want you in my office now!"

Vinson raised his gavel, then stopped himself. He looked at Macauley, who sat slumped in his chair, pale-faced, his eyes unfocused. "General, for myself I do apologize to you. You have been ill-used. So has this committee."

Macauley stared vacantly up at him.

Before Vinson brought the gavel down, another congressman interrupted, one who had heretofore said nothing and whom Dillon could not identify. "Mr. Chairman, point of personal privilege, if I may, sir. I do have one question for the witness. For General Dillon, that is."

Vinson sat back wearily.

"General Dillon, this committee is in your debt. Your simple demonstration spared us a mighty embarrassment, not to mention what it did for your air force colleagues. I just want to know how you got that typewriter sample? Forgive me, I'm curious. Between yesterday afternoon and this morning, how did you do that? Did the secretary of the navy just let you come right in and sit at the typewriter?"

"*Under* secretary of the navy, Congressman."

"Well, did he?"

"Undersecretary Weld, I think it is safe to say, was unaware of my interest."

"So how did you get it?" The congressman smiled ingratiatingly.

"May I know to whom I am speaking?" Dillon already knew something. At the sound of the man's familiar, flat accent, he had tensed.

"George Delahunt, Democrat from the eighth Illinois."

"That's Chicago," Dillon said calmly, but inwardly he raged at himself. Delahunt! He'd seen a dozen different case reports on Delahunt, a Kelly loyalist. How could he not have recognized him?

"Yes, General, Chicago. St. Rose of Lima. A few parishes over from yours, I believe."

Dillon said nothing.

"We have acquaintances in common, General. Or we did . . ." Delahunt's hesitation had the effect of marking this as an announcement. "I knew Raymond Buckley," he said quietly.

Buckley? Dillon waited.

Delahunt said, "Raymond Buckley gave me my start in politics."

Sean Dillon wanted to say, And have you followed in his footsteps? But he could not. Nothing would move. Raymond Buckley was still in Joliet prison, but it threw Dillon totally to have his image invoked here, as if Buckley were a source of Dillon's shame.

"Now will you tell us, General, how you obtained that typewriter sample from someone's private office overnight? For example, did you have a warrant?"

Dillon took hold of the back of the chair behind which he was standing. "My warrant?"

"Yes, General, your warrant. The legal basis for your search of another's property or premises."

Buckley? Warrant? "You are thinking, I suppose . . ." Dillon was like a stunned fighter, clinching, bobbing, holding on for an opening of his own. "That is, what body of law . . ."

The opening he needed was in himself. Buckley. Buckley. And then he had it: Buckley was the key. An opening not to shame but to indignation. Who do these bastards think they are? "My warrant was in the charge . . ." he brought an arm up, and it was weighted by his clenched fist. ". . . to counter the false and malicious misrepresentation of the actions of another, libelous detraction, slander, a calumny . . ." He was falling back instinctively on the first language he had learned, the language not of the law or the military, but of the Church. ". . . against one of the few true heroes of our nation and our time!" Dillon's arm shot toward Macauley. "Have you forgotten already what these men did for us? What they did for the world? This committee carelessly allowed their essential virtue to be called into question, and with theirs, our very nation's. My warrant, sir, is not the question. What was yours?"

Delahunt sat back against his chair, disinclined to answer.

The other members were silent, unsure what had just happened.

But Vinson was not so easily cowed. "Perhaps your warrant *is* a question, General. You entered the offices of the navy *when* exactly?"

"Last night. Near midnight."

"Accompanied by?"

"I was alone."

"Well, I know they don't just leave the doors ajar over there. Who opened the doors for you?"

"I opened them myself."

"Well, *did* you have proper warrant?"

Dillon almost said what was true. It never occurred to him to worry about a warrant. But then he recognized the vacuum in the law and instinctively moved into it. "No warrant is needed to enter a house if asked to do so by its owner."

"Which in this case means?"

"You, the Congress. My charter is a matter of statute. As director of OSI, I have authority to approve investigative access to any federal facility when a matter of the security of the United States Air Force is involved. Warner and Weld do not occupy private offices but public ones, and the typewriter involved is government property. My warrant to investigate such property is implicit, especially in a case like this. Calumny is one thing, Mr. Chairman, but the navy document also makes improper and illegal use of highly classified information about a top-secret weapon system. Whatever this committee in its wisdom chooses to do about those responsible, we in the air force intend to prosecute them for grave violations of the National Security Act."

"I can see, General, that the air force has a bulldog in you."

"No, sir." Now Dillon did look across at Macauley, meeting his eyes for the first time that morning. It was to the stunned Macauley and those other general-heroes who would hear from him that Dillon said simply, "Not a bulldog, just a cop."

All Dillon saw when he came out of the Old House Office Building was the dome of the U.S. Capitol across Independence Avenue. It shimmered brightly in the late morning light, and the backdrop of dull clouds moving against the gray-blue November sky made the dome itself seem to be falling toward him.

Spread before the Capitol was the formal park, bordered by a languid, curving drive, that ran across the hilltop plateau to the Library of Congress, which had *its* dome, shaped like a huge green lantern. A flock of pigeons swooped, like a single creature, from one dome toward the other, infiltrating the leafless branches of the huge old elms that an aging Thomas Jefferson was said to have planted.

Dillon watched the birds. The damn birds, he thought, as if he'd never left the stockyard. Birds were messengers of an independence he would never have.

He saw what he was looking for then, figures in the distant park of a woman and a child.

Cass saw Sean, waved and began to run toward him.

Richard, dressed in a blue cap, a blue coat, and flashing saddle shoes, stayed behind, playing in the grass. He was chasing the pigeons. Sean imagined scooping him up in the crook of his arm, bulling through the line, a touchdown. The thought of Rickie's laughter cheered him.

Cass. His eyes went back to her as he started to move, that lithe woman the very sight of whom released him. That she had come to him the night before meant they had done this together. What happiness it was to want, at last, to go not just to their son, but to her.

But then Dillon heard the sound of Randall Crocker's

wooden leg. The secretary came out of the building behind and took Dillon's arm. "Sean, Sean." Crocker steadied himself on Dillon to flourish his stick. "Patterson just told me we have the votes. For the first time ever, the air force has the votes. And you did it, Sean! You put us over! You're launched now, Sean! You're launched!"

Once Dillon would have been only grateful for such an affirmation from this man, but now ... now things were far more complicated. Crocker's delight inspired an entirely new thought, an upsetting one. Dillon was instantly cautious. "I appreciate your saying so, Mr. Crocker, but I still have a problem."

"What?"

"I meant what I said in there. We have to bring charges under the National Security Act against those responsible."

"We might do better to drop the thing, Sean."

"Then I have a question to ask you, sir."

"What?"

"Are *you* responsible?"

"What are you asking me?" Crocker let go of Dillon's arm.

"Were you behind that letter? The letter that I just exposed as coming from the navy? I had an uneasy feeling while I was testifying, but only now do I see what it was. I saw the expressions on the congressmen's faces as they realized they'd been set up, but now I wonder. Was I set up too? Exactly to finish off the navy. Set up by you."

"By me?" he said quietly, offended. "Sean, what can you be thinking?" Crocker pushed down on his stick with both hands. "You just *proved* where that letter came from."

"I established what machine it came from, not who typed it. I went into the navy offices in the middle of the night. You could have done the same thing, knowing I would go in on my own afterwards."

"What, burglarize Pentagon offices? Christ, I never thought you'd do that. It never occurred to me."

"Just answer the question. Did you write that letter or not?"

"No."

"Did you have it written?"

"No."

"The navy did it, as I just testified?"

"Yes."

"Then why would you drop it? Why wouldn't you prosecute?"

"Because someone has to stop this nonsense. We're not at war with the navy, whether they are with us or not. Don't start thinking like these people, Sean."

"You say I'm launched, but I ask into what? Have I already become one of them? Delahunt had his reasons for asking me about a warrant, but he also had a point. If it had been against the law, what I did last night, I wouldn't have cared. I was going to do it anyway. I was going to do whatever was required. And why? To save Macauley's reputation? Or to save the B-36? Or to save the air force? Why?"

"You were going to do what was required because I asked you to."

Dillon stared at Crocker, shocked to realize that what he'd said was exactly true. He saw what a huge investment the older man had made in him, and now it shamed him that he repaid it with—

Crocker finished Dillon's thought. "Yet now you're suspicious of me."

"I said once in front of you and the whole Air Staff that I believe in original sin. I believe we are all capable of a corrupting self-interest. That's what makes me suspicious. You hired me because of it."

"No, Sean, I hired you because you know the difference between lies and the truth. That is a rare knack around here. I'm telling you the truth now, and I expect you to see it."

"I do see it."

"I'll tell you one last thing, and I am only going to tell you this once. Maybe in some mad circumstance I would set up Macauley or others like him, but I would never do that to you."

Now it was Dillon who took the older man's arm, wanting to say he was sorry, but knowing not to.

"You were about to go to Cass. I see her there, across the avenue. You should go."

"Yes."

"Tell her what I said, that you are launched here, Sean. Tell her that bottomless faith she's had in you is finally justified."

Dillon smiled. "I couldn't tell her that."

"Then I will. Tell Cass this lonely old man wants an invitation to Sunday dinner. I want to get to know that boy of yours."

Dillon was startled at what he saw in Crocker then, the simple, open expression of a father's feeling for his son. How Sean wanted to be worthy of it.

"Now go."

Dillon turned toward Cass. It was true, she *would* understand the full meaning of his triumph, because it was her triumph too. But Dillon realized she would not understand the qualm it left him with, any more than Crocker did. That deep buried feeling—What have I done?—was his alone.

His eyes went to his son. How gleefully he played, dashing after one pigeon, then another, sending them aloft, then leaping with laughter, which seemed to carry all the way across to him.

Launched! Dillon's eager son was launching birds, carriers of his innocence, his absolute assumption that the world is, and always will be, only a delight.

Dillon saw that Cass was waiting for him on the far curb. An ache of love exploded in Dillon's chest as he left Crocker with an acknowledging wave and began to skip down the long staircase of the Old House Office Building. He ran toward her, crossing the street carelessly, flinging himself into her arms. She received him with a jolt of her own strength, halting the stampede of his feelings, stopping him absolutely—all but his eyes, which ran on wildly to Richard, as if the boy were in danger.

PART III

MEMORIAL BRIDGE

SIXTEEN

Historians would focus on 1963 and 1968 as years of the great American reversals, but the first half of 1965 was a turning point too. On the thirteenth of February of that year, the President launched the air war against North Vietnam, justifying it as an alternative to sending in GIs. Hardly more than a month later, because of guerrilla threats to the air base at Da Nang, from which Thunderchiefs, Phantoms, and Skyhawks blazed into the air, he sent in the GIs anyway. By April there were eighty thousand American soldiers in Vietnam. Announcement going one way, policy going another; inept improvisation shading toward deception—that quickly, the patterns of the entire war were set. Though the air force claimed its bombers "expended ordnance" only on roads, bridges, warehouses, trench lines, gun sites, river barges, trains, and odd "hooches," all they succeeded in permanently obliterating was the other future that young men of Richard Dillon's generation might have had.

That spring those young men had other things on their minds, of course, and had little reason to notice what was happening on the other side of the world. For Richard Dillon the first half of 1965 was nothing more than the second semester of his junior year at Georgetown. Not that he or his classmates were indifferent to large public events. Politics was a preoccupation among students, and so, after Kennedy, was the drama of government. As a Washington school tied in a particular way to the late Catholic President, a neighbor, Georgetown understood itself as a center of national consciousness. But a war in Indochina? Hadn't Laos been solved? And weren't things better in Vietnam too, once Diem was gone?

A fear of war had been a lively feature of student concern

since the missile crisis two years before, and that fear had been hammered into bone-melting terror by Kennedy's assassination. But exactly that dread—war, chaos, rampant enemies— had been soothed only the previous fall by Lyndon Johnson's victory over Barry Goldwater and then by the stunning promise of the Great Society. Now, in May, Dillon's class considered itself on the verge not only of an enchanted senior year but of a new hopeful era. After the world traumas of their first years at GU they felt frankly entitled to mark the boundaries of their concern for a while with the tidy walls of the college itself.

Dillon's feelings were somewhat less upbeat, perhaps, for after the inhibition of growing up a general's son in the literally guarded world of Bolling Air Base, life at the Jesuit college, with its strictures, had felt like more of the same. His father was a hero, of course, and throughout his boyhood Richard had reveled in his status. He had cruised around the base on his bicycle as if it were an old southern plantation and he were the owner's son. The pilots at Base Operations had bought him Cokes. The mechanics in the hangars had let him ride their dollies. The orderlies up and down Generals' Row had kept him in cookies, and in high school he'd made senior lifeguard at the Officers' Club pool. That Bolling had been his father's world had seemed no failing until he realized one day at Georgetown that he wanted a world of his own. Since by junior year he still felt like an interloper at the lively college, it had begun to seem to him that perhaps there would be no such place. At Bolling, as a general's son, he'd been regarded as a young lord; at Georgetown he carried himself like one of the guys, but in both places he felt like an outsider. Still, he wanted to believe that if he tried hard enough, in his studies, in some kind of school activity, and, of course, with girls, it was a feeling he could shake. He could belong.

So Richard Dillon was not obsessed with the fate of Vietnamese peasants that May. He was obsessed with the calculus course that jeopardized his three-point-oh; about refining his technique as a photographer for *The Hoya*, the campus weekly, to the senior staff of which he desperately hoped to get elected; and, above all, about his heartthrob, Rita Pinon, a Brazilian girl who was a sophomore in the School of Nursing and who, after putting the cold disk of her stethoscope against each of his nipples, had shrugged off her shirt and bra to let him do the same to her.

"Jesus, Cooney," he said, "if I told you what happened to me last night you wouldn't believe a fucking word of it."

"Fucking?" Cooney's eyebrows shot up, and he diddled his fingers at an imaginary cigar. They were two gangling kids loping across the brick quadrangle toward Healy Hall on a warm, sweet-smelling afternoon. They were dressed alike in chinos, blazers, and flying ties. Cooney was a reporter for *The Hoya*. Richard had his camera and light meter around his neck. They'd been dispatched by the godlike editor to cover some event at Gaston.

"Who says you can't tell me?"

Richard snorted. "If I tell you, you won't believe it."

"You mean I only believe what I don't know?"

"Via negativa," Richard said, and he began to laugh so hard that Cooney slapped his shoulder.

"Give me a hint," Cooney said, flashing his tongue.

"I'll give you one word."

Cooney stopped and faced his friend, forcing him to do likewise. Dahlgren Chapel loomed behind them.

"Stethoscope."

"Stethoscope?" A sly smile spread across Cooney's face. "Stethoscope?"

"Yeah."

"Where?"

Richard shook his head and started walking again.

"You shithead! You've got to tell me."

"Get yourself a nurse, Jerry. That's all I'll say."

"A nurse! You took the colored nurse out again?"

Now it was Dillon who stopped. "She's not colored," he said sharply. "Who the fuck says she's colored?"

"Well, spic then."

"She's Brazilian, you asshole. That's Portuguese, not Spanish."

"She's a piece, whatever she is. What'd you do with the stethoscope? Does her heartbeat have an accent?"

"You're an asshole, Cooney." Richard turned away and swung through the heavy arched door of Healy. This was the unornamented back entrance of the oldest building on campus; its soot-darkened Gothic spire punctured the Washington skyline as the Georgetown landmark. The door led directly to the main staircase, and Richard, feeling pissed and confused—Was she colored? Was that an issue?—began to take the stairs two at a time.

Cooney panted after him. "What is this meeting we're going to anyway?"

"You're the reporter, Cooney. I'm just snapping pix. Didn't you listen to Leo?"

" 'Teach-in,' " he said. "What the fuck is that?"

"Like a sit-in."

"So it's civil rights?"

"Yeah."

At the second-floor landing Dillon and Cooney wheeled out of the stairwell like a couple of firemen. They moved fast, not out of any real sense of urgency, but because that was how Georgetown men who mattered moved; they had appointments to make and checks to cash and speeches to give.

A pair of students bracketed the entrance to Gaston, each with an armload of leaflets. They brightened at the sight of Cooney and Dillon, who saw why. The auditorium behind them was nearly empty. Dillon took his leaflet and went in while Cooney paused to read it and then to ask questions of the students at the door.

A lone folksinger was on the stage, strumming his guitar, doing his best to sound like Phil Ochs. Dillon was a jazz buff himself—Brubeck, MJQ, Charlie Byrd. Folk music was too uncomplicated to be interesting. He felt the same way about rock 'n' roll, but wished he didn't. Even his taste in music made him feel out of it.

He approached the stage, uncovering his Nikon. From a position right below the singer he began to shoot. He liked the halo effect of the overhead light in the guy's hair, and as he snapped and cocked, snapped and cocked, he thought about the pictures he was taking the way he imagined Cartier-Bresson would.

A halo, an angel, a saint, an idealist: that's who these civil rights guys were. Richard admired people like that without understanding fully why he wasn't one of them. The singer's hair was almost as long as a girl's, so Richard knew he wasn't a Georgetown kid. He wore a leather fringed jacket, like Wild Bill Hickok, and Levi's. Not an angel, he thought then, but a lonesome cowboy singing his sad song, only instead of "Red River Valley," it was "The Times They Are A-Changin'."

Richard took a seat three chairs in from the aisle in the second row. He felt sorry for the singer, as he sensed that the others in Gaston were ready for him to finish. Scattered around the raked auditorium that could hold seven hundred were perhaps fifty people. On the stage, seated behind the singer, below the familiar bust of Dante Alighieri, were two scruffy-looking students. Each wore the mandatory jacket and tie but with a defiant carelessness that marked them as members of a small circle of misfits. Seated between the students was a white-haired priest, Father Gavin, who had taught Richard theology in his freshman year. He had never had a personal moment with the priest then or since, and he was certain the gaunt professor would not recognize him now. To Richard's knowledge Father Gavin had not been one of the Jesuits to go to Selma or otherwise involve himself with Martin Luther King. Maybe his being a civil rights neophyte was why the priest seemed so nervous as he listened to the mournful singer, then watched as one of the student organizers replaced the singer at the microphone. A few in the audience applauded the folksinger, but the priest only fidgeted with the cincture of his cassock. He glanced awkwardly at a sheaf of papers in his lap and then up and around at the venerable Gaston, as if Jesuit ghosts, their names emblazoned in gold around the ceiling—Loyola, Campion, Xavier, Marquette, Jogues—were about to judge him. Richard wished he'd brought his portrait lens as he lifted his camera, aimed at the priest and snapped.

"Welcome to the first all-university teach-in of the GU Committee of Concern—"

The microphone squealed suddenly, sending an ear-piercing screech through the hall. The student organizer jumped back with a faint yelp of his own. He was acne-faced and rumpled. Dillon sensed that he'd misread the guy's slovenliness as rebellion. He was just a slob, an incompetent slob. He had no idea how to deal with the runaway mike's feedback, and Richard found it impossible not to feel sorry for him too, even as he aimed his camera and snapped.

While the second student came forward to help tame the microphone, Richard opened the mimeographed leaflet he'd taken at the door. Only then, with a potent jolt of adrenaline, did he realize, from the bold words on the top of the page, what this meeting was. "A Teach-in," he read, "Against the U.S. Escalation of the War in Vietnam."

"Shit," he said under his breath, and he looked around for Cooney, who was just coming down the aisle toward him. Cooney was holding his ears against the feedback screeching which was intermittent now. When Cooney slid into the chair next to him Richard said, "They're peaceniks."

"I know. The priest is going to say the war is immoral."

"That's Father Gavin!"

"Huh?"

"You had him for religion, asshole. Freshman year. What do you mean, 'immoral'?"

"That's what the kid at the door said."

"What, he wants the Communists to—?"

"The Just War Theory. He's going—"

"Sorry, folks," the student organizer said. The sound system bucked once more, then settled down. The other student took his seat next to the priest. "Thanks for coming. We're really glad you're here. We know the turnout is down because of exams, but we wanted to hold this first teach-in anyway, because at campuses all over the country students and professors are meeting to consider the terrible realities of the . . ."

Cooney wrote furiously, trying to get down everything as the kid shifted into third.

Richard was struck immediately by the contrast between his appearance and his crisp, fluid expression. The kid was speaking without notes. Richard wondered if he was an organizer from another school.

". . . There are three questions to consider when we decide to inform ourselves more fully about Vietnam. One concerns Russia, one concerns China, and one concerns the nature of the conflict inside Vietnam. Is it a civil war or not? That is perhaps . . ."

Richard turned in his seat to quickly survey the hall. For the first time he noticed a tight knot of blue-clad students at the right side of the last three rows. They were a dozen ROTC cadets, and the sight jolted him. Except for the insignia on their epaulets, their uniforms were exactly like his father's, and Richard felt a rush of guilt for being there.

Strange how, when he faced forward, what sprang into focus in his mind was not the stage or the speaker but a clear image of his father's profile, framed against a dark automobile window beyond which, across the river, were the twinkling runway lights of National Airport. Richard was driving his father home from the Pentagon late one night, and they were cruising along the ridge of Anacostia Drive above the river valley. Serving as his father's occasional night chauffeur was a favorite chore of Richard's, and on this night, just a week before going off to Georgetown as a wide-eyed freshman, he had a question to ask. He always had a question for those rides, but this one seemed fraught.

"Dad, I have to decide something."

"About school?"

"Yeah."

"What is it?"

His father looked at him easily. Richard often had the sense that his father listened with a small part of his mind, the larger part having remained behind in the Situation Room where the JCS were staving off war in Berlin or Cuba.

"There's a form in the registration packet asking if I want to join the ROTC."

"Do you?"

Richard looked away from the road toward his father. Their eyes met.

"I don't know," Richard said, and it felt like a confession. He stared forward out the windshield again.

"Would it be air force?"

"They have all three. Air force, army, navy. There's a drill team. And the air force teaches cadets how to fly."

"You'd like that, wouldn't you?"

"Sure."

"What's the problem then?"

"Well, Rot-see, it's sort of like 'tin school,' isn't it? Compared to the Academy, I mean. Aren't reserve officers second class? Don't the regulars—?"

"Richard, that's a career issue." His father laughed. "Are you worrying about your career?"

"Yes."

"Rich . . ." He reached across the car to put his hand on Richard's leg. "It's your freshman year. You're just getting started. When I was your age I'd already decided to be a priest, and look at me now. I was way ahead of myself." His father's gesture, his free hand back toward his chest, was humorously self-deprecating, as if his general's uniform showed how far short he'd fallen. "Nobody expects you to make career choices now. You just concentrate on getting your education, and the Jesuits will see you get the best. I had the Jesuits, Rich. And you know how pleased I am you'll be at Georgetown. I want you to make the most of it. Big choices come later."

"But I have to decide about ROTC now."

"Make the decision based on now, then. Not on the rest of your life. Don't worry about Academy graduates looking down on you ten years from now." His father laughed again, and Richard realized condescension like that was something he had had to deal with. He could not imagine anyone looking down on his father.

"ROTC is a good way to get your commission. When you go in the service, whether as a career or not, you'll want to go in as an officer. But you can also do that through OCS later. Same with learning how to fly, if that's what you want."

"I thought you'd want me to do ROTC."

His father shook his head. "It's up to you, Rich."

Richard was silent for a long time. His father shifted in his seat and Richard saw in reflection on the windshield the flash of his gleaming silver stars, three on each shoulder. He was not sure, even, that his father was waiting for him to declare himself. At last, without daring to look across, he said, "I love the air force. You know that, Dad."

"I know."

"But I think I'll skip Rot-see for now."

His father nodded. "That's fine."

No problem. No fucking problem at all. Why then had Richard's immediate impulse been to find a sink and rinse out his mouth?

Richard raised his Nikon and discreetly aimed it at the cadets in the rear of the auditorium. He snapped a picture, then poked Cooney. "Look," he whispered. "Fly-boys."

Cooney swung around. "Jesus, what are they doing here?"

Richard faced the stage once more.

The student at the microphone was concluding his introduction. "So those are some of the questions. If it is a civil war, why are we interfering in it? If the Geneva accords said the boundary between North and South was to be temporary, how can we consider the North Vietnamese as foreign aggressors? And why wasn't the Geneva conference election held in 1956 when the boundary—"

"What about the terrorists in the villages?" a voice yelled

from the rear of the hall. "What about the Red murder squads?"

Richard did not have to swivel to know it was one of the ROTC cadets.

The student at the microphone was flustered at first, then, after glancing back at his comrade, began, "There will be questions and answers after."

"What about our obligation under the SEATO treaty?"

"And Ho Chi Minh was trained in Moscow!"

The student held up his hands, but instead of calming things, he shouted back, "Ho Chi Minh quotes Thomas Jefferson!"

The priest stood up at his chair while the cadets continued to yell at the student, but as the priest approached the microphone, even they fell silent.

The student looked sheepishly at the priest whom it had been his responsibility to introduce. This Jesuit was the only faculty member who would agree to appear at the teach-in. The student stepped aside for him, saying audibly, "I'm sorry, Father."

Father Gavin put the sheaf of papers on the lectern and slowly took his eyeglass case out from the mysterious folds of his cassock.

Through the lens of his camera Richard saw the flecks of dandruff on the priest's shoulders, and he remembered from theology class how Gavin had reeked of tobacco. His fingers were still yellow with nicotine, and now they shook slightly as he unfolded his glasses and hooked them around his ears.

By the time he began to speak, the silence in Gaston Hall was absolute. "Those of you who had my moral theology course know the distinction . . ." He peered out across the hall as he had over countless classrooms. A filmy vagueness in his eyes gave him an eerily distracted air, as if he weren't sure where he was. He looked old to Richard. ". . . between *jus ad bellum* and *jus in bello*. Moral reasoning about war requires two separate judgments: a judgment as to the justice of the war itself, and a judgment as to individual actions committed in the course of that war. Lacking full knowledge about the true character of the various aggressions in Vietnam—whether they derive from an invasion or a civil war, whether a violation of proper accords or fulfillment of treaty obligations—no one here is qualified to make an informed moral judgement as to *jus ad bellum*, but even a just war must be conducted according to the natural law which is manifest in positive rules of engagement, and on that score, in the matter of *jus in bello,* sad to say, the American government, mounting evidence suggests, is behaving barbarically!"

The priest's voice rose so shrilly on the last word that Richard heard Cooney gasp. Richard's camera sat in his lap, a dead weight. Father Gavin's abrupt display of feeling—so much dense emotion packed in that one condemning world—landed with such weight that Richard wanted to stand up and declare, I'm just here as a photographer. I don't buy this bullshit!

Father Gavin was holding sheets of paper over his head. "These are copies of letters," he said, "provided to the head of Clergy Concerned About Vietnam, letters from American soldiers, not statements by the President or the generals or polemic, for that matter, from irresponsible and unpatriotic radicals, but testimony from GIs themselves, men your age who are over there right now. They are the ones who lay bare the true character of this mismatch between the greatest power on earth and one of the poorest nations. Listen"—the priest found an exact page—"to this, from a young marine. 'The Vietcong aren't the only ruthless ones. We have to be too. Have to. You'd be surprised to know that a guy you went to school with is right now shooting a nine-year-old girl and her mother. Or throwing a Vietcong out of a helicopter because he wouldn't talk.' "

"Oh, bullshit," Richard said in a whispered exhalation, but the word carried and Father Gavin looked up abruptly to see who'd said it. Richard stared right back at him, formulating his rebuttal. The caption under his photo: "Priest Discovers War Is Hell." Big fucking deal. If GIs throw prisoners out of helicopters, then they get court-martialed, and fast. It is that simple. Richard Dillon knew better than this old-fart priest what the American military was about, and that certainly did not include shooting nine-year-olds and their mothers.

Father Gavin rifled his pages, then read from one. " 'In fighting over here I have seen things done that I know are war crimes. I have seen people killed that had their hands in the air. I have seen a man killed that was already hurt and had no weapons; the sergeant just cut his head off. Also a lot of people here are carrying around ears of people . . .' "

Richard stood up and climbed past Cooney, who was writing

furiously. He stooped to Cooney's ear. "Don't dignify that crap by copying it down. It's bullshit."

Cooney whispered right back, "He's a priest."

Father Gavin whipped his glasses off and fixed the two obnoxious students with a glare.

Once more Dillon looked right back at him. A priest should know better. Then, clutching his camera and meter, he turned and headed up the long aisle, aware that the faces of the other students were frozen with the shock they had in common. It was one thing to hear such accusations from an SDS kid ranting from a bench at Dupont Circle, but another entirely from this figure of the absolute.

Behind him Father Gavin resumed reading. " 'Before I start this letter, I want you to promise to forget it as soon as you've read it. Yesterday I shot and killed a little eight- or nine-year-old girl with the sweetest, most innocent little face, and nastiest grenade in her hand, that you ever saw. Myself and six others . . .' "

As Dillon approached the last rows of the auditorium, where the ROTC cadets were sitting, he looked over at them with contempt. Why are you letting him say this shit?

The cadets were cowed, shrunk in their chairs. One was blushing furiously, as if with shame, and that was too much for Richard. He stopped and leaned over the guy. "You don't believe him, do you? Why are you sitting here as if you believe him?"

The cadet looked up at Richard. There were tears in his eyes.

Richard shook his head, then wheeled toward the door. He saw the two leafleteers still standing there, and now he saw what he had missed on the way in: propped against a chair was a large poster of a Vietnamese child whose skin had been bubbled by napalm. Under the hideous photograph were the words "Why Are We Burning, Torturing, Killing the People of Vietnam?" Richard knocked the poster down as he went by it. It fell with a clatter. The two antiwar ushers leapt back. Richard gave one of them the finger, then looked toward the stage to see if, as he hoped, the priest had noticed.

Father Gavin was resolutely reading on. " '. . . isn't on one side. A week ago our platoon leader brought in three prisoners . . .' "

Richard started through the door, but when he heard the priest's next words he froze.

" 'This guy from intelligence had all three lined up . . .' "
Intelligence? DIA. His father. Sean Dillon, by now, was director of the Defense Intelligence Agency. Intelligence, that's Dad. Richard turned back to listen.

" 'One was a woman. He stripped her down to the waist and stripped the two men all the way. He had a little gadget I thought was a walkie-talkie or something. He stuck one end of this wire to the lady's chest and it was a kind of electric shock, because she got a read bad burn. From what she was screaming, my buddy and I could figure she didn't know anything.

" 'Then they took this same wire and tied it on the lady's husband and brother, but on their lower parts. I grabbed the damn thing and stuck it to the backass of the guy from intelligence.

" 'Ever since that day I've been sick to my stomach and haven't been out on patrol or anything. My sergeant tells me I'm suffering from battle fatigue and might get sent home.

" 'We wish we could send you a couple of those electrical gadgets to use on the powers that sent and keep us here. This must end soon or a lot of us will go nuts.' "
The priest had finished. The silence in the room had the feel of solid mass. The priest was staring at the ceiling, his glasses in his hands, communing with the ghosts, perhaps, of the dead Jesuits. Disapproval and despair, like dark angels, fluttered above him.

"Father?" Richard took a few steps down the sloping aisle. His hand was in the air, a dutiful petition.

Father Gavin looked toward him.

"Father, that's wrong, what you just did." Richard's voice, to his own ears, had an eerie calm. Was he nuts? "You can't slur military intelligence like that because of one—"

"What's your name?"

"Dillon."

"These are not isolated reports, Mr. Dillon. Merely graphic ones. U Thant asserts that more civilians are now being killed in Vietnam by American warplanes than by Communist terror. Our country may have begun with good intentions, but to achieve them we have begun to systematically commit evil acts. Have you had my moral theology course?"

"Yes, Father, I—"

"Do the ends justify the means, Mr. Dillon?"

"No, Father, but—"

"The evil our nation opposes in Vietnam does not justify the evil of our opposition."

"But, Father, American intelligence officers are not evil." Richard's voice had become too loud and he checked himself. What made the moment so strange, so "nuts," was the way it involved both an absolutely unprecedented act of defiance and a simultaneous, gut-reaction defense of the central principle of authority itself, the very spine of his life. "I won't let you just say that as if you were there, as if it's doctrine. American intelligence officers are not evil!"

"We are what we do, Mr. Dillon."

"That's right, Father. Including you." Richard turned. The poster showing the napalmed child was at his feet. He kicked it. Then he stalked out of Gaston Hill.

The cool evening air feathered Richard's hair as he cruised along with the top down. His car was a nine-year-old baby-blue Ford convertible, and even though he lived in the dorm at Georgetown he often drove back to Bolling. The Officers' Club had a dance band on weekends and Richard loved to take dates there, mainly because of Sergeant Foster, who had once been his father's orderly and now worked as a club steward. The sarge would greet him and his date just inside the awninged door as if they were VIPs. With the flourish of a continental maître d' he would lead them to a table on the edge of the dance floor. While the sarge got them drinks, no questions asked, Richard would take his girl into his arms and glide with her across the glassy parquet, waiting a few minutes before looking into her eyes, which would invariably sparkle with delight. At that moment Richard always felt something in him sag; what a phony he was to have brought her there, to have made her think it was his.

It knocked girls out, too, the way the helmeted air policemen at the main gate brought themselves to attention as Richard's car approached, then as he drove through, how they snapped off a salute. The sticker on the Ford's front bumper had three stars on it, just like the Lincoln, even though his father never drove the Ford and was rarely in it. The air policemen knew Richard and they knew he was no officer, much less a lieutenant general, but they always saluted anyway, and Richard always waved. When the top was down he usually said, "How you doin', guys?" But not tonight.

Tonight Richard waved feebly as he went through the gate, unable to come out from under the weight of the events in Gaston. The priest was one thing, but what he could not get out of his mind were the slanted, wet eyes of the little Vietnamese girl on the poster, eyes which had been pleading up at him just as he kicked it. The feeling was, he had kicked her.

He slowed down as he entered the tree-lined enclave of Generals' Row. Once an AP had pulled him over for speeding right in front of the vice chief's quarters. In the military such infractions were bumped up to the perpetrator's commanding officer, and in the case of dependents, like Richard, they were bumped to the father's commanding officer. It was an army brat's nightmare to get his father reprimanded. Richard would never forget the night his father had come home steaming after being called on the carpet by the secretary of defense himself. Richard realized later that the secretary had intended the sham rebuke over the traffic ticket as a joke, but it had been no joke at Quarters 64.

"64. Lt. Gen. Sean Dillon." The tidy sign caught Richard's eye as he approached the house. The sight soothed his rough feelings some. The house was exactly like a dozen others on the Row, and though it had seemed a mansion to Richard when he was growing up, he knew now it was nothing compared to the real mansions on Foxhall Road or in Georgetown. Still, it was the only place he remembered living in, and despite his complicated feelings about the base, he could not arrive at the house itself without a sense of relief. He pulled in behind a long black Olds. He knew that Olds, but it took him a moment to place it as the archbishop's. "Crap," he said, and his impulse was to turn right around and go back.

Coming here tonight was to have been like tagging-up. A quick touch of the bag was all he wanted, a glimpse of his father, the sharp crush of his mother's arms. With the friendly but formal archbishop here, Richard would have to sit down. He'd have to answer questions about his courses. At some point he'd have to reply to the archbishop's sly hint that he considered the seminary after Georgetown.

He opened the door as quietly as he could. Voices in the dining room. He went into the kitchen, and when he saw Sergeant Mack he put his forefinger to his lips. Sarge grinned at him silently while Richard tiptoed across the kitchen. They slugged each other's shoulders, an old ritual of greeting.

"Hey, Rich. How are you?" Mack's raspy whisper made Richard think of Louis Armstrong. The stocky Negro was built solid as a fist. It was easy to believe that twenty years before he'd been an all-army boxer. He'd started out as a mess hall cook, but now he'd been with the Dillons for nearly nine years, three full tours, which indicated how they prized him. Sean Dillon liked Mack because of his rough-edged manliness. Cass liked him because he neither ingratiated nor resented. She did not want a servant who seemed like one. She also liked him, though nothing was ever made of this, for being a practicing Catholic. Richard liked Mack for no reason, and had since he was fourteen. Sergeant Mack had taught him how to drive.

Those hours, his first at the wheel of the baby-blue convertible, which at the time was still his mother's car, formed the center of a set of cherished memories. With a kibitzing Mack at his side, he had bombed up and down unused stretches of runway at the naval air station adjoining Bolling, less a learner than a make-believe Sterling Moss. Mack had made him feel almost instantly, not that driving was easy, but that he, Richard, had a natural gift for it. For highway experience they took long drives out to Mount Vernon or upriver to Great Falls. Once, cruising aimlessly in the Virginia countryside near Leesburg, Richard had asked Mack how it happened that he was Catholic. The top was down and they'd had to speak loudly. Mack had shrugged and said his people, Kentucky farmers, had always been Catholic. When he'd sensed Richard's surprise—Negroes were Baptists, weren't they?—Mack had added easily, as if stating the most obvious and natural fact of all, "The people who owned us were Catholics."

"The people who what?"

"Owned us."

Richard felt the lumbering auto veer, and the sudden sense that he was going to crash the car frightened him. It took a moment for him to feel in control again. When he looked over, Mack was watching the corn fields pass, apparently expecting no reply.

"I'm fine, Sarge," he said now in a whisper of his own, and he had an impulse to tell him about the girl whom Cooney had called "colored."

"They don't know you're coming, do they?"

"No. The arch is here?"

"And Father Simms."

The archbishop's secretary, an effete priest who used too much cologne. It gave Richard the creeps to shake hands with him. Richard's theory was that the archbishop liked having Father Simms around because, by comparison, he looked like Joe DiMaggio.

"Who else is here?"

"Just the two."

"And my dad? He made it home?"

"Late, of course, which is why they're still at the table." The sarge picked up the coffee tray he had just prepared and offered it to Richard. "Surprise your mother."

Richard took his windbreaker off and crossed quickly to the orderly's closet to don a white waiter's jacket, then came back. "Right you are, Sarge."

Laden, he backed through the swinging door.

"Coffee, madame?" he intoned.

His mother sent up a shriek of pleasure. "Rich!"

She was the only one of the four to get to her feet, and he hated to turn her aside. "Careful, milady." He placed the tray on the sideboard. Then, with a young prince's panache, he gave her the hug she deserved, covering the pleasure he took in getting his with a hammy "Hi ya, Mom! How ya doing!"

The grave mood in which he'd driven across Washington seemed to have evaporated, so that when he turned to the others, his Joe College good humor had already brightened their faces. He shook hands with his father hungrily, glad for the unmistakable flash of the affection that bound them. Father Simms was as limp-wristed as ever, but he too seemed glad to see Richard. The archbishop clapped both his hands over Richard's, his way of deflecting the traditional kissing of his ring, not that Richard needed to be deflected. "My spiritual consanguino!" the prelate said, an old joke between them, referring to the mystical relationship supposed to exist between a priest and those he'd baptized.

Sergeant Mack appeared from the kitchen carrying a place setting which included a cup and a plate of the cake the others had finished. Cass patted the table, a place next to her. "Sit here."

Richard helped Mack serve the coffee before he did.

"To what do we owe this honor?" his father asked from the far end of the table. The question was put casually, but his father wanted to know. With a host's complete authority he had just laid aside whatever else they'd been discussing.

Richard sensed the intensity of his father's gaze. They hadn't seen each other in more than two months. Though Richard had come home for Easter dinner, General Dillon had been on an inspection trip; to Japan, Cass had said, but now Richard wondered, Had it been Vietnam?

"I needed a book." Richard smiled at Archbishop Barry. It surprised him, the pleasure to be had in a smooth, automatic lie in the prelate's very face. What a total shit I am, he thought happily.

"What book?" his father asked.

"Tertullian," Richard answered, on a roll.

"Ah, the Fathers of the Church," Father Simms put in. "Don't believe all that those Jesuits say about the Fathers." He winked. "They'll try to make you think Ignatius was one of them."

But his own father was not playing. Richard's nonchalance about schoolwork had long been a sore point with him. "You're not taking patristics this semester. You're not taking any theology course, are you?"

As if the word itself were a trap door falling open under him, Richard grabbed at it. "Theology?"

"Are you?"

"No, sir."

His father, staring at him coldly now, had cut right through the wall of counterfeit cheer behind which Richard had quite deliberately taken cover. A sledgehammer smashing through plaster would not have jolted him more, as he saw how close he'd come to pulling the sham off, home for an hour's cake and happy-talk, then heading out into the night and its secret, a true liar.

His father's eyes conveyed implicitly the command to come to the point, and perversely the image that flashed before Richard was that of Father Gavin staring at him across the stretch of Gaston Hall, like God.

"I came home . . ." he began, then faltered. Groping, he looked at the priest sitting next to him, then across at the archbishop. The crimson tab at the prelate's Adam's apple caught his eye, then the gold cord curving across his chest, the cross hidden inside his black coat. The clerical garb struck Richard for the first time as a uniform, just like his father's. He glanced along the table, three men in uniform; he saw his father's silver stars. "The world in uniform"—the line from *Gatsby* popped into his head—"and at a kind of moral attention forever."

His mother wanted none of this. She was happy just to have him home for a minute, no questions asked. He let his gaze rest on her. "I came home because I had some questions."

"What about?" she asked, but so sweetly and so full of womanly concern that he realized she'd misunderstood. He had told her on the phone the week before that there was a girl he wanted her to meet, and he sensed now that she thought that was what had brought him home. He wanted to reach to her and touch the wisps of reddish gray hair that floated by her ear. No, Mom, he wanted to say, not the girl. He knew how worried she was for him, that he get it right with girls, but that was because she thought he had inherited his father's perfect inhibition. Girls had as little to do with this as fucking Tertullian.

"What, darling?" she prompted.

"I don't think this is a good time . . ." It maddened him, how he had so preempted their concern. Was his need so obvious, so pathetic? They were waiting for him to explain. They were looking at him as if he were a hurt child. He was filled with loathing for himself.

His father said, "What's up, Rich?"

At last he turned toward him, but Richard saw a different image of his father. In his senior year at St. Anselm's, he had looked up from the mud of their opponent's end zone to see him—in that blue uniform, those silver stars—leaning against the fender of his staff car, smoking. His father had made it to the game after all! Had seen him score! The driver had pulled the car right onto the cinder track in front of the stands, the only car there. It didn't matter that when Richard looked over again a moment later—now from the huddle before the point-after play—his father was gone. That disappearance was part of what made the memory wonderful.

"Dad," he began, "I wanted to ask . . ."

His father's expression now, as at St. Anselm's field that day, was supremely self-satisfied, a manifestation to Richard not only of his father's absolute inviolability, but of his confidence that his son could simply never disappoint him.

". . . about Vietnam."

"What about it?"

For a moment Richard saw his father not as calm but as smug. *If this is so easy for you, why is it so hard for me?* To his surprise, what he felt again, as earlier toward the Jesuit, was anger.

"I want to ask you about intelligence officers and what they do to get their information."

"Well, I'm the man to ask."

His father's tone, if anything, was even more controlled, which made Richard feel crazy. Then, when he saw Archbishop Barry reach a sympathetic hand across to cover his mother's hand, he almost reached over to push it away.

"I'm talking about Vietnam."

"I know you are."

"Do intelligence officers try to make the Vietcong prisoners talk?"

"Sure." Sean Dillon nodded, still relaxed, but was there a faint charge in the way he reached for the sterling silver cigarette box? He tapped a Camel once, then put it in his mouth.

"Do they sometimes do things they shouldn't do?"

"Like what?" Sean Dillon snapped the lighter and took the flame.

"Pushing them out of helicopters."

"Helicopters?" Sean narrowed his eyes, perhaps because of the smoke. "You mean helicopters in the air? Airborne?"

"Yes."

"Don't be ridiculous, Richard."

"Do they use electric wires on people?"

"Electric wires?"

"Yes. Attached to their bodies."

"You mean torture?" Sean's breath rasped out of him, and it was clear that despite his earlier air of paternal omniscience, his son had stunned him.

"I guess so, yes. Torture." Now Richard was finding his own balance, and words which moments before had been literally unspeakable came out in a rush. "Do your people in Vietnam torture prisoners? That's my question. Do our soldiers kill women and children? Do our airplanes bomb schools and hospitals?"

"Richard!" Cass pulled her hand back from the archbishop's. "What do you—"

"Let him finish," Sean said.

"I am finished. You have to tell me, Dad."

The silence settled on the room, a vacuum. Their oxygen had been sucked away, especially the general's. He had been completely blindsided, and now was finding it impossible to pretend otherwise. The two clergymen had folded their hands on the table, mirroring each other. They sat now with bowed heads, pious and invisible. Cass glanced once at the door to the kitchen, afraid that Mack might have heard.

"You're right, Rich," Sean said finally. "I do have to tell you." His face was flushed. Though he tapped his cigarette as if pronouncing on the White Sox pennant chances, his voice had become tight and cold. "I'm glad you came home with this. I'm glad you came to me. Obviously some of the wrong people have been telling you—"

"A priest told me these things, and a lot besides. A priest!" Richard heard the note of triumph in his own voice, and underscored it by looking toward the archbishop. "A moral theologian! He said the escalation in Vietnam is immoral."

"On what grounds?" the archbishop asked sharply.

"The Just War Theory."

Sean Dillon waved his hand dismissively. "I can apply the Just War principles as well as anyone." He plunged into the argument with relief. Argument he could handle, discourse, dissertation. "It is immoral not to resist an unprovoked act of aggression. In order to apply moral principles, Richard, you have to start with accurate factual information. That's where these antiwar polemicists go wrong every time, including your so-called theologian. Where does he get his information?"

"He had letters from GIs. Letters they wrote home, letters to parents and girlfriends, describing terrible things. These were eyewitnesses. They said that intelligence officers—"

Sean shook his head so vigorously that Richard stopped.

"Terrible things happen in war, son. Some few soldiers disgrace themselves and bring shame on their country, but that in no way—"

"That's what I said, Dad. I defended you!"

"Not me, Rich. You didn't defend me. I don't need defending on this score. My people don't commit murder and they don't torture."

Shame? It shamed Richard to realize that having defended his father, he had just accused him. My people don't commit murder! It shamed Richard to have required such a statement from his father.

Son and father. Father and son. They sat frozen, locked together by what they were seeing in each other's eyes.

Finally Sean said, "I know all about those letters, Richard. The famous letters home. They are lies. They are fabrications. Some were written to congressmen, the gullible ones. They use information supplied by the Communists as part of their propaganda blitz. I've had to testify about it on the Hill."

"The letters are lies?"

"Where did the priest say he got them?"

"He didn't."

"Has your priest been to Vietnam himself?"

"No. I mean, not that—"

"DIA has charge of intelligence for this war, Richard."

"I know. That's why I—"

"And if murder or torture were committed by men in my command, do you think I would know it?"

"Yes."

"And what do you think would happen?"

"You would court-martial them."

"That's right. We interrogate prisoners, Richard. We don't coddle them. What armies learn from the men they capture saves lives. Do you understand that?"

"Yes."

"But there are rules. Strict rules. Rules set at Geneva. Rules we abide by absolutely. Do you think the other side abides by them?"

"I don't—"

"They do not. The Vietminh have murdered fifteen thousand village elders in the last year. The GIs who have been captured have been routinely tortured. The Reds torture our boys to death, Richard. They are a vicious, evil enemy. They are Communists. They have no morality. Saigon had just begun to make headway against them when the North Vietnamese came to the Vietminh rescue. Now there are tens of thousands of North Vietnamese regulars, fully equipped and heavily armed, in South Vietnam. What is the moral thing for us to do? Walk away? Pretend we don't know? Send flowers? Let the Iron Curtain close around another country? The South Vietnamese are people who have thrown off the Japanese and the French because of their love for freedom. Are we supporters of that freedom or not? You loved President Kennedy. So did I. What did he say?"

"He said we should support freedom."

"And that's what we're doing. We are supporting the South Vietnamese. The U.S. soldiers who are there are only guards at our bases. We don't send GIs or marines on offensive operations. Do you know that? And as for the air force, you mentioned hospitals and schools as our targets. That's slander, Richard, and it saddens me terribly to hear you repeat it. Pilots of ours, men only a little older than you, have died in antiaircraft fire they could have easily avoided if they hadn't been trying to make sure their bombs fell on military targets, and not on schools and hospitals. I know about this, Richard. Do you hear me? I—"

Richard said nothing. His father saddened? What Richard saw was his reined fury. His father had checked himself, but Richard knew what he'd been about to say: I know what targets our bombers hit because I help to pick them.

"Do you hear me?" Sean Dillon repeated.

"Yes." Richard answered miserably, feeling misused and misunderstood. To himself he added, It's what I said, it's what I said at Georgetown.

Sean snuffed his cigarette out and looked up at Cass. "Ring for coffee, would you?"

Instead of hitting the buzzer buried in the rug by her foot, Cass stood up and served the coffee herself. Once more a cruel silence had settled on the room. As she poured for Sean she leaned to whisper, "It wasn't him."

Unfortunately Archbishop Barry heard her, and her statement prompted him to raise his eyes, which fell on Richard. He asked, "Who was this priest?"

Richard felt the pulse in his head roar. "What? I'm sorry?"

"The priest who read these fabricated letters to you. Who was he?" The archbishop too was angry. Richard Dillon wasn't the only person whose baptism he'd presided over. Archbishop Barry had been associated with the President's daughter's conversion to Catholicism, and he was to officiate at her upcoming wedding at the Shrine. The archbishop considered himself a personal friend of the President's. Was he to take the news neutrally that a priest of his archdiocese was giving aid and comfort to the great enemy, not only of America but of God? "What is this priest's name?"

Richard looked helplessly toward his father. Sean Dillon said nothing. Not a muscle moved in his face. The backs of Richard's eyes began to sting, and to his horror he realized it was possible he would cry. But no. No.

He thought of crashing through the door behind him, but then Sergeant Mack would see him. No.

Somehow he summoned up an act of will. Looking back on this moment, he would understand that it had changed him. And no. He would not cry.

"I forget," he said, and he knew all at once that, despite his father's authority and the archbishop's, despite the anger that he himself had felt toward the hapless, duped Father Gavin—Priest Discovers War Is Hell—he would not now or ever tell his name.

"A moral theologian, you said." This was Father Simms, an effete detective. "At Georgetown?"

Richard shook his head. "I heard him at Dupont Circle this afternoon, a peace rally. The priest who spoke said he was from Massachusetts, I think. Or Minnesota."

"You were at a peace rally?" Sean Dillon asked quietly.

Richard looked at his father. He almost said, I was just there as a photographer, taking pictures. But that was the truth, and what he needed was another lie.

Richard had rarely felt this confused, so beaten silly by his own impulses, first this way, then that. For an instant he saw the face of that Vietnamese girl whose photograph he had kicked—of all things to kick! He believed that the people imaged in photographs were present in them somehow, what the Hopis believed. Photographs were like sacraments. What had possibly justified his violence toward that image especially?

"Yes," he said. "I was."

His father showed no reaction; not a muscle moved in his face, and his eyes were simply dead. But Richard felt, in his lie, that he'd kicked someone again. But his father? Oh, fuck.

His father, when he spoke, had purged his voice of feeling, which effectively, ironically, underscored his unhappiness. "You can imagine, I suppose, what I think of that."

Richard went inside himself, deeply and quickly, not replying.

"If you have problems with the war," he said, his voice soft as carpet, "you bring them to me."

But I just did, Richard thought.

"All right?"

"Yes." In Richard's sinking imagination, but only there, he heard his father say, Yes what? "Yes, sir."

SEVENTEEN

The Pentagon had a climate of its own. The temperature was kept at an even seventy degrees year-round, the only variable being the level of moisture in the air, which in winter was raised and in summer lowered.

July 28, 1965, was one of a string of sweltering days in Washington and the weather had made its citizens cranky and nervous. Inside the Pentagon, though, the men were unwrinkled and they moved through their concourses, corridors and ramps with the crisp feeling of expectancy. They were about to come into their own again, for this was the day on which the war they'd already begun fighting was going to be declared. Or so they assumed.

The President was addressing the nation at noon. Only the minuscule circle of his closest advisors had seen his text, but military men—the brass, but also JCS staffers and intelligence analysts, experts who had just accompanied the secretary of defense on his reassessment tour of Vietnam, compilers who had processed the daily dispatches from MACV, evaluators who had worked over the reams of indications data, summarizers who had drafted the mountain of follow-up white papers on force-level ratios, endurance estimates, morale assessments, North-South infiltration reviews, air interdiction effectiveness studies—all of these men knew already what the President was going to say, had to say, would go down in history for saying. "Stop swatting flies" was how a famous bomber general put it, "and go after the manure pile."

Shortly before noon Sean Dillon left his office on the third floor of E-Ring, the OSD area, Mahogany Row, and headed down to the windowless depths of the building. At a junction of two broad corridors a gate manned by a pair of armed Military Police officers marked the entrance to the JCS operations area. "Restricted," a bold sign read. "Warning. Unauthorized Entry Strictly Prohibited. JCS Credentials—Display Required."

Dillon had crossed into the area thousands of times in the previous four years, yet that, like the show of stars on his shoulders, counted for nothing with the stolid guards. He paused at their desk to sign the entry log and to produce his laminated security badge which he clipped onto the flap of his tunic pocket.

A long narrow hallway stretched ahead of him, its stout metal doors marked only with color-coded seals which alone indicated the activities going on behind them. One room was the secure conference chamber in which the chiefs of the services met, "the tank." It was there that Dillon presented the JCS each morning with his "All-Source Daily," the overnight intelligence summary.

Behind another door was the National Indications Center, referred to only as the War Room, with its panoply of communications equipment, projection screens, and computer consoles. Behind that door now, as always, a dozen men sat at monitors, tracking input from the unified commands and the warning systems.

As Dillon moved along the corridor officers passed him, colonels mostly. They were somber and tense, but they usually were here. They always moved, and did now, with the air of worried fans hustling to their seats as the game was beginning. None of these officers acknowledged Dillon, nor he them, but suddenly a four-star general cut across his path, Davidson, the air force vice chief.

"Dillon," Davidson said abruptly, coldly.

Dillon stopped. "Good morning, General." They were neighbors at Bolling, but Davidson had been on the job only a few months and they'd rarely spoken outside briefings. Davidson was a tall, thin man, remarkably like Dillon himself in physique, and as they stood facing each other the effect was mirror-like. Their blue uniforms were identical except for three crucial details. Where Dillon, even after all these years, had a single row of ribbons on his left breast, Davidson had half a dozen. It was in combat that men won military ribbons; Dillon's combat had all been in Washington. The space above the ribbons on Dillon's uniform was naked, but on Davidson's it displayed the bold silver wings and wreath of a senior command pilot. To the fliers Dillon was a "kiwi," a flightless bird. And, of course, to Dillon's three stars, Davidson had four.

"Your Interdiction Review was on the Air Staff table yesterday. We disapproved it, to put it mildly."

Dillon flinched despite himself. "That review went to General Wheeler and Mr. McNamara. It was not for the Air Staff to approve or disapprove."

"You completely ignored the findings of the air force itself. Don't you think the people assigned the mission have some idea whether they're succeeding at it or not?"

"Excuse me, General, but I did not ignore the air force findings."

"You dismissed them."

"Certain numbers, yes."

"You mocked them."

"The air force tally of 'structures' destroyed, I believe the figure was 6,912 in June alone. And those damaged, 1,947."

"The precision of our count bothers you?"

Dillon shook his head. He had to rein his impatience. He hadn't come down here for this. "Lack of definition, General, was the point of my criticism. What is a 'structure'? The target area is the Ho Chi Minh Trail, jungles and mountains, hundreds of miles of paths and unpaved roads. In evaluating the success or failure of air interdiction, what is the possible relevance of enumerating the demolition of huts?"

"Warehouses, not huts. Storage facilities. Depots."

Dillon stared at Davidson, wanting the stare itself to be his statement. But it wasn't enough. "Vietnam is not Europe, General," he said at last. "Of much greater relevance in determining the effectiveness of the air strikes along the Trail is the question of whether Vietcong supply levels have risen or dropped in the past six months. By every measure they have risen dramatically."

"Your report goes on about refugees as if you're the Red Cross or the Catholic Relief Service."

"Refugees are relevant not because we feel bad for them, General, but because in great numbers they can represent a critical mass of social disintegration. How could the air force assessment not even mention the fact that the bombing in Binh Dinh Province alone has put to flight eighty-five thousand people, one tenth its population?"

"We look at military effects, General. Isn't that what you're supposed to do? Aren't you military? And, for that matter, aren't you air force?"

Here it was, the nub of Davidson's complaint, and it surprised Dillon not at all. The DIA Interdiction Effectiveness Review had concluded that six months of the deadliest bombing since World War II had done little to stem the flow of supplies and soldiers from North Vietnam into South Vietnam. The air force, with Operation Rolling Thunder, had dominated the war to this point, and what it wanted was not the massive introduction of foot soldiers but an expansion of bombing, a shift of the target area from the obscure North-South jungle trails to the city of Haiphong, the Russian port of entry into North Vietnam, and to the far northern border across which supplies came from China. But the air force case depended on a faith in strategic bombing which the army had always denied and which the recent DIA report undercut. Now, with the President's imminent announcement of full mobilization, army troops would replace air force planes as the center of the American combat effort in Southeast Asia. To the men who lived with him at Bolling, Sean Dillon had stabbed his own branch of the armed services in the back.

"I am air force, yes."

"Well, you're carrying the army's water. All Wheeler wants is a piece of the action, but a land war in Asia? Is that what you want?"

"What I want isn't the issue, General. My job is to provide intelligence to OSD and JCS, and that is what I do."

"OSD, that's right." Davidson grimaced as if he'd just remembered something, that the water this son of a bitch carried wasn't even the army's. His clenched expression conveyed contempt, which, if articulated, would have been, You fucking civilian!

"I assume you're on your way to hear the President," Dillon said. He made a show of looking at his watch. "Isn't what he wants the issue?"

Davidson grunted and pushed past Dillon. At the door to the tank he looked briefly back before going in.

Dillon continued down the corridor, and to his own surprise his legs wobbled under him. Once he would hardly have registered such a parochial and patently self-serving outburst. As recently as the years under Kennedy it had been, for Dillon, no source of discomfort to be associated, even as a general officer, with the vested gray suits' effort to tighten control of the blue and brown uniforms. McNamara, early in his tenure as secretary, had regarded centralization of the services as his top priority, and the first large institutional step he'd taken in that direction—his main rule for managers at Harvard and Ford both had been to control the flow of information; in the Pentagon that meant intelligence—was the establishment of DIA under Dillon. Kennedy himself became DIA's main sponsor after the Bay of Pigs disaster destroyed his trust in CIA, and his commitment to Dillon's fledgling agency was solidified a year and a half later when it served reliably as his main source of information about missile sites in Cuba. No one faulted Dillon for disloyalty in those heady days of the long-sought showdown with Russia. And no one doubted, or for that matter complained, that civilians were absolutely in charge of the military, even if one of them was the attorney general.

But the Kennedys were gone; so was the energy they'd brought to the impulse to reform the government. And in the year since Tonkin Gulf things had changed even more. Despite his quick start, McNamara's frustrations with recalcitrant Pentagon turf-defenders were as pointed as Forrestal's had been a decade and a half before, but the hard-driving pragmatist was not one to turn those frustrations against himself. He tempered his challenges to the generals; he needed them more, anyway, now that the organization he intended to bend to his will was no longer the Defense Department but a peasant-dominated, Asian form of communism. Frustrations with what his whiz-kid staffers called the mad-dog military? Frustrations with the wily but insecure successor President? McNamara would vent them on Vietnam.

Dillon had been left to fend for himself. DIA had its legs by now as a huge agency with thousands of billets, but every extension of its reach had been accompanied by savage bureaucratic infighting mounted from outside the Pentagon by the CIA and from within by the fiercely jealous service chiefs. As director, Dillon operated the Washington-based mechanisms of intelligence analysis and distribution, but the "collection assets" around the globe still belonged to the commanders in the field and therefore to the chiefs. Agents carrying DIA credentials, signal equipment on spy ships, eavesdropping aircraft, eye-in-the-sky satellites, all generated initial raw data on which

DIA depended, but they remained in the direct control of the air force, the army, and the navy. In the first phase of his mission—collection—Dillon was at the mercy of military men who opposed him.

And in the last phase too. As an early compromise, McNamara had allowed, over Dillon's strong objection, ambiguous language to define the DIA chain of command. His victory on this issue at OSI had been the key to his first success, and his defeat on it here was ominous. The language in the charter undercut the secretary's own authority, making the DIA director responsible "to" the secretary of defense, but "through" the Joint Chiefs of Staff. With McNamara increasingly less inclined to oppose them, the service chiefs had succeeded in interpreting that definition to mean that they were a coequal master of the intelligence agency, the very raison d'être of which they, of course, rejected.

Dillon knew better than to blame the small-minded generals and admirals whose commitment to a unified, single-thrust national defense was ambivalent at best. Their inability to cooperate with him, as with each other, was ultimately the consequence of confusion and ambivalence not in the Pentagon but in the White House. What Dillon longed for—yes, as a bureaucrat defending his turf, but more as the American military officer he'd been for almost twenty years now—was the clear, forceful statement of national will that both the reform of the Pentagon and the conflict in Vietnam desperately required and that only the President could give. In Dillon's view the ambivalence of generals and admirals, as well as the easily exploited ambivalence of newspaper pundits and college students, all derived from the President's ambivalence. Kennedy had learned how destructive ambivalence can be at the Bay of Pigs, and that lesson had saved the nation and perhaps the world eighteen months later, at the Cuban missile sites.

As Dillon approached the red-coded door at the end of the operations corridor he stopped to steady himself, an uncharacteristic hesitation. His mind was suddenly taken over by a sequence of images that didn't belong there. Cass bent over her patch of zinnias in the yard at Bolling, a garden tool in hand; the family dog, Prince, leaping up at him by the door; Richard at the dining room table that night last spring, his eyes shimmering with the threat of tears; and, of all things, what Dillon saw then was the vast stretch of the old Chicago stockyards as seen from the air, a view he'd never had of it, the view an airmobile helicopter could offer, acre upon acre of muddy corrals, lines of bleating animals, a throng of men in soiled overalls passing through the Stone Gate and, in the distance, the spewing smokestacks of slaughterhouses. He closed his eyes for a moment, standing with his hand on the doorknob, and he found himself hoping—praying almost—that after all these months of so earnestly wanting it both ways in Asia and having it neither, President Johnson too had learned his leader's lesson about the dangers of ambivalence.

Dillon opened the door into a small anteroom where another guard sat at a desk. This one stood abruptly, at attention. No question of checking Dillon's credentials here. The door behind the guard was marked with the letters ISIC, which stood for Intelligence Support and Indications Center. Below the letters was a plate-sized silver and blue seal: "Defense Intelligence Agency," its legend read, above an arc of thirteen silver stars which crowned a torch growing out of a blue-green globe suspended in a pair of atomic ellipses. "The United States of America."

The guard, in bracing, had touched his fingertips to the sides of his trousers, the salute protocol required. Then he opened the door for the director.

ISIC was the DIA alert center, a compact version of the War Room. It had its own banks of equipment and walls of maps and screens. As he entered, Dillon relaxed. This was an area in which all the moves by now came naturally. It was his.

A dozen officers were present, half of them his senior staff and half the permanent crew that manned the center. If they served in DIA not precisely at his pleasure—assignments in and out of the agency were made by the JCS—these men were nevertheless devoted to the mission as he defined it, no one else. Dillon had never lost the ability—or the confidence in himself the ability gave him—to inspire loyalty in those who worked for him. What success he'd had at DIA, despite the opposition, depended on it.

Others in the room, the alert-center crew at their various stations, ignored his entrance, as they were trained to. They maintained focus on the communications and tracking equipment before them. But his staff, clustered in one corner in the eerie blue light of three television monitors, came to attention.

"Good day, gentlemen," he said, crossing to the swivel chair positioned in the central place. He sat, then they did.

Dillon exchanged a look with the only civilian present, Michael Packard, who'd come with him to the Pentagon from the Bureau eighteen years before and had been his special assistant both at OSI and DIA. A civilian's occupying the agency's second chair proved his detractors' point, but Dillon did not care. Packard was the only man in government he completely trusted. For one thing, he was the only man in DIA who served solely at Dillon's pleasure. For another, he was a friend, perhaps Dillon's only friend.

Packard handed Dillon a folder with a red "Secret" stamped diagonally on it. "Khanh's people claim to have snagged four Chicoms in Songbe. In Chinese uniform."

"Songbe?"

"In Phuoc Long, near the Cambodian border."

"They came in from Cambodia."

"If they did." Packard rolled his eyes. "None of our people have been allowed to see them."

"Who's following it?"

Packard glanced at the one-star general behind Dillon, Huber, the head of the Southeast Asia Task Force.

Huber said, "Clark should be in Songbe by now."

The television announcer said, "Ladies and gentlemen, the President of the United States." The ragged audio of the reporters coming to their feet had the effect of cutting everything else off. Dillon, having glanced inside the folder, closed it and rolled it into a tube with which he gestured. "Keep me up to the minute on this. Does Clark speak Chinese?"

Packard and Huber exchanged a look. "Vietnamese, yes," Huber said. "I don't know about Chinese."

"We're going to force Khanh to let us interview these people ourselves," Dillon said coldly. "Don't you think the language is relevant? If Clark doesn't have it, make sure he brings his own translator. If dialects are an issue, make sure he brings several. I don't want Clark depending on the ARVN interpreter. Is that clear? I want absolute confirmation, first, that there are four captives in Chinese uniforms. And second, that they are Chinese."

General Huber nodded his head, but not quite to agree. "We know there are Chicoms massed in Cambodia."

Dillon, his eye steady on one of the television screens, cut the discussion off. "Let's listen to the President."

The image of Lyndon Johnson solemnly at the podium filled the three screens on the wall in front of the DIA officers. The reporters in the East Room of the White House had settled back into their chairs. Johnson brought his eyes directly to the camera as it closed in on him. He stared through his glass prompting device with that peculiar lugubrious leer which Dillon assumed was meant to convey sincerity but which in fact, for Dillon at least, always conveyed the opposite.

Dillon glanced at the digital clock on the wall above the monitors: 1233. He turned to Packard. "Do we need all three of these screens?"

Packard promptly stood and reached to the controls, snapping off two monitors. "My fellow Americans," Johnson began, bending the words with the drawl that was always a surprise. "Not long ago, I received a letter from a woman in the Midwest. She wrote: 'Dear Mr. President, In my humble way I am writing to you about the crisis in Vietnam ...' "

Dillon was aware of the officers behind him shifting in their seats, eyeing each other: Oh brother. He pressed his fingers against his temples, forcing himself just to listen. But the President's handlers had neglected to give him paper to hold, stationery, a lady's letter. He was reading the letter from the prompter, making it seem false.

" '... I have a son who is now in Vietnam. My husband served in World War II. Our country was at war. But now, this time, it's just something that I don't understand. Why?' " Johnson paused, frowned, nodded to himself. "Well, I've tried to answer that question dozens of times and more in practically every state in the Union ..."

Reciting the familiar litany of reasons, Johnson explained the American presence in Vietnam once more. "We did not choose to be guardians at the gate, but there is no one else ... The pledges of three Presidents ... to convince the Communists that we cannot be defeated ... We cannot abandon those who trusted us."

Dillon accepted all of it, but he listened impatiently. His question wasn't why Americans were in Vietnam but how, and it made him uneasy that Johnson was once more loading up his announcement with the mind-numbing rhetoric of justification.

Finally the President came to it. "I have asked the com-

manding general, General Westmoreland, what more he needs
to meet the mounting aggression. He has told me. And we will
meet his needs."

Dillon leaned forward, and was aware that every officer in
the room, including the duty officers at their consoles, was
doing likewise.

"I have today ordered to Vietnam the Airmobile Division
and certain other forces which will raise our fighting strength
from seventy-five thousand to one hundred twenty-five thousand men almost immediately. Additional forces will be
needed later and they will be sent as requested . . ."

"Oh Christ," someone behind Dillon muttered, and someone
else let out a mystified "What the hell?" Another said, "A
five-foot leap over a seven-foot pit."

Dillon stiffened, and the men behind him checked themselves at once.

". . . necessary to raise the monthly draft call from seventeen
thousand to thirty-five thousand and for us to step up our campaign for voluntary enlistments. After this past week of delib-
erations I have concluded that it is not essential to order
Reserve units into service now . . ."

The President continued to speak—". . . steps the government of South Vietnam will take to reform itself and
strengthen its fighting force . . . Secretary Rusk and Secretary
McNamara available to Congress . . . to move from the battlefield to the conference table"—but the words registered only
vaguely with Dillon, as if he were hearing them at the bottom
of a swimming pool. The realization had hit with awful clarity
that Johnson was changing nothing. Notching up the draft,
deepening dependence on Saigon, sending in the famous Air
Cavalry as if this were the movies. No call-up of Reserves. No
mobilization. No declaration of a national emergency. Just another fifty thousand men. Not enough—as it was Sean Dillon's
job to know better than anyone—to do anything in Vietnam
but die.

Dillon had slumped back in his chair. The men with him
were as stunned into disbelief as he was. They stared blankly
at the television screen, seeing nothing but the beagle-like lying eyes—lying because it was unthinkable that Westmoreland
had asked for so little—of their commander in chief.

". . . a personal note," Johnson was saying. "I do not find it
easy to send the flower of our youth, our finest young men,

into battle . . . the most agonizing and the most painful duty of your President . . . what I've wanted all my life since I was a little boy . . . help every Negro and every American . . . all of our dreams for freedom, all, all—will be swept away on the flood of conquest. This will not happen. We will stand in Vietnam."

Dillon had to avert his eyes from Johnson's. He looked down into his lap, at his fists, and saw only then what he had done, strangling the tube of the top-secret memo on the Chicoms in Songbe into a twisted rod.

"Cass? Are you awake?" He leaned against the doorjamb, waiting.

She was turned on her side toward him, the bedside lamp still on, her book open on the blanket, an Allen Drury novel.

He approached, walking softly, then was unable to resist bending down to touch her. He let his fingers fall into her hair. "I'm sorry I'm so late."

He wanted her to wake up. He had decided on his way home to break his absolute and oldest rule. He had decided to talk to her. He had to talk to someone.

She stirred, then pushed deeper into the covers, apparently dreaming.

He took his hand away, and realized it would never work, after all these years. She wouldn't have a clue what to do if he confided secrets from the office, even if she didn't know they were secrets. If he described the surreal sequence of events at the Pentagon that had followed upon Johnson's speech or if, God forbid, he let her see the terrible effect it had had on him, she would think he was having a nervous breakdown, which he wasn't, not even close. But something had snapped in him, he did not know what, and that was all he'd hoped to say.

He straightened to stand over her, noting the lightness of her open hand on the pillow beside her cheek. His own hands had been in fists for hours, but not now. His fingers tingled from having touched her there, those wisps of hair which fluttered at her eye, her lips, each time she breathed. The form of her body under the summer blanket was so familiar, that curve of the hip, the fold of legs and the shadow between them which remained a mystery to him. The threat of pregnancy, of course, hadn't been an issue in years, but Cass's menopause had not released them from their inhibition. Sex, by then, was simply not a language they spoke to each other. If Dillon had a language of the body now, it was of his clenched teeth and tight fists, and those had nothing to do with her.

Cass was Sean's only woman, had always been. Like her, he took their bond for granted, as well as the marital tranquility which had been purchased at a cost neither was aware of. Sex had been repressed, but so had something else, what Dillon stood on the brink of acknowledging. The sight of his wife, blessed in sleep but also pulled by what dream away from him, filled Dillon with astonishment. The feeling was more than he could handle, and so he deflected the rare urge to speak plainly into the far safer, more familiar hunger of his simple, old sexual desire. That he knew how to stifle.

She stirred again, smiling in her sleep. He thought, Perhaps she is dreaming of me. She did not wake up. He turned the light off and went back downstairs for a drink.

By the time she woke in the morning he was already gone again. She found his note which read simply, "Hot time in the old towne. Came and went to shower and change. See you tonight. I'll make it home for dinner. Promise. S."

Dillon's appointment at ten was with the secretary, but when he arrived at the plushest suite in the Pentagon, he was directed down the hall to the office of the assistant secretary, William Basset, one of the bright young managers McNamara had brought with him from Ford. Dillon had misread Basset early on. He had so ferociously challenged the entrenched military bureaucracy, including those elements that had opposed DIA, that Dillon had taken him for a man whose main commitment was to an organizational ideal. But in fact Basset's reforming zeal had fallen off along the same curve as McNamara's, and Dillon realized that the assistant secretary's only commitment was to McNamara himself. Basset was still only in his late thirties, the age of Dillon himself when he'd been commissioned the youngest general in America, but youth no longer seemed a note of Basset's. The five brutal years had taken their toll, and it was during the last one—the year of Vietnam—that his hair had gone completely white. His skin had the permanent sickly pallor of flesh that never saw the sun, and his eyes were always red. That he did not stand when Dillon entered his small, unpretentious office seemed less a matter of the discourtesy that set the brass grousing than of simple weariness.

"I'm sorry, General. The secretary's on the Hill. Fulbright went ballistic over the President's announcement. Mr. McNamara asked me to see you and convey any message."

"I'm ballistic too."

"Not the way Fulbright is. He thinks the President's program goes too far."

"Look, Bill, I need a meeting with McNamara right away. He put me off last night."

"Negative, General. You won't see him. You have to deal with me."

"The President is not getting briefed properly. I found out what happened at the NSC meeting two days ago. General Wheeler failed to make the case for the Reserve call-up. Neither MacDonald nor McConnell made a peep. The JCS went into that meeting determined to demand full mobilization, but when the President asked for their opinion they said nothing."

"So did Mr. McNamara. And at one point he wanted the call-up too."

"I know. That's what I wanted to ask him about. What the hell is going on? Isn't our job to tell the President the truth?"

Basset shrugged, a gesture of sublime resignation which infuriated Dillon, who slammed his hand down on the desk that separated them. "Don't you know what this means, what Johnson announced yesterday? Fifty thousand more troops won't alter the balance near enough. Taking the Vietcong and the NVA together, there are two hundred and fifty thousand seasoned fighters in the South, commanded by Hanoi's best officers, including Tran Do, and equipped with rocket launchers and AK-47s. ARVN has already broken and run, and when our boys show up, even too few of them, the South Vietnamese will pull back even further. There is no way fifty thousand—"

"It's the Airmobile Division, General."

"That's even worse. That's my point! Does the President know what going to war without a declared national emergency means? It means that any soldier whose enlistment is up in the next six months will not ship out. Without the mobilization those enlistments cannot be extended. Does the President know what that means? Fifty percent of the famous First Air Cav will not be going overseas, and that means that green recruits will be going instead. The best-trained soldiers will be staying at Fort Bragg, and half of those going into combat will not have had any airmobile training! Does the President know that?"

"I don't know." The look on Basset's face said he himself didn't know it.

"Don't you think someone should tell him?"

"General, the President is the commander in chief."

"We are his military advisors! Jesus Christ, Basset, he can't make decisions about sending what he called 'the flower of our youth' into combat based on what Senator Fulbright tells him."

At last Basset stood up, mirroring Dillon from his side of the desk. The air between them curdled. "Look," he said wearily, "don't come in here ranting at me about this. General Cannon, the Air Cav commander, issued a statement saying he and his men were honored to be tapped and enthusiastic about going. I didn't hear him complaining about lack of training."

"Cannon and his men are combat soldiers and brave ones, no doubt. Their job isn't to shape policy. Ours is, yours and mine. We're not Wall Street lawyers looking for loopholes in the tax law so our client can squeak through without paying. We're supposed to help the President fulfill the public trust, and that trust begins with GIs. Our job is to help the President shape policy that doesn't waste the lives of ill-prepared or outnumbered American soldiers, no matter how valiant they might be."

"That's right. And it's a job that begins, whether we like it or not, with Taylor and Westmoreland, who aren't exactly famous for wasting the lives of GIs. The President's announcement yesterday embodied what they want."

"Maybe."

"Oh? You have reason to doubt that they're on board?"

"No. But they are under political pressure too, I assume. We're not."

"You say 'political' as if it's a dirty word."

Dillon stared at Basset impassively, but instead of the exhausted staffer's, for an instant he saw the face of Mayor Ed Kelly, Raymond Buckley's mentor.

"But politics isn't dirty, General. That's a blind spot you fellows have here. Politics is just getting people to work together, and when it comes to this kind of war, political programs are the key. This isn't war the way American generals have seen it before, that's all. I think Taylor and Westmoreland, for two, understand that."

"Do you think politics in Saigon is different from what it is in, say, Chicago?"

Basset laughed. "If Richard J. Daley were running the show in Nam, he'd call in some markers and that would be that."

"Maybe so." Dillon smiled, wanting Basset to think he'd won. Basset knew nothing about Daley, nothing about markers. These brilliant analyzers, these geniuses from Harvard, these smartest men in America who'd imposed themselves on Washington and on the government and on this war, they were just provincials of another kind, Dillon thought. What made them dangerous was their assumption that they knew everything already. Sean Dillon knew damn well that he didn't, and his first job now was to find out what was really happening. He leaned toward Basset and lowered his voice. "Look, I'm the guy who is supposed to keep the picture in focus. Get me over there. Cut me orders to Vietnam. This thing is getting away from us. Send me on fact-finding for OSD. You can do that."

Basset shook his head. "You know the policy, General. We can't risk someone with your clearances in a war zone unnecessarily. You could be captured."

"McNamara just went."

"Him and half of the Old Guard. You wouldn't have a regiment for personal security. It's out."

Dillon felt fevered. "That's not the reason, and you know it."

"It's one reason, General, and that's enough. You thinking of another?" Basset nodded smugly. "Collection assets are not in DIR-DIA's purview."

"I never conceded that."

"The secretary conceded it for you."

"Look, these are the squabbles of bureaucrats. The secretary won the first battle of DIA, and it was over that letter *D*. The chiefs wanted the agency called 'Military' Intelligence, but he insisted on 'Defense' as a way of building his own primacy right into the title. Well, I need him to assert that primacy now, and if I can't get on his schedule, I need you to make the case for me. If there's divergence between what the JCS sees happening in Vietnam and what Westmoreland sees, I'm the one who should find out what it's about. Get McNamara to send me."

"Westmoreland doesn't want you near the place, and neither do the chiefs. They don't want you out of Washington."

"What kind of military advice can the President be getting if the men charged with giving it to him are divided?"

"Nobody hears the President complaining about advice."

"Not now, he isn't, when he has unanimous NSC meetings. But he'll howl later when his policy is a disaster. Ask General Taylor. He was at bat when the JCS didn't tell Kennedy the truth about the Bay of Pigs. None of the military chiefs believed the CIA plan would work, but they never warned the President because they thought he'd bought it already. And now it's happening again. Not a flag officer in this building thinks the way to go in Vietnam is the piecemeal build-up the President described, and very few think stabilizing the regime in Saigon should continue as our priority. Saigon won't be stable until we get the North Vietnamese off its back. The working group is unanimous on this—hit Hanoi and Haiphong, now and hard. Preempt the Chinese. Push ARVN aside and take over in the South, a quick victory, in and out. It's the only way."

"You heard the speech. On the President's scale that's the extremist way."

"Right. I forgot. The Goldilocks principle: one too soft, one too hard, and one just right. The President champions the moderate course midway between the peaceniks and the warmongers."

"Not only the President, General. A unanimous NSC."

"Unanimous in seeing what Johnson wanted and giving it to him. There's a long tradition of that here. I know all about it, the goddamn chain of command, and 'chain' is right. Every military man's mind is shackled by it. His fate depends totally on pleasing the guy just above him, so the system rewards dishonesty and cowardice. People who finally make chief are just more adept at it than anybody else."

Basset shrugged again. "That's not Mr. McNamara's problem. Or Bundy's. Or Rusk's. Or Rostow's. None of them are military, but when the crunch came they saw things the way the President did at that meeting. In fact, General Dillon, that's how our system works. The President decides. The rest of us execute."

"Execute." Dillon nodded slowly. "Is that the word you'll use in drafting the secretary's personal letters of condolence to the families of KIAs? You'd better cut some stencils, because you're going to have to start using a mimeographed form letter when the Air Cav rookies hit the zone."

"Anything else, General?"

"Just tell the secretary I want to see him."

"He's very busy. You can understand."

"Funny thing, Basset. That is exactly what General Wheeler's exec said to me yesterday. Of course, he feels entitled, since by his lights, despite my uniform, I belong to the Office of the Secretary of Defense."

"Maybe you should get the message then."

"What message?"

"We all get DIA reviews and estimates. On Southeast Asia they have become utterly predictable, all too consistently negative. You glorify Ho Chi Minh's abilities, and denigrate Nguyen Khanh's."

"And I denigrated Big Mingh's before him, and Ngo Dinh Diem's before him, and pretty soon I'll be denigrating a tin soldier named Nguyen Cao Ky. Khanh won't survive no matter what we do for him. None of them will. If we keep our chips on Saigon's racketeer-politicians, we lose. It's that simple. DIA estimates are not what's negative. What's negative is what's happening over there."

"You should know that Taylor and Westmoreland both have recently disparaged DIA analysis. Mr. McNamara is worried that your inflexibility is costing you your effectiveness."

"I hear regularly from my air force colleagues how my reports let them down, but they are the only ones. Is it too much to ask why other critics of DIA don't bring their complaints to me?"

"In fact, Mr. McNamara, when I spoke to him this morning, asked me to raise the issue of negativity with you. He said he would hate to see you shut out."

Shut out. Dillon recognized the words for the threat they were, the ultimate threat for men like him. It's time to get on board, General, or the train will leave without you. Johnson himself—that's what his news conference had really been—calling down the track. All aboard! The men of the NSC had heard, Basset had heard, and now Dillon was hearing. Get aboard or else you'll be shut out. This was the first time in eighteen years Dillon had heard that threat directed explicitly at himself. Year after year he had been brought in, not shut out, and by no one more powerfully than McNamara. Yet here it was McNamara's own flunky delivering the tickle, and he knew that the process of his being eased aside had already begun, even if he was just getting the message now. He knew that, because he wasn't getting it from McNamara or one of the chiefs, or vice chiefs even, like Davidson, but from this punk Ivy League whiz kid. For the first time Dillon saw the condescending Basset the way his fellow generals always had: the temple eunuch whose specialty was introducing others to his own state of emasculation.

"One further item, Mr. Basset, that you can pass on to the secretary for me." If Dillon had been a different man, a politician, say, he'd have found it possible to smile ingratiatingly here, cloaking his hostility while nursing it. But his face was wooden. Inside he felt raw. He stepped toward the door, then paused to say, "The four Chinese soldiers captured in Songbe . . ."

"Yes?"

"All four of them are dead, each one with a bullet to his head, executed before my people could interview them."

"Christ, who did that?"

"Tran Kim Don, the ARVN chief of staff in Phuoc Long. He did it himself."

"Jesus."

"Oh, and tell Mr. McNamara another thing. They were not Red Chinese."

"What?"

"Ethnic Chinese, from Cholon probably, but they were Vietnamese citizens. Most Chinese in Cholon are third or fourth generation. Khanh had them killed so we would not discover that they were mannequins."

"But you discovered it anyway?"

"The four were wearing People's Republic uniforms all right, but also ARVN-issue underwear and dog tags. It was a setup, a little sweetener from Khanh for the President's press conference, evidence that the Red Horde is coming."

"Jesus Christ, CIA had given him the report before you did, but as hard fact: four Chicom officers, serving as advisors to the VC, captured, debriefed, confirmed. The President was primed to use it in the Q-and-A if Red China's involvement came up."

Dillon nodded slowly. "That's what I love about this place.

I had 'Dubious' stamped all over the DIA report. Dubious, Mr. Basset. Dubious."

He made it home in time for dinner. In twenty-four hours his impulse had reversed itself. He did not want now to talk to Cass about any of it. They sat in the dining room opposite each other, too far away to touch, not speaking except when Sergeant Mack came in to serve or clear. Then they both made the usual effort, the push for chat that social events in Washington often required.

—The Eastern Shore an hour closer, what with the new Chesapeake Bay Bridge. Crabs lost less on Maine Avenue now.

—Zinnias, the Officers' Wives' Club Garden Committee, the plantings at the chapel, brutal dry weather.

—Abe Fortas, who first refused the appointment to the Supreme Court, then accepted. No one refuses the President. Arthur Goldberg hated to resign from the Court for the UN.

—Maintenance should check the spot on the ceiling upstairs. The air conditioner is clanking.

Finally, when Mack came in with the coffee, Cass said, "Leave it here, Sergeant. I'll pour."

"Yes, ma'am."

And Dillon added, "You can go, Sergeant. Leave the rest."

"Thank you, sir." He collected the butter dish and the salt and pepper, then nodded at Cass. "Good night, ma'am."

"Thank you, Sergeant."

The door slapped repeatedly after him, *foop, foop*, on its swinging hinge.

At last Cass brought her eyes up and waited for Sean to look at her. "I watched the President's news conference yesterday."

Dillon stared mutely across the table, thinking how unlike her it was to introduce a subject that touched on his work.

Perhaps simply to deflect his mind from whatever it was his grave wife was going to say, he thought of Richard just then, of the time years before when he was expelled from the Benedictine prep school for some prank—that toilet bowl, wasn't it? How he and another boy had moved it under the chair of the statue of St. Anselm. The great Doctor of the Church taking a crap on the grassy circle in front of the school. Sean had had to leave the Pentagon in the middle of the day to meet the livid headmaster at the school on the far northeast side of Washington. The monk had actually begun by telling Dillon that his son would not be readmitted, and at first Sean thought surely Richard had done some heinous thing. But a toilet bowl under the grimacing saint! Richard was a boy who often failed to think things through. Sometimes Dillon thought their son had an undeveloped sense of the link between acts and consequences. But this time, despite himself, Sean Dillon had wanted to laugh, laugh out loud. A toilet bowl under a saint—it seemed more than a prank, a kind of parable, a lesson about human life, a good one. But the monk was adamant: this was a grievous violation, not just the desecration but theft, theft of the toilet. Sean couldn't believe what he was hearing. He knew already that the toilet was from a junkyard. Richard and his partner had paid a dollar for it. Every volt of the anger he'd felt toward his son all the way across Washington leapt now at the ridiculous priest. "Come, come, Father," he'd begun at one point, and within minutes he had cowed the headmaster, who relented. After the meeting, but still in the headmaster's presence, Sean had, as the situation required, sternly admonished Richard for his impudence. But also he had winked.

"Yes," Sean said to Cass, "I saw it too."

"I wanted to ask you something. Can I?"

Sean simply looked at her, not answering. He had yet to fully admit to himself how demoralized he felt, how confused about the meaning of his own situation. He was surrounded by addled headmasters of his own now, and it was far from clear he was going to be able to change their minds. He thought of the great bronze robed figure of the thirteenth century's greatest mind, sitting on a cracked modern toilet. But nothing in him now thought the figure humorous in the slightest.

"The President said they're going to double the draft calls every month." As Cass lowered her coffee cup her hand shook, and when she placed it on the saucer the china rattled.

"More than double," Sean said quietly, almost to himself. "Seventeen thousand to thirty-five."

Then she asked a question some version of which parents all over America were asking but which, in all honesty and to his instant shame on hearing it, had yet to occur to Sean Dillon. "How will the increased draft affect Richard?"

Dillon's heart sank at the thought of his son in jeopardy, like those Air Cav rookies. His son, the football player at St.

Anselm's; his son, Dillon's own football. He remembered running with the boy bundled inside his arm, Rickie squealing "Touchdown!" How they would pretend to be in the end zone then, and would sing together the Redskins fight song.

He forced himself to shrug. "Richard's still in college. He has another year."

"But then?"

"A lot can happen in a year."

"Could this war be over?"

"He won't be drafted, Cass. Once he has his degree, he's a shoo-in for OCS, if it comes to that."

Cass sat there, solemn and rigid, her eyes fixed unblinking on her husband.

"Has he said something to you? Is he worried about it?"

She shook her head. "It's me. I'm the one who's worried." She smiled then. "But that's my job, isn't it?"

EIGHTEEN

More than half a year later, Dillon's airplane crossed over the lush Mekong Valley which formed the soft belly of the country, separating it in the south from Cambodia. The craft was, even if temporarily, his own C-54, outfitted as a command plane, with a communications center tying him to ISIC in Washington. The plane also featured a dining salon that doubled as a conference room, a main cabin with a dozen rows of standard passenger seats and, aft, a section of six individually curtained-off berths for Dillon and his senior staff. In this airplane Dillon, his chief of staff, his field detachment chief, the assistant director for special activities and the assistant director for plans and programs, all flag officers, had traveled thousands of miles. In the sealed-off, fabric-on-metal world of that stainless steel tube the infinite ambiguities of the war bureaucracy did not exist, for Dillon alone held power here, over his commodore, his colonels, his brigadier generals, and even over the rated fly-boys at the controls. When, for example, they had taken off from Bangkok that morning Dillon had given the navigator his course, directing them inland, despite procedure that required unarmed aircraft to circle south and come in on Tan Son Nhut from the sea. Instead, they were making a beeline over the most hotly contested terrain in the country. He felt his stomach lurch as the plane dropped at the point where he'd told the pilot to swoop down across the Delta wetlands, overriding the air traffic controller if necessary with a claim of fuel-line problems. Now that Sean Dillon was finally here he was going to see as much of Vietnam as he could.

"Look at this, Mike." His gesture drew Packard over. Packard was the only one in civvies. His white suit had not stood up nearly as well as the military khaki the others wore, and now it was whipped-looking, his tie limp as a noodle, his shirt open above the wrinkled knot. On this trip his face always wore the shadow of his beard, as if the tropics made it grow too fast. His by now slovenly appearance was deceiving, though, because he was the one man on the plane with ready access to Dillon. There had been no need to make explicit the understanding according to which, from Andrews Air Force Base on, the others had sat at the far rear of the cabin, leaving the seats next to the director and those immediately behind him vacant. Packard's seat was in Dillon's row, but across the aisle. Periodically, at Dillon's gesture, he joined him, as now. He craned past the boss for the window.

"Jesus."

An unwavering column of intense black smoke rose into the still air from a neat angled cut in the green nubby carpet of the jungle canopy thousands of feet below. The fires that generated the smoke had peaked some time before.

"A box," Dillon said, referring to what they'd both heard described a hundred times in target briefings. A flight of six or eight B-52s in wingtip-to-wingtip formation unloads its bombs simultaneously on a "box," wiping out everything in a sharply defined rectangular area the size of downtown Washington, from the Mall to Dupont Circle, from the Capitol to Griffith Stadium.

"It seems like nowhere," Packard said. "What were they hitting?"

Dillon pointed to an area in the distance where the jungle thinned and ribbons of lights flashed along the silver dot-to-dot of canals and ditches branching out from the river proper. The rivulets fed paddies, the sure sign of settlement. "Chau Phu," he said. "So right below us must be the top of Ca Mau. There are NVA regulars positioned all through Ca Mau."

"It makes me nervous, Sean. I have to admit, looking down on the real thing. I've never seen a war."

Dillon looked over at his friend. "Admit it to me. Not to the others."

"You haven't either."

Without batting an eye, Dillon answered, "It doesn't make me nervous, Mike." He raised his hand to show Packard his palm. Dry. Once, his palms had become wet just in flying. He smiled. "You get to a certain age."

Packard looked out at the welt of cut jungle again. "It's like
the slash of a lumber harvest. Look, there's another. An old
one without smoke. And there's another."

The two men stared in silence as the plane went steadily
lower. Soon other details of the terrain were distinguishable, so
that more than the bombed swaths were evident. Along the
banks of the river itself the earth was charred, having been
stripped by defoliants and the flame-throwers from navy river-
boats. The spikes of jungle vegetation, thickets of bamboo and
leafy pole trees, shot up from the undifferentiated green. Dillon
squinted down as if to look for the menace in the air, but saw
only dikes, wet paddies, and, once the jungle broke, carefully
laid-out fields. He recognized the farming region above Can
Tho.

The villages of the Mekong Delta came into view, shadowless in the hard sun, at once alien and familiar to Dillon. He
knew the Delta from the air like this as well as he knew the
carpet of the yard behind the house at Bolling, pebbles marking the path. Cass's flower beds and strawberries, the pleas-
antly turned soil, the square of Richard's sandbox—

The sandbox had been gone for years now, long replaced by
a terraced brick barbecue. It startled Dillon to have called to
mind the tidy rectangle in which his child had so loved to play.
Dillon had often watched him, marveling from the second
floor, and what he saw now was his son banging his toy shovel
violently, an act of impatience that made Dillon want to scoop
his son up, bind him in the thatch of his arms, stopping him
and consoling him at the same time. He could not help for a
second seeing his own father bringing his hammer down with
like impatience on a recalcitrant machine. His father had been
so unhappy with his dark little life in the South Side car barns,
and it shocked Dillon to sense his son's capacity, despite the
sunshine in which he lived, for an unhappiness of the same
kind. In Dillon's memory such moments of his own acute
longing and worry were often associated with Richard. They
came unsummoned, a wound so secret that Dillon hardly understood it himself. His son was like a book that always fell
open to the same page—a page, he admitted now, that he himself had bent back years before; his own father had bent it
back before that.

He had studied hundreds of photos of the Delta terrain far
more carefully than he'd ever looked down from the second

floor on the yard behind his quarters, but now it struck him that the recon photos were always sepia. He had never seen the Delta colors, the dozen vivid greens as different from one another as red is from blue, the soured browns of bomb craters and scorched riverbanks, and, everywhere here, the silver-blue blades of water sparkling in the dry air of the time without rain.

Packard interrupted him. "Here's the briefing book on Lodge." He handed over the thin black folder. "You probably know it all, but you may want to refresh yourself before the meeting. I'm not sure what it means for us, him running the embassy now instead of Taylor."

"I knew Taylor. I don't know Lodge."

"That's to the good, though. Right?" Packard smiled. "It means he won't know you. DIA wasn't in the lineup when he was here last. He won't know where we fit in."

"Where do we fit in, Mike?" Dillon asked the question absently, leafing through the pages. Henry Cabot Lodge, Jr., his schools, his clubs, his jobs, his family and friends, his political connections, his money—everything Sean Dillon was not. Yet Dillon had taken Lodge's reappointment to the ever more crucial post of ambassador as a measure of Johnson's growing desperation. The Brahmin's embodiment of everything the Texas-bred poor-boy President so patently wanted to be obscured the fact that Lodge's mistake during his first tour in Vietnam was his nation's mortal one. Sean Dillon knew that, more than anybody, Lodge had sponsored the coup d'état against Ngo Din Diem in 1963. Diem's assassination—the crude American attempt to take control of the Saigon government itself—was the miscalculation from which every subsequent miscalculation had derived. Three coups later the government of South Vietnam was proving to be America's black hole. Dillon was no spiritualist, but he was still a Catholic, and Diem's murder loomed for him as the original sin. Even at the time, when he had yet to assemble DIA's fully staffed Southeast Asia Task Force, the assassination had sent an ominous shiver up his spine. It had occurred on All Souls' Day, the day of the dead, and when Diem's corpse was found it was garbed bizarrely in the robes of a Catholic priest. Diem's blood had seemed to splash back on America itself, an almost biblical moral consequence, for three weeks after approving Lodge's plan to eliminate Diem, Kennedy was himself eliminated. The gyre down into the abyss was set winding just as his successor, with the blood-spattered widow standing next to him, swore his oath.

"This bastard," Dillon said to himself, slapping the folder, "what is this bastard doing back here?"

"I'm sorry, what?"

"Lodge." Dillon tossed the briefing book back at Packard.

"He never committed to an appointment for you. It's the first thing we'll have to arrange. We've sent three cables. The Saigon embassy acknowledges, but they haven't picked up."

"That's good news, Mike. We don't need an appointment with Lodge."

"But that's our rationale."

Dillon's trip, now in its second week, was an exhausting tour of U.S. embassies in Asia, from Tokyo to Manila to Seoul to Taipei to Jakarta to Bangkok and only now to Saigon. From here he was scheduled to go on to Delhi, Teheran, and Tel Aviv before heading home. The official purpose was formally to effect the assumption of DIA control over the military attachés who were assigned to the major embassies, a recently won extension of the agency's mandate. Such attachés had always been intelligence operatives, although they were known around embassies mainly for the flair their formal uniforms brought to parties. Naval attachés, air attachés, and military attachés were now to be known as defense attachés, and as spies their orders would come from Dillon, not the individual branches in which they served. Dillon might anyway have decided to personally visit each embassy, meeting his new men and briefing the ambassadors, but he had been confirmed in his impulse when he realized such a trip would provide a cover for his journey to Vietnam. Vietnam was all he really wanted.

"Lodge can only cause me trouble, Mike. More than Taylor even, he'll be looking out for the company's interest against us. You know how CIA would like to keep us out of here, as much as those G-16s at State. I'm sure Lodge takes his cues from Hilsman and Bundy."

"But Christ, Sean, he's the ambassador. If you're not coming here to brief him, what are you doing here? How do you justify it?"

"We're covered because we sent the cables. We'll use the bureaucracy's rules against itself." Dillon smiled and shook his head. "It's like threading a mine field. Here's what we do." He ticked his fingers. "Don't take any further initiatives with Lodge. Fold the embassy attachés into a larger briefing with the DIA detachment at MACV. I'm here to see my men."

"Even if they don't know they're yours?"

"Arrange the session for this afternoon. I want it to take place before Westmoreland can stop me."

"But I'll have to do it through MacAuliff's office. You don't have line authority over DIA-MACV."

"Leave General MacAuliff out. He's supposed to be the link between us and MACV, but he's Westmoreland's man, pure and simple. I want this meeting, Mike, and I want it before Lodge or Westmoreland can stop it. DIA men, the collectors, the interrogators, the debriefers, are the sources of all our human intelligence on this war. They carry credentials with my signature. They may never have taken an order from me, but they know who I am and they know I wear three stars. That's what will count in the end. I outrank MacAuliff."

"You don't outrank Westmoreland. He'll be ripped when he finds out."

Dillon smiled. "In the seminary we used to have an expression: It's easier to get forgiveness after, than permission before. If I wanted to get MacAuliff's point of view, I could have stayed in Washington."

"You may wish you did."

"Just call the session when we get in, Mike. General MacAuliff and Westmoreland are busy men. We don't need to bother them."

"Westmoreland's another one, like Lodge."

"Another what?"

"Another mystery to me."

Dillon looked over at his old friend. For how many years had they been sending each other the signals of their disdain for Pentagon martinets? "Westy? No mystery there, Michael. LBJ gives him his head for three reasons."

Packard unfurled a finger. "He's a southerner."

"Right."

Packard had to think for a moment, then got it. "After his stint at the War College, he went to Harvard, didn't he?"

"Harvard Business School, with Mac."

The two men grinned. Harvard had been a joke between them for years. Packard was a Phi Beta Kappa graduate of

Michigan, but he'd gone as a night student to a downtown law school like Dillon.

"And the third thing that impressed Johnson?"

"Early success." Dillon's grin broadened. "He was the first man in his class to get a star. LBJ loves Westmoreland because he was a general at thirty-eight."

Packard slapped Dillon's leg. "Thirty-eight, that's old." He burst out laughing. "You were thirty-seven!" He glanced backward to see if the others in the cabin were watching them.

Dillon began to laugh too, letting his tension go in this rare indulgence. Like the free-spirited young men they'd been together an entire era ago—long before they'd found themselves snarled in the thickets of the bureaucracy—they laughed.

The first thing to strike Dillon from the top step of the aluminum stairway was not the savage noontime heat—heat had been the feature of their last three stops—but the apparent chaos at Tan Son Nhut; not the chaos of battle, scrambling jet fighters, incoming mortar shells, GIs ducking for cover, but of construction and transport. Immediately to his airplane's left a pair of huge Chinook cargo helicopters were banging into the sky with dun-colored, car-sized crates dangling beneath them. To the right a line of four C-130s were off-loading a shipment of Jeeps and trucks with all the bustle of a seaport. Across a vast flat valley road graders were extending runways; bulldozers maneuvering around stacks of burning brush were pushing back the jungle; huge mechanized concrete spreaders were blanketing the dusty red soil. Elsewhere the broad apron was paved with aluminum matting. A dozen different types of aircraft taxied back and forth as the heat of their exhaust wrinkled the air. Dillon's nostrils burned. Buzzing amid the planes like gnats were tractors pulling carts laden with boxes. The tractors swerved and cut to avoid sentry-like pallets piled high with cartons and sacks, some construction supplies and some PX goods emblazoned with brand names—L & M, Coke, Maxwell House, and Miller High life. Dillon knew that Tan Son Nhut was now the third-busiest airport in the world, but the commotion stunned him nonetheless. It was an unexpected measure of what the U.S. presence here had become, and would become yet.

He looked behind his airplane and saw, like a huge wall, a row of metal hangars and, more construction, the line of a dozen others half assembled. There were warehouses, office buildings, the control tower with outslanting green windows and, beyond those, the rooftops and water towers of the air base proper which amounted to a sizable new town. Only the smoke from the burning brush at the jungle's edge beyond the new runways evoked the feel of violence, but it did so vaguely. Even in the oh-so-domesticated Pentagon Dillon had never been able to forget that he was a general officer who had never been at war. To some, he knew, that anomaly remained the most distinctive thing about him. As he stood gazing out across the war capitol's airfield, the glimpse reminded him not of war but of Chicago's ever booming O'Hare.

He saw the army bird colonel waiting to greet him at the bottom of the stairs: a ruddy, jowly man built like a former linebacker. Dillon recognized him from his picture.

And quickly taking in the adjacent area, he saw another figure, a man in a seersucker suit and a Panama hat, and at once Dillon came even more alert. The man was standing twenty yards behind the colonel, near a pallet stacked with soft-drink cartons. The backwash from the Chinooks began to flap the fabric of his suit just then, and the man took his hat off. He was quite bald.

Dillon descended the stairs, donning his service hat; he took pains to avoid seeming to notice the man, but inwardly he cursed. CIA, he thought. Or Lodge, preempting him after all.

"You must be Flynn," he said to the army colonel.

As Dillon's foot hit the tarmac Flynn saluted. "Yes, sir. Joseph Flynn. Welcome to the zone, General Dillon."

Dillon returned the salute, then offered his hand. "Hello, Colonel. It's good to meet you at last." He smiled warmly. "I was happy when General Westmoreland gave me an Irishman as my man in Saigon."

"Thank you, sir." Flynn's handshake was firm, but he looked away too quickly, with a note of, Your man?

The figure in seersucker had been several steps toward them, but now had stopped.

Dillon turned to introduce Packard, whose tie was firmly at his throat now, reddening his face. Dillon knew that it wouldn't be long before Packard unbuttoned his collar again.

As the other officers came down, Dillon introduced each of them to Flynn.

The man in seersucker began again to approach. He had donned his hat once more and his face was in shadow.

Under his breath Dillon asked Flynn, "Who is this?"

There was no subtlety in the DIA local commander as he turned to gape at the newcomer. "I don't know," he said, blushing to hear from his own mouth the one answer colonels knew generals could not tolerate.

The man in seersucker approached directly now.

Packard stepped forward, as if to intercept a court official delivering a subpoena, but Dillon took Packard's shoulder, drawing him back.

"General Dillon?" the man said, taking his hat off again. "Excuse the intrusion, sir." He glanced at Flynn, an apology for a turf violation that confirmed Dillon in his intuition that the man was CIA.

"I am Colonel Peter Freeman." He reached inside his suitcoat, drawing out a credentials folder and displaying it. "OSI, sir."

"OSI?" Flynn blurted out, as if he were in authority.

Freeman glanced at him, nodding. "Air Force OSI, Colonel."

Packard could not help himself. "Pete Freeman, don't I know you?"

Freeman grinned. "Mr. Packard, you presented me with a commendation in 1956."

"You were on the Hans Dieter case."

"Yes, I was."

Packard touched Dillon's sleeve. "That was Wiesbaden, the Luftwaffe mole. Pete Freeman helped break the Dieter case open, forcing the Bonn indictments."

Dillon said, "You worked with Bill Turner?"

"Yes, sir. We miss Bill."

Dillon extended his hand. "It's good to see you, Pete. I miss Bill too. What in hell are you doing here?"

Freeman glanced at the other officers standing awkwardly by. Colonel Flynn looked particularly glum.

As an army man Flynn had had no direct contact with the air force security agency, but he knew very well General Dillon was its founder, and he had heard how OSI officers still regarded Dillon as one of theirs. OSI men, with their civilian clothes and their exemptions from the requirements of rank, were more than ever misfits in the military, resented even outside the air force. They were also, unfortunately, damn good investigators.

"I'm the commander of the local district, sir," Freeman said.

"How'd you know we were coming?" Dillon asked.

"We try to maintain your standard, sir, of knowing what matters." Freeman grinned. "I just came out to add my word of greeting to Colonel Flynn's." Again, Freeman offered the army man a deferential nod, but the wooden DIA commander did not respond. "And to say, General, that we would be honored, your schedule permitting, to have you inspect our facility at Bien Hoa. And to also say that OSI is at your service should there be—"

"Thank you, Pete," Dillon said with patent appreciation, but he cut him off too. It would not serve Dillon's purpose to show up the reticent and cautious Flynn. Dillon's in-field DIA people, men from all three services, were the ones whose devotion he needed now, and winning it had proved far more difficult than the air force agency's had ever been. Heartfelt as Freeman's gesture was, OSI was history for Dillon now.

Despite his civilian clothes Freeman took half a step back and saluted smartly. Dillon returned the salute. Dismissed, the OSI man turned and walked away.

Dillon nodded at Flynn and the group set off in the opposite direction, Flynn and Dillon side by side, leading the way across the tarmac. Dillon noted it when Colonel Flynn skipped subtly, tucking one foot briefly behind the other, to get into step with him.

"I expected to see body bags somewhere here," Dillon said as they walked. He had to engage this man, to smoke him out. It was an old act of cops' intuition to ask a frontal question that went right to the heart of things.

They were passing the C-130s. The noise of revving engines made it necessary to speak loudly, but also it isolated them.

"Body bags, sir?"

"Yes, Colonel."

"I doubt if they'd be that noticeable. We haven't been losing that many kids lately."

"We lost seven hundred in November and four-fifty in December."

"That was Ia Drang, though, General. Things have been going much better since Ia Drang."

Is Drang was the valley in the Central Highlands where the

half-rookie First Air Cavalry had been decimated in a series of disastrous battles that had begun within a few weeks of their much-touted arrival. When the Air Cav had been so dramatically staggered, the President had responded by immediately sending over another fifty thousand troops, but still without mobilization. More rookies, in other words.

"But the remains are sent home from here, aren't they?"

"Yes, sir. But you don't see bags on the flight line now, not since those photos ran in *Life*, the dead arranged in squad formation, waiting to be loaded onto C-130s. The body bags are kept inside the hangars now, and loaded from there."

"Who ordered it done like that?"

"You could assume, General, that Camus MacVie did."

"Who?"

The quick look Flynn gave Dillon had a note of panic in it. A mistake? Showing up the general? Referring disrespectfully to another? "General Westmoreland, sir."

COMUS-MACV. Dillon had never heard the acronym pronounced. "What's the total now, KIA?"

"1,757 as of Monday."

"And the rate projection is—?"

"As of now, 500 per month."

"But we're doing better than that?"

"Yes, sir." Flynn hesitated, then added, "So we're told."

"What do you mean by that?"

"U.S. casualty figures are out of our purview, sir. That's all I meant."

Flynn was clearly grateful to be able to cut into Base Ops then, the low-slung white building beside the looming control tower. Colonel Flynn led Dillon's party through the crowd of pilots and navigators, cargo masters and transport officers. Those men were uniformly young, with very short haircuts, lean bodies, cracking agitation. They stared openly as the line of senior officers passed through.

Outside, drawn up at the curb were four unmarked Citroëns, each with civilian plates and each with a Vietnamese driver standing by its door. The drivers were dressed in slacks and Hawaiian shirts.

Dillon approached the driver of the lead car. "Do you speak English?"

"Yes, sir."

"What's your name?"

"Tran."

"Tran, I want you to stay here and supervise the transfer of our baggage. Will you do that for me?"

The driver glanced at Flynn, who did not react.

"You can pick your car up at our quarters." Dillon offered his hand and the driver took it. "Thanks, Tran." The driver smiled then, and hustled back into the operations building.

Dillon turned to Packard. "You drive, Mike. Follow the other cars." And to Flynn he said, "Colonel, you ride with me."

Dillon and Flynn got in the backseat as Packard sat behind the wheel. The other officers loaded into the automobiles behind.

Packard let the second Citroën go ahead of him, then fell in behind it. As the cars pulled away Dillon's eye wandered across the sights of the teeming air base, the barracks and hangars, maintenance buildings and huge warehouses.

"It's like a boomtown," Packard said from his place at the wheel.

"It's incredible," Flynn replied with nervous enthusiasm, "how fast we've done this." He pointed to a factory-sized building that reminded Dillon of the tempos on the Mall. "That's the new MACV headquarters. It will be done in May. Pentagon East, they call it."

Packard glanced in the mirror, catching Dillon's eye. Westmoreland was moving his headquarters onto this base because not even Saigon was secure.

"Speaking of headquarters, General," Flynn began, "I've already arranged—"

"No arrangements with headquarters will be necessary for now, Colonel. I want you to work with Mr. Packard in putting together a meeting with your personnel this afternoon."

"My personnel?"

"The DIA detachment of which you are commander."

"All of them?"

"Yes."

"But General, some of my men are in the field, and they won't—"

"I'm especially interested in hearing from them. Get everyone there."

"But I—"

"If there's a problem with this afternoon, we'll have the

conference tonight. But I'd prefer it this afternoon. Mr.
Packard will work with you. I want a full-court briefing on the
current enemy battle order. I want to know current rates of
North-South infiltration. I want your assessments. I don't need
anyone outside DIA."

"General MacAuliff would—"

"Just my people, Colonel. My arrangement with General
MacAuliff and MACV is something else. I don't want you to
involve them at this point. Is that clear?"

"Yes, sir."

"I want DIA credentials displayed, no one else admitted. A
secure conference room outside the MACV compound."

"Our offices are in the compound, General."

"I know that. I want this meeting held elsewhere."

"But, sir, without notice there's no place else I could—"

"Colonel, there are ten thousand Americans in Saigon. Are
you telling me there is no secure conference room outside
MACV headquarters?"

"Sir, I—"

Dillon's eyes went to the rearview mirror, to Packard. "Get
on to Freeman, Mike. Tell him we'll take him up on his offer.
I want the meeting at OSI at Bien Hoa Air Base." He looked
at Flynn, whose upper lip had broken out perspiring. "Nineteen
hundred hours, Colonel."

Dillon paused before asking the question that President
Johnson habitually put to Westmoreland. "Can you do it?"

Challenged in that way, Flynn answered promptly, as he was
supposed to. "Yes, sir."

Dillon faced away from Flynn just as Packard followed the
lead car through the air base gate, out onto the road that would
take them into Saigon. Shacks and lean-tos with walls made of
flat pounded beer cans were clustered like barnacles on the
U.S. enclave. A stench hung in the air. Dillon's first experience
of the people he too was at war to save was of the maimed
half-naked men, the clacking boys with limbs missing, the
dull-eyed girls pumping their hands, all rushing the line of
sleek cars for the minute it took the drivers to accelerate away.

A moment later Dillon realized that without actually being
threatened by the Vietnamese beggars and whores, he had automatically raised his hand—his palm wet now—as if to fend
off a sudden swarm of crazed birds.

* * *

Display boards on a pair of easels dominated the front of the room. Colonel Flynn was standing between them with his pointer, winding up his presentation. Forty-one uniformed Americans, including Dillon, sat on metal folding chairs in front of Flynn. Packard was next to Dillon in the first row. Every man present wore DIA credentials pinned to his shirt. Mostly they were young, lieutenants, captains, a few majors.

One board was headed "Statistics, February 1, 1966," and it outlined in comparative figures the troop strengths of the allies and the Communists, the numbers to date of battalion-sized attacks, of bomb tonnage dropped, of acres defoliated. At the bottom, side by side, were the numbers of casualties suffered. The second board listed numbers also, under three headings: "Commando Hunt," "Market Garden," and "White Wing," which referred respectively to the interdiction efforts along the Ho Chi Minh Trail and along the coastal waterways, and to the big-unit winter offensive spearheaded by the 25th Infantry Division and the 101st Airborne Division. This board listed numbers of enemy trucks and tonnage of ammunition, supplies and rice destroyed or captured. Particularly highlighted were the numbers of NVA regulars deployed to the South by all routes.

With a flourish, Colonel Flynn whipped one board off its easel to expose another, "Projections: VC-NVA." Not numbers arranged in columns, but a graph on which a rising curve had topped out and begun moving down. Flynn slapped the graph dramatically with his pointer, the practiced gesture of a professional briefer. "Here is the key," he said. "We have a kill ratio going of two-point-six. We have cut the Communists' ability to infiltrate reinforcements by sixty percent. Main force Vietcong and NVA regulars are dying or being wounded now faster than they can replace themselves. The same downturn applies to supplies and ammunition. Those are the hard numbers on which our estimates are based." Flynn put his pointer on the easel's ledge and faced his audience once more, bringing his eyes confidently to Dillon.

Dillon was staring at the graph. The numbers differed slightly from what he'd seen, but the thrust of Flynn's presentation matched what his own briefers in the Pentagon had been saying for two months. Westmoreland, the JCS, the secretary of defense, and the CIA all seemed to agree that despite the high cost in American casualties, the commitment of U.S. ground forces had turned the tide. President Johnson had said as much on national television, describing as potentially decisive his recent order to increase U.S. troop levels one last time. Soon there would be three hundred thousand GIs in Vietnam.

"Very impressive, Colonel."

Dillon took a moment to light a cigarette, not because he particularly wanted one, but to avoid the air of a cross-examining attorney. "My hat's off to you and your men. It's easy to see why there's been a downturn also in the criticism we've been getting at DIA for being negative." He waved his match out.

Flynn let his weight fall onto one foot, relaxing. He acknowledged Dillon's compliment with a nod.

"I have a question or two," Dillon said, "but before I ask them, I'd like you to open the discussion to the floor. Does anyone present have anything to add—or for that matter subtract?"

Flynn raised his eyes to the room. No one moved.

Dillon slowly turned in his chair. Every man was staring at him. Their faces were impossible to read. Only moments before they had looked so young to Dillon, a roomful of Richards. But now, with their concealing masks in place, they reminded him of the robot-bureaucrats in the Pentagon.

Dillon said, "Then you're all agreed." He swiveled back to Flynn. "Tell me, Colonel, how you arrive with such precision at the enemy casualty figures. Communists killed in action, 37,784. Where do you get that?"

"Body counts, General, taken after every engagement. Men present in this room supervise ARVN counterparts in keeping track. It's the area in which discipline has improved the most."

"So you consider the KIA figure hard, not estimate."

"Hard as numbers get, General. Margin of error five percent or less."

"I see no figure for civilian casualties."

"No, sir. You requested battle order."

"11,430 trucks destroyed. Where do you get that?"

"That's an air force number. 'Commando Hunt.' I would consider that figure less hard, sir."

"Aren't our people debriefing pilots?"

"Yes, sir, but they have their own formulas and adjustments. It's likely that at least occasionally more than one pilot claims the same hit."

Dillon smoked in silence for a moment, studying the graph,

the downward curve. It was the perfect expression of the two-pronged American strategy. Seal off the battlefield with bombing. Then engage the enemy and attrit. Finally, he said, "The infiltration figure. NVA North to South. How is that exact?"

Flynn glanced at his board. "We have a variety of sources, sir."

Dillon waited.

"Electronic sensors seeded from the air along the Trail measure troop movement."

"Right."

"Observation posts at the DMZ, in the hills above Dakto, above Pleiku, above Banmethuot, and above Tayninh. Those posts are staffed jointly by ARVN soldiers and our people. Again, some of them are here. In the last year the web of jungle paths was transformed into a modern logistical system, as the Communists shifted from a mainly guerrilla force into a conventional army, but that means now they depend on roads and bridges, heavy trucks and storage facilities, all of which are vulnerable from the air, and more to our point, easier to observe."

"Electronic sensors and observations posts."

"Yes, sir."

"What else?"

Flynn hesitated, then said, "SOGs."

Study and Observation Groups was the innocuous name given to the highly secret teams of U.S. soldiers which operated along the Trail in Laos and Cambodia. Dillon knew that the talk of electronic sensors and observation posts was pure bullshit, what MACV put out for the press. The roving of teams of superstealth soldiers along the Trail were the main source for the key infiltration numbers on which everyone's recent optimism, from Flynn's to President Johnson's, depended. The essential evidence for that optimism could never be presented to the public because it involved illegal military incursions into two countries with which the United States was not at war. What made Dillon uneasy was the fact that, because of the operation's secrecy, that evidence could not be corroborated either, not even by him. SOGs were Special Forces units and they operated not out of DIA but directly out of MACV. Suddenly Dillon felt that he'd come all the way to Vietnam not for a breakthrough in measuring the reliability of the intelligence system over which he presided, but for a close-up view

of the very wall that made him blind. The key facts on which
the entire American prospect in Vietnam turned—could the
battlefield be sealed off or not?—were compiled not by
bureaucrats—finally, that's what he, and for that matter the
President, were—but by adventurous men whose faces were
smeared with black grease. Wall? Dillon was once more up
against Aristotle's old divide between men of thought and men
of action. Wars go wrong when that divide becomes absolute.
Unless Sean Dillon could go on patrol with the stalkers himself, it seemed to him that he would never know what numbers
to trust and what to reject as mere fantasy meant to please superiors. Go on patrol? Hell, he was fifty-six years old.

He was about to stand and thank Flynn, and give the men
what they thought they'd come for, a short motivating talk
about the importance of their mission, but then the door to
Dillon's right opened and a two-star army general walked into
the room. It was a violation of protocol—they were already in
the presence of an officer senior to the newcomer—but the
men came to their feet at once. Flynn braced himself like a
plebe.

Only Dillon and Packard remained seated. No one had to
explain to them that this was MacAuliff, Westmoreland's intelligence chief. He drew himself up in front of Dillon, who only
crossed his legs, continuing to smoke, waiting.

MacAuliff was a thick-necked, stocky man of medium
height. In appearance he reminded Dillon of another Scot,
Macauley, the air force bomber general who had at first opposed Dillon, then had become his strongest supporter.

MacAuliff said coldly, "This meeting is in violation of security, General. Whoever authorized it is out of order."

"I authorized it." Dillon stood up wearily.

Packard alone remained seated, wearing an air of, Fuck you
all.

MacAuliff was shaking his reddened face. "No, General, not
here, not in—"

But Dillon cut him off with a sharp order. "Get out." His
arm shot toward the door, his cigarette steady between his fingers.

MacAuliff, despite himself, fell back a step.

"This is a closed briefing, General. DIA only. Now get out."

MacAuliff took another step back. "I'm speaking for General Westmoreland—"

"I gave you an explicit order. I expect to be obeyed."

MacAuliff's eyes brushed Dillon's left shoulder, as if to confirm that decisive third star. Then he executed an about-face and left.

Dillon calculated quickly. It would take MacAuliff twenty minutes to get to Westmoreland's headquarters. He had less than an hour. He faced the room. "Sit down, gentlemen."

The officers sat, bursting for a few seconds in expressions of surprise and interest, then falling completely silent and looking up at Dillon with an attention they had not given him before.

"I'm going to dismiss you now. I am grateful for this chance to meet you. I appreciate the diligence with which you have applied yourselves to your mission. The entire structure of the Defense Intelligence Agency stands behind you, but our ability to provide the President, the secretary of defense and, especially, front-line commanders here in the zone with the intelligence needed to win this war depends absolutely on you.

"I have tried to think of what I might do to convey my personal appreciation, and here is what I came up with. I would be happy to make contact with your families for you when I return home. I will call them myself, any of you who'd like me to. I have asked Colonel Freeman for the loan of his office across the hall for the next few minutes, and I will be available there to meet you, to take any messages you might like me to convey. From my own selfish point of view, this is my chance to simply shake your hands and say thank you."

Dillon nodded, and the men stood as he turned and left the room.

The officers filed in to meet him one by one, a series of quick encounters. Dillon made a point to gesture at the door as each man entered, to have him close it. The small, tidy office—a desk, file cabinets, the OSI seal on the wall—had the feel to Dillon of a confessional. As warmly but also as efficiently as he could, he took each man's personal information, noting it on an index card. And then, before dismissing him, he asked each one the question "Do you have anything to add to the briefing we just had from Colonel Flynn?"

One after another, the officers answered promptly, "No, sir." Each time Dillon nodded, as if that were the response he wanted.

Then a young captain entered, perhaps the tenth DIA officer to present himself. He was blond but gaunt, a man who had

lost his good looks. The stench of stale alcohol radiated from
him, and when he turned from closing the door to shake hands,
Dillon noted at once the bloodshot eyes, the slight tremor in
his hand. His cheekbones protruded, making grottoes of his
eye sockets.

"Thomas Bowers, sir."

"Nice to meet you, Captain. How long have you been
here?"

"Eight months, sir. My cover is MAAG. I'm attached to the
ARVN office that runs joint analysis teams in I Corps."

"So you're in a position to know . . . ?"

"What we get from prisoners." Bowers dropped his eyes. "It
is not nice work, sir."

"I understand that." Dillon remembered Richard that night at
Bolling, the way the word "torture" had twisted his face.
Dillon's own quick denial that intelligence men used torture,
he knew now, had been much too facile. DIA men were not
supposed to participate in sadistic ARVN interrogations, but
they were expected to make full use of information, however
obtained. Dillon said, "Questions put directly to enemy soldiers give us the most important intelligence we have. What
you do is crucial, Captain."

"Thank you, sir."

There was a long silence then, and once more Dillon
thought of the confessional. When he'd dreamed years ago of
being a priest, mainly what he'd hoped to be was kind.

This captain in front of him, obviously at a personal limit,
an alcohol abuser, was the sort of man Dillon had ruthlessly
eliminated from his operations for decades now. But Dillon's
heart flowed toward Bowers, partly out of genuine compassion
and partly out of the sense that this man could give him what
he wanted. Dillon prodded quietly, "Something's bothering
you."

"Yes, sir."

"What?"

"I don't have more than a small piece of the picture, sir."
Bowers glanced back at the door, then stepped closer to Dillon.
"But what we see in I Corps does not square with the numbers
you just got from Colonel Flynn."

"What do you mean, Captain?"

"The enemy battle-order estimates are way off, General.

We're not killing half the VC that Flynn says we are, not in I Corps. And if you ask me, not anywhere."

"You heard what the colonel said. Those numbers are confirmed."

"Confirmed *bodies*, maybe. But not *soldiers*. We count civilians, General. That's why Colonel Flynn's summary didn't list civilians as a separate category. They have civilian casualty figures for *bombing*, but not for combat. Anybody killed in combat, even little girls, old ladies, villagers—they count them as VC. *That's* why the kill ratio has soared. I hear that ARVN has been faking body counts for years, and now we're helping them to do it. The numbers are what General MacAuliff wants, and it's what we give him."

"What troop-force indications do you get from prisoners?"

"That's what worries me. Captured VC and NVA regulars give us numbers that run the other way. Up, not down, in I Corps anyway. I've written several explicit memos on this myself. MacAuliff's numbers do *not* include self-defense units either, the VC auxiliaries who lay the Claymores and booby traps. We keep those numbers—SDUs are going up for sure—but they never make it onto charts or into briefings. We're not killing near as many as we say we are, and the Communists are sending in *more* than we say. We have North Vietnamese prisoners linked to nine separate NVA battalions, but MACV claims there are only four in I Corps."

"How can you be certain of that?"

"Believe me, General, by the time the poor buggers we have start to talk, they tell the truth."

Dillon thought of the letters home that Richard had heard some priest read, how he, Dillon, had dismissed them.

"And you've put all this in memos?"

"Yes, sir."

"To whom?"

"Colonel Flynn. And I've talked to my counterparts in III and IV Corps. It's the same everywhere, General. Not suppression, maybe, but being hooked on the most optimistic reports. When collators get contradictory feed, they just file the bad news under 'Dubious' or 'Unconfirmed.' Guys at my level know that the brass wants good news, so they just try to find it wherever they can."

"Every war has a version of that problem, Captain. No soldier wants to think his friends are dying for nothing."

"But they die when they shouldn't have to. That's my problem. I don't care if General MacAuliff needs happy-talk to send up the line to MACV and on to Washington. I don't give a damn what people think in Washington—no offense, sir. But the numbers Colonel Flynn gave you are what our guys take on patrol with them. In I Corps we've got grunts going into the jungle thinking Commie troop strength is half what it really is, and *that* it why our guys are getting blown away. We write ARVN soldiers off as cowards, but the reason they don't go charging into battle is because they know better than to believe what their intelligence officers tell them. Our guys are dumb enough to believe us."

Captain Bowers was leaning over Dillon with a wild look in his dark eyes. His fists were clenched in front of his chest. To Dillon, after all these months, he was like an apparition come with the message of his worst fear.

Before Dillon could respond, there was a single sharp rap on the door.

"Come!" Dillon said.

Colonel Freeman, the OSI chief, opened the door halfway and leaned in. "General Cobb is on the line, sir, General Westmoreland's exec. He wants to talk to you right now."

Dillon felt the pulse of his own blood, but he clamped it and showed nothing.

Freeman glanced at Bowers, undecided, but only for a moment. "I told General Cobb that you might have left already."

"You were right, Pete. I did leave. I'm gone already. Tell General Cobb that you heard me say I hope to meet with General Westmoreland tomorrow morning."

Freeman nodded and left.

Dillon looked at Captain Bowers. "I want copies of your memos."

Bowers leaned in on Dillon again. "I'll get them for you tonight. Will you show them to Westmoreland? Will you say they're not getting—?"

"Captain, you have to trust me to handle what you give me. I don't want you talking about it, that's all. I don't control your assignment here, but I need it."

"But *you* have to tell Westmoreland. He'll listen to you."

"I said, you have to trust me. You may not care about Washington, but that's where I can make a difference. I need your numbers. I want you to get your own current I Corps estimates down on paper for me, and if possible sound out your counterparts in the other sectors. I want regular reports from you. I don't want Flynn to know. I don't want him dumping you, or MacAuliff either."

"But General, what about the battle order? I can't just slip the real numbers off to you in CONUS while guys here keep getting the bullshit. *Here* is where our guys are getting killed. You're asking me to just go along with that?"

Richard again. Dillon kept seeing Richard.

"You're not going along with it now, are you?"

"No, sir."

"You're doing something about it by telling me, aren't you?"

"Yes, sir."

"Captain, you're going to have to trust me on this. It's my job to make the best use of what you give me. Will you trust me?"

After a moment Bowers answered. "Yes, sir."

Dillon nodded. "Colonel Freeman will channel your paper to me. He's OSI, not DIA, but he has full clearance. You have complete discretion to say anything you think. But the harder your numbers are, the better. What I need are data, anything you can get me about enemy numbers. I'm not *ordering* you to do this, because it involves irregularities that could cause us both problems. You just saw that in my response to Cobb. But I will promise you this: I will be out on the limb with you if anybody tries to cut it off."

Bowers laughed. "General, that's enough for me. I was hoping for this." His face darkened. "Desperately hoping."

"I sense that, Captain. Pull in on the desperation if you can. Cut back on the booze. I don't want you getting sent home on detox. I need you."

"Yes, sir," Bowers answered firmly. "All I needed was a reason to quit."

Dillon smiled, the kindly old confessor. "You don't have to quit, Captain. Just slow it down." He picked up a blank index card. "And what about your folks? Can I call them for you when I get home?"

"Yes, sir. Please."

"What's the name?"

"Dr. John Bowers, Fort Wayne—"

"Your father's a doctor?"

At first Dillon had no idea why that particular detail should have struck him with such force. But then he knew. Another man who'd trusted him, Riley, Richard Riley, the doc.

NINETEEN

"I can't believe he's really dead." Cass was looking away from Sean, out her window. She didn't want him to see that she was near crying again. The red-tinged leaves of the September trees passed in a blur. They were in Sean's long blue car, riding in back with a stretch of the soft gray upholstery separating them. Sergeant Kingfield was at the wheel. Richard was in the front passenger seat. He had graduated from Georgetown two springs before, and was a second-year law student at the University of Virginia now. As if it would help to fend her emotions, Cass looked at the back of her son's head. The fringe of his hair brushed the collar of his dark suit. Usually he wore his hair longer. She knew he'd gotten it cut for her, for this, not that she cared, really. He was her rock. She was so grateful to him for getting here.

They were on Michigan Avenue, passing the wooded vale at the foot of the hill on which the Old Soldiers' Home sat. Up ahead the Shrine had just come into view, the huge blue beach ball of a dome, the needle spire of the K of C belfry, the largest Catholic church in North America. Ordinarily Cass felt a lift on first glimpsing the great basilica, but this morning her heart sank. They were coming here for the funeral of the man who'd built it, her oldest friend in Washington, Archbishop Barry.

Sean reached across to touch her. Unconsciously, she covered his hand with hers, holding it on the seat. She was still looking at her son. "I was thinking last night of his baptizing you, Richard. He did it here. Do you remember that? At the Shrine."

Richard turned and looked at his mother. He smiled, but

with a touch of self-mocking solemnity. "What I remember is that I was just a baby, Mom."

"Archbishop Barry was the rector. He was the first priest we knew here. He made our coming from Chicago seem all right. He gave me . . ." Cass took her hand back from Sean to open her purse for a fresh Kleenex.

Richard glanced at his father. They saw each other rarely these days. It had been so long since they had talked that Richard knew there was no point in trying, here, to indicate anything. Should he say, for example, that his mother's sadness was upsetting to him, but that he hardly shared it? He had come from Charlottesville for her, not for Monsignor Barry and not for his father.

The silence into which his mother's grief had taken them drummed unpleasantly in Richard's ears. "Actually, Mom," he said, "my favorite memory of Monsignor Barry will always be when he went to give you that medal from the Pope, but he didn't know where to pin it."

Cass smiled wanly. "Archbishop," she said softly, correcting the title Richard had used. She went back to looking out her window.

Sean reached up to touch the back of Richard's seat. Richard was sure his father was going to find fault with him. For recalling a moment of the archbishop's awkwardness? For calling him Monsignor? For hair that was too long? But Sean said, "I'm glad you could get here." Richard turned around in his seat, unable to keep the surprise from his face. But then he remembered, it was not true that his father could read his mind. Perhaps his father did not know how alien he felt. He almost said something to explain himself, but instead he glanced at the driver, who was new to him. The driver's presence, like that of how many other drivers and orderlies before him, guaranteed that they would not speak of anything that mattered. With Mack he might have, but Mack was retired, and now Richard knew enough to measure what they had been to each other, despite the fondness, by the fact that he had never known Mack's first name. He had never known any of their first names.

Richard thought of those nights when he had been the one to drive his father home. He had not done so in more than a year now. He could see it: the two of them staring out into the moving lights of the darkened city, stone silent, as if they had each begun to believe that Richard too was the general's servant. It was their silence when they were alone that Richard had come to find unbearable.

At Fourth Street the driver steered the car into the Shrine's broad entrance circle. Policemen lined the curving drive like posts. The shadowless Romanesque church loomed above a row of arriving automobiles, many of them limousines. Senators, congressmen, lobbyists, Establishment lawyers and stars of the administration were leaving their cars and heading up the long flight of bright stairs.

Richard saw a four-star army general getting out of an olive-green staff car, and from a car behind, a pair of admirals. Archbishop Barry, with Cardinal Spellman of New York, had taken recently to staunchly defending the war in Vietnam. The more strident the war's critics had become, especially among the liberal clergy, the more pointed had become Barry's expression of support. No wonder the military brass were here. Richard wished for a way to set his father apart from them. My father knew this priest before he was a bishop, before my father was a general! Richard glanced back at the stars on his father's shoulders. When had it ever occurred to Richard that those stars would cause him to feel ashamed?

The mourners, moving in a steady stream up the stairs, all carried themselves like VIPs, except for the nuns and priests, who were alike in hiking their robes to go up. As Sergeant Kingfield slowed their car, Richard looked away from the church entrance. Beside the Shrine was an oblong green, a tranquil stretch of tidy lawn, and beyond that were the pseudo-Gothic buildings of Catholic University. He recognized in the distance the oblivious bustle of students going to and from classrooms. Richard envied them their rightful indifference to this event, but Catholic students were known for their indifference to civil rights and peace marches too. Did he envy them that? To Richard's surprise, though, he saw on a nearby sidewalk, opposite the K of C bell tower, a moving circle of twenty or thirty protesters who were carrying hand-lettered signs he could not read. Not students, he realized, but mature people, Quakers or *Catholic Worker* types probably. They were separated from the throng of funeral goers by a thin row of policemen, but unlike the ceremonial guard lining the driveway those cops had their nightsticks ready. To Richard's relief, neither of his parents seemed to notice the demonstrators, and to his further relief, once he'd left his father's car, none of the demonstrators seemed to notice him.

The familiar aroma of wax hit Richard's nostrils as he entered the church. Thousands of votive candles flickered eerily in the pale morning light at side altars up both sides of the length of the nave. More than any other detail, that smell evoked what was left to him of Catholic feeling. Adorning the concave wall at the far end of the church, dwarfing everything but the stone structure itself, was the sparkling mosaic of a Byzantine Christ. The figure's huge oriental eyes burned into everyone else's face, perhaps, but not Richard's. He remembered that the gaze of that Christ was famous for following the guilty no matter where they went in the vast space. But now the eyes seemed flat and unthreatening, like the religion itself.

Richard looked at his mother, knowing how wounded she would be to know her son was an apostate. He wished she could take it as a sign of his deep love, that he was not here for God either. He was here only for her. He squeezed his mother's elbow, sending her a pulse of affection and concern.

An usher recognized them and led the Dillons up the long aisle, directly to reserved seats in the fourth pew on the epistle side, well in front of Cabinet secretaries and national politicians, including the two senators Kennedy. Others already seated in the fourth pew included the former vice president, the heavy-browed Richard Nixon, Martin Donne, the wealthy Irish contractor who had built the Shrine and numerous other buildings for the archdiocese, and former mayor Robert Wagner of New York. Richard noticed that after genuflecting his father glanced back several rows at Secretary McNamara, who did not acknowledge him. To Richard it seemed that his father had just been snubbed, but that made no sense.

The first two pews were occupied by far more ordinary-looking people than the illustrious VIPs next to and behind the Dillons, and Richard sensed that they were the archbishop's relatives. The third pew, the one immediately in front of the Dillons, was vacant.

The organ was playing softly.

Cass sat holding each of her men by the hand. Behind them, well back along the aisle, mourners continued to file into the pews.

Finally, all was still except for the organ, and soon it too fell silent. The vast church, thronged by more than two thousand

people, was hushed. Nothing to do but float into the luminous
eyes of the mammoth Savior. Richard became impatient for the
procession to begin, but the sudden commotion came then not
from the distant rear, where the clergy and pallbearers had
gathered with the casket, but from the small doorway to the
left of the Dillons' pew. Three men in dark suits came swiftly
in, each darting down a different aisle. Two others entered, taking up positions in front of the first pews, staring out over the
congregation with such undisguised hostility that Richard
thought the show of it must be part of their strategy.

An ear-splitting blast of trumpets, coming on the heels of the
arrival of the Secret Service, made many in the congregation
jump. The trumpets sounded almost angry, and they were followed on the organ by an agitated liturgical flourish, which led
into the first bars of "Veni Creator Spiritu."

The congregation's attention flowed backward in a wave
toward the long line of clergy and the coming casket. Everyone
in the church stood like one huge stirring animal. Richard continued to watch the small side door, and it was just then, as
most heads had turned away, that two more agents came in,
leading the President and one of his daughters. They slipped
into the vacant pew and moved toward the aisle until they
were in front of the Dillons. The girl, the convert to Catholicism, knelt down for her brief prayer, but the President turned
as others had, to face the rear. He seemed to draw all the color
in the surrounding space to himself, even that of the towering
mosaic behind him, as if he were a Technicolor figure having
intruded by mistake on the set of a black-and-white movie.
Johnson's blue suit, his red tie, his tanned skin and the tiny
American flag in his lapel all shimmered brilliantly. Richard
had never seen him this close before, or any President, and he
felt ambushed by the power of the man's presence. Johnson's
lachrymose expression, reminiscent of the one he used on television to talk of the war dead, revolted Richard, but when his
eyes and the President's met for an instant, Richard nodded, an
act of pure, instinctive, affirming subservience for which he instantly hated himself.

Sean Dillon had his own reaction to the President's arrival.
He did not stare. All through the procession and the first part
of the liturgy he found it possible to act as if the man in front
of him were nobody, but inwardly Dillon felt the knot of his
frustration twisting, and from his own deep irrationality he

heard, as if it came from someone else, a cry of, Now! Now! Now's your chance to tell him!

When concelebrating bishops and priests had taken their seats in the sanctuary and the congregation had settled down for the readings, Dillon let his eyes park on the back of Johnson's head. While verses from Isaiah and from the letter of Paul to the Ephesians rolled out with soothing meaninglessness into the vast air above them, Dillon composed his own epistle.

"You are not getting the whole story, Mr. President."

Not an epistle but a speech, one he had been composing for months without knowing it. The reel of his mind spun it off, as if the back of Johnson's head were a prompting device.

"Mr. President, here, behind you. Listen to me. I'm on your side, Sir. I am one of your loyal officers. I'm trying to help you. Listen to what I have to say."

Sean Dillon thought of Johnson as a rational man, as a good man, but also as a man tortured by an inability to make crucial things happen, which was like Sean's own inability, Sean's own torture.

"Here is what is wrong," he imagined himself saying. "By the time intelligence estimates work their way to Washington the rough edges on all the numbers, the pits and flaws and imperfections, have been removed. And by the time they get to you, they are perfectly polished. But it is the pits and flaws and imperfections in those numbers that are killing us. When are you going to get angry at what we're telling you? You keep sending our kids over there, three hundred and twenty-two thousand of them now, and then we turn around and tell you it isn't quite enough. When are you going to ask us why we keep doing that to you? When are you going to get angry at what we are not telling you? Ask us, Mr. President, what the problem is! Demand to know! And some of us will admit we have one. We will explain it."

Dillon's impulse was to sit on the edge of his pew and touch Johnson's shoulder and whisper, "Mr. President, may I see you for a moment after?"

But if Johnson were to turn his face toward him, Dillon realized it would be uncomprehending, and he would have to add, "I'm your director of DIA. I'm one of the men who never gets near you. I put queries beside half the numbers I'm obliged to send you, but I know those indications of doubt are removed before you see them. You deal in summaries, but the summaries never include the questions that nag at men lower down the line or the dissenting footnotes of the few skeptics that are left at my level or even the cautiously expressed misgivings of men who are on the fringe of your circle. So the summaries on which you base your decisions—four hundred thousand now, five hundred thousand next? six hundred thousand?—never include the most important part, the fact that no one really knows what's going on in Vietnam. Between you and the real war stands a bureaucracy that blocks out that humiliating brutal truth. Well, for once no bureaucracy stands between us, Mr. President, so here it is."

Dillon's one fist was clenched at his side. His other was squeezing his wife's hand so hard it hurt her, but he did not know that. He did not know for certain, either, that he had not begun to speak these words aloud. They came with the fluidity of a crafted speech, not because his mind ordinarily worked that way, but because, in his unconscious, he'd been working these words over for a long time. The words unscrolled as on a prompter, and indeed, his lips were moving. If anyone noticed, perhaps they thought he was praying.

"I am presiding over the production of bad intelligence. My basic job for you, unlike CIA's or NSA's, is to count the enemy. That is the essential function of military intelligence, and I confess I am not doing it. I don't know how to do it. I would admit failure and resign, but no one else knows how to do it either, and I would be replaced by a sycophant general who regards the dogged skepticism of those below him as bad morale, instead of as a clue that must be followed.

"I used to think we were producing mere guesses for you, but lately I'm suspicious even that overstates what we are doing. We produce wishes for you in the form of data, wishes about the number of enemy dead and wishes about the number of enemy soldiers coming in from the North. Wishes that make you happy when you first hear them, but more and more, Mr. President, they've been making me nervous. What happens when they explode?

"In that light will we see that all our numbers had more to do with what we all thought you wanted than with what was actually out there in the jungle?

" 'Suspicious,' I said. I used to be a cop. In the Pentagon they still refer to me behind my back as a cop, but I've never considered it an insult. I'm talking about a cop's feeling now,

Mr. President, a set of unshakable intuitions about evidence, but my colleagues tell me you are not interested in suspicions or ominous intuition but only in facts. Everything else is defeatism and cowardice. Maybe so. Unfortunately I can't make this feeling of mine a fact. I've tried and tried but I can't get it into a form in which you or even I can use it. Someone else can, though, and someone else does. The kid from Sacramento or from Duluth or from Selma makes it a fact when he gets killed by an NVA soldier who by all our estimates does not exist. Then the fact we have is designated 'hard,' Mr. President, and why isn't it reason enough then to look again at our main assumptions: that we can seal off the South and win the war there; that we can do without full mobilization; that we can ignore the endless lines of Russian and Chinese supply, especially through Haiphong; or, the most basic assumption of all about this war, that we have to fight it. Asking such questions is not my job, but it should be someone's. Doesn't anyone tell you something else to do about that dead boy from Sacramento than to send his brothers over from Duluth and Selma, changing nothing else, so that they can become hard facts too?"

Dillon paused, as if the President were going to turn now and answer him. When Johnson did nothing of the kind, Dillon let his eyes drift up to the face of the mosaic Christ. It had never seemed so stern to him, and unforgiving. "Cowardice," Dillon repeated to himself.

His trance was broken when the congregation, cued by a gesture of the master of ceremonies, stood up for the reading of the Gospel passage. The choir intoned the alleluias with the forced joyfulness that marked the recently revised funeral liturgy. When Cass squeezed his hand Dillon knew she was thinking how the archbishop would have hated the new form of the Mass. The Dies Irae was gone, and so were the macabre black vestments, and so was the Latin.

The Gospel reading was about the Lord's raising of his beloved Lazarus from the dead, a happy proclamation of the good news if ever there was one. But Sean Dillon—defeatist?—seemed condemned to rebut everything with his doubt, and he found himself wanting to cry from the pew, "But Lazarus died again, didn't he? Where was Jesus then?"

Dillon did no such thing, of course. He sat demurely in his place throughout the liturgy, saying nothing, for that was what the situation required. And Sean Dillon, perhaps despite himself and certainly without fully meaning to, had become over the years the perfection of a man who did what was required. Silence and decorum; as the stages of the Mass progressed he experienced it as a sacrament of his entire life. The President of the United States was four feet away from him for more than an hour, and Dillon was powerless to reach him with his urgent questions. Sean Dillon had become one more of President Johnson's many underlings whose silence and decorum were efficiently and inexorably making Vietnam an American disaster. If he was different from the others, it was because he knew it.

"I repent myself . . ." Like an old refrain the line from Genesis began to roll by on the spool of Dillon's mind. Not in years had he thought of it, God's curse on his own creation, or had he felt it addressed so directly at himself. ". . . of ever having made him."

After communion, when those few in the congregation who received had returned to their places, there was a lull in the ceremony. Ordinarily the celebrant, having wiped the chalice clean, would say the last prayer and offer the blessing, and the recessional would begin. But the celebrant sat down instead. The others on the altar, bishops, priests, and servers alike, did the same. For some moments nothing happened.

Then the master of ceremonies moved a lectern to the center of the topmost step, adjusted the microphone and then walked down the half-dozen stairs to the center gate of the communion rail, which he opened. He nodded toward the President, who stood, left his pew, crossed to the communion rail and followed the MC up the stairs. President Johnson turned at the lectern, faced the congregation and began to speak.

Richard heard the President's words as if he were imprisoned in the crypt of that church; they were that unreal to him, that lost, in the stone echo of his own confusion. The President was saying something about his having come to this great church one night alone with Archbishop Barry, where they knelt in prayer together for guidance.

It took Richard a moment to realize he was actually talking about the war. He was talking about a decision he'd had to make about the bombing. President Johnson was talking—and later Richard would realize that this was what had made him snap—about how pained he, the President, was by the killing, about how he suffered with it more than anyone and about

how his dear friend the archbishop understood and bore the
burden of his pain and suffering with him. And now that our
boys had turned the last corner in Vietnam . . .

Richard had no sense of making an explicit decision to stand
up. His act was purely automatic. All that he was conscious of
doing was extricating his hand from his mother's. He never
looked at her. If he had, he realized later, he would never have
stood or slipped into the aisle or, just as the Secret Service
agent tensed, turned away from the President or begun the long
walk out of the packed church.

He became aware of what he was doing only in doing it. It
took forever. The lugubrious, despicable voice of the unaf-
fected President followed him, but what pounded in Richard's
ears was the defiant sound of his own footsteps. The people in
the pews stared at him, horror on their faces, and hatred. He
felt very small, vulnerable and afraid, but also he felt free.
Soon his movement down the length of the nave was not like
walking at all, but like flying, and Richard thought of himself
for a moment as the sparrow soaring through the great hall, the
story his father had told him years before. The eerie glow of
the votive candles struck him again as he recalled his father's
description of the sparrow's flight—human life—as an interval
of light between the two greater spheres of darkness.

But the light, real noonday light, blinding and brow-
piercing, was what awaited him when finally he pushed the
huge carved oak door open and left the church.

Word must have spread around the campus that the President was in the Shrine, because the small circle of peace demonstrators had grown much larger. Policemen were still
keeping it off to the side, and now they were wearing riot helmets. The picket line was moving in a broad oval along the
sidewalk, perhaps fifty strong now. Policemen and picketers
both were staring up at Richard, trying to decide if his appearance at the door meant the Mass was over. As he came down
the monumental staircase he drifted to the right, toward the
demonstrators. Having seen he was alone, they ignored him
now. Richard saw that in addition to the placards he had noted
before, some were carrying photographic blowups of war victims, and that was what decided him. He remembered the
photo of the napalmed girl which he had kicked at Georgetown
a long two years before. In joining the picket line he fell into
step with a gray-haired woman who was carrying a picture of

a mother bent over her dead baby. His emotion choked him.
The woman nodded at him and offered him the photograph to
carry. He took it without speaking or looking at the picture
again. He was relieved when the woman went off to get another for herself. He was afraid that he would cry.

When a few minutes later he picked his mother out of the
crowd that was spilling down the broad stairs—both the casket
and the President had been taken out the side doors—he pictured her not in black but in the tattered blue shirt, once his father's, that she always wore as a gardening smock. As a child
he had sat by the hour on the edge of his sandbox, a narrow
bench, watching her working at the flower bed, digging with
the hand spade, the tails of that shirt flapping behind her, filling him with the family feeling that he treasured. His father
now had his mother by the elbow, but she was leading, Richard saw, striding down the stairs at the angle that would bring
her to him.

Cass, for her part, had entered the eternity of pure feeling.
She was swollen by hurt and anger unlike any that a loved one
had ever caused in her before, much less Richard. Richard had
done this to her! She took the stairs blindly, seeing nothing but
him. The city of Washington, in the distance, was visible to
others from that height, but not to her. She could easily have
been in another city, another age. Once before she had felt
drawn out of herself like this, and she had charged then along
Exchange Avenue in Chicago, across from the Stone Gate of
the stockyards, stalking the man in the tavern who would tell
her what had happened to her Uncle Mike. The man who'd
told her was Sean.

Now Sean was holding her back. She pulled her elbow out
of his grasp and left him behind as she descended the last of
the stairs, brushing by a policeman who said, "Sorry, ma'am,"
and tried to stop her, but he could not.

Richard had stepped out of the moving circle of protesters
and was standing now, waiting with a child's panic in his face,
her adult son! Her law student! He held the oversized war photograph in front of himself like a shield, as if that would stop
her. The image of the anguished mother registered, but
vaguely—she would remember it in detail later—because she
was so intent on her son.

She closed the last dozen yards that separated them almost
running, in itself an extraordinary violation of decorum for her.

She drew her hand back as she moved, free of the impulse to speak because she knew there would never be words to express the betrayal she felt. He made no effort to turn away, but out of paralysis, not stoicism or courage. When the blow struck him, her open hand with all her might flat on his cheek, it stung even her, so sharply she seemed to awaken.

His head snapped away with such force she feared for an instant that she'd really hurt him. But he brought his face quickly back around and she recognized in his stunned expression, as only she could, a flash—she was sure—of gratitude.

When Richard at last found it possible to turn away from her, the God he no longer believed in, not finished with him yet, made his brimming eyes go immediately to the one face in the crowd on the basilica stairs that he truly wanted to avoid.

His father's.

His father was staring at him as from another world. If there was rage in his father at that moment, anything like his mother's, Richard could not see it. He knew he would never see it. What he saw instead and would always see now was nothing. His father's eyes—these were the eyes that would follow him everywhere—were simply blank, like a Greek statue's. The absence of expression in his father's face was so pure a form of personal negation that it cut through Richard like a chilling wind. The dead, he thought with a shudder. His father was staring at him from the world of the dead.

It never occurred to Sean Dillon anyway that he had time to brood about his son's behavior, but when he returned to the Pentagon that afternoon there was Michael Packard waiting for him.

Packard closed the door of Dillon's office behind himself, so that they were alone. He crossed to the desk just as his long-time boss was pulling up to it.

"What do you have?"

Packard held out a folder. "An ISIC bulletin."

Dillon took it and opened it, spreading it flat on the desk in front of him. Onto the center of an otherwise blank page three lines of ticker tape had been pasted. "1407/91267 Prior One," he read, "1407 DIA Estimates Officer, Captain John Bowers, USA, KIA 9-12-67, Area Da Nang. Rems Recovered. NOK Notfd."

Dillon stared at the strips of print, running his eyes over them again and again, waiting for the letters to rearrange themselves, to mean something else. When he looked up at Packard, finally, his deputy had turned away and was staring at the map of Southeast Asia that covered the nearby wall.

"What happened?"

"I don't know. That came in an hour ago."

"If the remains were recovered already and the next of kin have been notified, then there's no mystery. Why is this all we have?"

"Standard form, General. Casualty report won't come in until current dailies are posted."

"I want to know what happened to Bowers, and I want to know now. Cut through the dailies. Get back to Saigon, now."

Packard took a step toward the door.

Dillon stopped him. "Wait a minute. I'll do it myself."

"No, I'm—"

"I'm doing it, Mike." Dillon, clutching the folder, crossed ahead of Packard and out.

At the DIA alert center, the communications officer hurriedly and nervously sent off Dillon's demand. Dillon hovered behind him, waiting. In minutes the cipher machine sputtered out the tape of Saigon's reply. The officer read the tape, tore it and looked up at Dillon with an expression of distress. "No information, sir. Full reply pending."

"What do they mean, no information?"

"They must have—"

"Get me patched in to Flynn. Right now."

"I can't, sir. I'd have to go through Com Com MACV, and first I have to file a time request."

Without waiting for the officer to finish, Dillon turned on his heel and left the center. The Pentagon corridors through which he stormed were crowded with personnel. He cut through them as if they were shoppers on F Street. Packard hustled to keep up with him. When they hit a stretch of relatively deserted hallway Dillon said, "This summarizes my entire problem. Go through MACV, file a request, then route through the embassy, all to talk to my own man about what happened to another of my men!" Dillon stopped and faced Packard, poking him. "What did happen to Bowers? Do you know?"

"No, I don't. How could I?"

"They killed him. They killed him."

"Who did?"

Dillon stared back at Packard, unable to put his gut certainty into words.

Years before, Packard had felt self-conscious in calling Dillon General, and at first he had treated it as a joke. But then it became his customary way of addressing his boss, as it was everyone's. So it cut to the heart of their intimacy, of his concern, when he said now, "What, Sean? What are you thinking?"

Instead of answering, Dillon resumed his clipped pace along the hallway until at last he came to the suite of offices that had once been his. The director's office of the Air Force OSI.

Moments later, in the OSI communications center, Dillon stood with General Joe Hough, a protégé, while the OSI system went into play. Within minutes, a message came back from the OSI office at Bien Hoa. It was signed "Freeman" and it detailed what had happened to Bowers.

He went down in a transport helicopter shortly after it took off from the airfield at Da Nang. No hostile or friendly fire: a mechanical malfunction. The two pilots and all thirteen passengers, seven Vietnamese and six Americans, including a bird colonel, were killed. The chopper crashed in the jungle four miles outside the base perimeter. It took eleven hours to recover their bodies. Bowers's remains were now in the MATS morgue at Tan Son Nhut.

Between the OSI office and his own, Dillon stopped Packard. They were standing by a window overlooking the green courtyard that formed the center of the Pentagon, a target bull's-eye, the ultimate ground zero. Dillon looked out on the patch of grass, thinking as he often had before that grass was inappropriate for the place. It should have been paved, a parking lot for tanks. A heliport.

But grass. Grass evoked nearby Arlington, making Dillon think of the Pentagon as the largest tombstone in the world.

"Look, Mike. I want you to forget what I was thinking."

Packard laughed. "Boss, I'm good, I'm even very good. But I don't read your mind."

Dillon looked at him in surprise. "I didn't tell you what I was—"

"You said they killed him." Packard paused. "And I guess they did. The fates. The gods."

"It just shocked me, the plain fact of his being dead, but no details."

"And the details tell us a lot of men died. So we know Bowers wasn't singled out."

Dillon nodded. "Why do I feel relieved? He's still dead."

"You feel relieved because if your first instinct was right, it would mean the end of us."

"You and me?"

"The whole country."

Dillon nodded, then shook with a sudden shudder. He said quietly, "This thing is getting to me, Mike."

He led the way back to his office, Packard following. At his desk, Dillon swiveled absently toward the window, wanting a view to blank from his mind the image of the sterile grass courtyard. His eyes went to the needle in the distance, the Washington Monument, but he saw it as the K of C bell tower at the Shrine. He thought of Richard.

He wanted to call up Bowers's face, but he could not picture the man. Their encounter had been so short, so many months ago. He closed his eyes, trying for the image of the young captain, but when his mind broke free of his son, he saw instead the wrinkled, bloated drinker's face—Bowers was a drinker—of Richard Riley. Doc Riley. Trust me, Doc. Trust me, Captain.

Doc Riley's remains had never been recovered. And neither had Sean Dillon's ability to trust anyone but himself.

He opened his eyes and swiveled back to Packard. "Bowers's father is a doctor. When I call him he'll ask me exactly what—"

"General Hough said he'd have the autopsy by morning."

"I want to call Dr. Bowers tonight, from home. I'll want the autopsy carried out to him, in Fort Wayne. Send one of our people from the office here. Send Miller."

"Yes, sir."

"Do we have a photograph of Bowers?"

"I can get one from personnel."

Dillon opened the folder and read the strip message again. KIA: such innocuous letters, ruined for the language now forever. KIA, he thought. DIA. *Dia*. He'd never read it as the Greek word before. *Dia*: divided into two parts. He said, "I told Bowers I'd be out on the limb with him. But I wasn't."

"Hey, General, it was an accident. It could have happened on Shirley Highway."

Dillon shook his head. "He extended his tour for me."

"He knew it was important. You gave him a way to think that what he was doing was making a difference."

"But was it? What have I done with all that he sent me? What difference have I been able to make? The war goes on as if we could win it this way, but Bowers's numbers say we can't."

"There are all those other numbers, though. Everybody has his Bowers, General. They cancel each other out. Bowers's death isn't your fault, and neither is the confusion."

"Nothing's my fault. Nothing's anybody's fault. Damn it, everyone in this city is acting like the entire war is an accident! Somebody better start taking responsibility for it. I used to think the President was getting bad advice, but it's him! He has sold himself a complete bill of goods, and after hearing him at the funeral this morning, I see why. He thinks the only one suffering as a result of the war is him. And anybody who isn't ready to hold his hand and see it his way is sent out of the room. The President is dead wrong in the choices he's made, but he does not know it. From that first NSC meeting on, the men who know better have failed to tell him so. The only people who do are the crazies in the street, and they just make him all the more certain he's right. Compared to them, he is right. But compared to men like Bowers—" Dillon stopped, disgusted with himself. He picked up the cable. After a moment he said quietly, "I'm not letting Bowers die like this, for nothing."

"What can you do, Sean?"

"You mean, besides calling Dr. Bowers and telling him I'm sorry?"

"Yes."

Dillon was so accustomed to answering this question "I don't know" that he almost did so again. Instead, he put the cable down on his desk and touched the button on his intercom. "Helen, send Sergeant Kingfield to my quarters for a set of civilian clothes, a dark business suit, shoes, everything. Tell him to hurry. And Helen."

"Yes, sir?"

"Get me Randall Crocker on the phone."

He snapped the intercom off and looked at Packard. "I want

the file of everything Bowers has sent us. I want my own summaries and I want copies of what went to the White House after the CIA, JCS, and OSD worked my summaries over."

"That goes all the way back to March."

"I want it all."

"You can't go public with what Bowers was doing."

"What can they do to Bowers? He's dead."

"The file includes what the other sources sent too."

"Just Bowers's material, Mike. Isolate it. It's enough to make my point."

"It'll finish you."

"That I used the pouch with one of my own men?"

"In explicit defiance of CINCPAC's direct order."

"Look, Mike, they know from my reports that I had back-channel numbers. They don't care. They write me off."

"They'll care if now you try to flank them by bringing in someone outside of government."

"Mr. Crocker?" Dillon laughed.

"He's been out of government for years."

"Yes, like Averell Harriman has, and Chester Bowles and Dean Acheson and Clark Clifford. Look, Mike, the fact that we're losing this war is not a secret from the enemy. The VC and the NVA know what their numbers are. They know they can match us step for step if we keep the battlefield in the South, right up to a million men. The fact that we're fighting this war exactly the way they want us to is only a secret from the President. The President, Mike. I've been wasting my time with the secretary and the chiefs. The President—we have to bring him into the secret whether he wants to be there or not. He keeps saying the Communists are on the run. He wants it to be true so much, he thinks it is true. Listen, not two hours ago I almost grabbed him by the shoulder—Lyndon B. Johnson—in the middle of a funeral Mass. He was sitting right in front of me. If I'd known about Bowers, I would have grabbed him. It's just as well I didn't, of course, because he would have shrugged me off. But some men in this country he can't shrug off. And one of them is Crocker."

The intercom buzzed. When Dillon pressed it his secretary said, "Mr. Crocker on the line, sir." Dillon thanked her and picked up his phone.

"Mr. Crocker? This is Sean."

"Hello, Sean. It's good to hear your voice."

"Thank you, sir."

"How's Cass? How's my Richard?"

"They're well, sir. They're fine." A lie, a grotesque lie, but Cass and Richard were not the point, and anyway, the inquiry was form. If Crocker had family, Dillon would have asked of them now. Crocker lived alone in Gramercy Park. "I need to see you, sir. Right away."

After a long pause Crocker said, "I expected a call like this sooner."

"I wish I'd made it sooner. Can I come up today? I could be there in two hours."

"Come ahead then."

"At your office, sir?"

Crocker did not answer, and for a moment Dillon thought the line had gone dead. "I'm retired," Crocker said at last. "I don't have an office."

"Retired, sir?" This was news to Dillon. The last he'd heard Crocker was still active at his firm. Even if, in his late seventies, he'd slowed up, he'd have kept his office. Dillon glanced over at Packard, who was watching him deadpan.

"Meet me at the Metropolitan Club. We'll have a drink."

"My thought, sir, was something private."

"Where are you calling from, the Pentagon?"

"Yes, sir. My office."

"Look, General, I think I should say right here at the top . . ."

General? When had Randall Crocker ever called him General?

". . . that I'm not interested in discussing government business. I don't do that anymore. That's why there's no point in our meeting in private. But I'd love to see you for old times' sake." The warmth had returned to Crocker's voice. "It's been too long."

"Yes, sir. It has." Crocker had come to Bolling for dinner with Cass and Richard the summer before, but at the last minute Sean couldn't get home. Cass had not mentioned his retiring.

"Then I'll see you for drinks in the bar at the club? Shall we say five? Or do you say 'seventeen hundred' yet?"

Dillon laughed. Who besides Crocker knew the mental block he'd first had against the twenty-four-hour military clock? "Five o'clock, Mr. Crocker. See you then."

When he'd hung up the phone, Dillon swung back to Packard.

Mike Packard knew about that mental block. Mike had been there too. It was not true that Sean Dillon trusted no one but himself. He trusted Mike. He picked up a pencil and pointed at the phone. He exhaled a slow steady breath, then said quietly, "Crocker thinks this telephone is tapped."

New York's Metropolitan Club was on Fifth Avenue, but it had a discreet entrance off the busy avenue, on an inconspicuous side street: a wrought-iron gate, a cobblestone courtyard, a small paneled door. The club steward greeted Sean as "Mr." Dillon, not "general," and he was surprised how natural it seemed. In his dark blue suit, red tie, and cordovan shoes, his briefcase at his side, he knew he looked like every man who ever entered the place.

Inside there was nothing discreet about the Metropolitan Club. Opposite a huge fireplace, a sweeping marble staircase led up to the main rooms. Its balustrade featured miniature columns with ornate Corinthian capitals. The rooms themselves, both the dining rooms and the bar, had similar columns at entrances, in corners and spaced at freestanding intervals, but those pillars were oversized, not miniature, because the rooms, interiors soaring for three stories, were enormous. When the steward showed Dillon into the bar, he laughed to himself. The tables and chairs with huge winged backs were spread so far apart and, at that, were so sparsely occupied, there was no question of not having privacy here. Twenty priests could hear confessions, he thought, and at that moment he saw Crocker sitting in an especially isolated corner, waiting to hear his.

Crocker did not rise to greet Sean. The aluminum walker he used now, instead of a cane, was beside his chair. It was always a surprise to think of this man as a cripple. They shook hands warmly. Crocker patted the vacant chair next to him. Dillon sat. The chair had its back to the room. Because of its wings only Crocker could see him. Crocker could also see, without turning his head, the entrance to the bar. He had positioned himself as if he were a Mafia chieftain.

Dillon thought to make small talk while waiting for their drinks. "You brought me to a club of yours before."

"The Metropolitan in Washington. I recruited you."

Dillon nodded. "Everything follows from what you said to me in that club. Everything of mine, I mean."

"And much of mine, Sean. Much of what I'm proudest of." Crocker looked quickly and emotionally away.

Small talk? Sean studied his old friend, his mentor. Crocker looked far older than when Dillon had last seen him, perhaps six months before. It shamed Dillon that he had not been in touch with the man for his own sake. Now, instead of dressing fastidiously, Crocker managed only to dress with a nostalgia for his former style. He wore a good three-piece tweed suit but it needed pressing. His yellow bow tie, faded and wrinkled at the knot, still lent a touch of flamboyance to Crocker's appearance, but it was undercut by what to Dillon was a shocking show of dandruff on his shoulders.

"You look well, Mr. Crocker," Dillon lied.

"I wish I could say the same for you, Sean. Your taste in clothes has improved, but you look exhausted. You look lousy."

Sean laughed. "I need a vacation. So does Cass."

The waiter brought their drinks. They watched while the man placed their napkins and glasses of gin and the bowl of nuts. Then he left.

Dillon took a sip. The rush of alcohol to his brain released the first set of locks.

"What's wrong with Cass?"

Sean looked up sharply. "Who said anything about Cass?"

Crocker sipped his own drink, then put it down again and said nothing.

"We had an unfortunate scene this morning at the archbishop's funeral. The President was there and—"

"I heard about it."

Dillon was surprised. "Retired, but not off the tickler," he said lightly, but it made him angry to think the incident at the Shrine, his son's outrageous, insulting act, had been the subject of insider gossip all day. A hundred people present at the Shrine would have known not only who Richard was but who he was, a kind of godson, to Randall Crocker. Dillon shrugged with resignation, saying only, "Cass was devastated."

"And you, Sean. How were you?"

Instead of answering, Dillon lit a cigarette. He took his time. He waved his match out slowly. Finally he said, "Mr. Crocker, what happened at the Shrine is not what I'm here to talk about."

"You're here to talk about the war."

Dillon knew it had to be obvious. Still, he was surprised at Crocker's direct statement. He felt cautious suddenly and did not respond.

"You're here to tell me we're losing the war, and you want me to use my influence with the President's friends so they can get him to see that."

Dillon touched his briefcase. "Mr. Crocker, I'd prefer to let you draw your own conclusions. I've brought some material for you to read. It will make the point better."

Crocker pushed against his chair, scraping it back, an expression of shock on his face. He glanced quickly around the room, then said too loudly, "I'm not reading anything, Sean. You know I don't have clearances."

Dillon stared impassively at the only man toward whom he'd ever felt—he could call it devotion. What had happened to him?

Crocker then brought himself forward, and when he talked quietly now it made Dillon even more uneasy than when he'd been too loud. "I don't need 'material' to know the war is a disaster. I'm a lawyer. So are you. You could have been one of my lawyers. The first thing a lawyer does when he's offered a case is decide if it's a loser or not. He might take it anyway. But he's got to know from the start if it's a loser. Are you just discovering that Vietnam is a loser?"

Dillon smiled and exhaled his smoke. He still did not know what he was dealing with. He shook his head.

"Well, Sean, why are you up here in New York City offering me 'material'? Why aren't you showing them on E-Ring? Why not McNamara? Why aren't you telling him what you know?"

"I do tell him. I tell him in person at oh-eight-thirty hours every Tuesday and Thursday. And every morning, between black folders, I give him the numbers that MACV gives me. I flag those numbers with yellow every chance I get."

"For caution? Or for cowardice?"

"I'm sorry, what?"

"I was thinking of McNamara."

"McNamara knows better than anyone the hole we've dug for ourselves. He's paralyzed now because he also knows the

minute that he describes the true dimensions of that hole to
the President, he's gone. The Pentagon is full of ghosts now,
the ghosts of men who raised questions or expressed doubts.
So is Foggy Bottom. That's why I am here. The President
does not accept bad news from people who work for him. Our
problem has become that simple. That is why the President
thinks we're winning. I'm here looking for people who don't
work for him, to whom he might listen, people he associates
with Roosevelt ..."

Crocker was shaking his head with such a depth of feeling,
of sadness, that Dillon had to stop.

"I have a question for you, Sean."

"What?"

"Why aren't you one of those ghosts?"

Dillon said nothing.

"Why are you still a part of this thing? We've got American boys dying in jungles over there for nothing. You know
that. And you've known it for a long time. Talk about ghosts!
And you remain a part of it. Sean, I have to say I'm surprised.
The others don't surprise me, the chiefs, the field commanders, the admirals, the marines, the bomber generals, the
gung-ho and the can-do! But you, Sean. You weren't like
those others. That was the point about you. You were something else. And now you tell me that some of them are
gone—admirals and generals—gone because they told the
boss what he didn't want to hear. But you are still there, Sean.
Why is that? Because you deal in yellow flags? What about
red flags? Forgive me, I'm just trying to understand. Why are
you still there, Sean?"

Dillon said without hesitating, "I'm still there because my
work isn't finished. It's that simple."

Crocker shrugged elaborately.

"But you, Mr. Crocker, were the one who taught me about
complexity and compromise. I'm not pure, that's for sure. Nobody is who's had anything to do with Vietnam. But I was not
pure when I worked for you. David Lothrop? Sylvia Yergin?
General Macauley? Have you forgotten? Are you actually
asking me to explain about the necessity of staying with a situation even if it's politically or morally ambiguous?"

"Ambiguous? Forgive me for asking, General, but what is
your position on the war?"

Dillon answered coldly, "We are at war with Hanoi. We've

stopped them from cutting the South in two and we've made our own bases secure. But that's it. That's as far as we get in the present setup. Bloody stalemate now, which I oppose with every ounce of my weight. We should have taken it to Hanoi in the beginning. A strategy of attrition was wrong. We're the ones attriting, not them. A strategy of political reconstruction in the South was wrong. The South is a political shambles. Now it may be too late, for North and South both. Still, if only to justify the lives of the men we've already lost, I would try. We could win yet, but it would take full mobilization, a full invasion of the North, a total blockade of Haiphong. Shut off China and Russia, seal the whole country, and then fight them. If we can't sell that to the American people, then we get out right now. In or out, I don't care which. But whatever it is, we do it all the way. And I am going to stay in my job until one direction or the other is set. I'm not quitting, to be replaced by an intelligence chief who, when he sees an American funeral pyre, calls it the light at the end of the tunnel."

"You don't care which?"

"I care that the line we draw against communism is a line we will stand by. Where that line is? We elect people in this country to make decisions like that. People like me carry them out. I accept that. What nauseates me is a government that ducks the decision, that wants it both ways. So now we have it neither. And you're right, boys are dying in the jungle for nothing."

"How many have died by now?"

"Fourteen thousand seven hundred, plus. This morning one of my people died."

"That's why you're here. To justify what happened to him."

"Yes. I'm not interested in denouncing the war. I want to influence it! Fulbright doesn't affect policy and neither does General Gavin. But you could."

Now it was Crocker who took a stiff swallow. "You've come to the wrong place, my friend. If I had any power, this obscene war would be over now. Didn't we learn anything in Korea? You were on board for Korea! How can you think like this? Your notion of what to do would, if anything, be worse." Crocker's eyes widened. "Blockade Haiphong? Are you crazy? Are you all crazy?"

Crazy? Me? Dillon would have dismissed the thought, but then he remembered how that morning, when he'd heard that Bowers was killed, his immediate intuition was that CIA had done it because of Bowers's secret work for him.

Crocker drank again, compulsively, perhaps the way Bowers had, using alcohol to fend off terrors. Then his eyes swept the room quickly. To lean closer to Dillon, he used both hands to pick up the dead weight of his wooden leg and move it. "I have been arguing in my own circles against the war for months. A number of us have been, at some cost to ourselves. That's why I was moved out of my own office, at my own firm. I have offended some very powerful people. They say I've betrayed my country over this war, but I haven't. My country has betrayed me." Crocker stared at Dillon, his eyes like saucers.

Dillon could not breathe, looking at him.

Crocker said, "We tiptoe around the throne, all of us. You do it and so do we. We take precautions because we have to, all of us, for the same reason." Crocker had leaned forward and placed his hand on Dillon's arm, and now he was whispering. "Because the emperor is mad! Don't you see the effect that has on all of us? Lyndon Johnson was always an evil man, always. But now he is completely mad. I have reports. I have secret information. The President is clinically paranoid!"

Dillon's heart fell from a cliff into the abyss of a fear he didn't even know he had.

Randall Crocker believed the DIA director's phone was tapped. Randall Crocker, sending spooked eyes around a harmless room, acted like a surveillance subject in his own club. Randall Crocker thought his staid law partners had banished him for being a traitor to his country. Randall Crocker regarded the shrewd, megalomaniacal, ruthless President as clinically paranoid, but Sean Dillon grasped now, viscerally and horribly, that the paranoid was Crocker himself.

"We must not tell anyone. And we must not let him know that we know. Otherwise—" Crocker stopped as a cloud of fear darkened his face. He closed his grip on Dillon's arm so fiercely that it hurt. "You won't tell him, will you? You won't tell him what I said, will you?"

Dillon shook his head. He covered Crocker's hand with his own. "No, sir. I won't," he said. The image of James Forrestal came to the threshold of Dillon's mind, but he closed the door on it. Not Forrestal, no. He would not think of Forrestal. And he would not think of craziness.

He himself had been crazy for a moment, paranoid, only that morning. "In fact, Mr. Crocker, what I wish, on a personal level, is that you would come with me and stay with us, stay with Cass and me for a while."

"To Washington? No, I could never come to Washington now. Not to Bolling."

"You have friends there, sir. You know in what esteem the air force holds you."

"No, no." Crocker sat back, away from Dillon. "If I came to stay with you, Richard would think—"

"Richard?"

Crocker's face softened with embarrassment, a slip.

"Was it Richard who called you about the Shrine this morning?"

"He's a good boy, Sean. He reminds me of my son."

Crocker's poignant statement went through Dillon like a bolt, for he remembered the life-changing affirmation it was when he himself had been the one to touch Crocker there, in that wound. Crocker's son who died at the Rhine, leaving a crack in his father's heart that had opened then to a young man who stank of the Chicago stockyards.

But that crack had not healed, not in all these years. Times had changed otherwise. And now Sean was on notice that in Crocker's view he, Sean, was no better than the gung-ho killer generals whom once they both despised. Well, Randall Crocker was not who he had once been either. Life has a way of disappointing us; where is the surprise that we disappoint each other?

But Crocker was still a man of enormous magnetism and also, still—Sean saw this as for the first time—a man of enormous need. The thought of Sean's own son, his vulnerable, self-doubting Richard, being drawn into the crack of this old man's heart filled him with alarm.

Dillon remembered standing with Crocker on the steps of Congress, watching his little boy playing in the distance. He remembered feeling, without knowing why, that his son was in danger. What could it possibly have meant to him then, had he known, that the danger would be from the very man next to him, whom he had come to love? "What did Richard want?"

"He spoke to me in confidence, Sean. You can understand that."

"You didn't encourage him in this peacenik stuff, I hope. Did he tell you the effect of what he did on his mother?" At long last, anger at his son—his son not vulnerable and self-doubting, but cruel and stupid and selfish—overwhelmed Dillon. Did Richard think he was the only one in this family with a conscience? Did he think the President and the President's men didn't want peace? Did he think peace would ever come to Vietnam if Hanoi saw American students carrying Ho's picture in American streets? Dillon's own rage hit him as if it had been thrown by someone else, and for an instant he was knocked completely off balance by it—like a man falling inside a dead helicopter, and yes, for that instant, everything was upside down, and he saw himself as the crazy one, the paranoid, the man who'd lost the balance of his mind.

Randall Crocker, with a steady, sane eye, peered back at his one-time protégé. "And the effect on his father? The question I asked before, I think it is Richard's question. He knows how Cass was. You, Sean. How were you?"

TWENTY

Richard had his arms linked with a boy and a girl he had never seen before. He and Cooney had come here together, giving each other nerve, but they had become separated early on, during the speeches. Cooney was somewhere close behind, almost certainly. Richard hoped so, because he'd never believe this singing. That section of the vast throng was singing a Dylan song with the gusto of stadium drunks. "How does it *feel?*" they chanted. The driving rhythm of the music had them swaying in step as they slowly moved across the pristine white bridge, a knot of several hundred kids, complete strangers who'd come here from all different parts of the country, yet all wearing denim and cousin T-shirts in the warm October sun. They all knew the words, had known them forever.

In their minds, thrilling to the way they knew instinctively to claim that exact song as the day's anthem, they all supplied Dylan's whining harmonica and his scat-scat-scatting tambourine and his dynamite guitar.

Richard was taller than most; he stretched himself to his full height, looking back for his buddy, but Cooney, even with the flamboyant orange bandana tied hippie-fashion around his forehead, was not to be picked out from the mass of faces. The stream of marchers extended all the way back through the pillared bridge gate that featured the huge bronze pair of nude amazon horse handlers, their erect breasts, the horses' asses. Then the throng broke into half a dozen smaller streams on roads that fed Lincoln Memorial Circle. Halfway back was a huge, black-on-white, road-spanning, moving banner. "Support Our Boys In Vietnam," it read. "Bring Them Home Now."

A hundred thousand, one speaker had said. Jerry Rubin

swore there'd be a million, Cooney had instantly groused, but
what did Cooney want? Richard was awed by the mass of the
crowd, now that he had the whole bridge to measure it by.
Ahead, it disappeared into the fold of the Virginia hillside. A
hundred thousand! All linked to Richard himself through the
arms of these two on either side of him, all joined by words
they knew to sing, by wearing pants and shirts that showed
they had bodies, by not being afraid to touch each other. But
all joined first, today, he told himself, by how they hated this
fucking war.

Singing louder than he ever had before, Richard longed for
Cooney's back to slap, Cooney of all people, who once, when
a McLuhan-struck professor asked what binds the world together now, had piped up "Music!" and only the professor had
thought him wrong.

The boy next to Richard, without breaking stride, pulled his
arm free. Richard saw that the boy was accepting a joint that
had been moving through the crowd like the sacramental cup.
Still walking in rhythm to the song, the boy took a quick pull
on the marijuana, held the smoke for a moment, then, with a
practiced flourish, blew it through his clenched teeth. Grinning,
he passed the joint to Richard, who accepted it without hesitating, but also with a strange dual sense of the sacred and the
sinful. He took a pull of his own, his first hit of marijuana
ever, and the smoke went right into the bone hollows behind
his eyes. He held the two-inch cigarette in front of his face as
he had seen others do, taking in the sweet aroma which reminded him of the smell of the scorched air after small jet
planes took off from the runway at Bolling, on the weed-
ridden, off-limits fringes of which he had done his teenage
brooding.

"How does it *feel*?" they all sang and half cried.

And Richard, passing the joint along to the girl beside him,
cried back from farther down in his throat than his voice had
ever been—the dope?—"Great! It feels great!"

Why did he love this so much? On that bridge, with Lincoln's Doric temple behind him and Robert E. Lee's graveyard
estate ahead, with the towers of his uptight alma mater,
Georgetown, to his right and the blue water under him that
would flow in moments down to the riverside air base that had
been his only home, he felt at last that he was not on his own.
He had thought only he loved the Dylan lyric for that paradox,

how it celebrated loneliness while simultaneously offering in itself a way out of loneliness, but he sensed now that his whole generation felt that way about it.

"It feels great!" he yelled again, glancing left for Cooney, his one friend from all those years at GU, they should stick together more, they should stay in closer touch, he felt the rush of his affection, not understanding that the shot of dope smoke to his brain was freeing him from the grip of inhibition.

The feeling—oh the feeling—was he did have direction, and he did have a home. Not D.C. or GU or Bolling AFB, not UVA Law School either. These one hundred thousand friends were his direction. They would be his home. Bob Dylan himself was probably here; how could the Hibbing Hippie not be? Robert Lowell, the new-age foster father, was here, and so was SANE and Snick, the Student Mobe and the American Friends, Dwight Macdonald and Paul Goodman!

"Not Paul Goodman, love," the girl next to him said, and until that moment Richard had not known he was speaking any of this aloud. "*Mitch* Goodman."

"Who's he?" He laughed and accepted her offer of one more toke before she sent the joint along its sacramental route. Now he smelled her aroma, as well as the marijuana—Hindu incense and the perfume of sex.

"My name is Dylan!" Richard said hilariously. "No, really, honest to God. D-I-L-L-O-N."

She was so pretty. She had braided daisies into her flowing golden hair.

"I'm Sonja," she said.

He knew it wasn't her name, and the feeling was, Dillon was not his name either. He felt free, free.

When Richard slid his hand back inside her arm, he inadvertently brushed her supple breast under the thin cotton of her T-shirt, which was pale blue and featured the words "Diggers Free Store." The form of her breast kept the *r*'s of her shirt moving happily, and though the sight had struck him before, now it staggered him. His hand tingled to be touching that fabric; in his mind it felt like lingerie. He saw the form of her left nipple riding erect and proud. He felt wholly turned on, full of lust for that Sonja and for all the Sonjas around him, in their ass-hugging blue jeans and underwear shirts and the daisies in their hair.

And that quickly, the exhilaration of the Dylan song and the

march across the Potomac and the loosey-goosey feel of his
legs moving in step with two hundred thousand other legs, all
riding up in the hot-air basket of the dope bubble—the exhilaration became completely sexual. It was sexual, he realized,
for all of them. He laughed out loud again. Oh Sonja! He
hugged her, choked with happiness, tasting also, however, a
sweet distress at how close he had come, over weeks of worrying, to deciding he could not in conscience do this.

Only moments later he wondered what all that feeling, the
exhilaration and the lust and the freedom, had been. The marijuana? His namesake's song? The pretty Sonja, who then disappeared as the crowd surged at the end of the bridge, pushing
through the pair of majestic white towers under the guardian
eyes of giant eagles?

As Richard's section of the march wheeled through the traffic circle, turning upriver, he heard the roar rolling back from
those ahead, a deep, round, soccer stadium kind of sound. In
realizing what it was, he realized also that the high he had felt
there for a brief eternity was totally gone. The protesters ahead
were letting out their throaty shout in a steady back-flowing
wave as each rank advanced to the point where the four-lane
Jefferson Davis Highway rose at Boundary Channel, giving
them a view. Until Richard, on his toes, scanning the tops of
all those mother-displeasing scruffy heads, could see it too.
The Pentagon.

Like a dreamwalker then, Richard advanced as one of the
throng. He had never been a part of such a crowd before,
never, never, but to himself he was now radically alone. The
building became a point of fixation for him. All its most impressive aspects, its size in the flat river valley, the simple, yes,
elegance of its proportions and the becolumned grandeur, all of
this was familiar to him. What gripped Richard for the first
time ever, what he saw mounted above the mall entrance, taking up the space between the second and fifth floors in the
dead center of that side of the building, was the eye, wet and
veiny with blood, alive, the single huge Cyclops eye that was
staring hard at him. His father was in that building.

The eye was and would continue to be, had to be, he wanted
it to be, his secret. No one of the tens of thousands around him
could know or begin to understand what this moment was for
him. He was no longer linked to them at all. He allowed the
current of the crowd's movement to carry him. The main body

of demonstrators funneled into the vast north parking lot, where this phase of the rally was to take place. Speakers at the Lincoln Memorial had explained that government permits had been obtained for this second gathering, that it was perfectly legal. Those hoping to challenge the war by committing acts of civil disobedience would move on from the parking lot to cross the well-marked boundary onto the forbidden apron of the Pentagon proper. As they approached, Richard, still craning, saw that that boundary was marked by a length of yellow rope behind which stood a row of club-bearing military policemen. He saw their white helmets and knew, even from that distance, who they were.

Not Richard. He had not come here to get busted, and already he wanted to cry out, at the mystical eye that only he saw, what was now true, that he was not one of these people, that he had come here for reasons of his own, that while he too hated the fucking war, he did not hate the men who had to fight it.

You. I don't hate you, he said, perhaps aloud. He had his stare fixed on that spot on the side of the Pentagon, which was approximately where his father's office was. As he drew steadily closer it seemed to him he could distinguish among the numerous windows, picking out one window and drifting toward it.

Without realizing it, Richard's preoccupation took him to the edge of the crowd, away from the temporary platform in the middle of the lot on which a rock band was playing. Soon he found himself actually approaching the limit of the parking lot among a column of wild-hearted Yippie radicals who, it was quickly apparent, were here to make trouble. Just a few dozen yards ahead Richard saw kids taunting the stoical MPs. One was waving a small NLF flag directly in the face of an impassive black soldier, and several girls were dancing lewdly in front of another. Richard hard the catcalls and obscenities that the protesters were shouting at the soldiers, and he began to shout too, but against his fellow demonstrators. "No," he cried, "don't do that! Not like that!"

There were several hundred Yippies just there, where the embankment leading up to the building marked the limit of the parking lot. They were a knot of crude and, even to Richard, ugly young people, who then picked up the chant of "Out, demons, out!" Richard remembered that their leader, Jerry Rubin, had promised an exorcism of the war machine, but these kids were hurling themselves on the MPs as if *they* were devils. The idea of an exorcism had seemed like fun when Richard had heard it, but this frenzy—girls flaunting their bodies, boys waving enemy flags, shouting, "Out, demons, out!"— frightened him.

He decided to move away. But the crowd of chanters was thick and pressing him, and they forced him forward as the entire column moved steadily against the line of MPs.

"No!" Richard cried. "Stop this!" And he pushed roughly against a white kid whose hair was styled dramatically in an Afro. The kid punched Richard in the jaw, staggering him.

"Out, demons, out!"

When he'd found his balance again, Richard was facing the other way, his back toward the Pentagon, and he began pushing against the crowd, trying to get out. But it was impossible.

At one point he ripped out of someone's grasp another red and blue, yellow-starred Vietcong flag and quite deliberately threw it to the ground where it was immediately trampled under and lost.

The frontmost rank of demonstrators, no longer content with taunting the rows of MPs, broke and began running for the Pentagon, tearing the yellow cord down, scrambling up the embankment and, eluding the startled soldiers, actually crossing onto the broad paved apron. The crowd around Richard surged forward. The line of MPs was no match for it, and all at once hundreds of protesters were storming the Pentagon itself.

Richard, simply to stop himself from being carried forward, fell to the ground, one of the few who did, and one of the few easy targets, therefore, for the white-helmeted soldiers.

"You motherfucker!" an MP cried as he brought his club viciously down on Richard.

Richard covered his head just in time and took the blow with his shielding forearms. Instinctively he rolled away, scrambling to his feet and moving with energy and finesse, a halfback eluding tacklers. "Cheer for the Redskins!" The old fight song in his father's voice. Run me, Dad, run me!

Despite the shocking memory of his father's carrying him like a football, and despite the pandemonium around him, his brain snapped into focus, locked on one idea and held it as an absolute: not to get arrested. That was all. I cannot get arrested! But his instinctive move into open space had, in fact, taken him toward the Pentagon, not away from it. He was way over the line of what was allowed, but he was dodging everybody now. The Yippies were as much a threat to him as the MPs were. Cheer for the Redskins! Was it that memory that made him want to cry?

The first rank of radicals was just approaching the stairs leading to the river entrance proper, storming it like heroes. A Vietcong flag waved above them, and that drew Richard's eye just as the huge doors between the limestone pillars swung open. Out poured a company of countercharging troops, not white-helmeted, club-wielding MPs but combat soldiers in fatigues, armed with rifles. They stormed into and around the Yippies, who stopped cold, instantly overwhelmed. He saw soldiers repeatedly bringing the butts of their rifles down on the heads of the now panicked kids. Their cocky demon chant was transformed into screams of pure terror, and as they tried to fall back in retreat, the troops pursued them. Hundreds of combat soldiers continued to pour out of the Pentagon, chasing down the protesters, who in Richard's mind were transformed once more back into harmless flower children. "Don't," he screamed now, "don't do that!" But instead of at Yippies, he was screaming at a GI who at that moment was brutally clubbing a girl who had daisies woven into her hair. The girl was at the soldier's feet, writhing with the blows. Richard simply forgot his new absolute, that he could not be arrested, and he ran at the soldier. "Stop that, goddamn it!" He hit the GI from the side, with more force than he intended, and it stunned him that the soldier fell to the ground. Richard reached to help the girl. Blood was pouring from her head, and she was screaming hysterically, but instead of allowing Richard to lead her away, she pulled out of his grasp as soon as she was on her feet, and she turned on the soldier who was getting up. "Asshole!" she screamed. "You fucking baby-burner!" She stood over the stunned GI, just screaming at him, "Asshole! Asshole!" The soldier shook with confusion.

Richard took off. He ran as fast as he could, back toward the main body of the demonstration in the parking lot. The soldiers were scrambling after protesters, who were still scampering toward the Pentagon, not away from it, and so they ignored him. He cut through the crowd, more a halfback to himself than ever. By the time he hit the parking lot, the demonstrators there had turned their focus toward the battle on the embankment, and Richard was struck by the uniformity of expression on their faces: horror and anger. The huge crescent-shaped edge of the crowd stood watching the whacked-out Yippies take their beating.

Richard pushed through them toward the platform where the band had been playing, and he took up a position near the stage, amid a small and relatively tranquil group of demonstrators. There were older people here, men and women both, professors in corduroys and Wallabees, ministers in tweed coats and clerical collars, women in wraparound khaki skirts instead of blue jeans, as well as a sprinkling of long-haired earnest young men, hard-core pacifists who no doubt disapproved of the tactics of confrontation that threatened now to turn the entire rally into a violent rout. A minister was on the platform, speaking as if the soldiers and radicals were not battling each other a mere hundred yards away.

Richard tried to listen. Now that he had stopped, he realized how his heart was pounding and how his breath was coming in gasps. His legs were trembling. He felt nauseous. But he was surrounded here by people who seemed rooted, calm and serious. Gradually he felt their steadiness coming to him, and he found it possible actually to understand what the minister was saying.

"We are not here to defy the rule of law . . ." He was speaking from note cards, not ranting or extemporizing but presenting a firm, thought-out position. His voice was powerful above them, and to Richard the minister's evident self-possession seemed an antidote to his own inner quaking. ". . . but to redeem the system of constitutional government. We will no longer let the vulnerable young expose themselves alone to its fury, and that is why we join them in committing this act of direct resistance to the war and the draft. There are twenty-seven young men representing Resist groups from all over the country. They will come forward now to present to us the draft cards turned in locally by those groups, so that we in turn may present them, by prearrangement, to the chief marshal here at the Pentagon, and through him to the court of the United States. Those others of us who want to include their own draft cards are encouraged to do so. We will thus, in a simple ceremony, make concrete our affirmation of support for these young men who are the spearhead of direct resistance to the war and all of its machinery."

The group applauded, a subdued, polite reaction in marked contrast to the pitched battle still in progress on the slope between the parking lot and the river entrance.

The minister received several bundles of cards from the representatives who came forward solemnly, as in church. "Ceremony," he had said, and it was true. Richard felt that he was witnessing a holy ritual.

"Who is that?" he asked a woman next to him.

"Bill Coffin, the Yale chaplain. He just read Mitch Goodman's statement."

"Mitch Goodman?"

"The poet, the head of Resist."

Reverend Coffin held up a cloth sack into which the draft cards had been so liturgically placed. He announced, "Section Twelve of the National Selective Service Act commands that we shall not aid, abet, or counsel men to refuse the draft. But when young men refuse to allow their conscience to be violated by an unjust law and a criminal war, then it is necessary for their elders—their teachers, ministers, friends—to make clear their commitment, in conscience, to aid, abet, and counsel them against conscription. We too must be arrested, for in the sight of the law, we are now as guilty as you are." Coffin leapt from the stage to stand in front of it.

A second, more spontaneous procession began as other young men, and older men too, the professors and old lefties, filed forward to add their draft cards to those collected in advance. They dropped their cards into the bag with due solemnity; a few felt compelled by emotion to make brief, halting statements, but most carried out the act in silence.

Richard could hardly breathe, watching them. He stood on the edge, hugging his chest, which still ached from the exertion of his flight and from the pounding it was taking from his heart. No one looked at him, for which he was grateful. He felt quite naked and helpless, and like everyone else in that corner of the mad, desperate apocalypse of a demonstration, he was riveted by the sight of American men putting their entire futures in jeopardy for the simple sake of conscience.

Richard's hand went to his back pocket for his wallet. The movement was subtle, sly almost, but he was fully aware of it, and aware of its implication. Without fumbling in the slightest he withdrew the small stack of cards he carried, his library card, his UVA ID, his driver's license, his social security card and, on the bottom, his draft card. "Classification," he read, "2-S."

He was in law school, he admitted for the first time, only for the sake of that very number and letter, the precious exemption it offered. He felt ashamed of himself for the glib self-righteousness of his rejection of the war till then. It had cost him nothing, and he had risked nothing, while Vietnamese and Americans both were dying now in droves. His very acknowledgment of that disparity seemed itself a new kind of conscription, drafting from within him at last a rare sacrificial impulse.

He had joined the procession and found himself at the head of it, faced with the stern but steady-eyed Reverend Coffin, who was extending the sack toward him. Richard hesitated. The minister nodded and looked at him for an instant with such compassion, and also with such confidence, that his doubt evaporated. He dropped his card into the bag, then walked away feeling, despite having literally discarded something, more as if he had received, much more than he ever had at the communion of the Mass.

His path away from the platform took him toward the Pentagon for some yards, and his gaze quite naturally lifted to the place where before he'd imagined the Cyclops eye. The eye was gone. He no longer felt afraid. Not giddy either, or high, as he had on the bridge. He had never felt like this before, yet the feeling was familiar. *How does it feel?*

Like I am Richard Dillon, not someone's son.

For a while Richard would revel in the apparent contradiction—as if he were not meant to be both himself and his father's son—and he would love his sense of freedom from it.

If Richard had been able actually, from that distance, to single out the window of his father's office, he'd have seen that, like most windows on that side of the Pentagon, it was blank. Early that morning custodians had gone through the offices on the mall side, dropping Venetian blinds. In the VIP suites, like the DIA director's, there were also heavy serge draperies to draw across the windows, and in those rooms the outside world was thoroughly sealed off.

Since it was Saturday, General Dillon and his colleagues were dressed in mufti. They had begun the morning affecting a weekend nonchalance, but as the hours passed, even if they could barely hear it, they knew the huge demonstration was building to a climax. But the real urgency they felt had nothing to do with Jerry Rubin's psychopathic exorcism, or with the frenzy with which green, frightened GIs were holding off the ragtag army of nut-case radicals and spaced-out flower children outside.

Sean Dillon was closeted with his deputy director for JCS matters, his assistant chiefs of staff for technical application and for targets, the chief of the Southeast Asia Task Force and the chief of the Field Activities Division. Various other experts and analysts came and went from the DIA conference room as their viewpoints were required.

Dillon had called this meeting because of an unusual piece of human intelligence that had come in the day before. A Communist doctor who treated senior Hanoi officials, and who also served as a deep-cover DIA agent, had sacrificed his position to come out with his urgent report. The elite NVA 304th Division, which had led the assault on Dien Bien Phu and which had since served as the heart of the home guard around Ho and the other rulers of North Vietnam, had suddenly been withdrawn from its quite visible posting in the capital. Not only was the inner core of the government left vulnerable by this maneuver, but the famous division itself had all but disappeared.

When this word had come in the day before, Dillon had ordered a special new analysis of data from all sources that tracked the movements of troops from North to South. The most recent reports from the ground reconnaissance teams—SOGs—were not available yet because MacAuliff, in Saigon, still controlled them, but the evidence of aerial photography, infrared radar directed from airplanes, NSA signal intercepts that snatched the radio communications of Communist commanders out of the air and even the acoustic needle sensors sown along the Trail all suggested—but at most—a slight uptick in the levels of movement. Even that was occurring only along the northern stretch of the Trail.

"Khe Sanh," the JCS general said at one point. "Westmoreland is certain the Reds are preparing to take the bait at Khe Sanh."

A Marine Corps general, Bailey, snorted. The marines manned the remote garrison in the far northwest corner of South Vietnam. He objected not to the reference to the marines as bait, but to the fact that it was true.

Dillon eyed the marine. "This is the trap Westmoreland has been laying for months, hoping to draw the NVA into a big-unit siege once and for all. He wants Dien Bien Phu all over again. But this time we win."

The others said nothing.

Dillon toyed with a pencil. "Our job is not to second-guess General Westmoreland's strategy but to provide him with the intelligence he needs to make it work."

The JCS general said, "MacAuliff's urgent request, endorsed by General Wheeler, is for a redeployment of all-source collection to the Khe Sanh sector. They want us to focus on the DMZ, the area east of Tchepone and the routes into the valley itself."

"To do that we lose coverage of the Trail farther south, leading into the Central Highlands, II Corps and III"—this was General Hickox, the Southeast Asia Task Force chief— "exposing the populated heart of the country. We'd have to pull infrareds and eyeballs off the Sihanouk Trail, leaving Saigon a question mark. Why is Westy stuck on Khe Sanh?"

"Khe Sanh is crucial," Bailey said.

"Then why did the French abandon it without a fight, and why has it been ignored for years? It's an old outpost, high on a plateau hundreds of miles from anything that matters."

"Quang Tri matters."

"Gentlemen," Dillon said impatiently, "Khe Sanh matters because General Westmoreland says it does. It's where he wants to take on the enemy. Our question is simple. Has the enemy begun to accept the invitation?"

"What if it's a feint? We look toward Khe Sanh and he comes the other way."

Dillon nodded, and he touched the stack of briefings on the table in front of him. "First data suggests that the upsurge, if that's what it is, is restricted to the North. Here is what we do. We give the whole Trail a once-over, from Tay Ninh in III Corps to Dak To in II Corps. Eyeball, signals, sensors, everything. If there is still no change in movement south, then we go with MacAuliff, all the way. We move everything but the skeleton into I Corps, concentrate on routes into Khe Sanh. Westmoreland's strategy, gentlemen, depends on us. If Khe Sanh is it, and if there's going to be a difference between the Americans and the French, it's going to be that we could tell the soldiers on the ground well ahead of time exactly what the enemy was doing. And there are fliers in the air waiting on us as well."

From that day on, the various intercept devices and systems continued sending back signals of gradually increasing movement in the jungles of the North, nothing untoward in the South. Within weeks, SOGs confirmed the NVA 304th itself, a force of fifteen thousand crack soldiers, massed in the hills just across the Laotian border from Khe Sanh. In late November Sean Dillon authorized a fifty-thousand-dollar bribe to bring across from Hanoi a long-cultivated defector, who reported, among other things, that General Vo Nguyen Giap, vanquisher of France, had moved into Laos to take command of the forces of which the 304th was the spearhead. Its only conceivable target was Khe Sanh. That was enough for Dillon. Now mirroring Westmoreland, he deployed every available intelligence asset to I Corps, where fully half of the American maneuver battalions had been sent. In December President Johnson had a sand-table model of the Khe Sanh plateau and the surrounding valleys set up in the White House Situation Room. The President, his high-toned civilian advisors, and his generals were agreed in believing that the trap of Khe Sanh was finally going to justify the two and a half years of Vietnam agony.

The siege did not commence. Christmas came and went. The concentration of the American military leaders was more focused than at any prior point in the war. They had a strategy at last that showed every sign that it would work. Now if Giap would only move.

Not even the increasingly outrageous acts of antiwar protesters—Roman Catholic priests pouring ducks' blood on draft files!—could usurp the generals' attention or undermine their conviction that the surest way to the peace they longed for too lay in convincing Ho Chi Minh he could not prevail. Nor was Sean Dillon's attention diverted by the effective disappearance from his life of his son. Richard's absence, frankly, was a relief. As the weeks passed, Dillon was as obsessed and became, perhaps despite himself, as hopeful as anyone in the Pentagon—or in Pentagon East, for that matter. He presided with scrupulous, tireless devotion over the reception and analysis of data from all sources, the radar, the sensors, the signal intercepts, the airborne eyeballs, the face-painted recon teams. Each bit of hard intelligence had registered individually at first, as the movement of a single truck, say, then as the movement of a unit, then as a larger force, up to the size of a battalion. Then the incoming data along the northern leg of the Ho Chi Minh Trail registered as something else. After the new year—it was January 1968 now—the tempo of signals suggesting movement suddenly increased, like the first rapid clicks of a Geiger counter sensing radiation, pushing a needle up a dial, toward the danger zone, the red.

Through the night-reflecting prism beads of rain and the *slap-slap* of windshield wipers, Richard saw the figure of the air policeman step out of the spotlighted gatehouse. The white of his peaked hat was clouded by the plastic rain cover, and his long blue raincoat reached to below his knees, which gave him the silhouette, in Richard's mind, of a German storm trooper.

Richard slowed his car, reaching to the dash to notch his headlights down to the parking lights.

Instead of waving him through, the AP raised his hand.

Richard cursed. He hadn't thought of this when he'd scraped the base sticker from the bumper of his car. The three silver stars had always elicited heel clicks and salutes from these guys.

He rolled the window down.

The AP leaned to him, a neutral, acne-scarred face. He wore two stripes on his sleeve, an airman second, a kid, younger than Richard was himself.

"Good evening," the air force cop said noncommittally. "Would you state your business, please?"

"Hi. I'm General Dillon's son. I'm visiting my parents." Richard smiled in a friendly way, but he sensed that the airman knew how false it was. He noticed the AP's eyes checking out his hair, which was way too long for this place.

"May I see your ID, please?"

"I'm not his dependent anymore, I'm just his son." Richard hadn't thought of this either when he'd thrown out his air force ID card. He hadn't thought of a lot of things.

The air policeman nodded, then straightened up. "If you'll wait a moment, please. I have to call for authorization."

"Call who?"

"General Dillon's quarters."

"Wait a minute, wait." The rain was coming in Richard's window. He felt the cold drops on his face as he looked up at the AP. "It's a surprise," he said. "I haven't been home in a while. They don't know I'm coming."

The AP shook his head. "Without ID, I'm required—"

"Is Sergeant Briggs around? Does he still work the gate?"

"Sergeant Briggs is off duty."

"I know him, and I know Sergeant Kaiser."

The AP hesitated. "Sergeant Kaiser is on the other gate tonight."

"Could you call him? Tell him Rich Dillon just wants to surprise his folks. He knows me. He knows this baby." Richard patted the wheel of his car, the blue Fairlane.

The AP stepped back, looked the car over, then turned and went into the guardhouse. A moment later he came back out.

Richard's shoulder was wet from the rain coming in his window.

"Okay," the AP said, and he waved Richard through without saluting.

Once on base, it amazed Richard how instinctively the turns on those streets came, even at night, even in the rain. On one side, the theater, the bowling alley, the USO, the chapel, the commissary. On the other, the back ends of hangar after hangar, the Base Ops Building, the barracks, the headquarters of the air force band. As he gunned up the hill toward the Officers' Club—he saw the shrouded swimming pool and remembered those summers when he'd been a lifeguard—he stopped resisting the powerful flood of his nostalgia. This crisp, ordered world had once been so much his; he remembered feeling like a prince in a privileged kingdom. What hit him now, as he rounded the last curve into Generals' Row, was not the loss of the perfect order but the loss of the absolute sense of virtue he had so long associated with this world. The people here had been the guardians of the world's freedom, but now they—

He remembered listening from his lifeguard seat that last summer to a knot of laughing young fighter jocks lounging by the pool. One had been describing his first sortie over Vietnam with dramatic hand motions and sound effects. Every time he'd used the word "gook," he'd said "fucking."

Even in the months since he had been here, a number of the names on the signs in front of the generals' houses had changed. Senter was gone, so was Davis. Basel too. New names that meant nothing. The endless rotation of their neighbors had always seemed unfair to Richard growing up, how he had forever stayed behind at Bolling—his father alone never getting transferred, the great General Dillon, indispensable at the Pentagon—while other kids moved in and out. Now what reminders of that rotation evoked in Richard was anger at how the war machine just used up endlessly its supply of faceless, soulless men, who came and went without effect, doing what they were told.

As he approached number 64, he slowed down. Was he really going to do this? Did he really have to?

He stopped his car in front of the house, turned the engine off and slumped over the wheel, at the mercy of his despair. Yes, he had to do it. Yes, he would.

Moments later he was inside. He had opened the door quietly. His parents were in the enclosed porch beyond the living room where the television was. He heard the sound of the late night news. A weather forecaster was talking about the winter rains. He crossed the living room to the threshold of the porch.

Neither his mother nor his father had noticed him yet. He stood there for a moment behind them, studying them. They were on the couch, close to each other but not touching. His mother was wearing her glasses because she was knitting; his father sat with the sports page spread open on his lap, but he was looking at the TV screen.

"Hi," Richard said at last.

His mother was the one he was watching. The one he could bear to look at. Her eyes came right to his, and danced with surprised delight. "Richard!"

Her knitting fell as she started to get up, but she checked herself, glanced at Sean and sat back down. "Richard," she said again, but forlornly. The last time she saw him she had slapped him.

His father folded the newspaper.

"I'm sorry I've been so out of touch. I had a lot to get straight about."

His father said coldly, "Are you all right?"

"Yes. I'm fine."

His father stood and crossed to the television, to snap it off. He faced Richard.

Richard was surprised to find himself taller than his father. He'd been taller for years now, but he never pictured it so. "I can't stay long. I came by to tell you something."

"Of course you can stay," Cass said. "Where are your things? Here, sit." She made room for him on the couch.

"No, really. I'm only here to tell you something. I tried to write ..." Richard's eyes went directly to his father's. Half a dozen yards of open space separated them, pale blue air force–issue carpet.

"What?" Sean Dillon asked.

"I've been drafted."

"Drafted?" Dillon said, genuinely surprised. "Did you quit law school?"

"No. They reclassified me anyway. I've been 1-S since around Thanksgiving. I got my induction notice ten days ago. I'm supposed to report tomorrow."

"Where?"

"Anacostia." Richard laughed. "Up the river, like they say in prison movies."

Sean gestured at the chair in the corner. "Have a seat, Rich. Let's figure this thing out."

Richard did not move from the threshold. He thought of how, in earthquakes, the threshold is where it's safe.

Since his son didn't move, Sean didn't either. He was paying close attention to him, looking for signs of his distress, as if he were standing on a ledge. But Sean could read very little in his son. He seemed to be in some kind of shock.

Cass was the one to recognize how very much like each other Sean and Richard were at that moment. Her two men. Neither was moving. Neither was showing anything. She thought of that television program, *Gunsmoke*, a pair of gunslingers facing off in the street, daring each other to draw. She said with false cheer, "Anacostia! Well, that's all the more reason to stay over."

"No, Mom."

A ledge. Sean hated the thought of his son in such a position. He wanted to reach a hand toward him. He said, "We can meet in the morning, before you report to Anacostia. You have a lot of options. I'll help you look at them. I can send for OCS forms—"

"I'm not going for OCS, Dad." Richard had resolved just to declare himself, but the words were stuck in his throat. Finally he forced them out. "I'm not reporting for induction."

"What do you mean?"

"I'm against the war. It would be against my conscience. I'm not reporting for induction."

"You're not serious."

"It's against my conscience, Dad."

"Your conscience?" Dillon asked quietly, but the step he took toward his son was so charged with violence that he stopped.

Cass stood up abruptly, planting herself between them. "Stop this," she said.

"Did you know he was doing this?" Sean asked without looking at her.

"No, she didn't," Richard said fiercely, as if defending his mother from charges.

Cass put her hand on her son's chest. "We can still help you. I've thought about this. It's not that unusual now. You can apply for conscientious objector. They give that if fighting is against your conscience."

Richard shook his head. "I'm not against fighting, Mom. Just this war. This war is immoral, maybe not all war. They don't give COs for selective objection. You have to be a Quaker."

"That's not true," Sean said. "Catholics can obtain CO status."

Richard brought his eyes to his father again. "I'm not a Catholic."

Cass took her hand back from his chest to stand before him, deflated. "Oh, Richard," she said quietly.

"I'm sorry, Mom."

She stared at him, not angry but terribly, terribly hurt. Her eyes filled, but before they spilled over, she said, "I'm making some tea," and she went to the kitchen.

Sean and Richard remained frozen in place.

Sean said, "You have such a sensitive conscience, but you'll do that to her."

"If her religion is so important to her, it's because of what you've done, not me."

"What the hell does that mean?"

"Living with you, what else does she have, what else has she ever had but the Church?"

"She had a son."

"Yes. And her son grew up. It's what happens. And like it or not, he grew up the way she raised him."

Sean lifted both his hands, palms outward. "Wait a minute. Let's not do this."

"Do what?" Now it was Richard who took a step. "Tell each other the truth finally? How I hate your fucking war?"

"Don't you talk to me like that."

"Like what? Saying 'fuck'? Is that what's wrong? Saying 'fuck'? I guess if our pilots were flying over Vietnam with big loudspeakers attached under their wings, blaring 'Fuck! Fuck! Fuck!' all over the countryside, then you'd say the war is immoral, right? But as it is, what our pilots do instead is drop napalm on villages. Napalm! And they drop it on the villages that you pick out for them. Isn't that what you do? Pick the targets? Isn't it? Isn't it?"

"In point of fact, it's part of what I do."

"And you talk to me about the word 'fuck'!"

"Use the word again, Richard, and you leave this house."

"You have it all backwards, Dad. You really do."

"Not me. You say you want the war to end, right? Right?"

"That's right."

"But what you are doing prolongs it. I guarantee it. You and all your friends, with your demonstrations, your marches on the Pentagon."

"I was at the Pentagon that day."

Dillon knew that his son's announcement was intended to jolt him, and it did. "I suppose I should have known that, after what you did at the archbishop's funeral."

"I had the feeling, even in that huge crowd, that you were watching me with the same look of disgust you showed me at the Shrine."

Dillon shook his head slowly. "I guess after that I blanked it out. At the Pentagon I didn't allow myself to—" He stopped, and with a fresh push of anger asked, "Were you one of those who defecated on the stairs?"

" 'Shit,' Dad. Say 'shit,' for Christ's sake. Is the word 'shit' so offensive to you?"

"No, what's offensive is your flight from responsibility."

"I'm taking responsibility. Don't you understand that? Ever since that day at the Pentagon. No, I didn't shit on the stairs! What I did do was turn my draft card in."

Dillon nodded. "You're a fool, Richard. You have no notion that certain acts bring certain consequences."

"I accept the consequences of what I do."

"You don't even see the consequences. Were you one of those carrying the Vietcong flag? Do you have any idea what the consequences of that are? When the rulers in Hanoi see their flag on the steps of the Pentagon, don't you know there are consequences? They don't know what a bunch of badly raised, spoiled-rotten kooks you all are. They think you are their serious allies. Don't you see that, Richard? We're not trying to defeat the Communists in Vietnam. If we wanted to, we could obliterate them. What we're trying to do is get them to negotiate with us. We're trying to convince them that their war is futile, that they can't win. And we are very close to convincing them of that. This war could be over, and soon! It's my business to know this! We are on the eve of what could be the last battle right now! But do you know what could screw it up? Your so-called peace movement. You and others like you make the Communists think they can win. You are encouraging the enemy to hang on."

"They aren't my enemy, is the point."

"The hell they aren't. You are a naïve young man. People like you are put to death by Communists everywhere, and the Communists in Vietnam are the most vicious brutes of them all. They have already killed twenty thousand fine young American boys who didn't weasel out of the draft."

"Is that what you think I'm doing?"

"Of course it is, and I am ashamed of you. You're hiding behind a claim of conscience, but all you are is a coward."

Richard felt his knees start to go, and he thought, Now. Here. This is where I collapse. I knew I couldn't do this.

But somehow he braced his legs, did not collapse. "That's not true," he said, but weakly. "If I was a coward, I would not have come here to face you. Mr. Crocker told me—"

"Crocker! Have you been talking to Crocker?"

"He agrees with me. He thinks the war is wrong too. A lot of good people do, Dad. He thinks you've been too influenced by other generals."

"I forbid you to see him again."

"Dad, that's ridiculous. You don't 'forbid' me now. Especially not about Mr. Crocker, who happens to be devoted to you. He's the one who said I owed it to you to come here. Otherwise I'd have just split for Canada. You would never have seen me or known what—"

"That's the way you should have done it."

"Mr. Crocker was sure you'd respect me for—"

"Respect? Never. I want to tell you something. I want you to be very clear on this. If you refuse induction tomorrow, you needn't ever come back here again. Do you understand me?"

"Yes." Tears were running freely down Richard's cheeks, but strangely enough, he had never felt less like sobbing. He turned and walked back through the living room toward the front door. His mother was standing, beyond, in the threshold of the kitchen. He wondered, Could she have heard?

"You're having tea," she said.

"No, Mom." He opened the front door.

She crossed to him and took his arm. "You can't just leave."

"I have to, Mom. Don't you understand? I have to."

But she would not let go. Still holding him, she whipped around toward Sean, who was still an entire room away. "Tell him!" she cried. "Tell him not to go."

But from that side of the house no sound came, only a silence which had all the weight of a father's reply.

Richard kissed his mother, then pulled away from her and dashed into the black rain.

TWENTY-ONE

"They made total fools of us," General Dillon said. "And of me in particular, because frankly, I had my doubts about our strategy at Khe Sanh until it approached climax, at which point, like everyone else I became a true believer. I thought we had them snookered, but it was the other way around."

He was standing in his crisp uniform, stars gleaming, ribbons glowing on his tunic breast, a rubber-tipped pointer lightly in his hand. Beside him was an easel holding a large map of Indochina. Its legend read, "Enemy Offensive, Tet, 1968." The map was marked with two dozen red arrows of various sizes, cutting arcs across all of South Vietnam, from the DMZ to the Ca Mau Peninsula. The tips of the arrows punctured the major cities; half a dozen converged on Saigon alone. The attack had occurred during the traditional cease-fire at the end of January, nearly a month ago now.

Dillon was speaking to the special group of eminent elder statesmen. A shaken Lyndon Johnson had convened to review the entire war effort after the shock of an offensive that had sent the American ambassador, Ellsworth Bunker, fleeing in his pajamas. They were seated on one side of a long conference table in an ornate room on the second floor of the Executive Office Building next to the White House. They were men who'd spent their lives at such tables, and among them were the notables Averell Harriman, Dean Acheson, Omar Bradley, George Ball and Randall Crocker. It was exactly such a group of New Deal veterans, Johnson's heroes, that Dillon had hoped Crocker himself might convene when he'd approached him in the early fall, but what Dillon failed to accomplish, the Communist initiative had. Dillon's sense of Crocker's enduring influence as a counselor-to-power was confirmed by the President's appointment. Of course, their encounter in the fall, after Bowers's death—not to mention Crocker's outrageous, glib sponsorship of Richard's flight to Canada—guaranteed that wise man Randall Crocker would have no influence with Sean Dillon. But the collapse of his friendship with Crocker was not the point. The possible collapse of the American will was the point.

Lyndon Johnson's hypnotic—and despotic—attachment to good news was apparently broken, but would it be replaced by its opposite? Since their number included men already known to be critics of the war, like George Ball and Randall Crocker, it was clear that the panel had been gathered to summarize the bad news for Johnson. But Dillon wondered if they, like the media and the liberal politicians, were going to make an absolute of American failure, as, before Tet, Johnson had tried to make an absolute of American success.

Dillon knew that anyone inclined to do that would be able to find justification aplenty in the testimony it was his obligation to give. He had just laid out in fuller detail than even his critics from CIA had done the massive failure of his own intelligence operation. He knew that whatever else Tet meant, it meant the end, over the next months, if not sooner, of his career as the military intelligence chief. Already McNamara was gone as secretary of defense, and Dillon was certain that soon Westmoreland would follow him. Tet was the hole into which their personal futures had fallen, and it could yet swallow, since this was an election year, the President's too. Indeed, the self-anointed Eugene McCarthy had just come close to defeating Johnson in New Hampshire.

But the end of careers did not matter. What mattered now was getting the truth out, the truth of what they'd learned and the truth of what the war required yet. Dillon was in no mood to mince words, and hadn't. But throughout his presentation he had found himself unable to look Randall Crocker in the eye. Sean Dillon, it turned out, was incapable of feeling angry at his former mentor. Time had touched them too deeply for that, and in fact Dillon's heart had sunk when he first saw Crocker, how time had turned against him. The skin on Crocker's face had begun to come loose from its bones.

Dillon was summarizing now. "So instead of our blindsiding Giap in Khe Sanh, he blindsided us"—he touched the pointer to the various targets as he named them—"in Da Nang, Qui Nhon, Nha Trang, Pleiku, Saigon, and Hué. Civilian losses everywhere were staggering."

"How staggering?" a voice asked.

Dillon answered without hesitating. He knew these goddamned numbers very well. "14,300 civilians killed, 24,000 wounded, 27,000 displaced from their homes, 72,000 homes destroyed."

"All that?" the same voice pressed. "And the attack on Khe Sanh was for real?"

"Yes, sir. Two NVA divisions hit Khe Sanh."

"That part you saw coming, though? At Khe Sanh?"

"Yes, sir. And, of course, we held our ground there."

"But you foresaw nothing else?" It was Acheson, a longstanding supporter of the war.

"No, sir."

Then another voice piped up, "Ninety thousand enemy troops moving en masse throughout South Vietnam—and you didn't see it? I don't understand that, General."

What Dillon didn't understand was how the row of grayhaired old men could seem so uniform to him, and how in their speaking they could manifest so little of themselves that often, as now, he was unsure whom to address. All he knew for certain was whom to avoid—Crocker. He said, to the panel generally, "We didn't see them, sir, because we did not know they were there to be seen. It sounds anomalous, but it's that simple. It appears now, given the numbers of enemy troops we know were involved in the Tet attacks, that we have been undercounting the enemy in place in the South for two years. Frankly, at various times, we were afraid of exactly that, but we never confirmed it. And so by the time we were alerted last fall for some kind of offensive, we detected no increase in troop movements along the Trail into III Corps and IV Corps, because there were none. The enemy troops in huge numbers were already there. The movements we did detect were all into I Corps, so we thought Khe Sanh!"

"You had no notion of the undercount?" Dillon recognized General Bradley, whose voice was laced with incredulity bordering on contempt. The old man was wearing a baggy brown suit, his bald head with flaky skin close to the table surface. Not a four-star general like Westmoreland or Wheeler, Dillon remembered, but five, like Eisenhower.

Dillon answered carefully. "In fact, sir, in the spring of last year, we conducted a major military intelligence reevaluation of the entire enemy battle order. That reevaluation, over my signature and that of General Westmoreland's own intelligence chief, suggested that the estimates of enemy strength in South Vietnam could be off by as much as two hundred thousand."

"Under by two hundred thousand?"

"Yes, sir."

"And what happened as a result?"

"General Westmoreland's intelligence chief was replaced."

"But not you?"

"I serve at the pleasure, jointly, of the secretary and the Joint Chiefs, General."

Bradley nodded. "You're harder to replace."

"General Bradley, I must say that if I was certain General Westmoreland was wrong, I would have resigned. You of all people, sir, understand the importance attached to the views of the commander of armies in the field. Those views are properly regarded as having near absolute authority, and as it happened, sir, the hard numbers that might have alerted us to the reality continually eluded us—all of us. We had intuitions and fears. Some of us went outside channels to try to get reliable figures. But we couldn't. Numbers were ambiguous because the very definition of the enemy in this war is ambiguous. Do we count children as members of the VC battle order when they throw grenades at our soldiers? Do we count old women who plant punji sticks? We decided to restrict our count to uniformed soldiers subject to military command. Even at that, we suspected the enemy was being undercounted, but we finally decided the prudent thing to do was to go with what we could verify."

"What you could verify?" It was Randall Crocker's voice, angry and shrill, cutting through the tense air like electricity. Dillon slowly turned toward him. "Wasn't it instead that you went with what your seniors wanted to hear?"

"As it happened, yes, sir. We went with estimates that confirmed the commanders in decisions they had already taken."

"Like Khe Sanh. You told Westmoreland what he wanted to hear."

Dillon did not answer at first, because in his mind at that moment he could not reconstruct it. Was this true? Had he become just another sycophant? In the chain of sycophants that went right up to Johnson? He said at last, because he had thought it was the fact and now hoped it was, "Our estimates, at every point, were as honest as we could make them."

"And now you know that they were wrong."

"We do indeed, sir. But if I might add, speaking personally, I reject any suggestion that our numbers were arrived at with a view toward pleasing those up the chain of command. My concern always, sir"—Dillon's voice shot up in pitch and volume—"was with those *down* the chain, with soldiers in the field. I was supplying them with numbers, and to have done so falsely would have amounted to murder, the murder of our own—"

"General, General," Acheson soothed, "no one's talking about murder here."

Dillon fell silent, embarrassed at his own display. He waited.

"General?" Randall Crocker leaned back in his chair wearily. Dillon looked at him again. How tired Crocker seemed, how shrunken, how much older, even, than when they'd been together in New York. "We have been told that, despite the reaction of the Walter Cronkites and the Eugene McCarthys, Tet was a grievous defeat for the Communist side, not ours." Crocker's eyes floated around the ceiling, measuring its rosette of molded plaster. Perhaps he intended to be taken for a cagey cross-examiner, but his manner seemed wildly inappropriate.

"Yes, sir," Dillon said carefully. "I am familiar with the CIA analysis."

"That's right. CIA. Senior CIA people tell us we actually beat them at Tet. Except in Hué, the Vietcong and the North Vietnamese, despite initial successes, were thrown back rather quickly pretty much everywhere. Your own numbers agree with CIA—that half of the ninety thousand attacking Communists were killed, wounded, or taken prisoner. That does sound like a defeat, doesn't it?"

"Yes, sir. And more importantly, the Communists were expecting a popular uprising in the South. They thought the mass of peasants and refugees would join them in their moment of victory, but the population did no such thing."

"So you agree, the Communists failed at Tet."

"They did not accomplish what they hoped for."

"General Westmoreland says now that the enemy is vulnerable. He wants two hundred thousand more troops, and full Reserve call-ups. He says now he can win. What do you say?"

"That question is out of my purview, sir."

"Out of your purview, General?" Crocker's face flashed with sarcasm. Dillon had once watched him use sarcasm to humiliate martinet bomber generals. "I thought you were the director of the Defense Intelligence Agency. Is it out of your purview to tell this panel whether you think we can win this war or not?"

"I have my opinion on the strategic question, sir. But that's all it is."

"State it," Crocker said, a direct order meanly given. His fellow panel members looked at him uneasily.

"If Tet was a failure for the Communists," Dillon answered carefully, "it still exposed our failure, and that is what the Cronkites see so clearly. Tet demonstrates that our entire effort of interdiction of troops and supplies is a failure. The bombing of the Ho Chi Minh Trail, including the defoliation of the jungle canopy, the napalming of suspected staging areas, the obliteration of obscure targets along three hundred miles of remote mountainous terrain—that bombing, which has been under way for three years this month, is useless. And if it is useless, it is inhumane and should be halted. Tet means the United States cannot stop the movement of armies from North to South. North Vietnam still has at home a population of more than a million young men of combat age. Tet means the United States can do nothing to stop them from coming South. Tet means the United States cannot prevent North Vietnam from dominating South Vietnam. Therefore, the alternatives facing us now should not include a stepped-up continuation of what we are already doing in the South—Westmoreland's proposal. The alternatives are clear: either an immediate and complete American withdrawal, defeat; or a massive, full offensive against North Vietnam itself."

One of the panel members slammed back in his chair, muttering audibly, "Oh, Christ."

But Crocker was the one who bore into Dillon. "A massive offensive? Including atomic weapons?"

"Not at first. A massive but conventional air war against every major industrial, communications, transport and supply target in the North. The immediate mining of Haiphong Harbor. A total blockade of the entire country. Shut it off. In that case it would be sufficient to hold nuclear weapons in reserve."

Randall Crocker slammed his hand down on the table, startling those around him. "Sean! Listen to yourself! That's Russia! That's China! That's World War Three you're proposing! What have you become?"

Crocker's red eyes snapped, and the blood color spilled into his face, swelling it alarmingly.

Dillon stifled the instinctive concern he felt for his old friend, and he said firmly, "I have become what you first asked me to be, an American military officer. As such, my role is to help win the wars that others in our government decide to fight. I am convinced we can bring Hanoi to negotiation quickly, simply by indicating our resolve at this crucial point. Resolve is the issue. You asked me if we can still win in Vietnam, and I answer yes and indicate how. You have not asked me *should* we win, or whether the political risks of an expanded conflict are worth taking. That question does not belong to me." Dillon glanced along the table. The dozen distinguished men seemed confused suddenly, and also frightened. "In fact, gentlemen, given the commission you have from the President, I'd say the question belongs to you. I am a man in uniform. I have a narrow view."

"It's a narrow view that has ruined us in Vietnam!" The man next to Crocker put his hand on Crocker's arm, but Crocker shook him off. "Now you want atomic weapons! Have you no morality, sir?"

Sean Dillon was not capable of being provoked by Randall Crocker in that obvious state of distress. Such a question from anyone else would have generated a fierce reaction, but toward Crocker at that moment what he felt was, well, grief.

Have you no morality? He heard the echo of Joseph Welch's famous question to Senator McCarthy: "Have you no sense of decency, sir, at long last? Have you no sense of decency?"

Dillon recalled that he had watched the fateful encounter between the army counsel and the Red-baiting senator on the television in Crocker's office in the Pentagon. Together they had cheered Welch, then Crocker had called him.

Morality. The word echoed inside Dillon. In his view it had become a cheap word, banalized by the critics of the war, and by simpletons like his own sad son. Morality *ad bello*, he thought, remembering his Aquinas. Morality *in*.

He said quietly, "The immorality I am most aware of right now, Mr. Crocker, is the wasting of lives, American and Vietnamese both, for no purpose. A halfway war that has no chance of success is what is immoral. The VC and NVA offensives at Tet demonstrated that what has been immoral for three years is our refusal to engage Vietnam fully. To keep faith with the twenty thousand Americans who have died there, we should engage Vietnam fully now."

Crocker lurched out of his chair, knocking his walker over noisily. The gold chain of his watch fob, clutched in his fist, whipped in the air. "You want more dead? What about Richard? Think about your son!"

"My job," Dillon replied, "is to think about everyone's son."

"You have no—!"

The slam of the gavel cut Crocker off.

He blinked down the row of his oldest friends, toward Acheson. The expression on Crocker's face was of a man rudely awakened. The panel members stared back at him with a full range of worry on their faces. Finally they seemed to have noticed that something was wrong with Crocker. Very wrong.

Dean Acheson declared the session adjourned without a word of acknowledgment to Dillon, who gathered his papers and, with a baleful final glance toward Crocker, quickly left.

At Dillon's office in the Pentagon, Michael Packard was waiting.

"Good Lord, General, Randall Crocker—"

Dillon shook his head, brushing past his assistant. "It was awful. You wouldn't believe how he behaved—"

"No, I mean, they just called from the EOB. Mr. Crocker has had a stroke, a serious stroke. They've rushed him to the hospital."

Martin Luther King was assassinated little more than a month later, on Holy Thursday. By the middle of Good Friday afternoon, rampages of arson, looting, and street warfare had broken out in more than a hundred American cities, and the worst violence of all struck Washington. More than seven hundred fires were set there, and even by Sunday afternoon, Easter, the sky above the nation's capital was still marked by numerous faint ocher columns. The fires had been concentrated along Fourteenth Street Northwest, the quarter just above the White House, but black neighborhoods in Southeast, near Bolling, had been hit too. The air everywhere was sour and from most vantages in the city there was a view, at least, of smoke.

Sean and Cass, after Mass, had gone to the Officers' Club for brunch. The club steward had laid on a festive spread, but thoughtlessly, for he had set up the lavish buffet outside on the terrace, which was famous for its commanding view of the Potomac and, in the distance, of the capital skyline. The officers and their wives moved through the buffet line and took their tables quietly, uncheered by the idea of Easter or by the glorious spring weather, for just beyond the railing the view of Washington was of its shroud. The monument was in a fog of smoke. More than one of the officers felt as though he were stationed back at Tan Son Nhut or Bien Hoa. They were in an enclave of privilege and safety while, outside fences along which airmen in combat gear had been posted, a city was staggering under the effects of war. An American city! Washington!

Moving among the tables, pouring water and serving butter and rolls, were stoical black waiters. Cass, for one, felt like grabbing the sleeve of every colored person she saw and apologizing. She ate her omelet and potatoes listlessly, as little inclined to talk as Sean.

It was he who said finally, "After Washington, they say Chicago has been the worst."

Cass nodded. "I read that. There were fires 'back of the yards.' Strange they still call Canaryville that, since the yards are gone. Do you ever think of the yards?"

Sean shook his head, but he gazed toward the city as he did. Was he thinking of the yards now? Because of the smoke, the stench in the air? It was the single great triumph of his life that he'd left the slaughterhouses behind, but the feeling now was, Had he? He stared across the distance, trying to ignore the knot of pure fear twisting in his stomach. Fifteen thousand troops had been deployed in Washington. Machine-gun nests had been set up on the top steps of the Capitol and at the Supreme Court and inside the gates of the White House.

Cass said, "I also read what Mayor Daley said, about shooting looters. Shoot to kill, he said." She shivered with disgust.

Sean brought his face sharply back to his wife. "Actually, the order was shoot to kill arsonists, Cass. Not looters. A responsible order, in my view. These fires are killing people. An eleven-month-old burned to death in his crib in Chicago. I'd have shot that arsonist myself, if I'd had the chance."

Cass put her fork down, touched her napkin quickly to her mouth. "Oh, Sean, you're so . . ."

"So what? What?"

She only shook her head.

"Cass, do you understand how close to chaos we are in this country?" Sean bunched his own napkin and threw it on the plate in front of him. "Look, look at that. That's Washington! That's our Washington! And our Chicago is just as bad!"

"Is the answer to all that just shooting them? Is that really what you think?"

"Shooting arsonists, Cass. Arsonists!"

"Negroes is what Mayor Daley means, whatever you say he says. Shooting Negroes is what he means. My only thought is that we've shot enough of them now."

"Oh, Christ, Cass."

"No, really." Cass looked quickly around, shocked to realize they were arguing in public. They had not actually raised their voices, but crushed napkins sat on both their plates, and beside those plates their fists were clenched. Cass noted with relief that the subdued diners around them seemed intent on their meals, as uninterested either in speaking or listening as Sean and Cass themselves had been only moments before.

Sean leaned back abruptly to break their mood. He took out his cigarettes and lit up. Cass joined him in a rare smoke of her own.

He said quietly, wanting to disarm her, "I admit to being afraid for our country."

"I was just thinking of you." She leaned across to him, to touch his hand. "I think you are making things worse on yourself than they need be."

"What are you talking about?" He was sure that she was going to say Richard.

She said, "Mr. Crocker, I'm talking about Mr. Crocker."

He looked away.

"I want you to come with me, Sean. You should come with me."

Dillon inhaled his cigarette, then raised a finger at a waiter for the check.

"Sean, it's been more than a month. His condition is worsening. He would recognize you, Sean. He recognizes me, I'm sure of it. It would mean—"

"Cass, please, Cass. Take my word for it, Randall Crocker does not want to see me. It would be no kindness to him."

"But I've told you what the doctor said. His behavior toward you was almost certainly part of the effect of the undetected strokes he'd been having for months, the lashing out, the hostility, the paranoia. His brain was affected. Men in his law firm had their troubles with him too. You're wrong to take it personally, or to think that now—"

"It is not a matter of my taking it personally," he said, irritated. "We have a seriously divided government. I am totally identified with one side, he was—"

"Sean, he's sick." Cass leaned toward him again, but for the control it gave her. If she was speaking in a whisper, it was a venomous one. "And now he's alone. No one visits him but me. He has no family, Sean. He has no friends, not here anyway, this damn, heartless city."

"I'm glad you go to see him, Cass."

"His eyes move, Sean. When I read to him he nods at what he likes. I've been reading James Bond novels to him, Sean. You should be doing that, not me. You owe him more than I do."

"Maybe we owe him, both of us, more than you think."

His bitterness tipped her. "You can't blame him for Richard. Stop blaming Mr. Crocker for that. Richard made his own choices, and if he found someone he could talk them over with in Mr. Crocker, that's all the more we owe him."

"I don't see it that way."

"You don't see anything anymore. You make a judgment and then refuse to change it."

"Once you admired that in me. Once, Mr. Crocker did."

"I'm not talking about gangsters in Chicago or Raymond Buckley—"

She stopped. Suddenly her hands fluttered with nervousness. It was the first time either of them had mentioned Buckley in years. The name hung between them in the air like some foul word, some curse.

Dillon could not look at her. He dropped his eyes to her hands, which, as if independent of her, were compulsively twisting around each other. He noticed that her hands were not beautiful any longer. Rheumatism had knotted her long, tapering fingers.

"I just mean," she continued, "that now you might be wrong

in your judgment, Sean. The judgment you want to stick by. You might be wrong about everything. Has that occurred to you?"

"Everything?" he asked, and waited with gathering intensity for her to answer. When she said nothing, he repeated, "Everything?"

She clamped her hands together, stopping them.

"You mean the war, don't you?"

She was startled by his accusation and her face showed it.

"You mean the war," he repeated. "Are you going to start in on the war? Is that your point? Now you can join the line of experts on Vietnam. Everybody in this town knows what to do in Vietnam except those of us charged with doing it. Including you. Well, yes, Cass, it has occurred to me that I'm wrong. I've been wrong. And boys have died as a result! Is that your point?"

"I didn't mean the war," she said, but in a detached, impersonal tone. The war, like the riots in Washington, was an agony beyond her.

But Sean went on as if he hadn't heard. "But what if I am mistaken? I still have to act. Don't you understand that? I still have responsibility."

Cass shook her head. "I know nothing of that, Sean. But I do know this"—she indicated the two of them, their family—"and from what I see, you do not act, and you do not accept responsibility, and for all I know, it's the same in the Pentagon. What I see is a man who is only waiting, waiting for something awful to happen. Like your son to reject what you stand for, or your oldest, dearest friend to do that too. To me, you're like Mayor Daley, just wanting to strike out! Once you hated men like him. Now you defend him. Shoot to kill—that's not responsibility, and if that's all we're doing in Vietnam now, well then . . ." Her antagonism shocked even her, and she had to stop. With a shift back to the impersonal, she said, "I don't know anything about Vietnam. I deliberately refuse to think about it. But I know about you. And what I see from beginning to end when I look at you now is a man who has become paralyzed. You're stuck, Sean. You're as paralyzed in your way as Mr. Crocker is in his. But at least when he moves his eyes or squeezes my hand I get the feeling that he's still alive inside. I'm not sure if that's true of you anymore, Sean. I'm really not."

The waiter approached, bringing the check, and his reprieve. How Dillon welcomed it that he did not have to respond to her. He would never respond to her.

He signed his name, then snuffed out his cigarette, a gesture of adjournment. "I'm not letting you go over there today. It's not safe to leave the base yet."

Cass pushed her seat back from the table. "He's at the hospital at Andrews, Sean. You know that. Andrews is an air base just like Bolling is."

"You'd have to drive the Suitland Parkway. The rioters have been throwing debris down on cars from the overpasses. Suitland is one of the most terrorized areas. You're not going."

"And you're not telling me that. It's Easter, and Mr. Crocker deserves a visit. You can't stop me." Her anger had purged her of nervousness. Cass stood up and walked away from the table.

Sean watched her go. He had to admire the way she left the terrace, despite her fury, as if she were going ahead to use the powder room. She gave away only what she wanted to, and only to whom. From a distance there was no evidence of her coming rheumatism or the general slackness of her skin. His wife was fifty-four now, but still had a young figure and moved gracefully. That surface poise, he realized, had always been her strongest suit, but always too it took its power from the dark torrent of feeling that ran beneath it. Even after all these years she could still surprise him. Despite her denial of it, he knew damn well she had just challenged him precisely on Vietnam. Paralyzed, she had said. And of course he was. She had instinctively cut to the core of his situation. He had been powerless to influence events in Vietnam for years, standing by with nothing but timid queries, like every other man of his rank, while the endless supply of grunt heroes was fed into the maw of a war that was both too little and too much.

But not paralyzed, not paralyzed at all. He had been bumping futilely against first one wall, then the next. Not paralyzed, he wanted to call after her, but corralled, JCS on one side, OSD on the other, CIA and MACV and always, forever, the individual service branches which automatically undercut him every chance they could. The corrals and chutes of his permanent situation. The Pentagon. The stockyards. What he had so proudly—Chicago's Pride—left behind.

When Cass had disappeared through the open French doors,

sheer curtains billowed in the wind, pointing his gaze toward the distant river, across the flight line. His eyes seized upon a soaring V-shaped wing of birds. The Lord is risen, alleluia, he thought, the Lord is risen indeed. Never had he felt the need more for a robust dose of the resurrection, and never had the formulas of his faith seemed staler.

As he watched the birds winging north toward the black spire of Georgetown, he thought of St. Bede's sparrow. Into the hall, out again and gone.

Like her.

Sean stood, and as he crossed the terrace he was aware that the majors, colonels, and generals at the other tables had noticed him, but he sensed from their open glances and even, here and there, nods, that they had no idea of what had just passed between him and Cass.

He found her in a phone booth off the lobby, with the glass door closed. He waited for her to finish her call. She hung up the phone and came out.

"What was that?" he asked.

"I called a taxi," she said, and brushed past him, out the door.

Under the Officers' Club's fancy entrance awning he took her elbow. "Look, Cass, if I have problems with your driving across Suitland, I'm certainly not going to let you do it in some damn taxicab."

"What is this 'let' me? Since when do you 'let' me?"

He saw that he was going to lose this, so, still with her elbow, he pulled her toward their car. "All right, I'm driving you. You simply cannot go out there alone. That's all. I'm driving you."

They exchanged not a word for the twenty minutes it took to reach Andrews Air Base. They drove under a dozen overpasses on which they saw not one rioter or looter or arsonist, nor one Vietcong.

At the long circular drive leading up to the General Malcolm Grow Air Force Hospital, the flagship medical facility that was the air force's equivalent of Bethesda and Walter Reed, Dillon ignored the marked general officers' parking places to pull right up to the door. He stopped the car with more of a jolt than he intended.

Cass opened the door, then looked back at him. "You're really not coming?"

He shook his head no.

"Do you want me to tell him anything?"

And he shook his head again. "I'll wait here."

Cass got out of the car and slammed the door behind her. She went into the cool hospital, her heels clicking on the tile floor as she made for the VIP wing, without looking back at her rigid husband, resolving to forget him for the hour.

Mr. Crocker was quiet that afternoon, but he held fiercely to Cass's hand. Now and then his good eye snapped into focus and he seemed to register that she was by his bed. But he was free of the agitation and restlessness that sometimes made time with him so upsetting to her. The entire left side of his body was slack, his mouth drooped, his arm and leg lay in his bed as if unrelated to the rest of his body, like logs that the doctors used to reinforce the metal railing.

Cass propped the book against her knee with her free hand, and as always she read in a steady, quiet monotone. *Casino Royale* was the name of the novel, and the truth was, though she had spoken each word of its first two thirds aloud, she had little or no idea what it was about. It was the third James Bond novel she had read to him. Often she had decided he was not listening, and had stopped, but he had surprised her regularly by sending a protesting jolt of energy through his fist. Her custom was to read until he was asleep, then to sit there, still holding his hand, for the length of time it took to say her rosary.

She could not say that old friend of a prayer now without thinking continually of Richard, but she never felt that Mr. Crocker would mind. As she recited the Hail Marys and Our Fathers and Glory Bes, she replayed with like rote-mindedness a favorite sequence of quick memories: Richard's first laughter filling the halls of the Mellon Art Gallery as she tickled him; his staring in wonder at the Indian statues at the Smithsonian; a snow-suited Richard on his back on the hard-frozen reflecting pool near the Lincoln Memorial, flailing his arms and legs to make ice angels; a teenage Richard at the door one Mother's Day carrying a young but flowering dogwood tree by its dirt ball; the warm, powdered weight of Richard's infant body against hers, the liquid motion of the rocking chair; Richard at

seven or eight carrying a stick like a cane in emulation of Mr.
Crocker.

Mr. Crocker. She remembered the open admiration in his
eyes the time she'd sweet-talked J. Edgar Hoover on the
phone. She thought of his unannounced arrival at the crypt
church of the unfinished Shrine, the leather-bound Bible he
had brought for Richard, the Bible she had held for Sean when
he took his air force oath. She thought of the affectionate
laughter with which he'd say after some pointed comment of
hers, "You have an angel in you, Cass, but I think it's trying
to get out."

She blessed herself at last, her prayer at an end, and she put
her rosary away. She looked at him. His head had fallen to the
side of his pillow, and he was breathing with rough steadiness,
asleep. A line of drool hung from the dead side of his mouth.
She pulled her hand free of the clamp of his fist, then fumbled
in her purse for a tissue. She wiped his chin clean, then noticed
that his left eye had begun to tear, only his left one, and she
wiped it too.

"Dear, dear man," she said gently, and almost added, "Pa,"
which, when she realized it, shocked her. The ache it soothed
to be here for him was the oldest one she had.

She was not aware of Sean.

He was standing in the hallway behind her, looking in.

She did not move from Crocker's side. After a few minutes
Sean walked away from the door, to the window at the end of
the corridor. The view was of the tops of trees running off, a
carpet, into the hills of Maryland, but it was easy to see it as
the view from the Bethesda Naval Hospital, the view of Washington, the view Forrestal glimpsed one last time as he went
through his window. But then Dillon remembered that if he
were looking at the city skyline, it would now be smeared with
the smoke of smoldering fires.

A pair of F-105s leapt out those trees, screaming into the
sky. The Andrews runway was hidden in the distance. The
fighter planes were brown and black, sinister darts, killers.
Dillon had to stifle the automatic repugnance that still set him
apart from other air force men. Despite the effect of his daily
effort, especially his supervision of target selection, the actual
sight of warplanes dressed for combat, so thrilling to their pilots, who regarded every other kind of airplane as an effete
plaything, always made Dillon uneasy. It was alienation which,

ordinarily, he quickly fended, but not now. Instead, he stayed
with it long enough to let it open out into a far larger
alienation, a far more dangerous one.

What drives a man to suicide? Twenty years before, at the
time of Forrestal's, Dillon could not imagine. Suicide, he'd
thought then, could only be the act of a deranged mind, but
now he felt differently, far less smug and sure. Had Forrestal
simply perceived something more sharply than others had?
What if, in looking back on the arc of his life, public or private, a man saw only a bending sequence of grave mistakes?
What if the end product of a life was itself seen to be a grave
mistake? Sean Dillon knew that Randall Crocker and others
like him had become so enraged in the argument over Vietnam
because to them the war called into question the real character
of the postwar American order, the creation of which was the
climactic labor of their lives. Dillon had had no such experience regarding Vietnam—the order held for him, indeed he
was defending it, but he felt no smugness in that either. The
truth was he had not dared to look at the arc of his own life
with a view to judging it, and the two who had done precisely
that, Crocker and Richard, he had completely shunned.

He turned and walked back along the corridor to Crocker's
room, stopping once more in the doorway. He was fully aware
what a grave mistake it would be now, whatever came of his
fugitive son, if he were to let Randall Crocker die without
knowing how much he loved him.

Cass sensed his arrival this time. She stood and came to the
threshold. She took Sean's hand and led him to Crocker's bedside. The old man's eyes were open. Cass joined their hands.
The pressure of the grip with which they held each other
turned their fingers white.

TWENTY-TWO

"Man that is born of woman hath but a short time to live."

The gold-edged pages of his prayer book fluttered in the hot breath of the wind, costing him his place, but it had been decades since the old minister had needed text for this service. He folded the book into his arms, and his eyes moved to the coffin in front of him, the chasm below.

"He cometh up and is cut down like a flower; he fleeth as it were a shadow and never continueth in one stay."

A few feet away, in front of felt-covered folding chairs, Cass clutched at Sean's arm, staring hard at the flag-draped box, the end with stars. Behind them was a group of several hundred. Many of the men, like Sean, were in uniform. Cass's face was darkened by a veiling lace mantilla that made her look like a Spanish lady. Rosary beads slipped through the fingers of her free hand.

"In the midst of life we are in death; of whom may we seek for succor but of thee, O Lord?"

Without a cue from the minister, or an evident order from their officer, a squad of soldiers stepped forward for the flag. With rigid solemnity they uncovered the casket, folding the flag back into the traditional three-sided bundle. They passed it to their officer, who held it before his face, unmoving.

The minister took a small handful of dirt from the acolyte's tray and began to sprinkle it, rubrically, on the lacquered wood. "Unto God's gracious mercy and protection we commit you, Randall . . ."

When the prayer was finished, the officer crossed to Cass and Sean. With the stilted precision of a wind-up doll, he presented the flag to her. She pressed the thing against her bosom, as if damming a hole. Randall Crocker had expressly indicated that the flag be presented to her, as she knew, but still, it was a shock, one last loving gesture from a man who, despite all that made such a thing unthinkable, had become her one true father.

And not only hers.

The honor guard officer saluted.

Dillon returned the salute. He stood holding his breath, his face squared against the sky and shining trees. He had never seemed more the hard, spare man. The morning light glinted off the silver stars on his epaulets.

The rifle squad stood at a distance, and its first volley made the people jump.

Dillon stared hard across the river valley as the sound of the guns boomed across to the marble city. Three volleys of gunshot signified, originally, that the bodies of the fallen had been retrieved, and now the battle could resume. It was June 1, 1968.

They were gathered on an Arlington knoll two hundred yards south of the Lee mansion. Some of the mourners were of Crocker's generation—Harriman was present, in from Paris where the peace talks had just begun, and Acheson and William O. Douglas. The disgraced McNamara was here, and his replacement at Defense, Clark Clifford. So were Rusk and Rostow, the Joint Chiefs resplendent in their stars and ribbons, and two dozen other generals, especially of the air force. An exhausted-looking Hubert Humphrey stood on the other side of Cass. He had come in from California for this funeral, though he would go right back because of the campaign.

A lone bugler on a distant hillside began to play. *Fades the light . . .* Those sweet notes unlocked the last corner in which the sadness of all those men and women had been sealed. Cass had known better than to wear makeup on such a morning. Sean put his blue arm around her shoulder, but it braced him as much as her. The last mournful notes of "Taps"—*Leadeth all / To their rest*—floated into the air above them.

Most of the military men, unlike the civilians, stood at perfect attention, staring blindly. Their faces seemed dead. This was part of what they'd been trained to do. Their young colleagues died all the time and they had developed a system of their own—soldiers and fliers lived by systems and died by them—for dealing with a destiny that had become as mundane as it was tragic. They were *listening*, actively, intently. They were listening past the bugle for another sound, a sound of theirs.

It came at first as a faint low roar funneling at them from the south, up the river valley from Alexandria, from the mouth of the great Potomac. As the last echo of "Taps" faded, the roar grew quickly louder. The mourners turned toward what had become a screech, and saw swooping down from the blue yonder, wheeling in a wide arc away from the Jefferson Memorial and the Washington Monument, a flight of sleek fighter planes, four of them, with long thin fuselages, sharp as arrows, maneuvering on clipped wings, heading right at Randall Crocker's grave.

The missing-plane flyover was taken to be an honor, and Crocker was a rare civilian to receive it. But what those particular dignitaries recognized in the screaming airplanes was rage. Wouldn't those pilots see in the tormented, ineffectual government elite the enemy they could never see in fleeing, naked, almond-eyed children—that emblazoned, forever-photographed girl-child on the road, her Munch shriek—whose skin they'd bubbled with their napalm? The four Thunderchiefs pulled out of their dive at the last second, and as they passed perhaps three hundred feet above the hilltop, they rolled slightly in a perfectly synchronized wing dip.

When the planes had gone, climbing away into the Virginia sky, Dillon looked around and saw that he was the only man in uniform not saluting. His right arm still encircled his wife's shoulders, which moved gently with emotion.

The flag in front of Lee's mansion was being lowered to half-mast in strict silence. Every military eye was fixed upon it, as required. The flag at such a moment was the nation.

Dillon, even to offer the homage he most believed in, did not remove his arm from her. Instead, he pressed the woman of his life closer as softly, softly, the flag fell on its pole. He saw the other flag, the one she held against her breast, and he realized with a sharp, fresh pain that she was cradling it as if the flag were her baby.

Her baby. His. He thought again of their son, who didn't even know that Crocker had died. He remembered carrying Rickie in his arms like that, not a flag, a football. How he had loved to tuck the boy into his side and run. Now Richard did his running alone. He had been in Canada for months.

Then the ceremony was over, and Cass was clinging to her husband, whispering, "Oh, Sean!" Her mantilla rippled in the summer wind that snapped across the hillside, as if the backwash of the fighter planes had sucked it up from the languid river. Dillon felt he had an exotic dark flower in his arms, felt for the first time in years that he could hurt her if he pressed too hard—the black petals crumbling on one another—which was ridiculous. His wife was stronger than he was.

"You're a good woman, Cass."

She pulled back to look him in the eye. "He was a good man. He loved you."

Dillon wanted to say, I loved him too, but the old wall of his reticence stopped him. She settled into his embrace once more. He stroked her shoulder.

But suddenly he tensed. A human cry pierced the air from the valley behind them, and he heard it at once as having meaning for him.

The cry again. A man. A second man. Then, "Stop! Stop!"

The burial-truce was over, and instinctively Dillon thought again about Richard.

"Stop, you!"

"That's him!"

The others, like sleepwalkers, only turned their heads to look, but Sean began to move, leaving his wife's arms, walking down into the grave-littered hillside. In the valley, plainly visible, figures in dark suits were cutting between and around the line of blue and black staff cars that awaited the dignitaries. Four men, five, no, six. The military drivers, at ease by their fenders, were too surprised to join them. The men in suits, with a cry of "There!," broke out running onto the far hillside, a strike across the tombstones. Eight, nine of them spread out like a stain through the rows of white markers.

Then Dillon saw whom they were chasing. He knew his son at once, despite the distance: the lanky boniness, how his arms flailed as he ran, the way he clambered up the hill with the spunk and eagerness that had marked him since early childhood. The flying, wild hair was still unfamiliar, but it wasn't new.

His son, astray in the grass of Arlington, must have planted himself behind some tombstone, hoping to share, even that way, the obsequies of the old man he loved. But agents had talked Richard even here, and now they were going to arrest him.

Cass began moving too, watching with horror as she realized what was happening.

The agents closed in on Richard before he reached the crest of the far hill. They seized him roughly, yanked his hands behind his back and handcuffed him. Then, on him like beetles, they began dragging him back through the tombstones, down the hill to the valley road where their cars too had pulled into line.

Cass began to run. Her mantilla fell from her head and she had to clutch at it. She threw herself recklessly down the hill, well behind Sean.

Their son stumbled, but his captors hauled him up in a hurry, dragging him toward the road.

One agent had his gun drawn.

A second slapped Richard on the back of his head, to make him move faster.

Dillon was running hard; his outrage filled the air. "Stop! Stop!"

Richard fell across a tombstone as his father arrived, confronting the agent with the gun. "Holster that," he ordered. "Holster it now!"

The agent backed away, glancing at a colleague, who nodded. The agent put his pistol into the holster on his hip.

Dillon turned on the second agent. "Are you in charge?"

The agent reached into his coat pocket.

"What is the meaning of this? Don't you see what this is?"

The agent had his credentials folder out, but before he could open it, Cass stormed between them and slapped the thing out of his hand. She did not wait for the agent's reaction, but crossed to her handcuffed, bloodied son and embraced him.

"This is a funeral!" Dillon declared.

"We are apprehending a fugitive," the agent said coldly.

"With guns?" Cass charged. "He's a pacifist."

Dillon ignored his wife, and he had yet to look directly at his son. "We are burying a loved one up there. But you know that, don't you?"

Was it possible? He had been an FBI agent himself once. Could he have done such a thing as this? In the transformation of his roles, had he forgotten something? He had known what it was to spring a trap around a point of human need, but has he ever crudely exploited human grief to make an arrest?

"Does Hoover know you're doing this?"

The agent flinched, recognizing the question as a statement of the general's intent to *tell* Hoover.

The agent stooped for his credentials. He looked back at his colleagues, surrounding the kid with the long brown hair, the wire-rims, the faded brown shirt and blue jeans. "Move the woman away," he said. "Read the boy his rights."

"No. Leave him alone!" Cass clung to her son. She looked helplessly up at her husband. "Make them leave us alone."

The agent faced Dillon again. "He's in our custody. We're going now."

Another agent read from his Miranda card.

Dillon's inability to move, or even to look down at the rapt pietà of his wife and son, could only seem a stark refusal.

"Sean!" she said, glaring at him,.

Still he did not look at them. Instead, he asked the agent, "What's your name?"

"Sawyer."

All this bickering over their son as if he were a child. He was a twenty-three-year-old man. He had been living with the consequences of his cruel conscience for a long time now. It was crueler to him than to anyone else. Richard said softly, "Let go, Mom." With his hands cuffed he was powerless to move his mother away. He had a signifying mind, and that display of her paralyzing maternal love must have been unbearable.

Neither of the nearest agents moved against her.

"Really, Mom." His voice was weak, a hint of whine in it. She took his face between her hands. "Are you all right?"

Richard nodded. If his hands had been free, he'd have pushed the lock of hair away from his eyes, a characteristic tic, a way of keeping his fierce emotions at bay.

He said, "I was all right until I heard about Mr. Crocker." He stopped, choked. "I'm so sorry, Mom," he said, as if he had caused Randall Crocker's death. With a bird-like, darting movement of his head, he looked up at his father. "Dad?"

Instead of answering, Dillon stared across at the orderly hillside. Tombstones made it orderly; the dead were well behaved; cadavers never needed haircuts. The mystery of Sean Dillon's sorrow, what kept him from even the smallest expression of acceptance of his only son, was impenetrable. He was at a limit, that was all. For the first time in his life, there was simply nothing he could do or say.

When it was clear to all that the general was not going to reply to his son, the agent-in-charge nodded at his men. They firmly pulled the woman up, and then her son. As they led him off, he looked away from his father, a show of resolution, as if this had not been a moment of absolute, obliterating rejection.

When Sean faced Cass, her sore eyes were pinned on him, and for the first time since their beginning, the word for what he saw in an expression of hers was hatred.

Their beginning.

He refused at first to look away. The hatred in her eyes drew his eyes like a flame, and he knew it was hatred for him.

There were the slams of the Bureau car doors, and the sooty noise of their engines as they drove away.

Then that silence again.

No "Taps" now, no roaring flyover, no triple volley of guns. No muffled weeping either. The silence of pure aftermath.

Their beginning: Was this end implicit in it? That was the question he wanted to ask her. He turned to stare out at noble, spare Washington across Memorial Bridge, but saw instead all those door-shaped marble stones at his feet, ten thousand doors, which began to open slowly on the one long corridor of all the choices they had made.

He shook himself, and looked back at the other powerful men of Washington who had drifted down from the knoll, witnesses. The various expressions on their starched faces all said the same thing: You're lucky, General, this damned war being what it is, that all you've lost is your son.

By afternoon, since the cellblocks deep inside the courthouse were essentially unventilated, heat had replaced noise as the thing to hate most. It seemed that the sultry Washington air had infiltrated the double-lock doors in order to have the moisture baked out of it. There were perhaps four dozen cells on two levels, and each one, he assumed, was like his, a windowless cubicle not much wider or longer than the bunk, into the corner of which he had curled himself. A second bunk—unoccupied, thank God—crowded him from above. The two bunks, except for the jammed, overflowing metal toilet, were the only furniture, and even the narrow steel slabs, lacking mattresses, were more like shelves than beds. In fact, every surface in the closed space was cement or metal, which was why each sound bounced and bounced again, a cacophony of clanging doors, curses, barked commands, an endless series of outraged, self-canceling echoes. Several times an hour agitated men had been brought into the lockup from holding cells elsewhere in the building, or from jails, or, freshly arrested, from the street. Every such arrival, like every appearance of guards in the narrow aisle on the first level, had set off the noise.

He had sat for a long time with his arms around his head, trying to shut the din out. Because the heat seemed to drain the space around him of air, he had begun holding his mouth open until his jaw hurt, as if that would make it easier to breathe. The excruciating pain in his chest was perhaps a sign of mere suffocating and not, as he'd thought, of anxiety-induced heart attack. He brought his hands down from his head and unclenched them. They were gray. He used his hands to hoist himself off the shelf of his bunk into the two-yard-wide space beside it. He unfolded his lanky body and stood up, averting his eyes from the disgusting toilet, although the stink of the brimming foul liquid hit him again. He began to pace between the bars of the cell door and the wall to which the toilet was fixed, turning briskly every few steps, all in an effort to get the air moving across his face. Soon he found he could walk the few steps to and fro with his eyes closed, and he resolved on impulse to pretend he was a free man strolling outside in a garden. But the image that came at once to mind was the hemmed-in stretch of grassy park at the end of Generals' Row where he had always dreamed of playing football with his father.

He stopped his pacing and opened his eyes. The stark vertical bars of the cell door were a foot in front of his face, and all at once the pain in his chest intensified, the panic of claustrophobia. He felt sure he was about to explode like a pus-swollen beetle on the scalding summer sidewalk. He had to move with energy or burst, and in that small space only one move was possible. He turned and, stepping on the edge of the lower bunk, hefted himself neatly up onto the upper. He settled on his back. The stained ceiling was a mere three feet above his face. Until now he had shunned the upper bunk because it was mercilessly exposed to the naked light bulb hanging on frayed wire from the ceiling just outside the cell. The bars were harder to ignore from that bunk, and the light itself was infinitely more aggressive than the grotto-like shadow below. He stared up at the light bulb feeling dizzy, thinking of Camus' Meursault, who blamed the relentless Algerian sun not only for his indifference to the man he'd killed, but for his real crime, indifference to the fact of Maman's death. Heat and glare, the absurd, individual moral action against hopeless odds, exile, mad revolt and genuine rebellion—he loved Camus. Camus was his Moses. He pictured Dr. Rieux, who always appeared in his mind as a version of the French actor Yves Montand. He conjured the deep, curling voice in which his careful imagination rendered all French epigrams: To resist the pestilence is not heroic but a matter of common decency. Common decency, he repeated to himself as he shrank into the corner, where the steel shelf met the cinder block wall.

He closed his eyes and saw the face of his own mother, to whom he was in no way indifferent. He pictured her as she had been at the cemetery that morning, how she had turned on his father, demanding that he intervene. How she had held him; for a moment he had felt at peace in the old cradle of her arms. Yet once again, in the rough way the FBI agents had yanked her away from him, his mother had been the one whom he had caused to be hurt. Here was where the excruciating pain in his chest came from, an agony of guilt—how he had hurt his mother, hurt her and hurt her and hurt her again, when it was his father with whom he had his quarrel. But his father, as in the cemetery and as everywhere his whole life long, was too stolid to hurt.

From the main cellblock entrance at the far end of the narrow aisle came the clang, and its echo, of the huge steel door banging open. He could picture it, like the door of a bank vault, and he remembered how the first sight of its thickness had panicked him in ways the jolt of his arrest had not, not the handcuffs nor the booking procedure nor even the humiliation of being fingerprinted. The door had terrorized him because the door was going to close, as he thought of it, on his body, as if he were dead already. It was going to close on his future, and on his membership in every collective that mattered to him, when what he wanted, even more than such a door closing on, say, the war, was for a stout, transcendent door like that to close on the feeling he had of being so alone.

From Randall Crocker's funeral in Arlington Richard Dillon had been brought to the lockup in the bunker-like federal courthouse across from the clay tennis courts on which he had played several matches for St. Anselm's School, near the intersection of Pennsylvania and Constitution avenues. The Capitol itself was only two blocks up the hill from there.

By June of 1968 it was not unusual, of course, for young men like him to be hauled into such places, but not in the way that he was. Richard had attended his first peace march only months before, yet now here he was in jail!

The trauma of arrest in civil rights and peace demonstrations was supposedly mitigated by the fellow feeling of protesters, their bonds with each other and the rituals that preserved them—the singing and the linking of arms and the flashing of peace signs and, at climactic or fearsome moments, the hugging and the weeping. But Richard Dillon had gone to jail alone. Nothing had mitigated his trauma and now, hours after his arrest, with no clear sense of what he was charged with or when he would, if ever, get out, he was sinking deeper and deeper into a chasm of despair where only one thing was clear, that he had made a terrible mistake, because he could not do this.

The cellblock door banged shut, and prisoners in their cells began to hoot at the guards as they escorted a newcomer into the lockup. Richard listened as the footsteps grew louder, and he abruptly twisted around in his bunk and sat up as far as he could under that ceiling as he realized they were coming toward his cell.

A huge black man with his hands cuffed behind his back appeared on the other side of the bars. A pair of guards, both white, were on either side of him, each holding one of the man's arms. They were dwarfed by his size and they lacked utterly the mean cockiness that had so cowed Richard when they'd brought him in. The prisoner's forehead was freshly bandaged. His eyes flashed with hostility as he glared into the cell, right at Richard.

"Hate to do this to you, Quaker," one guard said as he applied a key to the cell door.

The black man only stared at Richard. Though Richard was perched on the bunk high off the ground, his and the new prisoner's eyes were on the same level. The man was nearly seven feet tall.

Richard did not blame black people for their rage, especially after the murder of Dr. King, but it was a nightmare now to be the object of it. He understood that to this new prisoner he, Richard Dillon, was no better than George Wallace or Lester Maddox or the man, for that matter, who had shot Dr. King.

One guard pulled the door open while the other removed the man's handcuffs. As soon as the man's hands were free, though, his arms shot out to grab hold of the door posts, and his huge body went rigid. "I'm not going in there!"

Because of me, Richard thought, and then he realized he was on the man's bunk. But that was crazy. The man had no claim to the upper bunk. But Richard didn't want the upper bunk, was the point. The lower bunk, with its soothing, concealing shadow, was his. But would he want this behemoth on top of him?

"I'm not going in there, motherfucker! Give me one with a head that works!" The man's stare was fixed on the brimming toilet, the foul urine on the floor around it.

"Get in there, you nigger fuck!" one guard said while pulling the nightstick out of its holster on his hip. In one quick movement he slammed the end of the stick into the prisoner's lower back. The prisoner cried out in pain, releasing one hand to press it against his spine. The second guard quickly slammed the door, which closed on the prisoner's other hand. The man shrieked.

"Hey," Richard cried out despite himself, "you've got his hand!" Richard sat completely up, hitting his head on the ceiling. "You've got his hand! Open the door! Open the door!"

The black man curled around the left side of the door where his hand was being mangled.

"Say 'sir'!" the guard ordered, vising the door shut even further, squeezing the fingers in steel.

The prisoner didn't hesitate. "Sir!" he cried. "Sir! Sir!"

The guard opened the door enough for the man to take his hand in, and collapse on the floor, groaning. Then the guard slammed the door shut, locking it. The guard with the stick poked it between the bars at Richard. "What's your problem, Quaker?"

Richard scurried back into the corner like a gerbil. "No problem," he said. "No problem."

The guard laughed. "That's what you think."

The second guard chimed in, "Enjoy your new roommate, Quaker."

They went off laughing.

Richard threw himself back across the bunk to the bars, grabbing one in each fist, as he'd seen a hundred cattle rustlers do in the movies. "When am I getting out of here? I'm supposed to have a lawyer coming!"

His cry was the cue for a fresh outbreak of obscenities and complaints from the other prisoners, who had until then, Richard now realized, fallen completely silent. "When am I getting out of here?" one voice cried, and another, "Where's my lawyer?"

"Balling your old lady, that's where!"

"Fuck you, pizza face!"

Richard pulled back away from the bars to his corner again, hugging himself, aware suddenly that his T-shirt was soaked through with perspiration.

His bunk shook a few minutes later when his cellmate lifted himself into the lower bunk. The man became absolutely still so quickly it alarmed Richard. He listened carefully for some moments but couldn't even hear the man's breathing. He crossed over the edge of his bunk to ask, "Are you all right?"

The man had his face to the wall, and made no reply.

"If you prefer this bunk up here, I'll switch."

Still the man said nothing. His body rose and fell in the easy rhythm of sleep. Sleep? It was inconceivable to Richard that the man could have gone to sleep.

Richard rolled back to his own wall, pressing the length of his body against it. He tried the not-moving too, the rhythmic breathing, but if anything the pitch of his anxiety rose. At one point he imagined that the man below him was his father, and to cauterize that fresh panic, he quite deliberately recalled a pleasant moment, the time he'd brought a new girlfriend home from Georgetown and his father had surprised them all by going out to the terraced garden after dinner and returning with a daffodil for her.

For a long time, like the man below him, Richard did not budge, on the animal theory that perhaps bad things happen only to those who move. Eventually the guards came back. "You, Quaker," one said. "Your name Dillon?"

"That's right."

"Surf's up." Both guards had their nightsticks out, ready for trouble; hoping for it, Richard sensed. One unlocked and opened the door, eyeing the motionless hulk on the lower bunk. "Let's go."

Richard hopped down to the floor with a jolt that shot right to his teeth. He quickly went through the door, ashamed of the stealth in his movement, an implicit throwing-in with the guards against the sleeping black giant.

But there was nothing conspiratorial in the way the guard handcuffed him. The two shoved him along. Out of the lockup there were stairs and a maze of corridors, progressively wider and more recently painted, more populated. Finally the guards led him into a large paneled waiting room and turned him over to a man behind a desk, a marshal. Richard became aware of his own filth. A door off the room was marked "Men" and Richard gestured toward it with his cuffed hands; only then did he allow himself to feel an acute need to urinate. "Can I go in here?"

"No way, bub," the marshal said, and another came then and took Richard by an elbow, leading him through an opposite door into a hearing room. A magistrate was seated at a dais on one side, and a collection of perhaps a dozen people were seated on fixed benches on the other. Richard refused to look at them because he knew at once who was and wasn't there.

Before he'd looked away he had glimpsed his mother, had seen in that instant her hand fly to her mouth, not quite able to stifle a yelp of pain at the sight of him. She was still wearing the black suit from the funeral, and it shocked him how old she seemed. Her clothes looked slept-in. For the first time in his life he'd seen her hair as gray instead of red. In sunglasses she'd looked like a woman in the magazines, yet he had known her in an instant. What he had recognized was the way she had of holding her face tilted upward, proudly, despite everything.

And who wasn't there, naturally, was his father.

"State your name and address, please." The magistrate did not look up from the ledger he was writing in.

"Richard Dillon, no address."

A clerk handed a sheet of paper to the magistrate, saying, "The government lists him at Sixty-four Westover Avenue Southeast, the District of Columbia. That's Bolling Air Base, your honor."

"Mr. Shaw?" The magistrate gestured toward a man at a

side table whom Richard hadn't noticed. He was completely bald, dressed in a searsucker suit.

"Ready, your honor."

"Mr. Dillon." The magistrate now looked up at Richard, frowning solemnly. "The purpose of this hearing is threefold: to present you with the charges as brought by the government of the United States, as represented in the person of Mr. Shaw there; to allow you to answer those charges by entering your plea; and to set the terms of your disposition between now and the time of your trial. Do you understand?"

"Not that last part."

"To set your bail." The magistrate looked toward the others in the room. "Are you represented by legal counsel?"

"Not yet, I . . ."

From behind him, a male voice announced, "Your honor, if I may."

And then, almost immediately, a different voice preempted the first. "Your honor, I represent Mr. Dillon."

Richard turned to see two men approaching through the narrow opening of the one low gate. It was clear that they were racing each other to the front, and from their appearance alone the stakes of their competition were obvious. One was gray-haired, tall, and crisply dressed in a blazer and gray slacks. He carried a leather briefcase. A mere glance told Richard all he needed to know about this one. The other, a shorter man and much younger, wore a brown corduroy suit which, already long rumpled, had wilted further in the steamy weather. The trousers of that suit hung slackly at the man's knees and so far over his shoes as to hide them. The man's hair seemed incongruously short and slicked back, but then Richard realized, as the man swung through the gate, that he had a ponytail long enough to brush his shoulders. One would have thought that, especially paired with the other, the younger man would have come off at once as an ill-kempt flake, but to Richard at least, his clothing and hair and even the tattered satchel slung on his shoulder combined with a virile flint of the eye and the carriage of a former athlete to give him an offbeat glamour, like a jazz musician's.

The gray-haired, distinguished-looking man spoke first. "I am representing Mr. Dillon."

The magistrate began to write. "And you are—?"

"Excuse me, your honor." The man in the ponytail tried to

squeeze between Richard and the other lawyer, who refused to move. Richard made way for him, but rigidly. He was staring at the magistrate, resolutely not looking at the people behind him. "I believe I am Mr. Dillon's attorney."

"Who are you?" the magistrate asked.

"I am David Cohen."

"I am Lloyd Macmillan, your honor, of Crocker, Wells and Birone. I was engaged by the parents of the accused."

Richard was startled by the man's announcement. The word "Crocker" had lifted Richard's spirit, which crashed immediately when he realized the word "accused" referred to him. Before he could react, Cohen put his hand on Richard's shoulder.

"I am here," he said firmly, "in response to Mr. Dillon's own phone call." Cohen looked across at his rival attorney with a kind of triumph. "He called us."

"And who is 'us,' counselor?" the magistrate asked.

Cohen, a short man, seemed to draw himself up by several inches as he answered with the single word "Resist."

The name of the notorious antidraft peace group stalled in the air, curdling it for most of those present, but the word resonated inside Richard. A certain public stiffening of his own spine seemed the reward for his having mustered the nerve hours ago—or was it weeks?—to squander the privilege of his one phone call on strangers. Instead of calling the D.C. number he knew by heart, he had dialed the number scrawled inside the matchbook he had carried with him from Toronto. It had never occurred to him that his parents would send a lawyer. Not his parents, he corrected himself. Despite what the man in the blazer had just said, Richard was under no illusion that his parents had responded. Only she had.

While the two lawyers fenced before the magistrate, Richard turned slightly to let his eyes flow toward the others in the room. Cohen had been seated with three other people, a man with a beard wearing wire-rims and two women gotten up like twins, in loose-fitting India print dresses and long unpinned hair.

He wanted to call his eyes back when they hit the vacant spot on the bench where Lloyd Macmillan had been sitting, but it was impossible. He knew already who had accompanied the lawyer. Richard's longing quite abruptly turned into the familiar nausea of guilt as his gaze kept moving and he allowed himself at last to look directly at his mother.

Cass felt she had been here before. While waiting for the proceedings to begin she had been drawn back against her will into an entirely different scene, seeing her husband in a room like this. But that was a long time ago, and he wasn't her husband then. He was a young stranger who had saved her, but in that room it had become apparent that he had lost Doc Riley, whose other name was Richard. She remembered Sean whispering in the ear of the frightened prosecutor while the smirking man who'd murdered both her uncle and Doc Riley leered at her from the raised platform of his chair. She remembered anger blowing her apart and the judge—no, coroner—banging his gavel, ordering her just to sit there quietly, as if she were stone or salt.

And now she was just sitting there quietly again. Her fists were clenched at her sides, pressing like stymied pistons into the cold wood of the bench. It was all she could do to keep from leaping to her feet and screaming, Leave my son alone!

But scream at whom?

The magistrate seemed as perplexed as she by what was unfolding before them as the two attorneys vied for the right to speak for Richard. There was no smirking murderer here, but Cass recognized the ill-groomed anti-Establishment lawyer as a deadly threat to her son.

"Your honor," he said, "let Mr. Dillon speak for himself. He has engaged us to represent him."

The lawyer Cass had hired was shaking his head vigorously. She knew nothing about him but that he was a senior partner in the Washington office of Randall Crocker's firm. The first thing he'd told her was that he had been at Randy's funeral that morning. He'd said that he would drop everything to help her son. He knew how Randy loved Richard.

"I have had no access to my client," he was saying now. "I must insist on it before the matter of representation is ruled upon. Mr. Dillon, to any extent that he has acted at all, has done so under duress."

" 'Ruled upon'?" Cohen protested. "There's no question of ruling here. My client has . . ."

Richard himself seemed oblivious of the fateful argument. Cass realized that instead of listening he was slowly turning toward her part of the room. She recognized as characteristic that vague-eyed drifting of the head, had seen it dozens of times at the dinner table and in church. She had heard teachers describe the way his otherwise gifted mind could just float right out the classroom window. Once his inability or refusal to pay attention had been a source of irritation, but now knowledge of it simply caught in her throat, like a qualm of her own. She waited, hardly breathing while his gaze swept steadily toward her. At the last moment she took her sunglasses off. Their eyes met through a mutual shimmering glaze.

The gavel came down hard. "Mr. Dillon," the magistrate said, "you must indicate which of these attorneys is to speak for you." The official had no need to put into words the fact of his own preference for Macmillan. He was looking for grounds on which to send the long-haired peacenik shylock back into his hole.

Cass sensed the reluctance—and guilt—with which Richard let go her eyes.

"It's true," he said timidly. "I called them. I asked them for help."

"You asked who for help?"

"Resist."

"Your honor," Macmillan said, "Mr. Dillon's parents will be posting his bail. Surely they—"

Cohen waved Macmillan off. "We're prepared to make bail, your honor. Provided it is reasonable."

Macmillan looked sharply at the other lawyer. "Do you always post bail for your clients?" He faced the magistrate. "That proves my point, your honor. Resist is a political organization seeking to exploit this young man for its own ends. Once they feed him to their publicity machine they will make a spectacle of him. That's all they want."

The magistrate peered at Richard. "Have you considered that?"

"What, that . . .?" Richard's voice trailed off, as if he had not quite grasped the point.

"I object to this, your honor," the Resist lawyer said. "It is of no relevance who posts—"

"Just a moment, counselor. I'm talking to you, Mr. Dillon. Have you considered what these people may expect of you?"

"Oh, please!" Cohen protested.

The gavel came down again. "Another word out of you and you're dismissed! Now, Mr. Dillon."

"They expect me to be against the war," Richard said calmly. "I am against the war."

"They expect you"—this was Macmillan and he was almost whispering—"to denounce your father."

In the silence that followed that statement Richard turned toward Cohen, who said, "That's not true."

But Macmillan pressed. "It's what they do, Richard. Ask him about the press conferences and television appearances he arranged in nine cities for another client, Leroy Kuttner, the army deserter."

"Kuttner wanted those press conferences! Your honor, why are you letting this—?"

"Ask him about Paul Cummings and Harold Diver and Jerome Travis."

"The same thing. They all wanted to make their statements. We didn't force—"

"They'll do whatever they have to, Richard, to get you on their wavelength. You are the catch of the year, the son of the head of DIA, the son of the man in charge of all military intelligence, the son of the man whose organization picks the bomb targets in North Vietnam! What they think they have is a son prepared to charge his father with war crimes! They have already contacted a producer at the *Panorama* show about your appearance."

Cohen shot a look at Macmillan of such enraged surprise that Richard saw at once that the accusation was true. He drew back from both men, shaking his head. "I can't do this."

"Mr. Dillon," the magistrate said, "you have to decide."

"I don't want either one of them."

From her seat behind him Cass saw the color rush to her son's neck, the band of skin between his T-shirt collar and the fringe of his hair, the scruffiness of which had once made her wild with anger and shame. How long ago that seemed now, and how ridiculous. She was half off the seat, wanting to stand and declare the meeting at an end. This is a mistake! This is my Richard! Let him come home with me!

"Are the boy's parents present?"

"Yes, your honor. His mother."

"Mr. Dillon, perhaps a short recess would be—"

"No!"

"—to talk to your mother about—"

"I don't need to talk to my mother. I don't need these lawyers. I'll be my own lawyer. Can't I do that?"

"If neither of these gentlemen is to represent you, the court shall assign your case to the public defender."

"I don't need anybody. I was a law student. You want me to enter a plea. I can do that. I don't deny what I did, but I'm not guilty of any—"

"Your honor, this is improper."

The magistrate waved his hand impatiently. "I know. I know. There is still the matter of your bail, Mr. Dillon. The government has asked me to set it at fifty thousand dollars."

"Your honor!" Macmillan said.

"The young man has already established his willingness to flee to avoid the obligation of law, counselor. The government is properly—"

But Richard cut through the squabbling again. "I don't want bail. Do I have to have bail?"

"You want to stay in jail until your trial?"

The prospect, so directly put, slammed Richard. At first he could not answer. Then he said slowly, "The jail where I am now?"

The magistrate shook his head. "You're in the court lockup now, not jail. You would be remanded to Occoquan. I would not recommend Occoquan for you, young man. You have an alternative not available to the men who are there. You should take it."

"Maybe that's the point," Richard said with fresh energy. "Dr. King didn't take bail when he was alive. The Vietnamese are not offered alternatives, why should I be? You people think . . ."

Cass put her sunglasses back on, but otherwise did nothing to conceal her distress. Richard had his back to her and could not see. She knew that he was speaking mainly now to her.

". . . you think I have some kind of hang-up with my father, and I'm only doing this because . . . I mean, you think I need to get back at him. But that isn't it. That isn't it at all." He turned slightly toward Cohen. "I'm not talking about my father. He has nothing to do with this. I am talking about the Vietnamese, those women and children, and those men too. I'm just not going to kill them, that's all. I'm not going to help kill them in any way." Now he turned to Macmillan. "This has nothing to do with my mother, either. This has to do with me."

Cass wanted to go to him and pick him up by his skinny ribs and bony elbows and swing him off his feet until he

squealed with pleasure. He was a foot taller than she was, and
it had been years and years since she had been able to do that,
but holding her Richard in her arms the way she used to was
all she could think of now. He had been such a beguiling baby,
and she had loved taking him everywhere in the magic city
that Washington was for young mothers after the war. He had
soothed her loneliness, then destroyed it. She remembered how
he could sit for long periods under the huge arching dinosaur
skeleton at the Natural History Museum, staring up as if counting the individual bones. On the grassy stretches of the river
park at Hains Point he had learned to walk as strangers
cheered him on. He had rarely seen his father in those early
years, but that was normal, for as enchanting as Washington
was for women, museum guards, and bus drivers, it was still,
for the powerful men of government like Sean, the center of
what had become the permanent world emergency.

Cass had told herself it wouldn't matter that Sean knew
Richard mostly from what she reported late at night. But as
Richard grew older he had seemed less consistently bright, and
then, once he started school, there had come those sporadic
hints of something missing. His first teachers used the label
"lazy." He refused to learn to tell time. He was the last second
grader to master reading. He didn't finish things. Eventually
she had known to take that lack of focus as a signal of his
lurking inner fear that his mother's well-behaved, infinitely
cherished only child, her good boy, was not nearly good
enough. Cass knew all about the cruel boomerang of
parenthood—how a well-brought-up child can come to believe
he is deeply loved not for himself but for being well-
brought-up. If her son feared he was not good enough, and if
what she was witnessing now was that fear finally ruining him,
Cass Dillon would be forever unable to say it had nothing to
do with her. After all, that exact fear was hers before it was
his, and who would dare claim that such things were not, despite all love and all effort, passed on, like freckles or bad
teeth or, for that matter, original sin. "This has to do with me,"
her son had just proclaimed with such fierce nobility. No, Cass
thought, you dear sweet silly. Not only you. Not only you at
all.

TWENTY-THREE

The workhouse in Occoquan, Virginia, was serving that spring as a spillover jail for the District of Columbia, since many of the men arrested in the disturbances after Dr. King's assassination still filled the D.C. Jail itself. It was a medium-security prison thirty miles south of Washington, a compound of buildings spread across thirty acres on a plateau overlooking the creek that had given the place its name. The Occoquan spilled out of Bull Run toward the tidewaters of the Potomac, cutting a mean, dark valley through the hills.

Two of Occoquan's buildings were new and housed, in college-style dormitories, trusties who did road work throughout that part of Virginia. But the central building, in which Richard and other pretrial inmates were held, was a sinister-looking structure dating back to the Civil War. Until the April riots emergency, it had been abandoned as obsolete. Built of huge granite blocks, long since blackened, the jail had a squat dome and four bastion towers at each corner. Inside, the cell-blocks were arranged as balconies ringing an atrium that was open all the way up the five stories to the concave black vault of the dome. If there had ever been windows, they had been long since bricked in, and now the only light came from naked bulbs that protruded at intervals above each balcony. Richard's cell was on the fourth level, and he shared it with five others. The men at Occoquan were an intimidating lot, either too poor to make bail or too criminal to have been offered it. As a group they behaved contemptuously, with endless shouting and cursing from their cells that guards made no effort to control and that echoed through the cavernous space all day long.

But Richard, in his own cell after the first terrifying night,

had found it possible to rein his fear. He had been relieved that
the cell was a large space, relatively, and that it had beds, not
mattressless bunks, and that they were lined up in a neat row
against the one true wall, giving the cell the feel, in Richard's
compensating mind, of a military barracks. There was even a
partition isolating the toilet and sink, both of which by some
miracle still functioned. And because six men shared the space,
instead of two, the threat of unwanted intimacy seemed far less
here than in the courthouse lockup. Richard's cellmates were
blacks who wore their hair in Afros and carried themselves
like militants, but they were alike in ignoring him. It was as if
his skin color had made him invisible, which was fine. All in
all, in other words, once he'd made it through that first night,
he'd found things to feel okay about.

But the days going by had seemed like months because this
crowded, ad hoc jail was understaffed and lacked an organized
routine and even minimal facilities for prisoners' work or rec-
reation. There were no radios or television, and no true library.
Kept in their cells, the inmates passed the daytime hours
stretched out on the beds, on which they then slept fitfully at
night. Absent the natural light of windows, time itself seemed
as imprisoned as the men. Richard would have paced the cell,
but he was afraid of irritating his cellmates, so he spent a lot
of time standing, leaning against the bars, his back to the men
who did not speak to him, looking out across the balcony cat-
walk and through the Cyclone fence that had been raised
above the old iron railing to prevent suicide leaps. He stared
either at the wall of dark barred cells across the cavern or
down at the scene below, the floor of the atrium, called "the
pit." It was an object of endless fascination for Richard, the
source of most of the noise and the only action. Milling prisoners transformed the pit into a plaza during their one-hour
shifts of "out-time," which, apart from thirty-minute forays to
the grim dining hall for meals, constituted their single break of
the day.

One morning, Richard's fourth day there, the bell marking
the first shift of out-time rang as usual, but the guards did not
file onto the balconies to escort the designated prisoners from
the cells down to the pit. The prisoners slated for the break began to protest with bar banging and curses—"Where are you,
motherfuckers?"—which inmates from all five tiers were soon
echoing. Still the guards did not come, and then the realization

spread among the prisoners that the guards were nowhere in evidence, not on the catwalks or on the scaffold stairways or on the floor below. That the guards had for some reason been withdrawn seemed ironically like a further deprivation, and that led to a redoubling of protests.

Now all five of Richard's cellmates were lined up at the bars beside him, and like countless others they were banging the iron rods with metal objects, contraband spoons and belt buckles. The noise grew to a crescendo, then fell, then grew again. Richard was paralyzed by the anarchy at first, but then began to let out a throaty roar of his own, and the relief he felt at once made him go all the way with it. He gave himself over to the mass anger, yet without letting go of his acute appreciation that these fearsome lawbreakers had summoned this rage to protest the infraction of what they regarded as the law of their schedule.

Still the guards did not come.

Where are the motherfuckers? Richard too wanted to know. Just as it occurred to him that the officers had abandoned him to these desperadoes, a guard showed himself in the pit.

The sound of their hatred soared as the redneck guard walked to the very center of the vacant floor, looking up at them. In his hands he carried a yellow battery-powered megaphone. This was unprecedented in Richard's short experience. There had been until then no announcements by the jail authorities or general communication of any kind. Gradually, as the prisoners registered the fact of the megaphone, the noise decreased. It never quite stopped, but when it had dropped to isolated curses and the bar banging of a few diehard hysterics, the guard raised the megaphone to his mouth.

"Even you assholes," the disembodied southern voice began, "ought to know this." He paused, then quickly announced, "Some motherfucker shot Bobby Kennedy in California, and this morning he died."

At that the guard lowered the megaphone and slowly moved his gaze around the great hall. Now, at last, for the first time except for short periods in the night, stillness descended on the jail, a simple stunned silence which itself grew and grew as each single prisoner proved incapable of breaking it, as earlier the noise had grown with each one's piled-on outrage.

First the President, then Malcolm, then Dr. King. Now Bobby? The silence grew through phases of, first, shock that

was familiar, then fear that was new, into a rare deeper silence
that was absolute.

And Richard Dillon decided at that moment, with a kind of
perverse relief, that none of this was really happening, and the
guard saying that about Kennedy—Bobby?—proved it. Richard decided that, in fact, he was crazy, that was all. He had finally lost his mind.

The visiting room at Occoquan was in the dining hall wing, a
drab one-story cinder block addition that had been grafted onto
the domed granite antiquity after the First World War. The visiting room itself, with its concrete floor and light bulbs dangling from cords, was as unfinished as a garage, but windows
were spaced across one wall and morning light cheerfully
splashed into the place. The shadows it cast included bars, but
what the men from the cellblocks saw was light. Visitors,
seated on their side of the rough fixed table that bisected the
stark room, always felt oppressed and claustrophobic, but the
jailed men, on being admitted here, always felt released.

Richard hesitated at the door, blinking like a boy stepping
into the bright street from a Saturday matinee.

Seven or eight prisoners were at the long table, apart from
one another. Across from them sat lawyers or girlfriends. The
pairs leaned toward each other but the table was too broad for
them to touch. The cryptic murmur of their whispers filled the
room.

Guards slouched against opposite walls at either end of the
long table, mirroring each other, even the way they cradled
shotguns. One of them tossed a look at Richard, then flicked
his head at a point on the table. Richard went to it. No sooner
had he hitched his legs over the bench and sat than the room's
other door opened, the one from the world, and his mother
walked in alone.

Not since Mr. Crocker's funeral—no, not since the bail hearing afterward had he seen her.

She was wearing a green summer dress; a broad yellow ribbon held her hair tightly away from her face. Sunglasses
blanked her eyes. Cass Dillon seemed to have drawn to herself
all the color of that drab room, and as she approached her son,
he beheld her as a kind of apparition. He was aware of it when
the eyes of the others went to her, but to them she could have

seemed only like an image from the movies or a figment from a dream. To him she was an epiphany.

But she crossed to the table with mundane efficiency and took her place opposite Richard.

"Hello, Mom."

"Hello, Richard." She removed her sunglasses. Her eyes were red, but from tiredness, he sensed, more than emotion.

Instantly they fell silent. Each had thought of remarks with which to open, but now neither could think what they had been.

Despite everything she'd intended, Cass felt herself slipping down into her pain. Yes, she was glad to see him, and yes, thank God he seemed to be all right. But also, yes, how hurt she was. The last thing she'd intended was to begin with accusations, but that unpredicted, pinging silence took her under. "Why have you refused to see me?" she asked.

He dropped his eyes. "It wouldn't have done any good. I knew you would just argue with me about the lawyer."

His direct statement jolted her because it was true. Since his arrest she had been obsessed with the question of his lawyer. Lloyd Macmillan had tried everything to get the court to assign him to Richard's case, but he had failed. In addition, Richard had refused to see the appointed public defender as well, and the court had upheld him in that too. What did the court care if he was an overstressed, too sensitive boy behaving self-destructively out of all too obvious complexes that made him completely vulnerable to the madness of the times? It was the times that were mad, Cass had insisted, and she had rejected Lloyd Macmillan's last proposal, to initiate proceedings to have Richard declared incompetent.

She said softly now, "I didn't come to argue with you."

"I'm glad you came again, Mom. I told them I would meet with you this time because of Bobby Kennedy. That really knocked me for a loop. Even here, it affected everybody. A lot of these guys are here because of going nuts after Martin Luther King was killed, and now Bobby . . . It made me . . ." He shrugged his shoulders, unable to explain, completely unaware that in that particular gesture was the life of another man.

Cass recognized Sean in her son's stolid muteness, that rise and fall of shoulders. How long had it been since either of her men had found it possible, once coming to this wall of inarticulateness, to push through? No wonder they were both such loners; she had never seen their resemblance in that light before. They were alike in how alone they were—even with her.

"He was so thin," Richard added incongruously, as if that note of Kennedy's physique explained a mystery, as if anything did.

"You're thin too, Richard. I've never seen you so thin." Cass paused, then went on, "I thought Bobby Kennedy was important to you because he was saying so much of what you believe."

Richard nodded, but looked down at his hands. "He was lately."

And Cass wondered, Was Kennedy's death serving in this way everywhere now, to bring children together with their parents? In the way typical of her kind, Cass had long admired and been proud of the Kennedys and had even felt a real love for Jack, especially when he'd singled out Sean as one of his special men. But Bobby had taken over a corner of her heart without her even knowing it. The same was true, obviously, for Richard, and it was those corners that now had overlapped.

Cass said, "Did you read what he said when he was shot?"

Richard shook his head. "We don't have any newspapers to read. I haven't read anything. All I know is that he's dead." He blinked at his mother, trying to place himself. "What did he say?"

"After he was shot, he was lying on the floor of that hotel kitchen. Four or five other people were shot too. Did you know that?"

Richard looked up, appalled. "No."

"They aren't going to die. He was the only one to die. What he said was, 'Is everybody all right?' Those were his last words. 'Is everybody all right?' "

After a moment she reached into a pocket for a tissue. As she did, she glanced along the table toward one of the guards.

"What did Dad say?"

"He was just . . . like everyone. Very sad. Very worried. We were at the cemetery yesterday, so soon after Mr. Crocker's—"

"Yesterday? For Bobby's funeral?"

"No. The funeral was Saturday. Yesterday it was just people filing past the grave. Half of Washington, I think. A lot of colored people were crying, just crying and crying. Everyone was. They buried him just to the side of the President. Your father and I stood in line, like everybody. We wanted to. It took us three hours just to—"

"You waited three hours? You and Dad?"

"Did you think we wouldn't feel this?"

"But Bobby was against the war. He said the war was criminal. I would have thought Dad would regard him . . . as a traitor."

Cass shook her head, so sadly. "He doesn't regard you as a traitor either, if that's what you think."

"At Arlington, at Mr. Crocker's funeral, when the agents were arresting me, you asked him to intervene for me and he refused. I saw that."

"I was very upset. There was nothing he could do. I understand that now. Your father is a lot like you are, Richard. He sees only what he sees."

"That's not like me." Richard grinned with unmistakable, and quite sane, self-mockery. " 'You see things; and you say, "Why?" But I dream things that never were; and I say, "Why not?" ' " He laughed. "George Bernard Shaw. *Back to Methuselah*. Bobby's favorite quote."

But Cass nodded quite seriously. "That's true. You are different from your father in that way."

"We're opposites."

Cass smiled. "I don't know if I'd say that."

"I would."

"Then you don't know him. He's a good man," she said simply.

Richard flushed. "I know how much you admire Dad, how proud you are of him."

"Does that mean I can't be proud of you?"

Richard had to look away from her.

"I know you care so much about your father, what he thinks. Do you want to know what I think?"

"About me? About what I'm doing?"

Cass nodded.

Richard realized only then how afraid his mother was that compared to his father's judgment hers meant little or nothing to him. Was it that he didn't care? Or that he'd taken hers for granted? He felt his face redden, and his hand went to the place on his cheek where she'd slapped him at the Shrine. "Yes," he said. "I do want to know."

"Then look at me."

He did.

"I think you are strong and honest and good, Richard. You surprise me because your conscience is so much your own. At first that angered me, and foolishly I let it hurt me, but now I am proud of you for it. And I am sorry it has taken me this long to tell you so."

Instinctively Richard put both his hands into the forbidden middle space of the table. "You think that? Really?"

She nodded, twisting her Kleenex. "I think the war should end, just end right now. A lot of wives think that. And I think you were brave to refuse the draft."

He could hear the "but" coming. Strangely he did not dread it. There was an incipient "but" in him too.

"But I don't understand, Richard, about this." She let her eyes, their quick circuit of the sterile room, explain her statement.

" 'This' is where I should have been in the first place, Mom. Instead of Canada. Dad told me I was a coward for taking off, and I see now that he was right. He said I should face the consequences of my choice, and that's what—"

"But, Richard!" Now she stretched toward him, reaching across to his hands.

"No contact!" boomed a guard's voice. "No contact!"— another guard, so filling the room it was impossible to tell which of the two had spoken.

Cass reacted immediately, jerking her hands back and looking from one guard to the other with fear twisting her face.

"It's okay, Mom." Richard had not jumped. He smiled. "You get used to it."

She shook her head fiercely. "I can't stand it, Richard, thinking of men like that over you."

"It's all bluster. The guards are like that because they're as afraid as we are. They're victims too."

"You're the only victim I care about. I want you to come out of here, Richard. I've never asked you for anything before. I want you out of here, please. Please, Richard, come out."

"I can't, Mom. I'm stuck. The feeling is, I'm stuck."

"Then, see your father," Cass said, falling automatically back, despite every reason not to, on her lifetime's one refuge. "Talk to him."

"About what? He's as stuck as I am. Isn't that the problem?"

And, of course, it was. Her problem, her child's problem. Could she possibly leave it at this?

"He'd never come here, Mom."

"If you asked him to, he would."

"You don't believe that."

"I do, Richard. I know your father better than you." The strange, awful room around her seemed silent, as if everyone were listening to them.

She decided he was not going to say anything else.

But then he said, his voice hardly more than a whisper, "Well, would you ask him for me then? Would you say I need him?"

He spoke as if the words made him ashamed.

It was early afternoon by the time Cass arrived at the Pentagon. She rarely went there, and as she pulled into the south parking lot from Shirley Highway, it was impossible not to remember the night she'd waited here for hours and then he'd come, full of his secrets and his need. They had kissed, like passionate teenagers, before crossing the bridge back into Washington where, finally, they had parted.

Now, when she looked back on their life together, it seemed, more or less, a smoothly running stream, with swallows skimming its surface. She had long since adjusted to the fact that its strongest currents ran underground.

The long walk from the car to the river entrance gave her time to collect herself, but in her mind she returned to that water image of her life. It seemed a harsh desolation: she was just a floating twig, bent and black and very frail, tossed from one thicket of dammed branches to the next, but never catching.

Security at the entrance surprised her. Always before she'd been able to gain admittance with her dependent's ID, but now, since the demonstrations, it wouldn't do. Not even as a general's wife could she get in.

It was embarrassing. All around her, uniformed young men and women paraded by while she had to stand at the guard's table as he telephoned. Someone had to come down from Sean's office and sign her in. She waited.

At last Michael Packard came. The sight of his bright, smiling face relieved her, and when he opened his arms, she went into them as if that hallway were the platform of a train station. How did he know she needed to be welcomed? For twenty-five years Michael had been their friend, obviously far more Sean's than hers, but Cass felt a rare dose of her fondness for him. She had an impulse to confide in him, but she instantly recognized it for what it was—a wish to recruit Michael as her ally.

"What's wrong?" Packard asked after signing her in and while leading her into the Pentagon.

"I have to see Sean right away."

"About Richard?"

"Yes. I've just come from Occoquan."

"Is he all right?"

"How could he be? That place is a dungeon."

"So is this place, Cass." Packard said this without slowing down. He had Cass fiercely by the elbow. "The President finally replaced Westmoreland. They just announced it. He'll be coming home week after next—but guess what? He's the new chairman."

"What?"

"That's right. Chairman of the Joint Chiefs. Westmoreland! After Khe Sanh!"

The siege of Khe Sanh, begun at Tet, had gone on until April. Five thousand bombs a day had been dropped around Khe Sanh, "the most concentrated bombing in the history of warfare," as Westmoreland put it. For two miles in every direction the once lovely hills had become a moonscape. When at last the enemy had lifted the siege, Westmoreland had stunned every man in the American military by ordering the "anchor base" abandoned—the base for which more than ten thousand men had died. To civilians Tet had revealed the absurdity of the war, but to soldiers Khe Sanh had.

But Cass was not thinking of Khe Sanh. "Westmoreland? But the war goes worse than ever. There are a thousand men a month being killed now."

"You know your numbers, Cass."

"Every mother knows them."

Packard stopped her. Military men continued to flow past them, parting slightly, like a current of water around an obstacle. "The war is not my point just now, Cass. I'm talking about Sean. I wouldn't have brought it up to you but, well, here you are. McNamara is gone. Clifford has no interest in defending DIA against other agencies that have been trying to kill it since the beginning. And add to that Westmoreland, who will be Sean's direct superior now, after what they've been through."

"You want me to worry about Sean? Is that why you're telling me this? How can you expect me to worry about Sean?"

"Somebody has to. They're going to scapegoat him, Cass. The Tet postmortems landed on military intelligence as the key failure, Sean's failure. Not Westmoreland's. Not Johnson's. As if Sean hadn't continually raised questions and sounded warnings."

"I think Sean accepts his part of the responsibility."

"That's my point. Everybody is covering his ass except Sean. He's the only one not desperately trying to protect himself. And so he's vulnerable. Between CIA and JCS they're going to eat him alive, and OSD, under Clark Clifford, will let them. Sean is alone here now. Totally alone."

"Here? Here? He has you, Michael, doesn't he?"

"Until the finish, yes. But I'm just—"

"Then he has more than some others I could name."

"You mean Richard?"

"For one." If they stood there, a pair of stanchions in the stream of humans, for a hundred years, she would not have added, "And for another, me." But also, for a hundred years—an eon of self-pity—she would have thought it.

At Sean's office Packard opened the door for her, but he remained outside. Two other officers, who'd been looking at charts spread on the conference table, took their cue from Sean's dismissing toss of the head and left. When the door closed it was just the two of them.

"I've seen Richard," she said.

Sean came around the table to pull a pair of chairs together. He held one for her and she sat. Then he sat next to her, away from his desk and away from the table. At their feet, woven into the rich blue rug, was the DIA seal: the earth, the torch of knowledge, the two atomic ellipses and the olive branch for peace.

Sean asked quietly, "He agreed to see you?"

Cass nodded.

Sean, waiting for her to explain, lit a cigarette.

She said, "Aren't you going to ask how he is?"

"How is he?"

"He's good. He's better than I thought he'd be."

"I'm glad."

"You don't seem it. You don't act like he's anything to do with you."

"Look, Cass, you arrive at my office unannounced, I automatically assume there's something wrong. I'm waiting for you to tell me what it is."

"Richard sent me here to ask you something."

"What?"

"He wants to see you. He asked me to tell you that he needs you."

Whatever Sean's reaction was, he hid it by putting his cigarette to his mouth. The smoke obscured him further.

"Well?"

"What do you mean 'well,' Cass? What can I possibly say to that?"

"You can say, 'My son needs me. I'll go to him.'"

"But you know better than anyone how impossible that would be."

"Your only son is in a terrible jail, and the rest of his life depends on how his trouble is resolved, and he's asking you to help him. Which is impossible. Everything is impossible, Sean. Don't you see? Which means now you can do what you want to do."

"You're talking nonsense, Cass." Dillon stood abruptly, crossed to his desk and leaned to his intercom. "Send in some coffee, Jane, would you please?"

Cass watched him as he went to the window, to stand there looking out, his back resolutely toward her. To his left was a gold-tipped flagstaff from which hung the blue and silver flag of his rank. In another age that flag would have followed him into battle. She waited.

The secretary entered with the coffee service, placed it on the conference table and, with no direction from either Sean or Cass, left.

Sean ignored the coffee.

Cass stood, crossed to it and poured. She carried his cup and hers over to the window. Without a word she handed him his.

They stood side by side, looking silently out the window, toward the river and Memorial Bridge. Cass, speaking almost absently, said, "Before we ever came here, you did something that was against your conscience. I never asked you to do it and we never talked about it, but you did it for me."

"You mean Buckley, the lies I told to get him."

"Of course."

"This is different, Cass."

"I know. You don't have to arrange someone's imprisonment this time. Quite the opposite."

But Sean was shaking his head. "By my lights Richard is giving aid and comfort to the enemy. Until he's prepared to renounce his association with people who are helping Hanoi, I can't have anything to do with him."

Cass put her cup onto her saucer. The clink of the china resounded, aural punctuation. "Then I've been wrong all these years."

"What?"

"About you. I've been wrong. I've thought you acted against Buckley for me because of what he had done to my uncle. But now I see you did it for yourself. You lied to the priest. You used my illegal transcripts. You manipulated the law. But it wasn't for me. You did it for yourself."

"Why are you saying these things?"

"Because if you won't violate your precious conscience for your son, you certainly wouldn't have for me. What I see, Sean, is that you've never cared about anyone but yourself, and that's the awful truth behind the shell of your famous integrity. Otherwise you would jump at the chance to go to your son when he asks for you."

"But he's guilty, Cass. He's a draft dodger. Nothing I do can change that. His future is at stake, yes. But he's in charge of it. He's not our little boy anymore. He has chosen to defy the government in a way that the government simply cannot allow. The government has to land on him. Its ability to field an army depends on the Selective Service System holding. Richard has to go to jail. He should go to jail."

"And you would not consider asking Mr. Hoover or Ramsey Clark to intervene, this once, for—"

"Of course I wouldn't."

"It's that 'of course' I hate in you."

"It has always been there, Cass."

She shook her head. "Once it wasn't."

Cass turned and crossed to the conference table and put her cup down on the tray. She did so carefully, without flamboyance. Then she picked up her bag and started toward the door.

"Cass?"

She stopped, her back toward him.

But he could not think what he wanted to say.

She left.

Dillon's colleagues returned to the room and they resumed their discussion of the current deployment of North Vietnamese regulars in the South. The assessment was crucial for Averell Harriman at the peace talks in Paris. But Dillon's mind was only half focused on the charts and maps before him.

It was after three o'clock before he broke free to call her. "Look," he began, "you said some things I need to answer."

"Sean, I suggest you drop it. I'm not interested in—"

"I can't drop it. Now listen to me. You brought up Buckley. And I've been thinking. You were right. I didn't do it for you. I set him up because I hated him. I hated him for what he'd done to your uncle." Dillon saw the flash of an image, a pale mangled corpse dripping beside the blood pit. "And for what he'd done to Doc Riley. But you're right, it was my hatred. And I acted on it as I did because, if the law protected him, it was wrong. It seemed that simple to me. If the law protected Buckley, the law was wrong. And Cass, do you know what? I do not regret having manipulated the law to get him. And if I lied, I haven't regretted that either. Buckley died in prison after more than twenty years. I'm sorry the doctors couldn't cure his cancer because he deserves to be in prison still. That's the first thing I wanted to tell you."

Dillon moved the phone receiver to the other side of his face, from the hand that was wet to the one that was dry. He was standing in that same window, looking out at the river and the bridge. The black spire of Georgetown in the distance reminded him of the old Jesuit, of the sparrow in the hall.

"And the second thing is, you were wrong when you said I'd never put aside my conscience for you. Cass, you are my conscience. From the very beginning, you've been that to me. Are you listening?"

"Yes. Then I have to ask you something, if that's what I am to you. Something I swore I'd never ask."

"What?"

"How can you continue to be a part of this war?"

Silence. Dillon knew she'd never have dared ask him that if they'd been face to face.

"The war, Sean. You hate it as much as Richard does. How can you still be a part of it?"

"Cass, I have no choice."

"You do! You do! You could resign!"

"Cass, the peace talks are on in Paris. What happens there can justify all that's happened up till now, all the killing, everything! I'm part of that still, don't you see? I help with those talks. I keep our people on top of what the other side is really doing. My work has never mattered more. Don't you understand? The peace talks are what will end the war. Not protests. I don't resign, because if I did, I wouldn't be quitting on President Johnson or General Westmoreland, but on hundreds of thousands of men who are still in terrible danger. They're the ones I think of now. If it was in my power to just bring them home today, I would. I helped get them there. I have to help get them home."

"Get them home by denouncing the war."

"That would give Hanoi another reason not to settle. I can't be a part of that. Besides, critics of the war are a dime a dozen."

"So are subservient generals, Sean. I hate to say it, but you are kidding yourself."

"Maybe so, Cass, maybe so. But it's not subservience I'm known for lately. I've seen everything I've believed in and given my life to not only corrupted but betrayed. And it breaks my heart. Do you hear me?"

"Yes."

"We're nearly drowned in lies over here. I know that better than anyone. Mostly, we've lied to ourselves. Well, that is something it's still my job to change. For me to walk away to preserve what little is left of my own integrity, as if I'm better than these others, would be a last betrayal. I have no illusions, Cass. But there are peace talks on in Paris. They are the best chance we have. That's why I stay."

"In Paris, all they do is argue over the shape of the table."

"That's not true. That's all the press sees happening. It's a potential breakthrough, Cass, take my word for it."

"And you want to see it through because of the boys."

"That's right."

"And what about *your* boy?"

"That's why I called you. I've been thinking about it. And I think there is something I can do, something you suggested."

"What?"

"Go to Hoover. Ask him to get the case against Richard dropped. I'm on my way there now."

"That's not what Richard would—"

"He'll never know, Cass. It's the best thing I can do for him. The government has plenty of discretion in these cases. They don't prosecute every violator, and there's no reason Richard shouldn't be one who draws a bye. Once he's out, *then* I'll see him."

Cass did not respond at first, her feelings were so complicated. But finally this was what she wanted, wasn't it? Richard out of that hateful jail? What did it matter, compared to that, that Sean was otherwise so wrong?

The Justice Department on Ninth Street—how many countless times had he entered it, always with a clip in his step? After the Pentagon, it seemed a modest building. Even on Pennsylvania Avenue, with the temple-like National Archives looming to the east and the massive Victorian oddity, the old post office, to the west, Justice hardly registered as grand. But to Dillon, the halls of that building, unlike any other in Washington, were hallowed. Even now, when so few of his illusions remained intact, he could not enter the Justice Building without feeling a rush of affirmation. How different his life would have been if he'd remained here as a Bureau man. He would not have been an outsider all these years, for one thing. And his exercise of power would not have been thwarted at every turn by small-minded military turf-defenders.

But Dillon laughed, chiding himself at once. Exercise of power? If he'd stayed in the Bureau, he'd have had no problem with that, since he'd have had no power. Work for Hoover? Not a chance.

But working *with* him had been something else. Hoover and Dillon each occupied chairs on the President's Foreign Intelligence Advisory Board, where their intimacy had been implicit. Even as the aging FBI director had become a parody of himself, obviously ill equipped for the era of civil rights and political dissent, Dillon's respect for him held. Compared with the intimidated military men who made every decision with a furtive eye up the chain of command, Hoover's cantankerous willingness to offend seemed precious to Dillon.

The wall at the elevator was decorated with bronze bas-relief panels portraying the great lawgivers of history: Moses,

Hammurabi, Justinian. As familiar emblems of the system to which he was devoted, the figures reassured him. Though he had come here explicitly to bend that system to his own benefit, he felt remarkably at peace. Unlike nearly everyone else in that city, Dillon had never cashed in a chit for himself, as Hoover would know better than anyone. Yet to do so now seemed wholly right. Hoover regarded himself as Dillon's mentor. It would please him to be asked for help, and to offer it. Dillon rode the elevator up to the director's floor, full of confidence.

At the door to Hoover's outer office, he hesitated for a second to savor the difference it was to come here in the uniform of a three-star general. To young agents, this same door could seem a gate of hell.

Miss Gandy greeted Sean with twinkling affection, but she stunned him then by saying that Hoover wasn't there.

"But you told me yourself not an hour ago that he would see me now."

"That was before, General. The director had to leave. He said that you should go into Mr. Peterson's office and talk to him."

"Peterson?"

Walt Peterson was the deputy assistant director of domestic intelligence, a position Dillon himself had held at the end of the war. Dillon barely knew Peterson. As he left Miss Gandy, he fended the certainty that he'd just been shunted aside. He knew damn well this had happened before. His current troubles at the Pentagon had begun when McNamara started sloughing him off to deputies. At Peterson's office, the secretary was ready, and she showed him in with nervous efficiency.

"Hey, Sean, how are you?" Peterson came at him with outstretched hand, like a salesman.

"I'm well, Walt. Nice to see you."

The two men took chairs opposite each other.

"The director was called away, I guess. He asked me to see you. What's up?"

Sean shook his head. "Not much point in my raising the thing with you, Walt. It's personal. I indicated as much to Miss Gandy, and I have to assume the director knew that. It makes no sense that he referred me to you."

"Unless it involves your son."

Peterson's direct statement caught Sean off guard. But then

he understood how obvious it was. Hoover's refusal to see him was already a refusal to help Richard.

Dillon lit a cigarette to calm himself. "Why the referral to you, Walt? My son is a two-bit draft dodger, not in DI's purview. I'd have expected to be passed along to the fugitive section."

"Actually, these recent draft cases are on our docket. There's a difference between a draft dodger and a resister. I'm sorry to say, Sean, your boy mixed himself up with some of the wrong people. He's involved with a subversive group."

"What the hell are you talking about?"

"It calls itself Resist. It has cells in cities all across the country. It's an out-and-out revolutionary organization, committed to the overthrow of the entire Selective Service System. And we have reason to think it is an organization run by foreign operatives."

Despite a wave of nausea, Dillon laughed. "Foreign operatives! Walt, listen to yourself. You think Moscow is behind all these kids taking off for Canada? Jesus, Peterson. Who are you getting your briefs from? Herb Philbrick?"

"You wouldn't be amused if you saw the material I see."

"Then show it to me. Show me what implicates my son with subversives, what sets him apart from ten thousand other boys who have refused to report for induction."

"I can't. You know that."

"Why, because my clearances aren't up to level?"

Peterson looked away from Dillon, not replying.

"Then why isn't he charged with violations under the Smith Act? Subversion, acting as an agent of a foreign power, conspiracy. Why aren't those the charges? You have him for one lousy count of failure to report, and another of unlawful flight. Why are those the charges if he's so dangerous?"

"We can't bring our sources into court, that's why. But we're using what open violations there are to bring this movement to a halt. You know how it goes. Unfortunately, your son got caught in the first phase of our full-court press. I've no doubt he's just been duped, Sean. But he *is* active. His first phone call from jail was to Resist. He was active with Resist in Toronto."

"Which you have infiltrated, right? That's how you knew he would be at Randall Crocker's funeral."

"That was badly handled. I admit it."

"Badly handled! Christ, it was a funeral! Where do you get your agents now? The Cosa Nostra? They're the ones who make their hits at funerals."

"I said it was badly handled. What do you want?"

"I want the charges dropped against my son. Whatever you have going with this Resist operation, he's peripheral to it."

Peterson shook his head. "The indictment's been handed down."

"Hoover could have it quashed in an hour, and you know it."

"Mr. Hoover expressly told me, Sean, to convey his regrets on this. He'd like to help, but he can't. This is a national security case, and you should—"

"Don't give me that crap." Dillon's anger brought him to his feet. He leaned over Peterson. "This is my son. This is me. Whose side do you think I've been on for thirty years? I'm not accepting this from you. Hoover will have to tell me to my—"

A brusque voice from behind cut Sean off. "No, he won't, General."

Dillon turned to see in the side doorway the figure of Clyde Tolson, Hoover's alter ego. He'd obviously been listening to everything. "Mr. Hoover won't see you on this."

"He'd better see me, Clyde, because I don't think you can make clear to him how strongly I feel about this. I've never asked for *anything*, once! Nothing for myself, ever. I came here to ask, but now I'm telling! This is me! This is my son! And I won't let you dump a load on him that belongs to someone else. Do your work. If you have a case against Resist, develop it. If you have Soviet penetration in the antidraft movement, expose *that*. Don't pretend these easy-to-arrest, long-haired, hippie peaceniks are national security threats, especially not my son!"

Dillon had crossed to Tolson, always a sycophant. But now he seemed weak and old. In Tolson's flinching, Dillon saw something else. "Or is it especially that he *is* my son? Is that it? You land on him *because* of me? What, to prove how serious you are, to send Resist a message? Or who, the Kremlin?

"Well, I have a message for you, a message for the director. Tell Hoover I won't stand for it. Not *my* son! You don't do this with *my* son. The Bureau used to take care of its own. He taught me that. Well, in this I'm still a Bureau man and I take care of my own. You tell him that, Tolson!" Dillon poked him

once, firmly. "I'll be the Bureau if you won't be." At that
Dillon walked out. Not Moses now, but St. Paul, having
shaken from his clothes the dust of the road to Damascus.

St. Paul, he thought, looking at the imposing figures of the
bas-relief on the wall at the elevator. He saw not Justinian now,
nor the barons of the Magna Carta, but Saul of Tarsus. Dillon
had never felt less like a saint; it was the idea of reversal that
had seized him.

He remembered from his lessons years before that Saul was
a leading rabbi whose conversion turned him against the religious Establishment. His conversion marked him from then on
as a misfit, a heretic, and a criminal. Like Richard.

Dillon's blue car was waiting for him on Ninth Street.
Sergeant Kingfield craned back at him from the driver's
seat.

"Take me to Occoquan, Gus."

Kingfield hesitated.

"It's the prison complex south of Fort Belvoir, out Route
One."

The driver's face clouded over as he faced forward. Automatically, his eyes found the general's in the mirror. "I know
where Occoquan is, sir. I had a cousin there."

"My son is there, Gus."

"I know that too, General. I'm glad we're going out there."

Kingfield pulled the car into traffic. "I only met your Richard that once, when we went to the Shrine for the archbishop's
funeral. But the other sergeants, they all tell me he's a good
man."

"Thank you, Gus. I think he's a little lost, though, if you
know what I mean."

"Yes, sir."

Kingfield drove in silence then.

Dillon watched the features of the city slide past, then those
of the commercial highway, then of the deep Virginia countryside. He thought of Paul, to whom on that road God appeared
as a lightning strike. The flash of light made Paul blind. But
blind, he saw more clearly than he ever had before. He saw
that his great enemy had all along been his friend. He saw for
the first time the real meaning of his life.

Richard. Dillon thought of his son. Now everything depended on Dillon's ability to deflect the government's assault.
Not against my son, you don't.

Dillon forced himself to think about what to do.

The first problem was, what lawyer? Not the genteel Macmillan. Richard would need a cutthroat attorney, an Edward Bennett Williams or an F. Lee Bailey. And once he had the lawyer, what part could Dillon himself take, in all discretion, to help prepare him? What could he reveal of what he'd just learned in Peterson's office?

It shocked Dillon to realize that he felt somehow bound by the secrecy of the Bureau's dubious assessment of Resist. He recognized his readiness to protect their operation, even now, as a measure of his lifelong habit of personal renunciation. And it seemed perverse to him.

The fine points of the draft law would be key; what cutthroat attorney would see that? Dillon took the subtleties for granted. He thought of that bastard Raymond Buckley, and the use of that law he himself had made years before. "The goddamned draft," he said aloud. He laughed, but felt a throaty nudge of despair. The circle his life had made. "The goddamned draft."

TWENTY-FOUR

It was late in the afternoon, and less than thirty minutes remained of visiting hours, even for lawyers and court officials. The last thing the guards behind the thick plate glass at the gatehouse were prepared to deal with was some asshole's father.

But those guards were service veterans to a man, and by that point in that year, they were incapable of squelching a feeling of reverence at the sight of a uniform like Dillon's. The blue, the stars, the embroidery on the visor of his hat—to them he was the flag come to life.

The supervisor himself escorted Dillon through the double-door chamber. A short, dark hallway took them to another door, which brought them outside again, into the broad open space behind the high, old wall. The newer buildings were to the left. The Civil War–era bastion was farther away, up a hill to the right. As Dillon and the guard crossed toward the ancient jail, they passed the trusties' playing field. Spectators were knotted around a football game, forty or fifty denim-clad men. The raucous ball game stopped as inmates noticed the general passing by, like an apparition. At first they fell silent, watching him, then a few began to feign salutes and call out—"Semper fi," "Up we go, fly-boys," "Fuck the army!"—until guards began to whistle them down. That set off the remaining prisoners, who hooted and jeered as Dillon and his escort moved away.

The isolated granite jailhouse was somber and quiet by comparison. Another double-door chamber brought them inside, where the combined stench of fungus and disinfectant jolted Dillon. He followed the guard with a dead feeling in his stomach, staring straight ahead, ignoring the silent, shackled inmates seated on benches that lined the hallway. They were waiting for admittance to an infirmary, he realized, and he thought of the stockyards dispensary. This place revolted him, like that one had. Yet it was as easy to imagine himself confined here as it was Richard—no, easier.

The makeshift visiting room was crowded. Every place at the long, broad bisecting table was taken, and perhaps that was why Dillon's arrival was such a disruption. That uniform; who would be made to move aside for him? The commotion of the competing talk broke off abruptly, as all became aware of the threat he was. Every head in the room fixed on him for a moment. The privilege and power implied in his appearance seemed an affront.

Dillon's escorting guard tapped the shoulder of an old woman, but it was to the prisoner she was visiting that he said rudely, "Time's up, bud." The prisoner threw his mother a kiss and, with only a sneer at Dillon, got up and left. To Dillon's surprise, the woman did not protest either. He said, "I'm sorry," when she brushed past, but she ignored him.

No sooner had Dillon taken his seat than a far door opened, and Richard appeared. He was in prison denims too, and he was handcuffed.

Jesus Christ! Dillon was staggered by how awful his son looked. His bones protruded through the rough fabric of his jail clothing. His hair was pulled away from his face in a ponytail so tight it stretched the skin of his face into a translucent pallor. While a guard uncuffed him, he seemed indifferent and inert. Only his eyes moved, searching the visitors' table; his pupils darted weirdly, like a frightened animal's, from within the cave his brow made.

Oh Christ, Dillon repeated to himself, as he watched his son move slowly toward him, rubbing his wrists, hardly bothering to lift his feet off the floor. His eyes seemed incapable of focusing, even after they'd found Dillon. Where is my bright boy? Dillon wanted to know. Where is my laughing child? My Rich, my football?

"Hi, Dad."

Richard approached his side of the table and sat down.

"Hello, Rich."

"Gee, you're in uniform."

Dillon opened his hands, indicating himself, but he said nothing.

Richard cast his eyes around the visiting room, the armed guards, the shadows of bars falling across the floor, the other prisoners. "Probably haven't been that many silver stars in here."

"Sheriffs' badges," Dillon said. He was not going to leap with his son to the subject of shamed uniforms.

"Listen, Dad." Richard's voice seemed so weak. Once more the ache of his concern washed over Dillon. What are they doing to my boy? Then he thought, Hoover. What is Hoover doing to my son? The weight of the entire misguided government had landed on Richard, and had broken him.

"I feel bad about causing all that trouble at Mr. Crocker's funeral. I'm sorry, I just wanted—"

Dillon cut him off. "Randall Crocker loved you. And he was proud of you. He defended you, even to me. He was completely on your side. It was right to go to his funeral. No one's presence, including all those big shots, would have pleased him more than yours. The agents had no business arresting you there. So don't apologize to me again about that, all right?"

"But at the time, you seemed so . . . you looked right through me."

Sean listened to the sounds of the other prisoners talking. He had no trouble recalling the exact feeling he'd had that day at Arlington, having buried Crocker, having felt the hot wash of the Thunderchiefs swooping down on him and all those others who had made the war, having chased his fugitive son right to the edge of what? A pit of blood. The feeling had been that his entire life—his work, his love—had come to nothing, worse than nothing.

"I've had a lot to figure out, Richard." How even begin to speak of it? He had just told his son not to apologize. Yet Dillon's every impulse was to do exactly that himself. Not apologize, rather confess. But it is a law of nature, isn't it? A father does not confess to his son. "Frankly, I've had more linebackers blindsiding me than I can handle. Perhaps someday I'll give you a full account of it, and you can tell me how it was for you." Dillon knew what a sham his show of dignity was, but it seemed a saving show. He was here for his son's sake, not his own, and what his son needed was strength. "But for now we should settle for the fact that we're together at this able, and we're discussing your situation. Can you settle for that?"

"Yes."

"Good. Me too. I . . ." Dillon stopped at another wall then—walls inside of walls, the corrals and chutes of a lifetime's feelings—for his impulse was to—Is there a law of nature against a father's thanking his son?

"Richard, I'm glad you asked me to come here."

"I didn't want to ask you."

"I know. But I'm here to help. First, I hope you'll reconsider your decision not to accept a lawyer."

"Yes."

"Good. I've been thinking about it—"

"You, Dad."

"What?"

"I want you for my lawyer."

Dillon stared at his son, unable to speak.

"You're a lawyer, aren't you? I mean, weren't you?"

The screen of Dillon's mind had been taken over by a scrolling list of all that made such a thing impossible. Himself, his son's lawyer? He was the director of DIA, an active-duty general, whose commitment to policy, despite everything, held. He'd resolved to protect his son, but from a distance, from his usual distance.

The list scrolled quickly past, leaving his mind blank until a new question posed itself. Why didn't I think of this? Of course I should be his lawyer. I know better than anyone how to defend him.

And then he saw that his son was not broken at all. He saw the reserve of courage out of which this desperate, life-changing stroke had come.

"I'm honored, Rich, that you would ask me that."

"Will you do it?"

"Yes. I'm still a member of the bar."

For the first time, light returned to Richard's face.

Sean went on immediately, solemnly, "The first thing a lawyer and a client have to do is settle on terms."

"You mean, what I have to pay?"

"In a way, yes. I have a couple of conditions."

"What?"

"First, timing. This is June. As of now you're scheduled to

come to trial week after next. I would enter a motion havin
the trial put off until August."

"August! Why?" Richard's stomach twisted at the though
of weeks more in the Occoquan jail.

"Because in August the eyes of this city will be on Chicago
for the convention. More to the point, every news hound wil
be there, and for that matter anybody whose inclination is to
set himself up as a moral prophet on the war. Chicago will be
the showdown with Eugene McCarthy and poor old Huber
Humphrey. No one will know or care what goes on in a low-
rung D.C. courtroom."

"And so they won't notice that you're there, you mean?"

Dillon wondered, Was that it? Crazed Lyndon Johnson
would personally strip him of rank if he made news in an antiwar courtroom. But no. Lyndon Johnson was not the issue,
and the court case didn't have to be about the war. "I'm not
thinking of myself, believe it or not. Your case won't be
helped if it becomes a cause célèbre. We want the judge to feel
absolute and unfettered discretion, which they never feel if
there's publicity. I know that, as a rule, the people you follow
thrive on publicity, but you have to take my word for it: in
your case it wouldn't help." Dillon watched as his son sank
into sullenness, and he couldn't keep the irritation from his
voice as he added, "You don't see my reason?"

"It seems sort of beside the point, to worry about what people think."

"What people think?" Dillon asked quietly. "I thought that
was the entire point. What the people think is the object of the
contest between your side and mine, isn't it?"

Dillon waited. Richard refused to answer. Both felt the
gloom of a coming failure. This was impossible. How had either imagined they could do this?

Dillon purged his voice of defeat to say, "My thought, and
I presume yours in asking me to defend you, was perhaps to
leave our 'sides' out of this. Am I wrong? The newspapers
would love a general and a draft dodger in court together, the
Pentagon and the peace movement. A soap opera, two great
symbols of the generation gap. Is that what you want? Or can
this be plain Richard Dillon and plain Sean Dillon? Is it my
uniform and title that are important to you? What did you
want, Richard, when you asked me to be your lawyer?"

Very quietly, "You."

"Well, that's what you've got. And in court, by your side, I'll be my plain self, in civilian clothes, because the air force, my part in it, has nothing to do with this." Dillon watched his son for a moment, and he saw clearly the edge onto which the boy had placed himself. "Tell me what's bothering you."

"August. You said August."

"Which is a long time in this place."

Richard nodded abjectly.

And Dillon was glad for the signal that his son was not so far gone as to like it here. "Lucky for you, my second condition takes care of the Occoquan hellhole problem. You have to accept bail and come out."

It was no surprise to Richard how easy he found it to yield at once to his father's authority on this. Jail had never been essential to his position, and he hated it so. "But, Dad, I couldn't live at Bolling. I can't go back to Bolling again."

"I understand that, Rich. You're an adult. You live where you want. That's not my issue."

"And, Dad, when it comes to my trial, I'm not going to deny what I did. But I'm also not pleading guilty. I don't think I'm the guilty one."

"You can plead nolo contendere. No contest. Just what you said. You wouldn't be denying what you did, and you wouldn't be admitting guilt. You simply refuse to answer the government's charges."

"I'm not interested in plea bargaining."

"I don't know what they taught you at UVA, but a plea of nolo is treated by most courts exactly as guilty, but you get no credit for a show of remorse. It's slightly defiant."

"I'm not making any deals, that's all. You have your conditions, okay, but I have mine. I want a jury, and I want to take the stand before them so that I can say what I believe. I'll be speaking for thousands of guys who feel like I do. We aren't traitors. I want to put a decision about the war to the jury. I feel obliged in conscience, after all of this."

"I understand."

But this was the one thing Sean Dillon would not be party to, speaking of conscience. He would not enable the delivery of one of their simplistic, war-prolonging speeches, not even Richard's.

But if he said as much now, he sensed his son and he would be at the wall again, on opposite sides of it. Having come here and having seen Richard, and, more, having felt the tug of his old desire to protect him, Sean Dillon did not want to scare his son away. Alone, Richard would be at the mercy of a government that had, in this instance, lost its conscience. Dillon sat there for a long time, in stark silence. But not uselessly. He was thinking.

"All right," he said at last. "I'll accept that, if you accept what I propose."

"Which is what?"

"Every criminal trial begins with a motions phase in which rules for evidence and procedure are set."

"I know that."

"Good. Then you won't be surprised when in that first phase, before jury selection begins, I move to dismiss the case."

"On what grounds?"

"Government malfeasance."

"Malfeasance? Because of the war?"

"I won't define it now. The point will be that before you broke the law, the government did. If the judge denies my motion—and they usually do—then you get your jury and I will call you to offer whatever testimony your conscience requires."

"But if the judge grants it?"

"The case is dropped and you're free."

"Completely free?"

"Yes. Except for a promise I want you to make to me right now, for your mother's sake."

"What?"

"If you are freed from these charges, you will still have to deal with your draft board. I want you to promise me that you will put in for CO status and that you'll file the statements necessary to get it."

"You mean apply on religious grounds?"

"If that's what it takes."

Richard did not answer at first, but neither now did he lower his eyes or show other signs of vacillation. Sean realized what a strong, soul-centered man his son had become, despite the ravages of his anxiety.

Sean said, "If you thought it was useful, I would help you with that too. I'm sure we can describe your position in ways that are true to you, but that also satisfy the board's requirement. Eligibility for CO status is a subtle point of the law, and most local board members—they tend to be potbellied legionnaires—are not theologically sophisticated, to say the least. I have no doubt the intention of the law was to respect the conscience of men exactly like you. I think together we could establish that."

Richard smiled. "Together? We should be able to. Weren't we both trained by Jesuits?"

Dillon didn't answer, and they were silent for some moments. Then Richard asked, "Government malfeasance?"

Sean shook his head once, briskly. "I'm not explaining that until I have it more sharply in my sights. You have to trust me."

"Because you're my lawyer?"

"No, because I'm your father."

Sean saw himself, dressed in dark clothing and basketball shoes, moving through a darkened corridor, guiding himself by the feel of his fingertips on the wall.

Only the sensations of the moment registered—the smooth, cool tile broken at regular intervals by ridges of mortar, the muffled sound of his own footsteps and his careful breathing, the shapes around him of the shadows that marked doors he was passing. He was counting the doors. Somehow he knew the seventh on this corridor would be his.

He found the knob, and below it, the lock. Quickly he took a key from his pocket—a key? from whose belt?—applied it, turned the knob, opened the door and went through. From another pocket he drew a small flashlight—from that cop's belt!—and snapped it on. As he expected, he was in another corridor, a shorter, narrower one off which other doors led.

He pushed on the first door and it opened. Even in the darkness, the structure of the room was evident. Beyond a set of six typewriter tables and a supervisor's desk was a wall of filing cabinets.

Typewriters, filing cabinets.

Dillon began to cross the room, aiming the narrow beam of the light at drawer labels, at the trademarks of the typing machines.

He made his moves easily, his mind purring along. He opened a cabinet drawer, and the sight of a bundle of letter folders exhilarated him, though he did not—

He froze.

The sound of voices behind him, voices carrying in from the short corridor outside. But it was the middle of the night. No one was—

Not voices, he realized, but one voice.

He crept back to the door of the room, and after listening for a moment, opened it a crack.

A gruff male voice coming from the office at the end of the corridor. A man talking on the telephone. But in the middle of the night? The man's voice carried an urgency, something of panic and fury both, and Dillon realized that it was a voice he knew. But who?

Raymond Buckley. Randall Crocker. J. Edgar Hoover. Lyndon Johnson.

Dillon realized that he was not wearing gloves. He was leaving fingerprints everywhere!

He heard the door open at the far end of the corridor. The man was coming.

Dillon dashed back across the room for that file of letter folders. His hands shook as he pulled the folders from the drawer. They began to spill. He tried to stop them from falling. He banged the drawer closed, and the noise gave him away. The door opened behind him, and he faced the man whose room this was. A man in uniform. A general. Four stars on his shoulders. But old, very old. And angry. Like God.

Dillon woke up.

His fists were clenched in the sheet. Cass, with her back to him, was still asleep. He blinked at the clock. It was twenty past two.

He sat up, aware at once of what had happened.

A burglary, the third burglary of his life.

Not Buckley's office, and not the navy's. Despite the fright with which he'd wakened, Dillon laughed to himself. He was fifty-nine years old, and at his exalted place in life, he could do his sneak-thief night work without leaving bed.

And then he knew who the old coot general was, General Lewis B. Hershey, the head of Selective Service since 1941, when Dillon first knew him. Still hanging on, he was an exact peer of Hoover's, and a fossil like Hoover—and, Dillon realized, a file keeper like Hoover too.

Hershey's files. They were what his dream had given him. Sean Dillon knew what he had to do now. He had just burglarized himself.

TWENTY-FIVE

Richard woke up and saw a naked girl standing by the foot of his bed. She filled the narrow space by the card table that he used for a desk. Beyond her the curtain, a tacked-up tie-dyed sheet, lifted in the warm morning breeze. Outside the window there were the traffic sounds of P Street, as cars crossing from Georgetown accelerated up the hill toward Dupont Circle.

Jeannie. With the dark brown hair, which fell in a straight drop to a point below her shoulder blades. She was turned two thirds away, and he saw her mostly from the rear. He watched, without her knowing, as she lit a cigarette, then, inhaling, went up on her toes with pleasure. That movement pulled the line of muscles taut from her calves through her thighs to her biscuit-like ass. The sight stirred him. As she came down on her heels again, waving the match out, her breasts shook.

"A room with a view," he said, propping himself with a pillow.

"Hi, sweet." She faced him, smiling. Her eyes were bright as the light coming in under the makeshift, garish curtain.

He raised a hand toward her. She came back to the bed. "I dream of Jeannie," he said, his old joke. They kissed, but with sated tenderness. He cupped her left breast and kissed it also. "What would I do without you?"

"Self-abuse."

"You're crass." He laughed, but in fact she often caught him off guard like that.

"No, I'm cold. I need a shirt." She stood. Two steps took her to his closet. She opened it. "Gee, what's this?"

He looked past her into the dark closet space, most of which was taken up by a stack of cartons, his books. There were no shelves in the room and he didn't plan to be there long enough to build them. Next to the boxes his clothes were hung on hooks, but one item hung on a heavy wooden hanger.

She lifted the blue sleeve and asked again, "Rich, what is this?"

"My suit."

Jeannie turned toward him, still holding the sleeve. The shock on her face surprised him. "Your suit? What suit?"

Richard laughed. "My UVA moot court suit. I went home yesterday and got it."

"Home?"

"To Bolling." He looked away.

"I didn't know you were going to wear a suit."

"Jeannie, I have to wear a suit. There will be a jury. They will be average people. They won't listen to me if I look—"

"Like what you are? You'll look ridiculous in that suit. What about your hair? You can't wear a blue suit with a pony-tail." Then she saw what the sudden color in his face was telling her. "You're getting your hair cut? Jesus Christ, Richard. Did your father—?"

"My father has nothing to do with it. He didn't mention my clothing."

"Your mother, then."

"Jeannie, my parents and I are way past that shit with each other. It's just a question of my wanting to communicate with people. Like if I was ringing doorbells for McCarthy."

"Oh, Christ." She fumbled in his closet, past the suit, for a shirt and put it on, a faded brown workshirt with tails. "McCarthy. That's my point. Did you hear what he said yesterday in Chicago, about Czechoslovakia? It's 'no major world crisis,' he said. Jesus, Richard, the Russians send tanks to Prague, and McCarthy shrugs. He shrugs about the war by now."

"McCarthy wasn't my point." Richard pulled the sheet up higher on his body. She wasn't naked anymore, neither would he be. "Communicating was."

"But you're getting your hair cut?"

"I didn't say that."

"Well are you?"

"I . . . I hadn't decided."

"Your trial's tomorrow. When were you going to decide?"

"Today."

"And you're wearing a suit? A tie?"

"Why are you so uptight? Why does it matter so much to you?"

Jeannie shook her head, not that she didn't know, but that she would not tell him. He was startled to see a sudden flow of tears in her eyes. "Jeannie . . ."

"No. You're right. It's none of my business." She crossed to the other side of the bed, to the chair where she'd put her own clothes the night before. She took her underpants and her jeans and her own shirt and went into the bathroom. She closed the door.

In the night she had made him feel that she understood him better than anyone ever had. He had told her everything. She had been the only person in the world. When they made love she had crushed him to her with her arms and legs both. She had cried out, her feelings for him spilling everywhere like the juices of their two bodies. He had never felt so free, so happy. He had felt they would be together always.

He heard the toilet flush.

He tossed the bed sheet back, hopped out of bed and pulled on his Levi's. He went to the table for a rubber band he used to hold his hair back, and with one deft movement he gathered his hair and fixed the rubber band at his nape. He reached for a cigarette, lit it, lifted the purple curtain away from the window, saw trees in the distance of drowsy Rock Creek Park, let the curtain fall and snapped on the cheap plastic radio. "Hey Jude," Paul McCartney sang. The tune was everywhere that month.

She came back into the tiny room, and when Richard faced her he felt claustrophobic. There wasn't room for one in that shithole, much less two. How could it have seemed their perfect little space capsule the night before? Their trip to the moon.

Dressed now in her T-shirt and bell bottoms, she held his brown shirt out to him. "Thanks," he said.

He took the shirt but did not put it on. He stood there barechested.

The Beatles were screaming now, a feature of the song. Richard turned the volume down to nothing.

"Can I ask you something?"

"Sure," he said.

"Do you love your father?"

He didn't answer at first. He knew she wasn't really asking that. She wanted him to declare himself politically to her; was he loyal to the movement or not? To their generation? To the pure and bright throng, much of which, even then, had descended on Chicago? Was he loyal to her?

"I thought I told you that last night."

"We talked about a lot of things last night."

"But I said what it meant to me, didn't I? That he agreed to defend me?"

"But he put all these conditions on you."

"No, he didn't." Richard stepped toward her, smiling suddenly. "Except making me come out of jail. Which is why I met you."

"I just think you should be who you are with them, Richard. You should be strong. If you try to take the edge off what you believe, it won't cut through all the bullshit they keep piling on us. Like McCarthy, he's the same as Johnson and Humphrey now."

Richard took Jeannie by the shoulders. He realized that this was the other side of her fierceness as a lover. She had pressed things out of him he hadn't known were even there, and maybe—verbally—she was doing it again. "I think this is a good country," he said. "I believe in it, you know? I think Americans want to do what's right. They just don't understand what's happening now. I want to tell that judge and jury about the Vietnamese! Who talks about the Vietnamese? They're the ones getting mauled. They're the ones we have to make those jurors think about, or the judge at least. Judges could declare the war unconstitutional! I don't want them to be able to write off what I say because I look like—"

"One of us."

He shook his head. "I'm not getting my hair cut, Jeannie. I just decided."

"It wasn't your hair that bothered me, it was your suit."

"Why? Why is that so important to you?"

"Because I made you a shirt."

"What?"

"For your trial."

"A shirt?"

"Yes. A cotton shirt, embroidered around the collar." She looked away from him. "Now I feel foolish."

"Where is it?"

"In my pack. I was going to give it to you today."

"Can I see it?"

She hesitated, then went to the card table, pulled the chair aside and stooped for her knapsack. She took a package out. It was wrapped in tissue. She brought it to him timidly.

"I can still have it?"

"I made it for you."

He carefully unwrapped the package, put the paper aside, then held up an undyed muslin shirt with blousy sleeves and a high, plain collar edged in blue thread by a careful border of tiny crosses.

"It's beautiful. Really beautiful. You made it?"

"Yes. I made it for you because I love you."

Richard pulled her shirt on over his head, then fastened the three buttons at his chest. The buttons, too, were homemade, wooden disks. "Jesus Christ, Jeannie, I love it."

There was a cracked mirror on the near wall, and Richard turned toward it. "Holy shit," he said, "I look like Thomas Jefferson!"

She laughed, throwing her hands back. "God, you do!"

"Maybe now they'll listen to me." He struck a pose. " 'Indeed, I tremble for my country when I reflect that God is just.' "

He turned back to her, full of happiness and hope. He put his hands on Jeannie again, and drew her close.

The joke of his resemblance to Jefferson—a particular statue of the young farmer in the rotunda at Charlottesville, the sleeves loose like his own, the hair tied back—changed into something else, a charged, and charging, gravity. After a moment's silence in which their two bodies settled against each other, he said quietly, " 'And for the support of this declaration, with a firm reliance on the protection of divine providence, we mutually pledge to each other our lives, our fortunes, and our sacred honor.' " He pulled back to look at her. "Or should we just fuck?"

"The whole world is watching! The whole world is watching!"

That night in Grant Park, across the street from the hotel where the McCarthy and Humphrey campaigns were headquartered, ten thousand demonstrators had gathered. Thousands of others milled about outside the convention hall across vast parking lots that had once been a corner of the stockyards,

Chicago's Pride. After World War II the meat-packing industry had been transformed by frozen foods, and the stockyards had been closed now for more than a decade. Still, on warm, humid nights like that one, the old stench of the slaughterhouses rose from the pavement. Delegates and demonstrators from outside Chicago did not know why the air, even inside the hall—it had been built mainly for showing livestock—seemed rotten.

The peace plank, a direct challenge to Johnson's war, had been roundly defeated that afternoon after not only Humphrey but even McCarthy declined to speak in favor of it. The terrible contest that had begun in New Hampshire half a year before was over, and the opponents of the war had lost. Now they were in the parks and streets of Chicago. The police, who'd been invited by Mayor Daley in April to shoot to kill, were in those parks and streets too, twelve thousand of them, together with another twelve thousand hastily deployed and heavily armed GIs.

The clash was inevitable and had now come.

"The whole world is watching!" The demonstrators chanted, desperately pointing at TV cameras and lights while helmeted policemen ran through the crowd swinging clubs and firing off canisters of Mace and tear gas.

Prague. This was Prague again.

Policemen with bullhorns could be heard replying with curses to the taunts of the hysterical kids. The throng kept falling away and circling back each time knots of policemen charged.

Bloodied students were hauled toward police wagons. At intersections along Michigan Avenue combat troops had mounted machine guns, and sinister-looking army vehicles blocked the movement of fleeing, dazed demonstrators. Smoke and tear gas wafted above them, and many had covered their faces with their shirts. Cries and popping noises, sirens and chanting crowds—"Join us! Join us!"—filled the air.

Policemen could be seen clubbing the inert forms of people who'd fallen to the ground.

The whole world was—or was not—watching, but Sean Dillon was, sitting alone before the television in his quarters on Generals' Row at Bolling Air Base.

Cass had found it unbearable and had gone upstairs.

Dillon's mind was half taken up by the flashes on the television screen, the jumping images, the screams and curses, the melee; and half by the flashes of his own memory, the stockyards, with swarms of sparrows picking at the dung; the amphitheater and the Stockyards Inn outside which—on that pavement there!—Raymond Buckley had been arrested; blood overflowing the gutters of a slaughterhouse, the animals stampeding inside their corrals, the shriek of terror rising above the city as thousands of cattle, sheep and hogs gouge each other to death.

Chicago's Pride.

What he had built an entire life thinking he had left behind. He sat dead-still in the chair of his television room in the grip of a nausea he had not felt in years. The eerie blue light from the screen flickered over him mercilessly. He would have turned it off and gone upstairs too, but the images of a human stampede, the ungodly shriek, brought back what he had so fiercely shut out. There was no shutting it out now.

Not any newfound sympathy for the hateful nihilism of the protesters, but something older, almost forgotten about the forces of control, those policemen, those men in uniform, the same old hatred and violence. Chicago policemen.

Chicago politicians.

Now he was a policeman.

The television images switched from the streets to go inside the convention hall where a nearly equivalent chaos had apparently taken hold. The galleries high above the floor were filled with screaming demonstrators, but instead of "The whole world is watching," they were chanting "We love Daley!" and bouncing placards that read, "Daley Forever."

Richard J. Daley.

The camera went to him, sitting imperiously by the huge "Illinois" sign not far below the podium. Daley's face was twisted with rage. The men around him were standing shoulder to shoulder, sealing the mayor off from the wild arguments in other delegations. One Daley henchman in particular caught Dillon's eye, a stocky man whose head was bald but for his temples where the gray hair stuck out like handles. Dillon's memory tossed his name up, George Delahunt, the former congressman, the one who'd sent a tickle past Dillon when he'd testified against the navy twenty years before. Even from the dais Delahunt had mentioned Raymond Buckley, acknowledging a debt to him. Now Delahunt was sneering up at the speaker on the podium a mere twenty feet away.

The speaker was tall, gray-browed Abraham Ribicoff, looking more like a general than a politician, but a general in the heat of battle. His voice fairly cracked with emotion as he brought his fist down, bouncing the microphone at the climax of denunciation: ". . . Gestapo tactics in the streets of Chicago!"

The camera caught Daley half out of his chair. "Fuck you, kike!" The mayor's lips moved with precision around the awful words.

Whether the whole world was watching, Sean Dillon was.

Richard J. Daley in a free fall of hatred.

But Dillon saw something entirely other in the flickering blue light of his short-circuiting mind: Edward Kelly, Daley's long-dead predecessor, the gangster mayor who had embodied, for the young Dillon, a demonic corruption of his city.

"Out, demons! Out!"

Dillon could not watch Chicago that night, the war come home, and recognize himself on either side of it. But to his great surprise he realized, nevertheless, that if he were born thirty years later, he would certainly have been in those very streets defying Daley and Lyndon Johnson, denouncing the callous arrogance by which they claimed the right to rain clubs and bombs upon the heads of those they disapproved. Dillon thought of Eddie Kane, who had changed the meaning for him of the word "policeman."

But now he, Sean Dillon, was a policeman.

When he went upstairs at last, Cass was asleep. He nearly woke her. Carefully, instead, he lay down beside her, knowing he would never sleep. He lay there trembling for his country and for himself.

In the morning, after washing, he went to his closet, intending to dress in his lawyerly pin-striped suit, but his hands went automatically to his uniform. He took it out of the closet on its hanger and dropped the hook over the doorknob. Without having thought of doing so before, he removed one set of three silver stars from the left epaulet, and then the other from the right.

Six silver stars, a set in each hand, which he then closed, squeezing the sharp points until they hurt.

To turn them in, at last, far too late, a resignation not out of

any standing-in-judgment above what had been done—twenty-
five thousand Americans dead, ten times that many Vietnamese, America herself morally napalmed, and for what?—but
out of a judgment from below of his own essential contribution
to the massive self-deception. There was nothing of which he
could accuse the President, Rusk, Westmoreland—or even
Daley?—that he could not accuse himself. And his refusal until
now to resign? An act of cowardice after all? Was he just like
the others in that too? He had no idea. Virtue or cowardice? He
had no idea.

He opened his hands and saw blood. Blood. He had helped
build an Asian slaughterhouse. And he should leave now because it stinks? He could not walk away from the war until it
was over; that was all he knew.

Dillon wiped the blood from his palms with a handkerchief,
and then pinned the silver stars back on the shoulders of his
uniform jacket.

Then he had a fresh impulse, another response to Mayor
Fuck You Daley. Instead of dressing in his lawyer's suit, as
he'd told his son he would, he donned his uniform, taking
more care with it than ever. If the President and his men, including Daley and Hoover, found him insubordinate now, that
was their problem.

And three hours later, looking like what he was, resplendent
in his blue creases, his stars and his ribbons—the Distinguished Service Medal, the Legion of Merit, the National Defense Medal—he entered the United States Courthouse on
Pennsylvania Avenue where his wife and son were waiting.

In a hallway like this—high, ornately molded ceilings, mahogany benches lining the walls, polished terrazzo floors, frosted
glass double doors, court functionaries idling by huge
windows—a young Sean Dillon had pronounced a first vow:
"I owe Doc Riley." His first Richard. "I owe him you."

Dillon walked quickly, sharp-eyed, aware of the faces turning toward him as he passed, aware also that none of the faces
were the ones he wanted.

Until he came to the rotunda, the domed, open center of the
building, where benches were backed against the railing of a
high balcony. On one of those Cass was sitting, and so was his
second Richard, his only son. They both stood as Sean ap-

proached, and he saw surprise sweep into their faces like a cloud.

Sean, with a twist of his palm, indicated Richard's blue jeans, his hippie shirt and long hair. He had to stifle a burst of impatience at his son's getup. "No one will take you for the lawyer," he said.

Richard grinned, hugely pleased to be able to rebut his father. "You either, General."

Cass put a hand on each of their arms. "You both look fine to me."

Sean snapped his wrist out of his sleeve, to check his watch. "It's time. Let's go."

With Cass between them Sean and Richard walked, in step, into the courtroom. There were two men at the prosecutor's table, the stenographer was at her machine in front of the bench, a bailiff waited by the judge's door in the far corner. No one else was present. The jury box, three long elevated benches behind an elaborate balustrade, was vacant. Cass took her seat on one of the spectators' benches. Sean ushered Richard through the rail to the defendant's table. When they sat there together, the two prosecutors stared openly, then leaned to each other to confer.

At an order from the bailiff, all rose, and the judge entered, a thin, bald man with a wizened face dominated by rimless eyeglasses. Sitting, he too registered the sight of a general officer forward of the rail. The bailiff recited the "hear ye's" and announced the case, and as soon as he was finished the judge, with an impatient curl of his hand, barked, "Approach."

Richard sat. Sean and the two prosecutors went forward to the right side of the bench where the judge, glaring at Sean, asked in a low voice, "What's the meaning of your uniform?"

"I am an active-duty regular officer of the United States Air Force, your honor. I am also a member of the Illinois and District of Columbia bars. I am representing Richard Dillon in this matter, as a private citizen."

"Are you with JAG, or what's the military connection here?"

"Richard Dillon, my son."

The senior prosecutor shook his head, "Your honor, this is impossible. We can't have this uniform before the jury."

Dillon answered sharply, "This is a case involving questions of national service, patriotism, and loyalty. The defendant's

background as having been raised in the American military is
relevant."

"He's in rebellion against it," the prosecutor said.

Now Dillon looked at him. "That's the point, Mr. Repucci.
If the defendant's actions could be dismissed as mere rebellion,
I would not be here. You're going to have to make a better
case than that."

"All right, gentlemen. All right," the judge said, then fixed
Dillon with a glinting stare. "General, I do not want it ever
said that a serviceman's uniform was unwelcome in my courtroom. Nevertheless there is a problem here, and before we begin to seat the jury I am going to have to rule on it."

"My uniform before the jury may not be an issue, your
honor. I have a preliminary motion I'd like you to hear."

"I would too, if I were you. With what's happening in
Chicago"—the judge glanced toward Richard, the beau ideal of
a hippie troublemaker—"I'd move to postpone."

"My motion, your honor, is to dismiss."

The judge exchanged a look with Repucci, who rolled his
eyes.

"All right." The judge pushed back in his chair, ending the
sidebar conference. "Let's hear it."

On his way back to the defendant's table, Sean noticed a
man who'd slipped into the courtroom and was now seated in
the rearmost row. Sean noted his close hair, his civilian clothes,
the pad on one knee. He thought of Hubert Humphrey, how
Johnson's agents trailed him everywhere in the campaign, taking down whatever he said, to be sure he did not criticize the
President's war policy, even slightly.

A moment later Dillon was on his feet at the table, his papers spread, Richard seated beside him.

"Your honor, I move to dismiss the charges against Mr.
Dillon in this case on the grounds that this prosecution is con-
sequent to a response by the United States government to Mr.
Dillon's admitted, initial violation of the law that is itself illegal. I have a brief here . . ." Dillon handed a pair of folders to
the clerk, who had come forward for them. He carried one to
the judge and the other to Repucci. While Dillon spoke, the
judge and prosecutors read. "On October twenty-first of last
year, Richard Dillon did knowingly part with his Selective Service registration, his draft card, in violation of Section 172B of
the Selective Service Act. Since Mr. Dillon's registration, to-

gether with one hundred and twenty-seven others, was delivered to authorities representing the attorney general, there was no effort to hide or deny the violation. The attorney general was bound to prosecute that violation according to procedure outlined in the law, but instead, on October twenty-third he forwarded Mr. Dillon's registration to the office of General Lewis B. Hershey, director of the Selective Service Administration. General Hershey, in further violation of the law, issued a directive on October twenty-sixth addressed to Mr. Dillon's draft board, ordering its members, first, to reclassify Mr. Dillon from 2-S to 1-A and, second, to conscript him forthwith into American military service. This represents a perversion of the Selective Service for purposes of punishment and of political control. The government's implicit claim to be defending Selective Service against . . ." Dillon veered, in order not to mention the targeted group, Resist. It would not serve his purposes to cross Hoover's line. ". . . is false. The government's action itself represents the threat to Selective Service. As such, it strikes at the heart of a system that exists by explicit act of Congress solely for the purpose of raising an army to defend the interests of this nation."

Dillon had taken the court by surprise. His preliminary motion had become a speech, but so far neither the judge nor the prosecutors had mustered an objection. It amazed him how easy this was, quick turns on the shiny surface of the language. At this—if not his own work—he was a natural. He should have been lawyering all these years.

"My client rejected the government's act of conscription because, for his own reasons, he did not recognize it as having proper authority. Whatever his reasons, he was right. The government should have prosecuted him for failure to maintain in his possession his Selective Service document. Instead, it improperly reclassified him—he was still eligible for student deferment—and drafted him. His refusal to report for induction and his subsequent flight to avoid prosecution are both rendered moot by the fact that his conscription was illegal."

The judge slowly began to shake his head. "In order to dismiss on these grounds," he said, "I would have to see evidence of direct causation, linking the conscription order to the young man's draft card burning."

"He did not burn the card, your honor. He turned it in to a government official."

"I still need the link."

"It is available, your honor." Dillon lifted two more pages from his table. The clerk again carried them to the judge and the prosecutors. "I am going to subpoena these official government records. As you will note, of the one hundred and twenty-seven other men who turned in their draft cards on October twenty-first, one hundred and fourteen of them were reclassified and drafted within weeks. Of the thirteen who were not, six were already classified 4-F and two were already classified CO."

The judge peered toward Dillon without responding for a moment. Then he curled his hand. "Approach, please, gentlemen."

Dillon and the two prosecutors once more went to sidebar.

The judge cupped his hand over the small microphone, the stenographer's supplementary recording device. He leaned close to Repucci. "What's the government's disposition on this material?"

"Your honor," Repucci whispered, "correspondence internal to a defense-related agency is privileged—"

"That's ridiculous," Dillon said, eyeing the man directly. "If you have problems with providing those communications, it's because you see it will undercut government cases against one hundred fourteen other men, and probably many others." Dillon faced the judge. "The issue here is crucial, your honor. The Selective Service System is being perverted."

Dillon did not say it was being perverted in precisely the way he himself had perverted it in Chicago twenty-eight years before.

The judge was ignoring Dillon to glare at the prosecutor. "I'm going to have to rule on this, if this case proceeds. I'm going to need this material."

"Your honor, I . . ." A line of sweat had broken out on Repucci's upper lip. This was to have been a third-rate slacker case. Repucci was out of his depth, and showed it.

The judge said, "If you want a short recess to . . . consider the issue . . . I'll grant it."

"Yes, your honor. Please."

The judge reached for his gavel, lifted it, then stopped. "General, you state in your outline that this correspondence is on file in dated folders at Selective Service headquarters. How do you come by that information?"

Dillon did not flinch. "We have sources inside the Selective Service administration who object quite strenuously to its perversion."

"Who?"

"That is privileged information, your honor, and irrelevant." Dillon's authority matched the judge's. "The records in question are easily available to this court, and will speak for themselves. You could have the file from headquarters this afternoon."

"Nevertheless—"

"Your honor, as a young attorney in 1940 I participated personally in the drafting of the original Selective Service legislation. I represented the FBI, and I know from my own experience there were some in the Bureau who wanted to use the draft as a way of extending government jurisdiction over nefarious mobsters. But it was clear the American people would accept conscription—this was in peacetime—only if its purpose was absolutely restricted to raising an army. It is a principle that must be protected in a free society."

Dillon knew full well what a hypocrite this speech made him. The hypocrisy was implicit in the very arc of his life.

The judge did not react for what seemed a long time.

Finally he said once more, to the prosecutor, "I'm going to have to have this material." He brought his gavel down sharply once, facing the open court. "Short recess!" He banged the gavel again and stood.

"All rise!" the bailiff called as the judge left.

Richard and Sean remained at their table after the prosecutors had hurried away.

Richard couldn't help himself, the amazement he felt, the twin thrills that his father was doing this for him and that his father was so good. He leaned across, cupping his mouth. "We have a source in Hershey's office? God, Dad, how'd you come up with that?"

Sean looked at his son. "I didn't," he whispered.

"What do you mean?"

"There is no source."

"You just said ... Isn't that perjury?"

Dillon shook his head. "Nothing a lawyer says in court is under oath. Only witnesses are sworn. You know that."

"But Christ, it never occurred—"

"Law school is where you learn how it's supposed to be. In

court you learn how it is. Lawyers are always making things up."

"How'd you know for sure about the files?"

"I don't. I'm guessing. If I'm right, they won't want to produce them. I'm sure Hershey ordered your conscription and that of your friends. I'm not sure he's dumb enough to have kept copies of the letters he sent to the local boards. But he may be." Sean's grin returned. "Think of it, kid, a numbskull four-star general!"

Richard laughed out loud, and for a moment the two men were bound by their secret. Sean recognized his son, the renegade outsider, as *his*, and Richard saw in his father, for the first time in years, a flash of the man he hoped to be himself.

Richard, finally, leaned back to his father. "Hey, Dad," he whispered.

"Yeah?"

"Cheer for the Redskins."

Twenty minutes later the court reconvened, as sparsely attended as before, although once again, the observer had taken his seat in the rear.

The judge eyed Repucci. "We have a motion to dismiss before the court. Does the government have anything to say about it?"

Repucci stood, fussing nervously with his notes. "Your honor, if it please the court. The United States would like to enter its own motion for the court's approval of dismissal . . . a preceding one."

The government's dismissal! Richard had to bite his tongue to keep from yelping. His dad had pulled it off!

Repucci said, "Rather than compromise the integrity of internal defense-related communications, the United States is reluctantly prepared to move to quash the indictment in this case."

The judge peered across at Dillon, who said at once, "On the condition, your honor, that the termination of prosecution is with prejudice, so that the government cannot recommission the charges"—Dillon waited for Repucci to look over at him and nod—"the defense withdraws the prior motion."

Repucci, still reading from notes, entered the motion to dismiss, then brought his face up, raising his eyebrows expectantly.

The judge picked up the gavel, but asked Dillon, "For the record, do we have assent from the defense?"

Dillon stood. "Your honor, before assenting, my client would like to address the court."

Richard, startled, scooted forward on his chair, staring up at the judge, who only then seemed to take notice of the anxious young man next to the general.

The edge in the judge's manner softened as he said quietly, "We'll hear it."

Sean sat down, unsure himself why he had enabled his son's speech, or what his son would do with it. He glanced back toward the agent in the rear. Whose? he wondered. Westmoreland's? Clifford's? Hoover's? Johnson's himself?

Richard stood up slowly. "Your honor, I'm not sure what others think is happening." He glanced over at Repucci, who, red-faced, showed as much impatience as he dared by turning his palms out, and only then sitting down.

Thomas Jefferson, the ponytail, the shirt. Richard remembered a kid on the stage at Gaston Hall—where this all began for him—saying that Ho Chi Minh quoted Thomas Jefferson.

But whatever others made of him, Richard Dillon was no revolutionary to himself at that moment. He said almost timidly, "I wanted the chance to say what I think is happening. I love this country . . . I know what's happening in Chicago . . . I guess we all do." Richard looked hard into the judge's face. His legs felt rubbery and his voice seemed caught in his lungs. The faint whine of air conditioners could be heard in the room. "What I love about America is how it keeps trying to correct itself. It makes mistakes like other nations, but someone rises up to point to those mistakes, like Martin Luther King did. And now, in Chicago, and, well, maybe, here in the courtroom, average people are rising up . . .

"I understand that my father . . . I mean my lawyer . . . has found a technical mistake that the government has made in bringing this case, that it drafted me instead of going right ahead and putting me in jail. But the mistake I care about is not technical." Suddenly Richard's voice broke free of his shortness of breath, and the sponginess disappeared from his legs. The air of timidity fell away. His hand came up in a fist protruding from the blousy sleeve of the colonial shirt.

"It's the mistake America has been making in Vietnam. That's the one I wish you would rule against, your honor. Not the pseudo-injustice that has been done to me or some other draft resisters, but the brutal injustice that is still being done to the people of Vietnam."

Richard swept his flamboyant arm toward the vacant jury box. "I came here thinking I wanted to address a jury about this, but, your honor, you are a judge. In our system, you are the protection against the misbehavior of our government, which is my father's point. But he brought before you the wrong malfeasance. You could do something about it right now. You have power to speak to and for America that no one in Chicago has. Vietnam is the malfeasance! Vietnam is the crime! It is an illegal, unconstitutional, and unjust war. Would you rule against that, your honor? I beg you, please."

Richard sat down abruptly.

The judge did not move. Was it true, what he could do?

The silence had a hollowness to it, as if the words that had just been spoken remained in the room, floating above it, a kind of shell within which an echo bounced. The young man had evoked a sense of the presence, in that very space, of whom? Others like him? Or of the human beings elsewhere on the earth who cried only "Stop!"

Sean Dillon was thinking of those long black envelopes, aligned like dominoes, on the apron of the air base at Tan Son Nhut.

He lifted a deferential finger to the judge, who nodded.

Sean stood up. "Your honor, if it please the court."

The judge made no move to stop him.

"Obviously, my son and I are in complete and total divergence in our views on two matters. First, the conduct of the United States government in this case is not a mere 'technical' mistake, but an assault against the very core of our democratic system, and it must be checked. Secondly, the American effort in Vietnam is not in my view a 'mistake,' much less a 'crime,' but a purpose undertaken for the best of reasons, to limit the unjust aggression of a Communist power."

Dillon shifted his weight, a subtle act of inclination toward Richard, but also an act enabling a glance toward the agent in the rear. He wanted that bastard to be taking this down, and he was.

He said, "It must seem very clear to all of us now that, regarding Vietnam, we are at a crossroads, and if we make the wrong choices here, then the words 'mistake' and 'crime' will fall short of describing what we have done. The behavior of authorities in Chicago, like the behavior of the government in this case, indicates how at risk our society is. People in authority, in uniform, if you will, are not infallible. Nor are we immune to the viruses of disorder that seem to be in the very air now. In such a situation, what will see us through is a rededication both to the principles of law and to the commitments we have made as a nation. We often say that the end does not justify the means, but in Vietnam only the end—a stable, free and democratic government in Saigon—will justify the terrible means we've had to use. But such an end abroad will not be achieved by an American government that ignores principles of freedom and democracy at home. That, your honor, is why your ruling in this case is so important. Don't rule against the war in Vietnam. Help end it justly by ruling in favor of the Constitution of the United States."

Dillon lifted his hand and placed it on Richard's shoulder. "And your honor, if, before offering our formal assent to the motion to dismiss, I may add one further, personal note."

"You may, indeed, General."

"Thank you, your honor." Dillon squeezed his son's shoulder, but did not look at him. "I said we're at a crossroads. Perhaps, at some previous crossroads, we took a wrong turn in this country, without knowing it. The impasse over Vietnam tells us that the way we've been doing business in this country is not working, and by 'we,' I mean men like you and me, sir. And it seems to me our only hope is if our successors begin to make decisions that are radically different from ours. If they don't, then the world is finished. Unsettled as I am by it, what I recognize in my own son is the uncompromising will to change the direction in which we are headed. He and I disagree, as I said, on almost every particular, but on the level, as my Jesuit teachers would have called it, of the universal, it is not that we disagree. It is that I learn from him, and as a nation, my hope is that we can learn from all the people like him."

Thirty feet behind Sean and Richard sat Cass. If her husband was describing a crucial recognition, she was having one of her own. A recognition not of something in Richard and not of something new. She was recognizing in Sean an explicit manifestation of what she'd first sensed in him one desperate night on a corner in Canaryville across from the Stone Gate. She had, in the first instant of her feelings, been right about him, and that knowledge justified, fulfilled and, in some way, to her, sanctified the whole life they had had together.

Sean Dillon sat down.

The judge tapped his gavel on its disk almost gently. "This case is dismissed," he said.

All rose. Everyone left the courtroom except Sean and Richard and Cass.

Sean and Richard, awkward, turned away from each other and stepped toward the railing where they met Cass. She embraced them in turn, Richard first. Still she was what they had in common, and as if once more her expression freed theirs, they faced each other at last.

Richard, staring directly into his father's eyes, said, "This is not how I wanted it."

"There was no chance he'd rule against the war."

"But Dad, he didn't even rule against the Selective Service abuse. He let the government off the hook. What about all those other cases? Did you just bring them up to force the issue?"

Sean shook his head. "No. What Hershey is doing is wrong, and I'd like to stop it, stop it all. Daley and Hoover too. But I can't. To stop the abuse in your case, I'm willing to let go of the others. That's all."

"But Dad, you said—"

"I've said a lot of things, many of which I regret. What matters most now is ending the war. Isn't that how you feel?"

"Yes."

"Believe it or not, it's how I feel too. No one is sicker of this thing than I am. And if I am still going back to the Pentagon after all of this, it's to help stop the killing, and get our boys home."

"Then just stop it, Dad. That's how to end the war. Just end it."

"It's not that simple, Rich. That's how we still differ."

"You said we differ on the particulars, but not the universal. All I see are the particulars, Dad. The bodies. The rest of it is bullshit."

"You are wrong. Someday you will see that."

For the first time ever, in an exchange on this subject, they spoke to each other without anger. That seemed a miracle to Sean, but instantly he corrected himself. Not a miracle, but the result of hard work, his and Richard's, and also Cass's. A victory, yes. But not yet something to celebrate. Dillon felt as deflated as his son so clearly did. They stood in silence, peering into each other's eyes, seeing flecks of the same refusal. Truce was not the same as peace. Sean turned and led the way out of the courtroom.

In the corridor he saw the hovering figure of the agent; now Dillon noted the man's blazer and gray slacks. He crossed toward him. "Identify yourself, please."

The man began to back away toward a corner. Sean pressed him. "Who sent you?"

Instead of answering, the man tried to push past Sean into the corridor proper, to get away, but Sean took his arm. It was impossible to know who'd sent him. Though the man's shoes were highly polished, plain-toed military issue, he could still be with the Bureau. The JCS. The air force. The White House. It didn't matter. "Whoever you're reporting to," Sean said, "I want you to add something. Say: General Dillon is not resigning. Don't misunderstand what he did here today. He's in this, fulfilling the oath of his commission until that commission is withdrawn. Tell them that. Tell them they'll still have to deal with me. Got it? I'm still here."

Sean released the man, who found it possible to muster his dignity and to walk away without running.

Cass came up from behind, to put her arm around Sean's waist. "I'm still here too," she said.

Sean looked at her and smiled sadly. "We won't be here for long, sweetheart."

"Do you suppose we'll have to go back to Canaryville?"

"Nope, not there either. A *real* move this time."

Cass shrugged. "I'm ready. I've been saving cardboard boxes for a while now."

Sean laughed. "You have no way of knowing this, but even if they fire you, the U.S. government provides the boxes."

"They may not—for you."

And then they both laughed.

Finally Sean looked over at Richard. "I could use a lift back to work."

"What about your driver?"

"I released my driver a couple of weeks ago. I use the motor pool. I wanted to arrange a promotion for Sergeant Kingfield while my recommendation still carries weight."

"You've seen this coming?"

"What's that song of yours say, about not having to be a weatherman? What about a lift, Rich?"

Richard realized his father was inviting him to revisit one of their most precious forms of intimacy, Richard as his father's driver, those late night rides home, when they crested the ridge above the Potomac, the blue and red runway lights of Bolling and National both gleaming magically.

But it was impossible. All those particulars. He shook his head sadly. "Not to the Pentagon, Dad. I can't drive you there."

Cass saw the awful hole beginning to open up between them again. She touched both their elbows. "I was hoping we might all three stop at Arlington. We could say that prayer we never finished . . . for Mr. Crocker . . . and for . . . everyone."

Sean said, "I'd like to do that." He would walk to the Pentagon from there, across the fields of the dead. It would concentrate his mind.

Cass looked at her husband gratefully, but she saw now added to his clenched teeth and tight fists a vacancy of the eyes, as if he were seeing already the last destruction of his hopes. What would it be like, watching him retreat into an even greater solitude?

Richard was focused on Cass. He thought of Stephen Dedalus, who refused to pray with his mother, and of Meursault, who refused to mourn his. He knew at last not only that he lacked any such capacity, but that he didn't want it. "So would I," he answered.

The three left the courthouse then. They squeezed into the front seat of the old baby-blue convertible, Cass in the middle. They rode with the top down, glad for the wind in their faces, for a reason not to speak. They went the length of Constitution Avenue, around the Lincoln Memorial and across the bridge.